DARK WITCH TRILOGY

CHILDREN OF THE GODS SERIES BOOKS 83-85

I. T. LUCAS

Published by Evening Star Press

EveningStarPress.com

ISBN: 978-1-962067-63-8

CONTENTS

ENTANGLED FATES

JASMINE

J asmine pushed the pile of Fritos away from the edge of the table. "It's a shame that you ladies cannot stay longer and win back some of your losses." She collected her playing cards, reshuffled them a few times, and then returned them to their cardboard box.

As Lina translated what Jasmine had said into Russian, her two other poker buddies regarded her with mock animosity. Grabbing a handful of the winnings, Jasmine stuffed the chips into her mouth while mock-glaring back at the two and crunching loudly.

Lina was the only one of the three who was semi-fluent in English, but Jasmine had a feeling that the other two understood more than they were letting on.

Panya snorted and released a string of words in Russian that made the other two laugh.

"What did she say?" Jasmine asked Lina.

The girl's cheeks reddened, which happened often because her skin was so pale that it appeared almost translucent. "Panya said that if you keep eating your winnings, you are going to get thunder thighs, and it will serve you right for cheating."

Jasmine frowned. "I'm not cheating. I'm just good."

The two older women snorted derisively, and then Panya released another rapid-fire string of Russian words.

Lina translated, "She says that mind reading is cheating even if you are not doing it on purpose."

Panya must have gotten the idea that Jasmine could read minds from Amanda's visit to the lounge the other day.

Rumors about Jaz's uncanny streak of poker winnings had reached the neuroscientist who specialized in paranormal abilities. She had gotten curious and had come down to the staff lounge to test Jaz for telepathy and precognition.

The results had been unimpressive, and when Amanda had insisted on bringing others to test her further, the results remained underwhelming.

So, Jasmine might have fudged them just a little to avoid suspicion, but not by much. She really wasn't a telepath or a seer.

She was something else. She was a conduit for the divine spirit of the goddess.

Right.

It sounded good, but was it true?

Probably not.

Jasmine was just exceptionally good at reading people without having to peek into their minds.

"I'm not a mind reader. I'm a body language reader, and as much as the three of you try not to project what you are thinking, you still do."

After Lina translated into Russian, Panya retorted again, but this time her tone sounded more good-natured than derisive.

Lina translated. "She doesn't mind losing because it doesn't cost her anything. Even the potato chips are free. She says that playing with you teaches her how to guard her expressions and body language so that when she gets back home, she will win real money playing with her friends."

"I only play for fun." Jasmine cast Panya a mock glare. "Tell her to have mercy on her friends and not play for money. It will only bring her bad luck."

Under the table, Jasmine curled her thumb between her index and middle fingers, forming the *malocchio* sign to shield against negative energies and ill intentions.

Playing poker professionally could have made her rich, but after all the lectures she'd heard from her father about how it could get her in trouble with bad people or even killed, she only played for fun, or in this case, for Fritos and information.

Not that the Russians were particularly forthcoming. The bits and pieces she had collected so far were pitiful compared to what she could usually gather with nothing more than a few charming smiles and several carefully spaced questions.

As much as she was grateful to these people for rescuing her from the cartel and giving her a ride back home, she was dying of curiosity about them, and all the secrecy they insisted on was just ridiculous.

She was stuck in the crew quarters, not allowed to go to the upper decks, and no one was willing to tell her anything.

Panya waved a dismissive hand as she rose to her feet with Lina and Anya following her. "Nevezeniye—eto yerunda," she said before heading toward the door.

Lina translated, "She said that bad luck is nonsense."

"It's not," Jasmine murmured under her breath.

It was no use trying to convince the stubborn Russian that bad luck was very real. She would find out soon enough.

Jasmine munched on the last of her winnings, walked over to one of the plush couches in the corner, sat down, and stretched out her long legs.

With the kitchen staff leaving to start working on tonight's wedding dinner, the lounge was emptying, and the place that was usually bustling with activity and lively chatter was turning depressingly quiet.

Ever since Jasmine was brought on board, she'd been observing the same exodus happening every afternoon, but usually some of the staff remained because not everyone worked all three shifts.

Today, though, she'd heard rumors that someone very important was getting married, but no one would tell her who they were or even why they were important.

Well, since Lina and Marina were the only ones who spoke English, they were the only two she'd asked, and both had refused to answer, saying that it was classified information.

Whatever.

It didn't matter who was getting married. What bothered Jasmine was that with the staff gone, she was about to be the only one left in the lounge. The rescued women who occupied some of the cabins on this level only left their rooms to eat in the crew's dining room and never visited the lounge, but even if some of them decided to brave it, they only spoke Spanish, and she didn't.

The truth was that Jasmine hated being alone, and she hated being stuck in places with no windows, but the staff quarters and facilities were all below the water line, and she was not allowed to venture to the upper decks where the Perfect Match Virtual Studios management mingled with the distinguished guests, who were all former users of the service who had found true love in a Perfect Match adventure and were getting married on this super-secretive, exclusive cruise. Not that she knew any of that for a fact, but she had gathered enough tidbits of information to deduce that.

The other thing that Jasmine hated was sleeping alone in her tiny, window-less cabin, but it didn't seem like she would be able to find anyone to share it with for the last three nights of the cruise. The number of male staff members was pitifully small, and they were either too old, too young or in committed relationships.

Jasmine sighed, her fingers drumming an idle rhythm on her thigh. If only she could venture to the upper deck and mingle with the guests, she could perhaps find the handsome helicopter pilot whom she'd flirted with during the boat ride from Modana's yacht to the ship.

Edgar had been enchanted with her, and he seemed like a nice guy. The two guards who had collected her and the others were not bad looking either. In fact, she wouldn't have minded a tumble with any of them, but none had come down to see her, not even to say 'Hi, how are ya?'

Had she lost her touch?

Maybe they had been told to stay away from her?

It was ridiculous how tight-lipped everyone was about the whole Perfect Match thing. So what if the couples had met through the company's exclusive dating service?

If anything, it would make a fantastic PR opportunity.

Jasmine would love to become part of that PR effort, perhaps as the spokesperson in their commercials, or a character in one of their adventures. After all, they based their avatars on real people, or at least that was what she'd been led to believe.

Some sneered at the service and its users, but not her. It would be nice to have the computer find her the perfect guy. After the disastrous results of consulting her tarot cards on matters of the heart, Jasmine was much more inclined to trust artificial intelligence to find the perfect man for her.

The damn tarot had promised her a prince, and she'd foolishly believed they had meant Alberto, only for her so-called prince to turn into an ugly, wart-covered toad.

Jasmine's stomach churned at the memory of how easily she'd been fooled by the handsome, charismatic guy pretending to be an honest, well-to-do business-man. Alberto had swept her off her feet with lavish dinners, extravagant bouquets of flowers, and charming smiles. She'd been so sure that he was the prince the tarot cards had foretold, but instead of a happily-ever-after, she'd found herself snared in a nightmare.

Shaking off the painful recollections, Jasmine sat up and pulled out the worn velvet pouch nestled in her purse. Despite their disappointing guidance as of late, she cherished those tarot cards above all of her other possessions.

They had been her constant companions since she was a young girl, an unin-tended gift left behind by her mother.

Or intended, as she chose to believe.

Her mother had left the cards hidden inside a secret compartment in her jewelry box, which she must have known would go to Jasmine after her death.

With no one to instruct Jasmine on how to use them, they had initially been just a collection of pretty pictures, a reminder of the mother she'd lost, and a secret treasure hidden from her father. But when Jaz got old enough to be allowed access to the internet, she'd found all the instructions she needed.

Over the years, Jasmine had come to rely on the cards' guidance, finding comfort in their cryptic messages and, more often than not, finding out that they had been right. But sometimes, she had done so to her detriment.

Well, only once.

They had never steered her wrong before leading her to that scumbag Alberto. May his dark soul rot in hell.

Glancing around to ensure that she was truly alone, Jasmine pulled the deck out of the velvet pouch and began to shuffle. A smile spread over her face as the familiar motions relaxed her better than meditation, yoga, or just about anything else.

Well, save for sex. But that wasn't in the cards until she got off the ship.

Jasmine snorted. Not in the cards—now that was funny.

She closed her eyes, focusing her energy on the question that had been plaguing her since she was brought on board.

Was her prince on this ship?

Was that why the cards had led her to Alberto, so she could end up here where her prince awaited?

With a deep breath, she laid out the first card, The Six of Cups. The image of two children exchanging gifts stared back at her, a symbol of innocence, nostalgia, and the promise of a new beginning. Jasmine's heart skipped a beat. That card hadn't popped up before. Could this mean that her prince was someone from her past? Perhaps it was a guy that she'd met in school and hadn't noticed back then but who had admired her from afar? And who was also secretly a prince?

Jasmine chuckled. Talk about romantic fantasies. She sounded like a character from one of her period romance novels. She'd never really thought that the cards were promising her an actual prince. They must have meant a prince of a man, and she would be more than happy with that.

The next card was The Lovers. The naked figures of Adam and Eve were intertwined beneath the watchful eye of an angel, the image relaying a profound connection and a union blessed by the divine. After pulling that one, she knew what the final card would be even before laying it down, the same way she knew when she was about to get a winning hand.

And there it was—The Knight of Cups, a dashing figure astride a white horse, holding out a golden chalice as if in offering. The embodiment of romance, chivalry, and the arrival of a suitor. And behind him, rising from the horizon like a beacon, was a castle.

Her prince.

The first few times the same sequence had unfolded, Jasmine had been so excited that her hands had trembled, but now, it seemed more like a curse than a blessing.

It was nothing, a fluke, a cruel joke that some malicious spirit was playing on her.

Her father had warned her against relying on the cards, and at the time she thought he was being superstitious, but maybe he'd been right. After all, cartomancy had only been her introduction to the occult. Since then, she had delved into more serious stuff, but she still had a lot to learn about being a proper witch.

The devil's playground, her father called anything he considered witchcraft, but he was wrong. Hellish or divine, it all depended on the practitioner.

2

KIAN

Kian left Margo's cabin and headed toward the elevators, intending to finally have a long overdue chat with Jasmine.

When she'd been brought to the ship, he hadn't paid her much attention because he hadn't deemed it necessary. After all, the woman had just been someone whom Margo had befriended, a magnet for trouble who had gotten Margo entangled with the cartel. But since day one, people around him had been talking about Jasmine as if she was someone special, and that included Syssi and Amanda, whose opinions he valued.

According to his wife and sister, Jasmine had an uncanny ability to read the most minute changes in expression and body language, which allowed her to excel at poker. She'd won against Amanda, who was an excellent player herself. That and her likability led them to believe that Jasmine might be a Dormant.

Given the way the Fates worked, Kian had no problem believing that she had found her way to the ship with their guidance, but the skeptic in him was still very much to the fore, and before he accepted the supernatural explanation, he needed to make sure that Margo's befriending Jasmine in Cabo had indeed been a coincidence, and that the woman wasn't a plant.

Stopping by the elevator, he considered for a moment calling Anandur and Brundar to accompany him. Protocol demanded that they be with him in all meetings outside the village, but since the ship was under his control, it was like an extension of the village, and therefore he didn't need bodyguards to be with him when he visited the woman.

Not that he would have needed protection from the human under any circumstances, but he had vowed to follow his mother's rule in that regard, and even though he used every available loophole to avoid dragging the brothers everywhere with him, he never disregarded it completely unless he had no choice.

Besides, the two were enjoying themselves at Onegus's bachelor party, and Anandur was most likely drunk by now. Not that it would make the Guardian any less effective. Anandur was lethal even when inebriated, but Kian was loath to pull either of the brothers away from the festivities.

As he pressed the button to summon the elevator, it occurred to him that he didn't know where to look for her. He knew where the clinic was located, but other than that, he wasn't familiar with the crew quarters, which was where she was staying.

Kian could call the security office to ask, but it was a little embarrassing to admit that he didn't know his way around his own ship. Syssi would know where Jasmine could be found, but she was in the pool with Allegra and he didn't want to disturb her, which left Amanda.

His sister was at Cassandra's bachelorette party, but that shouldn't prevent her from answering him unless the party was so loud and boisterous that she didn't notice it.

His phone rang a moment after he'd sent her the text.

"Why do you want to know where to find Jasmine?" Amanda asked without much preamble.

"I'm intrigued. Isn't that reason enough?"

She chuckled. "It is. I'll come with you."

Kian frowned, glancing at his watch once more. "Are you sure? I don't want to pull you away from Cassandra's celebration. It would be rude for you to leave in the middle of the party."

Amanda laughed, the sound light and breezy. "Don't worry about that. Cassandra is indulging in a bubble bath, and her mother and sister have every-thing under control. Geraldine and Darlene are getting ready to attack Cassan-dra's hair, and Eva has her bag of tricks with her, although I doubt Cassandra will let her touch her face. The female is gorgeous, and she knows how to use makeup to her advantage. She doesn't need Eva's help."

Kian stifled the urge to roll his eyes. "I'll take your word for it."

Amanda laughed again. "Too much information?"

"You could say so. Makeup is not my field of expertise."

"I get it. Where are you now?"

"Outside the elevators on Margo and Frankie's deck."

"What are you doing there?"

He'd just finished updating Margo about the successful evacuation of her parents and her brother and his fiancée from their homes, but Amanda wasn't aware of the latest crisis, and he didn't want to tell her about it while waiting for the elevator.

"I'll tell you on the way to the crew quarters. Meet me next to the staircase on the promenade deck."

"See you in a few," Amanda said before ending the call.

As Kian made his way to their designated meeting spot, his thoughts drifted back to Margo. He hoped that her transition symptoms were not a false alarm and that she was indeed turning immortal. He also hoped that no Doomers would show up at her parents' and brother's houses so her family could return to their homes.

Right now, they were on their way to the clan's mountain cabin with Turner's team to keep watch over them.

Kian didn't like that the cabin's location had to be compromised for Margo's family and that there was no one there to thrall away the memory of where it was from all the humans involved, but he'd had to come up with a location on the spot, and the cabin was his go-to safe house.

Lost in his musings, Kian didn't notice Amanda approaching him until he heard the clicking of her high heels on the marble floor. She looked fantastic in an elegant cocktail dress reminiscent of the fifties. If he wasn't mistaken, Audrey Hepburn had worn something similar in one of her iconic films.

"You look distracted." She leaned toward him and kissed his cheek. "Everything okay?"

Kian started down the stairs, which were thankfully deserted. "Margo may be transitioning, and we had a close call with her family." He proceeded to tell Amanda about Carlos Modana showing up with two Doomers at his brother's mansion and then the two talking about Margo. "We got her family out and installed cameras to monitor both houses. I hope no one shows up so they can return home, and we don't need to relocate them permanently."

"What a mess." Amanda sighed. "It's like the Fates are constantly throwing challenges at us. Couldn't they have given us a break during this ten-day cruise?"

"My thoughts exactly, but then we have been gifted two new Dormants during this vacation, so perhaps it could be called a good trade. Maybe three if Jasmine proves to be one as well."

"True." Amanda slowed down her pace and stopped on the landing. "But Frankie and Margo are mated to gods, and they are not part of our clan. I don't see why we all had to suffer so the gods would get a boon."

Kian turned to his sister. "I don't know, but I'm sure the Fates had a good reason."

Amanda smiled. "What a transformation you have gone through. My jaded, skeptical brother has faith now."

"I do, and I don't. It depends on my mood on any given day." He continued down the stairs.

Amanda followed. "And what is it today?"

"That still remains to be seen."

3

JASMINE

As Amanda entered the lounge with a man who could only be described as a god, Jasmine got a little lightheaded.

Was that what swooning meant? She'd always wondered about that word when it appeared in the historical romances she favored.

His features were chiseled, his eyes a piercing blue, and his presence seemed to fill the room with tangible energy.

"Jasmine, this is my brother Kian," Amanda said. "Kian, this is Jasmine."

Jasmine pushed to her feet, but her knees refused to lock, and her heart fluttered in her chest. Could this be him? The prince the tarot cards had promised, the one who would sweep her off her feet?

Except, unlike most men, Kian seemed indifferent to her charms. His gaze was cool and reserved, and as he inclined his head in greeting, there was no spark of interest and no flicker of attraction in his eyes.

Confused and a little hurt, Jasmine tried to mask her disappointment.

She really should stop relying on the damn tarot. They had either lost their potency, or all their prior successes had been flukes.

As if reading her mind, Amanda smiled knowingly. "Kian is Syssi's husband. They have the most adorable little girl named Allegra." She opened her purse and pulled out her phone. "I have to show you her picture."

Jasmine felt like knocking on her own head to check if anything was loose in there. She'd been so stupefied by Kian's looks that she'd forgotten that Amanda had introduced Syssi as her sister-in-law.

Then again, Amanda could have more than one brother, right?

"Here is the little princess." Amanda thrust the screen in front of Jasmine's face.

"Absolutely adorable." Jaz smiled at Amanda, silently thanking her for the reprieve she'd given her by showing her the picture. She then turned her smile on Kian. "She is a mixture of you and your wife." She pushed aside the foolish notions of princes and destiny. "But I'm sure that you didn't come down here to show me pictures of your daughter."

"I did not. Let's sit down." Kian waved a hand toward the couch and then lowered himself to a sitting position with more grace than a man his size should have been capable of. "As you know, Julio Modana was convinced by my associate to abandon his evil ways and embrace God."

She chuckled. "Kevin's hypnotic ability is mind-boggling."

"It is." Kian offered her a tight smile. "Julio's brother Carlos was obviously not happy about the one-eighty pivot his brother had made, and he paid him a visit. Fortunately, we'd planted listening devices around the estate, and we heard two of Carlos's goons talking about Margo and you. They even knew that Margo's family was under the impression that she was in the witness protection program."

Jasmine's eyes widened. "Why would they think that? Margo was supposed to board this ship, and her family knew her plans. They wouldn't have wondered where she was."

Kian looked at her as if she was dimwitted. "Margo was reported missing from her hotel room by her sister-in-law, and all of her things remained there. Her family was not informed of her finally being able to board the ship, and they also didn't know which ship she was supposed to board because we kept those details confidential on purpose." Kian turned to his sister with a smile tugging on his lips. "This time, you have to agree that my paranoia had merit."

Amanda winced. "I'm not sure that Mia kept the name of the ship from her friends. I just hope that Frankie and Margo didn't repeat it to their families."

Letting out a long-suffering sigh, Kian briefly closed his eyes. "I should never have agreed to allow Frankie and Margo on the ship. Evidently, I'm not paranoid enough."

Jasmine listened to the exchange, waiting for a break so she could ask what was going on. The level of secrecy Kian insisted on implied something more serious than protecting the identities of famous guests.

"Why was it important to keep the name of the ship a secret? Is something illegal going on here?"

Suddenly, Jaz remembered the poor women in the other cabins and wondered whether they really had been rescued from traffickers. What if they were being trafficked?

"Don't worry." Amanda leaned over and patted her thigh. "Our unfortunate entanglement with the cartel is all Margo's fault and has nothing to do with why we needed to keep the ship and its guests secret. We need to keep the paparazzi off our trail. You have no idea how resourceful they can be, how tenacious, and how low they are willing to stoop to get a story." She smiled. "But then, if Margo hadn't tried to help you, we would have never known that you were trafficked, and no one would have come to your rescue, so it's all good, right?"

"Now I feel guilty." Jasmine sighed. "If I hadn't gotten involved with Alberto, none of this would have happened. It's all my fault, not Margo's."

Kian lifted his hand. "Let's not play the blame game. Since the thugs mentioned you, we are concerned that they might go after your family as well as Margo's. They know how to locate Margo's family because her brother's fiancée filed a missing person's report, and they can find all the information they need by following her trail. We got her parents, brother, and future sister-in-law to a safe location. How easy will it be for them to locate your folks?"

"Why would they go after our families?" Jasmine asked. "What do they hope to gain by that?"

"Leverage," Kian said. "That's the cartel's mode of operation. They take hostages to pressure family members to give them what they want, whether it's money or information."

"I see." Jaz tucked a lock of hair behind her ear. "I'm not too worried about them finding my family. I use a stage name and I legally changed my last name years ago. My father and stepmother live in New Jersey, and we rarely see each other or even talk on the phone. If the cartel people check my records, they will see that most of my calls are to my agent, my acting coach, and my friends."

Jaz didn't have many friends, and she rarely talked with them on the phone, but it would have sounded pitiful if she'd only mentioned her agent and her coach.

"What about your brothers?" Kian asked. "Margo told me that you have two stepbrothers."

Jasmine snorted. "I see them once a year on Christmas at our parents' house, and we never call each other. There isn't much love lost between us."

"Good." Kian nodded. "I mean, not good that your relationship with your family is strained. It's good that we don't have to worry about it."

"Yeah." She winced. "Sometimes having an unhappy family is an advantage rather than a disadvantage."

"To quote Tolstoy's Anna Karenina," Amanda said, "all happy families are alike, but each unhappy family is unhappy in its own way."

4

KIAN

When Jasmine had explained her family situation, Kian couldn't shake the nagging suspicion that something was off about her story. She was hiding something, but then it could be just family drama that had nothing to do with him and the safety of his people.

He studied her carefully, noting the way she forced her eyes to stay focused on his, and smiled pleasantly when he knew that he was making her nervous.

Not that her reaction to him was surprising.

Kian made most people uncomfortable, even gods and immortals, and Jasmine was just a human female. She was beautiful, which no doubt contributed to her self-confidence, but she was also an actress, and she knew how to hide her tells remarkably well.

"It's a shame that you are not close to your parents." He offered her a smile. "Family is very important to me." He cut a sidelong glance at Amanda. "Sometimes they drive me crazy, but most of the time, I'm grateful for having them in my life."

"Ooh, Kian." Amanda batted her eyelashes and put a hand over her heart. "That's as close as you've ever gotten to telling me that you love me."

He frowned. "Really? I must have told you that I love you hundreds of times."

"Maybe when I was little, but you stopped when I became a teenager."

"That's because you were a hellion."

Jasmine's eyes darted from him to Amanda and back. "What's the age difference between you? You don't look more than five years apart."

Amanda laughed. "Kian only looks young. His soul is at least two thousand years old."

He wanted to kick her leg to make sure she was more careful about what she was saying in front of Jasmine, but there was no way he could do that without Jasmine seeing.

"So, about these paranormal talents of yours," Kian said before Amanda had a chance to make another comment that she shouldn't. "My sister and my wife are very impressed by your ability to read people."

Jasmine shrugged, a coy smile playing on her lips. "What can I say? I've always been good at picking up on the little things. Body language and micro expressions are all there if you know what to look for. People call it a sixth sense or female intuition, but it's just good observational skills." She leaned forward. "I call it the 'staying quiet and letting others talk' skill."

"That's very astute. Did you learn it from your acting teachers?"

Jasmine nodded. "My coach's number one advice was to observe people. The more I learn and store in my mind, the more I have to draw on when I need to build a character."

"Interesting." Kian crossed his arms over his chest. "When did you discover that you could use your observational skills in poker?"

"It was a gradual process. I joined the drama club by the end of middle school, and I discovered poker when I was an adult, but I didn't have such well-developed observational skills back then. Not until I got professional coaching. So, I think that it was a self-feeding loop. Better acting meant more poker wins, and more poker wins made me a better actress." She leaned back to reach into her pocket and pulled out a deck of cards. "Would you like a demonstration?"

He arched a brow. "You want me to play poker with you?"

"Yeah, why not. Amanda can join us, right?"

Amanda glanced at her watch. "I don't have a lot of time, but I would like Kian to see you in your element."

Kian was not a great poker player. In fact, he tended to telegraph his emotions and had a hard time keeping them in check.

"I'm a very mediocre poker player," he admitted. "You two will have no problem beating me."

Jasmine grinned. "Good, then I should take advantage of your supposed lack of skill. If I win, you will let me onto the upper decks and allow me to attend the weddings."

Kian arched an eyebrow, amused by her audacity. Eva would have called it hutzpah, and she would have been right on the money.

Not many people would have dared to challenge him so directly.

"Did you really expect me to agree to that?" he asked.

Jasmine sighed dramatically, leaning back against the plush cushions. "It was worth a try." She fixed him with an assessing look, her head tilted to the side. "I hate being cooped up here with no windows to the outside, and I really don't

17

understand why Margo gets to be up there while I have to stay down here." She pouted. "I will sign whatever NDA you want me to sign, and I will not breathe a word about the celebrities getting married on this cruise." She put a hand on her chest. "I swear it. I'm just dying of curiosity. I want to hobnob with the rich and famous and experience the glitz."

The woman didn't seem intimidated by him even in the slightest, which made Kian doubt her self-preservation instincts, but at the same time there was something refreshing about her irreverence and lack of fear, even if it was all an act.

Was she flirting with him? Or was she just using her charm to soften him up?

She was undeniably beautiful, and there was also a spark, a vibrancy to her that he found appealing in a completely nonsexual way.

Was that the affinity that Amanda had talked about?

Probably. It couldn't be anything else.

Kian was a happily mated male, bound heart and soul to Syssi, and the only thing he could feel for Jasmine was friendliness, which most likely stemmed from affinity.

Perhaps Jasmine was feeling that, too, but was misinterpreting it as attraction. If she were an immortal female, she would have sensed his bonded status immediately and never dared to approach him with even a hint of flirtation.

He waved at the deck in her hand. "Shuffle the cards, and let's play."

Jasmine shook her head. "We need something to wager, and I don't play for money."

That was strange. If she was as good as everyone was claiming, then she could make a killing playing poker professionally.

"Ever?" Kian asked.

"Ever. It's dangerous. I play for fun."

He supposed that it could turn dangerous if she played with the wrong kind of people. Criminal types were usually sore losers.

"That's smart. What do you usually wager with?"

"Chips, popcorn, crackers, grapes, etc."

"I'll get some chips." Amanda pushed to her feet and walked over to the vending machine.

While Jasmine shuffled the cards and Amanda collected bags of chips from the dispenser, Kian was tempted to delve into Jasmine's mind and search for a hidden agenda.

It would be so easy to reach out with his power, to slip past her mental defenses and pluck the truth from her consciousness. Except, it was against the rules to thrall a human without just cause, and curiosity didn't count.

5

AMANDA

"I win." Jasmine pumped her fist in the air and gathered her winnings, several flavors of Pringles Grab & Go packed in small individual containers.

Kian shook his head. "I'm positive that I wasn't telegraphing anything. How did you know that I had a crappy hand?"

Poor guy. He didn't even know how bad he was.

"You are a terrible poker player." Amanda patted Kian's knee. "You took one look at your cards, and your eyes narrowed like you wanted to shoot lasers at them and incinerate the useless hand, and the cloud over your head didn't clear as the game progressed, so Jasmine and I knew that you kept getting bad cards."

"I was narrowing my eyes not because I was angry at my cards but because I was looking at Jasmine and wondering if she had an amazing memory and incredible math skills. Usually, those are needed to be a good poker player."

Jasmine laughed. "I'm terrible at math. My memory is okay, but nothing special. It was just intuition and observation." She pushed to her feet. "If you'll excuse me, I need to visit the ladies' room." She glanced at Amanda. "Do you want to come with me?"

"No, thank you, darling." Amanda smiled. "I'll wait for you here. The truth is that I should be heading back to the party, but I want us to play one more game so Kian can win back the chips he lost."

Her brother waved a dismissive hand. "Contrary to what you think about me, I don't have to always win."

"I'll be right back." Jasmine rushed out of the lounge.

19

Kian cast Amanda a sidelong glance. "Did you have anything to do with her sudden need to visit the ladies' room?"

She shrugged and assumed an innocent expression. "I might have projected the suggestion to see if she picked it up."

"That was clever." Kian regarded his sister with appreciation. "Did you suspect that she was faking her underwhelming results with your tests?"

Amanda nodded. "She's unnaturally good with cards, so I suspected that she'd fudged the answers. Anyway, while she's gone, I wanted to suggest that you ask Edna to take a peek at Jasmine's psyche. Edna's talent is more akin to empathic reading than thralling, so it's totally within the rules."

"It is, but it's also not subtle. Jasmine will know that she's being probed."

"It's either that or thralling, which I don't mind doing if you are too squeamish about breaking the rules. You know that I don't believe in strict adherence to them, and since no one ever checks, I see no harm in taking a quick look. Jasmine wouldn't even feel it."

He tilted his head. "Why is this so important to you? Do you suspect that something about her is not as it seems?"

"Not really." Amanda sighed. "She's hiding things, but that's not an indication of anything malicious. We all have things we hide, old pains that we don't want others to see, shame, and guilt. But I want Jasmine to mingle with our eligible bachelors, and I know that you won't let her onto the upper decks without making sure she's harmless. So, we need Edna to take a peek, or I can do that and break the rules for a good cause." A sly grin lifted Amanda's red-painted lips. "Since Jasmine obviously has some paranormal talent, and the Fates brought her to us, we have an obligation to check whether she's a Dormant. I have a strong hunch that she is."

Kian surprised her by nodding. "I agree. Even I like her, and you know me. I rarely take a liking to new people."

Amanda snorted. "Generally, that's true, but in the case of gorgeous ladies, you are a bit more flexible."

"What are you talking about?" He glared at her. "Her looks have no effect on me. How can you even suggest that?"

"Relax." She put a hand on his arm. "I'm not suggesting that you are attracted to her, only that you find her pleasing to look at. It's natural, and you don't need to get defensive about it. Even little kids prefer pretty teachers to the ones less fortunate in the looks department. That's how humans are wired, and given who our ancestors are, you shouldn't be surprised. Gods are obsessed with beauty and physical perfection."

Kian dismissed Amanda's theory with a wave of his hand, not because it was untrue but because it was irrelevant to their discussion. "The cruise is almost over, so I don't see the point in sending Edna to test Jasmine. Before she disembarks, we will thrall her to forget about us, and while we are at it, we can take a look at whatever she is hiding."

"You forget the Doomers," Amanda said. "We can't just send Jasmine home, and we can't let her return to her job. We need to get her somewhere safe for a couple of weeks until we are sure that the coast is clear."

"True." He sighed. "I did forget about that. I'll talk to Edna, but it still won't change the fact that we have only three days left."

"We can do a lot in three days, even if you don't allow Jasmine to go up. I'm going to tell Max that he needs to keep an eye on her up close and personal."

"Why Max?"

Amanda shrugged. "He's been a groomsman but never the groom for too long, and it's his turn. Jasmine might not be the one for him, but he deserves first dibs."

6

JASMINE

Jasmine sat on the toilet and waited for her full bladder to empty, but instead of the gush she'd expected, there was only a trickle.

"Oh, crap. I hope I don't have a UTI or a bladder infection."

An intense urge to pee without much to show for it was a sure sign of one of those.

Nah, that was unlikely. She had drank plenty of liquids and hadn't been intimate with anyone since Alberto.

She was just nervous.

It wasn't smart to get the big boss annoyed, which would surely happen if she won again. Men didn't like losing to women, even more than they didn't like to lose to other men.

Fragile egos, one and all.

When she was done, Jasmine washed her hands, combed her locks with her fingers, and smacked her lips to plump them up.

Kian was a married man, and he wasn't interested in her, but it was always good to leave a good impression.

Satisfied with her appearance, she headed back to the lounge.

"I'm sure the queen would have loved to see her granddaughter and her great-grandchildren," Kian was telling Amanda as Jasmine entered. "It's a shame that's not possible."

"I'm not sure about that at all," his sister said. "The royals are a stuck-up bunch who won't approve of us."

Jasmine's heartbeat accelerated. No wonder they were so secretive about the passengers. There were royals on board.

The tarot had been right after all, and her prince was on board the ship.

"Which royals are you talking about?" She tried to sound nonchalant. "Anyone I know?" She walked over to the couch and sat down at the same spot she'd occupied before.

Amanda waved a dismissive hand. "Oh, it's a small, unimportant monarchy you have probably never heard of."

"Are they on board the ship? Is that why such extreme security measures are being employed?"

The brother and sister exchanged looks, and then Amanda shook her head. "I'm sorry, but it's confidential information."

"Oh, please." Jasmine rolled her eyes. "Who am I going to tell?" She leaned closer to Amanda. "Is there a single prince looking for a bride? Tell me just that, and I won't bug you anymore." *For now.*

Amanda laughed. "No, there are no single royal princes on board."

Jasmine tried to conceal her disappointment with a joke. "Of course not. Why would there be a prince for me?" She sighed dramatically. "Poisonous frogs seem to be my lot. It would have been nice to get a prince for a change. I mean, not a literal royal prince. Just, you know, a prince of a man. Someone kind and brave and true. Not like that scumbag Alberto who only pretended to be that kind of man." She lifted her gaze to Amanda. "Do good men even exist?"

"Sure they do." Amanda wrapped her arm around Kian's broad shoulders. "My brother is one of the best men I know, and so is my husband and many of the other men on this cruise. I should introduce you to some of them."

Jasmine's eyes widened. "You would do that for me? That would be awesome. I need someone sweet to wash away the rotten taste left over from Alberto."

Amanda grinned. "I have just the guy for the job." She leaned closer and whispered conspiratorially, "I won't tell him that I'm setting him up. I'll just tell him to keep an eye on you, and the rest is up to you."

If the tarot were right, her prince was awaiting her, but that didn't mean she couldn't have fun with a nice guy until she found him.

"That would be wonderful. Who is he?"

"Someone I think you will like, but if he's busy, I might have to send someone else, so I don't want to use any names."

"Understandable. Thank you." Jasmine took the card deck and started shuffling. "Are you up for another game?"

Amanda glanced at her watch. "I should have returned to the party by now, but I guess I can squeeze in another short game."

7

KIAN

The wistfulness in Jasmine's voice and the hope in her eyes tugged at Kian's conscience. She must be very lonely if she was so excited about Amanda's matchmaking, and in that moment, she looked young and innocent, a far cry from the confident, flirtatious woman who had been bantering with him and Amanda and handing them their asses at poker.

He also couldn't shake the feeling that she was important somehow and that the Fates had brought her into the clan's path for a reason.

When Jasmine had dealt the cards, Kian cleared his throat. "I'll consider your request to be allowed on the upper decks."

Amanda's head whipped toward him. "Who are you, and what have you done with my brother?"

He smiled. "I took into consideration what you said before. Besides, since Jasmine is not going home at the end of the cruise, the window of opportunity is longer than three days, especially if we put her up in the keep."

A smile spread over Amanda's face. "Good plan, brother of mine. I like it."

"I'm not going home?" Jasmine asked, looking surprised.

"I might not have been clear before, but the cartel thugs who are a potential threat to you and your family might come looking for you at your residence. We have a place in the city where you can stay until the danger is over."

Jasmine swallowed. "I have a job that I need to return to. It's not much, but it pays the bills, and I can't afford to lose it."

Kian leaned forward. "I was told that you work in customer service between the occasional acting jobs in commercials. How much do they pay you?"

She swallowed, looking embarrassed. "A little over minimum wage."

"Do you enjoy your job?"

"Not really."

He leaned back. "Then don't worry about it. If you lose it, I will find you something better."

Her eyes sparkled. "I would love to work at Perfect Match. Being a spokeswoman in their commercials would be a dream, but any other job would be great. I heard that employees get to be beta testers, and I would love to have access to the service without having to pay for it."

Kian smiled. "I happen to be very close to one of the owners. I can ask her on your behalf."

"Thank you." She reached for his hand. "Thank you so much."

He let her clasp it for a split second before pulling it out of her grip. "Don't thank me yet. Wait until I get you the job."

"Oh, my goddess." She fanned herself. "Perhaps I read the cards all wrong, and you are my prince."

Kian recoiled. "I am definitely not. I'm a married man."

"I didn't mean it that way." She squeezed her eyes shut for a moment. "Would you at least let me explain before biting my head off?"

Kian took a steadying breath. "I'm listening."

"I sometimes consult tarot cards for fun, and lately, I've been getting the prince card a lot. I thought that it meant I was going to meet my Prince Charming, but I might have interpreted it wrong, and the prince was not meant to be my romantic interest, but someone who would help me get a leg up in life."

"I see. Yes, well, I don't know much about tarot." He looked at Amanda. "Do you?"

"I don't know how to read them, but I've been to a fortune teller once or twice for a reading."

"Really?" Kian frowned at his sister. "Why would you consult someone who pretends to see the future in cards?"

She gave him a haughty look. "The cards are just a tool, a way for the gifted to channel their power. There are many charlatans, of course, but here and there, you can find real talent." She turned to Jasmine. "Are you a Wiccan?"

"Sort of. I don't belong to any coven, and the only Wiccans I know are in my social media worship group."

"Do you worship the goddess?"

Jasmine clutched the cards in her hand. "We are not idol worshipers or anything like that. We just revere the feminine aspect of divinity."

"That's very cool." Amanda put her cards down. "I dabbled a little in Wicca too, and I would love to chat more about it. But I should get back to the party before Cassandra sends out a search party for me." She pushed to her feet.

Kian glanced at his watch. He had less than an hour to get ready. For him, it was plenty of time, but not for Amanda. Also, Edna wouldn't be able to see Jasmine today.

Jasmine put her cards down as well. "Thank you," she said to Amanda, and then turned to Kian. "It was nice meeting you, and I'm sorry if I made you uncomfortable. I really didn't mean anything by it. You are very handsome, but I would never flirt with a married man." She scrunched her nose and looked at him from under lowered lashes. "Not seriously, anyway. Sometimes I just can't help myself."

"I know the feeling." Amanda patted Jasmine's shoulder. "You remind me a lot of myself a few years back, when I was still a single lady." She laughed. "I loved to flirt, and I loved the power I had over men, but I don't miss those days. Having Dalhu and Evie is so much more fulfilling than the endless chase after new thrills." She turned to Kian. "Are you coming?"

He'd hated the hunt, but then he was much older than Amanda and had been at it for too many years to count. Syssi was a boon from the Fates, for which he thanked them daily.

"Yes, I am." He looked at Jasmine. "I might send over a lady who has a talent similar to Kevin's to examine you. She has the ability to assess a person's intentions, and if she clears you, I will allow you to come up to the upper decks."

Grinning like she had just won the lottery, Jasmine reached for his hand but then reconsidered. "Thank you. I have nothing to hide, and I will do almost anything to be allowed to mingle with the guests. I can sing if you need additional entertainment."

They didn't have any entertainers other than the DJ. "I'll take it into account."

"Awesome." Jasmine clasped her hands, maybe to avoid reaching for his again. "What's the lady's name? The one who will come to assess me?"

"Edna. She will not have time to see you today, though. It will have to wait until tomorrow."

"Oh." Some of Jasmine's exuberance dimmed. "I hoped to attend tonight's wedding. Oh, well, there are two more to go, right?"

"That's right." Amanda hooked her arm through Kian's. "We need to go."

8

PETER

Peter adjusted his bowtie in front of the full-length mirror in the cabin's small foyer. Beside him, Jay did the same.

"I love weddings, but I hate these penguin suits," Jay grumbled, stretching his neck. "How about we suggest a new wedding tradition with no tuxedos, no suits, and no starchy white shirts?"

Peter cast his roommate an amused sidelong glance. "At least we don't have to wear high heels and tight dresses, so stop complaining and man up. Besides, you look dashing." He batted his eyelashes and put a hand over his chest. "Larissa is going to swoon."

Jay looked a lot like the young Beckham, and women went gaga over him.

His roommate snorted. "Instead of commiserating with our female partners, we should liberate them as well. No high heels and no corsets."

Peter frowned. "Do they still wear those? I mean, aside from wedding gowns."

Jay shrugged. "Sure they do. They are just made with better fabrics now. Don't tell me that you've never bedded a girl wearing Spanx."

"If I did, I didn't know what they were."

The brand name, which he assumed Spanx was, evoked memories of women's undies with cutouts for the ass cheeks to make them easily accessible for spanking. Naturally, thinking about it had a predictable effect, and he adjusted himself.

"They are not sexy," Jay said as he noticed what Peter was doing. "They make women's bodies look like sausages, and they are really hard to take off. I hate them."

"Are you okay?" Peter turned to face his friend. "You are usually not this grumpy."

Jay was a ladies' man, so it couldn't be because he was nervous about his date with Larissa. If anyone should feel nervous, it should be the girl.

It would be her first time attending a party as a guest, not a server, and there was also the language barrier. She spoke very little English, and Jay spoke even less Russian.

"I'm fine." Jay collected his phone from the table and put it in his pocket. "I hope Larissa will have a good time. Marina was a nervous wreck when she accompanied you to Vlad and Wendy's wedding, and she's much more confident than Larissa."

"Marina and I will stay close in case you need a translator."

"Thank you." Jay's lips curved up on one side of his mouth. "But I might not need help. I took a crash course in Russian over the past three days. I'm far from fluent, but at least I will understand what she's saying."

Peter hadn't known that. "That's a lot of effort for a girl you are not going to see after the cruise ends."

Jay shrugged. "Knowing another language is an asset. Besides, many of the Kra-ell are still struggling with English, and knowing Russian will help me communicate with them." He opened the door. "I can't wait to see Larissa's face when I greet her in Russian."

"Good luck." Peter followed him out the door.

When they reached the girls' cabin, Jay rang the doorbell, and a moment later, the door swung open to reveal Larissa, looking lovely but a little overwhelmed in a flowing purple dress and a pair of sensible black flats.

"Hello," she said with a bright smile as she stepped out of the tiny cabin.

Jay immediately launched into a string of Russian phrases, his accent passable, if a little overly enthusiastic, and Larissa's eyes widened in surprise and delight.

Craning her neck to look at Jay, she responded in English, "I can talk a little bit, too."

"Larissa needs to practice." Marina stepped out from the cabin in a figure-hugging, short black dress that showcased her long, toned legs. "She finally has an incentive to learn English, so don't start talking Russian to her."

Peter knew that dress. It was a loaner from Jessica, and he made a mental note to thank his cousin again for her generous donation to Marina's evening wear arsenal.

Jay's face fell. "I studied so hard so I could communicate with Larissa, and now you are telling me that it was for nothing?"

As Larissa's eyes darted between Marina and Jay, her smile turned strained, and she clutched her small fabric purse while shifting from foot to foot.

"It wasn't for nothing," Peter said, wrapping his arm around Marina's waist. "You can teach each other." He started toward the elevators.

"You look incredible," he whispered in her ear.

Her vivid cobalt-colored hair looked like a bolt of electric energy against the backdrop of her pale skin and black dress, and the red lipstick provided another vivid splash of color.

A self-conscious smile tugged at her lips. "Thanks."

Was it his imagination, or was there a tension in her jaw and a tightness around her eyes?

"Hey," Peter whispered, leaning closer. "Is everything okay? You seem a little out of sorts."

Marina's smile faltered, just for a second, before she hitched it back into place. "I'm great," she assured him. "Just excited about the wedding tonight. Onegus is an important guy, right? The chief Guardian and all that."

Peter doubted that was the reason. "Did you speak to Amanda about your wish to move into the village?"

She nodded. "She told me to wait until I get back to Safe Haven and ask either Eleanor or Emmett to request the transfer on my behalf."

"That's what I suggested."

"I know. I just hoped that Amanda being Kian's sister could wave a magic wand and make it happen instantaneously, so I was a little disappointed."

As Peter pressed the button for the elevator, Jay and Larissa caught up to them.

"Onegus's wedding will be just like all the others," Jay said.

"Not necessarily." Peter held the door open for everyone before getting in. "Cassandra is a hotshot art director, so she might have put her own spin on the decor."

That seemed to pique Marina's interest. "An art director? For what company?"

"Some big cosmetics brand," Peter said with a shrug. "Something with fifty shades, like the movie."

A blush colored Marina's cheeks. "Did you see it? I mean, the movie?"

"No. I heard it was awful."

"It was," Jay confirmed. "I heard that the books were much better."

9

MARINA

M arina's stomach was churning as she walked alongside Peter, her arm linked through his. She knew she needed to come clean, to tell him the truth about her initial motivation for pursuing him, but it was so damn hard. Larissa was right, though. Secrets had no place in a relationship.

On the other hand, Peter had made it very clear that he was not interested in having a relationship with her when she moved to the village, so why bother?

On the remote chance that he would change his mind?

But why would he? She had maybe two more decades of being attractive, if that, and then she would look old.

It was so damn depressing.

Why couldn't she be like Sofia?

Sofia's mother was a hybrid Kra-ell and her father was a human, which was a rare combination. In fact, she was the only human whose mother was a hybrid Kra-ell, and as it turned out, the longevity came from the mother's side.

Well, in Marina's case both her parents were human, so she had nothing of the kind.

Besides, Peter might never forgive her and dump her even before the end of the cruise.

Oh, dear Mother above. It was almost over. They were almost over.

"Are you okay?" Peter asked. "You seem tense."

Marina forced a smile, hoping it didn't look as brittle as it felt. "I'm fine. You know how uncomfortable I am mingling with your kind."

He frowned. "I thought you'd gotten over that. You survived one wedding and even got to enjoy yourself. Why the sudden nerves?"

She scrambled for an answer. What she'd told him hadn't been entirely untrue. She still felt like an imposter, playing dress-up in a world she didn't belong in. But that wasn't the reason she was so tense.

"It's the chief Guardian's wedding. Are you sure he won't mind having an uninvited guest at his party?"

Peter lifted her hand to his lips for a kiss. "You are an invited guest. You are my plus one."

Marina stopped. "What do you mean? What's plus one?"

He chuckled. "I keep forgetting that you know so little of the outside world. When people receive an invitation to an event, they need to respond and inform the host whether they are coming or not and how many people are in their party. When it's just the guest and their partner, they respond with plus one."

Marina looked confused by his explanation, but she nodded. "I think I get it. But you couldn't have responded with a plus one because you didn't know about me."

"I was speaking metaphorically." Peter led her to the main promenade bar and swiveled a stool for her so it was easier for her to slide on top of it.

Vasyli, who was the barman on duty tonight, gave her and Larissa a bright smile. "You both look so beautiful," he said in Russian.

"Thank you," Larissa said in English. "Can I have a glass of vodka with orange juice, please?"

Marina had had her memorize that one sentence, and she'd said it perfectly.

Vasyli's eyes widened. "When did you learn to speak English?"

Larissa's cheeks got red. "Only a little bit."

He turned to Marina. "What can I get for you?"

"The same."

He looked at Peter. "And for you, sir?"

"Nothing for me or my friend. We have to leave shortly." He lifted his wrist to look at his watch. "The ceremony will start in ten minutes." He leaned in to kiss Marina's forehead. "I'll come get you as soon as the doors open."

She nodded.

Humans were not allowed in the dining room during the ceremony, and Marina tried to imagine what secret stuff was happening behind the dining room's closed doors. Were the immortals conducting some sacred ritual that no one was allowed to see?

She would have preferred to wait for Peter in the kitchen like she had done the first time he had taken her to a wedding. Being elbow-deep in dirty dishes and preparing canapés would have kept her occupied and distracted from the gnawing anxiety in her gut.

It was better than sipping on her cocktail and trying not to fidget while the weight of her impending confession pressed like an anvil on her chest.

"You're making a mess of that napkin," Larissa remarked, nodding at the shredded paper beneath Marina's restless fingers. "What's going on with you?"

Marina took a fortifying sip of her drink, but the burn of the alcohol did little to calm her nerves. "I'm scared," she admitted, her voice barely above a whisper. "I'm a gutless worm who is terrified of telling Peter the truth." She sighed. "I don't even know why. It's not like what I did was so terrible. Women do those things all the time. Men too."

Larissa's eyes softened with understanding. She reached out, covering Marina's hand with her own. "If Peter truly cares for you, he'll understand, and he'll forgive you. And if he doesn't, then he's not worth your love."

The word love prompted her to take another fortifying sip from her drink and then another. She loved Peter, but he didn't love her back. Not enough, anyway.

"Hello, darlings." Amanda glided into the bar with her husband, looking like a movie star in a silver floor-length gown. "I have five minutes before I need to escort the bride to the altar, but I'm in desperate need of a drink." She cast Vasyli a charming smile. "I need something quick. Apple martini?"

"Coming up, miss."

While Amanda was all charming smiles, her husband was an intimidating mountain of a man, with bulging muscles that strained against the confines of his tuxedo and a stern, almost forbidding air about him.

"You two look absolutely stunning," Amanda drawled. "Stand up so I can get a better look at you."

"Thank you." Marina pushed to her feet. "You look as amazing as always."

The immortal was the most beautiful woman Marina had ever seen, and she was also super nice, which was surprising on several counts. Amanda was not only gorgeous, but she was also the leader's sister and a council member. People like her were usually stuck-up and condescending, but she wasn't like that at all.

In fact, Marina had expected all the immortals to be as haughty and full of themselves as the Kra-ell purebloods had been, but most were nice and friendly and treated the staff serving them with respect.

Amanda waved off the compliment and snatched the martini from Vasyli.

Taking a sip, she fixed her gaze on Larissa. "You, my dear, are a vision in that dress," she said in Russian. "I knew that you would look marvelous in purple."

Larissa blushed, smoothing a hand over the fabric. "I can't thank you enough for lending it to me. I feel like a princess."

"You look like one, too," Amanda reached for a lock of Larissa's hair. "Did you style it, or did Marina do it for you?"

"Marina did my hair and makeup," Larissa said.

"I must say, Marina, you've done an exquisite job." Amanda put a hand on her shoulder. "You can sit back down." She smiled at the bartender. "The martini is excellent, thank you."

"You are welcome, miss." Vasyli bowed his head.

Amanda's husband didn't ask for anything and remained standing behind her like a protective boulder.

A pang of jealousy pierced Marina's heart. She wanted a man like him who would stand guard over her. Not that she needed a guard now that she'd been liberated, but back when she'd been in the compound, helpless to object to any demand from the Kra-ell, she'd often fantasized about having a strong protector like that.

Amanda turned to her husband and offered him a brilliant smile. "Would you like a drink before we have to go?"

"No, thank you." He looked at her with so much adoration in his eyes that Marina's jealousy inflated into a big, ugly, dark balloon.

NEGAL

"There is nothing for miles around," Margo's mother said. "Your father and I have just taken a walk, and the air was so fresh and crisp. It's good to get out of the city once in a while."

"I'm glad that you are enjoying your time off," Margo told her mother.

After her family had been given a secure line, Kian had also allowed their new contact information to be added to Margo's phone so she could call them.

The problem was that her family had been given her contact information as well, and so far, her mother had called five times and her future sister-in-law had called twice, putting Margo's brother on the line for all of thirty seconds to ask how she was doing.

Her mother sighed. "It's nice for a day or two, even a week, but we don't know when we will be allowed to go back. Do you have any updates on how long we will have to hide out here?"

"I've already told you. Hopefully, less than two weeks. I have to go, Mom. Someone needs to talk to me."

Negal smiled at the small lie and moved his lips, pretending to be talking, and making Margo choke on a chuckle that came out sounding like a cough.

"Are you sick?" Margo's mother sounded worried. "Why are you coughing?"

"Just a dry throat. I need to drink something."

"Okay. Call me when you can."

"I will." Margo ended the call and dropped the phone with a sigh. "I love them to pieces, but they are driving me crazy. I'm tired and achy, and I don't have any patience, but if I tell my mother how I feel, she will start freaking out, and I really don't have the patience for that either."

Smiling, Negal gathered her into his arms so she was nestled against his chest. "Rest, Nesha. If they call again, I will answer for you and tell them that you are asleep."

Margo chuckled softly. "Then they will want to know who you are." She turned to look up at him. "What do I tell them about you?"

"That I'm your fabulous new paramour, and that you are madly in love with me, and that we are going on an expedition to Tibet."

She snorted. "Yeah, and that will fly so well with them. They will think that you are manipulating me and demand to meet you." She sighed. "I'm never that rash, and they know it. I take weeks to plan a weekend in Vegas."

Negal hadn't known that about her, but he should have. Margo was cautious in every aspect of her life, not just who she took to her bed.

"I hope Aru gets an extension from your commander," she said. "He promised that he would try if I start transitioning, and I have." She scrunched her nose. "At least, I think I am. I hope I am. Otherwise, I will get really worried about what's wrong with me."

"You are transitioning, my love. Even Kian said so, and he's the biggest skeptic I know."

The truth was that Negal was almost certain that Margo was transitioning, but he wasn't a hundred percent sure. He was waiting for Frankie and Dagor to leave for the wedding and for Margo to doze off so he could give her a transfusion of his blood.

Dagor had told him where he'd stashed the rest of the disposable syringes he'd pilfered from the clinic, so all that was required now was the right opportunity.

As Dagor and Frankie's bedroom door opened and the two stepped into the living room, Margo tried to whistle, but all that came out was a whoosh of air.

"You two look hot," she said. "I wish I could come with you."

"You can." Frankie patted the elaborate up-do she'd created. "You can put on something comfortable and spend the evening sitting in a chair. You don't have to do anything strenuous."

"It's okay." Margo smiled. "Negal and I will watch the wedding from here. They are broadcasting it live."

"I know." Frankie grinned. "I was in your shoes not too long ago."

Dagor wrapped his arm around his mate's waist. "We need to go, or we will be late. They lock the doors as soon as the bride walks in, and we will not be allowed in."

"Yeah, I know." Frankie cast one last sad look at Margo. "Feel better, bestie." She blew her a kiss and then flounced toward the front door with Dagor.

When the door closed behind them, Margo pulled the blanket up to her chin and yawned. "I'm so tired."

"Then sleep." Negal shifted her so her head was on the pillow, and then lifted her legs so she was supine.

"I don't want to miss the ceremony." She waved a feeble hand in the direction of the television. "Can you please find the channel they are broadcasting it on?"

"Of course."

She'd dozed off several times during the afternoon, but she'd refused to go to the bedroom and get a proper sleep as long as the others were around, and since her family had kept calling her, she wouldn't have gotten much sleep anyway.

Negal perched on the edge of the couch beside her. "I'll wake you up when it starts. You've been taking catnaps for the past couple of hours, and they seem to help you."

Margo nodded and then yawned again. "It's about to start shortly. I can sleep after it's done."

That was true, but he wasn't sure she would be able to keep her eyes open for much longer. Besides, he was itching to be done with the transfusion. The sooner she got it, the sooner she would get better.

"I wish Jasmine could at least watch the weddings on the screen." Margo curled on her side, facing the television. "She must be going out of her mind down there, all alone without even the staff to keep her company."

"I'm sure not everyone is working, and some people stayed behind." He reached for the remote and turned the television on. "She'll be fine."

Margo's concern for those she cared about was one of the many things he loved about her, but in this case, her worry was misplaced. Jasmine was safe in the staff area, and if Negal was being honest, he wasn't entirely sure he trusted the woman with her overly charming smiles and calculating eyes. Her scent was fresh and devoid of any undertones of deceit, but emotional scents were not the equivalent of a truth detector. Sometimes, they lied.

Margo didn't look entirely convinced that her friend was fine, but she allowed herself to be distracted as the screen filled up with a sweeping shot of the dining room.

"Wow, look at that," Margo breathed. "The place looks completely different every night. It's amazing what a transformation they can create with just the help of colorful lighting."

More than that went into decorating the ship's grand dining room and turning it into a space worthy of a gala, but she was right about the strategically placed colorful beams of light being the most impactful.

As the camera panned over the glittering tables and the array of immortals in their finest attire, Negal's thoughts drifted to the transfusion.

It wouldn't be enough for her to fall asleep for him to do the deed. As soon as he injected her, she would wake up from the needle jab, and he would have to explain what he had done and why.

Negal needed to thrall Margo whether he liked it or not, and the thought made his stomach twist with unease.

It was a betrayal of her trust, even though it was necessary.

Kian was not willing to compromise on the issue of letting any more people know about the miraculous healing powers of a god's blood, and even though Negal didn't answer to Kian, he answered to Aru, and Aru had promised Kian to guard the secret.

Besides, Kian was the Anumati heir's son, and even though he could never become an heir himself because he was a hybrid, he still deserved Negal's deference.

Mind made up, Negal took her hand and looked into her eyes. "Margo, my love."

She turned to him. "Yes?"

"Nothing." He smiled. "I just love looking into your eyes."

He reached inside her mind and gently wove the suggestion to sleep into her thoughts, his mental voice a soothing whisper against the edges of her consciousness.

"You're so tired, my love," he murmured aloud while making her feel her eyelids growing heavy, her limbs slacking and relaxing.

Nothing would rouse her from this slumber save a sweet kiss from her mate's lips.

He watched Margo's eyes flutter shut and a small, contented smile curve her lips. She looked so peaceful, so serene, that he was tempted to lean down and kiss her, but his kiss was what would wake her up, so he had to stifle the impulse and continue with his plan.

Retrieving the syringe from Frankie and Dagor's room, he tore the wrapping off on his way back to the couch.

Negal sat down, uncapped the needle, and positioned it against his inner elbow. By now, he was a veteran at this, and as he jabbed the needle into his vein, he didn't even flinch. After withdrawing about half an ounce, he took Margo's hand and moved the needle to the same spot on her inner elbow.

One quick prick, and it was done. Negal watched as the small quantity of his blood flowed into Margo's vein, and when there was nothing left, he withdrew the needle and pressed his finger to the spot. Then he licked it, sealing the tiny puncture, and was happy to see that the spot in Margo's inner elbow looked pristine.

With the procedure done, he collected what he had used and took it to his and Margo's bedroom. He couldn't risk anyone discovering the evidence in the trash bin, so he put the syringe back into its wrapping and stashed it in a pocket of his suitcase to discard later.

The transfusion was a small deception, a white lie told in service of a greater truth, but it still sat heavy on his chest.

Pushing the feeling aside, Negal returned to Margo's side. As his hand ghosted over her cheek in a feather-light caress, she stirred slightly at his touch, her lips parting with a soft sigh. He leaned down and brushed his lips against hers, the contact sending a jolt of electricity humming through his veins.

Her eyelids fluttered open. "Mmm," Margo murmured, her voice husky with sleep. "Did I miss anything? Has the wedding started?"

Negal forced a smile, hoping it didn't look as strained as it felt. "Not yet, my love. You dozed off for only a few minutes."

Margo lifted a hand to her face and rubbed her eyes. "That's strange. It felt like such a deep sleep. I've never slept so deeply for such a short time before."

A pang of remorse lanced through him, but he pushed it down, burying it beneath a layer of practiced nonchalance.

"Your body is going through a major change, and it needs rest, but you are fighting it because you are adamant about watching the wedding ceremony in real time. You know that you can watch it later, right?"

"I know, but it's not going to be as impactful as seeing it as it happens. I'm so curious to hear Onegus's vows. He's such an enigmatic guy."

Negal's jealousy flared. "In what way?"

Margo shrugged. "He's the chief Guardian, which I assume is like a general, but he looks and acts like a politician, charming and smiling and all that."

"Yeah, you're right. I've never thought of that. I think he's also a council member, so maybe he has some political aspirations."

"Is the clan a democracy? Could he run for office and replace Kian?"

Margo sounded worried, which was interesting. She didn't know either of the males well, but she'd spent some time in their presence, and it seemed that she had a preference for Kian.

"I don't think so, but I'm not part of the clan, so I don't know its inner workings."

Margo's gaze drifted to the television screen, and Negal's followed just as the camera panned over the assembled guests.

"They are all so pretty," she murmured. "Look, that's Frankie and Mia."

"I see them." He shifted his eyes to his mate, whose face was alight with excitement. "And I see you, my beautiful Nesha. My soul."

11

ONEGUS

Onegus stood at the altar, waiting for the female he loved more than anyone and anything in the world to enter and join him in front of the goddess.

He still remembered his reaction to her the first time he'd seen her at the fundraiser gala. She'd stood out from the crowd in every way possible. Confident, elegant, statuesque, and with ferocious eyes that could pierce through armor. They had certainly pierced through his.

Up until that moment, he had never believed in love at first sight, but he was a believer now. With one look, he had fallen head over heels, but it had taken him a few days to convince his brain of what his heart had known from that first connection formed from a distance in a crowd of over one thousand guests.

Come to think of it, the gala had been a much grander venue than his and Cassandra's wedding in the ship's converted dining room, but what it lacked in luxury and opulence, it made up with heart, and there was no competition. He would choose to be here a thousand times over. Almost his entire clan was present, their familiar smiling faces turned toward the entrance through which his bride was about to walk in.

As the music swelled and the guests rose to their feet, Onegus felt his breath catch in his throat. There, at the end of the aisle, Cassandra stood tall in a one-of-a-kind gown that seemed to have been crafted from liquid pearls. The dress lacked any of the embellishments so many of the other brides had favored. There was no lace, no tulle, no beading, just simple satin that flowed over Cassandra's gorgeous statuesque frame. Barely-there straps held a cowl neckline, and although he couldn't see the back, it seemed like it was exposed.

Her hair was swept up in an elegant twist, with a few wayward tendrils left loose to frame her beautiful face, and her luminous, expressive eyes held Onegus's gaze.

There was joy, love, and determination in her big brown eyes, and as her lips lifted in a smile that seemed to be just for him, he lifted a hand to his heart and patted the spot, letting her know without words what seeing her on the other end of the aisle was doing to him.

Cassandra glided toward him with her mother on one side and her sister on the other, and as she reached the altar, Geraldine placed her daughter's hand in his. He squeezed her fingers gently, and she rewarded him with a radiant smile before turning to face the Clan Mother.

Annani regarded them with a serene smile, her ancient, wise eyes, which belied her youthful appearance, shining with affection and approval.

The goddess raised her glowing arms and waited until the guests' excited murmurs quieted.

When the hall was utterly silent, she lowered them. "My beloved family and friends," she said in her melodious voice. "Tonight, we are gathered to celebrate the union of two souls, two hearts that have found each other across a room not much different than this one." She waved a hand over the dining hall. "Onegus never imagined that the gala he chaired would not only raise millions for our charity but also bring him the love of his life."

As Onegus felt Cassandra's fingers tightening around his, he ran his thumb over her knuckles in a soothing caress.

His groomsmen were worried about her getting overly emotional and unintentionally blowing something up, but he knew his bride well, and positive emotions did not cause her inner power to rise.

Hopefully, all of tonight would be joyful for her, and nothing would irritate her.

Annani shifted her gaze to the two of them and smiled. "Onegus and Cassandra. You are both highly accomplished, powerful people, and together, there is no limit to what you can achieve. I have no doubt that your love story will be told for generations to come." She smiled brightly. "And I cannot wait to see the children your union will produce."

As laughter mingled with murmurs of agreement, Onegus cast Cassandra a sidelong smile, which she returned. They were too busy to have children anytime soon, but when they did, he knew that they would be spectacular.

"Onegus," Annani said, drawing his attention. "You have given selflessly to the clan for many centuries, leading the Guardian force with a strong hand but also with devotion and compassion. Your people love you, and that is the highest honor a commander could hope for. You have more than earned the boon of a fated mate the Fates have bestowed upon you. None other than the granddaughter of my cousin Toven."

Onegus dipped his head.

Cassandra was even closer to her godly source than he was, but he never really thought about it. He loved her for who she was and not the blood coursing through her veins.

"Cassandra." The Clan Mother turned to his bride. "Your strength, resilience, and your dedication to those you love is as inspiring as that of your mate. You have faced challenges that would have broken a lesser woman, and yet you have emerged stronger, brighter, and more successful. You are a true winner."

As Geraldine sniffled, Cassandra gracefully inclined her head. "Thank you, Clan Mother."

Annani smiled. "Cassandra and Onegus. You have each made sacrifices to support those you care about and have proven that love can conquer all. Love knows no boundaries, it can overcome any obstacle, weather any storm, and emerge victorious on the other side."

She paused, signaling to their guests that it was okay to clap, cheer, and hoot, and when she lifted her arms, everyone quieted again. "Before I bless your union and pronounce you bonded for life, would you like to recite your vows to each other?"

"Yes, we would," Cassandra said.

12

CASSANDRA

Cassandra had never considered herself overly emotional. She'd prided herself on being pragmatic, assertive, and as far from a softie as could be. And yet as she stood at the altar with her hand clasped firmly in Onegus's, she was overwhelmed, and not just because she was officially marrying the male she loved above all.

So much had happened since that first meeting at the gala. She had discovered that her forgetful mother, whom she had been taking care of since she was a young girl, was a demigoddess who had suffered a traumatic brain injury that would have killed even an immortal. She also discovered that she had an older sister, a grown-up nephew who was a gifted hacker, an uncle who was a demigod who had been helping her and her mother since day one, and, to top it all, her grandfather was a god.

It was all so unbelievable that she often expected to wake up one morning and realize that it had all been a dream because stuff like that just didn't happen to normal people. But then, Cassandra had always known that she was different. Normal people couldn't blow things up with a thought or stop someone's heart, but she could, and she had done both.

Oh boy. Talk about inappropriate thoughts at a time like this.

Turning to her groom, her mate, the love of her life, she saw the same emotions reflected in his smiling, blue eyes.

"Onegus, my love. When I first met you, I thought I had you all figured out. I thought I knew exactly who you were—just another rich, charming playboy looking for his next conquest."

A ripple of laughter went through the crowd, and Onegus's lips twitched with amusement, his eyes sparkling with mirth.

"But you are so much more than that. You are kind and generous and so unbelievably patient. When you decided that I was the one for you, you took the time to get to know me, to understand me, and to love me for all that I am, flaws and punch bowls blowing up and all."

She paused as another wave of laughter swept through the crowd. "You have become my sanctuary and my home. You believe in me, support me, and you love me with a fierceness that takes my breath away."

Onegus's hand tightened around hers, his eyes shining with love.

"And so, today, I vow to be your partner in life, to stand by your side through every triumph and every challenge, to love you with every fiber of my being, and to cherish every moment we have together. You are my heart, my soul, and my forever. And I promise to spend every day of our forever showing you just how much you mean to me." She pulled her hand out of his and extended it to her sister, who handed her a ring. "I, Cassandra, daughter of Geraldine, granddaughter of Toven, take thee, Onegus, son of Martha, as my forever mate, to love and to hold in this world and the next." She slipped the simple gold circle on his finger. "I'm never letting you go."

As she finished, a single tear escaped down her cheek.

Onegus reached up with his free hand to brush it away. "Cassandra, my love, my light. From the moment I first saw you, I knew that you were unlike anyone else I've ever encountered, and given how old I am, that's saying something." A few chuckles sounded from the crowd, but he continued. "I knew that you were a force to be reckoned with, a woman of strength, intelligence, and incredible beauty, inside and out."

Cassandra smiled as she felt her heart swell with love and gratitude for this incredible male who had swept into her life and changed everything.

"Winning your heart has been the greatest adventure of my life. Our love was explosive from the very start." He paused to let the crowd clap and cheer. "You've brought so much excitement to my life, and given what I deal with day in and day out, that's saying something as well." He cast a sidelong glance at the crowd. "Being with you is a joy and a blessing that I thank the Fates for every day." He lifted their joined hands to his lips, pressing a kiss to her knuckles. "And so, today, I vow to be your husband, your mate, and your best friend. I vow to support you in all your endeavors, to catch you when you stumble, and to celebrate every victory by your side. I vow to love you fiercely, passionately, and unconditionally for all the days of our lives."

Cassandra's vision blurred with tears, her heart so full she thought it might explode.

Oh boy. Don't think about explosions.

"You are my everything, Cassandra. My reason for being, my guiding star, and my home. And I promise to spend every moment of forever cherishing you, honoring you, and loving you with every beat of my heart." He pulled a ring out of his pocket. "I, Onegus, son of Martha, take thee, Cassandra, daughter of Geraldine, granddaughter of Toven, as my forever mate, to love and to hold in this world and beyond." He slipped the ring on her finger.

As he finished, Annani stepped forward once more. "By the power vested in me by the Fates and in the presence of your loved ones, I pronounce you bonded mates, partners in life, in love, and in all things. You may now kiss."

As Onegus pulled Cassandra into his arms, his lips meeting hers in a passionate kiss, she hooked her arms around his neck and kissed him back.

13

PETER

Peter cast a sidelong glance at Jay, who was clapping, whooping, and whistling, enthusiastically adding noise to the ruckus the Guardians were making in honor of their chief's nuptials.

Not wishing to be outdone, Peter stuck two fingers in his mouth and emitted a whistle loud enough to rouse a firehouse.

The cheering went on during the kiss that the newlywed couple performed for their audience, and it didn't quiet down until Onegus took Cassandra's hand and led her to the dance floor for the first dance of the evening.

Peter glanced at the doors to the dining room, and when he saw them open, he clapped Jay on his back. "Let's go. Our dates are waiting for us."

The Clan Mother had departed through a secret passage that took her to one of the staff elevators that had been blocked off just for her.

Jay shook his head, looking like he'd awoken from a daze. "Yeah. Wow, that was something else." He shook his head. "I would have never imagined Onegus could deliver such a mushy speech."

"Mushy?" Peter arched a brow. "It wasn't mushy. Compared to the others, it was damn funny. I laughed so hard when he talked about Cassandra blowing up the punch bowl. At first, he covered up for her, but later, they both admitted that it was her doing." He started toward the exit.

"I remember." Jay fell into step with him. "I wasn't fond of Cassandra at first. She seemed a little standoffish, but later I realized that it was a defense mechanism. She lived in constant fear of accidentally blowing things up and harming people."

"Yeah, must have been tough. She didn't know what the hell was wrong with her."

Peter still thought that Cassandra was a little snooty, but if she made Onegus happy, which she obviously did, then he had absolutely no problem with her. He thought about Marina and her shifting moods. She'd been a little off today, probably shaken by her admission that she wanted more from him than he could give her.

He would have loved nothing more than to invite her to live with him in his house, but what would be fun in the short term would be excruciatingly painful in the long run, and he had to be smart about it.

As they approached the bar, the sound of laughter drifted to meet them. But there was an edge to it, a brittle quality that set Peter's teeth on edge.

Rounding the corner, they found Marina and Larissa, where they had left them less than an hour ago. They were still perched on the same barstools, but now their cheeks were flushed, and their eyes were a little too bright.

"Peter!" Marina's voice was screechy and loud. "And Jay! You are finally back." She leaned over to her friend. "Larissa and me, we thought that you forgot about us."

"Never," Peter said.

As he walked over to her, Marina started to slide off the stool, but wobbled precariously, and as he caught her, she fell into his arms with a giggle and a burp. "Sorry." She put a hand over her mouth and giggled again.

"Someone had a glass or two too many," he murmured. "How many have you had?"

Marina waved a dismissive hand. "I don't know. Ask Vasyli."

Beside them, Jay was helping Larissa off her own stool. He looked concerned even though his date didn't look half as inebriated as Marina.

Peter turned to the bartender. "How much did Marina have?"

"A lot." Vasyli smiled sheepishly. "I tell them both it was too much," he said in heavily accented English. "But they don't listen."

Marina's head whipped around, her eyes narrowing into a glare. "You're such a lousy bartender," she accused, her words slurring slightly. "You just broke the sacred trust between a customer and their barman. You released confidential information to a third party."

Peter bit back a smile at her drunken indignation. Even three sheets to the wind, his girl was a firecracker.

"I'm hungry," Larissa announced, leaning heavily against Jay. "Let's go inside and have dinner," she said in Russian, probably forgetting that Marina wanted her to practice her English. "The kitchen is serving beef Stroganoff tonight, and it's my favorite."

Jay seemed to understand what she'd said and started toward the dining hall but then stopped and looked over his shoulder. "Are you coming?"

"You two go ahead. We'll catch up in a bit."

Peter tightened his hold on his unsteady date. "Hey." He brushed a strand of blue hair off her forehead. "How about we step outside for a little bit? Some fresh air will do you good."

"Great idea." She nodded. "It might help, or I might puke over the railing. One of the two."

Peter chuckled. "Throwing up will be good for you too. You will feel better after that."

He glanced over at Vasyli, who was watching the exchange with amusement in his eyes. "Do you have any bottled water back there?"

When the bartender nodded and reached beneath the bar, Peter held up two fingers. "I'll take two, just in case. And a bunch of napkins, please."

He hoped Marina wouldn't throw up, but if she did, he wanted to be prepared.

As Vasyli handed over the bottles and the napkins, Peter stuffed the items into the pockets of his tuxedo jacket.

"Come on, sweetheart," he murmured, wrapping an arm around her waist and guiding her towards the terrace doors. "Let's get you some fresh air."

As they stepped out into the cool night and leaned against the railing, the salty tang of the ocean filled their lungs, and the night breeze caressed Marina's flushed cheeks.

The tension in her shoulders eased, and she tipped her head back to gaze up at the star-strewn sky. "It's beautiful out here," she whispered. "Peaceful."

Peter hummed in agreement, his own eyes drinking in the soft glow of the moonlight on her face. "Not as beautiful as you," he said, the words slipping out before he could stop them.

Marina's gaze snapped to his, her eyes wide and shining in the darkness. For a long moment, they stared at each other, the air between them crackling with tension.

He lifted a hand to cup her cheek. "What's wrong, sweetheart? Are you nervous about attending the wedding party?"

Marina opened her mouth to answer but then lurched forward, her hand flying to her mouth. "I'm gonna be sick," she mumbled, her words muffled behind her fingers.

Springing into action, Peter spun her towards the railing, one hand gathering her hair back while the other rubbed soothing circles between her shoulder blades.

Marina retched, her slender frame shuddering as she emptied the contents of her stomach into the dark water below.

When she was done, he turned her to face him, fishing a napkin out of his pocket and wiping her mouth as gently as he could and handed her a bottle of water to drink from.

"Thank you." She gurgled with some of the water, spit it out over the railing, and then drank the rest.

"Feeling better?" he asked.

Marina nodded, her eyes glassy with tears and something that looked a lot like shame. "I'm sorry." Reaching into her purse, she pulled out a box of mints and popped a bunch of them into her mouth.

Peter shook his head. "It's not a big deal. Happened to me on more than one occasion." Actually, he'd never gotten drunk enough to puke his guts out, but he didn't want her to feel embarrassed.

"You don't understand," Marina murmured. "I ruined everything."

He frowned. "What are you talking about? You didn't ruin anything."

Was she referring to her earlier admission that she wanted to move in with him?

He pulled her into his arms, tucking her head beneath his chin and running a soothing hand down her back. "You couldn't ruin anything even if you tried."

The truth of his words reverberated in his mind against the backdrop of the distant strains of music drifting out from the dining room and the crash of waves against the hull filling the night air.

Peter wanted Marina in his house just as much as she wanted to be there. He just hadn't had the guts to admit it or to act on it.

14

MARINA

The cool night air washed over Marina, helping clear her mind while Peter's arm around her waist provided a steadying presence. She leaned into him, grateful for his solid strength, for the way he seemed to anchor her even as the world tilted and spun around her.

She hadn't meant to drink so much. She hadn't planned on drowning her sorrows in endless glasses of too-sweet cocktails. But watching the gorgeous bride and her bridesmaids get ready to enter the dining hall, resplendent in their designer gowns and glowing with joy, had triggered an ache inside of her that was too difficult to overcome.

She'd hoped the alcohol would help, which was stupid because it never did. It only made things worse.

Marina was happy for the bride and groom and wished them all the happiness in the world, but she wanted what the bride had—the beautiful dress that was precisely what Marina would have chosen for her own wedding if she could afford it, and the wonderful, loving groom waiting for her at the altar and feeling like the luckiest man alive because this amazing woman had chosen him.

But that wish felt further out of reach than ever before, a distant mirage shimmering on the horizon of a cloudy future.

Marina didn't have a wonderful groom waiting for her at the altar. Her fiancé had dumped her for another woman, and she didn't even have a boyfriend. What she had was a web of lies and half-truths, a house of cards that was about to come tumbling down the moment she confessed her scheming to Peter.

And she would confess because she had to, and not just because she'd promised Larissa she would do it. A sort of morbid curiosity urged her to tell Peter the truth and witness his reaction.

Would he forgive her?

Or would he use it as an excuse to dump her right now?

The thought of watching the warmth in his eyes turn to hurt and betrayal was terrifying, but evidently, she was a masochist, and not just in bed.

Mother of All Life, help me do the right thing.

Tears stinging her eyes, Marina blinked them back furiously. She was tired of crying, tired of feeling defeated and unworthy.

Peter's arm tightened around her, his fingers splaying over her hip. "Hey," he murmured, his breath warm against her temple. "What's going on in that head of yours?"

Marina shivered, not because she was cold but because it was time, and she was terrified.

"You're shivering." He slipped out of his jacket and draped it over her shoulders.

The fabric was warm from his body heat, the scent of his cologne clinging to it, and Marina had the silly urge to bury her nose in it like a lovesick fool.

"Talk to me, Marina." Peter hooked a finger under her chin and turned her to face him. His hands came up to frame her face, his thumbs sweeping over her cheekbones. "Are you angry at me? Disappointed in me? What did I do?"

Marina squeezed her eyes shut. "I'm not angry or disappointed at you." A ragged breath left her lungs. "I'm angry at myself."

Peter's brow furrowed. "Why?"

"I'm scared that if I tell you, you'll hate me."

A shadow of apprehension crossed his handsome face, but he didn't pull away and didn't release her from the shelter of his arms.

"Try me," he said.

"I lied to you," the words tumbled from her lips in a rush. "When we first met, when I first approached you, it wasn't because I was attracted to you. Or, well, I was, but that wasn't the only reason."

Peter went still, his fingers tightening fractionally on her face. But he remained silent, his eyes fixed on hers with an intensity that stole her breath.

"I wanted to get out of Safe Haven. I told you that part. I was desperate to start over somewhere far away from the memories and the heartache, and I came up with a plan. If I could find an immortal who would fall in love with me, he might invite me to the village to live with him, and I would be set. I scanned the dining room during every meal, searching for the perfect candidate, and you caught my attention because you looked sad like I was. You needed someone to shower you with love and attention, and I figured that you wouldn't be too discriminating and might accept a human with blue hair and a nice smile."

She trailed off as shame and self-loathing rose like bile in her throat. Mother of All Life, saying it out loud made it sound even worse, even more manipulative and cruel.

"I used you," she whispered, hot tears spilling down her cheeks. "I used your kindness and open heart for my own selfish ends. And I am sorry for that, but in the end, I was the fool because I fell in love with you, and you don't feel the same about me. So once again, I'm the one holding the short end of the stick."

A sob tore from her throat, and Marina buried her face in her hands, her shoulders shaking with the force of her anguished confession. She waited for Peter's arm to fall away from her, waited for him to say something polite but final, but neither happened.

Instead, his arms tightened around her, pulling her into his warm, solid chest. "Oh, Marina," he murmured, his voice a low rumble against her ear. "My sweet, beautiful Marina." His heartbeat thrummed beneath her cheek as he stroked a hand down her back in long, soothing passes.

She lifted her head, blinking up at him through a veil of tears. "You're not mad at me?"

Peter's lips curved in a rueful smile. "Oh, I'm angry, but not at you." He brushed his fingers over her cheek. "I'm angry at the circumstances that made you feel like you had to resort to deception. I'm angry at your ex-boyfriend and the Kra-ell before him who made you doubt your own worth. But most of all, I'm angry at myself for pushing you away."

Marina shook her head. "None of this is your fault. I'm the one who schemed and deceived, who..."

"Who did what she had to do to make her life bearable," he finished for her. "I understand why you did it, and I'm not mad at you for that. We all have our ulterior motives for going after someone. Have you stopped to consider that all I wanted from you was a few tumbles in bed? Is that any better than what you wanted? More noble? If anything, it's worse. And just like you, I fell prey to my own scheming. Instead of seducing a sexy, beautiful woman, having my wicked way with her, and then forgetting all about her when the cruise was over, I fell in love with her, and I don't want to let her go."

Fresh tears spilled down Marina's cheeks, but this time, they were tears of relief.

He was right, but that didn't diminish the sweetness of his admission.

"Do you really mean it?" she whispered, curling her fingers into the fabric of his shirt. "Do you love me enough to keep me even though I'm just a human?"

He leaned down, his forehead pressing against hers. "I love you, Marina. That's all I can say. I don't know how we will make it work, but we have to try because I can't think of life without you."

The sob that escaped Marina's lips was part relief that he wasn't pushing her away and part despair because they really didn't have a future together. Surging up on her toes, she captured Peter's mouth and poured every ounce of her love for him into the kiss.

Peter banded his arms around her waist and lifted her off her feet, kissing her like a man possessed.

When they finally broke apart, chests heaving and hearts racing, Marina felt lighter than she had in years. The weight of guilt had lifted off her shoulders, replaced by the buoyant, effervescent joy of love requited. Her happy cloud had a big rock tied to it, but at this moment, the buoyancy was strong enough for her to soar despite the weight dragging behind.

"I love you so much," she whispered. "I will spend every day trying to be worthy of you."

Peter's eyes shone with a happiness that took her breath away. "You already are, Marina." He pulled her into another kiss, this one softer, sweeter, a promise of forever sealed with the press of his lips.

Marina felt a sense of peace settle over her. She was where she was meant to be, which was in the arms of the man she loved, or rather the immortal who, against all odds, loved her back.

15

AMANDA

When Onegus had swept Cassandra into his arms, the cheering and hooting had gone for much longer than it had for Amanda and Dalhu, and even though Alena and Orion hadn't gotten that much applause either, it still irked.

Amanda hated feeling petty and jealous, but she couldn't help it. So yeah, Onegus was the chief Guardian, and his people respected and appreciated him, but she was the princess, the clan's darling, the one who had set them on the path of finding Dormants who, in turn, had become life-long partners. If not for her, Onegus would have never suspected that Cassandra could be a Dormant, and she would have become just one more conquest in the endless string of them.

Oh, well. Amanda let out a sigh. She had a job to do and another happy couple to match.

Her gut was telling her that Jasmine was a Dormant, and even though Amanda had been wrong about that before, this time she was sure she was right because of the extraordinary circumstances of Jasmine finding her way to the clan. The more bizarre and unlikely the path was, the stronger the indicator for the Fates' intervention.

Craning her neck, she swept her gaze across the crowded ballroom, searching for Max. She spotted him by the bar, his blond head and boisterous bearing setting him apart from the other patrons waiting to be served by Bob.

He was so perfect for Jasmine. She seemed like a fun-loving, easygoing person, and that was Max to a tee. Opposites might attract, but similar personalities made relationships stick. The best ones had a little bit of both.

Her Dalhu hated attention while she thrived on it, but they both had an eye for art and shared similar views about the world at large. In fact, the only thing they had ever argued about was how to raise Evie, but they had sat down, had a talk, and reached a compromise like a civilized couple should, so it was all good.

Leaning toward her mate, she cast him a bright smile. "I love you." She planted a kiss on his cheek. "I'm going to have a quick chat with Max and come back. Do you want me to get you something from the bar?"

"I'll come with you." He stood and offered her a hand up. "I'll order us drinks while you have your chat."

"Good plan." She let him pull her to her feet.

He wrapped his arm around her waist and started toward the bar. "Are you going to talk to him about Jasmine?"

"Why else would I want to talk to him?"

Dalhu shrugged. "I don't know. You don't tell me everything."

She arched a brow. "That's not true. I don't keep any secrets from you."

"It's not intentional. Sometimes you think that I'm not interested in this or that, so you skip over the things you think bore me, but you shouldn't. I find everything you say and do fascinating." He leaned and brushed his lips over the side of her mouth. "I just love listening to your voice and seeing the sparkle in your eyes when you get excited about something. You are so full of life and energy. So passionate."

"Oh, darling." She leaned into him. "You say the nicest things to me."

"I love you." He let go of her as they reached the bar. "Make it quick." Leaving her standing next to Max, Dalhu strode to the other end of the bar.

"Fates, I love this male," she murmured, taking a moment to admire the breadth of his shoulders and his tight ass. "Perfection." She tore her eyes away from her mate, plastered a smile on her face, and turned to the Guardian she'd come over to talk to. "Max, darling. I need a word with you."

He inclined his head. "I'm always at your service. What can I do for you?"

She shifted her weight to her other stiletto-clad foot. "I'll cut right to the chase. I think that our rescued damsel in distress is a potential Dormant. I've spent some time with her, as have Syssi and even Kian, and we all believe that she has a paranormal talent. In fact, I'm sure of it." She leaned closer and whispered conspiratorially, "I thought I should tell you first that there is an available Dormant on the ship before it becomes widely known and there is a stampede of males vying for her attention. You've been the groomsman for too long. It's time you became the groom."

"I'll pass." Max surprised her. "If Jasmine needs guarding, I'll go, but I'm not interested in her otherwise."

Amanda blinked. "Have you seen her?" she asked, not even trying to stifle the incredulity in her voice. "She's a stunning woman, and she's lonely, just waiting for someone to talk to. Right now, she's all alone in the staff lounge. You can go, have a little chat with her, and see if there is any attraction. If there is, great, and if not, someone else will gladly take your place."

Edgar, who was standing next to Max, turned around and lifted his hand. "If he won't, I will. Jasmine is one hell of a catch. She's beautiful, friendly, and not full of herself as so many beautiful women are."

Had his remark been directed at her?

Amanda pursed her lips. "I'm not stuck-up."

Edgar blanched. "I didn't mean you. Never. I meant human women, and it was a generalization."

She waved a dismissive hand. "You don't need to apologize. I might not be stuck-up, but I can admit to being vain." She smiled. "If I didn't have any flaws, I would be perfect, and that's boring." She shifted her gaze back to the obstinate Guardian. "Last chance, Max. If you don't want to go, Ed will."

Max shrugged. "I've seen Jasmine through the surveillance cameras, and she's beautiful, but she also reminds me of someone who I lost a friend over, someone who wasn't very discriminating with her affections and chose to indulge me when she knew my friend was in love with her. I was an ass for not realizing the depth of his feelings for her, but she wasn't blameless. I know that Jasmine is not her, but she is similar enough in character and looks that I can't help the aversion I feel."

It was silly to think that just because Jasmine looked like that woman, she was like her in other ways, but Amanda had to admit that Jasmine was a major flirt, so there could be more to the similarity than met the eye.

"I would love to go," the pilot said. "I would have visited Jasmine before, but we were told to stay away from the crew quarters because of the rescued women and their fear of men."

That was true, and she'd forgotten about it, but the rescued women had their own section of the staff quarters, and as long as Edgar didn't go to that area or to the staff dining room, it should be okay.

"Jasmine spends most of her time in the staff lounge, and the rescued women never go there. If you stay away from the staff dining room and their section of cabins, it should be fine."

Ed rubbed a spot behind his left ear. "What if I go down there and Jasmine is not in the lounge? She could have gone to bed already."

"Then you can try again tomorrow. She doesn't have a phone. Otherwise, I would call her and ask her to meet you there."

"I can check for you." Max pulled out his phone. "We have surveillance cameras in the lounge." He typed on his screen and then nodded. "She's there, watching television, and Amanda was right. She's all alone."

Edgar's face lit up. "Awesome!" He practically bounced on his feet. "I'll go right now."

Chuckling, Amanda held up a finger. "Don't you want to stay for the wedding dinner?"

Edgar's eyes widened, a look of inspiration crossing his face. "That's a great idea!" He snapped his fingers. "I'll load up two plates and take them down to the lounge. Jasmine and I can chat over dinner and get to know each other."

"Just be careful," Amanda cautioned. "Jasmine still doesn't know who we are, and it needs to stay that way, at least until Edna probes her. I was supposed to wait until after Edna had a chance to get a read on Jasmine's intentions, but I got excited by the idea of making another match." She cast an accusing look at Max. "I didn't expect my gesture to be refused."

"I'm sorry." Max smiled apologetically. "I can't help it. Just looking at her irritates me."

"Don't sweat it." Amanda let him off the hook and turned back to the pilot. "Jasmine thinks that this cruise has been organized by Perfect Match for its management and top employees, and that the secrecy surrounding it is to protect the privacy of some high-profile clients who met through the service and are getting married on the ship."

"Got it," Edgar said. "I can talk a mile about Perfect Match. I've been on six solo adventures so far, and it was amazing."

Max clapped a hand on Edgar's shoulder. "I hope Jasmine is the one for you."

"Alright." Amanda waved a hand at Edgar. "Go forth and conquer, Romeo."

"Thank you." The pilot sketched a mock salute. "Wish me luck!"

16

EDGAR

Edgar discovered that loading up two plates at the buffet table required careful maneuvering, and it also annoyed the people standing in line behind him because he was taking so long to decide what to load for Jasmine.

Succulent slices of roast beef or beef Stroganoff, creamy mashed potatoes or Persian rice, crisp green beans or mushrooms with onions. He didn't know what Jasmine liked, but he figured variety was the key. The problem was that he had only two hands and could maneuver only two plates.

He loaded each plate with different things with the intention of letting Jasmine choose what she wanted, and he would eat the rest. Edgar couldn't care less what she left for him to eat as long as she didn't dismiss him.

She wouldn't be rude, he knew that, but she could come up with a polite excuse that she wasn't hungry, or that she was bone tired and on her way to bed, or any other gentle letdown she could think of.

Ed wasn't like the hulking Guardians that women found irresistible, but being a pilot had its own allure as well. A civilian helicopter pilot was not as sexy as a jetliner captain or a military fighter pilot, but it was still better than having a boring desk job.

Hopefully, Jasmine would remember him fondly from the boat ride, and would welcome his company.

Ed had been lusting after Jasmine from the moment he'd first laid eyes on her back on Modana's yacht.

Those lush curves and that dazzling smile...

Fates, she could make any male salivate.

Well, except for Max, who was acting like an ass, but his loss was Edgar's gain.

With her long, olive-toned limbs, ample hips, flowing dark hair, and flirtatious eyes that sparkled with mischief and intelligence, Jasmine was a knockout. And that seductive voice of hers that had wrapped around him like warm honey…

As his erection punched against the zipper of his slacks, getting lodged in an uncomfortable angle, Edgar groaned.

With a loaded plate in each hand, he couldn't adjust himself, which meant that he was going to show up at the staff lounge with tented pants.

Dear Fates, have mercy on me.

Jasmine was every male's sex dream come to life, and he'd been the lucky guy who had happened to be in the right place at the right time.

Walking out of the dining room, he headed to the bar instead of taking the elevator down to the staff decks or the stairs. Now that the party had started, no one would be there, so he could put down the plates and adjust the angle of his shaft.

When it was done, he let out a sigh of relief, hefted the plates, and headed down to the staff lounge.

The truth was that Ed didn't care whether Jasmine was a Dormant or not. He was young, and he wasn't looking for his one and only. He had centuries stretching out before him and endless opportunities to find his fated mate. All he cared about right now was seducing or being seduced and spending the night between those lush thighs.

He found her curled up on one of the plush couches with a book in her lap, and as he entered, she lifted her head and smiled.

"Edgar." She set the book aside and rose to her feet. "Are you lost? Or are you looking for me?"

"I'm not lost." He lifted the plates he was carrying higher for emphasis. "Amanda told me that you were all alone down here, and I had the brilliant idea to share dinner with you. I hope that's okay."

"It's more than okay." She reached for one of the plates. "I'm so glad to see you. I wondered why you didn't come to visit." She cast him an accusing look and walked over to the nearest table. "I thought that you forgot about me." She put the plate down.

"You are unforgettable, Jasmine. I was told to stay away from the staff area because of the rescued women who occupy several cabins down here. They are scared of men."

"Oh, yeah. I've been told to be super gentle with them. The women eat in the staff dining room, and some of the staff are men, but I guess the rule applies only to the guests. It's easier to ensure that the staff behaves than the guests, right?"

If they were human, she would be right. But that wasn't the reason.

Jasmine looked at him with anticipation, and only when he put his plate down did he figure out why.

"Damn it. I forgot to bring silverware. I need to go back and bring some, along with napkins and glasses and something to drink."

He'd been so excited about the opportunity Amanda had given him that he hadn't thought about all the details. Or, more accurately, he'd been too busy imagining Jasmine naked.

She laughed. "We have everything we need down here." She rose to her feet and sauntered over to the bar area of the lounge.

He had to force his mouth to close as he watched her ass sway enticingly from side to side, her dark locks reaching just above the start of the curve, and what a curve it was. He'd never thought of himself as an ass man, but he was now.

Jasmine collected all the missing items from behind the counter and returned to the table.

"Now we can eat."

As she put down a napkin next to his plate and put a fork and a knife on it, Edgar took a deep inhale, and her scent almost knocked him out.

Was she aroused just from being near him?

That was how it worked for males, but usually not for females. They needed much more than the sight of a handsome male to get all hot and bothered.

Perhaps she'd been entertaining naughty thoughts before he got there?

He remembered that she had been reading a book when he'd walked in. Was it one of those raunchy romances with lots of sex in it?

As she finished setting up the table, he cast a quick glance at the book that was lying splayed open on the couch, both the front and back cover visible but not clearly from the angle he was looking at it. Still, he could discern a woman in a Victorian dress with a dark-haired guy standing behind her.

"What are you looking at?" Jasmine asked.

"Your book. What is it about?"

She laughed. "It's a silly romance. Nothing a manly man like you would be interested in."

17

JASMINE

E d had interrupted a particularly steamy part in the book when he'd arrived in the lounge, but Jasmine didn't mind. She would rather have the real thing instead of reading about it any day of the week and twice on Sunday. It was Saturday, so perhaps twice on Saturday as well.

The pilot didn't emit the bad boy vibes that usually were her Achilles heel, but he was handsome and charming enough to compensate for the lack of spice.

She'd learned a long time ago that appearances could be deceptive, but he just didn't have that aura. Kian had it in spades, but he was taken, and Kevin even more so, but he was taken as well. Jasmine wondered what type of women managed to lasso such dangerous men. Syssi seemed mellow and shy, so maybe the old adage about opposites being attracted to each other was true. Then again, Jasmine didn't have a mellow or shy bone in her body, but she still liked edgy men, so maybe it wasn't true.

Edgar grinned. "A manly man? I hope you meant it as a compliment."

"Of course. Why wouldn't it be?"

He shrugged. "Nowadays, it's hard to tell. As long as manly man does not mean toxic masculinity, I guess I'm good."

She laughed. "There is nothing toxic about you. In fact, the only danger I could think of is you being too sweet."

His face fell. "That for sure is not a compliment. Sweet is not sexy."

"I disagree." She smiled suggestively. "Give me a fresh creampuff, and I'll show you how sexy it is to me."

As a pained groan escaped Edgar's throat, his eyes started glowing.

Was he crying?

Some men experienced excruciating pain when their arousal couldn't be immediately relieved, but usually that afflicted only very young men, and Edgar was in his late twenties or early thirties.

Perhaps she should take mercy on him and ease up on the flirting. "Let's dig in before this lavish feast gets cold." She lifted her knife and fork.

"Yes, indeed." He swallowed. "I didn't know what you like, so I piled different things on each plate. If there is something you like on mine, it's yours."

"I'm not a finicky eater," she said. "I'm perfectly happy with what's on my plate." She scooped some of the buttery mashed potatoes on her fork and found herself sighing with pleasure at the first bite.

The roast was also divine. "This is perfect," she murmured around a mouthful.

Glancing up at Edgar through her lashes, Jasmine expected to find him equally engrossed in his meal, but to her surprise, he was just watching her with those strange, glowing eyes.

"What is it?" she asked, suddenly self-conscious. "Do I have mashed potato on my nose?" She lifted a napkin and dabbed at it.

Edgar shook his head, his smile widening. "I just enjoy seeing you eating with such delight. It's so rare to see a beautiful woman with a healthy appetite. Food should be savored and enjoyed. It's one of life's pleasures, but so many women think that they should look like sticks and starve themselves." He leaned in closer. "Me? I love a woman with curves."

"You are like a decadent sundae, Edgar. You know all the right things to say to me."

Jasmine had every intention of inviting Ed back to her cabin once they were done with dinner, but first, she needed to pump him for information about Perfect Match and the mysterious guests whose privacy was so tightly protected.

"Those are not come-on lines," he said. "I'm just saying what's in my heart."

"I know, and that is what makes them even more precious to me." She set down her fork and fixed him with a coy smile. "Amanda and Kian visited me earlier, and Kian said something about sending a woman named Edna to probe me. Do you know what that's about?"

She watched Edgar closely, looking for any sign of recognition, any hint that he knew more than he was letting on. And sure enough, there it was—a slight tightening around his eyes, a barely perceptible stiffening of his shoulders.

"Edna, huh?" he said, his voice carefully casual. "Yeah, I know her. She's one of our special consultants."

Jasmine leaned forward, her eyes wide with feigned innocence. "Special how? What kind of probe does she use? Is it some kind of high-tech compatibility test?"

Edgar hesitated, and for a moment, Jasmine thought that he might clam up and change the subject, but then he shook his head. "Edna has a gift. She doesn't need any fancy equipment to see into people's hearts and souls. It's like a sixth sense. She can determine a person's intentions and innermost desires, and I'm not talking about desires of the flesh. I'm talking about desires of the soul."

Jasmine's breath caught in her throat, a thrill of something that might have been fear or excitement or both zinging through her veins. Was Edna a seer or a psychic?

Could it be that she was a fellow witch?

Would Edna be able to help her with the tangle of answers her divination had produced?

Jasmine had tried to connect online with other practitioners, and most had been eager to help, but their advice didn't improve her results. Some tried to give her alternative meanings, which had been somewhat helpful, but in her gut, she knew that the prince was not an idea but someone real that she had to find.

18

EDGAR

E dgar wondered where he had come up with that crap. Well, come to think of it, intentions and aspirations were desires of the soul, right? Still, Jasmine looked much too shaken by his description of Edna's ability than was merited.

"Desires of the soul?" she whispered. "What do you mean by that?"

He remembered her talking about her acting career and how she only got to play a few minor parts in commercials.

"If you are consumed by a burning need to become a movie star, Edna will see that in your soul even if you don't tell her anything about yourself. She might not know precisely what you want, but she will know that you desire fame, acceptance, recognition, or whatever else your inner motives for wanting to be a famous actress might be."

There was disappointment in Jasmine's eyes, as she picked up her knife and fork again. "That doesn't sound as scary as a probe. I was afraid that she could read my thoughts." She cut off a piece of roast beef and put it in her mouth.

Edgar was having a hard time formulating his thoughts as he looked at her mouth and imagined all the things he wanted her to do with it.

When she was done chewing, she regarded him with a small smile. "I've never thought about what motivates me to want to be an actress, and the funny thing is that it's none of the things you mentioned. Well, that's not true. I want to be famous and make a lot of money, but that's not the main reason."

"Then what is it?"

She shrugged, forked a few green beans, and put them in her mouth, probably to give herself a few minutes to think.

63

"When I auditioned for the first musical production in middle school, it was because a friend of mine convinced me that I had the perfect voice for the part, and since the person who was supposed to play that part had dropped out, it was a sure thing. The thought of performing on stage terrified me, but I went to the audition anyway, not really expecting to get the part. I must have impressed the drama teacher, or maybe she was desperate because it was so late in the production, and I was in."

She smiled, her eyes assuming a distant look as she walked down memory lane. "I found a home in the theater club, a community of like-minded people. I loved the camaraderie and the grueling schedule of rehearsals, and I loved finally being good at something. I wasn't a brilliant student, but I was a good singer and actress, and people who hadn't given me a second look before were suddenly smiling at me, congratulating me on my performance, and wishing me luck. I became addicted to the rush." She sighed. "Regrettably, my amazing career didn't extend beyond high school. I got accepted to one of the most prestigious acting programs in the country, but my father didn't have the money for the insanely expensive tuition, and he said that there was no way he was taking on debt for a degree in acting."

"That's harsh, but I can understand his reasoning."

Jasmine nodded. "Yeah, so did I, but it didn't make it any less disappointing. Anyway, I went to a community college that had a drama program and continued my studies, but I was no longer the star of the show the way I was in high school." She speared a bite of roast beef with her fork. "But enough about me. Tell me about yourself and why Perfect Match Virtual Studios need a helicopter pilot."

Ed suppressed a groan. He wasn't really an employee of the company, but he had gone on enough virtual adventures to talk about it with a degree of expertise.

The only problem he had was lying to Jasmine. He didn't mind skirting the truth, but he didn't enjoy fabricating tales from thin air as he was about to do.

"Some of the virtual adventures involve piloting a helicopter, and that's where I come in. They record hours of footage of me flying the simulator, and this footage is later used by the artificial intelligence to create realistic scenarios for clients. They are developing adventures that are all about piloting a helicopter, a fighter jet plane, a commercial airliner, a submarine, etc."

Perhaps he could suggest that they actually do that, so it wouldn't be a lie.

She looked at him with awe. "That sounds like a dream job."

"It is. But I still love the real thing more." He leaned closer to her. "There is one adventure I want them to develop, which you would be perfect for."

"Oh yeah? Do they use real people in their simulations?"

"Of course. The two participants, but that's not what I'm talking about. You would be a perfect avatar for Aladdin's Jasmine." He chuckled. "You even have the same name." He reached for her hand. "But if they ever make an Aladdin Perfect Match adventure, I would love for you to partner with me as yourself, no avatar needed."

She grinned. "Let me guess. You'd be Aladdin."

He arched a brow. "Would you prefer Jafar?"

Jasmine laughed. "No, not Jafar, but I kind of had a thing for the genie."

19

JASMINE

E dgar's eyebrows shot up. "The blue balloon-like cartoon genie? No way."
Jasmine shrugged. "He made me laugh, and he had really big biceps. Aladdin looked like a sixteen-year-old boy."

"So? How old were you when you first saw the movie?"

"The first time, I was a little girl, and I was so excited that I was named after the main character and also looked a little bit like her. Then I watched it a couple of times as a teenager, and I didn't really click with Aladdin. As an adult, I kept dreaming about finding the magic lamp and having the genie at my command."

Ed shook his head. "Do I want to know what you wanted to ask the genie for?"

Jasmine leaned forward. "I'll make you a deal. You'll tell me your preferred version of the story, and if I like it, I'll tell you mine."

He made a face. "That's not fair. I asked first."

Jasmine affected nonchalance. "Take it or leave it. That's my final offer."

He huffed out a breath. "You are a tough negotiator."

"So I've been told." She cut off another piece of meat and lifted it to her mouth.

"By whom?"

Jasmine paused with the fork suspended in midair. "Stop stalling. I won't tell you anything until you enchant me with your story first."

At this point, she was more curious about that than what Edgar could tell her about Perfect Match. Besides, if everything went well, he was going to spend the night with her, and she could ask him more questions over breakfast.

Her core twitched pleasantly at the thought.

Edgar was a delicious morsel of maleness, with clear blue eyes, a chiseled jaw, and a sensuous mouth that promised sinful kisses in all kinds of places.

Edgar smiled, the mischief and mirth in his eyes making him look even more handsome. "Princess Jasmine..."—he spread his hands theatrically—"is the most beautiful and desirable woman in all of Agrabah. Her sultry eyes and luscious curves have men falling at her feet, but she's bored with all the stuffy princes and dignitaries vying for her hand. She craves adventure and a man whose hands are callused from hard work and not smooth like a baby's ass."

Jasmine laughed. "Let me see your hands."

He shook his head. "This is my fantasy, not my reality. I don't have any calluses. I'm a pilot, not a woodcutter."

Jasmine smirked. "Oh, so you are Aladdin, the dashing street rat who's going to sweep me off my feet and show me the world?"

"Exactly." Edgar winked. "I'm the charming rogue who catches your eye in the marketplace. There's an instant spark between us, an undeniable chemistry that makes the air crackle with tension."

"Ooh, I like it."

Jasmine felt a thrill run down her spine and heat pooling low in her belly. Edgar was a good storyteller, but his story would have probably been less effective if Jasmine hadn't been reading a steamy book only moments earlier. She was still primed.

"Wait, the good bits are yet to come." He leaned back and crossed his arms over his chest. "When we meet in the market, I promise to visit you at the palace. You tell me not to come because it's dangerous. You reveal that you are extremely well guarded, and you are worried that I will get caught and executed on the spot. You can't stand the thought of losing me when you have only just found me."

Jasmine pushed the plate aside and leaned her elbows on the table. "So, it was love at first sight?"

"Of course." Edgar uncrossed his arms and leaned toward her, so their noses were almost touching. "I tell you that I would rather die than never see you again, but not to worry. I am an accomplished thief, and I won't get caught."

Jasmine smiled and picked up the storyline. "I wait for you every night, yearning for you to come but also dreading it. But as the nights pass and you don't show up, I start to worry that something has happened to you. I tell my handmaiden to bring me a commoner's cloak so I can slip away from the palace again, and just as she leaves to get it, I hear a knock on the terrace doors." She extended her hand, motioning for him to continue.

"Your room's balcony overlooks an inaccessible and therefore unguarded cliff, but I have a magic carpet that I got from the genie, and I use it to fly onto your terrace." Edgar's voice dropped an octave, taking on a seductive edge. "You open the doors for me and fall into my arms, sobbing with happiness. As I lift you into my arms and carry you to your enormous circular bed, you pepper my face with kisses."

Jasmine canted her head. "Why would a princess need a huge round bed?"

He rolled his eyes. "It's my fantasy, so let me tell it."

"Fine." She waved a hand. "Please, continue."

"You are draped in silks and a sheer gown that leaves very little to the imagination, and as I lay you down on the bed, your eyes darken with a hunger that matches my own."

Jasmine swallowed, her mouth suddenly dry. "And then what happens?"

Edgar's breath ghosted over her cheek. "My hands roam over your lush curves, caressing you through the thin fabric until you're trembling with need and begging me to undress you."

A soft moan escaped Jasmine's throat as his words conjured up vivid images in her mind. Tangled limbs, sweat-slicked skin, her pleasure coiling tighter and tighter.

"I tell you to have patience while I worship your body with my mouth and hands, and you are moaning my name. You tell me to lock the door so your handmaiden won't be able to come in, and when I do, you take off your clothing and wait for me naked, so magnificent that I'm frozen in place for a moment."

"I call your name," Jasmine said. "And I cup my breasts, teasing my nipples. I tell you to get rid of your clothes and join me in bed."

As Edgar's breathing became labored, he reached for her hand and brought it to his lips for a kiss. "I do as you command, and when you see me naked, you lick your lush lips and tell me that I'm a dream come true. I climb onto the bed and dip my head between your spread thighs, asking your permission to taste you."

Jasmine clenched her thighs together, her core throbbing insistently as desire pulsed through her veins.

"I grant your wish."

"I pleasure you with my tongue and fingers until you're writhing beneath me and begging me to take you. When I finally slide deep inside you, joining us as one, it's like magic, like flying over an endless diamond sky."

"You paint a vivid picture." Jasmine could practically feel everything he'd described, and she wanted it. She wanted his hands on her, his hard body pressed against hers.

"You're my muse." The words were low and rough, laced with raw desire that made her shiver. "Say the word, Princess, and I'll show you a whole new world."

She lifted her eyes to the surveillance camera mounted near the ceiling, which was pointed right at Edgar's head. "Should we continue the story in a more private setting?" With a smoldering look, she rose to her feet and offered Edgar her hand.

She had no idea if he would be as skilled a lover as his fictional Aladdin, but she couldn't wait to find out. After all, every princess deserved to be thoroughly ravished by her street urchin at least once in her life, and if Edgar's performance was half as good as his imagination, she was in for a wonderful magical ride.

20

PETER

As Peter led Marina inside the grand dining room, the music and laughter seemed oddly distant, a muted backdrop to the storm of emotions raging in his heart.

He had surprised himself when he told Marina that he loved her and couldn't live without her. It was the truth, but he had never intended to voice it, not to himself and not to her.

Now that it was done, though, he felt at least a hundred pounds lighter. Keeping his feelings locked inside had been as bad for him as the guilt Marina had harbored had been bad for her. They had both lied to themselves and to each other, trying to protect their hearts but only hurting themselves more.

Admitting the truth and accepting the consequences was so incredibly liberating, but it was also daunting, because now what?

Hope for a scientific breakthrough that would make Marina immortal?

The notion wasn't as farfetched as it sounded. Perhaps over the next two decades, Kaia and Bridget would uncover the secret of immortality.

They found Jay and Larissa seated at the table and enjoying the wedding dinner. Their heads were bent close together as they talked and laughed, and Peter couldn't help but smile at the sight. They were somehow managing to communicate with her broken English and his rudimentary Russian and were having a good time together.

As he and Marina approached, Larissa's head snapped up, her eyes widening with concern as she took in Marina's disheveled appearance.

Marina was still wrapped in his jacket, which looked like a coat on her, and her hair was a mess.

He should have told her that she needed to fix it before they went inside, but he'd been too busy freaking out inside his own head to think straight.

"*Chto sluchilos*?" Larissa asked in Russian, her brow furrowed. "*Ty v poryadke?*"

Marina waved off her friend's concern with a somewhat shaky smile. "*Ya v poryadke,*" she assured Larissa. "*Luchshe, chem v poryadke, na samom dele.*"

At Larissa's questioning look, Marina elaborated in English. "Everything's fine, Larissa. Better than fine, actually. I just had a little too much to drink on an empty stomach, that's all." She reached for a piece of bread from the basket on the table, tearing off a small chunk and popping it into her mouth. "I think I'll stick to bread and olives for now," she said to Peter. "And water. Lots and lots of water. But you should fill your plate from the buffet before your friends and family finish it all."

Peter squeezed her hand under the table. "I'll get both of us plates."

Marina shook her head. "I don't think it's a good idea for me to eat anything other than bread. Maybe later, I'll try something else." She smiled up at him. "When you go for seconds."

"As you wish." He pushed to his feet.

"I'll come with you." Jay looked at Larissa with affection in his eyes. "Do you want me to bring you another serving of beef Stroganoff?"

Her eyes sparkled. "Yes, please."

As Peter made his way towards the buffet table, Jay fell into step beside him. "I love watching Larissa eat. It's so erotic. She eats so daintily, and she looks like she's orgasming after every bite. I've been as hard as a rock the entire time you were outside."

Peter shook his head. "TMI, my friend. TMI."

Jay laughed. "Yeah. I have no filter. Is everything okay with you two?" he asked quietly, his gaze darting back to where Marina and Larissa were sitting, heads bent close together as they talked.

Peter hesitated for a moment. Soon, Marina would move in with him, so their love wouldn't be a secret anyway. Besides, he was a male in love, and he wanted to shout it from the rooftops, not hide it just because everyone he knew was going to think that he had lost his fucking mind.

"We're good." He let out a sigh. "Better than good, actually. We're in love."

Jay's eyebrows shot up, his expression shifting from surprised to skeptical. "You are in love with a human?"

Peter ran his fingers through his hair. "When it hits, there isn't much you can do about it. I don't know why the Fates chose a human for me, but I hope they know what they are doing and that it's not punishment for something I have done." He looked over his shoulder back to where Marina sat, her blue hair gleaming like a beacon. "She wants to move in with me."

Jay's eyes widened. "Kian will never agree."

"Why not? Marina knows who we are, and she wouldn't be the only human in the village. Several of those who served the Kra-ell moved into the village from Safe Haven, and Kian is contemplating inviting more. Atzil needs people to work in his bar, Callie needs servers and assistant cooks for her restaurant, and there are many other jobs that our people don't want to do."

Jay remained silent for a long moment. "What about you, Peter? What happens when she grows old? There is a good reason we don't form long-term relationships with humans, and it's not that we think of ourselves as superior."

Peter closed his eyes, a dull ache blooming in his chest. "I'll take whatever time she can give me, and I'll cherish every moment. And who knows? Maybe we'll decide to part ways after a while. It's not like we are fated mates. We can't be. So, it might end like it ends for many humans."

Even as he spoke the words, Peter was aware of the lie. Deep down, he believed that Marina was his one and only truelove mate.

Kagra's words echoed in his head again, "You are enamored with love, Peter. You are lying to yourself."

Was he?

Not really. He would be lying to himself if he denied what he felt for Marina.

There would be no parting ways, no amicable split. He was hers and she was his, and they were bound together by a force that transcended their differences, but he couldn't say that, not yet.

Instead, he clapped Jay on the shoulder. "Let's get some food. I'm starving."

21

MARINA

As Peter and Jay made their way to the buffet table, Larissa put her fork down, leaned back and regarded Marina with a knowing look. "Okay, talk. What happened?"

Marina leaned in close. "I followed your advice, and I confessed everything."

Larissa's eyes widened. "And? What did he say?"

Marina felt a smile bloom across her face. "Peter forgave me and told me he loved me and didn't want to let me go, no matter what. He wants me to move in with him. Can you imagine? It's everything I wanted."

A squeal of delight escaped Larissa's lips, and she reached across the table to embrace Marina. "I knew it! I told you he would forgive you. Peter is so in love with you that anyone could see it besides you."

Marina ducked her head. "I hoped so, but I didn't dare to believe. Heck, I still can't believe it."

"I'm so happy for you," Larissa whispered. "But what's next? You need to plan for the future."

Knowing what her friend was going to say, Marina grimaced. "What future? I'd rather not think about it."

Larissa sighed. "You can enjoy a few years with Peter, but you shouldn't stay with him for more than five years. Save up some money, maybe even study in an online university, and when you are ready, leave and find a human man to marry and have kids with. You don't have much time if you still want to have them."

Marina felt like she'd been doused in ice water, the harsh truth of Larissa's words hitting her like a physical blow despite having the same thoughts herself.

Somehow, it felt more real when someone else voiced them. Humans were very good at shoving unpleasant thoughts and consequences to the back of their minds. It was a coping mechanism, and right now, Marina would have loved to do that, but Larissa was right about the life she had imagined with Peter being a beautiful but fleeting dream.

Mother of All Life, have mercy on her soul. The thought of leaving him, of walking away from the most perfect relationship she'd ever had with a male, was like cutting her heart in half.

She just wouldn't survive it. To be with Peter, she had to give up other dreams.

"I'm not stupid. I had the same thoughts, but then I realized that not everyone has to have kids. We don't get to have everything we want, Larissa. And if I want to keep Peter, maybe I need to give up the idea of having children." She took a deep breath. "Did you know that in the Western world, as well as most countries in Eastern Europe, there aren't enough live births to keep the population from shrinking? Many people are not having kids at all. On average, women only have one and a half kids, which is way below the replacement ratio needed. The world population is going to decrease significantly in the next few decades."

Larissa rolled her eyes. "So what? You can't change that, and having kids isn't going to reverse the trend. You need to do what's good for you, not what's good for the planet."

"I want to have children," Marina said, even as the words rang hollow in her own ears. "For me, not for the planet."

Larissa threw up her hands, a look of frustration passing over her face. "A moment ago, you said you didn't want kids, and that many women chose not to have any. Then you said that the planet needed women to have more children, and that you want that too. Make up your mind."

The truth was that Marina didn't know what she wanted. The only certainty she had was her love for Peter.

Her gaze drifted to where he stood in line, his broad shoulders and tousled hair making her heart ache with longing, "I just want to be with him. I don't want to worry about anything else, about the future or the consequences or anything. I just want to live in the moment and not think about the future." She looked back at Larissa. "Is that so wrong? To want to be happy, even if it's just for a little while?"

Larissa's expression softened. "It's not wrong at all. The Mother of All Life knows how little joy we get in our miserable existence, and we need to grab whatever sliver of happiness we can get our hands on. If this sinfully handsome immortal makes you happy, then hold on to him with both hands for as long as you can."

22

EDGAR

Edgar had had easy conquests before, but never with a stunning beauty like Jasmine. And yet, here he was, holding her hand as she led him down the narrow corridor leading to her cabin.

Seducing her had taken almost no effort.

Hell, who was he kidding? He hadn't done the seducing, she had. Well, they both had.

Could she hear the pounding of his heart?

If Jasmine were immortal, she probably could, but she was human, so his secret was safe.

Well, not for long. He would have to thrall her soon so she wouldn't notice his fangs and glowing eyes, which he was barely managing to hold control of.

Edgar hadn't been with a woman in over two weeks, which was a long time for an immortal male, especially since he wasn't a fan of self-pleasuring. It was no fun having to bite a pillow or a towel to empty his venom.

It would take a lot of restraint for him not to harm Jasmine when he was going in that hot.

When they reached her cabin door, she gave him a bright smile as she fished the keycard from out of her purse. Her hands were steady as she pressed it to the reader and opened the door.

"Welcome to my humble abode." She waved at the tiny interior.

Edgar wanted to reach for her, wrap her in his arms, and kiss her until they were both breathless, but he held himself back, waiting for her cue.

Jasmine was in charge, and given his experience with her so far, she had no problem with that. The lady knew what she wanted, how she wanted it, and she wasn't bashful about her needs and wishes.

He admired that more than words could convey.

The cabin was tiny, with barely enough room between the narrow single bed and the desk and chair on the other side of the room. It couldn't be more than eight by ten feet.

"Most of the staff cabins are not as small as this one, but they are doubles, and this is a single." She put her purse on the desk and waved at the narrow bed. "This is a far cry from the princess's enormous round bed, but the mattress is surprisingly comfortable, and most importantly, there are no cameras in here. I checked."

So, was that why she'd said they should move to somewhere more private to continue their story? The surveillance cameras in the staff lounge bothered her?

Perhaps she had meant it literally, and all she wanted was to continue the story?

"Yeah. That's good." He suddenly felt too hot, claustrophobic.

Removing his tux jacket, he pulled out the lone chair and draped the jacket over its back. Not sure what he should do next, he sat down.

How had he expected her to invite him to her bed when they hadn't even kissed yet?

He'd been delusional.

As Jasmine looked at him, though, her eyes sparkled with mischief, and Edgar felt a surge of molten lust course through his veins. Fates, she was stunning, all lush curves and golden skin, her dark hair tumbling around her shoulders in soft waves that he couldn't wait to rake his fingers through.

Tilting her head, Jasmine put a hand on her hip and bit her lips. "It has been a long day of doing nothing, but I feel like showering. Would you like to join me?"

Fuck me. Edgar swallowed hard, his erection swelling to uncomfortable proportions in his pants. "I would love to." He rose to his feet and pulled her into his arms. "But I have a rule."

"What is it?"

"Before I get naked with a woman, I have to kiss her first."

She laughed, a throaty sound that sent shivers skittering down his spine. "I like your rules. Do you have more?"

"A few." He raised his hand and wrapped his fingers around her neck, threading them through her luxurious ebony locks. "But let's start with this one." He tilted his head and leaned into her, hovering his mouth a fraction of an inch away from hers.

Jasmine closed the last of the distance, fusing her lips to his, and then he took over, lashing his tongue against the seam of her lips and being granted immediate entry.

As he dipped his tongue into her mouth, he sent a light thrall into her mind, making her ignore the sharp points of his fangs and his glowing eyes.

Her arms closed around his body, and she brought him closer, her hardened nipples rubbing against his chest through two layers of fabric.

Three, if she was wearing a bra.

Jasmine pulled away, breathless and a little dazed. "You are one hell of a kisser, Edgar."

23

JASMINE

What had just happened?

Why was she feeling dizzy?

The kiss had been spectacular, and the hard muscles Jasmine had felt under Edgar's shirt had her blood pumping, but she wasn't prone to fainting spells like Margo, and she rarely felt dizzy.

Was the ship swaying more than usual?

"Are you okay?" Edgar steadied her with a hand on her hip.

"Yeah. I've never been bespelled by a kiss before." She licked her lips. "You didn't slip something into my water, did you?"

The horrified look on his face was the best answer he could have given her. "I would never do something like that." He reached for his jacket. "If you think I'm capable of such a despicable act, I'd better leave."

"Relax. I was just joking." She took the jacket from him and draped it over the back of the chair. "You are taking everything much too seriously."

"How can you say that? You were a victim of such a travesty only a few days ago."

Jasmine grimaced. "You are nothing like Alberto. I know that you would have never taken advantage of me." She reached for the hem of her top. "Let's play a game to lighten the mood. For every piece of clothing I take off, you have to take one off too. Deal?"

Edgar nodded, a sly smile making his handsome face look boyish.

"I'll go first." Jasmine pulled her top over her head in one smooth motion and tossed it over the desk.

Left with her lacy black bra on, she waved a hand at him. "Your turn."

"You are breathtakingly beautiful," he murmured as his eyes roamed over her exposed skin.

"I'm waiting." She playfully tapped her foot on the floor. "I'm not getting any younger here."

The dizziness had passed by now, and she was enjoying the game she'd come up with, even though it was tormenting them both by prolonging the anticipation.

Edgar started on the buttons of his shirt, going slowly and dragging it out as she looked on with fire burning in her eyes.

When he finally shrugged the shirt off, she sucked in a breath. "How many hours a day do you spend in the gym to look like that?"

The look of smug satisfaction on his face was priceless. "None. I spend a few minutes every day training at home."

"I hate you." When the horrified look returned to his eyes, she lifted her hand and laughed. "You are so literal. I'm just envious, that's all."

"Why?" He closed the distance between them with one step, wrapping his arms around her and pulling her to his bare chest. The feeling of skin on skin was incredible. "You are perfect." He kissed her.

When he let her up for air, she pushed on his chest. "Next item."

They continued their seductive game of strip poker, each revealing more and more skin until they were both completely naked.

Edgar seemed to have trouble breathing. "You are a goddess." The reverence in his voice did something to her chest.

Something eased inside.

Why had she allowed Alberto to erode her self-confidence with his snide comments about her hips being too fleshy, her stomach too rounded, and her nipples too big and too dark?

As always, she had shoved those uncomfortable thoughts into a corner of her mind where all the dark moments of her life were imprisoned, but Edgar's appreciative gaze had released them and then pulverized them.

He made her feel beautiful.

"You are not so bad yourself." She let her eyes roam over his body, stopping at the enormous erection jutting from between his hips.

Thankfully, she wasn't a dainty woman, and the size of him titillated her rather than worried her.

Edgar's skin was so much lighter than hers, and other than his head, he was almost hairless. If she hadn't gotten all of her body hair removed with laser treatments, she would have been more hairy than him.

Stop it. No self-deprecating remarks from you today. Or ever.

She walked into his arms, his skin hot and smooth against hers, and as their mouths met in another searing kiss, passion rose swiftly and sharply between them.

Somehow, they managed to stumble into the tiny bathroom without breaking the kiss. Fumbling blindly for the taps, Ed turned the water on, and the spray of water was so shockingly cold at first that Jasmine screeched and clung to his hot body until the water warmed up.

In the confines of the narrow stall, their bodies were pressed together from head to toe, slick and slippery as they explored each other with eager hands—soaping, massaging, stroking.

"I want you," she panted against his lips. "I want you now."

24

EDGAR

J asmine was just as gorgeous in the nude as Ed had imagined, but the reality of her was even headier—the hot silk of her skin, the intoxicating taste of her mouth, the way she moved against him, her lithe body straining closer, seeking more.

"I want you," she breathed. "I want you now."

He groaned, his erection throbbing almost painfully between them, and as she dipped her hand between their bodies and wrapped her palm around his shaft, his hips bucked into her hold as if they had a mind of their own. He nearly came right then and there.

That wasn't how he'd envisioned the encounter. If he climaxed now, he wouldn't be able to refrain from biting Jasmine, and that would send her on a euphoric trip that could last hours. He could wait for her to wake up and then have her again, but he didn't want to wait, and he didn't want to shortchange their pleasure by ending their shower interlude in under thirty seconds.

"Don't." He placed his hand over hers on his shaft. "I don't want it to be over before it begins."

She looked into his eyes, gold flecks swirling hypnotically in her irises, and after a moment, her grip on his happy handle slackened, and her lips curved in a smile. "Should I switch the temperature to cold?"

"No need, beautiful." He started going down to his knees, his hands sliding down her sides, caressing the smooth, silky, golden skin. "Just let me worship you first."

"Oh, goddess." She let out a throaty groan and leaned against the fiberglass wall.

"Yes, you are." He smoothed his hands back to cup her bottom and leaned in to plant a soft kiss on the top of her hairless mound.

She must have had her pubic hair professionally removed because the skin was flawlessly smooth, and her scent...

Fates, her scent.

He was getting lightheaded.

"You smell divine."

She emitted a throaty chuckle. "That's because I'm a goddess, right?"

"To me, you are." He slid a finger inside of her while pressing his mouth over her clit to suck it in.

"Fuck me!" Jasmine hissed.

He let go of her clit and looked up at her with a grin. "I will, just not yet." He wedged a second finger inside her.

Her hips churning, she lifted her hands to cup her ample breasts, rubbing her thumbs over her nipples as she gyrated over his fingers.

He berated himself for not giving them the proper attention and vowed to remedy the neglect as soon as he was done getting his fill of her feminine nectar.

Clamping his hands on her ass, he held her in place as he kissed her tender bud, soft kisses that were more teasing than satisfying. She tried to grind herself over his fingers and his mouth, and even though his hold on her was unyielding, she kept fighting despite the futility of it.

Stubborn woman.

He liked strong females, and her stubbornness only spurred his arousal.

As she burrowed her fingers into his hair and tugged hard, he groaned against her throbbing clit and rewarded her with a flick of his tongue.

"Yes, just like that," she encouraged. "It's so good."

It was, but it would be even better in bed. The shower had seemed like a good idea, but it was way too small. On the other hand, it meant that everything was within reach.

It was the work of a moment for him to turn off the water, grab the towel, and wrap Jasmine in it.

"What are you doing?" she finally croaked when he lifted her into his arms.

"The bed will be much more comfortable."

"I've never seen anyone move so fast." She wrapped her arms around his neck.

"Pilot training." He laid her on the narrow bed using one hand while tugging the towel with the other.

Her large amber eyes grew even bigger. "How come you are so strong?"

Toweling off, he laughed. "Next, you'll ask why my teeth are so long."

Hopefully, his thrall made sure that her brain couldn't process seeing his fangs, but she must have sensed that something was off and that she was in the presence of a predator because a shudder went through her.

"Are you cold?" he asked, tossing the towel into the small bathroom.

She shook her head. "I'm serious. I'm heavy, and you lifted me with one arm like I weighed no more than a feather."

He prowled over her. "Lots of weightlifting." He cupped her breasts and then lightly pinched her nipples.

Jasmine narrowed her eyes at him. "You said that you don't go to the gym."

If she was this coherent, he wasn't doing a good job of pleasuring her.

"You said that you only…"

Lifting her by her waist, he twisted her around before the last syllable left her mouth.

His hand on her nape, he pushed her down so her face was on the mattress and her ass was high in the air.

Jasmine turned her head and looked at him over her shoulder. "What are you doing?"

"What does it look like I'm doing? I'm still worshiping my goddess."

Bending down, he extended his tongue and gave her wet slit a long lick. "Delightful." He smacked his lips before diving in for more.

25

JASMINE

As Edgar's tongue speared into her from behind, Jasmine gasped. It was so erotically wicked to be licked like that, and so was the feel of his strong fingers digging into her fleshy bottom.

It didn't take long until she was spiraling toward an orgasm, and as much as she tried to hold on so it could climb even higher, she was powerless to do anything about it. The climax erupted from her like a volcano, and she screamed something incoherent into the mattress.

Edgar kept gently licking her quivering flesh and pumping his fingers in and out of her until her tremors subsided, and then he flipped her over and looked into her eyes.

"Gold," he whispered.

Still dazed from her climax, she wasn't sure what he was talking about, but then it occurred to her that he was referring to the gold flakes swirling around her pupils.

He closed a warm palm around her breast, feathering his thumb over her nipple. "Are you ready for more?"

She reached between their bodies and took hold of his length. "Does that answer your question?" she purred, stroking him softly and maddeningly slow. "I need you inside me, but first..." She stretched her arm and retrieved a condom packet from her nightstand. "Protection."

With deft fingers, she tore the wrapper and sheathed him with practiced ease. "Now."

He entered her in one smooth thrust, his shaft sliding inside her wet heat with ease and sheathing himself to the hilt.

They both gasped at the intensity, the incredible feeling of being joined.

The fit was so perfect that she had an absurd thought about Edgar being her promised prince.

He surely looked and made love like one.

Even his weight on top of her felt perfect, his smooth, muscled chest pressing into hers and flattening her breasts. At first, his hips retreated and surged forward slowly and gently, and as he increased the tempo and strength of his thrusts, he did so in small increments as if testing how much she could take.

Did he think she was made of glass?

She was far from delicate, timid, or shy, and she could take much more than what he was giving her.

"More." Jasmine arched up.

He didn't comply right away, exhibiting uncommon and truly admirable restraint as he ramped up his thrusting, and for some reason that brought tears to her eyes.

Well, Jasmine knew precisely why she appreciated that so much. Most of the men she'd been with hadn't been as careful with her, even those she'd been in long-term relationships with, and this stranger was gentler than those who had claimed to love her.

Pausing completely, Ed lifted his head and looked into her eyes. "Am I hurting you?"

"No. You are perfect."

"So why are you crying?"

She wasn't. She was sure that not a single tear had spilled from her eyes. How did he know that the tears were gathering before even looking into her eyes?

Intuition?

Or had she made a sound without being aware of it?

Lifting her hand, Jasmine cupped Edgar's cheek. "I'm just a little emotional. Thank you for being so careful with me."

He lowered his head and pressed his lips against her in the softest of kisses. "You are precious," he murmured between kisses. "And you deserve to be treated as such."

The man didn't know her, so if he thought that she was precious, he must think that all women were, and that made him even more special to her.

So many men thought of women as vessels for their pleasure, to be used and abused. Most were not malicious, though, just careless and selfish.

"You are a rare jewel, Edgar, a prince among men."

He smiled and then, kissing her softly, resumed his slow and steady rhythm.

Watching her carefully, he soon set up a tempo that had her careening toward the edge of the cliff again.

She met him thrust for thrust, her nails raking down his back and her breathy moans and cries spurring him on.

It was raw and primal, but she still had a feeling that he was holding back. It was evident in his tense shoulders, the hard set of his jaw, and the perspiration on his brow. But as much as she tried to spur him on by churning her hips and moaning in his ear, he wasn't releasing all that pent-up power.

His tongue flicking over her neck was what drove her over the edge, and as another climax washed over her like a tsunami, she heard him hiss, and then twin points of searing pain stole her breath before fading away. The momentary pain was replaced by another earth-shattering orgasm, and as his hot seed jetted out of him, another climax thundered through her.

When her convulsions finally eased up, relaxing her muscles and leaving her boneless, euphoria spread throughout her mind and body, carrying her on its wings to a place of bliss where nothing negative existed.

Was it heaven?

Did she just die from too much pleasure?

Jasmine couldn't care less as she soared above the clouds, light as a thought and free as a bird.

26

EDGAR

Stars exploded behind Edgar's eyes as he followed Jasmine over the edge and emptied himself inside the damn condom.

Still, despite the hated prophylactic, it was the best sex he had ever had by a wide margin. Clinging to Jasmine, he retracted his fangs and licked the puncture wound closed, but he didn't stop there. He pressed soft kisses to her damp temples, her cheeks, and her lush, kiss-swollen lips that were lifted in a blissful smile.

"You are incredible," he murmured, even though she couldn't hear him. "A fantasy come true."

Letting himself catch his breath and enjoy the feel of this incredible woman in his arms, he turned to his side, bringing her with him, and almost fell off the narrow bed. He knew that he couldn't stay like this forever, but for a few more minutes, she could be his Princess, and he could be her Aladdin, and the real world could wait.

Caressing her rosy cheek, Ed chuckled. His definition of the real world was very different from Jasmine's. Would Kian allow him to tell her about their world?

He'd allowed that for Frankie and Margo just because of a few weak indicators that they might be Dormants, so why not Jasmine?

If Amanda had wanted Max to check her out, she suspected that Jasmine was a Dormant as well, and she must have a good reason to think it.

Damn, he hoped that Max wouldn't change his mind and decide that he wanted to pursue her. The Guardian was an impressive guy, and Jasmine might decide that she preferred his hulking masculinity to Edgar's more slender and less macho form.

With a sigh, Ed carefully untangled himself from Jasmine's arms and pulled out slowly while holding on to the top of the condom so it wouldn't spill inside of her.

He didn't have much practice with those, and he wondered why he hadn't thralled Jasmine to forgo it. His standard modus operandi was to thrall his partners to ignore his fangs and glowing eyes, to think that he'd used a condom when he hadn't, and to forget the venom bite. He had thralled Jasmine with all save one.

Come to think of it, his subconscious had saved him from making a huge mistake. If Jasmine was a potential Dormant, he could have accidentally induced her without her consent.

She had to be told about her potential first and then decide whether she wanted to be induced and who she wanted her inducer to be. He couldn't assume that she would choose him.

Hell, she could potentially want to sample all the eligible clan males before deciding on the one who would induce her. Something told him that Jasmine wasn't the kind of woman who settled on the first option presented to her.

Rising to his feet, Edgar discarded the condom in the bathroom trashcan and turned on the shower faucet again. The towel they had used had slipped to the floor, and when he picked it up, he realized that it was still a little damp, but it was the only one she had.

As he stood under the spray, he thought about Max. Perhaps he needed to have a talk with the guy and ask him to stay away from Jasmine. If he hurried, he might even still catch the Guardian at the wedding party.

But did he have the right to make such a request of the guy?

Jasmine wasn't his girlfriend, let alone his mate, and tomorrow, she might decide to invite someone else to her bed. After Edna cleared her, which he had no doubt she would, Jasmine would be able to mingle with all the bachelors on the upper decks and have her pick of the crop. Why would she limit herself to him?

It wasn't as if they had formed an emotional connection. As amazing as the sex was, it had been purely physical.

For the first time in his life, Edgar bemoaned not spending more time with a woman and getting to know her before taking her to bed. He should have formed a closer connection with Jasmine before engaging with her sexually.

The thing was, though, Jasmine had taken him to her bed, not the other way around.

27

KIAN

Syssi leaned her head on Kian's shoulder and whispered, "What time is it?"
He glanced at his watch. "It's five minutes after midnight. We should start making our exit soon."

The wedding party was still in full swing, and they had plenty of time until the telepathic meeting between his mother and her grandmother, but before leaving, they needed to congratulate the newlyweds and say goodnight to people. Syssi also wanted to get out of her evening gown and put on something comfortable before heading to his mother's cabin.

Scanning the room for Aru, Kian found the god dancing with his mate, and when they made eye contact, Kian lifted his wrist and looked at his watch again. Getting the hint, the god nodded.

It still boggled Kian's mind that Aru and Aria could create an instantaneous mental connection while separated by hundreds of light years. The implications were so profound that it made his head ache just thinking about them. It was proof that consciousness was not bound to the material world and its rules, at least not in the way he understood the laws of physics and space-time.

Kian put down his coffee cup, pushed away the small plate with the half-eaten cake, and put his hand on Syssi's thigh. "You look tired, my love."

It was her cue to start pretending that she was exhausted so they would have an excuse for their early departure.

The queen of Anumati expected the connection to be established by one in the morning Earth time, and the meeting would start whether he and Syssi were there or not.

The truth was that it wasn't really necessary for him to be with his mother when the meeting commenced.

It wasn't as if Kian feared for Annani's well-being when alone with Aru. First of all, she could take care of herself, as Toven had reminded him time and again, and secondly, she had her Odus with her, and not even Aru's immense strength was a match for two Odus who were charged with protecting their mistress.

Still, his mother appreciated the moral support. Besides, Syssi had volunteered to transcribe everything that was being said, and he couldn't argue with her logic that the best way of keeping the notes an absolute secret was writing them by hand.

In today's hackable world, recording things with pen and paper was the only hack-proof method, provided that the records were well hidden and well guarded, which he would take care of as soon as they got back to the village.

Syssi sighed loudly and turned to Kian. "My feet are killing me. Are you ready to call it a night?"

Across the table, Amanda lifted a brow. "Leaving so early again? What's your rush?"

"It's not that early," Kian forced a casual tone. "Syssi has been dancing for hours, and she's tired."

"So were you." Syssi grimaced. "Just not in high heels. I'm dying to take my shoes off."

"You can dance barefoot," Amanda suggested. "Many do." She waved her hand at the dance floor.

"True, but they are not shorties with giants for mates." She cast a fond look at Kian. "Kian would look like he's dancing with a little girl."

He snorted. "No one would mistake you for a girl." He leaned closer and nuzzled her neck at the spot he planned on biting later tonight. "You are all woman."

Amanda rolled her eyes. "Oh, please. You should have said that you were eager to take your wife to bed from the get-go."

Predictably, Syssi's cheeks reddened. "It's not that. I am really tired, and we also need to go pick up Allegra from your mother's. We don't want to keep her up too late."

Suspicion flashed in Amanda's eyes.

His sister was sharply perceptive, always had been. It was part of what made her such a great researcher. She never accepted things at face value and always asked why.

Kian's jaw clenched at the need to hide things from her, but Aru insisted on keeping his ability to communicate with his sister a secret, and Kian had given him his word.

"I see." Amanda's tone was carefully neutral. "Well, don't let me keep you." Her gaze cut to Syssi, a silent question in their blue depths.

Syssi leaned over the table and clasped Amanda's hand. "The decorations were beautiful tonight."

Amanda shrugged. "Not my doing. Cassandra did all that on her own. I didn't even help with the menu. Geraldine insisted on doing it. Not that I minded." She leaned forward to whisper in Syssi's ear. "It left me free to do some matchmaking." She turned to Kian. "By the way, did you remember to talk to Edna about Jasmine?"

"Not yet. I'll speak with her first thing in the morning."

Amanda's eyes narrowed. "Don't put it off too long. I've already put the rest of the plan in motion."

"You did?" He glanced at the dance floor where Max was dancing with Darlene.

Amanda followed his gaze. "Oh, not with Max. He declined the offer. Something about Jasmine reminding him of someone he disliked."

"Then who?"

"Edgar."

That surprised Kian. He hadn't seen that coming. Edgar was still a kid in immortal years, but he had a reputation for being a ladies' man. Like most immortal males, he was handsome, but in a more boyish way than Max. He didn't have the heft and swagger of the Guardian.

Kian wasn't sure how he felt about the pilot pursuing Jasmine. It wasn't that Edgar was undeserving of a mate. It was just that he was still young and there were many who were more deserving.

Jasmine being a Dormant was not a certainty, though, and at the moment, it was only a theory.

"We still don't know what Jasmine is about, and having a Guardian befriend her would have been better."

"I know," Amanda admitted. "But Ed overheard me talking with Max, and when Max declined, he jumped on the opportunity to take his place. I couldn't say no."

"You could, but I assume it's too late?"

She nodded. "He took her dinner and didn't come back up yet."

"If he returns after we leave, question him about her."

"Yes, sir." Amanda saluted him. "Goodnight, you two, and kiss Allegra for me."

"We will." Syssi pushed to her feet and stopped by Amanda to give her a hug. "Enjoy the rest of the party."

After a round of congratulations and goodnights to the groom and bride and to their families, Kian and Syssi walked out of the dining room.

The music and laughter faded behind them as they entered the elevator, and as soon as the doors closed behind them, Kian pulled Syssi into his arms. "Can I steal a kiss from my wife?"

"Always." Smiling, she lifted on her toes, cupped his cheek, and pressed her lips to his.

Kian leaned into her touch. "I hate all this damn secrecy. It feels wrong to lie to my sisters and keep this from them. They should know." He couldn't say more in the elevator that had a surveillance camera located in a discreet spot.

"I know, love." Her thumb stroked over his cheekbone. "But it's not up to you. It's Aru's call, and I can understand why he's being so paranoid about it." She waited until they stepped out of the elevator on their deck, where the surveillance cameras were off for the next few hours. "If word got out about Aru's sister and her work with the queen, it could spell disaster not just for her but for the queen, the oracle, and the entire resistance."

Nodding, Kian opened the door to their cabin and drew her into his arms. "I love you," he murmured into her hair as he held her close, breathing in the scent of her and letting it soothe his jagged edges.

"I love you, too." She kissed his cheek lightly. "But we should hurry up and change. We have five minutes to be at your mother's."

He sighed. "That's a shame. If we had fifteen, it would have been infinitely better."

Snorting, Syssi playfully slapped his arm. "Do you ever think of anything other than getting me in bed?" She started walking toward their bedroom.

"I do. I think about getting you in the closet, in the shower, on the kitchen counter…" He stopped to catch the pillow she chucked at him. "Oh, this is going to cost you, young lady."

Syssi laughed, the husky sound fueling his budding arousal. "I'm looking forward to it, big guy."

28

ANNANI

Annani stood in front of the door to the cabin's terrace and looked up at the starry sky. Somewhere out there, hundreds of light years away, was Anumati, the home world of the gods, the corner of the galaxy her father had come from.

In the enormous, incomprehensible scale of the universe, Earth and Anumati were not only in the same neighborhood but on the same street. Maybe even in the same apartment building. She did not know enough about astronomy to know the actual scale, but since they were in the same galaxy, probably even in the same spoke of the wheel, it was considered close.

They called themselves gods and believed that they were the masters of the universe, but that was as misguided as humans thinking the same thing. Somewhere out there, in a different galaxy, there was probably a species of beings even more powerful than the gods, but the distances were so vast that there was no way to physically traverse them. The only way contact could be made was through connected consciousnesses like Aria and Aru's.

Somehow, their minds were entangled like quantum particles.

Vivian and Ella had a similar connection, probably created by the same mechanism of quantum entanglement. The question was whether beings who had never touched each other, physically or otherwise, could be conjoined.

Theoretically, it was possible.

After all, the entirety of matter and all of energy in the universe had supposedly been created in the Big Bang, so every particle in all of creation had at one time touched all others.

Everything was intertwined.

Annani lifted a hand to her temple. She was giving herself a headache by thinking and theorizing about things she did not know enough about and had no patience for learning.

Sometimes, she suspected that she suffered from what humans called attention deficit disorder. She had all the classic indicators, starting with poor impulse control and continuing with a dislike of learning anything that required concentrating for a long time.

Oh, well.

No one was perfect. Not even the royal heir to the throne of the Eternal King. Annani was a powerful goddess, the most powerful being on Earth, and deep down she knew that she had not explored the extent of that power.

Toven kept telling her that, and she kept dismissing him, saying that after five thousand years she knew perfectly well what she was capable of, but it was a lie. The truth was that she was afraid to look too deeply inside herself and discover that she was more powerful than her father or even more than her grandfather.

It was terrifying.

Annani did not want to rule Anumati any more than she wanted to rule Earth. She had not even wanted to rule her own clan, entrusting her children to manage it for her, and they did that splendidly without her.

As for humans, even if she was interested in governing them, they would never accept her as their ruler, and by taking over she would do more harm than good, which was the reason why she had never considered it.

Working from the shadows and trying to improve their condition as much as she and her clan could was the best option for the divided and fiercely tribal humans.

But Anumati was different, and it was possible that she was the only one who could liberate trillions of beings from the oppressive rule of her grandfather.

Or conversely, cause mass loss of life and destruction.

A soft sigh had her turn to look at her sleeping granddaughter. Allegra shifted in the portable crib that Parker had brought to Annani's cabin with Okidu's help.

The sweet child always brought a smile to her face.

Annani had hundreds of grandchildren, great-grandchildren, and many times removed great-grandchildren, but Allegra had a special place in her heart.

When the doorbell rang, the child whimpered in her sleep but did not wake up.

As Kian and Syssi entered along with Aru, Annani walked over to them and welcomed each one with a warm embrace.

"Are you okay?" Kian regarded her with a frown.

"I am very well, my son. I have been pondering the universe, and it has made me feel melancholy for some reason. But then I gazed upon the face of my granddaughter, and my heart swelled with so much love that I became emotional. But do not mind me." She waved her hand at the couch. "Let us all get comfortable before the meeting begins." She turned to Aru. "Is Aria ready?"

"She has not opened the channel yet, but I assume that she will at any moment."

"Indeed." Annani offered him a fond smile. "In the meantime, please help yourself to the refreshments my Odus have prepared."

"Thank you, Clan Mother."

As Aru reached for a teacup, Ojidu immediately rushed to lift the carafe and pour into the young god's cup.

When each one of them had a cup in hand, Aru closed his eyes, and Annani's heartbeat accelerated.

There was something she desperately needed to ask the oracle, and hopefully, her wish would not be denied by her grandmother or the seer.

29

QUEEN ANI

A ni settled into her cushioned seat, excited anticipation filling her chest as she prepared for another telepathic meeting with her granddaughter. The connection, which was made possible through the extraordinary abilities of the twins Aru and Aria, had become a lifeline for her, a bridge over the vast distance between Earth and Anumati so she could get to know her beloved son's daughter and share the wisdom of her years with Annani, the young goddess who might be the answer to the future of their people.

Sofringhati slanted a look at her. "You look amused. Care to share?"

Ani smiled. "I was thinking of Annani, and to me, she is a young goddess, but she thinks that she is ancient at her mere five thousand Earth years."

"It is a matter of perspective, my dear friend. She lives among humans whose lives are so short that they are a mere blink of an eye to us. And yet, they pack so many experiences into their short lives to take with them to the beyond."

Ani frowned. "You said that you cannot see beyond the veil. So how do you know that?"

Her friend's lips twitched with a smile. "I cannot see, that is true, but sometimes I get impressions." She leaned closer to whisper in Ani's ear, as if anyone could hear them.

Aria was there, but she was already privy to all of their secrets, so there was no need to whisper around her. Sometimes, Sofri just liked to be dramatic.

"The mighty gods would not like to hear this, but beyond the veil, they are no different than the created species they look down their noses at. In the realm of the spirits, no one being is worth more than another." Sofri leaned back.

Ani nodded. "That is what the scriptures say, but I doubt it. Do you know why?"

"Enlighten me."

"Patterns. The universe is made of patterns, and things repeat themselves. So, if there is a hierarchy in the physical world, there is also a hierarchy in the spirit world. They might not use the same criteria for who is better than whom, but I am sure they have them. Besides, can you imagine how boring it would be without any intrigue and backstabbing?"

Sofri shook her head. "You are as incorrigible and irreverent now as you were when we were girls. You just mask it with a lot of royal attitude."

Ani canted her head. "I am a free thinker, Sofri. I never accept dogma."

"I know." Sofringhati reached for her hand. "That is why you are the unofficial leader of the resistance; its beating heart."

Ani squeezed her friend's hand. "That was very nice of you to say." She glanced at Aria. "Is it time?"

The young goddess dipped her head. "Yes, my queen. I will check if Aru and the heir are ready."

"Annani likes to be called the Clan Mother," Ani said. "I think it says a lot about her."

Sofri nodded. "It does. She is a shepherd at heart."

Ani hoped that she and Sofri were not projecting their wishes onto Annani and making her out to be someone she was not. What if she was more like her grandfather than they realized?

They did not need another Eternal Queen who would do everything to stay in power, no matter who she needed to murder to do that.

From what Aru had told them, though, Annani had left the leadership of her clan to her children and functioned more as a spiritual figurehead than an active ruler. It indicated that she was not power-hungry.

But who knew?

She might develop a taste for it like her grandfather had. El had been a brilliant leader who had united Anumati's factions and brought peace and prosperity before his heart had turned to stone.

"They are ready, my queen," Aria said.

"Send my warm greetings to Annani, her son, and his mate if they are with her."

Aria closed her eyes for a moment. "They are, and they send their warm greetings as well. Your granddaughter awaits her first lesson on Anumati's history."

There was so much to tell, so much history and knowledge to impart. But where to begin? How to condense the complex, often turbulent story of their world into a narrative that would both inform and inspire?

Ani took a deep breath, casting her mind back to the earliest days of Anumati, to the tales passed down through the generations of gods and goddesses, some of them recorded by oracles from the past, some by scribes and scholars.

"Not much is known of the early days of our kind's creation. There are legends, of course. The Kra-ell believe in the Mother of All Life who created every living being in the universe, and they claim that we believed in her as well before we lost our way and severed our connection to the land, deciding that we were gods—the creators of our world and many others."

She sighed. "But I am getting ahead of my story."

"When our civilization was young, millions of years ago, our lifespans were not endless like they are now. On average, we lived about a thousand Earth years, which is long compared to your humans, but a blink of an eye compared to our lifespans now. There were conflicts, as in any civilization, power struggles, and wars, but there were also long periods of peace, during which we lived in harmony, exploring the boundaries of our abilities and shaping the world around us. As the eons passed, our numbers grew, our technology advanced, and space travel became a necessity, first for the harvesting of resources and later for colonization. Naturally, power struggles and differences in opinions created division. Factions arose, each with their own vision of what Anumati should be and how its people should live and govern themselves."

Ani twined the chain of her pendant around her finger. "Most of the struggle was political and economic, and the leading families who owned the large manufacturing conglomerates became the royalty of Anumati. They controlled the genetics labs and dictated who got which traits. Those who had the means invested in their children's future, giving them a genetic advantage over those with lesser resources, and over time, a huge divide formed between those who called themselves royals and those who they called commoners."

30

ANNANI

"So that was how it began," Kian murmured as Aru paused to listen to his sister Aria's telepathic relay. "The divide between the glowing and non-glowing Anumatians."

"I wonder if that schism was the start of the resistance," Syssi said.

Annani had a feeling that even more complex political machinations had been at play in those early days of their ancestral civilization. Regrettably, it seemed to be a universal constant that in every society there were leaders and there were followers. And more often than not, those who rose to power came from the privileged echelons, even when they claimed to champion the cause of the downtrodden masses.

It was almost never about the masses. It was always about power and wealth.

The simple truth was that the underprivileged were usually far too preoccupied with the daily struggles of earning a living and providing for their families to have the time or resources to organize a rebellion.

"Each of the royal families amassed their own power bases," Aru continued. "Alliances and coalitions were forged, consolidating their power primarily through strategic marriages between the leading houses. It was an imperfect system, but it worked."

Aru went on to relay the queen's explanation of how the ruling families installed vast networks of administrators who were tasked with overseeing public affairs and enforcing the dictates set forth by their masters. While each dynastic conglomerate had its own particular set of laws and customs, there was a great deal of commonality between them. By and large, the system functioned adequately, and the majority of the population, commoners included, enjoyed a reasonable degree of prosperity.

"But periodically, the leaders of one faction or another would grow dissatisfied with their allotted share of wealth and power." Aru paused for a moment. "Or they would feel slighted by some real or imagined offense from their rivals. In such cases, localized conflicts would erupt, disrupting the peace. In an effort to break the cycle of internecine violence, the heads of two of the most influential royal houses convened a summit, where they conceived of a governing council intended to serve as a forum for the peaceful resolution of disputes. They presented their idea to the heads of the other families, who agreed to the proposition, and thus the first Anumati Council was born.

"Each family was granted the right to appoint a single representative to the Council, regardless of their relative wealth, territorial holdings, or the size of the population under their dominion."

"A surprisingly egalitarian provision," Annani said, "given the generally oligarchic nature of the power structure. I wonder how effectively it worked in practice."

Aru nodded. "Her Majesty believes this is a suitable place to conclude for today. She has provided you with a broad overview, which she will continue to expand upon in the subsequent meetings. After that, she intends to circle back and delve into more specific aspects of Anumati's sociopolitical evolution. Are there any other questions you would like to present before we adjourn?"

Annani glanced at her son, knowing that he would not like what she was about to ask next, but she was going to ask it anyway. "Actually, my question is more in the nature of a request. I was hoping that the Supreme Oracle might be able to shed some light on a particular event from our own history, one that has haunted me for millennia."

She braced herself as she awaited the response, hoping against hope that the oracle might be able to help her.

"The oracle would love to help, but regrettably, Earth is shielded from her sight," Aru relayed. "She cannot penetrate the barrier to glimpse its past or future."

Annani's heart sank, but she had expected as much. The queen had said so last night, but Annani had hoped that there was a loophole she could use. "Is it certain that this limitation applies to all of Anumati's oracles?"

"I am afraid so, my dear granddaughter," Aru relayed the queen's answer. "But I am curious to hear what you wanted Sofringhati to divine for you."

Annani cast another glance at Kian, and given his somber expression, he knew what she wanted to ask. "After your revelation about the assassins the king sent to kill my father and the realization that Mortdh might not have been the one responsible for the annihilation of my people, it occurred to me that perhaps he was not responsible for my Khiann's death either. For five thousand years, I have been haunted by the horrific account of my mate's supposed demise at Mortdh's hands, an account I have never before had any cause to doubt. But now I cannot help but question it."

She closed her eyes against the sudden sting of tears. "My father made numerous attempts to placate Mortdh and defuse his hostile intentions. When all of those overtures failed, I fear Ahn may have resorted to a far more ruthless stratagem. He dared not have Mortdh assassinated outright, for it would have been all too clear who was behind the act. But if he could convincingly lay the death of a god at Mortdh's feet, the effect would be much the same in terms of neutralizing the threat."

Annani's hands curled into fists. "Ahn was a cold and calculating ruler, as you well know. But I refuse to believe that he would have conspired to murder my mate solely for the purpose of framing Mortdh. What I suspect is that the witnesses who originally reported Khiann's death to my father may have simply informed him that my love and his retinue had fallen victim to the catastrophic earthquake that cleaved the desert. My father might have seized the opportunity and compelled the witnesses into claiming Mortdh had murdered Khiann in cold blood. That is what I hoped the Oracle could ascertain. Because if Mortdh did not, in fact, behead my beloved, then there is a chance, however small, that Khiann still lives. He might be in stasis, trapped beneath the desert sands, waiting for me to find him and bring him home."

Annani's voice broke on the last word, and in her peripheral vision, she registered Kian shaking his head.

If Kian had known Ahn, he would have realized that exploiting his own daughter's devastation for political gain was absolutely consistent with his character.

She could just imagine her father rationalizing it to her mother, saying that Annani's grief would make the deception all the more believable. He would have added that he had raised his daughter to be resilient and that, in time, she would recover from the loss.

It was even possible that he had intended to send a search party for Khiann once the threat of Mortdh had been eliminated but never got the chance to do it because of the assassins the Eternal King, his own father, had sent to kill him.

Such an ugly tangle.

"The Supreme Oracle sends her deepest regrets," Aru said. "She would gladly scour the desert sands in search of your mate were such a thing within her power, but the veiling of Earth has ever been an inviolable barrier to her sight."

Annani swallowed past the lump in her throat and nodded. "I understand. Please convey my gratitude to Queen Ani for the fascinating lesson in Anumati's history and let her know how eagerly I await our next session."

31

KIAN

As Aru's telepathic connection with his sister ended, Kian turned his gaze to his mother. She avoided his eyes, but he could see the stiffness of her shoulders and the stubborn tilt of her chin.

Annani feared that he would dismiss this latest theory of hers as more wishful thinking and quash her hope again.

The prophecy she'd gotten five thousand years ago had kept that flicker of hope alive in her throughout the millennia, despite all the evidence stacked against it. He knew that, even though his mother didn't talk about it. Or maybe she did, just not with him. Perhaps she'd confided in Alena.

The thing was, she should have trusted him to be open-minded and listen to her because what she had told the queen actually made perfect sense. In fact, he couldn't understand how none of them had ever considered the possibility of Ahn manipulating the witnesses.

His grandfather had been a powerful compeller and a ruthless leader. If he wanted to eliminate the threat of Mortdh, Khiann's untimely demise in the earthquake would have provided him with the perfect opportunity to frame Mortdh as his murderer.

Kian couldn't understand how Ahn could have been so cruel to Annani, but then he himself was very different from his grandfather. He would never have sacrificed his own daughter on the altar of politics.

Hell, he would have killed Mortdh himself and screw the consequences.

Syssi reached out and touched Annani's arm. "I know you are disappointed that the oracle couldn't help you, but perhaps I can help search for Khiann. If there's even the slightest chance that he is alive, I will do everything I can to find a clue to his whereabouts. After all, if I could find David's parents by inducing a vision, I might be able to find out the truth about Khiann's fate as well."

Kian hated it when Syssi did that. It was one thing when the visions came to her unbidden and another thing when she forced herself into a trance and invited them.

Every time she delved into the mists of time and possibility, she emerged drained and disoriented, sometimes taking days to fully recover. The thought of her subjecting herself to that again made his protective instincts surge to the fore.

True, he told himself that she wasn't pregnant now and that there was no risk to her health, but he was still wary of the damn visions. Where did they come from? Was it from the Fates or from some malignant force that could leave its residue on Syssi's soul?

Kian didn't like anything that he didn't understand, and out of all the paranormal abilities, seeing events that hadn't happened yet or even past events that were unconnected to the seer had no logical explanation.

Still, he didn't say a word.

The desperate hope his mother was trying to mask slew him, and if Syssi could help her, he would never stand in her way.

Annani turned a grateful smile at Syssi. "If you wish to try, by all means, but there was a reason I did not turn to you first, my sweet child. Your visions are about the now or the future, not the distant past. Jacki might have been able to take a peek if I had anything of Khiann's I could give her to hold, but regrettably, I have nothing of his."

Kian frowned. "Why not? Didn't you take some mementos from your time together when you fled to the north?"

"There was no time. I knew that I would need to start a new civilization and to do that, I would need knowledge I did not possess. My first priority was to find Ekin's tablet and steal it." She sighed. "I took some jewelry to barter with, and I used it wisely over the years. Keeping my children and grandchildren fed and sheltered was more important than keeping Khiann's gifts. I have never assigned much value to possessions." Her eyes suddenly widened. "What about the Odus? They were also a gift from my Khiann. I could ask Jacki to touch them."

Syssi pursed her lips. "Jacki can definitely try, but I doubt it will work with the Odus. Then again, Jacki saw what happened to Wonder just from touching the little statue someone had made of her as Gulan, so maybe she can pull it off." Syssi cast a sidelong glance at Kian. "It's a shame the amulet is depleted of power. Jacki could have used it to amplify her ability."

Annani shook her head. "That thing was evil. Even if it still held its potency, I would not resort to using it for this purpose. My Khiann was all bright light and love. To seek him through an instrument of darkness would be an affront to his memory."

Kian nodded in agreement. "I wouldn't use that thing either. I hope that Kalugal stored it somewhere safe so no evil can find it and use it to amplify its darkness."

His mother cast him a loving smile and reached for his hand. "You might not be Khiann's son, but I named you after him not just because I wanted to honor his memory, but because I saw so much of him in you, even when you were still a baby. You grew up to be just like him in so many ways. Your strength, compassion, and sense of justice, even your sense of humor. You also love your wife as fiercely as he loved me."

Kian felt his throat tighten with emotion. "Thank you. I'm honored to carry his name, and I hope Syssi or Jacki can help find him or at least find out what fate befell him."

Annani squeezed his hand. "I know it is not easy for you to watch your mate surrender to the visions, and I appreciate it."

Syssi leaned back in her chair. "If it wasn't so late, I would do it now, but I'm tired, and it's never good to summon visions when I'm not fully rested."

Aru, who had listened to the exchange without saying a thing, pushed to his feet. "If my services are no longer required, I would like to retire for the night."

"Not yet," Kian said. "There is a matter I need to discuss with you before you go."

32

ANNANI

Annani had not expected Syssi to volunteer to induce a vision about Khiann, so she was not disappointed that her daughter-in-law did not wish to do so right away.

Well, not majorly disappointed.

When Annani had asked the oracle for help, she had been aware that Earth was obscured from her vision, but she had hoped that some events from the distant past were accessible to the Supreme Oracle of Anumati, and hearing that they were not had been deeply disappointing. In comparison, Syssi's delay in doing so was inconsequential.

Annani had no doubt that her son's mate would do everything in her power to assist her. In fact, she would probably do more than she should and exhaust herself.

Leaning over, Annani took Syssi's hand. "Promise me to pace yourself and not force too many visions. If Khiann has waited five thousand years for me to realize that he might be alive, then he can wait a few more weeks."

Syssi nodded. "You know me too well, Clan Mother. I promise not to overdo it. If the Fates are willing, they will show me Khiann, and if they are not, no amount of pressure will force them to do so."

Aru had waited patiently for her to finish talking before turning to Kian. "What did you want to discuss?"

Kian raked his fingers through his hair. "It's late, so I will cut straight to the chase. I'm not comfortable hiding things from my sisters and sneaking around behind their backs. This connection is monumental on so many levels, and they are the leaders of this community as much as my mother and I are. If you want us to someday house the headquarters of the resistance, they and everyone else in my clan will have to be told, but everyone can wait. Right now, I just want to tell my sisters."

Aru's eyes blazed with anger. "I thought that I was clear on that. You've already betrayed my trust by telling your mate, and now you want to tell your sisters?"

"If I'm talking with you about it, I'm not betraying your trust. I know that you want to protect your sister, but you are being irrational. At some point, we will have to share this with them, and you know it. Does it really matter if we do it now or in a few months? The only thing we will achieve is mistrust. My sisters will not be happy to discover that they have been kept in the dark for so long."

Closing his eyes, Aru let out a breath. "What about their mates?"

Kian met his hard gaze with an equally hard one of his own. "My sisters and their mates are one and the same. None of them will betray you."

Indecision clouded Aru's eyes. "I did not tell my mate about my connection with my sister. If we are to include your sisters and their mates, then I will have to tell Gabi as well. She is my partner, and I cannot in good conscience keep this from her while sharing it with your entire family."

"Of course," Kian said. "I don't know why you kept it from her so far."

Aru's brows went up, and the look he gave Kian had her son avert his eyes. What was that about? Was it about Kian keeping from Syssi the knowledge of what a god's blood could do?

Annani would find out later, but right now she needed to find a compromise that would keep Aru from losing his mind. "I have an idea," she said. "If it would set your mind at ease, I could use compulsion to ensure the silence of my daughters and their mates on the matter. I do not like controlling the minds of others, least of all my children, but I am willing to do so to alleviate your concerns."

"That is an interesting proposition," Aru said. "How strong is your compulsion ability, Clan Mother?"

"Strong," Kian answered for her.

"What about Toven?" Annani asked. "He might be crucial to the success of our future goals, and he should be in the know as well."

Aru's expression turned pensive. "Can you compel Toven?"

"I've never tried," she admitted. "But he is a very strong compeller in his own right, so I probably have no power over him, but I trust him implicitly. Ultimately, however, I leave the decision in your hands."

Aru was silent for a long moment. "Let's keep Toven in the dark for now. We can always include him later when we actually need him. The same is true for your daughters, Clan Mother, but I understand that family dynamics might become problematic if we keep this from them."

"It is not about family dynamics," Kian said. "In the grand scheme of things, this affects everyone in the clan."

"I could host a family lunch tomorrow," Annani suggested before turning to Aru. "You and Gabi are invited, of course, but perhaps it would be a good idea for you to inform Gabi beforehand. She is your mate, and she might feel slighted at not being told first."

"You are right, Clan Mother. I will speak with Gabi beforehand."

"Is there anything else we need to discuss?" Syssi glanced at her watch. "It's nearly three o'clock in the morning."

"I believe we are done." Annani looked at Kian, and when he nodded, she added, "I will make the arrangements for lunch tomorrow. Will one o'clock in the afternoon work for you?"

When Aru nodded, Kian turned to Syssi. "Did you make any plans for tomorrow?"

She smiled. "Other than chasing a vision of Khiann? No. I didn't." She walked over to Annani and embraced her. "If he's alive, we will find him. I promise."

33

JASMINE

J asmine woke up alone.

She hadn't expected Edgar to spend the night in her narrow bed, but she'd hoped he would stay despite the cramped space. He could have spooned her or held her to his chest, and in the morning, they could have shared breakfast in the dining room.

With a sigh, Jasmine turned on her back and draped her arm over her eyes. She was no stranger to disappointment, and as usual, she found a way to look on the bright side.

Edgar couldn't have joined her for breakfast because he wasn't allowed in the staff dining room, where the rescued women ate. Not that it made any sense to her since the male staff members used the place, but that was the rule, and he couldn't break it.

Poor women, though. It wasn't hard to see that something terrible had happened to them. Their eyes were haunted, hopeless, and Jasmine found it painful to look at them.

Thank the goddess that she hadn't chosen a career as a therapist or a social worker. She would have sucked at it. There were only two ways Jasmine knew how to make people happy. One was acting or singing, and the other was sex.

She also sucked at finding love, but that was beside the point. She should be glad for everything that the goddess had given her.

With a sigh, Jasmine dragged herself out of bed and went through her morning routine, trying to shake off the lingering sense of melancholy. As she made her way to the dining room, she wished she had a phone, just so Edgar could call her and tell her that he missed her or that he had a great time last night and couldn't wait to see her again.

She would have even settled for a half-assed excuse explaining why he hadn't stayed with her.

After getting dressed, Jasmine stepped out of her cabin and headed for the dining room, but then decided to skip it and go to the lounge instead. Her mood was low enough without seeing the poor women and getting nauseous thinking of what had been done to them or getting chest pains from trying not to think about it.

There was so much evil in the world, and there was so little she could do to make things better.

Besides, she wasn't hungry, probably because of the late dinner she'd eaten last night, and she could get coffee at the lounge.

The place was quiet when she got there, the usual bustle of activity conspicuously absent. After pouring herself coffee from the commercial pot, Jasmine settled herself on one of the plush couches and grabbed a glossy magazine that someone had left behind. Flipping through it, she looked at the celebrities caught on camera doing this or that and tried to ignore the hollow feeling in her stomach that wasn't about hunger.

From the corner of her eye, she saw a couple enter the lounge, but since neither of them was Edgar or one of her friends, she ignored them and kept flipping through pages of gossip about the rich and famous.

Jasmine would have loved to be on those pages, but that was a dream that she had given up on a long time ago. Now, she just wanted to act in quality productions and get paid enough to make a decent living. Except, even that modest dream was out of reach for most actors, including her. The best she could hope for was getting a part in the occasional commercial and satisfying her acting bug performing at community theaters for free.

When the couple approached her couch, she couldn't ignore them any longer and shifted her gaze to them. The woman looked a little drab but was pretty in a forgettable kind of way, and the man was a hunk who looked like he could bench-press a car. She hadn't seen either of them before, so they were either lost guests or they were looking for someone.

Jasmine put on a charming smile. "Can I help you?"

"Hello," the woman said. "My name is Edna. Kian sent me to talk to you."

Oh, crap. The one with the probe, whatever that meant. She'd forgotten all about it.

Jasmine rose to her feet and offered the woman her hand. "I wasn't expecting you so early in the morning."

A tight smile lifted the edges of Edna's thin lips as she shook Jasmine's hand. "It's after ten in the morning, so I wouldn't call it early." Her pale blue eyes bored into Jasmine's, but there was no malice in them, just curiosity and piercing intelligence.

Wow, she hadn't encountered anyone with quite that look before. Later, she would practice it in the mirror. Was it possible to act out an intelligent look, though?

Jasmine shook her head. "I didn't know that it was so late. I don't have a phone, and it's difficult to assess the time down here." She waved a hand at the windowless walls.

Edna scanned the room and nodded. "I would be uncomfortable in these surroundings." She glanced at the hulking man next to her. "Does the lack of windows make you uncomfortable, Max?"

"Not at all. It's cozy down here."

The man was the very embodiment of masculine beauty, and his deep voice sent a shiver down Jasmine's spine. Except, he hadn't spared her a look yet, so he was either gay or one of those dudes who thought that they were all that and that women should fall at their feet and worship them.

Not this woman. She was the one who should be worshiped, and Edgar had.

"Hello, Max." A coy smile tugging at her lips, Jasmine offered him her hand. "Are you here to make sure that I don't escape Edna's probe?"

He finally looked at her. "You've got it. Are you going to run?"

The dude was looking at her as if she had something nasty stuck in her teeth.

Turning to Edna, she asked, "Do you always travel with a bodyguard?"

"No, not always." She lowered herself to the couch. "Please, sit down, and let's get it over with."

Perhaps Max was Edna's boyfriend? The two didn't look like they even liked each other, but perhaps they had gotten into an argument on the way.

"How long have you been together?" Jasmine asked as she sat down next to Edna.

"We are not together," Max said. "I'm just an escort."

A chuckle bubbled up from Jasmine's throat. "I bet you are pricey." She waved a hand at him. "What with all the muscles, you must be in high demand."

As Edna snorted, sounding like a donkey, Max's neck went a very satisfying shade of red.

"I'm not a bodyguard," he clarified. "Nor am I Edna's boyfriend or her paid escort. I'm here as a representative of the clan, and my job is to ensure that you behave."

Jasmine had to bite her lip not to pick up that line and run with it.

But then it occurred to her that he'd said 'clan.' What clan?

Before she could inquire further, however, Edna lifted her hand to put a stop to the banter.

"Before we begin, tell me a little bit about yourself."

Edna's pale blue eyes were unnerving, and Jasmine wondered if she was a powerful hypnotist like Kevin. Come to think of it, why hadn't Kian sent Kevin to talk to her?

If the guy could convince Modana to be born again, he could get her to tell him anything he wanted.

Maybe she wasn't important enough to bother Kevin with.

The truth was that she had nothing to hide except her witchy ways. They were harmless, but some people thought that they were evil or dangerous, while others scoffed at all Wiccan practitioners, regarding them as lunatics.

Come to think of it, Kian had decided to send Edna to probe her after Jasmine had admitted to him and Amanda that she was Wiccan. But then Amanda had also admitted to dabbling a little with the occult, so maybe they had no problem with it.

Still, maybe it was better to preempt any potential criticism by explaining why she'd chosen that path to follow and the solace and comfort it provided her with. She should tell Edna about that in her own words instead of the woman picking up some odd ritual and thinking that Jasmine was a devil worshiper because she saw a pentagram in there.

"First and foremost, I'm an actress," Jasmine said. "Acting is my passion and what I enjoy doing the most. I'm not famous, and I can't make a living doing what I love, so I work in customer service to pay the bills. I'm also a Wiccan. I know that some people have negative preconceptions about Wiccans, but for me, Wicca has been a blessing and a solace. The embrace of the Mother of All Life, the connection to nature and the divine feminine have helped me through some tough times." She smiled. "The life of an actor is full of rejections, and everyone deals with that in their own way. I think mine is healthier and more nurturing than most."

To her surprise, Max suddenly seemed very interested in what she had to say. "Did you say Mother of All Life?" It sounded like an accusation.

Jasmine nodded, taken aback by his tone. "Yes, she's one of the central deities in Wicca. Why?"

Max shook his head. "Nothing. Go on."

He sounded dismissive, which was so aggravating because so many people made fun of witches.

"Wicca is listed as an official, legitimate religion by the government, with recognized holidays that practitioners can claim." Jasmine's tone was a little sharper than she'd intended. "It's not some fly-by-night cult."

Max snorted, his expression turning derisive. "Yeah, because the government is always such a great arbiter of what's real and what's not. Your so-called religion is just another sham organization that calls itself a faith to get tax-exempt status."

Why was he being so hostile?

What had she ever done to him?

Jasmine bristled, anger and indignation coursing through her veins. "Wicca has no churches," she snapped, "and no one makes money off of it unless they run a store, which wouldn't be tax-exempt anyway. We don't have any central authority or hierarchy. It's a personal, individual path."

There were covens, but they were usually small, ten to fifteen people, and Jasmine didn't belong to any. She was still a rookie witch who didn't know enough to even ask the right questions.

Max looked like he wanted to argue further, but Edna held up a hand, silencing him with a pointed look.

As she turned back to Jasmine, the woman's expression was one of gentle curiosity, with no trace of judgment or condemnation. "Tell me, Jasmine, has your practice ever produced any tangible results for you? Any instances where you felt like your spells or rituals had a real, measurable impact on your life?"

Jasmine nodded, a smile tugging at her lips as she remembered the countless times her incantations had seemed to work in her favor. "Absolutely. I always do a special ritual before going on auditions, and more often than not, I end up getting the part. It's like the universe is conspiring to help me succeed."

Edna's expression turned thoughtful, her head tilting slightly as she regarded Jasmine with a piercing gaze. "So, would it be fair to say that you've never auditioned for any truly major roles? No leading parts in big-budget productions or anything like that?"

Jasmine felt her cheeks heat up, a twinge of embarrassment mingling with the ever-present sting of self-doubt. "Well, no," she admitted. "But that's because I knew those parts were out of my reach."

"From divination?" Edna asked.

Jasmine nodded.

Something like understanding flickered through Edna's eyes, shaded by a hint of sadness or pity. "Perhaps it would have been better if you hadn't consulted your cards or your crystals whether you should audition for bigger parts. It's possible that you channeled your doubts and lack of belief in your own abilities into your divinations, producing the results you expected to see. And those results, in turn, only fed back into your insecurities, creating a self-fulfilling prophecy."

Jasmine stared at the woman as the truth of her words sank in. She had never stopped to think that her own fears and doubts might be influencing the very tools she relied on for guidance and reassurance.

"I've never thought of it that way, but you might be right. Do you really think that my own mind could have been sabotaging me?"

Edna reached out, her hand coming to rest on Jasmine's arm. "The mind is a powerful thing, and our beliefs, whether positive or negative, have a way of shaping our reality in ways we might not realize."

Max, who had been watching the exchange with a skeptical expression on his infuriatingly handsome face, leaned forward, his elbows coming to rest on his knees. "So, what else?" he asked, his gaze darting between Jasmine and Edna. "If her divinations were just a reflection of her own doubts, does that mean there's nothing to this whole Wicca thing? No real magic or power at all?"

Before Jasmine could jump to the defense of her beliefs once more, Edna spoke up again.

"I wouldn't be so quick to dismiss the validity of Jasmine's beliefs," she said. "Just because her divinations may have been influenced by her own thoughts and emotions doesn't mean that there isn't real power or truth to be found in the Wiccan path. The divine feminine, the connection to nature, the belief in the inherent sacredness of all life, are all powerful ideas with roots that go back thousands of years."

Jasmine felt like hugging the woman, but instead, she glared at Max. "Yeah, what she said."

Edna smiled. "The key is to learn to quiet the mind and trust your intuition and inner strength rather than relying solely on external tools for validation. Your power comes from within, Jasmine. You need to learn to tap into that."

As Edna's words washed over her, Jasmine felt a sudden sense of clarity. All this time, she had been looking outside herself for answers, for guidance, for proof of her own worth and value. But the real magic had been inside of her all along if only she knew how to reach it.

But wasn't that why she had turned to the occult in the first place?

She'd always felt that there was a reservoir of something powerful inside of her, but she didn't know how to tap into it.

Jasmine let out a breath. "That's the trick, isn't it? To learn how to use what's inside. The thing is, I don't even know what I've got inside." She put her hand on her stomach.

Edna reached for her hands and clasped them. "I can help with that. Look into my eyes and let me in. Don't try to fight me, or this will be more difficult than it needs to be."

As Jasmine looked into Edna's strange, wise eyes, she felt the world recede. "Are you going to hypnotize me?"

"Something like that."

34

ARU

The weight of the secret Aru had been keeping from his mate sat heavily on his shoulders.

It was strange how it hadn't bothered him before. He and Aria had been hiding their abilities since the day they realized that their connection was more than the typical twin intuition. They had kept their telepathic communication from their parents, their teachers, and their friends, and if the oracle hadn't discovered them, they would have kept it a secret from everyone still.

Having a truelove mate was a game changer, though.

It wasn't just about the fairy tales claiming that bonded mates could not keep anything from each other. For Aru, it had been a physical strain to keep the secret from Gabi, and in a paradoxical way, he was grateful to Kian for forcing his hand.

Now he had no choice, and it was like a two-ton boulder had been removed from his chest and he could finally take a deep breath.

"What time is the lunch at Annani's?" Gabi asked as she removed a freshly brewed coffee cup from the machine.

"One." Aru sipped on his tea. "Why?"

"Karen was released from the clinic last night, and she is back in her cabin. I want to visit her."

She sat on the stool next to him. "I'm not going to stay long. Just a few minutes to see how she's doing."

"Did she have her test yet?"

Gabi shook her head. "Karen doesn't want one. She says that all she has to do is look in the mirror to know that she's immortal. The fine lines around her eyes are gone."

He chuckled. "Smart woman. Although I have to say, rituals have their place. Maybe she should have the test done anyway just so it's videotaped, and she can show it to her grandkids one day."

Gabi rested her head on his shoulder. "Not everyone is sentimental, and apparently, Karen is not."

Taking a deep breath, Aru wrapped his arm around Gabi's shoulders, pulling her attention back to him. "There is something I need to tell you. A secret that I've been keeping from you."

She lifted her head, and the look of worry that flashed across her face made his gut clench. "Is something wrong? Do you need to leave?"

He hurried to reassure her. "It's nothing bad, but it's important, and I need you to vow that you will not tell anyone. Not even Dagor and Negal know, and it's important that it stays that way."

Gabi nodded. "Just tell me. The anxiety is killing me."

"First, I want you to know that I kept it from you not because I didn't trust you but because I was protecting my sister. It is something that Aria and I have been hiding our entire lives, but I was forced to share our secret with the Clan Mother, and, by extension, Kian. And now, with recent developments, I must also share it with Kian's sisters and their mates. But you deserve to know first."

Gabi swallowed. "What's going on, Aru? You are scaring me."

He tightened his grip on her hand. "Aria and I share a telepathic connection that allows us to communicate instantaneously regardless of distance. Over the past two nights, we've been facilitating contact between Queen Ani of Anumati and her granddaughter Annani. That's why I needed to leave the weddings every night to be at the Clan Mother's cabin at precisely one o'clock in the morning for the nightly meeting."

"That's incredible, Aru. Why is it such a dangerous secret, though?"

He sighed. "I told you about my home world and the king ruling it. His wife is not his fated mate, and she is not his ally. She is the heart of the resistance, and she's grooming her granddaughter, the only legitimate heir to the throne, to one day take his place."

"Oh my." Shock rippled across Gabi's face. "Now I get why your sister is in so much danger. But Dagor and Negal are part of the resistance. Why do you need to hide this from them?"

"So no one can pluck the information from their minds. The Eternal King's spies are everywhere, and they might even infiltrate the resistance. Some of them are rumored to be mind readers. No one is safe, not even inside their own minds, unless they keep their shields up at all times, the way Aria and I have learned to do. Telepathy of any kind is a rare and highly sought-after skill on

Anumati, and even rarer is the ability to communicate verbally mind-to-mind like Aria and I can. If we had been discovered, we would have been either eliminated or conscripted to the king's spy service. That's why we hid it from everyone, even our own parents."

Gabi's fingers tightened around his. "If you kept it a secret, how did you end up working for the queen? Did you and your sister offer the queen your services?"

"I wish we were that brave or that altruistic." Aru's mouth quirked in a sad, wistful smile. "The Supreme Oracle found us. Queen Ani tasked her with finding people with our specific talent, and as soon as our abilities manifested, the Supreme sensed us. But she waited, biding her time until we were old enough to be properly brought into the fold."

He went on to explain how he and Aria had been recruited into Ani's service. "We were brought to the sacred temple that stands as one of the only bastions of safety from the King's spies. Aria was hired to become the Oracle's personal scribe, her telepathic bond with me allowing her to relay messages and information instantly and securely. I was drafted into the interstellar fleet, and my posting on the patrol ship tasked with monitoring the sector where Earth resided was not a coincidence. It was all part of the queen's plan, a gambit to find a trace of the exiled gods. Again, Negal and Dagor have no clue about any of that. They wonder why I was chosen to be the team commander despite my youth and inexperience, and they suspect some nepotism, but that's it. It's crucial that they never find out."

"This information will never leave my lips." Gabi reached up to cup his cheek, her thumb brushing gently over the curve of his jaw. "If you want, you can thrall me to forget all of this. I don't need to know."

He shook his head. "There should be no secrets between bonded mates. Telling you has lifted a heavy weight off my chest."

Gabi's eyes suddenly widened. "Did the Queen know that you would find her granddaughter on Earth? Did the oracle tell her that?"

Aru shook his head, a rueful smile tugging at his lips. "For some reason, Earth is veiled from the Oracle's sight. That is why the queen needed to have boots on the ground, so to speak. She hoped to find out if any of the exiled gods had survived and made a life for themselves on Earth. Discovering that the beloved son she had lost had fathered a daughter and his legacy lived on was as much of a surprise to the queen as it was to us. A very joyous surprise, I might add."

"Naturally." Gabi's eyes shone with tears. "That is such a tragic and heartbreaking story, but also so full of hope and love."

He glanced at his phone and noted with a start how much time had passed. "I think you will have to wait to visit Karen after the luncheon with the Clan Mother and her family. It's almost time for us to head over there."

KIAN

"Here you go, sweetie." Kian put the tray over Allegra's highchair while Syssi put a bowl of cooked veggies in front of her.

Allegra regarded the peas and carrots with such distaste that Kian could barely stifle a chuckle.

"Tha!" She pointed at the breadbasket.

He turned to Syssi. "Can I give her a piece of baguette to chew on?"

"Only if she eats at least some of the veggies."

Allegra slumped in the highchair with an air of resignation that would have made a surly teenager proud, gave her mother an accusing look, and then picked up a piece of carrot and stuffed it in her mouth.

"Good girl," Syssi encouraged. "Eating your veggies is important. Try the peas, too."

Struggling not to laugh, Kian turned his attention to Amanda and Dalhu, who were similarly engaged with Evie. Their daughter was much more amenable than Allegra and didn't make a fuss as Dalhu fed her some mush from the bowl. But then, she was younger than Allegra, and her personality might still change. So far, she seemed to take after Alena more than Amanda, but she still might develop a forceful personality like her mother. No one could have ever accused Amanda of not being assertive.

Shifting his gaze to his mother, Kian was happy to see her basking in the joy of her granddaughters.

Good times.

If only all the moments of their lives could be so peaceful and happy. Some might say that would be boring, but Kian would have welcomed it with open arms.

There was always something to keep him on edge. Now it was the developing saga with the Doomers in Mexico, and Syssi's promise to his mother to induce a vision about Khiann.

She hadn't yet, but she planned to do so when Allegra took her afternoon nap. The problem was that their daughter was not always cooperative in that regard, and sometimes instead of sleeping, she chose to rest in her crib awake.

He wondered what she thought about when she lay quietly with her wise eyes open and her blanket clutched in her small hands. Was she pondering the mysteries of the universe? The meaning of existence?

"Did Edna probe Jasmine already?" Amanda's question pulled him out of his reveries.

Turning to his sister, Kian nodded. "She did."

"And? What did she find? Did Jasmine click with Edgar?"

"According to the guys in security, Jasmine took Edgar to her cabin, and he stayed there for a couple of hours before returning to the wedding party." Kian wasn't happy about sharing that information with his family, but he knew that Amanda wouldn't rest until she got it out of him. Resistance was futile, and it was faster and easier to just report things as he knew them.

Amanda grinned. "I hope that it was more than just sex, and they clicked. Did Edna say anything about it?"

"She didn't report anything about Jasmine having feelings for the guy, but she might not have looked for them, or they might have been absent. I didn't ask."

"I like how assertive Jasmine is," Amanda said. "She knows what she wants, and she isn't afraid to take it. What else did Edna say?"

"Edna seems to think that Jasmine is harmless. There are some painful shadows in her past, probably childhood traumas that Edna didn't explore, and she's a Wiccan, which we already knew, and she believes in the Mother of All Life, which we did not know." He chuckled. "I wonder if that's another influence of one of the Kra-ell's early settlers."

Amanda's eyes sparkled with excitement. "That's probably a coincidence. Many of the ancient civilizations worshiped the Mother. Anyway, I'm so happy that Jasmine is a practicing witch. If she turns out to be a Dormant and joins the clan, I'll have someone to play with."

Syssi groaned. "Promise me that even if Jasmine joins the clan, you won't start a new tradition of forming witch circles and chanting in the nude inside the village. The place is not big enough to ensure your privacy, or rather to ensure that those who shouldn't see a bunch of ladies dancing in the nude under the moon are not exposed to it."

"I don't mind who sees me." Amanda leaned back in her chair. "It's liberating, and it works."

Dalhu wrapped his arm around Amanda's shoulders. "The Fates work in mysterious ways, and it seems like they chose to deliver you a playmate." He leaned and kissed her temple. "You can chant in the nude as much as you want, just not without proper safety measures. While you and your lady friends are busy having fun, I and the other mates should secure the perimeter."

Kian shook his head. "I can't believe that you are taking this so seriously, Amanda. Doing it for fun is one thing, but to actually think that it's effective is crazy."

"Oh, really." She gave him a haughty look. "It worked every time."

"Coincidence."

Amanda looked down her nose at him. "If it makes you more comfortable to think that, be my guest."

"Thank you." He mockingly dipped his head.

"You're welcome. So, are you going to allow Jasmine on the upper decks?"

"In light of Edna's findings, or rather lack thereof, I don't see why not. And if Jasmine bonds with Edgar, I will allow him to tell her the truth so he can ask her consent to be induced. In the meantime, though, I'll instruct everyone not to talk about immortals and gods around her, and I'll have her kept under close watch."

Annani, who hadn't said much until now, nodded. "In case Edgar is not the one for her, it will be good for Jasmine to interact with more people."

"Precisely." Amanda dabbed at Evie's mouth with a napkin. "You still didn't tell us what this lunch is about. You wouldn't have asked us to come earlier if it was just a regular family get-together."

His mother's idea was for the two couples with young children to come a little earlier so the girls could finish eating before the rest of the adults arrived.

"Patience, my daughter." Annani leaned over and patted Amanda's hand. "We have important issues to discuss, and I did not want us to be interrupted. Once the girls are done with their lunch, Ojidu can watch over them in the bedroom while the adults talk, but we need to wait for your sisters and their mates and for Aru and Gabi to join us. It concerns all of you."

"Now, I'm really worried." Amanda crossed her arms over her chest. "Can you at least give me a hint?"

Annani smiled. "It is big, but no one is in any immediate danger."

"Thank the merciful Fates." Amanda let out a breath. "By the way, how is Margo doing?" She looked at Kian. "Is she really transitioning?"

"I don't know," he admitted. "I haven't checked on her this morning."

"Perhaps you should call her before the others get here," Amanda suggested. "She'll be so happy to hear about Jasmine being allowed on the upper decks."

Kian turned to their mother. "Is it okay with you if I call Margo now?"

"Of course. I am also curious about her transition."

Kian pulled out his phone and scrolled through his contacts until he found Margo's. He could have used a voice command like all the young gods were doing, but he liked doing things the old-fashioned way.

Margo answered on the second ring, sounding breathless. "Hello, Kian. What a nice surprise. How can I help you?"

"I have some good news, and I also want to know how you are feeling. Did you experience any changes? Are there any new developments?"

"I'm feeling great. Bridget came to check on me earlier, and she said my fever and blood pressure have both gone up, which, according to her, are good signs that the transition is progressing as it should. Surprisingly, though, I don't feel weak or dizzy anymore."

Kian had a strong suspicion regarding Margo's sudden improvement. Negal had most likely given her his blood, and he just hoped that the god had exercised discretion.

"That's fantastic news, Margo. Is Bridget moving you to the clinic, or is Karen still there?"

"Bridget said that Karen is doing well enough to be released and that I can move in whenever I want, but I'm not in any rush. I told Bridget that Negal had been glued to my side, fussing over me and functioning like my own personal nurse, and she agreed that I could stay in the cabin for now. If things get worse, Negal will take me to the clinic."

"That's good." It was unusual for Bridget to agree to leave a transitioning Dormant in the care of her partner, but she must have had her reasons.

"So, what's the good news you were calling about?" Margo asked.

"I cleared Jasmine to roam around the upper decks. She can visit you, spend time on the Lido deck, and she can attend the weddings, but only after the ceremonies are concluded. I want to keep her exposure minimal, so we won't have as much to thrall away in two days."

"That's wonderful. When can she come up?"

"As soon as she wants, but she doesn't know yet. I need to send someone to inform her. Regrettably, we don't have a spare phone we can give her."

"I can ask Frankie to go down there and get her if that's okay with you."

"Of course. It will save me the trouble. But you need to remember not to say anything about your transition. You will have to tell her that you are just sick. As I said before, the less she knows, the less we will have to erase."

"Don't worry," Margo said. "I totally get it, and I won't breathe a word about anything she doesn't need to know. Thank you for letting her out of the lower decks."

"My pleasure." He ended the call.

36

AMANDA

O nce Kian was done with the call and had slipped his phone back into his pocket, the sound of the door chime announced the arrival of more guests. Amanda pushed to her feet as Ojidu opened the door and greeted her sisters and their mates with hugs and kisses. When the greetings were done, everyone took their seats at the table, which was now complete save for the two empty chairs reserved for Aru and Gabi.

It was like the game 'find the Thing That Doesn't Belong.' Why were Aru and Gabi invited to a family lunch?

Usually, when the close family got together, it was for more than just the feels. News and updates were delivered in an unofficial manner, and advice was provided just as unofficially.

The reason that Aru and Gabi had been invited was probably that they had news that pertained to the family, which meant something about Anumati.

Oh, well. Amanda would have to wait and find out, along with the others, what this was all about.

When the doorbell rang again, and Ojidu opened the door for Aru and Gabi, their pinched expressions made Amanda's hackles rise.

She leaned over to Syssi. "Something big is about to happen," she murmured conspiratorially, her eyes darting between her mother, who had lost her easy smile, and the anxious-looking couple. "I can smell it in the air."

Syssi's only response was a slight nod.

"Good afternoon, Clan Mother." Aru bowed to Annani. "I apologize for us arriving last."

"No need to apologize, Aru. You are right on time. The others have arrived a little early."

"That's good to know," Gabi said. "Thank you for inviting us."

As Annani inclined her head magnanimously, the couple followed Ojidu to their seats and sat down.

Annani scanned the faces of her guests with a soft smile lifting her lips. "Now that everyone is here, we can start."

Amanda held her breath as she waited for her mother to reveal what the meeting was about, but Annani just lifted her hand to signal to her Odus that it was okay to bring out the food. The babies had been situated in the bedroom with a kids' show to entertain them and an Odu to watch over them.

As the Odus began to serve the fragrant dishes, the adults dug into the delicious pesto pasta and Caesar salad, and the conversation around the table turned to the latest developments, with Kian filling the others in on Karen's and Margo's progress.

"It's a pity that Frankie and Margo are going to leave right away," Alena said. "I bet Mia is disappointed. She hoped they would join her in the village."

"It's problematic." Kian spread a napkin over his knees. "Negal and Dagor can't join the clan for security reasons, and the same is true for you, Aru." He looked at the god. "Nevertheless, we need to extend our umbrella of protection to them. There should be no unaffiliated immortals out in the human world even if they have three gods to protect them." He shifted his gaze to Gabi. "You need a community. Especially if and when you have children. You already have family in the village, so it's a given, but I will have to talk with Margo and Frankie about their status."

She gave him a bright smile. "I thought that it was a non-issue, and that I could visit anytime I wanted, but thank you for the official welcome."

When their mother regarded Kian with pride in her eyes, Amanda wondered if that was what they had been assembled for. Except, Kian did not need their approval to welcome new members to the clan. If he thought that approval was necessary, he should have called a council meeting and put it to a vote.

Perhaps he wanted to make sure that the family was on board beforehand?

David chuckled. "You should have a 'Welcome to Oz' banner at the glass pavilion for the newcomers, and a yellow brick road painted on the floor."

Amanda lifted her hand. "I volunteer to be the witch, but I don't know which one, the Wicked Witch of the West or the Wicked Witch of the East, or one of the good witches. I need to read up on them again." She had read the original book version, which had four witches, two good and two wicked, but Amanda didn't remember who was who and what each was responsible for.

Kian groaned. "Again, with the nonsense about witches?"

Sari narrowed her eyes at him. "What nonsense?"

"Turns out that our rescued guest fancies herself a witch." Kian shook his head. "Jasmine is an active Wiccan who is convinced that she's destined to meet a prince. I wonder if Edgar fits the bill or if he's just a placeholder until she finds her dream royal."

Amanda snorted. "Edgar is a sweetheart, but he's no Prince Charming. I mean, he can be charming, but he is…" she glanced at her mother "not very discriminating with his affections, and very active."

That was common for young immortals, and until not too long ago, Amanda had been just as bad or just as good, depending on how one regarded raging promiscuity. She'd used to refer to herself as a slut, but it had become politically incorrect to do so because it was supposedly shaming. Except, she had always worn the title with pride.

Oh, well. She was a college professor, which meant that she was surrounded by the current generation of whiny ninnies who found every other word offensive but had no problem bullying whoever did not fit their extremely narrow and misguided worldview. The ignorance was just staggering, but thankfully, it wasn't as bad in her department. Scientifically inclined minds were a little better trained to ask questions and a little less susceptible to herd mentality, though not by much.

Amanda stifled a sigh. Her job wasn't to teach them right from wrong. That was their parents' job. She was there to teach them about the brain.

As the conversation turned to Wicca, Amanda discovered that Sari knew more about it than she did. Her sister had not taken part in any rituals, but she'd studied the subject because several of her people had gotten into it. She explained about altars, the different deities they believed in, and the tools they used to channel energy.

The soothing sounds of conversation mingled with the clatter of silverware and the clink of glasses, and even Aru and Gabi cracked a few smiles, the good mood around the table managing to break through the anxious veil that seemed to be hanging over them.

Something about Jasmine's prince quest prickled Amanda's mind, but before she could catch the string of thought, her mother distracted her with a comment about brainwaves that she had to respond to, but even though Annani nodded and smiled, it was obvious to Amanda that she wasn't really listening.

The glint of anticipation and excitement in Annani's eyes sent a shiver down Amanda's spine.

The luncheon wasn't about welcoming new immortals into the clan or even about Jasmine. It was about something else.

Leaning forward, Amanda asked, "What's going on, Mother?"

Annani smiled, the gleam in her eyes making Amanda's heart race. "Patience, my darling," she murmured. "All will be revealed soon. But first, let us enjoy coffee, dessert, and wonderful company."

37

ANNANI

As the Odus cleared the dishes and then served coffee and tea, Annani watched Amanda's growing impatience, her leg bouncing beneath the table and her fingers tapping its top.

She had always been such an inquisitive child. Annani should have known that she would one day become a researcher despite the years of partying and losing herself in the pleasures of the flesh to drown out the crippling grief that had followed her son's death.

It was any mother's worst nightmare, and Annani regretted having this in common with her daughter. She did not know what was worse, losing Lilen, who had been an adult and whom she had gotten to know and appreciate as a grown man, or losing a little boy and all the unrealized potential of who he might have been had he lived.

Death was a terrible thing, but hopefully it was not the end, and beyond the veil, Lilen and Aiden were together, perhaps they had even joined Khiann, if he had indeed been murdered by Mortdh and was not in stasis under the desert sands as she ardently hoped.

Across the table, Aru and Gabi sat in silence. Annani could not see their hands, but she was sure they were clasped tightly together under the tablecloth as they sipped their coffee and avoided the curious gazes of her children and their mates.

As the minutes ticked by and the coffee cups emptied, the tension in the room grew thicker, and Annani knew it was time.

"I can see the curious looks you're casting my way, and I know that you are all wondering why I have called you here today. There is a secret I am about to share with you, but I want you to know that I kept it from you only because it was not my secret to reveal. Kian and I have convinced Aru that you can be trusted with it, but to ease his fears, I also offered to compel you all to secrecy, but I will never force it on you. If you do not wish to be compelled, you can leave now before I speak of it."

Amanda snorted. "After such a preamble, wild horses couldn't drag me away." She waved a hand. "Please compel me and then tell me what the big secret is before I die of curiosity."

This was such an Amanda response that Annani could not help the laughter that bubbled from her throat. "Does everyone here share Amanda's opinion?"

As heads bobbed all around, Annani closed her eyes for a moment to gather her power.

When she opened them, her family were looking at her with so much awe that she knew she must be glowing like a star. Glancing at her exposed arm confirmed her suspicion.

"My dear family, my son, my daughters, and their mates. What Aru and I will tell you in a moment can be shared only between those seated around this table. The only one who can choose to share it with whomever he pleases is Aru because this is his secret."

Hopefully, she'd closed all the possible loopholes, and if modifications were needed, she could alter her compulsion as needed.

As her glow receded, Aru bowed his head. "Your power is immense, Clan Mother."

"Yeah." Alena rubbed her belly. "I hope it didn't do any damage to the baby."

"He or she will be privy to the secret and will have to keep it," Amanda teased her sister. "After all, your child is seated around this table."

"Not funny," Alena grumbled. "We don't know what compulsion does to the brain, and especially to a developing one."

"He is going to be fine." Sari reached for her sister's hand.

Alena frowned. "How do you know it's a he?"

"I don't, but I have a hunch. Kian and Amanda got girls, so it's your turn to have a boy. You also have many more girls than boys, so a boy is statistically more likely."

"It doesn't work that way," Amanda murmured. "There are many factors that determine a baby's gender."

Annani lifted a hand. "Let us not get distracted." She turned to Aru. "Would you like to share your story, or should I?"

"I will start." Aru rose to his feet.

Annani felt a flicker of apprehension twist in her gut. She knew that the revelation of his connection to the queen of Anumati and the communication that was enabled thanks to him and his sister would come as a shock to her daughters and their mates, but the bigger shock would be when they understood the implications.

"I have guarded this secret since I first became aware of it, and it has shaped the course of my life and my twin sister's. Not even our parents or my teammates know, and it's imperative that they never find out. It is not because I don't trust them but because this knowledge is so dangerous, and the king's spies are everywhere." He scanned their faces. "Except here. Earth is shielded from the oracles, and the only vessel passing through this sector is the patrol ship I arrived on."

Annani was not sure that Aru was right about that. Had the assassins who had come to destroy the rebel gods arrived on a patrol ship? Or had the King sent a smaller, faster vessel with a few well-trained, well-armed, trusted operatives?

"My sister and I have a special telepathic connection," Aru continued, his words hanging heavy in the air. "You have a similar duo in your clan, a mother and daughter who can talk to each other mind-to-mind. What you might not have realized is that distance does not affect telepathic communication. I can talk with Aria, who is on Anumati, as if I was talking to any of you on the phone. It is instantaneous."

Even though everyone was aware that Vivian and Ella possessed a similar ability, a ripple of shock went around the table, gasps and murmurs of astonishment mingling with the clatter of silverware and the hush of held breaths. Annani kept her gaze focused on her daughters, her heart preparing for their hurt expressions.

"That's amazing," Amanda said. "I understand the need for secrecy given that you are part of the resistance, and I assume that your sister is part of it too, but why was it necessary when you were growing up?"

Aru sighed. "Duos like ours are hunted on Anumati. The Eternal King does not want a mode of communication that he cannot tap into. We are either recruited to work for the king or sent to a colony to meet with unfortunate accidents. Aria and I were lucky that our connection bloomed when we were old enough to understand that we should keep it a secret. But that's just the tip of the iceberg, as the Earth saying goes. The queen of Anumati discovered Aria and me a long time ago and recruited us to work for her.

"My sister serves the Supreme Oracle, who is the queen's closest friend and coconspirator, and I was inserted into the interstellar fleet and through careful maneuvering stationed on the patrol ship bound for this sector.

"The queen hoped to find some survivors who could tell her what had really happened on Earth and how her only son had died, but she didn't expect to find a living granddaughter, her son's only legitimate heir, and therefore the only legitimate heir to the throne of Anumati."

Aru turned to Annani. "Would you like to tell the rest of the story?"

She nodded. "Thank you, Aru. I can take it from here."

38

ARU

As Aru sagged in his chair, Gabi reached for his hand and squeezed it. Hearing himself talk about his connection with his sister had been terrifying, and his confession hadn't brought about any of the relief he had expected.

The cruise had done what Kian and the heir had hoped for, which was to bring Aru and his teammates into the fold without inviting them to join the immortals' community. By now, they were almost like family to him, and he knew he would do everything to protect them, like he had done everything he could to protect Aria, but he still felt as if he had betrayed her even though he had not.

Well, maybe he had.

He hadn't asked the queen's permission to tell all of Annani's children, their mates, and his own mate about the communications between the queen and her granddaughter, which was most likely the most important secret in all of Anumati and its countless colonies.

The resistance needed the queen, and it needed Annani to step into her grandfather's shoes after he had been forced to vacate them. But the truth was that they would need the help of all of Annani's children to achieve that, and it couldn't be done without letting them in on the secret.

The Clan Mother, as the royal heir of Anumati liked to be referred to, scanned her children's faces. "The Queen, my grandmother, was delighted to find out about me. She suggested that we meet through Aru and Aria, who would function as the channel between us. We have had two such meetings so far, both at one o'clock in the morning, which necessitated Kian and Aru leaving the celebrations before they were over." She glanced at her daughter-in-law. "Syssi knew about Aru and Aria from a vision she had about the queen and her best friend, the Supreme Oracle. Once she saw Aria's face, it was clear to her that she was Aru's twin sister, and the rest of the puzzle pieces fell into place. That is why she joined our meetings and transcribed by hand what was being said so nothing would be lost."

The heir paused, letting her words sink in.

"The queen of Anumati," Orion murmured, "hundreds of light years away, is talking to you here on Earth. What did she tell you?"

"In the first meeting, she asked me many questions, probably to assess my worth. Our second meeting was used by the queen for a broad history review of Anumati, which was a little more political in nature than what Aru already shared with us. She intends to continue the overview tonight, and then go back and describe things in more detail."

"To what end?" Sari asked. "Just for your general knowledge?"

Sari was a smart female, and she must have guessed what was behind the queen's interest in her granddaughter. Aru's emphasis on her being the only legitimate heir to the Anumati throne must have given that away.

The Clan Mother nodded. "The queen wants me to learn all there is to know about Anumati's social structure, its politics and economy. Her plan is to impart an intimate knowledge of the main movers and shakers, so one day, when the resistance manages to take down the Eternal King, I can take over and prevent chaos from destroying Anumati. The population will accept me as a rightful ruler, and the transition of power will be smooth."

"That's insane," Alena said. "Why did you allow her to convince you to take part in this?"

The Clan Mother sighed. "I did not commit to anything yet. I do not wish to rule, but I am starting to realize that if I refuse, I may be condemning the people of Anumati, along with all the hybrid species they have created over millions of years, to endless war and chaos, which would happen if the resistance takes down the king and there is no one to replace him who can unite them. Still, it might take thousands of years of resistance to get to that point, and in the meantime, I am worried about what my grandfather will do to Earth once humans advance beyond what he is comfortable with. This is a male who had no qualms about killing his own children. Do you think that he would hesitate even for a millisecond before he gives the order to destroy Earth?" Her voice rose in power as she got emotional. "The only way to save Earth is to take him down before he finds out, and that means that I have to push the timeline of the resistance."

"How long have you known?" Amanda directed her question at Kian.

"Not long."

"Before the cruise or during?" Amanda asked.

"During. Aru told me first."

"You should have insisted that we all learn of it as soon as you found out," Amanda said. "It was wrong to keep it from us."

"I know, but it wasn't my call."

Amanda turned a pair of angry eyes at Aru. "Thank you for finally confiding in us, but I truly don't understand why you felt the need to keep it from me and my sisters. Once you told Kian and our mother, there was no point in hiding it from us."

Kian lifted his hand. "Enough. This is not the time for accusations or recriminations. Aru has risked everything to share this truth, and we should be grateful to him and Aria for providing this channel of communication that wouldn't have been possible otherwise."

Amanda snorted, her eyes flashing with anger. "It would have been better if they hadn't. I don't want our mother to get involved in the biggest uprising in the freaking galaxy. Chances are that she won't survive it, and neither will Earth. Instead of plotting insane coups, we should adopt the same strategy that has helped us survive against the Brotherhood. We need to find a way to hide Earth and its capabilities from the freaking Eternal King."

39

ANNANI

As Amanda's words hung heavy in the air, Annani felt a ripple of unease pass through her assembled family. She could see the conflict playing out across their faces, the struggle between the desire to protect the mother they loved and the sense of duty to do the right thing.

"Amanda has a point." Sari's eyes drifted to meet Annani's. "In the grand scheme of things, we are nothing. We can't even obliterate our enemies at home. To think that we can move the needle against the Eternal King is too ambitious even for you, and frankly, it's delusional. And I mean no offense, Mother. I'm just stating the facts."

"It is not ambition, my child." Annani's heart clenched at the fear in her brave daughter's voice. "I understand your concerns, my darling, and I would be lying if I said I didn't share them. But here are the facts. This is not the clan's fight or even mine. I will have one job in this grand scheme, and it is to become a figure-head the people of Anumati can unite around." She smiled. "I do not intend to lead armies into battle or challenge my grandfather to a duel to the death."

Sari shook her head. "The moment he learns of your existence, it's game over for you and for all of us, including every human on Earth."

Annani swept her gaze over the faces of her children and their mates. "That is a valid point, but I cannot let fear dictate my actions. I cannot hide from the truth of who I am and the responsibility that comes with it."

Orion leaned forward, his brow furrowed. "But is it really your responsibility, Clan Mother? The Eternal King is the ruler of Anumati and its colonies, and he might be a tyrant, but he is out there, and you are here, and until not too long ago, you didn't even know that he existed. Why should you risk your life and ours and the safety of our entire world to overthrow a tyrant on a planet hundreds of light years away?"

Annani sighed. "Because it does not matter if he knows about me or not. Sooner or later, his gaze will turn to Earth, and when it does, he will not hesitate to eliminate this planet we call home if he perceives humans as a threat. We cannot wait and hope that he will one day disappear and that the threat will be gone. There is a reason he calls himself the Eternal King. He has all the time in the galaxy to find us and destroy us. If we do nothing, we are as good as dead."

She turned to Amanda. "Hiding was a good strategy against the Brotherhood, and still is, but it is not an option against the Eternal King. Not in the long run. The only way we can prevent Earth's destruction is to make sure humans never achieve interstellar flight capability. Do you really think we can do that?"

Kian nodded. "Mother is right. We cannot bury our heads in the sand and hope that the storm will pass us by. I've seen enough human leaders adopt that approach and get wiped out. History forgot about them."

"But at what cost?" Alena whispered, her hand coming to rest on the swell of her belly. "Are we really willing to risk everything, to put our children and our future in jeopardy, for a war that is not our own and might never get here? The Eternal King has declared Earth a forbidden planet whose name was erased from Anumatian records. He might have forgotten about us."

Aru cleared his throat. "The fact that he sends a patrol ship every seven hundred years or so indicates that he has not forgotten about Earth. In fact, he probably keeps closer tabs on it than many of the colonies that are in the records."

"It's because of the Kra-ell," Amanda said. "He's afraid of the damn royal twins…" Her eyes widened. "The prince and the princess, the son and daughter of the Kra-ell queen." She looked around the table, a smile forming on her face. "Jasmine is obsessed with finding the prince that her tarot cards keep promising her. She even hooked up with Alberto because the damn cards told her to. What if the Fates are steering her toward the Kra-ell prince?"

Syssi chuckled. "Of all of your harebrained ideas, that is the wackiest. We talked about seeing patterns where there are none. It's nothing more than projecting your wishful thinking onto things and connecting dots that don't connect."

Annani was grateful for the change of subject.

Jasmine's preoccupation with tarot cards and royalty was a much lighter topic of conversation than the threat of the Eternal King and Annani's aspirations to save the home planet of her people and Earth along with it.

Kian shifted and put his hand next to hers on the table. "Are you okay?" he asked quietly as his wife and sisters continued arguing with Amanda about her latest hypothesis.

"Yes, my son." Annani drew herself up, her shoulders squaring and her chin lifting in resolve. "I am the daughter of Ahn, the granddaughter of the Eternal King, and even though I may not have sought this destiny, it has found me, and I will not run from it. I will not hide from the truth of who I am and what I must do."

The Eternal King might be a formidable foe, a tyrant with an iron grip on the galaxy and a heart as cold as the void of space. But Annani was not weak, even though her heart was full of love. Maybe that was why the Fates had chosen her. She was all about love and hope, while her grandfather was all about cruelty and despair.

4 0

MARGO

Margo stretched out on the couch, feeling more energetic than she had in days. The fatigue and dizziness that had plagued her since the onset of her transition seemed to have vanished overnight, to be replaced by a sense of vitality that had her itching to do something, anything, other than lying around.

So what if she had a little fever and her blood pressure was elevated? She didn't feel it, and if Bridget was allowing her to stay in her cabin instead of hooking her up to the monitoring equipment in the clinic, she wasn't worried about her suddenly losing consciousness either.

The phone call from Kian had also been a major mood boost. She couldn't wait to show Jasmine around the ship. Well, her cabin would have to do for now, but maybe tomorrow she could take her to the Lido deck and they could share a drink.

Regrettably, there was no way Negal was going to let her go down to the staff decks to look for Jasmine, and leaving her alone to go himself was also not going to happen.

Frankie wasn't back yet from lunch, so Margo couldn't ask her to do it. Maybe instead of waiting for Frankie to come back, she could call her and ask her to stop by the staff lounge before returning to their cabin.

When she reached for her phone, Negal frowned. "What are you doing, Nesha? You should be resting."

"I'm calling Frankie. I want to ask her to find Jasmine and bring her up here."

His frown deepened, concern etching lines into his handsome face. "You should be resting. In fact, you should be in bed."

Margo waved off his concern with a smile. "I feel great, Negal. Better than I have in days. And it's all thanks to you."

He tensed, his eyes widening slightly. "Why me?"

She laughed, reaching out to pat his arm. "Your godly mojo, of course. I wouldn't be transitioning with such ease if I'd been induced by a mere immortal's diluted venom. Yours is a miracle drug."

Negal shifted uncomfortably, looking like he wanted to say something but thought better of it. "Still," he said after a moment, "hosting a party might be pushing it. You don't want to overtax yourself."

"It's not a party," Margo said. "It's just a little get-together, Jasmine, Frankie, and maybe Mia if she's free. Does it really matter if I'm on the couch watching television or talking to my friends? One does not require more energy expenditure than the other."

He looked like he wanted to argue but then nodded. "Fine, but you are staying on the couch. I'll make them coffee or tea or whatever you want to serve them. Deal?"

"Deal." Margo smiled as she pressed the star next to Frankie's number.

"What's up, Margo?" Frankie asked. "Did you change your mind about lunch? Dagor and I are on our way out, but we can stop by the kitchen and bring two packed lunches for you and Negal."

"Thanks, but we are fine, food-wise that is. I need to ask you for a favor."

"Anything," Frankie said. "Are you feeling better? Do you want me to sneak you out to the Lido deck while Dagor distracts Negal?"

Margo laughed. "I might take you up on that offer tomorrow. Today, I was hoping you could go down to the staff lounge and tell Jasmine that Kian cleared her for the upper decks and bring her here. As you know, she doesn't have a phone, so someone has to go get her, and Negal won't let me off the couch."

"No problem," Frankie said. "Dagor and I are heading down there right now. See you soon."

"I love my friends," she murmured as she called Mia.

The phone rang a few times before her friend picked up, sounding slightly out of breath. "Hey, Margo, is everything okay?"

"Everything's great. Are you busy?"

"No, not really. I was just doing a little exercising."

Trying to imagine her wheelchair-bound friend doing sit-ups or push-ups, Margo frowned. "Lifting weights?"

Mia chuckled. "Lifting one weight. Me. I brace my arms on the armrests and lift myself off the chair. It's like push-ups in reverse, if that makes sense."

"That sounds difficult. How are your feet coming along? You keep hiding them, so I don't know if you are growing toes already or not."

"I am. Bridget says they will be complete in no more than two weeks. I can't wait to walk again."

"I can imagine." Margo sighed. "I want to celebrate your first steps on your own two feet with you, but I probably won't be there." She shifted her gaze to Negal. "I'm progressing so fast through my transition that Aru won't need to ask their commander for a few more days before they head to Tibet. I will be fine to join them."

Smiling, Negal sent her an air kiss.

"I'll pray that you do, and if you have to miss my first steps on my brand new feet, I'll have Toven film it, and you can watch it live."

"That's an awesome idea. You do that."

"I will, but enough about me. How are you doing?"

"Great, and that's why I'm calling. I was wondering if you wanted to come over for a bit. Kian approved Jasmine to be on the upper decks now, and Frankie is bringing her up to our cabin. I thought we could all hang out together. I mean, as long as it doesn't interfere with your bridesmaid duties."

"Mey didn't invite me, so I don't have any. I don't really know her all that well. I'd love to come over."

"Awesome. See you soon." Margo ended the call and tossed her phone aside. "I'm so excited that Jasmine is coming." She opened her arms. "Come give me a hug."

"You're lucky you're so cute," Negal said as he leaned over her and kissed her lightly on the lips. "Otherwise, I might have tried to talk some sense into you."

She laughed, reaching for his hand and twining her fingers through his. "Admit it," she teased. "You love it that I'm stubborn."

"I love everything about you." Negal's voice dropped an octave as he lifted her hand to his lips. "Even when you're driving me crazy with your stubbornness."

41

JASMINE

T he sound of the doorbell echoed through Jasmine's tiny cabin, startling her out of a very romantic part of the book she was reading.

It was the third time she was reading it, and yet she still teared up when James went down on one knee and declared his undying love to Annabel.

"I'm coming." She scrambled off the bed, smoothing down her hair and checking her reflection in the small mirror above the desk.

It was probably Margo. She hadn't seen her or heard from her in what seemed like days, and she was starting to worry about her.

Or maybe it was Edgar, come to apologize for leaving last night with not so much as a note.

Satisfied that she looked presentable, she pulled it open, a smile curving her lips. But instead of Margo or Ed, she found Frankie standing in the corridor with a breathtakingly handsome guy towering over her petite frame.

What was it with the insanely good-looking people on this cruise?

"Hey, Jasmine!" Frankie said. "I have great news. You've been cleared to come up to the upper decks, and Dagor and I are here to escort you to our cabin, which we share with Margo and Negal."

Jasmine's eyes widened, her heart doing a little flip in her chest. "Really? Did Edna clear me?"

Frankie shrugged. "Margo only told me that Kian was okay with you coming up and to come get you."

The niggling feeling of worry that had been hovering in the back of her head came to the fore. "Is Margo alright? I haven't seen her in days, and now she sends you instead of coming down here herself."

Frankie waved a dismissive hand. "She's just a little under the weather, and Negal is fussing over her and not letting her move from the couch. She wants to see you. We can all hang out together."

"Awesome." Jasmine turned back into the cabin. "Do I need to put on something fancier for the posh upper decks?"

Frankie shook her head. "Nah, you look great. We're just going to Margo's cabin. No need to get all fancy."

"Then I'll just get my shoes and my purse." Jasmine cast a smile at Frankie's boyfriend. "I'm so excited to finally be allowed up there." She chuckled. "Talk about feeling like Cinderella."

As they stepped out into the hallway, Jasmine was practically bouncing on her toes in her eagerness to get to the upper decks and see all the wonders hiding up there, but as they got to the stairs, a familiar figure rounded the corner, his blue eyes lighting up when he saw her.

"Jasmine!" Edgar grinned. "Where are you off to?"

"I've been cleared to go up to the upper decks, and I'm going to visit Margo in her cabin."

His eyes widened. "That's fantastic." He reversed direction and climbed the stairs beside her. "I can finally show you around and give you the grand tour."

"That sounds great." She reached for his hand and clasped it. "But I will have to take a raincheck. I need to go see Margo. Frankie said that she was not feeling well, and I wanted to make sure she was okay. I haven't seen her in days."

Edgar nodded. "Perfectly understandable. Mind if I tag along?"

Jasmine glanced at Frankie and then at Dagor. "Is that okay with you?"

Frankie hesitated for a moment, annoyance flickering across her face too quickly for Ed to notice. "Sure." She affected a bright smile that didn't quite reach her eyes. "The more the merrier, I guess."

An uncomfortable silence fell over the group as they made their way up the stairs, and Jasmine didn't like the tension in the air.

Ed shouldn't have invited himself, but was it really such a big deal?

"Why are we taking the stairs instead of the elevator?" she asked, to fill the silence.

"Our cabin is on deck three," Frankie said. "It's faster to climb the stairs than to wait for the elevators."

As they stepped into the lushly appointed hallway of Frankie and Margo's deck, Jasmine pushed the thought aside and took in the decor.

She approved.

It wasn't gaudy or over the top as she'd expected. Instead, the style was of understated elegance. Plush carpets, gleaming wood panels, and works of art that might have been originals or fakes—she didn't know enough about art to tell the difference.

42

AMANDA

While the discussion around the table continued to revolve around modern witchcraft, fields of energy, and how quantum physics could explain paranormal phenomena, Amanda pushed aside thoughts of her mother becoming the ruler of the galaxy because, frankly, it was just crazy.

Instead, she thought back to the fun times she'd had with leading her mostly made-up witchy rituals.

She had always been fascinated by alternative spirituality and connecting with the divine feminine, but she had only superficial knowledge of Wiccan practices and had never delved too deeply into the specifics of modern witchcraft. It had always been about fun for her—a way to bond with her female friends over something different and naughty. She'd had a blast scandalizing Syssi by coercing her shy sister-in-law into dancing in the woods in her birthday suit.

Amanda stifled a smile at the memory.

Across the table, Syssi let out a long-suffering sigh. "I will never forget how you roped me into the ritual you did for Vivian."

"I was just thinking about the same thing," Amanda admitted. "It was so much fun."

"For you," Syssi grumbled.

Amanda chuckled. "After you got over your excessive modesty, you enjoyed it too. Besides, it worked beautifully, so it was worth a few minutes of embarrassment. Vivian stopped thinking that she was cursed and embraced her relationship with Magnus."

Sari cast Amanda an amused look. "Since the curse only existed in Vivian's head, the ritual probably had a placebo effect. She believed that it worked, so it did."

Amanda pursed her lips. "Maybe you are right, or maybe the combined positive energy of fourteen females did the trick."

Syssi laughed. "It was an impressive theatrical production, so it looked convincing. Although I doubt that Vivian was impressed with the wizard robes we wore. They came from a costume shop."

"Why fourteen?" David asked. "I've heard of a circle of seven or thirteen but never fourteen. Is there more power in doubling up on seven?"

"Humm." Amanda tapped her finger on her lower lip. "I should have thought of that explanation when we ended up with fourteen instead of thirteen witches in our circle, but that wasn't it. It's actually a fun story." She looked at Syssi. "Do you want to tell it, or should I?"

Syssi waved a hand. "Go ahead. I'm sure that your version will be much more entertaining than mine."

"Fine. So the plan was to assemble thirteen females, but since I knew that not everyone would be on board with nudity," she cast Syssi a pointed look, "I got fifteen. Syssi said that there was no way she was getting naked and that she would offer her support from the sidelines. Kri, who was there in a Guardian capacity, was armed to the teeth, so she couldn't join in either because of her weapons. That left me with thirteen, which was what I needed."

"We looked so ridiculous," Syssi said. "I had my clothes on under the wizard robe, but Amanda, Carol, and many of the others were naked underneath."

Amanda shrugged. "We looked fabulous, but after we each shared our life force energy with Vivian, it was time to disrobe, and before you all think that I was being eccentric or silly or just wanted to torment poor Syssi, I will have you know that nudity is a legit requirement of the Wiccan ritual. You can look it up if you don't believe me."

Syssi let out a sigh. "You made a very convincing argument back then, and I'm often reminded of it. It was about how we clothe ourselves in customs, ideology, and comforting illusions in our everyday lives. The naked body represents the truth, and by shedding our material and spiritual garments, we proclaim our loyalty to the truth."

"Nicely said." Sari nodded.

"That's how Amanda convinced me to participate," Syssi said. "That and the speech about how we are all perfect in our own way and have nothing to be ashamed of. When I agreed to shed my clothes, I became the fourteenth female in the circle that had been supposed to have only thirteen."

Kian shook his head. "You are a bad influence, Amanda."

He'd heard the story before, probably more than once, so he was saying that to tease her. Fine, she could play his game.

She gave him a haughty look. "I beg to differ. I think that I'm a wonderful influence. All the women who participated in that ritual felt energized and empowered by it, and Vivian no longer thought that she was cursed. It was a win-win for everyone involved."

Not only that, but they had created a memory they would carry with them forever. How many of those did people have? Most of life was mundane, with one day resembling the next and nothing to distinguish it from all the others. People remembered the highs and lows. Since lows were usually unplanned and just hit them over the head at random, it was important to build an arsenal of highs, and that didn't happen without planning.

Syssi leaned toward Amanda. "Do you remember the incantation?"

"More or less." Amanda cleared her throat. "We are gathered here in a circle of fourteen powerful women to beseech the Goddess's help for our sister Vivian. With her divine light, the Goddess will destroy the malignant energy within Vivian's soul and free her from her curse. Let us all join our voices in the chant. Please repeat after me. Great mother, the supreme mistress who lives in our hearts and guides our way toward love and compassion, honor and humility, mirth and pleasure, bestow upon us your power tonight, chase away the darkness and replace it with your light, so our sister Vivian can worship and honor you by freely accepting love and pleasure without fear."

Leaning back, Syssi crossed her arms over her chest. "You totally made that up."

"I did," Amanda admitted. "But you can't deny the energy we all felt that night. That wasn't made up."

"It's true." Syssi looked at Kian. "We talked afterward, wondering if a group of males could have produced the same energy."

He chuckled. "Don't expect me to try it, and if you somehow convince thirteen males to do a witchy or wizardry ritual in the nude, there is no way I'm letting you watch it in the name of science or anything else."

"Don't worry, my love." She cupped his cheek. "The only male I want to see in the nude is you."

"Oh, wow." Amanda fanned herself. "Who are you, and what have you done with my shy sister-in-law? The Syssi I know and love would have never said that in public."

As Syssi's cheeks got red, Annani came to her rescue. "So, if I understand correctly, modern Wiccans worship the feminine."

"Not exclusively," Sari said. "Wiccans believe in a dual deity system, with a goddess and a god representing the feminine and masculine aspects of divinity, but because Wicca is about honoring the natural world and the cycles of life, it has a more feminine slant than the traditional religions, and it appeals more to females."

"What about the magical aspect of it?" Gabi asked.

Amanda lifted her hand. "I can answer that. The Wiccan magic is not the fantasy version of turning misbehaving princes into beasts or growing giant trees from magical beans. It's about focusing intention and energy to bring about positive change on the individual and global levels."

"Those are lofty statements," Aru said. "But how does that work in practice? How can a ritual or a spell influence reality?"

Sari leaned over so she could face him. "In the same way that meditation and prayers do in other spiritual traditions. Wiccans believe that by aligning their intentions with the natural energies of the world, they can tap into a deeper power and create change in accordance with their will. Given your connection with your sister, you shouldn't be so skeptical. There are forces and energies in the universe that are impossible to explain based on what we know."

Aru dipped his head. "Well said."

David, who so far had been satisfied with just listening, put his hand on Sari's shoulder to get her attention. "You don't have to work hard to convince me that this is all real, but with harnessing such power comes great responsibility. How do those who practice the Wicca religion ensure that it is used ethically?"

Sari let out a breath. "The Wiccan guiding principle is the Rule of Three: Whatever you release into the world will return to you trifold, so be sure that you do no harm."

Amanda nodded. "What it's basically saying is that everything a witch does comes back at her, so cursing someone or wishing them ill will cost the witch dearly. It's a good incentive to only cast good spells."

Kian looked like he'd had enough of the discussion. "As fascinating as I find all this talk about witchcraft, what we should focus on is what Jasmine believes in and if she can actually do what she claims she can."

"Very true." Amanda smiled at her brother, who had been very patient up until now. "I should talk to her about it."

43

JASMINE

As they neared Frankie and Margo's cabin door, Jasmine watched Frankie pull out her phone and aim it at the lock.

"That's so cool. I only have a simple keycard." It figured that even that small convenience was reserved for the guests of the upper decks.

As the door swung open, Margo rushed over, her face split by a huge grin. "I'm so glad that you are here."

Pulling her friend into a hug, Jasmine was careful not to squish Margo, who looked a little pale. "I finally get to see where you've been living."

Margo laughed, ushering her into the spacious cabin. "This place is bigger than my apartment and much nicer. I don't know how I'm going to go back to living like a pauper."

"You won't," Frankie murmured.

Jasmine wondered what she meant by that. Was Margo moving in with Negal? If so, they were moving a little too fast, but who was she to judge?

Everyone had their own timelines for things.

"You weren't kidding about this place being swanky." She turned in a circle, taking in the professionally decorated living room portion of the cabin with its floor-to-ceiling sliding doors that overlooked a spacious balcony and the ocean beyond.

"Mine is just as nice," Edgar said from behind her.

Crap, she'd forgotten that he was there. Plastering a smile on her face, Jasmine turned toward him. "You remember Edgar, Margo, right?"

Margo offered him her hand. "Of course. How could I forget the pilot who brought me Negal?"

"It was my pleasure." Edgar shook what he was offered.

Margo pulled him into a quick one-armed embrace. "I'm glad that you two found each other." She let go of Ed and regarded him with curious eyes. "How have you been?"

"I've been good, but I'm even better now that I was allowed to venture down to the staff quarters and reunite with Jasmine." He took her hand and brought it to his lips for a kiss. "As you know, males are banned from the lower decks because of the rescued women, but Amanda convinced Kian to let me visit."

"I'm glad." Margo sat down, looking exhausted just from standing for a few minutes.

Joining her friend on the couch, Jasmine regarded her with a frown. "What's going on with you? You look like a ghost."

Margo grimaced. "It's nothing. Probably a bug I caught while on shore, or maybe the whole kidnapping ordeal is finally catching up to me. How about you? Are you okay?"

Margo was so sweet, always worrying about others.

"Honestly? The whole thing feels surreal. I keep waiting to wake up. First, it was Alberto turning out to be a scumbag, but that wasn't such a big surprise. I was starting to suspect something was off about him long before I met you, but I had no idea how bad it was going to get. Then I got kidnapped, dragging you along into the abyss, and then Edgar flew a team to our rescue." She smiled at Ed. "But ending up on this ship almost makes it all worth it."

"Really?" Margo arched a brow. "Even though you were restricted to the staff decks?"

"It wasn't all bad." Jasmine crossed her legs. "I made new friends, met interesting people, and I even got tested by a neuroscientist and a probe lady." Jasmine chuckled. "The wonders never cease." She waved her hand over the cabin. "And now this. I plan to explore the upper decks and all the luxuries they have to offer."

Frankie perched on the arm of the chair Dagor sat in. "You will need to hurry up with your explorations. The cruise is almost over, so you don't have much time left." She sighed. "I'm going to miss this ship with all its comforts, especially the dining room. I love having all my meals prepared for me."

When Negal finally emerged from the bedroom, Jasmine was reminded how incredibly handsome he was. Edgar was a good-looking guy, but next to Negal, he looked almost plain.

"Hello, Jasmine." Negal smiled at her. "I'm glad that you are finally free to visit. How are you feeling?"

"Great. I was just telling everyone how it all feels surreal."

"I bet." He turned to Edgar, who squeezed in next to Jasmine and sat down on her other side, and arched a brow. "Hello to you too, Ed."

"I'm here with Jasmine." Ed clasped her hand. "We are together."

"I see that." Something unreadable flickered through Negal's eyes. "I wish you the best of luck. Can I offer you a drink? Tea or coffee?"

"What do you have?" Ed let go of Jasmine's hand and rose to his feet.

"Let me show you," Negal said.

As the guys were joined by Dagor at the kitchen counter, Jasmine leaned toward Margo. "Things look serious between the two of you."

"They are," Margo whispered conspiratorially. "Negal is amazing."

Frankie snorted. "He's like a mother hen, fussing over Margo and not letting her move an inch. I'm glad my Dagor is not such a fusser."

Margo snorted. "Right, says the girl whose boyfriend was so anxious to see her that he couldn't wait for the boat to get to the ship, jumped into the water, and swam the rest of the way."

As Frankie's lips quirked in a half smile, Jasmine leaned back and crossed her arms over her chest. "Now, that's a story I want to hear all the details of. What was Dagor doing in a boat, and why was he so anxious about you?"

Frankie slid into the armchair that Dagor had vacated. "I got shot."

Jasmine's eyes widened. "Really? How? When? By whom?"

Frankie cast a quick look at the men before leaning forward and whispering, "I'm not supposed to talk about it, but did you wonder where the rescued women came from, and who rescued them?"

A shiver ran down Jasmine's spine. "I thought they were just given passage like I was."

"There is more to it," Frankie said. "It all started with a cursed amulet."

Jasmine laughed. "I knew you were pulling my leg, but I'm always game for a good story."

The doorbell ringing stopped Frankie from telling the rest of it, and as Dagor opened the door, Mia drove in, exchanging quick greetings with the guys before joining the girls.

"I'm so happy you are finally free." She returned Jasmine's hug. "We can now plan a get-together on the Lido deck. Did you bring a swimsuit?"

Margo chuckled. "It's not a suit. I first met Jasmine by a pool, and what she had on was a skimpy bikini that would have made even Amanda blush."

Jasmine pretended to be offended. "That's a huge exaggeration. My bikini is not scandalous at all. It's not my fault that I'm generously endowed."

Margo cast her a fond smile. "I wasn't talking about the front. I was talking about the back. I didn't even know that thong bikinis were a thing until I saw you in one. But I have to say, you look damn good in it."

147

44

EDGAR

A surge of possessiveness swept through Edgar as he watched Jasmine laughing with her friends. She was so damn beautiful, and it wasn't only about her physical attributes. Jasmine was vivacious, and it was the first time he had ever used that word to describe a woman because he'd never met one who fit that adjective so well. Her eyes sparkled, her smile was bright, and her laughter wrapped around his shaft as if it were her hand.

He wanted to pull her into his arms, carry her out of Margo's cabin, and lock her in his until the end of the cruise.

The problem was that she would not be on board for that. Ever since they had arrived at Margo's, Jasmine had been distant, her attention divided between him and the others, which usually wouldn't have bothered him, but he had a niggling sense he couldn't quite shake that she wasn't into him as much as he was into her.

He tried to tell himself that it was just the excitement of finally being allowed on the upper decks and getting to spend time with Margo and Frankie, but it seemed like Jasmine was doing her best to avoid his eyes, and her laughter sounded a little too loud, too forced, which led him to believe that she was nervous, but he didn't know why.

Was she intimidated by Dagor and Negal's presence?

That wasn't likely. Jasmine didn't know that they were gods, and she didn't seem like the kind of woman who got nervous around attractive men. On the contrary, that was where Jasmine was in her element.

"So, what changed Kian's mind about letting you up here?" Margo asked.

Jasmine flipped a dark lock of hair behind her shoulder. "He sent a woman named Edna to probe me. She's a hypnotist like Kevin but with a slightly different ability. She can determine people's inner motives and intents. She must have arrived at the conclusion that I was harmless, but she definitely didn't come in thinking that way. She brought a hunky guard with her, a guy named Max, who did his best to intimidate me."

Edgar felt a hot spike of jealousy pierce his gut, and it only got worse when Frankie and Margo started peppering Jasmine with questions about her interactions with the Guardian. Edgar tried to tune them out, but it was difficult to hear Jasmine gushing over Max's impressive muscles and piercing eyes.

The jealousy was irrational. Jasmine sounded like she was describing a movie star, admiring his attributes but not saying anything that would indicate that she was attracted to the guy, and Max had assured him last night that he had absolutely no interest in her.

Edgar had returned to the wedding party to catch the Guardian and have a talk with him about staying away from Jasmine. It also hadn't hurt that Max could smell her on Edgar. He might not be one of Max's buddies, but he knew the guy wouldn't go after a woman he was interested in. It was a matter of honor.

Still, males might claim to adhere to a code of honor only to throw it out the window when an attractive female caught their eye. Shamefully, he had been guilty of doing that once or twice, but then neither he nor his friends had been pursuing females for anything other than a tumble between the sheets.

In fact, that's how he should think about Jasmine instead of getting all worked up about her. He had no right to claim her or feel possessive or territorial about her.

Easier said than done after the incredible, mind-blowing night that had left him aching for more.

He'd thought that it meant something to her and that the connection he'd felt wasn't just in his imagination. But watching her with her friends and seeing the way her eyes kept darting to the door as if she was waiting for someone else to arrive, Edgar felt a sinking sensation in his gut that Jasmine did not consider last night a preamble for more.

She probably saw him as a convenient stepping stone, a way to pass the time until someone better came along. Someone like Max, with his chiseled jaw and rippling muscles and aura of power.

Edgar clenched his fists, fighting back the urge to punch something.

He was just a civilian pilot, a glorified chauffeur in the grand scheme of things, but he was fun to be with, and he had a much better sense of humor than damn Max. Females loved Ed, as evidenced by the endless parade of beautiful women who had graced his bed.

He needed to take a step back and breathe and give Jasmine space to figure out what she wanted. If he wasn't the one for her, so be it.

The world was full of beautiful women. But beautiful women who were also Dormants were rare, and there was a slight chance that Jasmine was a Dormant.

Nevertheless, he wouldn't make a fool of himself, even if it meant watching her flirt with other men. He would grit his teeth and smile through the jealousy that clawed at his insides and pretend that he was fine with it.

That didn't mean that he wouldn't fight for her, though. Just that if he lost to someone else, he wouldn't be a sore loser.

Even if she was just a human, Jasmine was still worth fighting for, if for no other reason than to prove to those macho Guardians that charm and wit were no less important than bicep size.

When there was a slight pause in the chatter, he leaned over and put a hand over Jasmine's thigh. "Can we talk out on the balcony for a minute?"

Jasmine glanced at her friends, hesitated for a moment, but then nodded and rose to her feet. "Lead the way."

Margo and Frankie regarded him with twin puzzled expressions, but the knowing looks in Dagor and Negal's eyes told him that they understood what was going on.

When they stepped out to the balcony, he closed the sliding door behind them and pulled Jasmine into his arms. "I need to kiss you."

She giggled. "Is that what you wanted to talk about?"

"Yeah. More or less." He wrapped his palm around the back of her neck and kissed her hard, pouring all of his uncertainty and pent-up possessiveness into the kiss.

When he finally let her go up for air, she was breathless. "Wow." She brought a finger to her lips and rubbed it over them. "Whatever you wanted to talk about, that was a very convincing argument."

He chuckled. "I'm glad that we have that settled." He took her hand and turned toward the sliding door.

"Wait." She tugged on his hand. "Is that really all you wanted? To kiss me?"

He hesitated for a moment. "I wanted to remind you how good it is between us, just in case you forgot while drooling over Max's biceps."

"Oh, Ed." Jasmine laughed. "I'm not interested in Max, and he's not interested in me. I think he doesn't like me for some reason. He was borderline rude to me and kept looking at me as if I had dog poo stuck to my shoe."

Now, that made Ed angry almost as much as hearing that Max had flirted with her would have. "I'll talk to him. He has no right to regard you with anything other than respect."

"Oh, sweetie." She lifted her hand and cupped his cheek. "That's so chivalrous of you, and here I was thinking that chivalry was dead."

He felt his chest puff up even though he hadn't commanded it to do so. "I'm glad to restore your faith in my gender."

She leaned in and feathered a soft kiss over his lips. "As much as I appreciate the gesture, please don't talk with Max about me. You don't need to risk your friendship with him over a silly thing like that. Besides, I'm a big girl, and unless I've been drugged and kidnapped by a drug lord, I can take care of myself."

45

MARGO

After Jasmine and Edgar left to explore the ship, Margo leaned back on the plush couch, listening to Frankie and Mia talk about Karen.

"Gabi told me that Karen doesn't want to do the test," Mia said. "I need to have a talk with the woman and explain that it's not about making sure she has transitioned, but about tradition. All transitioned Dormants do it. It's like a rite of passage."

Frankie shrugged. "Karen strikes me as the practical sort, and she doesn't need the proof, so why go for it?"

"That's what she says." Mia let out a breath. "Karen told Gabi that the disappearance of her fine lines was proof enough that it worked."

As her friends debated the merits of Karen's decision, Margo's mind drifted to her own situation. Bridget believed that her symptoms were consistent with the transformation, and Negal was convinced of it, but part of her still doubted. What if they were all mistaken and something else was responsible for her symptoms?

Frankie's test was a simple cut on the palm of her hand that had healed in a matter of moments. The ceremony around it had been a much bigger deal than what was needed for the test.

Margo wanted the certainty that came with concrete proof that she was truly becoming immortal, and as she listened to the others talk, an idea began to form in her mind.

A brief moment of pain was worth it, to know for sure, and she didn't even need the doctor for that.

"I need to visit the bathroom." Margo put her teacup down on the coffee table.

Mia smiled at her. "I should go. I promised Toven that I wouldn't stay long. He wanted to go to the Lido deck."

"I think Dagor and I will join you," Frankie said. "Jasmine and Edgar headed there." She cast a glance at Margo. "Do you want to come? You can lie down on a lounger, and it will be like being on the couch here, just out in the fresh air. Am I right?"

"Maybe tomorrow." Margo pushed to her feet and gave Frankie a quick hug and then another to Mia. "I'm sure that by tomorrow, I'll feel well enough to go out there, but today, I'd rather take it easy."

She walked by Dagor and Negal, who were sitting on barstools in front of the tiny counter, sipping on bottles of that potent beer that the immortals liked.

She pecked Negal on the cheek. "I'm just going to the bathroom. I will be right back."

He nodded and got to his feet to open the door for Mia.

So far, so good.

Margo felt like a teenager sneaking away to smoke a cigarette where her parents wouldn't find her.

Negal would be furious if he found out what she was about to do, but she needed to know.

After locking the bathroom door behind her, Margo rummaged through the drawers but found no scissors, no clippers, and not even a razor. Negal used an electric shaver, and she had forgotten to buy a disposable blade for the few stubborn armpit hairs that no amount of laser treatments had managed to obliterate. Not that it was such a big deal. The hairs were blond and barely visible, but they annoyed the heck out of her.

She should just tweeze them away.

Well, what do you know? She could use the tweezers to make a scratch, right?

The cool metal felt slightly ominous in her hand, and she hesitated for a moment, not because she was afraid of a little pain but because she was debating the wisdom of her plan.

When Frankie was transitioning, Bridget had claimed that she had to wait to test her until Dagor's venom cleared her system because Frankie's body had been saturated with it, so the wound could have healed because of that and not the transition.

That wasn't the case with Margo. Negal had bitten her only once, so if she healed faster than normal, it would be a sign that she was transitioning.

Taking a deep breath, Margo hiked up her skirt, exposing an expanse of her thigh. She needed to make the scratch somewhere inconspicuous in case it didn't heal faster than it should, and she would be stuck with the evidence of her subterfuge.

With a shaking hand, she pressed the tip of the tweezers against her skin, wincing at the sharp sting of pain. It wasn't a deep cut like the one Bridget had given Frankie, but even a scratch would normally take days to heal on Margo's fair skin.

Transfixed, she watched as a thin line of blood welled up along the shallow wound, the deep red a stark contrast against her pale flesh. It didn't happen right away, and she was starting to despair, but then the blood flow stopped, and then the edges of the scratch started knitting together before her astonished eyes. It took long minutes until the wound vanished entirely, but it was still a miracle.

Normally, she would have never healed so fast.

A giddy laugh bubbled up from her throat. There was no more doubt. It was happening. She was truly transitioning.

Bursting out of the bathroom, she ran to the living room in a whirl of excitement and launched herself at Negal, who was sprawled on the couch. "I'm becoming immortal." She peppered his astonished face with kisses.

He let out a startled grunt, his arms coming up automatically to catch her as she clung to him like a koala. "Did you doubt it?"

She nodded.

A slow grin spread across his face as he took in her elated expression. "Of course you are, Nesha. But what has changed in the last five minutes?"

Margo's smile turned sheepish, a blush staining her cheeks. "I needed to see it for myself. I needed to know that this was really happening."

Understanding dawned in Negal's eyes, followed quickly by a flash of concern. "What did you do?" His gaze roamed over her body as he searched for injury.

Margo shook her head, pressing a reassuring kiss to his lips. "Just a little scratch to see how fast I would heal."

Negal's frown deepened, his hands tightening on her hips. "Margo, you shouldn't be doing stuff like that. Your body is going through enough changes as it is, and it's too early for testing. You should have waited for Bridget to determine the right time."

She sighed, resting her forehead against his. "I needed to do it, Negal. I needed proof. The anxiety of the uncertainty was making me sick. I feel so much better now that I know for sure."

He softened, one hand coming up to cup her cheek. "I understand," he murmured before taking her lips in a kiss. "How much stronger do you feel?" He whispered against her ear.

"Much, much stronger." Margo pulled back to look at Negal's eyes, which were sparkling with mischief. "And I feel like celebrating."

His gaze darkened with desire, his hands sliding down to cup her backside. "And what exactly did you have in mind for your celebration, Nesha?"

Margo grinned, pressing herself against him in a way that left no doubt as to her intentions. "Oh, I can think of a few things," she purred.

Negal's answering growl sent a shiver down her spine, and then he was lifting her into his arms and carrying her toward the bedroom with single-minded purpose.

As he laid her down on the mattress, his body covering hers in a delicious weight, Margo wrapped her arms around her mate and held him to her. "I love you."

"And I love you, my soul."

He began worshipping her body with gentle hands, lips, and tongue, and as he brought her to the heights of pleasure, Margo let herself get lost in the sensations.

Later, when she lay quivering and boneless in his arms, she looked into his beautiful blue eyes. "What about you?" She reached between their bodies and took hold of his hard length through his pants.

He shook his head, removed her hand from his erection, and brought it to his lips for a kiss. "I don't think I should give you more venom while you are transitioning. In fact, I'm sure that I shouldn't. Bridget told Frankie and Dagor to abstain until Frankie was out of the woods."

She smiled sheepishly. "That doesn't preclude a hand job."

"It does because I'm too tightly wound up to refrain from following up with a bite. I can survive one more day."

"I love you." She lifted her hand to cup his cheek.

Negal smiled, his hand coming up to cover hers. "I love you too, Nesha. More than I ever thought possible to love someone." He pressed a kiss to her temple. "But now, you need to rest."

"I do." She let out a breath and nestled into his embrace, letting the steady beat of his heart lull her into a sense of peace.

46

KIAN

"Join us." Syssi wound her arms around Kian's neck. "Allegra loves playing in the pool with you, and you are supposed to be on vacation, not working all the time."

Usually he brought work with him on vacations, but this time he'd intended to do as little as possible and enjoy time with his family. Obviously, the Fates had different plans for him.

He kissed the tip of her nose. "You know that I'm not a great fan of public pools."

That's why he had a private lap pool at home for his exercise.

Kian was the leader of his community, and he had to maintain a certain distance whether he liked it or not. No one would bat an eyelash if he showed up on the Lido deck in his swim trunks, but he wasn't comfortable doing so.

Besides, he needed to talk to Turner before Yamanu's bachelor party.

"You don't have to go into the water if you don't want to." Syssi pouted. "You can just chat with my father over a drink. You know how much he enjoys talking to you."

Syssi's parents had come over earlier to take Allegra to the pool, and Syssi had stayed behind for a few moments to put her swimsuit on and gather a few things. Allegra loved her granddaddy, and Adam adored Allegra, but Kian had no doubt that his father-in-law would love some adult conversation. Regrettably, he couldn't oblige him today.

"I love chatting with your father as well, but I haven't checked with Turner about Margo's parents' place yet, and then I need to get ready for Yamanu's bachelor party."

Yamanu was one of the oldest Guardians on the force and one of its most valued members. His bachelor party was not one that Kian wished to skip.

"Fine." Syssi let go of his neck. "My dad is going to be disappointed, but he will understand. Enjoy the party, and I'll see you when you get back."

Syssi looked a little disappointed herself, but it couldn't be helped. Besides, she was meeting her parents and Andrew and his family, so she and Allegra would have plenty of company.

"I love you." He dipped his head and kissed her cheek. "Give Allegra kisses from Daddy."

"I will."

When he closed the door behind Syssi, Kian pulled out his phone and called Turner.

Turner answered after several rings. "Good afternoon, Kian."

"Good afternoon. I hope I'm not interrupting. I just wanted to know if you've heard any news from your teams in regard to Margo and her family's residences and workplaces. Did anyone come snooping around?"

"I've just got off the phone with my assistant. So far, no suspicious activity has been recorded."

Kian was glad that there was no activity but only because he didn't have Guardians in the area to take care of it.

Things were going to change once they returned home.

"Keep me posted if anything changes."

"As soon as I hear anything, I'll let you know."

"Thank you, and I'm sorry about making you work on your vacation."

Turner chuckled. "Don't be. I've realized that I don't enjoy long vacations. I get bored. I like doing what I do too much to want to be away from it for too long."

"I know what you mean, and we are both certifiable. Try to enjoy the rest of the day."

"Same goes for you," Turner said.

Ending the call, Kian sank into his chair and rubbed a hand over his face.

Unless Carlos Modana and the Doomers he was working with had decided to drop the investigation of what happened in Acapulco and what had made Julio change his stripes, they would want to have a talk with Margo and Jasmine, if only to cover their bases.

Now that Margo was transitioning, one problem was solved. She was not going back to her apartment and her old job. She was most likely going to accompany her mate on his journey to Tibet.

Her family was still a big problem that needed to be resolved, though, and naturally, it was up to him. They needed new identities and new jobs, and that was going to cost a bundle.

Perhaps he could get Toven to take care of that. After all, Margo and Frankie were on the cruise at his personal invitation.

Jasmine would be much more difficult to hide and protect.

Her customer service job was easy to replace, but she also had a modest acting career, and that made her face recognizable, so hiding her would be tougher.

Or maybe not?

She could get a new name, a new agent, and maybe, with Brandon's Hollywood connections, better parts.

That wasn't smart, though. Putting Jasmine in front of cameras was too risky. Her looks were too distinct to be forgettable, and not even plastic surgery could do much about it. Besides, the woman didn't need anything done, and she wouldn't want to change what she was given by the Fates.

He needed to find something else for her that would keep her out of the public eye, at least for a couple of years until Modana and the Doomers forgot about her.

The easiest thing would be to put her up in a hotel and ask her to stay put for a few weeks. After that, Toven could arrange a Perfect Match job for her. Given her experience in customer service, that wouldn't be a problem. Those departments always needed new people.

47

AMANDA

Amanda scanned the dining room for Jasmine and Edgar. "I don't see them." She turned to Dalhu. "Do you?"

She was wearing flats, so he had a good half a head or more over her.

"I don't. Maybe they went to the Lido deck."

Frankie had said that Ed had taken Jasmine on a tour of the ship, but the only public spaces were the dining room, the gym, and the bars on the promenade deck and the Lido deck.

Amanda cast a sidelong glance at her mate. "Do you want to grab something to eat before we go up there?"

They had eaten brunch at her mother's, but that had been an hour ago. She wasn't hungry, but Dalhu might be.

"I'm full." Dalhu adjusted Evie in his arms. "Let's go."

They only got as far as the elevator. As soon as the doors opened, Jasmine and Edgar stepped out along with several other passengers.

"Amanda!" Jasmine spread her arms and hugged her as if they were the best of friends. "Thank you. You freed me."

"You're welcome." Amanda patted her back. "Are you heading to the dining room?"

"Yes." Jasmine beamed happily. "I'm curious whether the food up here is better than the food down in the staff dining room."

"Why would it be? It's cooked in the same kitchen."

Jasmine looked surprised. "Really? I thought there was another kitchen down there adjacent to the dining room."

159

"There is, but most of the cooking is done in the main one." Amanda turned to her mate. "Dalhu, this is my new friend Jasmine. Jasmine, this is my husband Dalhu and our daughter Evie."

"A pleasure to meet you both." Jasmine gave Dalhu one of her flirty smiles, but by now Amanda knew that didn't mean she was actually flirting with him. It was just the way she was, and she probably couldn't help it.

Evie regarded the woman with shy curiosity and after a moment gifted her with a small smile before ducking her head and hiding her face in the crook of Dalhu's neck.

"She is adorable," Jasmine said. "And she looks like a mix of the two of you. More like you, Amanda."

Dalhu kissed the top of Evie's head. "Thank the merciful Fates for that."

"Have you eaten already?" Edgar asked.

"We did, but we will come to keep you company." Amanda threaded her arm through Jasmine's. "I want to ask you a few questions about your Wiccan practice if that's okay."

"Of course." Jasmine leaned into her. "What would you like to know?"

Amanda slanted her a smile. "I'm fascinated by the occult, and I'm an amateur practitioner, but I never had the time to study the rituals and spells. I'm also interested in the deities you honor and your guiding beliefs."

More than that, Amanda wanted to understand the woman herself and get a sense of the person behind the tarot cards and the talk of princes. She had a feeling that there was more to Jasmine than met the eye.

The woman's face lit up, her eyes sparkling with excitement. "After acting, that's my second favorite topic, but I only talk about it with people who have at least some knowledge about it and don't think it's devil worship." She grimaced. "Like my father."

Amanda had a feeling that there was a story there, but it was better reserved for another time.

They found a table, and once Dalhu had set Evie down in a highchair, he and Edgar went to the buffet to collect a sampling of the dishes.

"I've already eaten," Amanda said. "So I'm not hungry, but if you want to go get something, I'll wait."

"It's fine." Jasmine waved a dismissive hand. "I trust Edgar to get me things I like."

Amanda arched a brow. "When did he have the time to learn your culinary preferences?"

Jasmine chuckled. "He didn't, but I'm not very choosy with food. I can eat anything."

That was unusual for someone who was pursuing a career in acting, but

Jasmine seemed to be unconcerned with Hollywood's unrealistic beauty ideals and was comfortable in her own skin.

Amanda put a hand on the woman's upper arm. "The more I get to know you, the more I like you."

Jasmine grinned. "Ditto."

"So, Jasmine," Amanda said, leaning forward with a conspiratorial grin. "Tell me more about your Wiccan practices."

"I'm a beginner witch myself, and I learned what I know from the internet, other practitioners on social media, and books. So far, I like that Wicca is all about honoring the cycles of nature and the interconnectedness of all things. I believe that by attuning myself to the rhythms of the universe, I can tap into a deeper wisdom and power that can guide me." She looked at Amanda from under lowered lashes. "Does that sound like a load of crap to you?"

"Not at all. That's how I feel as well."

Jasmine looked relieved and then glanced around to check who was listening to their conversation before leaning closer to Amanda. "One of my favorite rituals is the Drawing Down the Moon," she said. "It's a powerful invocation of the Goddess's energy, a way of connecting with the divine feminine and bringing her wisdom and guidance into our lives." She continued to describe a few more rituals, but her main tool of divination seemed to be tarot cards.

Amanda nodded along. "I've never paid much attention to tarot reading, but you mentioned that the cards have been pointing to a prince in your future. Can you tell me more about that?"

"It started with a simple three-card spread," Jasmine said in a near whisper. "The first card was The Six of Cups, which represents innocence, nostalgia, and the promise of a new beginning. The second was The Lovers, which speaks of a deep, soulful connection blessed by the divine. And the third was The Knight of Cups, the embodiment of romance, chivalry, and the arrival of a suitor."

She paused, letting the significance of the cards sink in before continuing, but since Amanda wasn't all that familiar with tarot, it was all pretty meaningless to her. The few times she had gone for a reading, she paid more attention to the lady interpreting the cards than to the cards themselves.

"Together, they painted a picture of a profound, fated love and a connection that would transform my life. If it was a one-time occurrence, I would have dismissed it, but the same cards continued to come up."

Jasmine's excitement was contagious, and Amanda felt a flicker of it in her own heart. "Was that it, or did you get any more clues from the cards?"

"Not yet," she admitted. "The cards are frustratingly vague on that point. But I trust that when the time is right, he will reveal himself to me. Until then, I just have to keep my heart open and my eyes peeled."

Amanda shifted her gaze to the men who were heading back with loaded plates.

"Could the prince be Edgar?" she asked quickly.

"Maybe." Jasmine shrugged. "Maybe the card meant it metaphorically." She chuckled. "Instead of the knight in shining armor arriving on a noble steed, my knight arrived in a shining helicopter and brought along two noble saviors."

As the guys put the plates down, Amanda smiled at Edgar. "Are you planning on inviting Jasmine as your date to the wedding tonight?"

Edgar's face split into a wide, boyish grin as he trained his eyes on Jasmine. "Of course. That was the main reason Jasmine wanted to be allowed on the upper decks."

The smile slid off Amanda's face as she remembered that Jasmine was not allowed full disclosure. "Just as a reminder, Jasmine will have to wait to come in until after the ceremony." She looked apologetically at the woman. "I know it's disappointing, but that's the way it has to be."

"Why is that?" Jasmine leaned forward with a quizzical frown. "If you're practicing some kind of witchy ritual, you know that I'm totally on board. I love learning about new traditions and practices."

Amanda shook her head. "We have other reasons for the secrecy that I'm not at liberty to disclose. It's nothing personal, and you are not the only one who has to wait until after the ceremony to be allowed inside. Marina and Larissa will also be waiting in the bar for their boyfriends to escort them into the dining hall, so the three of you can keep each other company."

48

YAMANU

Yamanu sprawled on a lounge chair and surveyed the group of males gathered around him with a contented smile playing on his lips. The balcony of his cabin was filled with the rich aroma of cigars, laughter, and, most importantly, camaraderie.

Looking at the faces of the males who had stood by his side through countless missions, he felt a surge of gratitude. Arwel, Bhathian, Anandur, and Brundar were like brothers to him, and Kri a sister, and it was a damn shame that she had bowed out, saying that she didn't really belong with the boys. She was the youngest Head Guardian, and he was so damn proud of her.

She should have been here.

Then there was Onegus, the chief, and Kian, the big boss. The Clan Mother's son was a good leader, fair and just, and no less importantly, the guy had an uncanny knack for business, which had them all living in style and armed with the best weaponry money could buy and William could produce.

Julian was the odd one out in the group. The young doctor wasn't a Guardian, but he had joined the force on several missions and had proven himself to be coolheaded and capable under fire, which was admirable for a civilian.

Yamanu had befriended Bridget's son when he had started volunteering at the halfway house for the survivors of trafficking, running the weekly karaoke night. Julian was charged with managing the place, and he did that remarkably well considering that he had never managed anything before. Having a mate who had been a victim of trafficking herself probably made Julian better suited for the position than most.

Yamanu had found himself looking forward to those karaoke nights. Bringing the girls joy through singing was a different path for him to make the world a slightly better place. As a Guardian, he protected his clan and saved victims of trafficking when not running missions against the clan's enemies. His singing was just something he enjoyed doing, while his powerful thralling and shrouding abilities were weapons in the clan's arsenal that he had spent centuries honing and developing through great personal sacrifice.

Celibacy had enabled him to channel all of his energy into his massive thralls and shrouds, diverting hordes of marauders away from his people and enabling countless missions that would have been impossible to pull off without it.

And yet, the Clan Mother had been willing to give up that protection just so he could find happiness in the arms of the female he loved. As it turned out, his abilities had not disappeared when he had broken his vow of celibacy, but the goddess couldn't have known that, and he would be forever grateful to her for encouraging him to mate Mey.

He had never expected to find love, had never even dared to dream of it, but the moment he'd seen Mey for the first time, Yamanu had known that she was the one, the missing piece of his soul.

His talents had not diminished after their union but had only grown stronger, as if Mey's love had unlocked some hidden reserve of power within him.

He had never been happier, and he owed it all to Mey, Annani, and the group of friends gathered on his balcony.

Smiling to himself, Yamanu pushed to his feet and lifted his whiskey glass, the amber liquid glowing in the soft light of the setting sun. "To Mey." He raised a toast. "My one and only, my mate, who became the owner of my heart and gave me a reason to live. And to all of you, whom I'm honored to call brothers, thank you for always having my back."

After they had all clinked their glasses and emptied them in one go, Arwel grabbed a bottle and refilled them. "To Yamanu." He lifted his glass. "We all owe you big time for sacrificing so much to protect our sorry hides."

Arwel had sacrificed himself plenty and was still sacrificing almost daily, but Yamanu didn't think this was the time or place to mention it. He planned on toasting his brother-in-arms at his own bachelor party, which would happen tomorrow, the last day of the cruise.

Nodding, Kian rested his cigar on the lip of an ashtray. "I don't even want to speculate about what would have befallen our clan if not for your immense shrouding and thralling abilities, Yamanu. And you did that all while keeping secret the great sacrifice you were making to be able to do so."

Yamanu felt self-conscious. "That's precisely why I kept my vow of celibacy a secret from you all. I didn't want this." He waved the hand holding the cigar. "I

164

didn't want to be treated differently and put on a pedestal. Each one of you would have done the same given similar circumstances."

As the others averted their gazes, Yamanu laughed. "I know what you are thinking. No way would you have given up sex to grow your power, but I assure you that you would have done it if you knew that your sacrifice would save your loved ones from annihilation by our enemy or by humans. After all, what are our lives worth without those we love to live it with? Nothing."

A few moments passed as each of the males contemplated his words and tried to imagine themselves in his position.

"I agree," Kian said. "When I was still a bachelor, I would have sacrificed everything to protect my clan. But now, I'm not so sure. My wife and daughter will always come first, then the clan, and lastly, my own needs."

"I'll drink to that." Yamanu lifted his glass again. "To our mates!"

Onegus waited until they all emptied their glasses before opening another bottle of fine whiskey and refilling them. He raised his glass in a final toast. "To Yamanu and Mey and their everlasting love and commitment to each other and to the clan."

Yamanu clinked glasses with everyone before downing another shot. Fine whiskey was meant to be savored, and it was a shame to drink it like that, but it was for a good cause.

Julian raised his glass, his eyes shining with mischief. "Now that the toasts are done, it's time for a song." He bowed to Yamanu. "I believe that the one about the bonny lass in the blue dress is most appropriate for the occasion."

It was one of the favorites on karaoke nights, and the girls asked for it each time.

"That's a fine one, indeed." Bhathian wrapped his arm around Julian's shoulders. "We will join you for the chorus."

Yamanu grinned. "Aye, 'tis a fine choice." The song was more funny than romantic, but the melody was lively, and it always put everyone in a good mood.

He cleared his throat, and as he began singing, the others joined in, their strong voices blending in a harmonious chorus despite some of them slurring their words. Bhathian's deep, rumbling bass provided a solid foundation, while Julian's smooth tenor wove a melodic counterpoint. Anandur added his rich baritone, and Brundar tapped his foot to the beat, which made Yamanu stupidly happy because Brundar never actively participated in things of that sort.

The chorus swelled, and the men clapped their hands and stomped their feet in time with the tune. The sound carried on the breeze, and soon, more voices joined them from the other balconies.

As the final notes faded away, the men erupted in laughter, and applause sounded from the other balconies.

"Thank you!" Yamanu called out to his impromptu audience.

"A toast!" Onegus leaned over the railing, raising his glass high to the specta-tors from the other balconies. "To all the bonny lasses who've captured our hearts!"

49

SYSSI

"Sweet dreams, my precious." Syssi kissed her sleeping daughter's cheek. After exhausting herself and her granddaddy in the pool, Allegra had fallen asleep in Syssi's arms on the way back to the cabin. The girl needed a bath, but Syssi knew better than to wake her up for that.

Allegra was a sweet child, but if anyone dared to wake her up before she was good and ready, she was cranky for the rest of the day and had a hard time falling asleep again at night.

The good news was that she would not wake up during the next two hours, so Syssi could use that time to summon a vision about Khiann and his fate, but the bad news was that Kian wasn't there, and he didn't like it when she induced a vision without him watching over her.

It wasn't necessary, and Okidu could help her if she ended up needing it, but Kian wouldn't be happy with the butler doing that, and maybe he was right. After all, Okidu had limited executive functioning, and he might not know what to do.

Tiptoeing out of the bedroom, Syssi walked over to the couch and pulled her phone out of her purse. Amanda had watched over her during a session before, and Kian had accepted her as a good substitute, but she might be busy doing something else.

After placing the call, Syssi cradled the phone against her ear and loaded the coffeemaker while waiting for Amanda to pick up.

She answered after several rings, sounding a little breathless. "Hello, my favorite sister-in-law."

Syssi chuckled. "I'm your only sister-in-law." It suddenly occurred to her that

Amanda might be at Mey's bachelorette party. "Are you busy? Am I interrupting?"

"You are not interrupting anything, darling. Mey's party hasn't started yet."

Syssi frowned. "Yamanu's bachelor party has already started. How come hers hasn't?"

"Yamanu's groomsmen are going to have a break between the bachelor party and the wedding, while Mey's bridesmaids are supposed to stay with her the entire time. She wants them to get dressed in Jin's cabin and then escort her to the event hall from there. Not that I intend to do that. I'll excuse myself and join them for the ceremony."

"I can totally understand that." Syssi needed to decompress after social interactions, and going from one party to the next without a break would have exhausted her mentally and physically.

Funny how certain things hadn't changed after her transition, proving how strong the mind-body connection was.

"It's a busy day for you, so I'm hesitant to even ask, but is there a chance you can come over for half an hour to watch over me when I induce the vision I promised your mother about Khiann? Kian is at Yamanu's party, and if I attempt it without anyone here to monitor me, he will pop a vein."

Amanda snorted. "Yeah, he totally would, even though it's physically impossible for him. I'll be there in five minutes."

"Thank you," Syssi said. "You are the best."

"Oh, I know, darling," Amanda purred. "I know."

Syssi ended the call with a smile. It was the Amanda effect and one of the reasons she still worked at her lab. They weren't making much progress with the paranormal research, but they enjoyed spending time together, and being around Amanda was uplifting. There was rarely a day that Syssi came home from the lab in a bad mood, and when she did, it was because Amanda turned the radio on and listened to the news on the way back home.

Lately, the distressing stuff Syssi heard was so overwhelming that she tried to stay away from it, but then she felt like a coward for hiding her head in the sand. It was even worse now than it had been right before she met Kian. Things had gotten better for a few years, and her visions of doom had subsided, but she should have known that it wouldn't last.

Surprisingly, though, the visions hadn't returned.

Perhaps motherhood was shielding her from the darkness the world was spiraling into.

Was it Navuh's doing?

She had no doubt that he had a hand in it. The worldwide chaos had his signature all over it, and if he was indeed behind what was going on, it explained why he hadn't bothered the clan in a long while. They had assumed that he was busy breeding the next generation of smart warriors, but he hadn't been idle in the meantime. He'd been steering things via his drug and trafficking enterprises, enlisting the help of cartels and terror organizations to propagate his agenda of world domination.

Still, as evil as Navuh was, she doubted that he had a hand in child trafficking. His cohorts did that of their own accord.

Syssi let out a sigh. She wasn't helping anyone by getting depressed over the sorry state of the world, but she could help Annani, even if it was just to provide her closure.

The mystery of Khiann's fate had been weighing on her mind ever since Annani had first shared her suspicions about Ahn's possible subterfuge. If Annani's beloved mate was still alive, trapped somewhere in stasis, it would be a miracle. In a way, the unintended results of Ahn's machinations could have been the survival of his daughter and her mate.

Then again, if Ahn hadn't framed Mortdh for Khiann's murder and instead had sent a rescue team to dig out Annani's husband and the immortals who had been with him, the gods could have still been around because Mortdh would not have flown over the assembly with a deadly weapon in his small aircraft.

Well, not really.

The Eternal King's assassins would have found a way to destroy all the exiled gods and their descendants and blame it on the humans or some natural disaster.

They all needed answers, and Syssi was the only one who might be able to get them. Allegra's presence had enhanced previous visions, and since it hadn't affected her daughter in any negative way, Syssi intended to meditate in the bedroom next to her daughter's crib to give herself the best chance of getting those answers.

As the door chime pulled her from her thoughts, Syssi rose to her feet and went to greet her sister-in-law.

"Thanks for coming." She pulled Amanda into a quick, one-armed hug. "I'm sorry if I interrupted your afternoon nap."

Leaning down, Amanda kissed her cheek. "You didn't interrupt anything important." She walked over to the kitchenette and opened the fridge. "I'm making myself a drink. Do you want one before doing your thing?"

Syssi shook her head. "I don't want anything interfering with my concentration. I will do it in the bedroom and leave the door open."

"That's fine." Amanda pulled a container of orange juice out of the fridge. "I'm going to read on my phone and not make any noises to disturb you."

"Thank you."

Syssi left her sister-in-law in the living room and walked into the bedroom, where Allegra was still napping peacefully in her portable crib, her little face relaxed and serene, and her little mouth parted.

She was a vision of perfection, and Syssi felt a rush of love for her daughter wash over her. There were many types of love, but the strongest one in the universe was the love of a mother for her child.

Fighting the urge to bend over the crib's side and kiss Allegra's soft cheek, Syssi took a deep breath, sent a silent prayer to the universe, and settled herself in the armchair beside the crib.

She closed her eyes and let the world fall away as she slowly slipped into the quiet place in her mind and envisioned what she wanted to see. If Khiann was buried under the sand, she needed the location, and if he was gone, she needed to see his death.

Fates, she really didn't want to see that and then have to tell Annani that there was no hope and that Khiann was really dead.

With her concentration shot, she had to start deep breathing and clearing her mind again. She pictured Khiann as Annani had described him—tall, strong, and beautiful, with chestnut dark hair and bright blue eyes that shone with love and mirth.

For a long moment, there was nothing, only darkness and silence and the steady beat of her own heart, but then, slowly, an image began to take shape in her mind's eye, hazy at first but growing clearer with each passing second.

She saw a mountain steeped in heavy mist, its rocky slopes rising starkly against a pale, washed-out sky. And as she hovered up to the very top, she discovered that the peak was hollow. There was a gaping crater at its center, a deep, yawning hole that seemed to plunge down hundreds of feet into the earth.

The barren, rocky mountain and the gray sky above it couldn't be located in a desert.

She was being shown something else.

Her consciousness hovering over the gaping hole, Syssi peered into its dark depths, her mind straining to make out the details of what lay at the bottom. When the clouds parted for a moment, letting the sun's rays through, the light bounced back from the reflective material of a sleek object that was nestled at the bottom of the crater.

She couldn't see any details, but her mind conjured the answer to what she was looking at without having all the necessary visual data.

It was an alien pod.

If she could force her consciousness to float down into the crater, perhaps she could see more details, but the vision refused to let her move from the one spot she was hovering over.

Syssi couldn't dive down or move to the side. It revealed another clue, though. The weak sunshine managed to vaporize the mist just as four people crested the top and walked over to look down the crater.

Syssi recognized all four.

The three males were the gods Aru, Negal, and Dagor. The fourth member of their group was the most surprising one, though.

It was Jasmine, the woman who had crashed into their lives like a comet, trailing occult mysteries in her wake.

As the four gathered around the crater's edge, Syssi wondered where the gods' mates were and why Jasmine was with them. And then, as quickly as the vision had come, it faded, and Syssi's eyes flew open.

"Talk about strange," she murmured.

"Did you say something?" Amanda asked from the living room.

"Give me a moment." Syssi brushed her hair away from her face.

For some reason, the vision had decided to show her one of the missing Kraell pods instead of Khiann.

Poor Annani would be so disappointed.

Still, it was an amazing development, even though Syssi couldn't tell where that mountaintop was. There had been no clues about that, but it was clear that Jasmine was somehow connected to the pods.

AMANDA

When Syssi emerged from the bedroom looking pale and shaken, Amanda tensed. "What did you see?" she asked, even though she was afraid to hear the answer.

"I didn't see Khiann." Syssi sat next to her on the couch and let her head drop back against the cushions. "I'm not sure what I saw or why I was shown it."

Syssi's visions were often vague, and it wasn't the first time she hadn't been sure what she'd been shown or why.

Tucking one leg under her, Amanda shifted so she was facing Syssi. "Just tell me, even if it's nothing more than a stream of consciousness. We can reconstruct it together."

"I might have seen a Kra-ell pod, and Jasmine was there with the three gods. I don't know how she's connected to their mission or why she was there with the gods while their mates were not. She was standing over a crater, looking down, and pointing. I think the vision's purpose was to show me that she needs to go with them to Tibet."

The dots were connecting in Amanda's mind. "I think so, too."

On the face of things, Jasmine's obsession with the prince that her tarot were showing her had seemed like a silly fantasy, a whimsical notion born of reading too many fairy-tale romances and not enough real-world experience. But Amanda had already suspected that there was more to it even before Syssi's vision.

"It was?" Syssi turned to her. "Because it doesn't make any sense to me, and don't start with your silly theory about her tarot prince."

"It's not silly." Amanda tapped a finger over her lower lip. "Jasmine keeps seeing a prince in her tarot readings and other divinations, and it's such a recurring motif that she follows the hunch and accepts Alberto's invitation to take her out of the country even though she doesn't know him well enough to trust him. Jasmine is not stupid, and she's not reckless. She felt compelled to do so, and in a roundabout way, it was the right step for her to take to get closer to finding the prince because it got her on this ship, where she met the three males that could potentially lead her to him. She might be the key to locating the Kraell pods, and if her drive to find her prince is for real, it means that the twins are still alive."

"That's crazy." Syssi frowned.

"Not really." Amanda waved a hand. "Think about how improbable it was for Orion and Toven to find their way to our clan, or Geraldine for that matter. When the Fates are behind the steering wheel, anything can happen."

"True," Syssi conceded. "So what do we do with this dubious information?"

"We need to talk to Jasmine and get her to join Aru's team. It's obvious that her help is needed to find at least the one pod you saw in your vision."

Syssi shook her head. "Kian will never agree unless she is a Dormant. Jasmine's help being essential to finding the royal twins is too long of a shot."

"And he might have a point." Amanda slumped against the couch cushions. "We need to think about it a little more. Should we even assist Aru and his team in finding the twins? They might be so dangerous that it would be better to leave them where they are."

Syssi cast her an incredulous look. "Can you really do that in good conscience? Leave them buried alive when we can do something to help find and save them?"

"To protect my clan and Fates know how many humans, yes, I can. I don't like it, but sometimes the only option is to choose the lesser evil."

Syssi shook her head. "I'm glad that I'm not a leader and don't have to make those kinds of choices. I don't think I'm capable of that."

"You are still very young, Syssi." Amanda patted her arm. "That being said, I'm also thankful for being able to leave the decision to Kian."

Syssi smiled ruefully. "We are such big chickens."

"We are." Amanda shifted on the couch. "It's too early to tell whether Edgar and Jasmine are meant for each other, but he can't start inducing her without her consent, so she needs to be told about us anyway, and if we tell her that, we might as well tell her about the vision, provided that Kian agrees, of course."

Syssi grimaced. "Telling Jasmine that her Prince Charming is waiting in a pod will not go down well with Edgar, and he will probably decide to drop his pursuit of her. And if she's adamant about finding her prince, introducing her to other immortal males wouldn't be fair to them either. The two objectives are mutually exclusive."

"Not necessarily." Amanda tapped a finger on her lower lip. "Jasmine is more like me than she is like you, and she has no compunctions about having fun with other males while awaiting her prince. As long as she is honest with Edgar or other males who will volunteer their services, no one will get hurt."

"Perhaps we should talk to Edgar and Jasmine but not together," Syssi suggested. "Check how they feel about each other. What if they are in love?"

"It's too early in their relationship to know one way or another," Amanda said. "Even for fated mates, it takes more than one hookup to know."

"Really?" Syssi arched a brow. "When I first saw Kian, it was like getting hit by lightning. I knew he was my destiny. Maybe not in my mind, but in my heart."

Amanda smiled. "I know. I was there when it happened, remember?"

"How can I ever forget?" Syssi slanted her a look. "You were the one who made it happen."

"True." Amanda grinned. "Kian was such a stubborn old goat. He refused to meet you, but then the Fates forced his hand, or rather I did, and when he came to berate me at my lab, he saw you, and it was game over for him."

Syssi nodded. "Yup. He got zapped at the same moment I did. What about you and Dalhu? Did you know right away?"

Amanda scrunched her nose. "Dalhu terrified me the first time I saw him, but I felt the pull right away, which was quite telling given that he was my enemy and he was kidnapping me."

It had been confusing and exhilarating at the same time, and as much as she had fought against it at first, as much as she had tried to deny the truth of what she felt, she'd eventually come to accept that Dalhu was her one true mate.

But not everyone's journey was the same, and not every Dormant had the luxury of waiting for their fated match to come along. Some, like Eva and Eleanor, had transitioned after a random hookup and had found their mates later.

"We need to talk to Kian about this," Syssi said.

Amanda nodded. "We don't have much time. Send him a text and ask him to call you."

51

KIAN

t's not urgent, but when you have a moment, please call me, the text read.

Kian always had a moment for his wife, no matter what he was doing, but he had to find a quiet space to talk to her.

She probably hadn't waited and had induced a vision without him. Hopefully, she had called one of his sisters to monitor her in case she fainted. It wasn't only about her now. She needed to think about Allegra.

Leaving the balcony and the sounds of boisterous laughter and clinking glasses, Kian walked into the living room of the cabin, sat down on the couch, and placed the call.

"You didn't have to call right away," Syssi said. "But thanks for doing so."

"What happened? Did you induce a vision?"

"Amanda watched over me, and I didn't suffer any ill effects, but regrettably, the Fates decided not to show Khiann, and the vision was about something completely different."

"That's indeed regrettable." Kian's heart clenched with sorrow for his mother. "But the Fates must have their good reasons." He pushed to his feet. "What did they show you?"

"It was about the Kra-ell pods. Or rather one pod."

Damn. Kian hadn't expected that.

"I'm on my way. I'll be there in a few minutes." He opened the balcony door and stepped out.

"What about the party?" Syssi asked.

Kian glanced back at the group of males, some sprawled on loungers, others standing next to the railing and puffing on what little was left of their cigars.

The party was winding down, with the toasts and laughter giving way to quieter conversations and contemplative sips of whiskey.

"It's almost over," he said. "I'll just say goodbye to Yamanu."

"Amanda and I are waiting."

Kian ended the call, slipped the phone back into his pocket, and walked over to Yamanu, who was standing by the railing and chatting with Arwel.

He put his hand on the Guardian's shoulder. "I had a great time, but I need to go. I'll be back in time to escort you to the altar."

A big grin spread across Yamanu's handsome features. "I'll hold you to that." He clapped Kian on the shoulder.

"Do you need me to come with you?" Anandur asked Kian.

"No. I'm just going to my cabin. Stay and enjoy the party."

It took Kian less than five minutes from the time he had ended the call with Syssi until he opened the door to his cabin. He found Syssi and Amanda seated on the couch, each holding a cup of coffee, which was a good sign. If the news were bad, Amanda would be nursing a drink.

"Hello, ladies." He leaned to kiss Amanda's cheek and then Syssi's. "You don't look like you have seen a specter, so I assume that the vision wasn't about doom and gloom."

Syssi's visions were rarely about happy events, which was the reason she dreaded them so much and tried to avoid them most of the time. The only reason she occasionally induced them was when she was trying to help someone else.

Had she used Allegra's amplifying power?

The door to the bedroom was open, and through the doorway, he could see their daughter sleeping peacefully in her crib.

Hopefully, assisting her mother just by being around wasn't detrimental to her in any way.

"What did you see?" Kian sat down on an armchair, facing her and Amanda.

Listening to Syssi describe what she had seen, Kian had to fight his natural skepticism. If those words were coming from anyone else, he would have dismissed the story as a dream or a hallucination, but his mate had a perfect track record for prophetic visions that, in one way or another, had come to pass.

"Jasmine needs to be told," Amanda said after Syssi was done. "I wish we had more time and didn't need to make rush decisions, but the cruise is almost over, and Aru and his team plan to head out as soon as they can."

"I need to think this through," Kian said. "It's not as easy as just telling Jasmine about gods and immortals and asking her to join Aru's team. We don't know what methods she uses other than the tarot cards, and whether there is any way she can actually guide the team to the location of the pod."

"She was there," Syssi said. "That means that she knows, or will know, how to get there. I don't see any other reason for the vision to show me that scene if it wasn't about to happen." Syssi leaned toward him. "We have just one more day at sea, Kian. You need to decide quickly."

He nodded. "Perhaps I need to discuss it with Turner. He usually sees clearly through the worst of messes. We also need to tell Mother." He looked at Amanda. "She will be so disappointed that Syssi didn't see what happened to Khiann. It was a long shot, but she had her hopes up."

"I can try again," Syssi said. "I gave it a lot of thought, and there is one commonality between the royal twins and Khiann. They are all in stasis. Maybe that's why I was shown the twins instead of Khiann. I was thinking about him buried deep in the earth." She sighed. "But maybe it's not the reason, and the Fates just wanted to show me the pod so I would know that Jasmine was needed to find it. This makes me think that they will not show me anything other than the Kra-ell pod until we find it. After that's done, I will try again, and maybe then I will be granted answers about Khiann."

52

ANNANI

Annani had a pretty good idea as to the reason Kian had called her to invite himself, Syssi, and Amanda over with only an hour or so remaining before the wedding ceremony was to start.

Syssi had probably induced a vision, and what she had seen was not good.

When Ojidu ushered them in, Annani scanned their faces for signs of sadness but found cautious excitement instead.

Had Syssi found anything? Perhaps she had seen a clue about Khiann's fate?

Hope surging in her heart, Annani wanted to cling to it for a little longer, so she did not ask about that. Instead, her gaze shifted to Syssi's empty arms. "Where is Allegra?"

"She's napping," Syssi said. "She was so exhausted from playing in the pool with my father that she fell asleep on the way to the cabin, and I had to put her in her crib without even giving her a bath. You know how she is if someone wakes her up before she is good and ready, so I left her with Okidu to watch over. If she wakes up before we're back, he'll bring her over."

Annani nodded, a smile tugging at her lips. Her granddaughter had a formidable will, which would make her a good leader one day, but it was not making her parents' lives easy, especially Syssi's, who was sweet and softhearted.

As her visitors sat down, Annani regarded Syssi with a calm expression, one she had honed over thousands of years of hiding her emotions. "I assume that you have news for me?"

"Not the news you hoped for, Clan Mother. The universe has chosen not to show me Khiann's fate and instead showed me clues about the Kra-ell royal twins."

Annani was indeed disappointed, but not as much as if Syssi had told her that she had seen Khiann's murder and that all hope was gone, so in a way, no news was good news.

"We should not refer to them as the Kra-ell royal twins," she said. "They are my half brother and sister, half god and half Kra-ell, so we should drop the Kra-ell part." She sighed. "I wish I knew their names."

Their mother had even hidden that from her people when she had conscripted her children to the priesthood. Kra-ell priestesses were referred to as holy mothers and, before that, as acolytes, but since there had never been male priests before the prince, Annani did not know how he should be referred to. Perhaps a holy brother? That made sense since the only reason he could have joined the priesthood was being his sister's twin.

Annani had no doubt that the Kra-ell queen had done so to further protect them and hide them from their grandfather.

She gave her daughter-in-law an encouraging smile. "Please tell me what you have seen, my dear."

As Syssi spoke of Jasmine appearing next to the pod, Annani was surprised. She had not met the human, but ever since Jasmine had been brought aboard, Annani had a feeling that there was something special about her. Still, she could have never imagined that the woman would lead them to the twins.

"I'm so sorry that I didn't bring you news of Khiann," Syssi said. "But I promise that I will try again once this vision is fulfilled. Until then, I doubt I will be shown anything else."

Annani leaned over and patted Syssi's knee. "Do not fret, my child. The Fates work in mysterious ways, and they reveal only what they want to reveal when they want to reveal it."

Syssi let out a breath. "I'm glad you see it that way."

Annani nodded to her daughter-in-law and then turned to Kian. "I am considering telling the queen about the twins when I speak with her tonight. I do not know whether she suspects that they are Ahn's. After all, his legacy lives on in them as well."

Kian frowned. "The twins didn't know who their father was, and all they have is his genetic material. You are the only one who carries on his legacy, and I don't think it is wise to confirm the queen's suspicion. She must be aware of them because the Eternal King wouldn't have needed to eliminate them if they were fully Kra-ell, and she knows that was his intention. Still, she does not know for sure, and maybe we should leave it at that. We don't know how she will react and what she will do with the information."

Annani shook her head. "It is the right thing to do. Ahn's mother deserves to know about all of his children, and that includes Areana. I mentioned that my sister had survived, but the queen did not ask about her."

"I'm not surprised that she didn't," Kian said. "She must have assumed that Areana was a mere immortal, and despite her lofty ideals, the queen will never accept a hybrid. That's also true of the twins, so she might be well aware of them being Ahn's, but she just doesn't care."

Kian might be right, but Annani refused to leave it at that. The queen was not an emotional female, and everything she did was for Anumati. She might really not care about any of Ahn's other children who were not his legitimate heirs.

Annani hoped that they were all wrong about that, and that her grand-mother cared. "I told the queen that my father offered Areana to Mortdh as a substitute for me, and Ani knows that Mortdh would have never accepted an immortal. Only a full-blooded goddess could have been offered."

Kian nodded. "You are right, of course. Queen Ani is too shrewd to overlook such a detail, but her lack of interest in Areana is telling, and if she feels like that about a granddaughter who is a full-blooded goddess, just not a legit heir, I'm curious about the queen's feelings toward Ahn's half Kra-ell children. She might be conflicted about the twins and wish them ill as the king did, not because she's worried about them taking down the king, but because they might be a threat to you, the heir to the throne, the one in whom she places so much hope."

Kian was right. The queen's reaction to the news of Ahn's other children could be unpredictable. She might see them as a threat to be eliminated rather than a potential ally to be embraced, or she might simply ignore them and pretend that they did not exist.

"The queen might be right about the twins being a threat." Annani let out a breath. "I am not concerned about Areana posing a threat, and yet I am careful about what I tell her. I never reveal anything that can lead Navuh to us, and I hope that Lokan and Kalugal are just as vigilant when they talk to her. The twins are an enigma, though. If we give any credence to the Eternal King's suspicions, they are extremely powerful and, therefore, dangerous. Still, that does not mean that they mean me harm. They could become valuable allies."

"We need to prepare for both contingencies," Syssi said. "I will start summoning visions about the royal twins. We need to know if they pose a threat to the clan and if they are friend or foe."

Kian nodded, his jaw clenching, probably at the thought of Syssi summoning too many visions and draining herself. "Aru and the other two gods are physi-cally a match for the Kra-ell. They were engineered that way. But they weren't given protection against the twins' rumored compulsion power. They will need to be equipped with the special earpieces we developed to filter out compulsion, to protect themselves in case the twins are malevolent. Whoever accompanies them on the search will need those as well."

Amanda leaned forward, her eyes shining with excitement. "They will need reinforced handcuffs and tranquilizer darts as well."

A rueful smile tugged at Kian's lips. "Aru's team did not arrive on Earth empty-handed. They have all kinds of sophisticated weapons that Aru refused to share with me. The one thing they don't have, though, is the means to protect themselves from compulsion, which is both surprising and it is not. A society as technologically advanced as the Anumatians should have developed the means to protect its soldiers from compulsion, but that would have eliminated the Eternal King's grip on them. He wants everyone susceptible to his power and under his control."

Breaking the king's grip and freeing Anumati from the chains of oppression and tyranny would be no easy feat. It might even be impossible.

"We need to discuss this with Aru before we approach Jasmine." Kian pulled out his phone. "There is no time to do so before the wedding, but we can meet tonight an hour before the scheduled meeting. Is that okay with you, Mother?"

Annani nodded.

"Can I come?" Amanda asked.

Kian turned to look at his sister. "I don't have any objection to that, but your sisters might not appreciate being left out, and I don't think Aru will appreciate having to conduct the telepathic conversation in front of a crowd. I'm surprised he can do that with just the three of us there. A fourth person might not be a big difference, but he might be uncomfortable with six people in the room, all watching him as he talks with his sister in his mind."

53

EDGAR

Taking a deep breath, Edgar tugged on the lapels of his tuxedo, raised his hand, and rapped his knuckles on Jasmine's door. Unlike the cabins on the upper decks, the staff quarters were equipped with standard insulation and soundproofing so Jasmine would hear his knock loud and clear.

"Just a moment!" Jasmine called out, and then the door swung open, revealing a vision that stole the breath from his lungs and sent his heart racing with a surge of pure, unadulterated lust.

"Well, hello there, handsome." Jasmine gave him a once-over before ushering him in. "You look spiffy." She put a hand on the lapel of his jacket, her lush lips curving in a coquettish smile.

Her hair and makeup were done to perfection, and she was breathtakingly beautiful, but it was what she was wearing, or rather what she wasn't wearing, that made his blood run hot and his body tighten with need.

The short, silky robe clung to her curves like a second skin, the fabric so thin it was nearly translucent and left little to the imagination. She had no bra on, and the creamy swell of her breasts and the shadowed valley between them were pure temptations. Below, the hem rode high on her thighs, exposing miles of smooth, golden skin that seemed to glow in the soft light of the cabin.

Edgar swallowed, his mouth suddenly dry and his tongue feeling thick and clumsy in his mouth. He wanted to reach out and touch her, to run his hands over those lush, inviting curves and feel the heat of her skin under his fingers, but if he allowed himself to succumb to the tide of desire, they would never make it to the wedding.

"You look beautiful, but you are not ready," he stated the obvious.

"I just need a few more moments." She gave him a slight push. "Take a seat."

Edgar nodded, his jaw clenching with the effort of restraint as he lowered himself onto the edge of the bed, his eyes fixed firmly on the floor. He could hear the swish of fabric as Jasmine moved around the tiny cabin, and he could feel the heat of her gaze on him, which made his skin prickle with awareness, but he refused to lift his gaze to her.

She chuckled. "You can look, you know. You've seen it all already."

"I did," he admitted, his voice rough with barely suppressed desire. "But if I see it again, we won't make it to the wedding."

Jasmine laughed, a throaty, sensual sound that sent shivers racing down his spine. "Well, in that case, don't look," she said in a mock-stern tone. "I really want to attend that wedding."

"Can I ask you something?" He still refused to look at her.

He heard her pause and felt her eyes on him. "Of course. What do you wish to know?"

"That prince you mentioned, the one who keeps showing up in your tarot cards. What's that all about? I mean, am I just a placeholder until you find your Prince Charming? Or am I misunderstanding the situation?"

There was a moment of silence, a pause that seemed to stretch uncomfortably long. "You could be my prince." Jasmine walked in between his spread thighs and placed her hands on his shoulders. "Divining the future is not an exact science, and the signs can be interpreted in many ways. The cards might have meant a real royal prince, or they could have meant it metaphorically, like a prince of a man." She gave him a sultry look as she rubbed herself against him. "You were definitely princely between the sheets. I don't recall ever coming so hard and so many times."

Edgar tried to stifle a wince. He was a generous and skilled lover, but Jasmine's explosive orgasms had been the product of his immortal biology, so he couldn't take credit for them. It was the venom hitting her system that had induced the string of powerful climaxes and sent her on a psychedelic trip through the clouds. He had thralled her to forget the bite, to blur the edges of the euphoria that had consumed her in the aftermath, but he'd left the memories of the pleasure intact.

That was what she remembered.

Lifting his head, he looked at her beautiful face, and as he took in the sultry gleam in her eyes and the wicked curve of her lips, he couldn't help but wonder if that was enough. Could he be satisfied with just being her lover but not her partner, not her prince?

"I'm flattered," he said. "Although not surprised. I've been told that before."

She laughed. "Now you're making me jealous." She took a step back, dropped her robe, and gave him a mouth-watering view of her ass that was covered by such a thin strip of fabric it was like it wasn't covered at all.

And it was glorious.

She pulled on a tight dress that looked like a bandage around her delicious body, stepped into a pair of stilettos, and then turned around and struck a pose. "How do I look?"

"Like a goddess," Edgar breathed. "The goddess of carnal pleasures."

Jasmine chuckled. "I'll take it. Anything that is preceded by the word goddess is music to my ears."

5 4

JASMINE

J asmine felt a flutter of excitement as Edgar led her to the bar, her eyes widening at the sight of Marina and Larissa, both decked out in beautiful evening dresses. The women were accompanied by two hunky guys, who were hovering over them like bees over honey.

"Jasmine." Marina pursed her lips. "You look absolutely stunning. Are you attending the wedding tonight?"

"I am." Jasmine grinned. "Amanda convinced her brother to let me out of the lower decks dungeon. And I have to say that you ladies look gorgeous." She slanted a glance at Edgar. "Ed, these are my friends, Marina and Larissa. Ed is my escort to the party tonight."

He wrapped his arm around her waist. "I hope that I am much more than that."

"Of course, darling." She turned to kiss the side of his face. "But you are my escort tonight because I wouldn't be attending the wedding if you didn't invite me as your date."

He cast her an amused look before turning to the men. "Peter, Jay, this is Jasmine. The lady we rescued from the drug cartel."

"Everyone on this ship knows who you are." The dark-haired one who was standing next to Marina extended his hand. "You are famous, Jasmine. I'm Peter, and it's a pleasure to make your acquaintance. I'm glad that we got to you in time."

She put her hand in his and smiled. "Not as glad as I am. If not for Margo and your security team, my life, as I know it, would have been over. I would have become the plaything of a mobster until he tired of me and got rid of me, and by getting rid, I don't mean letting me go free."

Jasmine shivered.

She didn't like to think of what would have happened to her if she hadn't befriended Margo and been rescued along with her. One thing was certain. She would never have touched a tarot deck again or lit white candles asking for true love.

"I'm Jay." The blond guy, who looked a little like David Beckham, offered her his hand. "I'm glad that you are not going to be swimming with the fishes anytime soon."

Marina gasped at his crude comment, but Jasmine laughed. "Yeah, I'm glad too."

As she sat down next to the women at the bar, Edgar joined the two men, and the six of them continued chatting. Jasmine tried to rein in her flirtatious persona, but it was so second nature to her that she didn't know how to act differently, especially around men.

It was so easy and fun to engage in playful banter, so entertaining to make even the most stoic of males melt with a simple bat of her lashes or a well-timed laugh. She knew the power of her own charm and felt helpless not to use it.

Perhaps she could channel Edna.

After all, as an actress, she should be able to assume any role she pleased, but what was the fun in acting so dry and reserved? Edna was a young woman, but she acted as if she was ancient.

Jasmine meant nothing by her lighthearted banter, and it was too enjoyable to flex her flirting powers over men to stop.

Still, her charms seemed to be lost on Peter, whose eyes never left Marina's face. The intensity of his stare sent a shiver down Jasmine's spine. There was something there, a connection that ran deep, a bond that made her a little jealous.

Did Edgar look at her this way? Like she was the most wonderful creature in the world, and he was happy to bask in her glow?

Casting him a sidelong glance, she caught him looking at her with annoyance in his eyes instead of the adoration she'd hoped for. Obviously, Ed didn't like the way she was interacting with the other men, but he should have known that her flirting was harmless.

She smiled and cupped his cheek. "Can you be a dear and get me a drink, please?"

"Of course. What would you like?"

"A classic margarita, please. With salt."

As Ed turned to the bartender and placed the order, Jay gave Jasmine a suggestive smile, his gaze roving over her figure with an appreciative gleam that made her skin prickle with awareness.

If she wanted to, she could have him wrapped around her little finger in no time, but she wouldn't, and not just because she was with Ed.

Larissa's eyes followed Jay's every move, the longing and adoration in her gaze so plain and raw that it made Jasmine's heart ache. The poor girl was clearly enamored with the handsome guy, and her feelings were written all over her face for anyone to see.

Jay, on the other hand, was either oblivious or simply not interested in anything serious with her. Curiously, though, his attention wandered to Jasmine but not to Marina. It was probably because he considered Peter his friend and didn't wish to antagonize him.

Did it mean that Jay and Edgar were not on friendly terms?

Maybe there was some bad blood between them and that was why Jay was allowing himself to pay Jasmine so much attention even though she was with Ed?

"Here you go." Edgar handed her the margarita and then turned to the other two men. "We should go."

Jay glanced at his watch and nodded. "Fifteen minutes to show time." He leaned over and kissed Larissa's cheek. "I'll be back for you in about forty-five minutes to an hour. Don't go anywhere."

"I be here," she said in heavily accented English.

Peter leaned over Marina, but instead of kissing her cheek, he took her mouth in a passionate kiss as if he was leaving her for weeks and not less than an hour.

Ed was less inclined to make a public show of affection and just pecked Jasmine's cheek. "Be good," he murmured against her ear.

She laughed. "The term good can refer to a lot of things."

He didn't look amused.

As Edgar and the other men excused themselves, leaving Jasmine alone with Marina and Larissa, she lifted the glass to her lips and took a grateful sip.

"So, now that I'm finally allowed to attend a wedding, can you tell me who is getting married?"

Marina and Larissa exchanged looks, and then Marina shook her head. "I'm sorry. We can't tell you."

"Can you at least tell me if it's anyone famous?"

Marina hesitated and then shook her head. "Not that I know of, but I'm new to this country, and I don't know all the famous people here."

Jasmine was impressed. She'd thought that Marina had been in the US for many years. "Your English is very good. Where did you learn to speak it so well?"

"I started back in Russia, and I kept practicing for long hours after we got here."

Jasmine knew better than to ask again how they had found their way to the US and got work on the cruise ship. When she'd asked her poker buddies, she'd been told that it was confidential.

Even after being allowed on the upper decks, Jasmine still had a nagging sense that something wasn't quite right, and that she had no idea what was really going on. When she asked questions and tried to probe for information, she once again found herself running up against a wall of secrecy and evasion.

Looking nervous, Larissa said something in Russian to Marina while her fingers were plucking at the fabric of her dress, the same one she had worn the night before.

Marina laughed and clapped her friend on her back. "Larissa is not happy about wearing the same dress two nights in a row," she translated for Jasmine. "I told her that Jay doesn't mind."

Larissa mumbled something under her breath and blushed profusely.

"What did she say?" Jasmine asked.

"That Jay only cares about taking the dress off her."

As the three of them laughed, Marina turned to her. "So, how did you and the handsome Edgar meet?"

"He's the helicopter pilot who flew Kevin over to the mobster yacht. We talked a little on the way to the ship, but then I didn't see him until yesterday when he suddenly came down to see me and brought me delicious food from the wedding party."

Marina regarded her with a wicked gleam in her eye. "I've heard that he left your cabin early this morning."

"You've heard right."

"Good for you." Marina let out a whoop of laughter, her hand coming up for a high five that Jasmine met with a grin. "Life is too short to wait for pleasure."

"I'll drink to that." Jasmine lifted her margarita glass.

As they giggled and gossiped like schoolgirls, with Marina translating for Larissa, who was too tipsy to concentrate on finding the right words, Jasmine still couldn't shake off the nagging sense of unease.

There was something different about Marina and Larissa. Jasmine was no stranger to girl talk, and women usually had much more to say about their lovers, their friends, and their life in general than those two were sharing.

Maybe it was the difference in cultures.

She tried to probe deeper, to ask about their pasts, their families, the places they had come from. But each time, she was met with vague, evasive answers, a polite but firm deflection that left her feeling even more frustrated and confused.

"We're from a remote region of Russia that is near Finland," Marina finally said after being asked for the umpteenth time where they were from. "You've probably never heard of it."

Jasmine decided to let it go.

It was just no use.

And then there was the matter of the nondisclosure agreement that, for some reason, no one had mentioned to her.

Margo had told her that everyone on the ship was supposedly required to sign one and that she wouldn't be allowed to mingle with the guests without it.

And yet, Jasmine hadn't been asked to sign anything.

Heck, no one had even told her what she could and couldn't say about her time on board.

Things didn't add up, and the more Jasmine thought about it, the more worried she became. There were too many secrets and too many unanswered questions.

Thankfully, it wouldn't be long before the ship docked back in Los Angeles, and she would be back on solid ground and in control of her own life.

But what if the cartel was looking for her?

Julio Modana had been made to forget about her, but what about Carlos? Kevin hadn't hypnotized the other brother, who was supposed to be even more evil than Julio. What if he decided to come after her?

Jasmine shivered, her hand coming up to rub at her arm as a sudden chill raced down her spine. She needed to talk to Kian and find out what he knew. He seemed to be the only one with any real answers.

55

MEY

Mey's heart was full to bursting as she walked toward the altar. Yamanu was waiting for her with a huge grin on his handsome face and eyes that shone with love and adoration.

Keeping her senses heightened so she wouldn't miss even the most minute of details and commit everything to memory, she was acutely aware of the gentle sway of her gown, the soft rhythm of her steps, and the radiant smiles on her bridesmaids' faces.

She was about to wed Yamanu, her fated mate, the male who had captured her heart and soul with his big smiles, his enormous capacity for love, and his boundless kindness.

Just like his unparalleled thralling and shrouding ability, her mate did everything on a grand scale, and that included his love for her.

And yet, even as happiness swelled within her, Mey couldn't help but feel a twinge of regret that her and Jin's adoptive parents couldn't be there to witness this momentous occasion. They had been the best parents any girl could hope for, raising her and Jin to be resourceful, independent, powerful women and doing so with gentle words, lots of hugs and kisses, and endless love and patience.

They were the best people she knew, and given that she was surrounded by a clan of wonderful people, that was saying something. It was so unfair that they couldn't be here now to share in the joy and celebrate their adopted daughters' weddings.

Mey silently vowed to make it up to them with proper human ceremonies. Jin wanted that as well, and Yamanu and Arwel would do whatever it took to make their mates happy, including traveling across the globe and attending a traditional wedding.

But even as she made that promise, Mey couldn't help but wonder, for what felt like the thousandth time, about her and Jin's birth parents. Who were they? What had happened to them? Were they still out there somewhere, thinking of the daughters they had lost or given away?

The mystery had haunted Mey for as long as she could remember, lingering in the back of her mind like a persistent itch that she needed to scratch and didn't know how. Even though she was the older sister, she had no memories of her birth family and no clues as to their fate. The only things she knew about her biological parents came from her and Jin's genetic makeup. Their mother must have been a Dormant, and their father a hybrid Kra-ell.

Returning her focus to Yamanu, Mey felt all those thoughts evaporate like mist beneath the sun, or rather her mate's broad grin, which was warmer than sunshine and overflowing with love and joy because tonight they were being officially joined with nearly the entire clan witnessing the ceremony.

Yamanu would never admit it, but he loved the attention. He was a showman who hadn't gotten to perform much during his long centuries of celibacy when he had been forced to drink a muting potion and meditate daily to maintain his vow and continue honing his incredible powers.

The potion had muted more than his libido, though, and he had often kept to himself. But those days were over now that he had broken the vow with the Clan Mother's blessing.

Shifting her gaze to the petite goddess, Mey dipped her head in silent thanks. She would be forever grateful to Annani for being willing to lose one of the clan's most valuable assets and releasing Yamanu from his vow so he could be happy.

Nothing was more sacred to the goddess than the connection forged by destiny itself. Annani believed that to stand in the way of such a bond was to court the wrath of the Fates.

Thankfully, mating Mey had not diminished Yamanu's incredible ability to manipulate the minds and perceptions of others. His power remained unparalleled, and the clan hadn't lost the protection that had saved countless lives and turned the tide of battles time and again over the centuries.

Taking her place beside Yamanu at the altar, Mey slipped her hand into his, and as a sense of rightness settled over her, she gave his hand a light squeeze.

The Clan Mother smiled at them both, her eyes shining with love and joy, and then shifted her gaze to the gathered crowd. "My dearly beloved. We are gathered here today to celebrate the union of two beautiful souls. Yamanu and Mey's love story is so exciting and unconventional that it could be made into a movie." She chuckled. "I think it is the first time that international espionage was used by the Fates to weave the common thread in the destiny of two people who were meant for each other."

Mey smiled at Yamanu through the haze of happy tears. The Clan Mother had a way of turning the mundane into spectacular, and giving significance and meaning to events that were at the time far from glamorous.

"Yamanu." The goddess turned her gaze to him. "You have been a true hero to our people, a Guardian and protector who has always put the needs of others before your own. You have saved countless lives and turned the tide of battles, and for that you have our gratitude."

Yamanu bowed his head. "It's my duty, Clan Mother, and I'm honored and grateful to the Fates for giving me the tools to protect my people."

Mey couldn't be prouder of Yamanu. He had never been one to seek glory or acclaim, never been driven by ego or ambition. Everything he did, every sacrifice he made, was for the greater good, for the safety and well-being of his clan.

"You have acted above and beyond the call of duty, Yamanu," the goddess said. "But your greatest act of heroism was your willingness to give up your immense powers for love." The Clan Mother smiled at him fondly. "When the Fates brought you and Mey together, you were prepared to risk everything to be with your truelove mate."

Mey squeezed Yamanu's hand, her heart overflowing. She knew how much his powers meant to him. To be willing to give that up, to put their love above all else, was a sacrifice beyond measure.

"And Mey," Annani said, turning her warm gaze to her. "You are such a wonderful addition to our clan, and not just because you make Yamanu happy, or because you possess a talent none of us has. You exemplify strength, courage, and unshakable loyalty, you also embody grace, elegance, and entrepreneurial spirit. You and your sister make me, your mates, your clan, and your adoptive parents proud."

Mey felt a lump form in her throat, and tears threatened to spill down her cheeks. Hearing the goddess's words, she felt the love and acceptance of her clan enveloping her in a warm embrace.

"Yamanu and Mey," the Clan Mother continued. "Your love is a testament to the unbreakable bond between fated mates. You have faced countless challenges and obstacles on your path to this moment, but through it all, your love has only grown stronger.

"And so," the goddess said, "it is my great honor and privilege to bless this union, to stand as witness to the joining of two hearts, two souls, two lives. Yamanu and Mey, you have proven yourselves worthy of the great gift of fated love, and it is my deepest wish that your bond will only continue to grow and flourish in the years to come."

Mey felt Yamanu's hand tighten around hers.

The Clan Mother smiled at them. "And now, it is time for you to exchange your vows. Yamanu, Mey, please turn to face each other and join hands."

Mey turned to face her mate, her heart racing with anticipation. This was the moment they would pledge their lives and their love to each other in front of their entire community.

56

YAMANU

As Mey turned to face Yamanu, her eyes shimmering with unshed tears of joy, his heart swelled with love. He had never seen her look more beautiful than she did at that moment, and it had nothing to do with the expertly done makeup and hair or the exquisite wedding gown. It was the radiance of her spirit and the love that shone through her eyes.

Mey took a deep breath and squeezed his hands lightly. "Yamanu, my love. When I first met you, I knew that my life would never be the same. You were like a bolt of lightning, a force of nature that swept me off my feet and showed me what true love was all about."

Yamanu's throat tightened with emotion as he listened to her words.

"You have been my anchor and my staunchest supporter," Mey continued, her voice growing stronger with each word. "You have loved me unconditionally and believed in me even when I doubted myself. You have always put me first, even when it meant sacrificing your own needs and desires."

Yamanu swallowed hard, his heart so full that he thought it might burst. It was true that he had always put Mey first, but he had never seen it as a sacrifice or felt like he was giving up anything. Loving her and being loved by her in return was the greatest gift the Fates could have ever given him.

"I promise to love you, to cherish you, and to stand by your side through thick and thin," Mey said, her eyes locked on his. "I promise to be your best friend, your lover, and your soulmate. I promise never to take you for granted and to always remember how lucky I am to have you in my life. And I promise to spend every day showing you just how much you mean to me and how deeply and completely I love you."

Mey let go of his hand and reached to her sister, who handed her a ring.

"With this ring, I bind my life to yours." She slipped it over his finger.

Overwhelmed with emotion, Yamanu lifted Mey's hand and kissed the back of it while collecting his thoughts. He had written a dozen different vows, but after listening to so many others, he'd decided to keep it simple.

"From the moment I first saw you, my love, I knew that you were the one. You walked out of that room in the modeling agency, and I felt like I was zapped by high voltage. I was burning, and you were the only one who could save me." He smiled. "Luckily for me, you didn't shy away from the wreck that I was and embraced me, faults, warts, and all, with open arms and a wide open heart."

Yamanu lifted his hand and cupped her face, his thumbs brushing away the tears that had started to fall.

"I promise to love you, to cherish you, to stand by your side through the ups and the downs and everything in between. I promise to be your best friend, your lover, your greatest cheerleader, and your rock. I promise to always put you and your happiness first. And I promise to spend every day of forever showing you just how much you mean to me, just how deeply and completely I love you."

As he finished his vows, Yamanu leaned in and pressed his forehead against Mey's, their breath mingling in the space between them.

Reaching into his pocket, he pulled out a ring and slipped it on her finger. "We don't need rings to bind us to each other, so think of it as a symbol of my everlasting love and devotion."

The Clan Mother stepped forward and placed her hands on their joined ones. "Yamanu and Mey. By the power vested in me by the Fates, I now pronounce you bonded mates. Two souls united for all eternity."

She smiled. "You may now kiss."

Yamanu needed no further encouragement. He pulled Mey into his arms and kissed her with all the love and passion he felt for her, pouring his heart and soul into that most important kiss that served to seal their vows to each other.

As they broke apart and turned toward the cheering crowd of their friends and family, the love, happiness, and support that surrounded them led Yamanu to feel as if the Fates themselves were celebrating with them at that very moment.

57

JASMINE

As Jasmine stepped into the transformed dining room of the luxury ship, she was struck by its grandeur. She'd seen the place when it had been set up for lunch, but she'd been so overwhelmed by her newfound freedom and talking to Amanda that she hadn't noticed the details.

Above her, multiple crystal chandeliers hung from an intricately designed ceiling. The dining area stretched around a large dance floor, where several couples were already dancing.

The tables were draped in white linens and topped with fine china, sparkling silverware, and polished crystal glassware. Rich wood paneling lined the walls, contrasting beautifully with the soft, opulent decor, and one side was all glass, overlooking a large terrace and the ocean beyond.

A buzz of conversation filled the place, accompanied by the clinking of cutlery, while soft music was playing on the hidden loudspeakers.

"Would you like to dance?" Edgar asked. "Or do you prefer to sit down first and munch on some appetizers?"

She was hungry, having only eaten a snack in the staff lounge, but the dance floor offered her a great opportunity to look around and search for celebrity faces in the crowd of guests.

"Let's dance first." She smiled up at him. "Are you a good dancer?"

He leaned to nuzzle her neck. "I'm an excellent dancer."

As they walked by the tables, Jasmine smiled and made eye contact, but although everyone was incredibly good-looking, she hadn't spotted any celebrities yet.

In fact, most of the people she'd seen so far had features so striking and perfect that they seemed almost unreal like they had stepped straight out of a movie screen or a magazine cover.

Her eyes roved over the flawless skin, the chiseled jawlines, and the luminous eyes. It was like being surrounded by a sea of supermodels, each one more gorgeous than the last, and for the first time in her life, Jasmine felt inadequate.

Who were these people, and why were they all so damn perfect?

Suddenly, a thought struck her. What if Perfect Match wasn't really a virtual experience? What if the avatars that users interacted with in the so-called virtual experience weren't computer-generated at all, but real people, flesh and blood actors hired to bring the customer's fantasies to life?

The virtual experience promised to be indistinguishable from real life, and it wasn't because of the revolutionary technology but because it was a huge scheme. The clients were probably drugged and put in studios where their fantasies were enacted with a host of attractive actors.

It seemed implausible because the cost of producing the fantasies would be prohibitive, but perhaps the math worked somehow. With prices per person starting at thirty-five hundred dollars for a three-hour session and seven thousand for a couple, it could be possible to pull it off even if they had to pay actors to pretend to be the avatars for three hours.

Did she want in?

Could she act out someone else's fantasies?

Nah, that was too freaky even for her.

It would certainly explain the need for such strict nondisclosure agreements and the air of secrecy surrounding the entire operation. If word got out that Perfect Match was essentially pimping out its employees, the scandal would be explosive and the fallout immeasurable.

Jasmine shook her head. It was a crazy idea, a conspiracy theory that belonged in the pages of a tabloid magazine, not in the real world. And yet, as she looked around at the impossibly beautiful people that surrounded her, she couldn't help but wonder.

On the dance floor, Edgar pulled her closer, his hand resting on the small of her back as they swayed to the music. "Is everything alright? You seem distracted."

Jasmine forced a smile, trying to push down the unease churning in her gut. "I'm fine. It's just strange how everyone here is so incredibly beautiful that they look like animated mannequins."

Edgar nodded, his gaze sweeping over the crowd with a knowing smile. "A lot can be done with makeup and clothing. Even plain-looking people can be made to look exceptional."

She arched a brow. "Makeup and clothing can go a long way, but they cannot perform miracles. This place looks like a supermodel convention."

He laughed. "You're right, they are all incredibly good-looking. Perfect Match only hires the best of the best, the most talented and attractive people they can find. It's part of what makes the experience so immersive, so believable."

Was Edgar admitting that they were using real people in their so-called virtual adventures?

Jasmine hesitated, biting her lip as she tried to find the right words. "Don't you think it's a little strange?" she asked, her voice dropping to a whisper. "It's like they're all playing a role in some kind of elaborate fantasy."

Edgar's brow furrowed, a flicker of confusion passing over his face. "I'm not sure I follow. What do you mean by playing a role?"

He seemed genuinely perplexed, so perhaps she was wrong, and there was some other explanation for why they were all beautiful and seemed to be of the same age group.

Come to think of it, she should have been suspicious when Amanda and Syssi had come to visit her, and then Kian. Heck, even Edna and Max. The last two were not as gorgeous as Amanda and her brother, but they were still very good-looking, and they all seemed to be about the same age.

Jasmine sighed. "Ignore what I said. I'm being silly. I guess I'm just over-whelmed by all the grandeur. I feel like I've stepped into another world where everything is just too perfect to be real."

Edgar smiled, his hand tightening around hers. "We are in the business of fulfilling fantasies. Only the most beautiful, most talented people make the cut. It's like a club within a club, an exclusive inner circle that only a lucky few get to be a part of. It's a very rigorous screening process."

Jasmine frowned as she tried to reconcile what Edgar was saying with the wild theory that had taken root in her mind. It made sense, in a way. Perfect Match was a luxury service, catering to the wealthiest and most discerning clients. Of course they would want to hire only the best and the brightest, the most stunning and charismatic people they could find.

"I also noticed there aren't any children around," she said, giving voice to the other thing that bothered her about the crowd. "Is this an adults-only cruise? I mean, besides the obvious reasons for privacy and discretion."

Edgar chuckled, shaking his head. "There are children on board," he said. "Just not many, and during the nightly festivities, they mostly stay in the cabins with their babysitters. These parties start and end too late for children to be present."

Jasmine nodded, feeling a little foolish. "Oh, that's right. I remember now that I saw Amanda's little girl with her, and she showed me a picture of Kian's daughter when I first met him."

Of course, there were children on board. Not everyone who worked for

Perfect Match would be single or childless. Some of them probably had families, spouses, and kids waiting for them back home. And it made perfect sense that the ones who were on board would not be present for a late-night event.

She had let her imagination run wild with crazy theories and baseless suspicions instead of focusing on what she could gain from being here. This was the opportunity of a lifetime, a chance to be a part of something truly extraordinary, and she needed to get her head in the game and mingle like there was no tomorrow.

58

EDGAR

Edgar wasn't surprised that Jasmine was suspicious. Any normal person would be. The guests were almost all immortals, and they were all exceedingly beautiful by human standards. They also seemed to be the same age more or less, and the lack of elders and dearth of children was another clue. Still, all the oddities could be explained away by the Perfect Match cover story, which made it a stroke of genius.

He wondered who had originally come up with it.

It had probably been Toven's mate. When Mia had invited her best friends Frankie and Margo on the cruise with the promise of jobs as beta testers for the service's virtual adventures, she must have told them that they were joining a Perfect Match company ten-day cruise.

For now, he had to perpetuate the lie, but at some point he would have to tell Jasmine the truth about himself and his clan and ask for her consent to be induced into immortality.

If she agreed but didn't want to leave her life behind and immediately join him in the village, he would have to make her forget what he had told her and keep seeing her until she either transitioned or proved not to be a Dormant.

Naturally, he hoped she possessed the necessary godly genes, and his hope was not unfounded.

Jasmine had a modicum of paranormal ability that marked her as a potential Dormant, and in addition, she had a way of drawing people to her, which indicated affinity.

But as much as he wanted to believe that she was meant for him and that the Fates had brought them together for a reason, Edgar couldn't ignore the nagging doubts that whispered in the back of his mind. If Jasmine was truly his fated mate, his one and only, then why did her eyes wander so freely around the room?

Why did her smile light up for every male who made eye contact with her?

It bothered him more than he wanted to admit and more than he had a right to. He wasn't in love with Jasmine, but it wasn't only about lust either. At the moment, she was a potential that he wanted to explore, a female he was still examining his feelings for.

Still, he couldn't help the annoyance that flared in his chest every time her gaze lingered on another guy and every time her lips curved in a seductive smile that wasn't aimed at him. It wasn't jealousy, or at least he didn't think it was, but it was insulting. While Jasmine was with him, she should turn off her flirtatiousness because showing interest in other males while dancing in his arms was disrespectful.

How would she feel if his eyes kept wandering to other females?

So yeah, most of those present were either his relatives or mated to them, but Marina and Larissa weren't related to him, and although they were accompanied by Peter and Jay, he still had eyes and noticed that they were both attractive women. Not that he would have flirted with either. He knew better than to infringe on what the two Guardians considered their turf, even temporarily.

While Jasmine was with him, he wanted her eyes on him and her smile directed at him and him alone, the same way his attention was focused on her.

When the song ended, Jasmine looked at him with a tired smile on her face. "Can we sit this one out? My feet are killing me, and I need to take a break."

"Of course." He took her hand and led her to the table.

It was easy to forget that she wasn't immortal and that she couldn't keep up. She looked the part so well, and for a human, she was also surprisingly strong and resilient.

Frankie and Dagor were already seated at the table, their heads bent together, no doubt whispering sweet nothings in each other's ears. Aru and Gabi were still on the dance floor, and Margo and Negal were not attending for obvious reasons.

Edgar pulled out Jasmine's chair for her, the chivalrous gesture earning him a warm smile and a murmured thanks. As he took his own seat beside her, her eyes drifted to the empty chairs surrounding their table. "I hope Margo is okay. I thought she would be here tonight."

Frankie turned to look at her. "She's still a little under the weather. Dagor and I are going to bring them to-go plates later."

"What's wrong with her?" Jasmine frowned. "Is it serious? I mean, she seemed fine this afternoon, a little tired maybe, but nothing that would keep her from attending the wedding. Did the doctor check up on her?"

Frankie winced. "Yeah, she did. But you know how doctors are. She told Margo to rest, drink plenty of fluids, and call her if she didn't feel better in the morning."

Jasmine nodded. "I know exactly what you mean. If you are under thirty years old, they treat you dismissively. A friend of mine suffered for years from stomach pains, and her doctor told her that it was all because of stress and recommended therapy. Turned out she had irritable bowel syndrome."

"How did she find out?" Frankie asked. "Did she go to another doctor?"

As the two continued talking about human maladies and the various treatments available for them, Edgar exchanged a knowing look with Dagor.

Having a human mate or one that used to be human was a different experience, and he hoped Jasmine wouldn't direct any health questions at him. He really didn't want to add more lies to those he'd had to tell her so far, and besides, he didn't know enough about human ailments to lie convincingly.

"I feel bad for Margo." Jasmine sighed. "This is such a beautiful event."

Edgar draped his arm over the back of her chair. "Oh, I have no doubt that Margo and Negal are finding ways to entertain themselves."

Provided that her transition symptoms had not worsened since he had last seen her, Margo seemed well enough to partake in some one-on-one fun.

"I bet." Jasmine laughed, her eyes sparkling with mirth as she leaned into him, her shoulder brushing against his. "In fact, they might be having more fun than we are."

He leaned closer and brushed his lips over hers. "The night is not over yet, beautiful. I promise that there is much more fun in store for you."

5 9

PETER

Peter's eyes drifted between Marina and the newlyweds on the dance floor. On his other side, Jay was engaged in a lively conversation with Larissa, their voices rising and falling in a loud mix of Russian and English and their hands gesturing the things they didn't know how to say to each other. Marina interjected from time to time, helping to bridge the language gap between them.

He was still amazed at the speed she had taught herself English. Jay, an immortal with a natural aptitude for languages, was still struggling with basic Russian after spending hours in an online course. For a human, Marina's achievement was extraordinary. Peter would have been inclined to assert that her aptitude for languages was a paranormal talent and, therefore, an indicator of godly genes, but the absence of the most obvious indicators overruled that possibility.

Given how many times they'd had sex and how many times he had bitten her, she would have started transitioning already if she was a Dormant.

A crushing sadness overtook him as he thought of her short lifespan. It was a blink of an eye in comparison to his, and by staying with her instead of cutting off the relationship, he was only delaying the inevitable heartache by a few decades yet amplifying it immeasurably.

He was so damn selfish. He couldn't give her children because they would be mortal like her. The smart thing to do would be to let her go so she could find happiness with a human male who could give her what she needed.

A home and a family to call her own.

But the ship had sailed on that. He was in love with Marina, and in his self-ishness, he couldn't let her go.

Even the thought of her returning to Safe Haven without him for a short while was intolerable to him. Peter had never imagined that he could feel this way about a human, that he could form a bond so deep and so unbreakable with someone who wasn't even a Dormant.

How was it possible that he felt like he had found a missing piece of himself in her?

How could the Fates be so cruel and merciful at the same time?

Except, if someone asked him whether he would have preferred never to have met Marina, he would have replied that it's better to have loved and lost than never to have loved at all.

Peter wasn't angry at the Fates for bringing her into his life. He just wondered what they had been thinking.

What was the Fates' grand plan for him and Marina?

As an eternal optimist, he hoped that there was a solution down the line, and in the meantime his concern was how to ensure the minimal separation possible between them.

He didn't want to wait weeks for her transfer request to go through the proper channels.

Perhaps he could convince Kian that Marina was needed in the village because of her translation skills? Many of the village's new residents still struggled with English, and the Kra-ell knew Marina and would be comfortable with her helping them with the language barrier.

On the other hand, his approaching Kian directly could backfire.

Kian would approve Marina's transfer request if he believed she wanted to move to be close to the other former occupants of Igor's compound or for a different sort of work than what she was tasked with in Safe Haven. He might not approve of her transferring to be with Peter.

Immortals were discouraged from having long-term relationships with humans, and the term discouraged was putting it mildly. It was more like prohibited.

It would be better to tell Eleanor and Emmett about Marina's translation ability and have them add it to the transfer request. The problem with that was that it wouldn't be immediate, and if he tried to expedite it, he would show his hand.

He needed to pretend that his interest in Marina was no different than any he had before with human females. Perhaps Kian wouldn't care that Peter was planning to keep Marina with him and would think nothing of it, but Peter couldn't take the chance that Kian would have an issue with that and not approve her request.

In the meantime, he could take a few days off and join her at Safe Haven, or even better, he could ask Onegus to transfer him there for a couple of weeks. After all, Guardians were rotated between Safe Haven, the keep, and the village, so it wouldn't be anything unusual for him to request a particular post.

Leaning over, he hooked a finger under Marina's chin and planted a soft kiss on her lips. "I love you," he murmured against her mouth before leaning away. "But don't tell anyone," he added with a wink.

She frowned. "Why not?"

"Because it needs to remain our secret," he said in a teasing manner, so if Jay heard him, he would think nothing of it.

"If you say so." Marina looked deflated.

"Hey." He leaned closer. "No need to pout. Do you want to dance?"

He had to explain why he was acting this way and also to tell her his plan.

60

MARINA

As Peter led Marina onto the dance floor, she was once again assaulted by fear and doubts. She thought about the borrowed dress she was wearing and the immortal female to whom it belonged. Was she watching her and telling her friends about her charitable gesture?

Were they pitying the poor human who was trying to be one of them?

But then Peter put his hand on the small of her back and pressed his body close to hers, and she forgot about everyone else around them and focused on the way he made her feel.

She had no doubt that he loved her, but she was disappointed that he wanted to keep his love for her a secret, even though she could understand his motives. His family wouldn't approve of her as his mate, but if he pretended that she was just a passing interest, just another body to warm his bed, perhaps they wouldn't mind.

They swayed together to the music, their bodies molded together as if they had been made for each other, and as Marina let herself get lost in the moment and the feel of Peter's arms around her, she couldn't help but steal a glance at the other couples on the dance floor and the way they moved with such effortless grace and fluidity.

Especially the females.

Their bodies were lithe and supple, and their movements were fluid and seamless. They seemed to glide across the floor with their feet barely touching the ground as if they were floating on air.

Compared to them, Marina felt clumsy and uncoordinated, her own movements stiff and awkward next to theirs, but when she looked up at Peter and saw the way he regarded her, his eyes expressing so much love and adoration, Marina felt all her doubts and insecurities melt away.

She didn't deserve to be loved like that, and the intensity of his feelings terrified her, because she knew how badly it was going to hurt him just by being by her side as her life span would be over in the blink of an eye, while he would go on forever, young and strong and beautiful.

How could she let him love her, knowing that she would cause him so much anguish in the end? How could she be so selfish, so cruel, as to let him tie himself to her?

But even as those thoughts swirled in her mind, the guilt and shame threatening to overwhelm her, Marina knew that she couldn't let Peter go by pushing him away.

She loved him too fiercely, too selfishly.

Maybe that made her weak, and perhaps it meant that she didn't love him enough or wasn't strong enough to do what was best for him, but she couldn't bring herself to set him free to find someone who could give him the forever he deserved.

Letting out a breath, she clung to him, her arms wrapped even tighter around his neck and her face buried in the crook of his shoulder.

"I want to explain," he whispered in her ear. "Why I want my love for you to remain a secret."

"It's okay," she murmured into his neck. "I understand. Your family will not approve of you having deep feelings for me, but they might be okay with you having fun with the human for a little while."

"Yes, but I wouldn't have given a fuck about what they think if changing their perception wouldn't have jeopardized your transfer to the village. For now, I want them to believe that what we have is casual, so no one will think of putting roadblocks on your transfer."

A weight lifting off her chest, she kissed the spot on his neck that her mouth was pressed to. "Thank you for telling me this. It means a lot to me."

He tightened his arms around her. "There is nothing casual about my feelings for you, and to prove it, I'm coming with you to Safe Haven." He brushed his lips against the shell of her ear. "I'll ask to be stationed with the team of Guardians on duty there and stay with you until your transfer is approved. That way, we don't have to be apart for more than a day."

Marina pulled back to look at him. "I love you so much that it hurts."

He frowned. "Why does it hurt?"

She averted her eyes. "You know why. But I'm too selfish to let you go, so I'll take everything you are willing to offer and enjoy it as long as it lasts."

Lifting a hand, he cupped her cheek, his thumb wiping away a tear she hadn't realized she'd shed. "Let's not think about the future. Let's just focus on the here and now."

Marina nodded, her throat tight with emotion. Peter was right. There was no point in worrying about the future when the present was so wonderful and perfect.

61

ARU

Aru glanced at his watch, his heart quickening as he saw the hands ticking closer to midnight. He had seen Kian and Syssi rise from their seats a few moments earlier, making their way over to the newlyweds to offer their congratulations and farewells.

Now that Kian's sisters were in on the secret, they could cover for him and make his early departure seem less conspicuous. In a way, it was a relief to have more people in the know and not have to carry the weight of this burden alone, but it was also the main cause for the churning in his gut.

It was illogical to feel that way about people who couldn't reveal his and Aria's secret even if they wanted to, but it was so ingrained in Aru's psyche to guard the telepathic connection with his sister that he couldn't help but feel exposed and incredibly vulnerable despite the safety precautions the princess had provided by compelling her children and their mates to keep the information from leaking out of their small group.

"Go." Gabi patted his arm. "You don't want to be late."

Aru hated leaving her alone. "Are you staying or going to call it a night?"

Gabi smiled. "I'm staying. I'm going to spend some time with Karen, Gilbert and the rest of the family. Everyone is fussing over Karen, and I need to do my share of fussing as well. It's my duty as her sister-in-law."

Aru leaned in to press a soft kiss to her cheek, breathing in the sweet, familiar scent of her perfume. "Enjoy yourself." He brushed his lips against her soft skin. "And if anyone asks where I am, tell them that I had something I needed to take care of, but I didn't tell you what it was."

Gabi chuckled, her eyes sparkling with mischief. "I'll tell them that you are sick of attending weddings."

Aru shook his head. "Only if you make it sound like a joke," he warned.

She laughed. "Of course."

The truth was that he had attended enough weddings to last him a century. The princess's speeches were great, full of warmth and wisdom and heartfelt emotion, but even though she had tried to make them individual for each couple, there was only so much variety she could introduce and only so many ways to say the same things over and over again.

With a final squeeze of Gabi's hand and a murmured goodbye, Aru slipped away from the table and made his way out of the dining hall.

Thankfully, he didn't encounter anyone in the elevator, and as he entered the corridor leading to the heir's cabin, he glanced at his watch and saw that he had exactly two minutes left to get there on time.

Hurrying his step, he got to her door and was about to ring the bell, when he heard a cabin door open behind him, and as he turned around, he saw Kian and Syssi stepping out of their cabin, which was located on the other end of the long hallway.

Unlike the previous nights, they were still dressed in their evening clothes, most likely because they hadn't had time to change out of them.

Aru waited for them to catch up.

He had no idea what Kian wanted to talk to him about before the telepathic meeting took place, and he hoped that it wasn't about revealing his and Aria's secret communication method to even more people.

Kian looked aggravated, and as the couple reached Aru, he tugged on his tux lapels and pressed the doorbell. "Saying goodnight to all these people cost us valuable time. We only had enough left to grab Syssi's notepad and had to rush over."

The door opened, and the princess's Odu bowed. "Good evening, Mistress Syssi, Master Kian, Master Aru. Please come in."

"Thank you," Kian said before ushering his wife in.

Avoiding eye contact with the cyborg, Aru walked in behind them.

His aversion to the Odus was another illogical thing that he couldn't help, and he wondered whether it had been encoded in his genetics.

"Good evening, Clan Mother." He bowed to the princess.

She smiled and inclined her head. "Please call me Annani, Aru. If you do not, I will correct you every time you use my title until you get used to using my given name."

"As you wish."

He was not going to address the heir to the Anumati throne so casually. He would just have to perform verbal gymnastics to avoid addressing her directly.

They sat down, Syssi next to the princess and Aru and Kian each taking an armchair, more pleasantries were exchanged, and then the Odu served tea and coffee.

When each of them held a cup in hand, Aru turned to Kian. "So, why are we here early?"

"Syssi had a vision about the pods," Kian said without preamble and turned to his wife. "Would you like to tell it, or do you want me to do it?"

Aru was grateful on two counts. The first that Kian was not asking to let more people in on the secret, and second, that he wasn't wasting time.

"I'll do it." Syssi put her teacup down. "Bear in mind that visions usually should not be taken literally, and sometimes their purpose is just to hint at things. Also, I didn't ask to be shown where the pod with the royal twins was buried. I asked for something else entirely and was shown this instead." She continued to tell him what she had seen and what she and Amanda thought about Jasmine's role in the vision.

As Aru listened, he found it hard to believe that two intelligent females like Syssi and Amanda had put so much faith in tarot cards and Jasmine's ramblings about her promised prince. Not only that, but it also seemed that they had managed to rope Kian and his mother into supporting that questionable narrative.

Aru didn't want to offend Syssi, but he couldn't contain his incredulity. "Are you seriously suggesting that a human who bases her life decisions on tarot cards and crystal balls can help us locate the pod with the royal twins?"

Syssi smiled indulgently as if he were the one whose logic was skewed. "Tarot cards, crystal balls, and other instruments of divination are just conduits for the energy that is inside the individual. On their own, they are just inanimate objects with no innate power. Jasmine has something, a spark of potential that we can all feel. And besides, my visions are never wrong."

She had just told him that her visions shouldn't be taken literally, and now she was telling him that they were never wrong.

"So, let me understand what you are suggesting." Aru took a deep breath. "You want us to take Jasmine with us and have her direct our search for the pods?"

Syssi nodded. "What harm could that do? One more person on your team is not going to make much of a difference, but she might be able to point you in the right direction when you have no other clues."

"Jasmine is human," Aru said. "She will slow us down."

Syssi smiled again. "Yes, she will, but on the other hand, she might save you a lot of time by pointing you in the right direction."

He couldn't argue with that, but there was one more point he could raise. "What if we determine that she's useless?"

"She won't be," Kian said. "I have full faith in Syssi's visions. But if you decide that Jasmine is not helpful to your search, you can send her back home. We will cover the bill."

"Sounds reasonable," Aru agreed. "Did you speak with her about it? Maybe she doesn't want to go?"

"We've told her nothing so far," Kian said. "I wanted to check with you first. There are also a few other concerns that we need to address."

"Like what?" Aru asked almost defensively.

Kian lifted the teacup to his lips and took a small sip. "The twins are rumored to be powerful compellers, and your team will need the specialty earpieces William developed that block the sound waves carrying compulsion."

Aru shifted in the armchair and crossed his legs. "That would be much appreciated. Thank you."

Kian regarded him for a long moment. "Does the queen know that her son fathered the twins with the Kra-ell princess?"

"I believe so, but you need to understand that my interaction with the queen has been minimal, and my sister serves the oracle, not the queen. We provide information, but we don't get much back, and we can only speculate on what the queen knows and thinks. There were rumors that claimed a dalliance between her son and the Kra-ell princess, who later became the queen, but I don't think the Anumati queen believed them at the time. She probably thought it was more of the Eternal King's negative propaganda aimed at discrediting his son and painting him as a deviant. The Kra-ell queen was very good at concealing the twins from the public eye and shrouding the identity of their father, and even the Eternal King, with all his spies, wasn't sure that the twins were his grandchildren. It's common for the Kra-ell queens to hide the identity of their children's fathers, especially those who father the daughters that will rule one day, so no one thought much of it. On the other hand, the twins became acolytes at a very young age, so they must have raised a lot of brows at the time. That was very uncommon."

Kian nodded. "I keep forgetting that this is ancient history to you. We've only learned all of this recently, and the Kra-ell, who told us about the twins being in stasis for thousands of years, said it was recent history for them as well. The question is whether my mother should inform the queen of Anumati about this new thread that might lead to them."

Aru leveled his gaze at Kian. "There is nothing I keep from the queen. I don't share every thought and speculation I have, and I don't bother her with every unimportant detail, so I can refrain from telling her about this new line of inquiry until it is proven to be relevant, but if it is, then I need to inform her." He dipped his head toward the heir. "My apologies, but my first loyalty is to my queen."

Annani nodded. "I understand, and I appreciate your loyalty to my grandmother and your honest reply, but I have no intention of keeping this from her."

62

ANNANI

Annani suspected that Aru had communicated to his sister every important tidbit of information he had learned about her and the clan. She would not have been concerned, but there was always the possibility that the queen's part in the resistance would be discovered, and she would be tortured for information.

There was not much she could do about it at this point, though. Her resemblance to her grandmother had given her away, and the moment Aru had informed the queen about her, the cat was out of the bag, so to speak, and there was no way to put it back in.

If the Eternal King discovered Annani's existence, he would not hesitate to destroy Earth just to get rid of her, and since there was no communication with Anumati, and no one was officially allowed anywhere near it, the king could annihilate the entire planet without worrying about his reputation.

Annani sighed.

It was not easy to live with a tangible and ever-present existential threat, but it was nothing new for her. Annani's life had prepared her well to not only handle and cope but to thrive under adverse situations. She would find a way to weather this storm as well.

"The queen is ready to begin," Aru said.

Annani nodded. "So am I."

Beside her, Syssi reached for the yellow notepad and pen and got ready to transcribe the conversation.

Once the initial greetings and pleasantries were out of the way, Annani humbly requested to take the first turn and tell the queen about her family.

"But of course," Aru said for the queen. "I am very curious to hear about you and your family."

"I would like to begin with my half-sister Areana." It would be a good way to ease the queen into a conversation about the royal twins. "I mentioned her before. She was the one who volunteered to take my place as Mortdh's bride, and that was how she was spared. Areana was on her way to Mortdh's stronghold when the assembly was bombed, but I did not know that she had survived until very recently. To my great surprise, Areana had mated Mortdh's son Navuh, and he has been keeping her hidden in his harem for thousands of years."

Aru looked at her with shock in his eyes. "He kept a goddess in a harem with human females?"

Annani nodded. "Immortal females mostly, and some human, but it is a sham. As shocking as it seems, Navuh and Areana are fated mates, and he does not grace the beds of any of the others. He is devoted to Areana. But since he does not want his army of goons to know that his mate is a goddess who outranks him in status, he keeps her locked in his harem, and none of them know that he has a goddess in there."

Aru's eyes looked like they were about to pop out of their sockets. "Why does she allow it?"

Annani sighed. "She loves him. Areana is a sweet and gentle soul, but she is a weak goddess. Navuh might be only an immortal, but he is more powerful than she is, and with his strong compulsion ability, he is also more powerful than many of the gods on Anumati." She smiled. "After all, he is the Eternal King's descendant."

So was Areana, but somehow, she had not inherited any of their grandfather's power. Her mother's genes must be dominant in her genetic composition.

Aru shook his head. "It will take me a few minutes to explain all of this to my sister."

"Take your time." Annani lifted her teacup for Ojidu to refill.

The queen's response came several moments later. "It is a disgrace that a daughter of Ahn, even one who is the product of an unofficial relationship, is kept as a sex slave by the hybrid son of Ahn's nephew. I find this appalling."

Annani winced. "Something must have been lost in translation. Areana is not a sex slave. She lives in a harem, but she is surrounded by luxury and treated with love and respect by her mate. I cringe at saying anything positive about Navuh, but that is the truth. I do not wish to go into a lengthy explanation, but we were able to plant a spy in the harem and establish a mode of communication with my sister. The spy confirmed what my sister had told me. Areana is the undisputed queen of that harem."

Aru dipped his head. "My apologies, Clan Mother. There is no word in Anumatian for a harem, so my translation was inaccurate."

"I see." Annani tried to think of a way to explain it better. "What do the Kra-ell females call the males in their extended family unit?"

"It is a word that is similar to a tribe," Aru said.

"You can tell your sister that Areana is part of such a tribe, but instead of one female with several males, this tribe consists of one male and several females. She is Navuh's favorite, and he does not engage with any of the other females. He lets others impregnate them and claims their children as his own."

Aru looked like he had bitten on a lemon, but he nodded. "I will try my best to convey this to the queen."

Annani waited patiently for the response, sipping on her tea and thinking of how she was going to move to the subject of the twins.

"The queen says that Areana is unimportant in the grand scheme of things," Aru said. "She is a weak goddess, the result of a dalliance, and she is not in the line of succession. Queen Ani wants to know more about Navuh."

Annani felt a flare of anger at the queen's casual disregard for Areana, at the way she seemed to brush her aside simply because she did not fit into the neat, tidy line of royal succession. But then, as quickly as it had come, the anger faded, replaced by a flicker of understanding.

The queen seemed to assume that Areana was the daughter of a concubine whom Ahn had kept in addition to his official wife, and Ani might have felt disappointed that her son conducted himself in the same shameless way as his father did.

"Areana was born long before Ahn met Nei, my mother," Annani explained. "Since the moment my father met my mother, he did not look at another female."

Aru took a moment to convey the queen's words. "The queen is still not interested in Areana. She wants to hear more about Mortdh's son."

The queen was right. Areana was important to Annani because she loved her and appreciated her, but regrettably, her role in history was not nearly as important as her despicable mate's.

"Navuh is my sworn enemy, and he seeks to destroy me, my clan, and all that I stand for. While my clan and I strive to improve human society to promote progress, peace, and prosperity, Navuh wants to enslave humans and control them. I do not wish to go into a lengthy explanation, but Navuh managed to create an immortal army that is many thousands strong. They are brainwashed and compelled daily to hate, destroy, and kill indiscriminately. Human lives mean nothing to them. They are barbarians who thrive on cruelty as a way to intimidate and control, and there is absolutely no chance of peaceful coexistence with them or even some sort of compromise. It is either us or them." She sighed. "It pains me to even say that. I do not wish to destroy what is left of our people, but the longer this conflict lasts, the more I realize that there is no other option."

Come to think of it, the queen probably did not hold human lives in high regard either. If she did not deem her own granddaughter important only because she was a weak goddess and not in the line of succession, she certainly did not deem humans as having any value whatsoever.

"Navuh is a threat to your safety," the queen replied through Aru. "How are you protecting yourself?"

As Annani had expected, the queen had not reacted to Navuh's disregard for human lives, but at least she was concerned with Annani and her clan's safety. On second thought, she was only concerned with Annani, the heir to the throne.

"I assure you that I am more than capable of handling Navuh and his forces. I have done so for thousands of years. He may have a large army of immortal warriors at his command, but we have always been several steps ahead of him thanks to our superior technology and knowledge."

Annani went on to explain the role of Ekin's tablet that she had 'borrowed,' a treasure trove of knowledge that had allowed her clan to stay ahead of Navuh's powerful immortal army and the humans under his poisonous control.

"We did not decipher all of the science that is contained in that tablet, and I understand only a small fraction of it," Annani admitted. "One of my great-grandchildren, who is much cleverer than I, was far more adept at deciphering the complex equations and formulas that Ekin had inscribed upon its surface."

A long moment passed until Aru relayed the queen's answer. "Did your father or Ekin find the Odus I sent to Earth with the information of how to build more of them? They were meant to arrive before the Kra-ell settler ship and its cargo of assassins so Ekin could build an army of them to protect Ahn and the others."

Annani glanced at Kian. "We have guessed correctly. The queen was the one who sent them." She was sure that Aru had told Aria about the Odus, so the queen knew that they had found them. Her grandmother's question was about the blueprints that she had hidden inside their brains and whether they had found them.

Annani was not sure that she wanted to reveal that highly confidential information in front of Aru.

After the Odus had been used for warfare, the technology for building robotic servants was banned on Anumati. Aru was a rebel, so he did not care about the ban, but he was not fond of Odus. He had grown up on horror stories that the official propaganda had spread about the Odus so people would be terrified of them, and no one would dare to build them again.

"You might as well tell her," Kian said.

"We found them," Annani told Aru. "But the information about how to build them was only recently discovered following an accidental reboot of one of the Odus. We are still trying to figure out what he wrote down. The biotechnology on Earth is not anywhere near as advanced as what you had on Anumati all those thousands of years ago, and we will probably be able to develop only a much less life-like product."

"The queen says that it is a shame the Odus were not as useful as she hoped," Aru said. "She took a great risk by sending these seven to Earth. But now that you and your clan finally have access to the information stored in them, you can build your own army and protect yourself from Navuh's immortals. The queen wants to hear more about the conflict and why Navuh is so determined to destroy you."

Annani explained the long and bitter history of the conflict between her clan and Navuh's forces. She spoke of the way they had fought by proxy, using their influence and their knowledge to shape the course of human history, to guide and protect the mortals who looked to them for guidance and support.

"Navuh helps the humans he controls and uses them against the people we are assisting with our technological and ideological knowhow. And we do the same, using the humans we helped to elevate and advance to counter his moves."

It was a never-ending game played out across the millennia, and through it all, Annani and her clan had endured. But now, the royal twins might affect the balance of power and change the game.

The question was how.

63

QUEEN ANI

When Annani had spoken about her sister, Ani had listened to her words with a sense of detachment. She didn't really care about Areana, who had mated the enemy of her sister. She must be weak of character in addition to being weak in power to mate a despicable male like this.

But then Ani was mated to a no less despicable male who was not even her fated mate, and she was still married to him because it was a position of power that allowed her to mitigate El's schemes to some degree and slow down his plans.

She found it hard to believe that, at one time, she had convinced herself that she loved El. He had not always been a monster, had not always been the cruel and tyrannical ruler he had become. Once, a long time ago, he had been a visionary, a leader who had united their people and brought peace and prosperity to a fractured and war-torn world. But power had corrupted him, twisting his mind and his soul until there was nothing left but greed, paranoia, and an insatiable hunger for control. And now, after millennia of his iron-fisted rule, there was no hope of redemption or change.

Ani despised him with every fiber of her being but continued playing the role of the dutiful wife and queen, all the while working in secret to undermine him and to build a resistance that would one day overthrow him and restore freedom and justice to their world.

It was not all that different from what Annani was doing on Earth; except Annani did not have to pretend to care for Navuh.

As her granddaughter shifted the narrative to the Kra-ell royal twins, though, Ani's interest was suddenly piqued.

She had heard the rumors about Ahn's supposed affair with the Kra-ell princess, his counterpart in the rebellion, but she had never believed them.

To her, the Kra-ell were barbarians, only one degree above the animals they hunted for blood, and to copulate with one was just disgusting. Still, it was possible that El believed that Ahn had fathered the twins because he had despised his son and his progressive ideas.

The royal twins had always been a mystery, consecrated to the priesthood and shrouded in secrecy. Their faces had been hidden behind veils their entire lives, and there had been rumors of deformity and abnormality, but Ani had never been one to put much stock in rumors.

Now, however, she was forced to confront the possibility that there might have been some truth to those rumors after all. If the twins were indeed the product of a forbidden union between a god and a Kra-ell, not necessarily Ahn but some other god, then it was no wonder that their mother had kept them hidden and their features obscured.

Perhaps Ekin had been the father?

He had shared Ahn's ideology, and he had always been sexually adventurous. If anyone was capable of coupling with a Kra-ell savage female, it was him.

Ekin was not her son, and Ani abhorred El's hordes of concubines, including Ekin's mother, but she had always been fond of Ekin despite his unconventional beliefs that had been even more radical than Ahn's.

Ahn had always been more reserved than Ekin, more refined, and she found it hard to believe that he had violated the taboo on copulating with lesser species and fathered children with the Kra-ell princess, who had later become the queen.

When Aria was done relaying Annani's story, Ani chose her response carefully. "I always assumed that the rumors about the twins were baseless—malicious propaganda spread by the Eternal King. But if what you say is true, if they are indeed the children of Ahn and the Kra-ell queen, then they might be just as dangerous as the Eternal King thinks they are, and they should be approached with extreme caution."

"I am not sure that they are dangerous," Aria gave voice to Annani's response. "I think that the Kra-ell queen sent them to Earth not to undermine Ahn and take over. I think she sent them to their father because she feared for their lives. If anyone had discovered that they were half god, half Kra-ell, they would not have lasted more than a day. Their own people would have slaughtered them along with the queen who had committed the greatest transgression. The only place they could be safe was on Earth among the rebels who believed in equality and were led by their father. If they were as powerful as the king believed them to be, their mother wouldn't have been so worried for their safety."

It was a smart observation, and the queen was proud of her granddaughter's deductive ability, but it was very possible that Annani was wrong. She was a little soft-hearted, and she believed in people's good intentions.

It was naive.

"The twins are a wild card," Ani said. "And depending on the power they can actually wield, they can be a variable that could tip the balance of power in either direction. You must ensure that it tips in your favor." Ani paused for a moment, thinking about the role of the human Syssi had seen in her vision assisting the team of gods. "The human needs to be watched carefully. The Fates work in mysterious ways, and the role they gave that woman might not be as straightforward as your daughter-in-law's vision suggests."

6 4

JASMINE

E dgar leaned back in his chair and rubbed his stomach. "I'm stuffed." He looked at the half-eaten cake on his plate. "This is delicious, but I can't take another bite."

Jasmine chuckled. "We've danced off the calories, so it's not so bad."

She wasn't sure that the net effect was zero, but she'd made a valiant effort to make it so. She had danced until her feet ached, sampled every delicacy the buffet had to offer, and got Edgar to introduce her to a bunch of people. Regrettably, none of them specified their positions in Perfect Match, so she still didn't know who she needed to impress to get a job at the company.

Kian had promised to talk to the owners on her behalf, but she hadn't heard from him yet. Besides, he might have meant to ask about some entry-level job for her to replace the customer service one she was probably going to lose.

She'd told him that she dreamt about being a spokeswoman in the Perfect Match commercials, but she'd also told him that any other job would be great, and that was probably what he'd remembered from their talk if he remembered her quest for a job at the company at all.

Edgar draped a lazy arm over the back of her chair. "Ready to go?"

Jasmine looked at the dwindling crowd on the dance floor and the partially empty dining tables and sighed. "I enjoyed this evening tremendously, and I don't want it to end." She turned to him and smiled. "I feel like Cinderella at the ball. The clock has already struck a few times, and I'm anxious about it striking twelve."

He leaned over and brushed his lips over her cheek. "It's way past midnight, beautiful, and the fun doesn't have to end just yet." He trailed his lips down her neck, eliciting a delicious shiver. "I'm not tired. Are you?"

Jasmine chuckled. "My answer would be my place or yours, but since your place is probably much nicer than mine, it has to be yours."

The lascivious smile he sent her made her tingle in all the right places. "Let's go." He rose to his feet and offered her a hand up.

Guiding her to the newlyweds through the throng of well-wishers and lingering guests, he stopped to congratulate them and then paused to say goodbye to Marina and Larissa and their dates.

As they made their way towards the exit, Jasmine's gaze landed on Max, his tall, imposing figure cutting a striking silhouette against the wall he was standing next to. Almost without thinking, she smiled and raised a hand in a small wave, immediately regretting the gesture.

After the way Max had treated her, he didn't deserve to be acknowledged by her.

When Edgar's arm tightened around her waist, pulling her close against his side in a possessive display, Jasmine bit back a smirk. Let the stuck-up Max see that she was desired and appreciated by a good man who deemed her more than worthy of his attentions.

As they stepped out into the corridor and Edgar pressed the button to call the elevator, Jasmine smiled and leaned into his embrace. "I bet your bed is bigger and more comfortable than mine."

He looked at her with a slight frown. "Your cabin is private, though, and mine isn't. I have a roommate. Charlie has his own bedroom, but it's not like he wouldn't know that you spent the night with me. Knowing him, he's probably sitting in the living room and watching a movie even though he has a television in his bedroom."

"I don't mind," she said, her fingers playing with the lapel of his jacket. "If you haven't noticed yet, I'm not shy. But if you are, I can be quiet." A wicked grin spread across her face as she leaned in closer, her lips brushing against his ear. "Or I can try. I can't promise that I'll succeed."

She wasn't an exhibitionist, but she got a certain thrill from making public displays of affection.

Edgar's answering chuckle was low and deep, sending shivers racing down her spine. "You can be as loud as you want," he assured her, his hand splaying across the small of her back. "The upper deck cabins have excellent soundproofing. The moment I close the door, Charlie won't hear a thing."

"Awesome. I hope your ears aren't overly sensitive," she whispered in his ear.

The woman who was waiting for the elevator next to them smirked as if she'd heard what Jasmine had whispered in Ed's ear, but it was unlikely.

The doors to the dining room were open, and the music spilling from the inside was still quite loud.

As the elevator arrived, a thrill of anticipation coursed through Jasmine, but since they weren't alone in the cab, holding hands was all they could do, and when they stepped out on Ed's deck, the same woman got out as well.

By the time they reached Edgar's cabin, Jasmine's skin was practically humming with need.

65

EDGAR

E dgar pushed open the door, ready to make the introductions, and sure enough, Charlie was on the couch just like he had known he would be, with a beer in one hand, the remote in the other, and his feet propped up on the coffee table.

Seeing Jasmine, Charlie's eyes widened, and he scrambled to his feet, hastily buttoning his shirt and smoothing down his hair.

"Hello, Charlie," Ed said. "This is Jasmine. Jasmine, this is Charlie, my roommate and a fellow pilot, only he flies planes and I fly helicopters."

"Hi." She gave Charlie a little wave. "It's nice to meet you. I wish I could say that I've heard a lot about you, but Ed only mentioned you when we were on the way up here."

"I'm not surprised." Charlie flashed her a smile. "He only remembers that I exist when he needs something from me."

Edgar shot his friend a warning look, but Jasmine just laughed. "That's what friends are for, right?"

Shrugging, Charlie pushed his feet into his slippers. "Yeah, he didn't bother to introduce me to you at the wedding." He cast Ed a baleful look.

Ed lifted his hands in the air. "If you wanted an introduction, you should have approached us."

Charlie shifted his gaze to Jasmine and smiled. "You seemed busy, making the rounds and charming your crowd. Everyone was watching you."

"Oh, thank you." She put a hand over her chest. "That's so sweet of you to say, but with all the beautiful women in attendance tonight, I doubt many people noticed me. I plan to rectify that at tomorrow's wedding, though. If the couple is

225

agreeable, I will sing for them. I have a decent singing voice, and since I'm not an invited guest, I need to pay my way, right?"

Charlie didn't know what to say, and neither did Ed. It was a nice idea, but Jin and Arwel might object.

Jasmine didn't wait for either of them to approve or disapprove of her idea and continued, "If the big bosses like my voice, perhaps they will offer me a job. I would love to be part of the Perfect Match family and get free access to their adventures."

"Perfect Match?" Charlie's brow furrowed in confusion, his gaze darting to Edgar. "What does that have to do with anything?"

Ed's mind raced to come up with a plausible explanation. "Charlie has nothing to do with hiring for our company," he told Jasmine. "His job in Perfect Match Virtual Studios is with flight simulations; just like mine, only he simulates flying jets instead of helicopters." He slipped his arm around her waist. "He's helping the company develop flight simulators that are on par with the studios' other virtual adventures."

Understanding finally dawned in Charlie's eyes, and he nodded, a sly smile playing at the corners of his mouth. "The new simulators are top secret for now. It's very hush-hush because of the lucrative government contracts that are in the works, so don't tell anyone."

Who knew that Charlie was such a storyteller? He'd just run with the idea, making it more believable.

Jasmine's posture relaxed as she leaned into Edgar. "Your secret's safe with me."

"Well, it was very nice meeting you in person, Jasmine, but I think I should hit the hay. Goodnight." With a wink and a grin, Charlie ducked into his bedroom and closed the door behind him with a soft click.

Edgar turned to Jasmine with an apologetic smile. "Well, that was awkward. Can I get you a drink?"

Before he could finish his sentence, Jasmine pounced, her arms twining around his neck and her legs wrapping around his hips as she claimed his mouth in a searing kiss.

Bracing her weight with his hands on her ass, he carried her to his bedroom and kicked the door closed behind him.

The room was dark, with only a sliver of moonlight shining through the seam in the closed curtains, but Edgar had no doubt that his eyes would start glowing soon, and the additional illumination would be impossible to hide.

Jasmine had taken him by surprise, and even though he had good control over his fangs and the glow in his eyes, he could only maintain it for so long. Still kissing her, he delved into her mind and thralled her not to see oddities or rather to ignore them. He had done it so many times before, with so many women, that it required no longer than a few seconds, and once he was done, he tumbled onto the mattress with Jasmine on top of him.

She laughed, and he immediately started on her dress, eager to get to her skin and her lush curves.

"Careful," Jasmine hissed when he pulled down the zipper at the back of her dress. "My hair got caught in it."

"Sorry." He lifted her and turned her around so her back was to his front and freed the trapped strand from the zipper while trailing kisses down her back.

When they were both naked, skin to skin, Jasmine moaned and undulated her hips as he worshipped her, his hands and mouth mapping every inch of her exquisite flesh.

Impatient to be inside of her, Edgar got between her spread thighs, remembering at the last moment that he needed to protect her. He didn't want to induce her without her consent, and now wasn't the time for lengthy explanations.

The problem was, he hadn't thought that they would end up in his cabin tonight and hadn't prepared a condom.

With a groan, he dropped his forehead to hers. "I don't have protection."

Caressing his back, Jasmine chuckled. "It's in my purse."

He lifted his head and smiled even though his fangs were on full display by now. Jasmine was blind to them as if they didn't exist. "Thank the merciful Fates one of us was thinking." He slid off her and darted his gaze around the room in search of her purse.

"On the floor. Right there." She pointed.

He didn't follow her finger. Instead, he drank in the beauty sprawled on his bed. "You are a goddess, Jasmine. The goddess of love and lust and carnal desire."

She grinned. "Ooh, I love it, but you know what I'd love even more?"

"What?"

"For you to get the condom, put it on, and give me what I need." She reached with her hand to the juncture of her thighs and cupped herself.

Edgar nearly climaxed just from that, and when she lifted her other hand to her breast and started tweaking her nipple, he leaped off the bed, upended her purse, and found the packet among all the items that had tumbled out.

He was sheathed in two seconds flat and entered her with one swift thrust.

Jasmine cried out his name, but he knew it wasn't because he'd hurt her. She clung to him, her nails digging into his buttocks, urging him to move, and as he did, she wrapped her legs around his torso and let him dictate the rhythm.

With their moans and groans echoing off the walls of the cabin in a symphony of bliss, Edgar went deeper, harder, until her pleasure crested, and she threw her head back with a scream that even the cabin's impressive soundproofing couldn't contain. And when he erupted and bit her at the same time, she screamed and climaxed again and again until her voice gave out, and all that came out was a croak, and then she fell silent.

Edgar licked the puncture wounds closed, tenderly kissed the spot, and lifted his head to look at Jasmine's blissed-out expression.

She would be hoarse tomorrow, but hopefully, his venom would heal her injured throat enough so she could sing at the wedding.

6 6

KIAN

Kian leaned back in his chair, savoring the rich, bold flavor of the coffee Syssi had made for him. She might have only chosen the right pod to pop in the simple machine they had on board, but it still tasted fantastic because he was enjoying it with her.

The morning sun was casting a warm glow on her multicolored hair, making it look like gold, polished copper, and even a few strands that were so pale they looked like silver or platinum.

Allegra was spending the morning with her grandparents, so it was a rare pocket of time where they could simply be together as a couple and breathe. For once, Kian allowed himself to relax and bask in the simple joy of his mate's company.

"My parents are spoiling Allegra rotten," Syssi murmured, her fingers curled around her own steaming mug. "She's going to miss them so much when the cruise ends and they go back home." She sighed. "As amazing as the cruise has been, adventures and all, I'm ready to go home too."

Smiling, Kian reached for her hand. "Me too. I should have stuck to my original plan of making the cruise only a week long. Ten days is too much. Besides, I bet your main impetus for going home is the fancy cappuccino machine that you can't wait to get back to."

"Guilty as charged," Syssi admitted. "For the next cruise, I'm ordering one for the ship. I'm so spoiled that I can't live without it."

Kian raised an eyebrow, his expression skeptical. "You do realize that every bar on this ship is equipped with a state-of-the-art La Marzocco machine, right? You chose them."

Syssi shook her head. "It's not the same as having one to myself. There's just something about being able to fiddle with the settings, to tweak and adjust them until I get the perfect cup. It's an art, really."

Kian held up his hands in surrender. "Far be it from me to argue with the master barista," he teased. "I will admit, though, your cappuccinos are the best I've ever tasted."

"Thank you." Syssi's eyes sparkled with pleasure. But after a moment, her expression turned serious. "Do you want me to be there when you talk with Jasmine?"

"Of course. I'm going to ask her to come here." He pulled out his phone. "And after we talk to her and she agrees to help look for the prince, I will ask Aru to join us as well. I would have asked him to come over now, but I don't want to overwhelm her."

Syssi chuckled. "I don't think that Jasmine gets easily overwhelmed. I think she dissociates, but I'm not an authority on the subject. David could probably assess her better."

"What do you mean by that?" Kian knew it was a psychological term, but he didn't know what it described.

Syssi shrugged. "Jasmine always smiles like she is perpetually in a good mood. Some people are naturally upbeat, so that's not enough of a reason to suspect dissociation. But add to the equation her being lied to, manipulated, and betrayed by her boyfriend, the trauma of being drugged and kidnapped, and Edna's comment about old childhood pain, and you have a prescription for dissociation. After all that Jasmine has been through, she needed a coping mechanism, but I doubt she developed it recently. She was probably well practiced in that before her ordeal."

Kian let Syssi's words sink in for a moment and then nodded. "Do you think she's acting out a persona? That who she is underneath is different from what she shows the world?"

"She might be, but I'm not an expert, and what I know comes from a few articles I read a long time ago. David would know much more about it, but he will need to talk to Jasmine at length before he can give you his opinion."

"So what are you suggesting I do? Should I ask David to analyze her first? We have an expert on post-traumatic disorders at our disposal, so why not?"

Syssi shook her head. "It won't change the outcome. We still need her to help Aru find the pods. It was just an observation."

Kian nodded. "As long as she's not going to fall apart because of whatever psychological issues she is coping with, we don't need to fix her, right? I wouldn't even feel comfortable suggesting it unless it was pertinent to the mission." He opened his phone and started scrolling through his contacts. "It's so inconvenient that Jasmine doesn't have a phone. The only way I can find out where to locate her is by calling security."

The call was answered right away. "How can I help you, boss?"

"I need Jasmine's current location. One of the two humans we saved from the cartel boss."

The Guardian chuckled. "We have only one Jasmine on board, and we know who she is. Right now, she is in Edgar's cabin. She walked in with him last night after the wedding and hasn't emerged yet."

"Thank you. That will be all."

Next to Kian, Syssi smiled. "Jasmine is a fast operator."

"Good for her." Kian scrolled for Edgar's number. "Makes things easier for me. I can just call Edgar and have him bring Jasmine here."

Syssi arched a brow. "Do you want Edgar to hear everything we tell her?"

That was a good point. Ed had a high-security clearance, and the two were a couple. If things were serious between them, he would probably have to accompany her on the mission anyway.

"Edgar's security clearance is as high as the Guardians. I have no problem with him being here. And if there's a chance that Jasmine is his fated mate, then he will want to accompany her wherever she's going."

Syssi's eyes widened. "Do we have another helicopter pilot?"

Kian chuckled. "Eric can fly helicopters, and so can I, but I wouldn't want to be my own pilot."

"Why not?"

"I learned how to fly on a simulator. It's better than nothing, but I would rather have a pilot with real-life experience."

Kian pressed send, and a moment later, Edgar answered.

"Good morning, Kian. Do you need me to fly you somewhere?"

Naturally, Ed assumed that was why Kian was calling. "Actually, I'm not calling for you. I'm calling for Jasmine. I need her to come to my cabin. You know where it is, right?"

There was a short pause. "I do. Is she in trouble?"

"Not at all. I just need to discuss something with her, and it cannot wait. How soon can you get here?"

Edgar cleared his throat. "Is twenty minutes okay?"

"That's fine. I will see you both here." Kian ended the call and scrolled for Aru's number.

"Amanda should be here as well," Syssi said. "I know she's not essential, but she will be annoyed if we don't include her in this talk."

"You're right. Can you please call her?"

"Sure thing." Syssi rose to her feet and removed her phone from the charger.

"I'll call Amanda from the bedroom so you can talk with Aru without distractions."

JASMINE

"What was that about?" Jasmine yawned and turned on her side to face Edgar. "Where do we need to be in twenty minutes and why?"

They had just made love again, and she didn't want to be anywhere other than under the covers with him. She certainly didn't want to rush to be somewhere in twenty minutes.

"Kian wants to see you, and he didn't say why. We should get out of bed right now," Ed said but didn't move a muscle.

"Can you call him back and tell him that I fell asleep or something? I don't want to get out of bed."

Ed's lips tilted up in a smile. "Do you really want to get on the boss's bad side?"

She grimaced. "No, I don't."

It couldn't be anything bad because she hadn't done anything to violate the rules. No one had told her that she couldn't stay the night on the upper decks, and why would they? It wasn't like there were any secrets hiding in Edgar and Charlie's cabin.

Then, a thought occurred to her. Charlie looked surprised when Ed showed up with her at their cabin. Maybe he was the prudish type and didn't approve?

"Could Charlie have complained about me staying the night?"

Edgar laughed. "No way." He let his arms fall away from her body. "We are down to fifteen minutes. I suggest you get dressed."

Oh, crap. She hadn't brought a change of clothes with her, and there was no way she was showing up at Kian's place in the dress she'd worn to the wedding.

It didn't matter that he knew she had spent the night with Edgar. Appearances mattered.

"I have to go back to my cabin to change. I can't show up there in the dress I wore yesterday. "

"If we do that, you will need to do it super-fast." Edgar's lips twitched. "The other option is wearing something of mine. I can lend you a T-shirt and a pair of gym shorts."

She cast him an incredulous look. "Not happening."

Sliding out of bed, Jasmine rushed into the bathroom, took care of business, brushed her teeth with a finger, and tried to use Ed's comb on her hair, but it was no match for her thick tresses.

When she got out, Edgar was already dressed in a pair of jeans and a t-shirt, and he traded places with her in the bathroom without copping a feel on the way, which was a little insulting.

Well, they were in a rush, but still.

By the time she'd put on her panties and bra, he was already out of the bathroom and helped her zip up the dress.

She pushed her feet into her high heels, wincing at the pinch of the too-tight shoes, but there was no time to worry about comfort or fashion, not when Kian was waiting, his summons hanging over her head like a dark, ominous cloud.

"I would really love a cup of coffee." She pouted as they rushed out the door. "Maybe you can get me a cup from the staff lounge room while I get changed?"

"Of course." Edgar pulled her in for a quick kiss as they waited for the elevator.

"You don't need to come with me," she said as they rushed out of the elevator on the staff deck. "I can handle Kian on my own."

Edgar shook his head. "Kian expects me to be there, but even if he didn't, I wouldn't have left you to face this alone, whatever it is."

Something warm unfurled in Jasmine's chest. It was nice to have someone in her corner, someone who had her back. She'd never had that, not since she left home and not even before that. Her father had often been distant, and her stepmother just hadn't cared about her.

When the elevator door opened, they ran out. Ed was rushing into the staff lounge to get her coffee, and Jasmine headed toward her cabin.

Bursting through the door, she fumbled with the zipper of her dress as she kicked off her shoes. She stripped off the gown, tossed it on the bed, and reached into the closet for a simple, pull-on sundress.

She quickly ran a brush through her hair, wincing at the tangles and snarls that snagged on the bristles, but there was no time to untangle it gently and style it or to reapply makeup. Instead, she grabbed a makeup removal wipe, hastily scrubbing at her face until her skin was clean and bare.

When she got out, Ed was waiting for her with a cup of coffee. "I didn't know whether you wanted cream and sugar, so I put in both." He handed her the paper cup.

"Thank you." She took a grateful sip even though it was too sweet. "I needed that."

Edgar regarded her with a smile. "You're even more gorgeous without make-up." He lifted his hand and cupped her cheek.

Jasmine leaned into his touch, her eyes fluttering closed as she savored his reassuring presence for a moment.

"We need to hustle." She took his hand and broke into a light jog toward the elevators.

By the time they got to Kian's deck, Jasmine's palms were damp with sweat, and the churning in her stomach was making her nauseous.

Edgar rang the doorbell, and a moment later, the door swung open, revealing a stocky butler in a three-piece suit and a mannequin smile on his face.

Wow, talk about stereotypes. He was perfectly cast for the role of a British butler in an aristocratic house.

"Good morning, Master Edgar, Mistress Jasmine. Please, come in."

Jasmine was impressed that Kian had told his butler to greet her by name. Did it mean that she was a valued guest?

She certainly hoped so.

Kian was sitting in an armchair while Syssi and Amanda were on the couch. Both women smiled warmly, making her feel more at ease, and Syssi got to her feet, but Kian remained seated and looked even more imposing and unapproachable than the last time she'd seen him, which was at the wedding.

Jasmine swallowed hard, her mouth suddenly dry as sandpaper. But she forced herself to meet Kian's gaze and smile. "Good morning."

Syssi walked over to her and gave her a quick hug. "Can I offer you some coffee?"

"Yes, please. I would love some."

She had discarded the cup Edgar had made her in a trashcan by the elevators because it had been so sweet that it was undrinkable, and she desperately needed something to wet her throat.

"How about you, Edgar?" Syssi asked. "Would you like some coffee as well?"

"Thank you," he said. "If it's not too much trouble."

"It's not. Okidu will gladly make it. The simple pod machine we have here does not require any finesse."

That was kind of insulting to the poor butler. It was as if Syssi was implying that he was a simpleton and couldn't handle a more sophisticated coffeemaker.

Not that the guy seemed to care. With a wide grin and a bow to his mistress, he hurried into the tiny kitchen and got busy making coffee.

And what was the deal with him addressing everyone as master and mistress? What was this, the eighteenth century?

"Please, sit down next to me." Amanda waved Jasmine over.

Jaz cast a quick look at Edgar, who gave her a reassuring smile and headed toward the armchair next to Kian's.

When Jasmine sat down next to Amanda, Syssi sat on her other side. "I can't start my day without a good strong cup of coffee either, so I know how you feel." She smiled. "I'm sorry for the early wake-up call."

Jasmine didn't blush often, but she felt her cheeks heat up. "That's okay. Edgar and I just overslept. We stayed up very late last night at the wedding."

Amanda chuckled. "And I bet you didn't go to sleep right away."

"We didn't," Jasmine admitted with ease. She had nothing to hide or be embarrassed about.

When the butler returned with coffees for her and Edgar, the familiar aroma of the fresh brew and the ritual of stirring in the cream and sugar helped to ease some of the tension that was coiling in Jasmine's gut.

But the reprieve was short-lived.

"Amanda." Kian turned to his sister. "Do you want to do the honors? Out of the four of us, you are the best suited for the task."

Jasmine's heart stuttered in her chest, a creeping sense of dread washing over her. "What task?" she asked.

Amanda just smiled, her eyes sparkling with a strange inner light. "You are about to fall down the mother of all rabbit holes, so brace yourself." She snorted. "Except in your case, you won't find a queen, but you might discover a prince."

6 8

AMANDA

Amanda moved from the couch to a nearby armchair and settled in so she could fix her eyes on Jasmine's face as the other woman sat perched on the edge of the sofa, anxious and a little frightened.

She felt a smidgen of sympathy for her, but not more than that. Jasmine was about to be given a precious gift—access to the best-guarded secret on Earth, a chance of gaining immortality, and maybe even a prince. The truths Amanda was about to reveal would shake the very foundation of Jasmine's world and challenge everything she thought she knew about herself and her place in the grand tapestry of the Fates.

Jasmine was incredibly lucky. She just didn't know that yet.

Crossing her legs and steepling her fingers, Amanda assumed her teacher's voice. "What I'm about to tell you is going to sound incredible, but I need you to keep an open mind. Listen to what I have to say and try to keep your questions until after I'm done."

Edgar cleared his throat. "Excuse my interruption, but if what you are about to reveal is what I think it is, then isn't that the job of the partner to tell it to the Dormant?"

Amanda shook her head. "Not this time. I'm sorry to rob you of the privilege, but Jasmine's case is more complicated than the usual potential Dormant's. That's why I have to do it."

"What's a Dormant?" Jasmine asked.

Amanda lifted a hand. "I'll get to that in a few minutes. First, you need some background. The history of the world you are familiar with is not only inaccurate, but it is intentionally misleading."

She paused, letting her words sink in for a moment before continuing. "Have you ever noticed how similar the mythological pantheons of gods are across different cultures? How do the same twelve main gods seem to appear time and again, just under different names?"

Jasmine frowned, her brow furrowing in thought. "I guess so. I've always assumed that ancient civilizations just copied from one another, borrowed and adapted each other's deities to fit their own needs and beliefs."

Amanda smiled. "That's what most people think, and there is truth to it, but it's not the entire truth, and as you know, half-truths are often worse than lies, but I digress."

She leaned back. "The truth is that the gods were real people, and the impact they left on humanity was so great that stories about them were told all over the ancient world. They were a small group of exiles from a place light years away from Earth who called themselves gods, which in their language meant creators."

In her mind, Amanda had adapted the old, familiar story about their ancestors to include the new information that they had recently learned from Jade, Aru, and what her mother had told her about what she'd learned from the queen of Anumati.

"The gods were physically perfect, and their bodies were immune to disease and healed so fast that they were nearly impossible to kill. They also possessed incredible mind control powers over humans."

It had been done by genetic design so humans would be easy to control, but that was beyond the scope of what Jasmine needed to know at the moment.

Jasmine's eyes widened, but she remained silent, her gaze fixed on Amanda's face as she hung on every word.

"I got a little ahead of the story." Amanda lifted her coffee cup and took a sip to wet her throat. "I need to backpedal a little. These powerful aliens called themselves gods because they were masters of genetic manipulation, and they created numerous new species on the planets throughout the galaxy that they colonized with the intent of these species to serve them. On Earth, they used their own genetic material and combined it with that of an early hominid species, creating a new hybrid that would come to be known as Adam, the first human. At first, the new class of servants they created was made one at a time, but since it was inefficient, they were given the ability to procreate. What the gods didn't anticipate was just how fertile this new species would be and how quickly it would multiply."

"Is that the origin of the Adam and Eve story?" Jasmine asked. "The Bible talks about them being created by God or gods, and given the ability to procreate and fill the world with their offspring."

Jasmine should have waited with her questions until after Amanda was done, but it was a good question, so Amanda nodded. "Bingo. The story of Adam and Eve is a retelling of that original act of creation, a metaphor for the gods granting humans the ability to reproduce and thrive. But as their numbers grew and they evolved, the gods began to realize the potential threat that their creation posed and decided to cull the human population."

"The flood?" Jasmine asked.

"The flood came after they exhausted other methods. They used their mind control to create incredible myths and stories to make themselves appear even more fantastic than they were. And they used theology to shape human beliefs and behaviors and bring them closer to the state of the enlightened civilization they envisioned."

Jasmine snorted. "That must have been a big failure. Humans are still not civilized or enlightened. Well, most are not."

Amanda was surprised that Jasmine was not trying to refute what she was being told. There was none of the usual disbelief that most Dormants exhibited when first told the truth about their origins.

"I agree." Amanda sighed. "Too many are still barbarians, and regrettably, they have greater ability than ever to cause pain and destruction in their need to intimidate and dominate. But that's a discussion for another time. We are still in the distant past. Once contact with their home world was severed, the exiled gods realized that their limited numbers were not sufficient for genetic diversity and thus not viable for the continuation of their species, not to mention their urgent need to boost their numbers so they were less threatened by the exploding human populace." She leaned forward, her voice dropping to a conspiratorial whisper. "And that's another story that the Bible copied. The gods took human lovers and procreated with the very beings they had created to give rise to a new breed—the immortals."

Jasmine frowned. "The Bible said that those unions resulted in giants, not immortals."

Amanda was impressed. "You must have been raised religious to know those stories so well."

Jasmine shrugged. "Not more religious than most. I just liked the stories."

"You've probably read the English version, and as it happens all too often, things get lost in translation. In the original Hebrew version, the plural word used to describe the progeny of gods and humans was Anakim, and the singular was Anak. Do you know what other very famous ancient word sounds almost identical to Anak?"

Jasmine's brow furrowed. "No clue."

"Ankh," Amanda said. "The Ankh is one of the most important ancient

Egyptian symbols, representing life, vitality, and immortality, and it is often depicted in the hands of gods and goddesses, symbolizing their ability to grant eternal life. Coincidence? I think not."

"Oh, wow." Jasmine's eyes widened. "That's so cool. So Anakim meant immortals?"

"Indeed. The children born of unions between gods and humans were immortal and gifted with incredible abilities like enhanced strength, accelerated healing, and also the ability to manipulate human minds. But when the immortal descendants of the gods took human mates, their children were born mortal. As it turned out, the children born to female immortals with human males carried the dormant godly genes that could be activated, but the children born to immortal males and human females did not. From then on, those genes were passed on from a mother to her children, and from her daughters to their children, and so on."

Amanda paused to take another sip of her coffee and give Jasmine a few moments to process what she had learned so far.

Since she was not freaking out or trying to refute what she was being told, Amanda didn't mind her asking questions during the telling.

Jasmine frowned. "So technically, there could be many humans who carry those godly genes."

Amanda nodded.

"What happened to the gods?" Jasmine asked.

"Their fate wasn't good." Amanda put her coffee cup down. "There was a dispute, and one god found a way to kill the others with a weapon that originated in their home world. Almost all died, including the assassin."

"Almost all?" Jasmine asked. "Meaning that there are still gods living among us?"

Syssi chuckled. "You are taking this incredibly well. When I first heard this story, I couldn't believe it."

Jasmine's gaze swept over Edgar, Kian, Amanda, and then landed on Syssi. "I'm a practicing Wiccan. I have no problem with believing in gods and immortals' magic and mind manipulation. And I'm also starting to understand what is going on here. Kevin didn't use hypnosis on Modana and his men. He used mind control."

"Bravo." Kian clapped. "I'm impressed."

"Thank you." Jasmine dipped her head. "So Kevin is an immortal, and so are the four of you?" She leveled her gaze at Edgar.

He nodded. "Guilty as charged."

Letting out a breath, Jasmine closed her eyes. "So, that's why everyone looks young and gorgeous. This ship is full of immortals, and you have a staff of humans serving you who are mind-controlled to keep your identities a secret."

She opened her eyes. "Talk about mind blown. This would make one hell of a blockbuster movie."

"That will never happen," Kian said sternly. "It is essential that humans don't know about us."

"Then why are you telling me?"

Amanda smiled. "Because, my darling, we think that you are a carrier of godly genes that can be activated. There is a chance that you can become an immortal. And there is also the issue of your obsession with meeting a prince."

Jasmine shook her head. "Now you've lost me. Why do you think I have these genes, and what does my obsession have to do with anything?"

"Do you remember the testing I did?"

Jasmine winced. "I didn't do so well."

Amanda laughed. "On purpose. I know. I found a way to test you without your knowledge, and you definitely have paranormal abilities. Telepathy for sure, and maybe also precognition. Paranormal abilities are one of the strongest indicators of godly genes. The second one is affinity." Amanda leaned toward her. "That's a little more difficult to quantify, but let me ask you this, did you always feel like you were different and didn't belong?"

Jasmine nodded.

"And when you met Margo, did you immediately feel like the two of you could be best friends?"

Jasmine nodded again.

"Then you met Frankie and Mia, Syssi and me. Did you feel more comfortable with us than you did with anyone before?"

"That's affinity?"

Amanda nodded. "Like recognizes like. Dormants and immortals are drawn to each other, and so are Dormants and other Dormants."

"I'll be damned." Jasmine slumped against the couch cushions. "I can turn immortal? How, though? Is there a blood transfusion involved, gene therapy?"

"Venom and seed," Amanda said. "And Edgar can supply both, but he needs your permission to do so first. We try not to induce anyone without getting their informed consent. Sometimes it happens by chance, but we try to do it the right way when we can."

Jasmine shifted her gaze to Edgar. "You have my consent. Whatever it takes, I'm game. I want to be immortal, and I want to be part of this world." She shook her head again. "This is so much bigger than getting a job at Perfect Match."

Kian chuckled. "I would say. But we are not there yet. We need to talk to you about the prince."

Jasmine once again glanced at Edgar before shifting her gaze back to Kian. "What about it?"

241

"We are looking for a lost prince," Amanda said. "We think that you can help us find him." She turned to Syssi. "Do you want to take over from here?"

Syssi nodded, and as Jasmine turned to look at her, she smiled. "I get visions sometimes. They are mostly vague and often unpleasant, but in one way or another, they always come true. I had a vision about you helping us find the prince or, rather, the royal twins. A brother and sister landed on Earth in an escape pod when their ship exploded. The pod is lost somewhere, but the people inside might still be alive. They have a type of life support that we call stasis, and they can stay in that state for a very long time."

"How long ago did the escape pod land?" Jasmine asked.

"More than a hundred years ago," Kian said. "But the life support can go on indefinitely, or as long as the pod is not too damaged."

"Poor people." Jasmine swallowed. "Naturally, I'm willing to assist in any way I can to locate them, but I'm not sure how."

"I'm not sure either," Syssi said. "But you have a connection to the prince, and in my vision, I saw you standing over a crater and looking down at a pod, and you were not alone. You were with Negal, Dagor, and Aru. Did Margo tell you about her plans after the cruise?"

Jasmine shook her head. "How is she connected to this? And what have I to do with her and Frankie's boyfriends?"

Amanda was once again impressed with Jasmine's levelheaded response. "Margo is mated to Negal, who along with Dagor and Aru are on a quest to find the royal twins and other escape pods from the destroyed ship."

Edgar emitted a low growl. "The hell Jasmine is going after some Kra-ell prince," he snarled, his eyes glowing. "Those twins are rumored to be extremely powerful, and no one knows anything about them. They might be evil, twisted beings."

Kian shot him a warning glare. "Let Jasmine absorb what she's learned so far and come to terms with the truth of who she is and what she's capable of. We will discuss safety precautions later."

Syssi leaned over and put a hand on Jasmine's knee. "Your prince is not necessarily your romantic partner. Sometimes, the most important relationships in our lives are the ones we least expect. The prince could be your mentor or your spiritual leader. It could also be that you need to find him not for your personal benefit but for altruistic reasons. The universe works in mysterious ways and uses different methods of delivering its messages. The same way I'm used as a conduit for some things, you might be used as a conduit for others."

Across from them, Edgar relaxed, his aggressive energy subsiding.

Jasmine let out a breath. "I'm ashamed to admit that I've never considered the possibility that I was shown the prince for altruistic reasons. At first, I was focused on finding my dream guy, and when the cards kept showing me the prince, I was convinced that I was destined to meet one." She looked at Edgar. "But then I met you, and I tried to give it a different spin. I reasoned that the prince was a metaphor for a good man and that you might be the one I was supposed to find. My prince."

Ed chuckled. "I'm afraid that I will always remain a frog, but I don't mind if you keep kissing me in the hopes of turning me into a prince."

ARU

"Good morning, Master Aru," Kian's servant bowed. "Please, come in."

Aru forced a smile, not for the Odu's sake but for its owner. Kian was very fond of his servant, and so was the princess of hers, so Aru was doing his best to get over his aversion to them, but it wasn't easy.

Being wary of them had been hardwired into his psyche.

"Thank you for coming." Kian motioned for him to sit down on the armchair next to his.

Aru glanced at Jasmine and Edgar, who were huddled together on the couch. The woman looked pale but not as shell-shocked as he had expected to find her. Perhaps it was the pilot's reassuring arm around her shoulders and the way he looked at her that was easing her into her new reality.

She must feel like the ground had been yanked out from under her, and everything she thought she knew about the world had been turned on its head. Edgar's presence was probably the only solid thing she could tether herself to.

Given how Jasmine was clinging to the guy, Aru had a feeling that they would need to include the pilot in their expedition, and he hoped that Kian would be willing to spare him. Perhaps they could even use Edgar's services on the trail. Renting a helicopter or buying one in Tibet would eat up a large chunk of the team's remaining budget, but it might shorten the duration of the search.

Well, that was provided that the tip they had gotten about strange energy signatures in Tibet was true, and they weren't going on a wild goose chase. The equipment they had at their disposal couldn't verify the claim from across the globe or even from several miles away. They couldn't be much farther than a mile from the pod for the energy to register on their equipment.

If the pod was still sustaining life after thousands of years, its energy read-outs would likely be minimal and possibly critically so.

The truth was that he was basing the expedition to Tibet on a source as unreliable as Jasmine's tarot cards or crystal readings or whatever else she was using for her divinations. What Syssi had seen in her vision was the best clue he had gotten so far, but the mountaintop she'd seen could have been located anywhere, not just in Tibet.

Aru turned to Kian. "I still think that basing the search on tarot cards is questionable, but I know better than to doubt a seer. Besides, it could be that the vision and the tarot were not just about Jasmine but about Edgar as well. Perhaps the success of the mission depends on us having a helicopter and a pilot at our disposal."

Edgar grinned. "That's right. It could be all about me."

Amanda rolled her eyes. "Males. They always think that the world revolves around them."

Kian chuckled. "The smart ones know the truth."

"I was just joking," Edgar said. "I would love to accompany the team to Tibet. Never been there."

Aru was glad that the pilot was willing to join them, but he still needed to convince Kian to approve it and perhaps help with the cost of acquiring a helicopter. "Edgar flying us from one point to another would be extremely beneficial, especially now that we will need to accommodate Jasmine, who won't be able to keep up. We will need to get organized better, perhaps hire locals with pack animals so as not to exhaust her. Margo and Frankie are also not at full capacity yet while they are recuperating from their transitions, so they would need frequent rests as well."

"Their what?" Jasmine untangled herself from Edgar's arm. "What are you talking about?"

Had no one told her that her friends had transitioned into immortality?

Come to think of it, she probably didn't know that Aru was more than an immortal either.

Amanda leaned closer to Jasmine. "Remember what I told you about Dormants and that there is a way to activate their dormant genes?"

Jasmine nodded.

"Frankie and Margo were both activated. Margo doesn't have the flu. She is transitioning. And Frankie did the same thing a couple of days before her."

Jasmine slumped, her back resting on Edgar's chest. "That explains so much. What about Mia?"

"She did that a while ago," Syssi said. "But since she's re-growing her legs, she is still wheelchair-bound. Not for long, though. She's almost done."

"Unbelievable." Jasmine pinched her arm. "Ouch. That hurt, so I'm not dreaming."

Amanda laughed. "That's not a conclusive test. You could be dreaming about pinching yourself and experiencing pain."

"But I'm not dreaming, right?"

Amanda's eyes gleamed with amusement. "If I say that you aren't, does it mean that you are not?"

Kian lifted his hand. "Please, ladies. This can go on forever, and we have things that we need to settle." He turned to Aru. "You were saying?"

"I was saying that we can use a helicopter and a pilot, and Edgar here is perfect for the job. The problem is resources." Aru scratched his head. "Perhaps we can buy a helicopter and then sell it after the mission is done. The delta between the purchase and subsequent sale price of the craft shouldn't be too prohibitive."

"Don't worry about the money," Kian said. "The clan can help, and so can Toven. He would do anything for Mia, who wants her friends back as soon as possible, and in every meaningful way, Toven commands unlimited resources, some of which he will gladly extend to acquire means of faster travel."

Aru had hoped that would be Kian's answer. "Thank you." He glanced back at Jasmine, surprised to see the confident woman suddenly looking as if she was starting to fall apart.

Everyone had their breaking point, and evidently, Jasmine had reached hers.

Following his gaze, Amanda looked at her and frowned. "What's the matter, darling? What got you upset?"

"I'm just overwhelmed." She lifted a trembling hand to her lips. "It started like a pleasant drizzle and then turned into a deluge that's threatening to drown me."

Amanda smiled. "It's understandable. You've been incredibly open-minded about all of this, but it's a lot to take in, and we dumped all of it on you in one go. The best way to tackle something so big is to break it down into smaller, more manageable chunks."

JASMINE

More manageable chunks. That was good advice. Jasmine didn't need to absorb and understand everything all at once. She should address one problem, or rather one issue at a time.

"So, let me get it straight." She looked at Kian. "You want me to travel with a team of immortals to Tibet to help them find a life pod that contains two aliens who are royal twins because you think that one of them is the prince my divining keeps pointing to."

Kian grimaced. "When put like that, it sounds ridiculous, but I've learned to trust Syssi's visions. So yeah. That's what we want you to do, and we will pay you for your trouble, but it is up to you. We are not forcing you to do anything you don't want."

That was what Jasmine had thought. It seemed that Kian was implying they wouldn't activate her dormant godly genes unless she cooperated with them.

"So, my payment is the chance at immortality?"

Kian looked like she had slapped him and offended his mother. "Of course not. One has nothing to do with the other. In fact, you shouldn't attempt transition until after the mission because you don't want to become incapacitated while trekking through unpopulated areas. I was talking about monetary compensation. I'll double whatever you are paid at your current job."

He sounded truthful, and since Jasmine hadn't gotten the impression that he was a good actor or even a decent one, she was inclined to believe him.

"How is the transition induced?" she asked.

"I will tell you later." Edgar pulled her closer to him. "In private."

She turned to him. "Does it hurt?"

He shook his head. "Getting there is the most pleasant experience, but the transition itself is not easy. It can even be dangerous. That's why it is not advisable to attempt it away from our experienced medical staff and a well-equipped clinic."

Given how husky Edgar sounded and that he didn't want to explain how it was done in front of the others, the induction had something to do with sex.

"So?" Kian asked. "Is it a yes?"

"Say yes," Edgar said next to her ear. "It's going to be one hell of an adventure. Besides, you can't go back home or to your job until we are sure that the cartel is not looking for you. Instead of spending weeks in some hotel or a safe house, you could be touring Tibet."

Jasmine smiled. "When you put it like that, I have to say yes."

"Welcome aboard," Aru said. "The way I expect it to work is for Edgar to drop us off at the designated location, and while we continue on foot, he will head to the next refueling station. You'll be able to see each other probably every night but not throughout the whole day."

That was disappointing but not a deal breaker.

Jasmine turned to look at Edgar. "Is that okay with you?"

"I figured that's how it would have to work."

Aru leaned forward, his nearly black eyes fixed on Jasmine with a piercing, penetrating intensity. "I'm not clear on all the details yet, but we also might leave the other ladies with Edgar to watch over them while you, my teammates, and I trek through the mountains. To cover ground quickly and efficiently, we can't be weighed down by excess baggage, and hauling supplies for four is much easier than for seven."

Jasmine let out a breath. "Contrary to the impression I give, I'm not a spoiled brat. I don't need a suitcase full of clothes and makeup. But I'm not a fan of camping, meaning sleeping on the ground where all kinds of creepy-crawlies can get into my sleeping bag."

Aru smiled. "By the end of each day, we will try to reach a spot where Edgar can land and collect us. So, most of the time, we sleep in hotels and inns. But occasionally, we will have to sleep on the ground. We will get a small, fully enclosed tent for you so no bugs can get into your sleeping bag."

"Thank you." She dipped her head. "That also covers my next concern which was keeping clean. I can go without a shower for a couple of days, but more than that, I feel gross."

Syssi laughed softly. "If I were you, I would be concerned with wild animals and bandits, not bugs and showers, although those are not negligible concerns either."

Jasmine grimaced. "Thanks for pointing that out to me."

"You have nothing to worry about in that regard," Aru promised. "My teammates and I can take care of any danger we are faced with."

"Right." Jasmine smiled at him. "The mind control. You can get into the minds of humans and other beasts."

He nodded, but given the spark in his dark eyes, she had a feeling that mind control wasn't the only tool at his disposal.

"I still don't get how I'm supposed to help you," Jasmine said. "Will I be required to consult my tarots and my crystals on a daily basis?"

Aru's expression turned speculative. "I don't expect your divination to work like a scrying stick, but I will probably ask you to consult your divining tools to give us a general sense of where we need to go."

Jasmine pursed her lips. "Actually, a scrying stick is not a bad idea. My divining tools are just conduits for the energy that's already inside of me, and if I channel my energy into a scrying stick and ask the goddess to help me, it might point us in the right direction." She sat up straighter. "I can even make one myself and infuse it with my energy and intention."

Excitement thrumming through her, Jasmine was ready for this new adventure. Deep in her bones and in her very soul, she'd always known that her mundane life was just a prelude for something much greater. But unlike what she'd believed before shooting down this incredible rabbit hole, that something wasn't a Broadway stage or a Hollywood movie set.

She was a descendant of gods, and she was destined for greatness.

TWIN DESTINIES

1

KIAN

K ian leaned back in the plush limo seat. "I don't know about you, but I'm glad to be back on solid ground."

"I'm so happy to go home," Syssi murmured, keeping her voice low so as not to disturb their sleeping daughter.

Allegra was nestled in her car seat between them, the soft, steady vibration of the car and the muted whoosh of the tires against the pavement lulling her to sleep. She was dreaming, her lashes fluttering against her cherubic cheeks and her sweet rosebud lips moving as if she was sucking on a pacifier even though she hadn't had one for a while now.

Kian wanted to lean down and kiss her upturned little nose, fluttering eyelids, or even just her tiny fingers, but he knew better than to rouse his daughter. It was best to let her sleep and wake up naturally.

Across from them, Annani sat flanked by her Odus, her gaze on her grand-daughter and her lips upturned in a soft smile. "I adore this little spitfire," she said quietly before shifting her eyes to Kian. "I am surprised that Okidu agreed to relinquish control of the limousine to Anandur."

"I didn't give him a choice. My penthouse is already full, and I needed him to open Amanda's penthouse for the other two couples."

Coordinating the safe and discreet departure of so many people from the ship was a feat of logistical planning.

Shai and Bridget had worked to arrange most of the details, ensuring that clan members would not travel in large groups to the same destinations. That would have attracted unwanted attention, which needed to be avoided under normal circumstances and doubly so now, when there was a chance that members of the Brotherhood might be waiting for them to follow them back to their strongholds.

Thankfully, that didn't seem to be the case, but Kian didn't regret going the extra step to secure his people. For a change, Sari had agreed to follow the safety protocol without grumbling about him being paranoid.

She and her people were en route to the airport, their flights booked to different European cities before they eventually returned to Edinburgh. There, nondescript vehicles had been parked in prearranged locations scattered throughout the city, allowing them to slip back into their lives with minimal fuss.

The Alaskan contingent took similar precautions before arriving at several private airports in Alaska. They were later picked up by Oshidu, who had stayed behind in the sanctuary to fly them back home.

The last piece of the puzzle was the rescued women, who had been collected by bus to take them to Ojai. Kian authorized the temporary lifting of the village lockdown so Vanessa could leave and make the necessary arrangements for them.

So far, everything seemed to be working like a well-oiled machine, and Kian was slowly relaxing his death grip on the phone.

No calls meant no trouble, and the further the limo got from the port, the more he allowed himself to relax.

The cruise was supposed to have been a respite from his stressful life, but instead of ten days of celebrations, he had acquired new worries.

It was all good.

The Fates demanded recompense for the many blessings they had bestowed on the clan, and he was glad to pay the toll, especially when it involved rescuing a group of women from a fate worse than death and eliminating the maggots who had committed unimaginable acts of cruelty against defenseless villagers.

Still, it had been a most troubling surprise to find out that the Doomers were working with the Mexican drug cartels. By rescuing the women and destroying the Doomer team that had been responsible for the massacre, the clan had poked the hornets' nest.

All the civilians and most of the Guardians were safely on their way home, but he was worried about the human staff and the few Guardians who had remained behind to protect them.

Once they were done cleaning up and preparing the ship for her next journey, they would also be on their way, and Kian would finally allow himself to relax fully.

Still, despite the unexpected trouble and the stress, the cruise had been a great success in terms of its stated purpose. It had provided a safe environment for his clan to gather and celebrate the eternal bond between ten couples.

It had been a little too long, though, and Kian was happy to be heading home.

2

JASMINE

"It's so annoying." Jasmine took Edgar's hand as she stepped out of the taxi in front of the keep. "My sea legs are reluctant to adjust back to solid ground, and I'm still wobbling."

After days of gentle sways and the rhythmic rolling of the cruise ship, her first few steps on firm ground had been unsteady. However, the sensation of floating had started to dissipate as she entered the taxi, and she had thought that she was over her sea legs.

Not so. Evidently, her body needed more time to adjust.

Edgar pulled their suitcases from the trunk, put them down on the sidewalk, and wrapped an arm around her middle. "If you feel dizzy, lean on me."

"It's not that bad." She smiled up at him. "But I don't mind leaning on you." She kissed his cheek and then looked up at the imposing high-rises on both sides of the street. "Those look like office buildings. I never would have guessed that there are residences inside."

"Good observation," Edgar said. "Many of them used to be office buildings, but there is less demand for office space these days than for apartments, so they were converted." He leaned to whisper in her ear, "It's easy to get permits for a change of use when you can manipulate the minds of bureaucrats and alter city records."

It took a moment for Edgar's words to sink in, and when they did, she gaped at him. "Are you serious? All these buildings belong to your people?"

"Most of them."

No wonder they had so much money to spend on cruise ships and lavish weddings. These buildings would be worth a king's ransom.

Despite living in Los Angeles for years, Jasmine had never been to this area of downtown before, and as she and Edgar waited on the sidewalk for the other two taxis to arrive, she took the time to look over the broad boulevard. Well-tended trees adorned the sidewalks, and everything was spotless, as if it had been cleaned that morning. There were no homeless encampments like in so many other areas of the city, but then it was easy for the immortals to keep them away.

The ability to manipulate human minds was very convenient.

Jasmine was still trying to wrap her head around the fact that she was surrounded by immortals who were the descendants of gods and that her immortal lover had fangs and venom, which provided the best orgasms and psychedelic trips, and the secondary effects were improved health and vitality.

Her life had definitely taken a turn straight into *The Twilight Zone*, and the immortals weren't even the strangest part of it. Turned out that her tarot cards had been guiding her toward an alien prince who belonged to a people named the Kra-ell, and she was supposed to direct the immortals to where his pod had crashed.

It felt like she was living in a movie.

It wasn't what Jasmine had dreamt of when she'd imagined a career in Hollywood, but maybe that was where her life had been leading her all along.

When the other two taxis pulled up to the curb and the rest of their team got out, the nine of them headed inside the building.

As Kian's butler led their group toward the security desk, Jasmine took in the sprawling lobby with its high ceilings, sparse groupings of seating, and the café at the far end. "I like the minimalistic decor. It looks so elegant."

"Wait until you see the penthouse," Gabi whispered in her ear as they followed the butler past security and into the elevator. "It's stunning."

Margo and Frankie exchanged excited smiles and clasped each other's hands like schoolgirls on an outing.

They were adorable.

The elevator shot up, and when the doors opened on the penthouse level, and Jasmine took in the opulent vestibule, she squeezed Edgar's hand with as much excitement as Margo and Frankie had exhibited moments before.

It was like a miniature of the lobby in the Venetian hotel in Las Vegas, but instead of everything being made from painted plaster, the columns, the mosaic floor, and the mural on the ceiling were all authentic. This was just the vestibule, which was a fancy name for an entry hallway.

A round granite table dominated the center of the space, its polished surface reflecting the intricate mosaic patterns inlaid in the marble floor. On top of it was an enormous vase overflowing with vibrant fresh flowers.

Kian's butler opened one of the two sets of doors. "This used to be Master

Kian's residence, and across the vestibule is what used to be Mistress Amanda's penthouse apartment. The penthouses were leased out until quite recently," the butler explained. "Fortunately, both leases ended in time for Master Kian and Mistress Amanda to make them available for your use during your stay in the city." He smiled conspiratorially. "The previous tenant was a Saudi prince with four wives and numerous children."

Jasmine's curiosity was piqued. "A prince?"

The strange-looking butler smiled indulgently. "I was told that there are many Saudi princes. I do not know how important the one who stayed here was."

Jasmine nodded, trying to look unimpressed but failing. As she followed the butler and the others, her breath caught in her throat the moment she crossed the threshold into a world of luxury.

The first thing that struck her was the wall of floor-to-ceiling windows directly opposite the entryway, offering a breathtaking panorama of the city skyline. The view was spectacular, with the countless skyscrapers stretching as far as the eye could see.

The expanse of glass opened onto a sprawling rooftop terrace, where Jasmine could make out the shimmering surface of a long, narrow lap pool flanked by an array of stylish lounge furniture bordered by lush, meticulously manicured greenery.

The living room was designed in a contemporary style, blending sophistication and comfort perfectly. A trio of espresso-colored leather sofas surrounded a massive stone coffee table, its rough-hewn edges strikingly contrasting with the smooth, sleek lines of the seating.

Beneath her feet, the rich hues of the hardwood floor were softened by a vibrant area rug with a bold abstract pattern that provided a pop of color to the otherwise neutral palette. Like the floor, the walls were adorned with vivid large-scale artwork.

A contemporary fireplace anchored one end of the room, its clean lines and minimalist aesthetic a perfect complement to the oversized screen mounted above it. Large vases had been placed in strategic spots, brimming with fragrant blooms and beautiful colors to enliven the space.

Jasmine had no doubt that a professional had created the ambiance, and a crew of caretakers ensured that the building was properly maintained.

For a moment, she allowed herself to imagine living in a place like this, waking up every morning to that incredible view, spending lazy afternoons lounging by the pool, and hosting intimate gatherings with friends in the chic living room.

It was the kind of life she'd dreamt of when she had still allowed herself to fantasize about making it big in Hollywood. But as the years passed, that dream had seemed farther and farther out of reach, and now that she was about to embark on a new chapter in her life, that future would probably never come to pass.

Jasmine was still coming to terms with the incredible revelations of the past few days—the possibility of her turning immortal, her role in the search for the Kra-ell royal twins, and the budding relationship with Edgar.

It was all so much to process.

If she could have her way, she would stay in this opulent penthouse, living the life of the rich and famous and enjoying herself with the handsome pilot.

She didn't relish the prospect of leaving all this comfort to embark on a journey to Tibet, but what choice did she have?

She was only here because their group needed a place to prepare for their departure.

Edgar must have sensed her unease and tightened his fingers around hers. "Are you okay?"

She nodded. "It's a little overwhelming. I've never stayed in a place this fancy before. Even the presidential suite in the hotel in Cabo that Alberto put me in wasn't this high-end." She turned to Margo. "Am I right?"

Her friend was just as wide-eyed as she was. "No. It wasn't. The suite in Cabo was trying to look like this, but this is the real deal." She turned to Aru. "How rich is the clan?"

"I don't know," he admitted. "What I do know is that Toven is rich beyond measure. He's probably the richest person on the planet, and no one knows it."

"That makes sense." Margo leaned on Negal's arm. "He always acts as if money is no object."

"He does," Aru confirmed. "He's buying us a brand-new helicopter." He glanced at Edgar. "Do you know which model he's getting?"

Edgar shrugged. "I made a few recommendations, but it depends on what he can get locally. China controls Tibet, so nothing is easy to get over there."

Negal leaned down and smirked at Margo. "Do you want to see where we are going to sleep?"

Dagor cleared his throat. "About that. One of us needs to go across the vestibule to the other penthouse." He pulled a coin from his pocket. "Do you want to flip for it?"

Negal pursed his lips. "No need. You and Frankie can have this one. Margo and I will go with Jasmine and Edgar to the other one."

The butler dipped his head. "Very well. Please, follow me." He started to walk toward the door.

As Jasmine and Edgar followed the butler, she told herself this was only a temporary respite before the true adventure began. But that didn't mean she couldn't savor it and commit everything to memory, which reminded her that she still didn't have a phone and needed one as soon as possible.

"Can we go shopping?" she asked Edgar. "I need to get a new phone."

3

EDGAR

Edgar shook his head. "You can't just go out and buy a phone. You need to get a special-issue satellite clan phone that works anywhere globally."

There was still so much that Jasmine didn't know, and the type of phone she could or couldn't use was just the tip of the iceberg.

She had no clue that Aru and his teammates were not mere immortals but gods and that they had been sent from the distant planet of the gods to search for the missing Kra-ell pods. They had also been tasked with finding out whether any of the exiled gods or their descendants had survived after the bombing that had killed almost all of them five thousand years ago, but that was not something that she needed to know.

Or so he thought.

No one had told him what he was allowed to tell her, and Edgar wasn't taking any chances.

The question was whether he should wait until tomorrow for Kian's visit or find a quiet spot and call Onegus for guidance.

"You can use mine until you get a new one," Frankie offered, then frowned. "Now that I'm immortal, will the restriction on who I can call get removed?"

Dagor pursed his lips. "I hope so. William probably can do that remotely."

The butler cleared his throat, reminding them he was waiting by the door to show them the other penthouse.

Margo leaned to plant a quick peck on Frankie's cheek. "We will just put our things in our bedroom and return here." She looked at the outdoor terrace. "Maybe we can have coffee and tea out there."

Frankie grinned. "I'll get the coffee going."

"I'm curious about the other penthouse." Gabi glanced at Frankie. "Don't you want to see it?"

"On second thought, I do." Frankie threaded her arm through Dagor's and led him toward the door.

As they followed Okidu out of Kian's penthouse and across the vestibule to Amanda's residence, Edgar tried to remember if he had ever seen Amanda's penthouse. He'd been to Kian's place a few times while they had all still lived in the keep, but Amanda had her own place back then, a condo near the university, and she'd rarely stayed at her penthouse apartment in the keep.

As he'd expected, the layout was nearly identical, a mirror image of Kian's, but the decor had a distinctly feminine touch. Where Kian's apartment had been all sleek lines and masculine hues, Amanda's was softer, the colors more inviting, and many plush throw pillows were strewn over the couches.

Okidu led them through the space, highlighting the various amenities and features. The fridge and the pantry were well stocked, reinforcing Ed's assumption that a crew had been sent to prepare the penthouses.

"Dibs on the master bedroom," Margo called from down the hallway.

Jasmine frowned. "Shouldn't we flip for it?"

Edgar chuckled. "They have priority. Negal was here first." And he was a god, but that revelation was still pending. "Besides, we are only staying here a couple of nights, so it doesn't matter."

"Right." Jasmine pouted. "I would like to bask in the luxury a little longer than that."

When Okidu opened the door to the guest suite, Jasmine walked in and nodded in appreciation. "This is very nice."

The centerpiece was a massive king-sized bed piled high with fluffy pillows and draped in sumptuous linens. Floor-to-ceiling windows offered a view of the city skyline, and a small sitting area was strategically placed to take advantage of the view.

"Look at this." Jasmine walked into the closet. "This is bigger than my entire apartment."

Edgar rolled their suitcases inside and left them near the door. "I don't think we should unpack. We are not staying long enough."

"Of course we should." Jasmine walked over to a bank of drawers and started pulling them out one at a time. "Most of my things are unsuitable for trekking in the Himalayas. I will need to go shopping." She turned to look at him. "Who is going to pay for that, and can I leave my stuff here?"

"I don't know the answers to either of your questions." Edgar rubbed a hand over the back of his neck. "Kian will stop by tomorrow, and you can ask him about it. We can store our stuff in the underground facility if he wants to lease out this place again. "

"There is an underground facility?"

He might have said too much. "Yeah. Storage."

With a doubtful glance in his direction, Jasmine walked out of the closet. "I want to see the primary bedroom. I can only imagine how much more luxurious it is."

"Sure. I want to see it, too." He'd only seen Kian's living and dining rooms and had never seen the bedrooms.

Jasmine knocked on the master's open door before walking in. "Is everyone decent? Edgar and I want a tour."

Margo emerged from what Edgar guessed was the bathroom and waved them inside. "You've got to see this."

As Jasmine hurried to join her friend, Edgar stayed in the master bedroom and walked over to the glass sliding doors that opened to the terrace. The lap pool was calling to him, and he resolved to use it at least once before they shipped out.

Who knew how long this expedition was going to last?

It might be months before he got a chance to swim again.

4

KIAN

As the limousine's windows turned opaque a few miles before the entrance to the tunnel, Syssi's soft sigh drew Kian's attention.

"Part of me wishes we could just live on the *Silver Swan*," she said quietly because Allegra was still sleeping. "It was so nice to be with our family and friends, and we enjoyed spending time together."

Leaning over, Kian pressed a kiss to her temple. "Sometimes, I fantasize about moving the entire clan permanently to a cruise ship. But we would need a much larger one for that." He smiled. "Perhaps we can purchase a decommissioned aircraft carrier. Those things are the size of a city. We could remodel it to include gardens and all the other amenities we have in the village."

Syssi chuckled. "As if you don't have enough on your plate already. Besides, I don't want to live in a floating city, and the Kra-ell even less so. Just try mentioning another sea voyage to them and see their reaction. I think they would be less horrified about boarding a spaceship bound for Mars."

Kian didn't laugh. "I wouldn't mind settling on Mars. No Brotherhood and no threat from the Eternal King. Just our people finally living in peace."

Across from him, his mother smiled knowingly. "Without adversity, you would not know what to do with yourself, my son."

"Not true. I might finally have time to read all the books on my wish list."

Syssi cast him a skeptical look. "I love reading, but I can't imagine doing only that for the rest of our never-ending lives. Let's talk about sunnier topics, though. Jin and Arwel's wedding was a great finale to the cruise. For some reason, it was more boisterous than all the other weddings."

"The reason is obvious." Kian chuckled. "Everyone was overjoyed that it was the last one. Don't get me wrong, I love weddings, but this was like overdosing on too much of a good thing. After the marathon of ceremonies, I need a break."

Syssi patted his arm. "There's a long list of couples eager to tie the knot on the next cruise, so your respite is not going to last."

Kian groaned. "I need at least a year before we go on another sea voyage, and my new rule will be no more than two weddings per cruise."

Annani nodded, her eyes sparkling with mirth. "We will have to convince the other couples to have their parties in the village square, Sari's castle, or in my sanctuary. I think that my sanctuary is the most beautiful venue, and all future weddings should be held there."

Kian arched a brow. "And where will you house everyone? You don't have enough room to host the entire clan."

Annani shrugged. "We can always build an annex to the existing structure."

It was more challenging than she made it sound, but it was doable, and Kian liked the idea of having a well-hidden escape location that could house all of their people.

He wouldn't want to live there full-time, but having the option appealed to him, especially since the keep had been compromised. They were still using it and would probably continue until it became clear that it was too risky. Hopefully, it wouldn't come to that because moving the crypt would be a nightmare.

The gods and their mates were heading to his old penthouse in the keep, and Okidu was with them to open up Amanda's. There were only three bedrooms in each, and he needed rooms for four couples as Jasmine and Edgar were with them. They wouldn't be staying there long, but they needed a few days to organize everything for the Tibet trip.

Tomorrow, Kian planned to meet with Aru to discuss the expedition's logistics. The possible retrieval of the Kra-ell royal twins was a mission of paramount importance. If they were as powerful as the Eternal King feared, having them as allies could tip the balance of power in the clan's struggle against the Doomers and later against the king.

The bewildering part was that, somehow, the key to it all was Jasmine. Kian still had doubts about relying so heavily on divination and visions to guide the gods on their quest. His pragmatic nature rebelled against having so much faith in the intangible and unquantifiable, but he implicitly trusted his mate's visions.

Syssi's gift had proven invaluable and infallible time and again. If she believed that Jasmine was the linchpin to unlocking the secrets of the royal twins' whereabouts, then Kian would follow that path without hesitation.

5

MARINA

Marina felt drowsy as the bus rumbled down the highway towards Safe Haven. Leaning into Peter's embrace, she savored the warmth of his body and the comforting feel of his arm around her shoulders.

About an hour and a half had passed since they had boarded the bus at the port, which meant twelve more on the road, but with Peter right there with her, she didn't mind the long ride. Besides, a luxury bus with all the amenities on board was a good way to travel.

Onegus had approved Peter's request to accompany her to Safe Haven and be part of a team of Guardians who would be on duty there for the next two weeks.

Regrettably, Jay was not one of those Guardians, and Larissa hadn't taken the separation well. She'd been sniffling softly from the moment she and Jay had said their goodbyes, and since she was sitting in the row behind them, Marina couldn't help but hear the pitiful sounds, and her heart was twisting with sympathy for her friend.

Jay had promised to visit Larissa in Safe Haven, but Marina knew the likelihood of that happening was slim. Jay's promise had been meant to offer temporary comfort but held little weight. He wasn't coming, and Larissa knew it.

Guilt nibbled at the edges of Marina's happiness, a nagging sense that her joy was somehow an affront to Larissa's pain. She knew it was irrational and that her friend would not begrudge her the love she'd found with Peter, but the feeling persisted nonetheless.

Peter tightened his hold around her and drew her closer to his side. "What's on your mind, love?" he murmured, his breath warm against her ear.

Marina sighed. "I was just thinking about Larissa," she whispered to avoid being overheard. "She's hurting, and I feel guilty for being so happy when she's not."

"It's not your fault that things didn't work out as well for them as they did for us." He kissed the top of her head. "It just wasn't meant to be."

She and Peter weren't destined for each other either, but Marina wouldn't say that out loud. They were both pretending they didn't care about the future, and as long as Marina maintained that conviction, she was happy. The problem was that it was difficult to cling to a fallacy.

She rested her head on Peter's shoulder. "I just wish there was something I could do to help her." She lifted her head and looked into his warm, brown eyes. "What about the Guardians that came with us? Maybe you could introduce Larissa to one of them."

"I can do that, but let's not rush things. It's too early."

He might be right. Before starting a new one, Larissa needed to grieve the end of her relationship with Jay, no matter how brief it had been. On second thought, though, perhaps she shouldn't date any more immortals. Nothing good would come out of it, and she was probably better off finding a nice human to settle down with.

The problem was finding such a guy in Safe Haven—the bastion of free love and no committed relationships. They had been told about the community's structure before voting between settling there or in the village, but Marina hadn't given the particulars much thought.

She'd been sure that her partner would come from her community because that was how things had worked in the Kra-ell compound. However, she hadn't factored in the new liberties that allowed the import of new partners from the outside, especially the universities that some of the human offspring of the Kra-ell hybrids were attending, the way her ex-boyfriend had.

"Tell me about your lodging in Safe Haven." Peter changed the subject. "Do you have enough room for me?"

"Not really. Larissa and I share a small room that is only a little larger than the cabin we shared on the ship." Marina sighed. "Maybe I could alternate shifts with her, so you and I can be together when she's working."

Peter shook his head. "I'll get us a place of our own. They had a bunch of small bungalows built for a project that got abandoned, and as far as I know, they haven't repurposed them yet." He leaned down and nuzzled her neck. "As long as there is a bed large enough for all the wicked things I want to do to you, I don't care how small the rest of the place is."

As images of what he would do to her flitted through Marina's mind, a tingle of desire coursed through her, but she quickly tamped it down. They were on a bus, surrounded by her coworkers, and would be stuck there for many more hours. "Won't our cohabiting weaken the prospects of my transfer request?" she asked. "You're not supposed to seem attached to me."

Peter chuckled, a confident grin spreading across his face. "Don't worry about that. Eleanor and Emmett owe me, and they'll work with us to ensure your transfer goes through smoothly. Besides, no one will bat an eyelash at my need to be alone with you."

Marina's curiosity was piqued.

Tilting her head to the side, she regarded him with a questioning gaze. "Why do they owe you?"

Peter's smile turned into a wince. "It's a long story that's a tale for another time."

Marina huffed, shaking her head in mock exasperation. "You're just full of secrets, aren't you?"

"It's not a secret, and I'll tell you all about it when we get there. It really is a long story."

She hoped that it didn't involve a history with Eleanor.

Marina knew that Eleanor and Emmett were a couple, but Peter could have been with her before she'd met Emmett.

So yeah, she was jealous of any relationship that Peter had ever had, but she felt entitled to her jealousy, even if it was irrational.

He belonged to her.

The depth of emotion that had grown between them in such a short time felt surreal, but Marina didn't doubt it anymore. Still, she couldn't help asking, "Just tell me if there was anything between Eleanor and you."

He chuckled softly. "It pleases me that you are jealous of me. To be perfectly honest, there was a smidgen of attraction when we had to work together as a team, but it never evolved into anything more, and Eleanor is now happily mated to Emmett."

"So, she never shared your bed?"

"She did not, and before you ask if I shared anything else with her, I assure you that we were never intimate."

"Good." Marina leaned her head against Peter's bicep.

As the bus wound its way along the coastal highway, the sprawling expanse of the Pacific Ocean stretching out before them, Marina felt a sense of peace wash over her. With the endless canvas of blue meeting the distant horizon and the rhythmic rumble of the engine lulling her to sleep, she closed her eyes and dozed off.

6

KIAN

Kian sat down in his executive chair, a broad smile spreading over his face as he savored the familiar comfort of his home office. A portrait of Syssi with Allegra in her arms hung over the couch across from his desk, painted with Dalhu's skilled hand from a favorite photograph Kian had taken of them. The wall to his left was mostly glass, the large sliding doors letting in the sun and the greenery of his backyard.

It felt good to be home.

After the cruise, with its endless parade of weddings and the constant socializing required of him, it was a relief to be back in his own space, surrounded by the trappings of his daily life.

The serenity wouldn't last long, though. He'd invited Jade to give him a report about everything notable that happened in the village during his absence, and she was due to arrive at any moment.

He enjoyed a few more minutes of peace before a knock sounded on the door.

"Come in," Kian called out.

The door opened, and Okidu poked his head inside. "Mistress Jade and Master Phinas are here."

That was a surprise. He hadn't invited Phinas but didn't mind Jade's mate tagging along.

"Show them in, please." Kian rose to his feet and walked over to greet them.

"Hello, boss." Phinas extended his hand. "It's good to have you back."

"It's good to be back." Kian shook both their hands. "Please, come in and take a seat."

Jade had her long dark hair pulled back in her customary ponytail, and she wore her customary black combat boots. She was dressed in all black, and so was her mate. Their boots were nearly identical, making them look like they served in the same unit, but they didn't. Phinas was Kalugal's lieutenant, and Jade was the leader of the Kra-ell.

"Welcome back, Kian," she said as they sat down, facing him across his desk. "I trust the cruise was a success?"

Kian nodded. "It was, thank you. It was more eventful than I would have liked, but we still managed to celebrate ten weddings, so the objective has been achieved."

Phinas chuckled. "Never a dull moment, eh?"

"I'm afraid so." Kian leaned forward to rest his elbows on the desk. "So, catch me up. How have things been in the village?"

Jade straightened in her seat. "Nothing to report security-wise. The lock-down was maintained per your instructions, and no suspicious activity was spotted around the village or the area leading to it."

"I'm glad to hear that," Kian said. "How is the community service of the Kra-ell pureblooded males going?"

On the way to his house, Kian had noticed the trimmed bushes on the village pathways and the new flowerbeds that had been planted.

Jade smiled. "I'm sure you've seen their handiwork. I keep them busy."

"That's good," he said. "How are the rest of your people doing?"

The smile slid off Jade's face. "They feel cooped up. Especially the pure-bloods. They need large areas to hunt in and to run free. The village is a nice little place—emphasis on the little. They need space to roam."

"Yeah. I get what you are saying. We promised them field trips, but we haven't done so yet. Please start organizing small groups."

Jade nodded. "I will. But where would they go hunting? It's not like there is much in the Malibu mountains besides coyotes."

"We can take them to the mountains around the cabin, but I don't know how much wildlife they will find there. Perhaps you and Kagra should scope out the area first. Just stay well away from the cabin itself. I have humans staying there now, and I don't know when they will go home."

Margo's family was in the cabin, and a contingent of human security was safeguarding them. The Kra-ell were too alien looking to go unnoticed, especially when they were traveling together.

"I'll check with Onegus about organizing transportation to the cabin area. I might take a couple more people with me, though."

"That's fine." He rapped his fingers on the desk. "Anything else that you want to discuss?"

"That's all for now."

Kian debated whether to tell Jade about Jasmine and the search for the pod containing the royal twins, but then decided against it. Much as he trusted Syssi's vision, it might take a long time until it became a reality, and until then, there was no reason to share it with Jade. He would tell her once there was something to tell.

"Very well. Thank you both for safeguarding the village in our absence."

"It was the least we could do after all you and your clan have done for us." Jade pushed to her feet, and Phinas followed.

Kian rose as well and shook their hands again. "I'm glad that the Fates brought our people together."

Jade nodded. "As am I."

7

JASMINE

Jasmine stirred awake, her eyelids fluttering open to the soft morning light filtering through the floor-to-ceiling windows of the penthouse guest bedroom. For a moment, she simply savored the plush comfort of the mattress beneath her and the warm, solid presence of Edgar at her side, but then her mind shifted into gear, and she marveled at the turn of events that had brought her to this beautiful, professionally decorated bedroom in a multimillion-dollar penthouse.

But that was the small stuff.

Could things get more surreal than a boyfriend who was the immortal descendant of gods?

Yeah, they could. There was a possibility that she possessed godly genes and could turn immortal with his help. Edgar had explained what was needed, and it was as simple as having sex with him without a condom.

Given that she was about to travel to Tibet, they needed to stock up on many boxes of those. She had no wish to start transitioning while on a trek through the Himalayas, and she also had no intention of abstaining for longer than was essential.

Sex with Edgar was literally out of this world.

Lifting her hand to the spot that he'd bitten last night, she felt her core tighten and her nipples harden at the memory.

Rolling over, she propped herself on one elbow and studied Edgar's sleeping face with a smile. He looked so peaceful, his puffy lips parted and his dark lashes fanning against his sculpted cheekbones. It was hard to reconcile the innocent-looking young man with the vampire he turned into every night.

Well, every night they had sex, and every morning, if she had her way. The fangs didn't scare her, and the glowing eyes were kind of cool.

Now that she knew who and what he was, he didn't need to hide them from her like he had done before.

Sensing her gaze on him, Edgar stirred, his eyes blinking open and a sleepy smile curving his lips. "Good morning, beautiful," he murmured, his voice husky.

"Good morning, handsome." Jasmine leaned down to brush a soft kiss against his mouth. "Did you sleep well?"

"Like the dead." Edgar grinned and pulled her down on top of him for a more thorough kiss.

She laughed against his lips, her body molding to his as she lost herself in the heady rush of desire. They were both naked, and he was already hard beneath her, but she was no longer on vacation and had a mission to accomplish this morning.

Regrettably, sex would have to wait.

She pulled back, ignoring Edgar's groan of protest as she sat up and ran a hand through her tousled hair. "I need to borrow your phone."

"What for?"

She tilted her head. "I need to make a scrying stick, and I need instructions on how to make it. Since I don't have a phone or a laptop, I need to borrow yours."

"I thought that you knew how to make one." He grimaced. "And to be perfectly honest, the idea of a stick pointing us in the direction of the pod sounds absurd."

Jasmine shrugged. "I don't have any better ideas, and if I'm going to be useful in finding the royal twins, I need to sharpen my abilities one way or another. A scrying stick, a crystal ball, or divining from coffee grinds, it doesn't really matter what I use, as long as it helps me channel my innate ability."

Edgar looked skeptical, but he reached for his phone and took it off its charger. "Let's browse together. I'm curious about what we can find."

Jasmine didn't think that he was motivated by curiosity.

Despite the compulsion that Kevin had put on her to keep the existence of immortals a secret, Edgar didn't trust her even though she couldn't tell anyone about them if she wanted to.

It hurt, but she wasn't going to make a big deal out of it. Edgar was probably so used to protecting this enormous secret that it was second nature to him.

Huddling together over the phone, they scrolled through pages of search results on the lore. Most of the information on scrying was related to crystal balls, water basins, polished round stones, and other methods, and there was very little about sticks. The only two references they found claimed that a branch of a willow tree was the best material for that purpose, and both said that it needed to be imbued with the energy of the witch who wielded it.

"Here, take it." Edgar handed her the phone. "My eyes are getting crossed from reading this."

He hadn't added 'nonsense,' but she knew it had been on the tip of his tongue.

Jasmine spent the next half an hour making a mental list of all the items she needed to prep the stick so it would do what it was supposed to.

She handed Edgar his phone back. "Looks like we're going on a walk." She tossed back the covers and swung her legs over the side of the bed.

Edgar groaned, flopping back against the pillows with a sigh. "Can't it wait until after coffee?"

Jasmine laughed, leaning over to kiss his pouting lips quickly. "Nope. The early witch gets the willow or something like that. We can get coffee after we find a stick. There are several other items I need to buy as well, so we will need to find a store that sells them."

"Like what?"

"I'll tell you on the way."

Grumbling about needing coffee to function, Edgar hauled himself out of bed.

8

KIAN

Kian took his coffee to his home office, sat behind his desk, and dialed Turner's number.

"Hello, Kian," the guy answered right away. "I was expecting your call yesterday. What took you so long?"

Kian chuckled. "I thought I would give you time to catch up. It isn't easy to shift gears after a long vacation. I decided to take it easy today and work from home."

He planned to drive to the keep later and talk with the team, but that shouldn't take too long.

"Same here. Neither of us works less while we are in our home offices. It's just an illusion to think that the comfort of working in your sweats and flip-flops means that you are taking it easy."

"Ain't that the truth? Did you have a chance to speak with your people about Margo's family?"

"I did. So far, there have been several phone calls to the advertising agency where Margo worked, inquiring about her whereabouts. Also, someone was seen knocking on her apartment door, but they didn't attempt to break in."

Kian frowned, a prickle of unease crawling up his spine. "Have your people checked her car for tracking devices?"

"I don't think so," Turner admitted. "But I'll have them on it right away. It will be interesting to see if the Doomers considered doing that."

"Did your people happen to track the callers who asked for Margo?"

"No. If they were Doomers, we wouldn't be able to trace their calls because they use a private network like we do. So, what's the point?"

"It could have been the cartel people."

"They are just as sophisticated."

Kian let out a breath. "Things used to be so much simpler not too long ago. I used to love technological innovation, but I'm starting to be wary of it. It's getting harder and harder to hide."

"At least the Doomers are having the same difficulty. I don't know how much longer they will be able to hide their island."

Kian wasn't so sure. "They use old-fashioned bribery and threats to keep it hidden, not so much technology, and those methods will always be effective."

"True."

"Did anyone come snooping around Margo's family's homes?" Kian asked.

"There has been no suspicious activity near their homes or workplaces. We can let them return to their lives in a few days."

Kian weighed his options. On the one hand, he didn't want to keep Margo's family sequestered away indefinitely. But on the other hand, he couldn't risk their safety, not when the cartel and their Doomer overlords hadn't made their move yet.

"Let's give it another week." Kian swiveled his chair and looked at his walled-off backyard. "If there are no further developments over the next seven days, we can allow them to return home."

"Of course," Turner said. "I'll keep you updated on any changes."

When Turner ended the call, Kian leaned back in his chair with a sigh. There was always something to worry about. He had forgotten what it felt like to be unburdened.

Was there ever a time when he had been free of worry?

Perhaps when he was a little boy, still innocent and unaware of all the evil in the world.

A soft knock at the door pulled him from his thoughts. As he turned his chair around, the door opened, and Syssi walked in with two cappuccino cups on a small tray and a plate of cookies between them.

"I thought you could use a pick-me-up," she said, setting the tray on his desk. "You look like you are carrying the weight of the world on your shoulders. What's going on?"

"Nothing new." Kian smiled. "Seeing you is like balm to my soul, a reminder of all that is good and right in my life." He took one of the cups, inhaling the rich aroma with a grateful sigh. "You have no idea how much I've missed these." He took a sip and let the smooth, creamy flavor roll over his tongue. "You, my love, are a master barista."

Syssi grinned, a blush staining her cheeks at the compliment. "Flattery will get you everywhere, mister."

Kian chuckled, feeling the rest of the tension drain from his body. "Is that a promise?"

"Isn't it always?" Syssi teased, taking a sip of her coffee. "But first, tell me what's got you worried. Is it Margo's family?"

Kian nodded, setting his cup down with a sigh. "I just can't shake the feeling that we're not out of the woods yet. The cartel is like a hydra—cut off one head, and two more sprout in its place, and the same is true for the Doomers."

Syssi reached out, taking his hand and giving it a gentle squeeze. "It's all going to work out just fine. It always does."

It had so far, but Kian couldn't help but worry about their luck running out someday. As vigilant and as careful as he was, someone was bound to outsmart him, outmaneuver him, and what would happen to his people then?

It wasn't about losing money or being inconvenienced. It was, and always had been, about an existential threat. It was the life and death of everyone he cared for.

Shaking his head to dispel the gloomy thoughts, Kian forced a smile. "Have I told you lately how much I love you?"

Syssi's eyes softened with affection. "Only every day. But I never get tired of hearing it."

Pushing to his feet, Kian rounded the desk, pulled Syssi out of her chair, and sat on the other with her in his lap. "I love you." He wrapped his arms around her waist and buried his face in the crook of her neck.

Just breathing in her scent was intoxicating. "I wish I could take the rest of the day off and spend it with you."

"Maybe you can." She leaned away to look at his eyes. "What are your plans for after your trip to the keep?"

"I don't have any. How about I take you out on a date? We can go to *By Invitation Only*."

She laughed. "The answer is a resounding yes."

9

JASMINE

When Jasmine and Edgar left the bedroom and entered the living room, Margo and Negal were not there. Jasmine assumed they were still in bed, but it was also possible they had woken up early and crossed the vestibule to the other penthouse to join the two other couples for breakfast.

After Edgar pulled two bottles of water from the fridge and handed her one, they headed out the door and into the penthouse level's dedicated elevator.

"I feel like a celebrity." Jasmine leaned against the cab's wall. "There is luxury, and then there is a private elevator. That's a whole different level."

Edgar waved at the two security guards in the lobby, and they continued walking through the cavernous chamber and out the building's front doors.

The streets of downtown Los Angeles were still quiet. The usual bustle of traffic and pedestrians was absent because of the early hour, with tendrils of fog clinging to the buildings and hanging over the sidewalks. Trees dotted the pavement at regular intervals, their leaves glistening with dew, but most were the wrong species for what she needed.

Hand in hand, she and Edgar walked for several blocks while scanning the greenery. It seemed that all the trees were either jacarandas or ficuses and had been planted at the same time.

Finally, just when Jasmine was losing hope, she spotted a single willow tree at a tiny corner park, its slender branches drooping gracefully over a single bench.

"This is it." She crossed the street, tugging Edgar behind her.

They were almost across the broad boulevard when, suddenly, a shout rang out in the morning stillness, startling them both.

Jasmine whirled around, her eyes widening as she spotted a disheveled man across the street. His face was twisted in a snarl, and his hand was raised in a fist as he hurled barely coherent obscenities in her direction.

Edgar stepped in front of her, his broad shoulders blocking her from view as he leveled a stare at the homeless man. "Just ignore him," he said. "He's not right in the head, but he's harmless. And even if he wasn't, you have nothing to fear from him with me by your side."

Jasmine nodded, trying to slow the pounding of her heart. He was right, of course. With an immortal as her protector, what did she have to be afraid of?

But even as she clung to that thought, doubt crept in. The truth was that no matter how strong or skilled Edgar might be, he couldn't protect her from everything. She was still human and fragile, and painfully aware of that.

Her life could be snuffed out as easily as her mother's.

To this day, her father refused to tell her how her mother had died, but she'd been about Jasmine's age when she'd passed. In the back of her mind, Jasmine had always harbored the morbid thought that she wouldn't live past the age of twenty-seven, which was how old her mother was at the time of her death.

Shaking off the maudlin thought, she smiled and let Edgar lead her the rest of the way to the willow tree. With a quick glance to ensure no one was watching other than the homeless man across the street, he snapped off one of the dry branches.

"Your scrying stick, milady." He handed her the branch with a flourish. "May it guide you well."

"Thank you." Jasmine took the branch, running her fingers over the rough bark and feeling a tingle of energy dance across her skin.

It was gone almost immediately, and she wondered whether it had happened only in her imagination. Or had it been real?

"How long does your wand need to be?" Edgar asked.

"It's not a wand. From what I read, the size is not set in stone, and it depends on the preferences of the user and the specific traditions they follow. A scrying stick should typically be anywhere from six to eighteen inches long." She weighed the thin branch in her hand. "It's important for the stick to feel comfortable and manageable." She turned it this way and that. "Since we will be traveling, I'm inclined to go with the shorter recommendation so it can fit inside my backpack, but I'll let my intuition guide me." She smiled at Edgar. "I'll close my eyes and meditate when I cut it to size."

She'd meant it as a joke, but Edgar took her seriously. "Just mark the spot, and I will do it for you. I don't want you to cut yourself by mistake."

"Don't worry. I was just joking about closing my eyes. But I was serious about doing it myself."

"Can I at least carry it for you?"

"Sure." She handed him the branch and took his other hand. "We should take it back to the penthouse and then go out for the rest of my supplies."

Edgar perked up. "Can we have coffee and breakfast first?"

"Of course."

They turned their backs on the muttering madman and the misty streets then walked in the direction they'd come from.

10

PETER

As the bus finally pulled through the gates of Safe Haven, Peter felt a sense of relief wash over him. He hadn't missed the compound or the rugged Oregon coast, yet it was a welcome sight after the fourteen-hour journey from the port.

Marina had slept on his shoulder throughout most of the night, but all Peter had managed was a few minutes of shuteye here and there. The Guardians had taken turns driving the vehicle, and when it had been his turn, Marina had used his vacated seat to lie down curled up like a pretzel. When he'd transferred command of the wheel to the next Guardian, he'd taken the empty seat next to Larissa instead of disturbing Marina.

Thankfully, Larissa had also been asleep, so he hadn't been subjected to her sniffling and mumbling about Jay. Still, Peter had felt ridiculously relieved when Marina woke up and asked him to return to her.

He was either losing his fucking mind or she was a Dormant after all, because such a strong bond surely couldn't form between a human and an immortal.

As Marina stirred, lifting her head off his shoulder and blinking her eyes open, she turned to the window. "Finally. I thought this ride would never end."

He leaned over and kissed the top of her head. "Happy to be home?"

She yawned and stretched her arms over her head. "This is not home, but I'm happy to get off the bus."

As they disembarked, Peter took in the familiar scenery. On the face of things, Safe Haven hadn't changed much since his time there, but appearances were misleading. A whole new section had been built in the back of the property, and it housed a secret underground lab and a bunch of bungalows to house two groups of very distinct residents. One group was the paranormal talents who had been moved to Safe Haven from West Virginia, and the other was dedicated to the scientists who had worked on a secret project in the lab.

As far as he knew, those bungalows were unoccupied at the moment because no one was using the lab. Still, Emmett and Eleanor might have been using them as additional guest units for their spiritual and paranormal retreats.

Peter wondered how that was going. Had they identified any new potential Dormants?

Probably not, or he would have heard about it.

It seemed that the only way to find Dormants was to trust the Fates to deliver them to their doorstep, so to speak, because all the efforts to identify them had failed except the first two that Amanda had discovered through her testing, and not for lack of trying.

Amanda's research was still going strong but producing no results. William's computer game was producing winners, but none of them had scored high enough on precognition to merit interest. Eva's romance novel about people with paranormal ability was not particularly popular despite a large advertising budget, so the chance of possible Dormants contacting the author was dismal.

The Echelon spy system was showing some promise, though. It was spitting out lists of people who had triggered the algorithm by speaking or posting about paranormal phenomena, and a couple of them seemed promising, so maybe that would prove to be the best approach.

As he and Marina entered the main lodge, Larissa's shuffling footsteps sounded behind them, along with the shambling gaits of the other humans. They were crossing the central hall to the rear exit and from there to the staff quarters, but Peter led Marina to the administrative wing of the lodge instead.

She looked up at him with a raised brow. "You seem to know your way around."

"It's not my first time here."

"I've never seen you in Safe Haven before. I would have remembered you." She tilted her head. "Were Guardians posted here before we joined the community?"

As Peter thought of Marina eying the Guardians who had done rotations in Safe Haven, a flare of jealousy rushed through him.

"Oh, yeah?" He stopped walking and turned to her. "Did you check out all the Guardians who were stationed here?"

A faint blush colored her cheeks. "So what if I did? I'm a healthy female in my prime, and you are all incredibly hunky."

Peter saw red. "Did you speak to any of them?"

She shook her head. "I was too intimidated. Working on the ship and serving your kind in the dining room proved to me that you were decent people and that I have nothing to fear from you." She stretched on her toes and kissed the underside of his jaw. "But I like it that you get jealous over me."

He huffed out a breath and resumed walking. "I'm not usually like this. I don't know what's gotten into me."

"It's called love." Marina leaned into him. "I'm jealous over you, too."

"I've noticed." He leaned to kiss the tip of her nose. "You are cute when you are jealous. To answer your previous question, Guardians have been posted in Safe Haven long before your arrival for reasons that have nothing to do with your people. Leon and Anastasia are here permanently, with Leon in charge of security and Ana developing content for the retreats. The others rotate every two weeks."

When they reached Emmett's office, Peter knocked on the door. A moment later, it was flung open, and he found himself enveloped in Eleanor's arms.

"I haven't seen you in ages." She leaned away from him. "Thankfully, you don't change. Why haven't you come to visit?"

Eleanor had seen him in the village, and it hadn't been that long ago, so he didn't know what her deal was. As for him visiting Safe Haven, Peter didn't have fond memories of the place, but he didn't harbor any ill feelings toward it or Emmett either.

"Why didn't you come on the cruise?" he asked, deflecting her question.

Eleanor let go of him and waved a dismissive hand. "Someone needed to stay behind and run this place. I don't trust leaving it in Riley's hands for more than a few days. Besides, Emmett and I don't really belong with your clan."

Feeling Marina bristling behind him, Peter reached for her hand and pulled her to face Eleanor and Emmett. "I don't need to make introductions, right? You all know each other."

"Of course." Eleanor looked at Marina. "The blue hair and piercings are hard to forget."

Marina grinned. "That's the idea. Blending in is overrated." She let her gaze roam over Emmett, who was wearing all white as usual.

At least he didn't have his prophet's robe on today. Instead, he wore white slacks, a white button-down, and a white cardigan. His black hair was long and perfectly styled, fanning out over his shoulders in thick curls.

None of the Kra-ell, pureblooded or hybrid, had curly hair, so she knew it wasn't natural.

"Bravo." Emmett clapped his hands. "That's my philosophy as well. Why be like everyone else when you can be one of a kind?"

11

MARINA

M arina had never been to Emmett's office before, but mostly it looked like she'd imagined it would. The furniture was much too big and flashy for the modest size of the room and precisely the kind she would have expected to be owned by the hybrid Kra-ell, flamboyant performer, who was the face of Safe Haven.

She hadn't expected the large glass sliding door that opened to an inner courtyard.

The truth was that she didn't like Emmett, and not because he had Kra-ell blood in him or because of his need to stand out and attract attention. He acted too theatrically for her taste and tried to make himself appear larger than life. Still, she was grateful for his part in freeing her and others from Igor's oppressive rule. If not for him, the clan would have never known of their existence, let alone come to their aid.

As for Eleanor, Marina had liked her and her no-nonsense attitude until the welcoming hug she'd given Peter.

Despite his claim that he had never been intimate with Eleanor, there was a history between them. Marina had no doubt of that, but Emmett seemed either oblivious, or he simply didn't care. After all, he was a hybrid Kra-ell, and jealousy was not part of the Kra-ell vocabulary. They didn't form committed relationships with just one person, and it had always seemed strange to her that Emmett and Eleanor appeared to be a couple in every sense of the word.

"So, Marina," Emmett said in that booming theater actor's voice. "How did you enjoy working on the clan's first family cruise?"

Marina was surprised that Emmett Haderech knew her name, but then Peter had probably called him ahead of time and requested a meeting, so he must have told him what it was about.

She turned to Peter and smiled. "It was wonderful. I enjoyed it very much."

Peter helped her into one of the chairs facing Emmett's desk. "I would like to say that it was smooth sailing, but we encountered some rough waters, metaphorically speaking."

"Oh, yes," Emmett said. "I have heard about the altercations."

"Would you like some coffee?" Eleanor asked.

Marina was dying for a cup, but she would never presume to have Eleanor or Emmett serving her.

"Yes, thank you, I would," Peter said. "We had drinks and sandwiches on the bus, but it was all cold, and I would love a hot cup of coffee. I don't want to inconvenience you, though."

Snorting, Eleanor picked up the receiver of Emmett's landline. "I need four cups of coffee delivered to Emmett's office. Cream and sugar on the side, please, and also add a plate of cookies. Thank you." She put the receiver down. "That's as inconvenienced as I'm willing to get."

Marina stifled a chuckle. She liked the woman's assertiveness. Heck, she envied it. She also envied Eleanor's relationship with Peter, no matter how long ago it was and how inconsequential.

"How is Sofia doing?" Emmett asked as Eleanor perched on the corner of his desk. "Were she and Marcel one of the couples who got married on the cruise?"

"No," Peter said. "But I saw her dancing and having fun. She's adjusting well to life in the village."

Emmett leaned back in his chair. "I will never forget her standing in this office after betraying me to Igor." He shifted his gaze to Marina. "But all's well that ends well, right? Without her help, we wouldn't have been able to liberate your compound, or rather liberate it with almost no casualties."

Peter nodded. "It was the Fates' will."

Eleanor crossed her arms over her chest and looked between Peter and Marina. "As much as I'm enjoying all this reminiscing, I want to get to the point before Marina falls flat on her face from exhaustion."

Smoothing a hand over her hair, Marina wondered if she looked as haggard as Eleanor's comment suggested.

"I'm okay. I slept on the bus."

"Good." Emmett cast her a smile before turning to Peter. "Because I want to hear more about the cruise."

Peter was about to answer, but then a knock sounded on the door. A moment later it opened, and Shamia walked in with a tray.

She put it down on Emmett's desk and cast a quick, questioning look at Marina.

Marina just smiled and nodded, signaling that she was okay.

"Thank you, Shamia." Emmett dismissed her.

"You're welcome, sir." She dipped her head and then turned to Marina. "Welcome back."

"Thank you," Marina said.

Shamia looked like she wanted to ask her about the cruise but then thought better of it. "I'll talk to you later." She dipped her head again and hurried out of the office.

12

JASMINE

J asmine's stomach rumbled in response to the rich aroma of Chinese food that greeted her and Edgar as they returned to the penthouse after their shopping excursion to the Wicca store.

The rest of their team was gathered in the living room, already digging into the boxes on the enormous coffee table.

"Why aren't you eating in the dining room?" she asked. "Kian will be majorly pissed if you stain his super expensive leather couches and authentic Persian rug."

"How do you know it's authentic?" Frankie asked.

"I'm part Persian." Jasmine sat down on said rug and crossed her legs. "But just look around you. Does any of this stuff look like it's not the real thing?"

Frankie glanced at the wall with the huge modern art pieces; then her gaze shifted to the two statues perched on top of pedestals before returning to the rug. "Yeah, you're right. We need to be careful."

Edgar put the shopping bags behind Jasmine before joining her on the floor. "Did you order enough for us, too?"

"Of course." Margo gave them each a paper plate along with a pair of chopsticks. "So, where did you go? And what did you get?"

Jasmine handed Edgar her plate to fill up. "I found the perfect tool for stripping the bark from my scrying stick," she said, holding up a small, curved blade. "And some oils to anoint it with. Sandalwood for protection and clarity, and a moonstone elixir to open my psychic pathways."

Margo looked like she was choking on a laugh. "I'm sorry. I know that you are dead serious about this stuff. But I just can't help it." She snorted. "Moonstone elixir?"

It was so annoying to hear people disparage her beliefs without knowing anything about them that Jasmine decided not to mention the candles she'd bought and the large map of Tibet that Edgar had printed for her from a satellite picture.

"What does that even mean?" Margo asked. "How can you make an elixir from a stone?"

Jasmine looked down her nose at Margo. "Moonstone is a gem associated with the moon, and it is supposed to have healing and protective properties. When put in clean water, the vibrational qualities of moonstones are incorporated into the liquid and form the elixir."

Frankie's brows met in a deep V between her eyes. "So, you are saying it's a stone dipped in water?"

"More or less." Jasmine took Edgar's plate, which was piled high with an assortment of dishes from the boxes. "A high-quality moonstone that is genuine and has not been treated with any harmful chemicals is immersed in spring or distilled water to avoid impurities that might affect its quality. The stone needs to sit in the water overnight under moonlight to charge it with its energetic properties." She lifted a piece of chicken with her chopsticks and put it in her mouth.

She had to stifle a moan as the flavors exploded on her tongue.

"Good, right?" Negal asked. "We ordered from this place many times while we were staying here before the cruise."

Jasmine finished chewing. "It's either the best Chinese food I've ever had, or I'm really hungry."

"Both," Edgar said. "All the Guardians order from this place when they are stationed in the keep."

For a few moments, everyone got busy eating, and no one spoke, which was okay with Jasmine. She was hungry, and she wanted a full stomach before starting to work on her scrying stick.

Gabi was the first one to put down her chopsticks. She wiped her mouth with a paper napkin with a red dragon printed on it and turned to Jasmine. "How do you know that the elixir is real and had a moonstone sitting in it under the moonlight? What you bought could be a total fake. Just tap water in a nice bottle."

"It could be," Jasmine admitted. "That's why shopping for these things in a reputable establishment is so important. Other practitioners highly recommended the store we bought it from."

"What is the moonstone elixir used for?" Gabi asked. "I mean, besides opening psychic pathways?"

She didn't sound condescending, so Jasmine decided to answer: "It soothes emotional instability and stress, enhances emotional intelligence and intuition, and promotes inspiration. Some say that it can even assist with the menstrual cycle and improve reproductive health."

"Thank the merciful Fates, I don't get any more of those." Gabi smiled at Margo and Frankie. "That's one of the perks of becoming immortal."

That didn't sound like a perk at all. Not if it meant having no kids.

She canted her head. "Does it mean infertility?"

"Almost but not quite." Gabi cast her a sad smile. "Fertility is severely diminished after the transition, but it's still possible to conceive. We don't menstruate, so we don't waste eggs."

Jasmine wasn't sure she understood how that worked, but she didn't like how it sounded. Being a mother hadn't been a priority for her, but she'd always assumed that she would one day marry and have kids. Having the option taken from her was disturbing.

Perhaps she could wait to transition into immortality after having children?

Taking for granted that she had godly genes and could transition was probably a mistake because it wasn't a sure thing at all, but Jasmine was an optimist at heart, and she believed that she had what it took to become immortal.

Provided she understood things correctly, she didn't need to become immortal for her kids to have the godly genes. Any children born to her would inherit them from her whether she was still a Dormant or had transitioned already.

Had Margo and Frankie known about the fertility thing before turning immortal?

Glancing at them, she didn't see surprise or alarm, so she assumed that they had been told, and if they didn't seem troubled by it, maybe she shouldn't either. Maybe there was a solution to the low infertility that no one had mentioned yet.

Jasmine wanted to ask, but Aru and Negal were discussing the intricacies of high-altitude trekking. Since she knew nothing about it and couldn't contribute, she dug into the tasty morsels on her plate and listened to the conversation.

It occurred to her that she wasn't in the greatest of shape and that she would probably be a burden on the team of immortals. But then she was the witch, the conduit for the divine that would guide them to the alien pod, and without her, all their formidable abilities were worthless.

13

MARINA

M arina sipped her coffee with grateful abandon while the others chatted about the cruise's highlights and the future of the rescued women.

Peter put down his cup and leaned forward. "I requested this meeting because Marina and I got close during the cruise, and we would like to be together. Marina has spoken to Amanda about moving to the village, and Amanda suggested that she submit a transfer application. All I ask for is that you expedite it." He trained his eyes on Emmett. "As a personal favor to me."

Eleanor's brow furrowed. "You know the clan's stance on relationships with humans. It's not done to be cruel or restrict members' liberties but to protect both from heartache."

"I know," Peter said, his jaw tightening. "Which is why I think it's important that Marina and I downplay the depth of our relationship, at least for now. Let Kian and the others believe it's just casual and that she's moving in with me temporarily until she finds her footing in the village."

Emmett smiled indulgently. "I'm not sure that's the best approach, especially since it is easy to see that the two of you are in love. Kian's a romantic at heart and won't stand in the way of true love."

Eleanor shook her head. "Kian is also pragmatic, and he's more likely to approve the transfer if he thinks it's only for Marina's benefit and has little to do with Peter."

Marina didn't know which of them had it right, but Eleanor was the more sensible one, and she was immortal. She probably knew Kian better than Emmett did.

"I agree with Eleanor," Peter said. "I don't want to lie to Kian, but not mentioning me in the application is not lying. Marina's command of English is impressive, and she can help the Kra-ell in the village who are still struggling with the language. She can also serve as an interpreter or fill any other positions currently offered and desperately seeking applicants."

Emmett nodded. "Naturally, I will do as you ask." He looked at Marina. "Is that your wish? Do you want to move to the village?"

"Very much so."

"Then it's done." Emmett tapped his palm on his desk. "I'll fill it out today and submit it tomorrow."

"Do I need to sign it?" Marina asked.

"No need." Emmett lifted his coffee cup. "You will be invited to an interview, and your wish to transfer will be verified in person." He took a sip, carefully keeping his mustache and beard from partaking.

Marina swallowed. She should have expected that, but she hadn't, and the thought of a face-to-face meeting with Kian terrified her.

"Thank you for your help," Peter said. "And now to my second request. I'm stationed here for the next two weeks and would like to use one of the bungalows so Marina and I can be together. Are any still available?"

"They sure are." Eleanor slid off the desk, leaned over its other side, and opened a drawer.

Was she looking for a key?

"This is the list of codes for the locks on each bungalow." Eleanor handed Peter a piece of paper with a list of numbers. "Make a photo of it. You can choose any of the bungalows marked as available. At this time, the entire section is at your disposal."

Peter chuckled. "You are not that old, Eleanor. Why don't you have the list on your phone?"

She shrugged. "It's less time-consuming to just write it on paper, and this way, I know that no one can hack the info and get into one of those bungalows without my permission."

Peter rose, spread the page on Emmett's desk, and snapped a photo. "Thank you. We will look at one or two and let you know which one we've selected."

"Good deal. You can also use the paranormals' dining room if you wish. It's less crowded and more intimate. The Guardians prefer it to the one in the lodge or the staff dining room."

Peter dipped his head. "Thank you. Have we made any progress with finding paranormals among the seminars' attendees?"

Eleanor shrugged. "We found a few talents, but nothing spectacular so far." She trained her dark, small eyes on Marina. "How about you? Any paranormal talents?"

Marina shook her head. "I'm afraid not."

"What about the rapid language absorption?" Peter asked. "Couldn't that count as a paranormal ability?"

"It might." Eleanor still had her eyes trained on Marina. "We should get you tested."

Marina swallowed. "I don't see the point. If I were a Dormant, I would have transitioned already. Peter and I haven't been using protection."

Eleanor pursed her lips. "I've heard of Dormants who took weeks to transition. It might still happen to you."

"I don't think it will and testing me won't change that."

"As you wish." Eleanor stood up and offered Marina her hand. "I'll keep my fingers crossed for you."

14

JASMINE

After the meal had wound down and the coffee table was cleared, Jasmine rose to her feet. "I'm going to head to our bedroom," she told Edgar as she gathered her supplies. "I want to get started on my scrying stick."

Margo looked up at her. "How long do you expect it will take you to make it?"

Jasmine shrugged. "I don't know. Why?"

"Kian is dropping by this afternoon with William, and later, we plan to do some shopping for the trip. We need warm clothing and hiking boots. It's going to be freezing at night where we're headed."

Jasmine couldn't suppress a grimace. Cold weather was not her friend. She was a creature of sunshine and heat, and the thought of trudging through snow and ice and huddling in sub-zero temperatures sent a shiver down her spine, but it wasn't as if she had a choice.

She'd agreed to help look for the royal twins, knowing they were in Tibet. She just hadn't known much about the place.

Oh well, a little discomfort was a small price to pay for the chance of a lifetime to do something extraordinary.

"If I'm not done by the time Kian gets here, just let me know he's here, and I'll drop what I'm doing."

"Really?" Margo looked doubtful. "Don't you need to complete a ritual once you start it?"

"I do, but each step doesn't take long. It will be fine."

Edgar rose to his feet. "I'll come with you."

She put a hand on his chest. "I need to work alone, and you need to plan a trip. Stay."

He didn't look happy, but he nodded, planted a chaste kiss on her forehead, and sat back on the floor.

The door to the other penthouse wasn't locked, and as Jasmine entered, she took a moment to admire the view before heading to the bedroom with her supplies.

She covered the desk with a clean white towel, laid out her tools, and began stripping the bark from the willow branch.

The willow tree was known for its connection to deep waters and hidden things. It was supposed to be cut during the waning moon to enhance its receptive qualities, but she didn't have time to wait for the moon to wane. Hopefully, it would work just as well without it.

After all, it was just a tool to focus on her inner ability, and it would do what she believed it could.

As Jasmine worked, a sense of calm settled over her, and soon the scrying stick started taking shape beneath her hands. Jasmine lost herself in the repetitive motions, her mind turning inward, seeking the place of stillness and clarity that would allow her inner energy to flow as the smooth wood emerged.

It didn't take her more than an hour, and when it was done, she anointed the stick with sandalwood for protection and clarity and a drop of moonstone elixir to open her psychic pathways.

In a quiet corner of her room, she placed the candles in a large circle around the map of Tibet, closed the drapes, and lit the candles.

Sitting cross-legged inside the circle, her scrying stick laid beside her, Jasmine closed her eyes and took deep, measured breaths, each inhale deeper than the last, each exhale a release of worldly concerns.

As her body relaxed and her mind cleared, she imagined her thoughts drifting away like leaves on a stream. She visualized herself as a pool of still water, un-rippled and reflective.

Jasmine focused on sharpening her intuitive senses, and connecting her mind with the subtle energies of her scrying stick would help her amplify them. When she felt the energies swirling around her and recognized their nuances, she held the stick gently in her hands and felt the pulse of its energy. She focused her intent on locating the missing escape pod, tracing her fingers over the lines and contours of the map spread out before her.

As she passed the scrying stick over the map, her hand trembled slightly when it hovered over a particular region—Mount Kailash. Trusting her intuition, she marked the spot with a small stone.

Jasmine didn't know much about it, but she felt it was a spiritual center of some sort. The escape pod must have been guided there to seek its resting place.

Her heart raced with excitement at the discovery and the hope that her scrying had been true, but she wouldn't trust this one result. At least two more attempts were needed to confirm the location, and until she did that, she wouldn't even mention Mount Kailash to the others.

15

KIAN

"Do you want me to ring the bell, boss?" Anandur asked as their group stopped before Kian's old penthouse door.

"They know that we are coming," Kian grumbled. "But ring the damn bell anyway. They are the residents of this place for now."

Julian glanced at the bag William was carrying as he shifted it to his other hand. "Do you want me to carry that for you?"

William cut him an offended look. "Of course not. It's not heavy. It's just that the damn handle pinched the skin of my palm."

The doctor frowned. "Let me take a look at it."

William's ears reddened. "No need. I'm fine."

As Aru opened the door, the god's gaze flickered over the group, and when it settled on Julian and then Ella, he lifted a brow. "Good afternoon. Please, come in." He took a step back to allow them to pass. "I didn't expect the doctor and his mate." He looked at Kian with a questioning expression on his face.

"I'll explain why Julian is here in a moment. Let's move to the dining room where we can comfortably fit around the table."

Aru nodded. "As you wish."

Greetings were exchanged with the other members of the group, some casting curious looks at Julian and Ella, but no one questioning their presence, probably because they had all heard Kian tell Aru to wait for the explanation.

When everyone was seated around the large dining table, Kian took a position at the head of it, his gaze sweeping over the group. "I'm not much for speeches, so let's start with the tech first." He turned to William. "The floor is yours."

William rose to his feet and put his paper bag on the table. "I have satellite phones for Jasmine, Margo, and Frankie." He pulled three boxes out of the bag and distributed them to the three ladies. "The phones I gave you before have limited capabilities." He looked at the two friends. "These are much better. I would like the old ones back, please."

Frankie pouted. "What about all the pictures I took with that phone?"

"Everything you had in the old phone has already been transferred to your new one." William smiled indulgently. "You can check."

Her eyes sparkled as she opened the box and pulled out the device. A moment later, she confirmed that all of her photos were there.

"Okay," William said. "Next are the earpieces. Please don't lose them because I have only one pair per person, and they are not replaceable. Well, they are, but not easily where you are going to be. I would have to air ship them to you."

He pulled out the small pouches with the earpieces and distributed them to everyone around the table. "These will not only allow you to communicate between yourselves and us, but they will also protect you from compulsion. Under no circumstances should you approach the pod without these firmly in your ears."

He explained how they worked, the different machine voices that were now available, and how that made using the earpieces less awkward. "I've sent each of you a video explaining how to mold these to your ears. It's meant for those of you who are using them for the first time and those who need a refresher. Ensuring the earpieces are correctly inserted and perfectly molded to your ears is critical. The smallest gap will expose you to compulsion and make you a danger to everyone else in your group. Is that clear?"

As everyone nodded, William shifted his gaze to Jasmine, and his expression softened. "If you wish, I can assist you with your earpieces."

"Thank you." She smiled at him. "After that preamble, I'm terrified of doing it wrong."

Margo lifted her hand. "I need help too."

"No problem, ladies."

Kian waited patiently for William to be done with their earpieces, all the while aware of Aru's stare. The god was questioning the presence of Julian and Ella and waiting for an explanation.

When William was done, Kian rapped his fingers on the table to get everyone's attention. "I know you are all wondering why Julian and Ella are here."

When there were nods all around, Kian continued. "While going over the details of this mission with Toven and Turner, I realized how perilous the conditions are in the Tibet region where Aru will start the search for the pod. I'm not concerned for the gods and immortals, but Jasmine is human, and we can't risk her getting hurt without medical intervention available to her."

Aru cleared his throat. "It's not necessary. Julian can give us a crash course in first aid, and I'm sure Edgar has some medical training since he often works with the Guardians."

"I do," Edgar confirmed.

Jasmine canted her head. "Did I hear you right? Did you say 'gods'?"

Kian looked at Edgar. "You didn't tell her?"

The pilot cringed. "I didn't know if it was okay. I was waiting to ask you today."

Kian groaned. "Let's make this short." He turned to Jasmine. "Aru, Negal, and Dagor are not immortals like the rest of us. They are gods who came directly from Anumati, the planet on which our ancestors were born. They were sent to locate the missing pods and perform other clandestine tasks. You can ask Edgar or Margo later if you have more questions."

Looking shell-shocked, the woman nodded.

Aru cleared his throat. "I don't mean to question your judgment, Kian, but adding two more people to our team complicates things, and it does so unnecessarily."

Kian knew what Aru was trying to say. If Jasmine needed medical help, Aru was assuming that a donation of blood from one of the gods would heal whatever was wrong with her, but he was wrong. The blood couldn't reset broken bones, and that was a big concern given the terrain they were going to traverse.

"Julian is not a Guardian, but he has military training, so his value is not only as a doctor. You are traveling with a human, and if she breaks an arm or a leg, someone will need to reset the bone and secure it. That's also true for the immortals and perhaps even for you. If the bone is not reset correctly, it might fuse in a way that would disable the injured person, making it difficult or impossible for the team to continue the journey. Also, if you find the Kra-ell, they may be in bad shape and need immediate medical attention. Ella has undergone emergency medical training, and she can assist Julian. Besides, they are fated mates, and it's difficult for them to be separated for more than a few days. As a mated male yourself, I'm sure you understand."

"Fair enough," Aru said. "But how are we going to fit everyone into one helicopter?"

EDGAR

That was an excellent question, and the answer was they were not, not unless they could access a large-capacity specially designed military helicopter, which might attract too much unwanted attention.

The region's high altitude meant thinner air, which reduced lift and impaired engine performance, making it difficult to operate typical heavier, larger helicopters safely. Landing would also be challenging because of the rugged and uneven terrain. Larger crafts needed a corresponding sizeable flat area to land safely, and in these mountainous regions, that might be challenging to find. While larger helicopters could carry more crew and equipment longer distances, their size limited maneuverability and made them more susceptible to adverse winds and turbulence, which were common condition when flying in the Himalayas among large peaks. It could compromise their response time in critical situations.

Edgar's experience showed that smaller craft that could perform tighter maneuvers and land in confined spaces were more effective in navigating demanding conditions like those they were going to face.

"We are not," Kian echoed Edgar's thoughts. "We are getting a small craft specifically fitted for higher altitudes that will carry your team and Jasmine. Everyone else will have to stay behind." He smiled. "It explains Syssi's vision. After all, she saw only the four of you standing over the crater, not everyone on the team."

"Makes sense," the god agreed. "Can we use a large truck to transport the helicopter if there are still paved roads?"

Kian shrugged. "We are still working out the details. I hope that everything will be set up by the time you land in Lhasa, along with a licensed local tour guide."

"What do we need a tour guide for?" Edgar asked.

"It's a requirement of the Chinese government," Dagor said. "When it was just the three of us, we could go undetected and thrall our way through the bureaucracy. But with a group this large, we will need a cover."

"Thank you, Dagor," Kian said. "What else can you tell the others about the conditions in Tibet?"

Dagor leaned forward. "The altitude is the most significant challenge. Much of Tibet lies above three thousand meters, which can cause altitude sickness and affect overall performance. It's less of a problem for us, but immortals and humans will need to acclimatize gradually."

Negal nodded in agreement. "The terrain is rugged, mountainous, and very sparsely populated. We'll be trekking through areas far from settled regions, so we must be prepared for self-sufficiency."

"The weather is unpredictable," Aru said. "It can change rapidly and without warning. Sudden snowstorms, high winds, and extreme temperature fluctuations are common. Having the right equipment is crucial." He looked at Jasmine. "Especially for a human."

Edgar was starting to feel uncomfortable about the whole thing. It seemed like the mission was much too dangerous for Jasmine. "Can't we wait for Jaz to transition first? I think it's worth postponing our departure for another week if it means that she can travel as an immortal and not a human."

"We can't wait," Aru said. "Besides, it's not guaranteed that Jasmine is a Dormant. You could spend the next two weeks trying to induce her transition, and if nothing happens, we will be back at square one."

"We need to leave now," Jasmine said. "I feel it in my bones that we are running out of time, or rather they are. I mean the twins and whoever else is in their pod."

There was a long moment of silence as everyone absorbed her statement.

"I'm not going to argue with a witch." Kian smiled. "Do you often get premonitions like that?"

She shook her head and put her hand over her chest. "No, but I have this sense of urgency that I didn't have before."

Kian nodded before returning his gaze to the others. "You will need specialist gear. High-altitude tents, cold-weather clothing, portable oxygen, if necessary, etc. Julian, can you work with Shai to procure these items?"

Julian nodded, making a note on his tablet. "Consider it done. I can have everything delivered to our location in Lhasa. There is no need to haul it from here."

"Except for the clothing," Margo said. "We need to buy it here to make sure that everything fits. It's especially important with hiking boots. They must be comfortable and broken in, or they will be a source of grief."

"Agreed," Julian said. "We should all go shopping for those items later today."

"Indeed." Kian pulled a card out of his pocket and handed it to Jasmine. "Charge everything you need on this card."

She looked at the card and frowned. "That's not my last name."

"I know. We are getting you fake documents with a different last name. In case the cartel is still searching for you, it's better not to leave a trail of crumbs they could follow." He pulled a folded piece of paper out of his pocket. "Here is the travel itinerary. You will take a commercial flight to Chengdu, China, and from there, you will fly to Lhasa. From there, you will fly to Shiquanhe and travel overground following Jasmine's directions. We are still working out the last details, but I wanted you to have a general timeline."

Aru looked at the page. "This says that we are leaving in a week. Why so long?"

"Because we are not sure we will have everything ready for you before that. We are still negotiating the helicopter purchase and need to secure special permission from the Chinese government to fly it. If we manage to arrange things beforehand, we can push the flights forward."

"Tibet is heavily restricted." Aru sighed. "Permits are needed for everything, and it takes time to get them unless you are right there to thrall the bureaucrats."

"Don't worry about that," Kian said. "We are handling everything—Tibetan travel permits, alien travel permits, and possibly military permits. Kalugal is working with his contacts to secure all of these. Your cover story is that you are a group of environmental researchers studying the Himalayan ecosystem."

"Environmental researchers?" Jasmine asked. "Won't they check our credentials?"

Kian smiled. "We are creating backstories for each of you, and we will provide you with the necessary documentation and cover identities."

"Wow." She slumped back in her chair. "I feel like I have friends in high places."

"You do." Edgar leaned over to her and wrapped an arm around her shoulders. "Welcome to your new reality, where almost anything is possible."

17

JASMINE

Jasmine followed Edgar into their bedroom, her arms laden with shopping bags filled with the clothing and footwear they'd purchased for the expedition to Tibet, and that was just a small portion of what they had gotten. Edgar was carrying the lion's share of their loot.

It had been nice to shop with the credit card Kian had given her without worrying about card limits or having to pay the bill once the statement became due.

Edgar put the bags in the walk-in closet, lining them up against the wall, and then took hers and added them to the neat line.

The speed and ease with which he did things still amazed her, and as he straightened and turned around, he must have liked the awed expression on her face because a smirk tugged on his lips.

Reaching for her waist, he pulled her to him and nuzzled her neck. "We have some time before we need to reconvene with the others. What say you we put it to good use?"

It was tempting, but before she allowed herself to get lost in Edgar's sinful touch, she had to confirm her previous findings.

Leaning away, she cupped his cheek. "As much as I'd love to, I need to scry again to confirm the location I marked earlier and confirm the result before I can share it with the others. I didn't want to tell Kian about Mount Kailash because I wanted to double-check that I got it right before he made travel arrangements based on that."

Disappointment flickered in Edgar's eyes, but then he smiled. "We have over two hours. I'm sure that we can do both."

Jasmine laughed. "I'll tell you what. If we have any time left after I'm done, I'm game, even if it's only fifteen minutes."

He'd bitten her last night, so he could refrain from biting her now. It wouldn't do if she blacked out for hours and missed the meeting.

"You've got yourself a deal." Edgar leaned down and kissed her.

When he finally let her come up for air, they were both panting, and Edgar had to adjust the massive erection that was pressing against the zipper of his jeans. "Do you want me to leave you alone so you can focus?"

Jasmine chuckled. "The only place you can go right now is the bathroom." She lowered her gaze to his crotch. "You can't show up like that in the living room."

He followed her gaze and snorted. "Yeah, I need to cool down for a few minutes."

"You can stay here and watch, but you need to be very quiet. Can you do that?"

"Of course. But are you sure my presence won't interfere with your energy flow or whatever you summon into your stick?"

Jasmine shrugged. "I'm not sure about anything, but I must get used to scrying in company. I won't have the luxury of a private room while trekking through the Tibetan frozen tundra and snowy peaks."

"In that case, I'm happy to stay and watch you do your thing." He reached out to tuck a stray lock of hair behind her ear. "I'll be on the bed and keep very quiet. You won't even hear me breathe."

"Thank you."

Jasmine cast him a grateful smile before retrieving her scrying stick and the map of Tibet from where she'd left them.

Arranging everything the way she'd done before, she lit the candles and settled cross-legged on the floor.

It was harder to concentrate, knowing that Edgar was watching her. Still, as she closed her eyes and took a deep, centering breath, she looked inward and let her surroundings dissipate into the mist she pictured covering a mountain peak in Tibet.

When her mind was clear, she focused on the energy of the scrying stick in her hands and the tingle of power that danced across her skin as she ran her fingers over the smooth wood.

Slowly, she began to pass the stick over the map, moving her hand in small, deliberate circles. She could feel the energy shift as she moved from one area to another, a subtle pull drawing her toward a particular spot. When she opened her eyes, she was relieved to see that it was the exact location she'd marked before—the area of Mount Kailash.

The mountain was located in western Tibet, and many other jagged peaks surrounded it. Rivers snaked out from its slopes, carving deep valleys through the landscape. The map also showed two large bodies of water and several glaciers and snowfields.

Just thinking about how cold it would be there, Jasmine shivered.

"What's wrong?" Edgar asked.

"Nothing." She turned to look at him. "I got the same location as before, but I took a closer look at the map this time. The whole area looks like it is permanently frozen. I don't like the cold."

He turned on his side and propped his elbow on the mattress and his chin on his fist. "Well, the good news is that you got your confirmation. And as for the cold, I promise to keep you warm."

"That's very sweet of you." She blew him a kiss. "I think having a more detailed map of this area would be helpful." She tapped the spot with the scrying stick. "Do you think you can have one printed for me?"

"Absolutely. Do you need it now?"

Perhaps she needed to scry again before sending him on an unnecessary quest.

"Before you go, I want to try one more time, but since I know where it is even with my eyes closed, I need you to turn this map around when I'm not watching."

"I can do that." He slid off the bed. "Close your eyes, beautiful."

When she did, he kissed her, his tongue delving into her mouth and scrambling her brain, so when he pulled back, she had no idea which side was up and which was down.

"It's ready for you." He kissed the top of her head.

"Thank you. Kissing me was a great way to distract me from noticing you turning it."

"You're welcome."

Jasmine let her mind wander for a moment, trying to imagine what they might find when they finally reached the mountaintop that Syssi had seen in her vision. It wasn't Mount Kailash itself because it didn't have a crater at its top, but it could be one of the peaks in its vicinity or maybe somewhere else entirely.

Would the royal twins even be alive after all these years? Or would they find only their remains?

In either case, it would be better than not finding them. Their family, if they had any, would at least have closure, knowing where their final resting place was.

It was more than she had.

Jasmine didn't know where her mother was buried, and her father refused to tell her. Sometimes, she fantasized that her mother wasn't dead at all. That she had run away for some reason.

Maybe she'd found love in the arms of another man?

It was painful to think that her mother could have left her behind to pursue her own happiness, but Jasmine preferred that to the finality of death. If her mother was still alive somewhere, there was still a chance that they could be reunited.

Perhaps she could scry for her? Even finding her grave would be better than not knowing for sure what had befallen her.

Shaking off the morbid thoughts, Jasmine took a deep breath and centered herself once more, emptying her mind of all thoughts while passing the scrying stick over the map.

When her hand was drawn to a particular spot, she opened her eyes and was amazed that it had settled on the same spot, even though the map was turned upside down.

She turned to look at Edgar, who was watching her with an amused grin. "My talented witch. Would you like me to get you a map of the Mount Kailash area?" He glanced down at his watch. "If I hurry, we might still have enough time left for a quickie."

She nodded. "Yes, please. To both offers."

18

EDGAR

Edgar strode into the keep's security office with the rolled-up map of Tibet tucked under his arm. He didn't really need it. It would have been just as easy to tell the guys to zoom in on the Mount Kailash area, but he wanted to make sure that they printed the entire area Jasmine had circled.

The place was primarily staffed by humans, but one immortal was on duty at all times, except for the duration of the cruise, when keeping an eye on things had been done remotely through the security feed.

Naturally, the humans had no idea that they were working for a clan of immortals or that the officer in charge was anything more than a highly skilled security operative.

Edgar approached Gavin with a smile. "How are things going?"

They embraced and clapped each other's backs.

"Boring as usual." Gavin stepped back and looked at the map tucked under Edgar's arm. "Problems with the printout?"

"No. It served its intended purpose beautifully, but we must zoom in." He rolled out the map and pointed to the area Jasmine had circled. "Can you get this part enlarged to the size of the original map?"

Gavin nodded. "Shouldn't be a problem." He took it and handed it to one of the humans.

The woman nodded, turning to the computer to generate the new, zoomed-in printout.

"Do you want to grab coffee while we wait?" Gavin asked.

"Sure." Edgar wanted to be back with the new map as soon as possible, but printing it would take time, and it was evident that Gavin wanted to talk out of the humans' earshot.

As they entered the staff's breakroom, the Guardian turned to Edgar with a raised eyebrow. "Did it work?"

Edgar nodded. "Jasmine repeated the scrying several times, and the stick kept pointing to the same spot. That's why we want a larger map of the surrounding area. Maybe she will be able to get an even more precise location."

Gavin snorted, pouring coffee from the carafe into two paper cups. "I can't believe Kian and the Three Stooges are basing the expedition on what a wannabe witch says. You know as well as I do that witches don't exist. To tell you the truth, I get unpleasant flashbacks every time I hear the word witch. Too many innocent women died terribly because barbaric morons accused them of worshiping the devil."

Gavin was old enough to remember the witch hunts, but, thankfully, Edgar had been spared living through that dark era. Not that things were much better nowadays. The world was regressing again, overtaken by hordes of fanatics who championed death and destruction.

"Innocents die all the time." He took the cup Gavin handed him. "Politicians get rich, their sponsors get even richer, and the poor sods who are just trying to survive are paying the price with their lives and the lives of their children. There is nothing new under the sun."

"True. Sad, but true." Gavin took a sip of his coffee. "Still, following the word of a woman who claims to be a witch is ridiculous. Kian should know better, as should Aru."

Gavin's dismissive tone grated on Edgar's nerves. Jasmine wasn't a fraud. Besides, Kian trusted his wife's vision, which had foretold that Jasmine would find the pod.

"Jasmine has a real gift, and she uses the Wiccan set of beliefs and the tools they recommend to help channel and focus her innate ability. I would never put my trust in a stick made of wood, but I trust her intuition, especially since it is backed up by Syssi's vision. Or do you question that as well?"

Gavin held up his hands in a placating gesture. "I meant no offense. I was just voicing my opinion. But if you say Jasmine is the real deal, I believe you."

Edgar took a deep breath, forcing himself to relax. "No one is certain that it will work, least of all Jasmine, but we have nothing to lose except time. Aru and his team were heading to Tibet, following a rumor about strange energy readings somewhere. They didn't tell us where, to avoid influencing Jasmine's results, but if the two match, that would be a good indicator that she's onto something."

Gavin nodded. "That makes sense." He finished the last of his coffee and tossed the cup into the recycling bin. "The map should be ready by now."

Edgar followed his example and threw away his cup before returning to the security office.

"It's ready." The human staff member looked up from her monitor and rose to her feet with a pleasant smile. "I zoomed in as much as possible on the area you marked." She handed over a freshly printed map. "It's a satellite picture, but I added names and colored topographical details and landmarks to make it easier for you to orient yourself."

"Thank you." Edgar took the map, unfurled it, and scanned the intricate lines and contours. It was precisely what Jasmine needed: a detailed view that would help her refine her search. "This is perfect," he said, flashing the staff member a grateful smile. "Thank you so much for putting in the extra effort."

"It was my pleasure." She dipped her head and returned to her station.

With the map in hand, Edgar bid farewell to Gavin and the other security staff and then returned to the penthouse.

He found Jasmine exactly where he'd left her, sitting cross-legged on their bedroom floor, meditating.

Not knowing whether he should disturb her, he placed the rolled-up map on the floor next to her.

Her eyelids fluttered for a moment, and then they were up. He was once again mesmerized by her gorgeous brown eyes with gold flakes swirling inside them.

"Did you get it?" she asked.

"Of course, I did." He pointed at the cylinder resting beside her. "A super-detailed, zoomed-in map of the area around Mount Kailash, courtesy of a security person named Heather."

He knelt beside her and spread out the map on the floor.

Her eyes widened in amazement. "This is incredible." She traced her finger over the contour lines that marked the valleys and ridges of the mountain range. "She's even colored it for clarity. I didn't know that could be done with a printout."

"I hope the amount of detail will help you zero in on the exact location."

"I pray to the Mother of All Life that it does." She picked up her scrying stick and began to pass it over the paper, moving her hand in slow, deliberate circles.

It was a little jarring to hear her invoke the Kra-ell deity, but apparently, the Wiccan also believed in her. Only the Wiccan goddess was a purely benevolent deity. At the same time, her Kra-ell namesake was a reflection of her believers—cruel and vengeful toward those who strayed from her path but generous with her rewards toward the true believers who adhered to her teachings and followed the heroes' path, or something like that. He had never delved too deeply into the Kra-ell's belief system.

Watching Jasmine do her thing, though, he could see a marked difference between her expression when she had done this before and now. Instead of the look of calm focus he'd seen on her face before, Jasmine's expression was pinched and uncertain. Her hand wavered as she moved the stick, and after a few moments, she let out a frustrated sigh and opened her eyes.

"I'm not getting anything," she said, sounding defeated. "Maybe I was deluding myself before, and I can't do this."

"Hey," he said, crouching next to her. "It's okay. This is a new map with a new level of detail. It might take some time for your mojo to adjust to it."

Jasmine shook her head. "But what if it's not that? So much is riding on my supposed ability to locate the pod." She traced her finger along the contour lines that marked one of the valleys. "I just hope we're not too late," she murmured.

"Listen to me." He took her hand. "I've seen what you can do. Your gift is real, and it will only get stronger with time and practice. Perhaps you overworked yourself and exhausted that special something that guides your hand. You need to give it a rest and come back to it later."

She frowned. "You might be right. Syssi said something about paranormal abilities diminishing with use and needing to let the mind rest."

Edgar smirked. "I have the perfect method for resting the mind."

19

JASMINE

"Oh, yeah?" Jasmine rose to her knees, wrapped her arms around Edgar's neck, and leaned into him. "I need an immediate demonstration of this method of yours." She pressed her lips to his.

He took over the kiss, wrapping his arms around her, and pulled her closer against his body. In a show of impressive strength, he pushed up to a stand and carried her to the bed.

"I have two variations," he said as he tumbled with her on the mattress. "One is slow and the other fast. You choose."

"Fast." She reached for his shirt and tugged it over his head. "We don't have much time." Her hands roamed over the contours of his chest, marveling at the ripple of muscle beneath his skin.

He grinned with a pair of elongated fangs. "That was the right answer."

Her clothes had somehow survived his attack, but she wouldn't have minded if he had torn them to shreds. Something inside of her was unleashed, and she felt feral with desire.

His eyes began to glow with that otherworldly light she had come to expect, and as he hovered over her, his elongated fangs gleamed in the dimness of the room.

Jasmine felt a thrill of excitement race through her, an anticipation for a repeat of the marvelous things he had done to her with those fangs.

Edgar didn't scare her, and she only regretted having missed out on those parts of immortal lovemaking when he had still needed to hide his true nature from her.

She reached up to his face, her fingers brushing lightly over the razor-sharp points of his fangs. Edgar shuddered at her touch, his eyes fluttering closed momentarily as he savored the sensation.

"I love seeing you like this," Jasmine murmured, her voice low and thick with desire. "The real you, no holds barred."

Edgar's eyes snapped open, the glow intensifying as he gazed down at her. "Oh, sweetheart. The holds are barred. You can't take what I can dish out. Not as a human."

"Try me," she challenged.

He shook his head, his hungry gaze softening. "I will never risk hurting you." He lowered his body over hers and wrapped his arms around her, holding her close as he kissed her gently. "You mean so much to me."

"Oh, Ed." Jasmine lifted her hands to cup his cheeks. "You mean so much to me, too." She kissed him, careful of his sharp fangs.

The word love had been on her tongue, but she'd refrained from saying it because it would have been a lie.

She liked Edgar a lot, but did she love him?

It was too early to tell, and she was in no rush. They had weeks or even months to explore their feelings for one another.

Dipping his head, he flicked his tongue over first one nipple and then the other. "I love your breasts." He ran his hand over the side of one swell and down the dip of her waist. "I love everything about you, Jasmine. You are femininity personified."

Was he trying to tell her that he loved her?

Not likely. It was just lust, which was perfectly fine with her. She didn't want anything more.

She ran her fingers through his short hair. "You say the nicest things."

"I mean it." He snaked his hand under the thick curtain of her hair and closed it over her nape.

Taking her lips, his tongue slipped into her mouth, and as it dueled with hers, she surrendered to the kiss.

His confidence and dominance were sexy, especially since they were tempered by his dedication to satisfying her needs and not pushing her to do anything she wasn't comfortable with.

Edgar was a skilled, generous, and considerate lover.

Under her fingers, his muscles felt tense, but the way he touched her was gentle. His hand brushed over her breasts and belly and then hovered over her center.

"The scent of your desire is like a siren call I can't resist." He kissed her again while his fingers dipped between her wet folds, teasing, caressing, and when he worked two into her, she groaned into his mouth.

She needed him inside of her, which meant it was time for a condom.

As if reading her mind, Edgar stretched his arm out to reach for the drawer in the nightstand where they had put the condoms and fished out a packet.

He handed it to her. "Put it on me."

"Yes, sir." She tore it with her teeth, removed the rubber, and sheathed him.

As he entered her, they both groaned and then he was moving, his hips retreating and surging forward in an ever-increasing tempo and power until he was ramming into her again and again and driving her up toward the edge of the cliff.

The world fell away as they lost themselves in each other, the pleasure building and cresting until it consumed them both. Jasmine cried out Edgar's name as she shattered in his arms, waves of ecstasy crashing over her one after the other.

He followed her over the edge, releasing with a primal roar that echoed through the room, but he didn't bite her.

They clung to each other, their sweat-slicked bodies entwined and their hearts pounding in sync.

"I'm glad that you didn't bite me, but I also regret it," she whispered into the crook of his neck. "I love the feeling of euphoria washing over me and the trip that follows."

He lifted his head and looked at her with a smile on his handsome face. "You would have been out for hours, and we are supposed to go talk to the others and show them what you found."

"I know."

He smirked. "Don't worry. I plan on making love to you again when we return here tonight, and then I'm going to bite you."

As a new thrill of desire rushed through her, Edgar groaned. "Don't do this to me, woman. I won't be able to get out of bed."

"I'm not doing anything." She moved her hands to his sculpted ass and dug her fingers in the muscle.

He was already hard again, and if they had a little more time, she could have enjoyed another round, but it would have to wait for later.

20

MARINA

The sounds of the ocean and the salty tang of the breeze were soothing, but Marina was too tired to enjoy either of them as she and Peter made their way towards the bungalow area.

She shuffled her feet and concentrated on not falling on her face and on keeping her eyelids from drooping. It sucked to be a human, especially when paired with an immortal who looked as fresh and energetic as if he'd slept the entire way from Long Beach to the Oregon Coast.

He wrapped his arm around her middle, propping her up, while his other hand pulled his suitcase with her duffle bag balanced precariously on top of it. Everything she owned fit into that one bag that wasn't even full. She was still trying to overcome the embarrassment of him seeing the room she'd shared with Larissa and how meager her belongings were.

Marina had caught the pinched expression on Peter's face when she'd collected her things and hugged Larissa goodbye. He hadn't commented on anything, but he had seen and internalized that he had fallen in love with a real Cinderella who had next to nothing to her name.

When they reached the first bungalow, Peter stopped and looked down at her. "Do you want to check this one out?" He nodded towards the door.

Looking up the street and the ascending line of bungalows, she shook her head. "I want the top one." Surprisingly, no one had thought to use the abandoned facilities to house more guests. They could have commanded a premium price. "It has the best view, maybe even of the ocean. It's on the top of the hill, so its windows should clear the lodge's steep roof."

Peter glanced up at the hill, then back at Marina, his brow furrowing. "Are

313

you sure you can make it up there? You look like you're about to fall asleep on your feet."

He wasn't wrong, but she was stubborn, and she wanted that bungalow. "I won't. I can do it."

Peter chuckled, then turned around and crouched down. "Hop on," he said, patting his back. "I'll give you a piggyback ride the rest of the way."

Marina hesitated momentarily, glancing around to see if anyone could see them, but the area was deserted, and the five hundred feet uphill looked daunting.

"Thank you. You are the best." She climbed onto his back, wrapping her arms around his neck and her legs around his waist. Peter stood up with ease, hoisting her higher, and grabbed the suitcase and bag with his free hand.

As he began to climb the hill, Marina couldn't help but laugh at the absurdity of the situation. "I'm so glad that no one can see us. It's like a scene from a romantic comedy or *The Twilight Zone*."

"I get the romantic comedy, but why *The Twilight Zone*?"

"It's just creepy that this entire resort section is unoccupied. It's so quiet and dark out here."

"Perhaps, but it works perfectly for us." Peter kept climbing the hill. "We can sleep in a different bungalow every night until your transfer request is approved."

When he reached the top, he set her down, pulled out his phone, and checked the photo of Eleanor's list with all the lock numbers. After a moment, he found the right one and entered the combination.

Peter reached inside and flipped on the lights as the door swung open. When Marina made a move to step in, he blocked the doorway with his body. "Isn't carrying the lady over the threshold a human tradition?" He swung her into his arms.

"It used to be, and only for brides."

"Well, I like it." He walked in and deposited her on the couch. "Don't move. I'll just get the luggage and close the door."

The bungalow was small, but it had everything, and it was perfect. There was a little kitchenette with a stretch counter that held a stove, a sink, and a coffee maker. The refrigerator was tall and narrow, and there was a microwave oven.

Peter brought in their luggage, closed the door behind him, and purposefully strode toward the couch. "Ready to see the bedroom?"

"Yes." She started to push to her feet but found herself in his arms instead.

"Another threshold," Peter explained as he dipped his head and kissed her lips.

The bedroom door was nestled between the kitchen and a dining nook, and

314

as Peter pushed it open, Marina saw the large bed in the middle. There was also a dresser, two narrow nightstands, and a desk under the window.

"This is amazing." She looked up at him with a happy smile. "It looks so small from the outside, but it has everything we need, and it's so cozy and pretty."

Peter grinned. "I love it too, and we didn't check out the bathroom yet."

He put her down, took her hand, and led her into the bathroom.

Flipping on the light, Marina felt her jaw drop as she took in the glass-enclosed shower and the deep, inviting bathtub. "Oh, wow." She ran her fingers along the cool porcelain. "I love having a tub. I only indulged in one at your cabin on the ship."

Peter wrapped his arms around her from behind, resting his chin on her shoulder. "I'm glad you approve."

"Approve?" Marina backed against him. "I more than approve." She turned in his arms, looking up at him with a smile. "You know, this is the first time in my life that I've had a place of my own. I could see myself living here with you, and I don't even mind my boring maid job. We could just stay here. Can you ask to be permanently stationed in Safe Haven?"

Peter cupped her face in his hands. "I could, but I won't unless Kian doesn't approve your request for some reason." He kissed her forehead, then pulled back to look into her eyes. "My house in the village is much bigger, and there are so many more opportunities for you there. You could study while interpreting for the Kra-ell or just babysitting here and there. You don't want to spend the rest of your life changing sheets and cleaning bathrooms. Nothing is wrong with that, but you are so talented with languages that it would be a waste. You will be happier in the village. I promise."

Marina bit on her lip. She had been so excited about moving to the village with Peter, but now that she was here, in this perfect little bungalow, she wasn't so sure. After all, Larissa and her other friends were here, and although she wasn't particularly close to any of them, she would miss them.

On the other hand, she wasn't so thrilled about the other humans in Safe Haven. It wasn't nice to think negatively about the community members who had welcomed her people with open arms, but she wasn't a fan of their chosen lifestyle.

Then again, living in a village of immortals where she was at the bottom of the food chain wasn't so great either.

"What's the matter?" Peter asked. "Are you having second thoughts?"

She nodded. "There are advantages and disadvantages to both places, but all I care about is being with you. I'll be happy wherever you are."

He brushed his thumb across her cheekbone. "If you want to stay here, in Safe Haven, then I will put in a request to transfer here permanently. We can keep this bungalow and make it our little paradise, but I suggest that you sleep on it. You shouldn't make any decision while you are so bone tired."

21

JASMINE

alf an hour later, when Jasmine and Edgar walked into the other penthouse, holding hands and with the map of Tibet tucked under Edgar's arm, the afterglow of their lovemaking was still thrumming through her veins. Still, she did her best to erase the stupid smile from her face and assume an impassive expression.

From her experience, people took those who talked calmly and rationally more seriously. Given that she was about to provide them with information that would determine where they were going, and that said information was based on an unproven method that they all questioned, she needed to appear level-headed.

The rest of the team had already gathered, sprawled on the plush couches and armchairs.

Aru looked up from the tablet he'd been studying, his brow furrowed in concentration. "Ah, there you are," he said, setting the device aside. "We were just going over some of the logistics for the trip. Did you have any luck with the scrying?"

Releasing Edgar's hand, Jasmine pulled the rolled-up map from under his arm. "I did. I was able to locate a general area where I believe the escape pod might be located, but when I tried to zero in and pinpoint the location, I was unsuccessful." She spread the map on the coffee table, smoothing the creases with her fingertips.

The others leaned forward, their eyes scanning the terrain.

Jasmine tapped a finger on the area she'd marked. "It's somewhere near

Mount Kailash. I couldn't get a more precise location, but I'm hoping that once we're there, I'll be able to sense it more clearly."

Dagor frowned, studying the map intently. "Mount Kailash is a pretty remote area even by Tibetan standards. It's not going to be an easy trek."

"No, it won't," Aru agreed. "We will need to upgrade the specs of our equipment."

Margo leaned back in her seat, her arms crossed over her chest. "What kind of conditions are we talking about, exactly? I mean, I know Tibet is located at a high altitude and all that, but what else should we expect?"

Negal glanced over at her, his lips twitching in a half-smile. "Cold, for one thing. Even in the summer, temperatures can drop below freezing at night. And the air will be thin, which can make physical exertion challenging." He shifted his eyes to Jasmine. "For a human. The rest of us will be fine."

She rolled her eyes. "Yeah, yeah. I know. But what can I do? We can't wait for me to transition." She sat down on the couch next to Margo. "Although, given how quickly the two of you transitioned, I might have been able to do that during the week we are supposed to wait for Kian and Toven to finalize the arrangements."

Margo let out a breath and smiled apologetically. "Edgar is not a god, which means that his venom is not as potent as a god's, so it might have taken you much longer than us to transition, and maybe not as smoothly."

Edgar had explained to her some of the differences between gods and immortals, and the distinctions didn't seem very meaningful to her. He'd also told her that some immortals were more powerful than gods. The three gods present couldn't compel like Kevin, an immortal, and Yamanu, who was also just an immortal, could make realistic illusions convincing thousands. The gods couldn't do that either.

But those were the outliers.

Edgar didn't belong to that exclusive group.

Frankie bit her lip, looking worried. "Is it going to be dangerous? I mean, I'm immortal and can heal fast, but if we are buried under an avalanche, what will happen to us?"

Dagor shook his head. "If that happens, which is unlikely, we will enter stasis and get revived once the rescue teams dig us out. But then we will have to thrall all their memories of finding us in that state."

"It's going to be fine," Negal said. "As long as we're careful and take the proper precautions. We'll have the right gear and acclimatize gradually to the altitude so none of us gets lightheaded when we are up there." He glanced at Aru. "Like what happened to you."

"What happened?" Gabi asked.

Aru waved a dismissive hand. "I learned the hard way that taking things slow and careful is better. In the end, it's a faster route."

"So, how do we get to Mount Kailash?" Jasmine asked, looking around at the others. "And what do we do once we're there?"

Negal leaned forward, his elbows resting on his knees. "We'll fly into Lhasa first, as planned. That's the capital of Tibet. From there, we'll need to arrange transportation to get as close to the mountain as possible. Probably a combination of jeeps and hiking, depending on the terrain."

Aru nodded. "We'll need to be careful not to draw too much attention to ourselves. Tibet is a politically sensitive area, and we don't want to raise any red flags with the authorities. A good cover is essential, and research sounds good. Perhaps we should read about geology a little. We should be able to sound professional when asked questions."

Jasmine felt a flicker of apprehension in her gut. "Make me the researcher's girlfriend who doesn't know anything. I'm not good with learning things fast."

Edgar cast her a smile. "Most people will assume that everything we say about the subject we are supposed to be experts on is fact, and they won't challenge us. People are quick to surrender their common sense and critical thinking when presented information by a source they have reason to consider authoritative. In other words, we should be able to BS through any interaction as long as our credentials are solid."

Jasmine didn't know how to do that, but she could pretend to be mute and let Edgar do the talking.

Negal tapped his chin. "Once we get to the area, we'll have to rely on a combination of Jasmine's scrying abilities and our equipment. If the pod is giving off any kind of energy signature, we should be able to pick it up on our scanner."

Margo sighed, running a hand through her hair. "It's like looking for a needle in a haystack. A really, really big haystack. It looks small on the map, but that's probably a big area." She looked at Jasmine. "I hope that you will be able to better pinpoint the location."

"I hope so, too." Jasmine sighed. "I'm just not sure that we will find them alive." She rubbed a hand over her belly. "I have a bad feeling about that."

Everyone around the table went quiet suddenly.

"What do you mean?" Edgar asked. "And when did you start having this bad feeling?"

They were all taking her so seriously that it was unnerving. "It's nothing." She smiled. "I'm probably more nervous now that I'm starting to realize how difficult this will be. It's not like the tarot told me that something bad will happen." She squinted. "Actually, I should do a reading." She looked at the faces of her teammates. "For all of you."

Dagor lifted his hands. "I'll pass."

"Why?" Frankie asked. "Don't you want to know your future?"

"No, not particularly. I prefer to be surprised. It makes life more interesting."

22

EDGAR

As Jasmine started to rise, Aru lifted his hand. "Let's keep the entertainment part of the evening for later. There is still a lot we need to discuss regarding the trip."

Edgar cast Jasmine a sidelong glance and wasn't surprised that Aru's words offended her.

When she sat back down, Jasmine's exuberant expression soured. "Tarot is a divining tool. They are not purely for entertainment."

"Apologies." Aru dipped his head. "I didn't mean to offend you."

She sighed. "It's okay. Most people think of tarot that way, and they are usually right."

Margo, who had been scrolling on her new phone and oblivious to the exchange between Aru and Jasmine, suddenly lifted her head. "Did you know Tibet is often called the 'Roof of the World'? The Tibetan Plateau is the highest in the world. The average elevation is almost fifteen thousand feet, the height of the tallest mountains in the continental USA." She lifted her head. "Can you imagine that? That huge plateau, which is almost one million square miles, is taller than Mount Whitney. Only Alaska has mountains that are taller than that."

"That's incredible." Frankie looked at Dagor. "Now I get why you were talking about trouble breathing up there. I thought you were exaggerating." She turned to look at Jasmine. "I'm worried about you."

So was Edgar.

Dagor shook his head. "As I said before, it's manageable when done correctly, so you don't need to worry. As long as we ascend gradually and give Jasmine's body time to adjust, she can adapt to the high altitude. We'll just need to be careful and watch for signs of altitude sickness."

"Good to know that the condition is manageable," Edgar said. "But you should be mentally prepared to do most of the trekking on foot. The helicopter might be pretty useless in such thin air."

That got their attention, and everyone's expression soured.

"What should we do then?" Aru asked. "Should we scrap the idea of a chopper altogether?"

Edgar realized his mistake. If they decided not to get a helicopter, they would have no use for him and most likely leave him behind. There was no way he was allowing Jasmine to slip away from him, probably straight into the arms of her damn prince. "A chopper can still be useful, even crucial, to the mission. I meant that its utility might be more limited than you hoped."

Frankie sighed. "I have a feeling that we will be separated for longer periods than we initially anticipated. Do they even have hotels and inns there? How many people live in Tibet?"

Margo looked down at her phone. "I don't know about inns and hotels, but it says here that the entire Tibetan population consists of about three million people and most of them are ethnic Tibetans. But there are also a lot of Han Chinese and other ethnic groups living there."

Dagor nodded. "That's true. The region has a complex political history, with a lot of tension between the Tibetan people and the Chinese government. It's an autonomous region of China, but many are not happy with that and want Tibet to be independent or at least have greater autonomy. As for accommodations for tourists, I'm afraid there isn't much outside popular tourist areas like Lhasa, Shigatse, and Gyantse. Smaller towns and rural areas might have guesthouses and inns that provide basic accommodations. In trekking areas, though, camping is the most common option. In some places, monasteries offer rooms for overnight stays, but we never took advantage of that. We always preferred camping."

Jasmine groaned. "I thought I could shower at least every other day, but it doesn't seem feasible."

Negal cast her an apologetic look. "I'm sorry, but it's going to be rough."

"Where is Mount Everest located?" Gabi asked. "Is it anywhere near where we need to go?"

"Not really," Aru said. "Mount Everest and Mount Kailash are not very close to each other. Mount Everest is located on the border between Nepal and Tibet and is part of the Himalayan range. Mount Kailash is situated more to the northwest of Tibet and is considerably remote. They are about five hundred miles apart, but it's not like you can travel to one from the other. You would need to return to a major city like Lhasa or Kathmandu and then proceed to the other destination."

"What about culture?" Gabi asked. "Isn't Tibet where the fabled kingdom of Shambhala is?"

Jasmine's eyes widened. "A hidden kingdom? What if that's what I'm supposed to find? Is there a missing prince in the legends about Shambhala?"

Dagor shrugged. "The legends of Shambhala are pretty vague and open to interpretation. According to some, it is a mythical kingdom that is hidden somewhere in the mountains of Tibet. It's described as an enlightened place ruled by a succession of wise kings who preserve ancient wisdom. It's only reachable by those destined to find it through their virtue and wisdom. Others say it is not a physical location but a state of enlightened consciousness achievable through rigorous spiritual practice. The prophecy associated with Shambhala suggested a future era of peace and enlightenment, emerging from global turmoil."

Jasmine rubbed her forehead. "Maybe that's my mission. The world is in terrible turmoil right now, worse than anything I can remember, and we desperately need Shambhala."

Dagor smiled indulgently. "You're forgetting Syssi's vision. She didn't see you standing at the gates of a magical kingdom. She saw you standing over a crater with something smooth and metallic at the bottom."

"Right." Jasmine let out a breath. "Compared to finding Shambhala, finding the royal twins seems easy."

Edgar would have been much happier with Jasmine finding a mythical land than some prince who might be the one destined for her.

He reached for her hand. "We'll be focusing our search around Mount Kailash, which is considered a holy site by multiple religions, so maybe the two are connected?"

Margo glanced at her phone again, her eyebrows raising. "It says here that Mount Kailash is believed to be the earthly manifestation of Mount Meru, the center of the universe in Hindu and Buddhist cosmology."

Dagor nodded. "The area around Mount Kailash is considered a powerful spiritual vortex, with some strange and unexplained phenomena reported by visitors. That's precisely the type of clues we are investigating, and Jasmine's scrying added validity to the location."

23

JASMINE

As the plane descended into the Gonggar Airport in Lhasa, Jasmine pressed her face against the small oval window, eager to catch her first glimpse of Tibet. The landscape below was breathtaking, a patchwork of rugged mountains, pristine lakes, and vast expanses of grassland stretching out as far as the eye could see.

She felt excitement as the plane touched down on the runway, bouncing a little before rolling to a stop. They had finally arrived in Lhasa, the capital city of Tibet, and the starting point of their incredible journey.

They had waited for more than a week as Kian and Kevin, aka Kalugal, Turner, Shai, and others, had worked tirelessly to make all the arrangements for them, with Mia's mate footing the bill for the expedition.

Jasmine couldn't even start to imagine how much money had gone into the mission and how much time everyone involved had put into the preparations, and it was all because of her.

Talk about pressure.

If she failed them, she would be crushed.

"Come on, beautiful." Edgar pulled out their carry-ons from the overhead compartment. "Let the adventure begin."

She smiled up at him. "My adventure began in Cabo and has been gathering momentum ever since."

As the group deplaned and made their way through the airport, the air-conditioned terminal provided a temporary respite from the thin, crisp air outside, but Jasmine knew that she would soon feel the effects of the high altitude. Lhasa was one of the highest cities in the world at nearly twelve thousand feet.

In the luggage area, a man holding a sign with the name of their fake research team was waiting for them.

He was tall and slender, with a warm smile and kind eyes. As they approached him, he greeted them with a traditional Tibetan welcome: "*Tashi delek*. I am Tenzin Dorjee, your guide. Welcome to Lhasa, the city of sunshine and the heart of Tibet."

Margo grinned at Tenzin. "*Tashi delek*! We're so excited to be here. I've been reading about Lhasa on the plane and can't wait to explore the city."

Tenzin smiled back at her. "I'm sure you will love it here. Lhasa is an extraordinary place, with a rich history and culture unlike anywhere else in the world." He put the sign away and pulled a bunch of white scarves from his satchel. "These are called khatas," he said as he draped the white silk scarves around each of their necks. "They are a symbol of goodwill and respect."

After collecting their luggage, they followed Tenzin to the waiting minibus that would take them to their hotel in the city center.

Looking out the window, Jasmine marveled at the unique architecture of the buildings they were passing. Many houses and shops were painted in vibrant colors and adorned with intricate designs and patterns, presenting a perfect blend of traditional Tibetan style and modern influences.

As the minibus stopped in front of the luxurious St. Regis Lhasa Resort, Jasmine was impressed by the unique beauty of the building. It was designed in the style of a traditional Tibetan palace, with sweeping curves, ornate carvings, and a grand central courtyard.

"Wow," Ella breathed as she stepped out of the minibus. "This place is incredible. I feel like royalty just standing here."

Julian chuckled and wrapped an arm around her shoulders. "You are my queen, so you should be treated as one."

After checking in, they headed to their rooms for a quick bathroom break, and then they regrouped in the lobby to begin their tour of Lhasa.

The objective was to spend a couple of days in the capital so Jasmine would get acclimatized to the high altitude before starting their travels. Still, everyone who hadn't been to Tibet before was pleased to have the excuse to see the city.

"The first stop is the iconic Potala Palace, the former residence of the Dalai Lamas and the symbol of Tibetan Buddhism," Tenzin said.

As they approached the massive structure, Jasmine was struck by its sheer size and grandeur. The palace towered over the city, its white and red walls gleaming in the bright sunlight.

Tenzin led them up the many steps to the entrance. "The Potala Palace was built in the seventh century by the Tibetan king Songtsen Gampo," he explained as they climbed. "It has served as the residence of the Dalai Lamas since the seventeenth century and is now a museum and a UNESCO World Heritage Site."

They explored the many rooms and halls of the palace, with its rich colors and intricate designs of the murals and tapestries that adorned the walls; the air was thick with the scent of incense and the soft murmur of chanting monks.

After the Potala Palace, they visited the Jokhang Temple, the most sacred temple in Tibet. The place was bustling with activity, with pilgrims from all over Tibet and beyond coming to pay their respects and offer prayers.

"King Songtsen Gampo also built the Jokhang Temple," Tenzin said. "It was erected to house a sacred Buddha statue brought to Tibet by his Chinese wife, Princess Wencheng."

Walking through the temple complex, they passed pilgrims prostrating themselves on the ground, their foreheads touching the stone floor as they murmured prayers and mantras.

"The temple is the spiritual heart of Lhasa and the most important pilgrimage site in Tibet," Tenzin explained.

Their final stop for the day was the lively Barkhor Street, a bustling marketplace and pilgrim circuit surrounding the Jokhang Temple. The narrow, winding streets were lined with stalls selling everything from colorful prayer flags and traditional Tibetan clothing to yak butter tea and momos, a kind of dumpling that made Jasmine's mouth water.

"How are you feeling?" Edgar asked. "Is the altitude bothering you?"

Jasmine chuckled. "I was so busy sightseeing that I forgot about it."

"Good." He squeezed her hand. "So, you are not dizzy or anything?"

"No, I'm good."

Smiling, Gabi leaned to whisper in her ear, "Don't get adjusted too quickly. I want at least another day here, and if you are good to go, Aru might push up the timeline."

"Got it." Jasmine gave her the thumbs up.

Given the smirk lifting Aru's lips, he'd heard their exchange, but he was pretending that he hadn't.

As they wandered through the market taking in the sights, sounds, and smells, Jasmine thought about the journey ahead of them, and she wasn't eager to begin it. It wasn't because she was worried about the discomfort of camping or the rigors of the trek—not even the lack of a daily shower.

It was the fear of failure.

Negal and Margo stopped by one of the stalls and started haggling with a vendor over a beautiful, hand-woven rug. Jasmine and Edgar joined Julian, Ella, Frankie, and Dagor in sampling yak butter tea.

"This is an acquired taste." Frankie wrinkled her nose. "But when in Tibet, right?"

Dagor chuckled and took another sip. "It's not so bad once you get used to it. And it's supposed to be good for you, especially at high altitudes."

"It's disgusting," Ella whispered. "Is there anywhere I can pour it out without anyone noticing? I don't want to offend anyone."

Julian took the cup from her. "I'll take one for the team." He drank half of the liquid before returning the mug to the vendor.

Jasmine smelled the tea and decided to pass on it as well. "I hope they serve regular food at the hotel. I'm hungry and afraid to sample the local fare and suffer the consequences."

"We should head back soon," their tour guide said. "And yes, you will be happy with the cuisine at the hotel."

Jasmine felt her cheeks redden. She'd thought he hadn't heard her.

That evening, as they gathered for dinner in the hotel's elegant dining room, Aru invited Tenzin to join them so he could share more details about what lay ahead.

"Tomorrow, we will continue the tour of the city, and the day after that, we will take a short flight to Gunsa Airport in Ali Prefecture. From there, we will have two drivers pick us up and take us to Darchen, the starting point for our trek."

She leaned toward Edgar. "Is Tenzin joining us on the search?"

Edgar shook his head. "Not likely. I'm sure that Aru will take care of this."

Meaning he would thrall the guide and leave him behind whenever it was possible.

24

EDGAR

E dgar stepped out of the Jeep, his boots crunching on the gravel as he surveyed the small town of Darchen. The two vehicles that had collected them from Shiquanhe Airport were now parked in front of a modest hotel, which would serve as their base for the time being.

Darchen was a small, unassuming town with simple buildings and dusty streets. But it had a certain charm, a sense of timelessness and spirituality that permeated the air. In the distance, he could see the snow-capped peaks of the Himalayas, their jagged silhouettes cutting into the clear blue sky. Somewhere out there, amidst those towering mountains and deep valleys, the Kra-ell pod lay waiting to be found.

Edgar took a deep breath, feeling the cold air filling his lungs and nipping at his skin. He glanced over at Jasmine, who was bundled up in a thick coat and scarf, her cheeks flushed from the cold.

She seemed to be struggling to catch her breath, and Edgar felt concerned.

"Are you okay?" He wrapped his arm around her.

"Yeah, I'm fine." She smiled at him. "I just need to stretch my legs after the long ride."

"It was damn bumpy." Margo stomped her feet. "I feel like taking a walk around. Do you want to join me?"

Their guide must have overheard her because he came rushing their way. "We need to check into the hotel. In the meantime, I will reserve a table at the restaurant."

Edgar cast a questioning look at what Tenzin called a hotel. He wouldn't even call it a motel, but as long as it had running water, preferably hot, and a bed, he didn't care.

And heating. At night, the temperatures in this place plummeted even lower.

As the drivers unloaded their luggage, they gathered their belongings and entered the hotel.

The ladies' faces looked apprehensive, echoing Edgar's. The accommodations were basic at best, with simple rooms and limited amenities. But they had all known what to expect when they signed up for this mission, and no one voiced their reservations. The other option was to erect a tent encampment for the group, which would probably be the cleaner route, but Edgar preferred a real toilet to a field one, and he had no doubt that Jasmine felt the same.

As they put their things in the room, Jasmine eyed the bed with suspicion. "What do you think about using our sleeping bags on the bed?"

"That's an excellent idea. But we should eat first." He took her gloved hand and led her out of the room.

The hotel restaurant, as their guide had called it, was housed in a large tent, but it was warm inside, and the aromas were appetizing. The menu was limited, with dishes like yak meat stew, steamed dumplings, and yak tea.

"Is everything here made with yak?" Frankie asked quietly. "Even the dumplings are stuffed with yak meat."

"That's what they have here," Ella said. "I love trying local cuisine, and since I don't need to worry about food intolerance, I can be adventurous, but I just can't stomach their tea."

After they ordered, Edgar turned to their guide. "When can I check out the helicopters?"

"Tomorrow," Tenzin said. "One was already delivered, and the pilot got a ride back to get the other one."

"Thank you." Edgar leaned back as the first course was served.

It was a steaming dumpling soup that seemed hearty and smelled delicious.

As they ate, he considered getting an aerial reconnaissance of the area. The plan was to scope out the region by hopping by air in ten-mile intervals, with Jasmine using her scrying abilities to guide them at each landing site. It would be time-consuming, and once they progressed beyond the hundred-mile radius, they would need to move their base forward to continue due to the helicopters' limited range. It would be tents and field toilets from there on.

Both choppers were small because of the expected need to navigate rugged terrain, steep slopes, and possibly tight spaces. Plus, once they moved their base out of the small town, one of the helicopters would be used to shuttle fuel to the other, allowing them to extend their range and continue their search.

As the meal ended, Edgar noticed that Jasmine looked even more uncomfortable, and her breathing was becoming shallower and more rapid.

He leaned over to Aru, who was seated on his other side. "I think Jasmine's having trouble with the altitude," he said quietly. "She doesn't look good."

Aru glanced over at Jasmine and frowned. "You're right. Julian can give her oxygen."

Jasmine shook her head. "I'm fine," she said, but her voice was strained. "Just a little tired after the long ride, that's all."

Edgar shook his head. "Don't be silly. Pretending that you are fine is not doing anyone any good. Let Julian help you."

Jasmine hesitated for a moment and then nodded. "Okay."

As Aru got Julian's attention and pointed at Jasmine, the doctor frowned, pushed away from the table, and walked over.

He checked her pulse and breathing. "You're feeling the effects of the altitude," he said, reaching into his bag and pulling out a small oxygen canister. "Here, breathe this in. It'll make you feel better."

Jasmine took the canister and inhaled deeply, closing her eyes as the pure oxygen flooded her lungs. Almost immediately, the color returned to her cheeks and her breathing became more even.

"Thank you." She handed the canister back to Julian. "I feel better, but that was a temporary fix. What if I need more oxygen?"

Julian smiled. "I brought plenty, and they also sell them here in the general store, so don't worry about it."

Edgar nodded in agreement. "You should pack some canisters in your backpack while trekking."

Aru cleared his throat to get their attention. "Tomorrow morning, Edgar, Jasmine, Dagor, Negal, and I will take one of the helicopters and start our aerial search. We'll fly to the first location we marked on the map and continue in ten-mile intervals. Hopefully, Jasmine's unique research method will point us in the right direction, and if we get lucky, our equipment will pick up the rest."

Aru was mindful of the other guests and staff who were within earshot, and that was why he was using the terms he had. A shrouding sound bubble wasn't advisable when it was obvious that they were being spied on. Their group suddenly going silent would have been even more suspicious than the mention of scrying sticks and alien technology.

Aru turned to the others. "The rest of you will have to stay here, ready to provide support if we need it."

Edgar couldn't imagine what support they could provide, but Aru had probably said that just to make them feel less useless. The only reason that Gabi, Frankie, and Margo had joined them was that they were all newly mated and couldn't stand being away from their mates. Ella had the slim excuse of having emergency response medical training and her ability to assist Julian if needed. Still, the real reason she was here was because of her mate.

Edgar didn't mind—on the contrary. Traveling with a large group was more fun, and the ladies made it look less suspicious.

25

PETER

A week and a half had passed since Peter had arrived with Marina in Safe Haven, and things had settled into a comfortable routine. He was making the rounds, patrolling and taking turns in the surveillance room while she worked in the lodge, preparing it for the next retreat that was supposed to start on Friday.

Standing on the sandy shore, he pulled out his phone and thought of an excuse to call her. Perhaps he could tell her the joke Malcom had told him that morning. It was stupid, but Marina would laugh anyway because she did so at all his jokes, and he loved hearing her laughter.

She did that much more often now that she was feeling more secure in their relationship.

"Hello, love, how is work?" he asked when she answered.

"Larissa and I are scrubbing the tiles in the bathrooms. Do you want to help?"

He chuckled. "No, thank you. If you had said you were scrubbing by yourself while wearing a naughty French maid outfit, I would have come running."

"You're such a perv."

"I know. That's why you love me."

It felt so good to say that without thinking twice about it and knowing that Marina would respond in kind.

"I do," she admitted. "And the idea of wearing what you suggested makes me feel all tingly in the right places."

Peter groaned. "You are killing me, woman. I'm on duty, patrolling, and now I have to do the three-legged shuffle."

She laughed. "You started it."

"I did."

"So, what did you call me about?"

"I wanted to tell you a stupid joke I heard."

"Tell me."

"So, this guy goes to see a marriage counselor," Peter said, grinning as he watched the waves crash against the beach. "He tells him that he thinks his wife is poisoning his tea. He even took the tea to a lab, and they confirmed it. The counselor tells him that he needs to go to the police, but the guy refuses. He loves his wife, and he wants to find out why she's trying to kill him."

On the other end of the line, Marina chuckled. "That is a terrible joke," she said, but he could hear the amusement in her voice.

"Wait, I didn't get to the punchline yet," Peter said, his grin widening. "The counselor promises the guy that he will talk to the wife. A week later, the guy comes to see him and asks if he talked with her. The therapist says, 'I did. I was on the phone with her for four hours and couldn't understand what she was trying to say. She was all over the place, and I couldn't get her to stop talking so I could guide her.' So, the guy asks, 'What should I do? I love her, and I can't live without her.' The therapist sighs and says, 'Just drink the tea.'"

Marina burst out laughing, the sound filling Peter's ear and making his heart skip a beat. "This is one of the worst jokes I've ever heard," she said. "And it's so human. I thought that all of your immortal buddies adored their mates."

"They do. It's something one of them heard on the radio. He thought it was funny."

"Well, it is. But that's because it's so bad."

"Fine, I'll search for something more amusing to tell you." Peter affected an offended tone.

"Did I insult you?" Marina asked.

"A little," he admitted, but he couldn't keep the smile from his face.

"I'm sorry. Where are you now?"

"On the beach. Why?"

"I'm coming over to kiss you and make it better."

"That worked even better than I planned. I'm waiting."

As he ended the call, Peter took a deep breath of the salty air, letting the ocean breeze ruffle his hair. The sun was high in the sky, casting a warm glow over the sandy expanse, and he couldn't help but feel a sense of peace wash over him.

When he heard footsteps approaching, he turned to see Marina walking toward him, dressed in the ugly pastel-colored uniform the lodge's staff was required to wear but looking beautiful despite it.

"Hey there, handsome," she said, wrapping her arms around his neck and pulling him in for a kiss.

He savored the softness of her lips and the warmth of her body against his, and when they pulled apart, he rested his forehead against hers, breathing in her scent. "I missed you," he murmured.

Marina chuckled, her fingers playing with the collar of his shirt. "It's only been a few hours," she teased, but he could see the happiness in her eyes.

"A few hours is a long time to be away from you. I don't know how I will survive when we're back in the village, and I have to go on assignments that will keep me away from you."

Marina cupped his face in her hands. "Hopefully, I will be just as busy, so I will not be alone in the house while you are gone. Otherwise, the missing you part would be intolerable."

He pulled her closer, burying his face in the crook of her neck. "I love you," he whispered.

She held him tightly, her fingers threading through his hair. "I love you, too," she murmured.

For a long moment, they remained wrapped in each other's arms as the ocean waves crashed against the shore, but duty called, and they each had their tasks to perform.

Marina pulled apart first. "I promised Larissa that I wouldn't be gone for long. I have to go back."

"I know." He smiled. "Three more hours."

She lifted three fingers. "Three more hours."

26

JASMINE

J asmine sat cross-legged on the floor of the hotel room, the enlarged map of Tibet spread out before her. It was night outside, and the room was dimly lit. The only source of illumination came from the bedside lamp, which was nothing more than an exposed lightbulb screwed onto something resembling a vase.

She'd wanted to bring candles with her for the ritual, but given the practical considerations of space and weight, not to mention the prospect of doing so in a tent, she'd opted to use incense instead.

The sweet, heavy scents of sandalwood and juniper weaved through the stale air of the small room, curling in whispers of smoke from a flickering stick nestled in an incense holder by the window.

The fragrance clung to the threadbare curtains and seeped into her clothing and bed linens, which given the smell in the room was a big improvement.

Jasmine took a deep breath, trying to clear her mind and focus. She imagined the Kra-ell pod, with twenty people inside of it. Now that she had been given more details, it was easier to visualize the alien craft, and hopefully that would help her scrying.

Except, it didn't.

The more she tried to focus her inner energy into the stick, the less response she was getting from it.

With frustration and disappointment welling up inside her, tears stung the back of her eyes, further obliterating her concentration. She closed her eyes, refusing to admit defeat and let Edgar see her breaking down.

Finally, after what felt like an eternity, Jasmine sighed heavily and slumped forward, her head hanging low. "It's no use," she admitted, her voice barely audible over her breathing. "I've tried everything, but I just can't get a read on the location."

Edgar was by her side instantly, wrapping his arms around her and pulling her close. "Hey, it's okay," he murmured, pressing a gentle kiss to her temple. "You're doing the best you can, Jaz. Spiritual stuff is finicky. You said so yourself. Sometimes it gives you what you ask for, and sometimes it doesn't."

It was true that she had said that, and yet, she couldn't shake the feeling of failure that clung to her like a layer of stinky tar. Turning in Edgar's embrace, she buried her face in his chest and sighed. "I hate letting everyone down."

Edgar held her tightly, one hand rubbing soothing circles on her back while the other cradled her head. "You are not letting anyone down, and this defeatist attitude is counterproductive, especially for this kind of work. You need to believe in yourself, or you will surely fail."

She chuckled. "Your pep talk sounds more like an accusation, but it's working." She lifted her head to look at him. "If I gave up every time I failed at something, I would never leave my bed."

A smile teased his lips. "I could work with that."

He was such a flirt. Surging up, she captured his lips in a kiss.

Edgar took over instantly, his mouth moving against hers with a hunger that ratcheted her own. Hands roaming and breaths mingling, they lost themselves in each other for a few precious moments, but then the familiar tightness in her chest forced her to pull away, gasping for air.

She still wasn't doing well in the high altitude, and the smallest exertion resulted in her struggling to catch her breath, spots dancing before her eyes.

Edgar sprang into action, reaching for the canister of oxygen that Julian had given her. "Take a few deep breaths." He held the mask to her face.

Jasmine inhaled gratefully, feeling the oxygen flooding her lungs and easing the pressure in her chest. When her breathing began to even out, she put her hand over his and pushed the mask aside. "I'm good now."

Edgar brushed a strand of hair back from her face. "You are always good. Especially when you are being bad."

Jasmine felt a flush of heat rush through her. "I would love to be bad with you, but I'm afraid I will pass out."

He smiled. "I can think of several ways to pleasure you that will not require you to move a muscle."

Jasmine had a good idea what those methods were. "Are they bad, though?" she teased.

"Absolutely wicked." He lifted her by the waist, carried her to their bed, and set her down. "And they come with the added benefit of a venom bite that will make you feel much better tomorrow." He leaned down, grabbed a pillow, and put it behind her. "Lie down, sweetheart."

As she did what he asked, he hovered over her for a long moment, his eyes roaming hungrily over her body while he traced the contours of her face with a feather-light touch.

"You're so beautiful," he murmured.

"You are not too bad yourself." She reached up to cup his face in her hands.

As their lips met in a hard kiss, Jasmine lost herself in the sensation of Edgar's body pressed against hers. His hands roamed over her skin, stripping her clothes off and leaving trails of fire in their wake.

When he kneeled on the floor, she lifted on her forearms and looked at him. "I don't want it to be just about me."

"Don't worry." He unzipped his pants and pulled out his shaft. "I'll do the honors for both of us."

There was something so sexy about what he was offering. "The good news is that we will save a condom."

"That's the only good news?" He leaned down and swiped his tongue over her slit.

Her eyes rolled back in their sockets. "That's good news as well."

He licked her again and then entered her with two fingers. "How about this?"

She could barely talk, and it wasn't because she was starved for oxygen this time. "Yeah, that's also good. Very good. Keep going."

He chuckled against her wet folds, the vibrations adding to her heightened state of arousal. "Oh, I intend to."

Jasmine wished she could watch him pump his shaft in sync with his licking and fingering, but his head was blocking her view. Still, she could hear the lurid sounds he was making, and that was sexy as hell. Closing her eyes, she let his skilled fingers and wickedly talented tongue wind up the tight coil of her pleasure.

When the sounds of his hand sliding up and down his shaft became frantic, so did his assault on her core and her clit, and as the coil sprang, she felt him sink his fangs into the tender skin of her inner thigh. The searing pain prompted her to scream, but she turned her face and pressed her mouth against her inner arm to muffle the sound, and when the venom entered her system, she climaxed again.

Lost in ecstasy, she shot up to the sky, and the world receded into a distant hum.

2 7

EDGAR

E dgar stepped out of the hotel and squinted against the bright morning sun. The air was crisp and cool, the same as when they had arrived the day before, but things warmed up later, only to cool down again in the evening. He had expected much harsher conditions and was pleasantly surprised to discover that the weather wasn't nearly as extreme as he'd been led to believe.

Perhaps it was the mild season on the Tibetan Plateau.

He took a deep breath, filling his lungs with the thin, dry air, and surveyed his surroundings. The arid landscape was ruggedly beautiful. The terrain was a patchwork of earthy hues, with expanses of sandy soil broken up by tufts of hardy grass and low-growing shrubs. Not so far in the distance, the snow-capped peaks of the Himalayas loomed large.

Still, he knew that the pleasant weather could deteriorate rapidly and drastically. The Tibetan Plateau was known for its unpredictable weather patterns, with strong winds and sudden storms that could appear seemingly out of nowhere.

Hearing footsteps on the gravel behind him, Edgar turned around and saw Tenzin walking toward him. Today, the man was dressed in traditional Tibetan clothing, with a long, dark robe and a colorful sash around his waist.

"Good morning, Mr. Edgar." He greeted him with a warm smile and a slight bow. "I trust you slept well?"

Edgar returned the smile. "Good morning, Tenzin. I slept fine, thank you. And please drop the mister. Simply Edgar is fine."

"As you wish." The guide dipped his head.

"I'm eager to get started," Edgar said.

"Of course. That is why I am here." Tenzin gestured for Edgar to follow him.

It took them about fifteen minutes to get from the hotel to the outskirts of the tiny town, where two small helicopters were parked along with a truck loaded with fuel containers and crates of unmarked medical equipment that contained the provisions Julian had ordered.

Two men stood by the truck. One was dressed like Tenzin, and the other wore Western clothes but looked to be a local.

"Edgar, allow me to introduce you to Norbu," Tenzin said, pointing to the man in Western clothing. "He is the pilot for the supply helicopter."

"A pleasure to meet you." Edgar offered the man his hand.

Norbu's grip was firm as he shook it. "Good morning, Mr. Edgar," he said, his English heavily accented but clear. "I am honored to serve a distinguished scientific expedition."

Edgar glanced at Tenzin, wondering what the guide had told the other pilot.

Tenzin looked a little uncomfortable. "Norbu asked why you needed to make so many trips. I told him that you would be flying a group of geologists who needed to collect samples from various mountain locations."

That was the cover story, but since Edgar hadn't read the brief, he hoped neither of the guys would ask him questions he had no idea how to answer.

Norbu looked at him as if he was a celebrity. "Which university is doing the research? Is it one of the famous ones like Stanford or MIT?"

Edgar felt a prickle of unease.

That was a particular question that only seemed innocent. He had been warned that they would be spied on, and Norbu was a prime suspect.

He shrugged, affecting nonchalance. "I'm just the hired pilot, so I don't know. I think that it's a collaboration between several institutions. Given how expensive this kind of research is, it makes sense for them to share resources."

Norbu looked impressed. "I hope they mention Tenzin and me in the research paper when they publish it."

Edgar shrugged again. "I don't know if that's something that is done, but I can ask."

The pilot grinned. "If they do, I will be very grateful. I will show everyone I was part of an important scientific project."

Edgar noticed that Norbu's eyes kept darting to the sky as they continued chatting. "What's the matter?" he asked. "Are you expecting something, that you keep looking at the sky?"

"The weather looks good for now," the pilot said. "But that can change quickly. You have no experience here, and it's my duty to let you know if the conditions change. The winds can pick up fast here, and the mountains can create their own conditions."

Edgar nodded, his gaze scanning the horizon. "I've heard that. I'll stay alert and adjust our course as needed." He glanced at the truck. "How much fuel do we have?"

"It will be enough for the next four days. Then we will need to send the driver back to bring more."

28

JASMINE

As Jasmine watched the guys loading the equipment onto the small, precarious-looking helicopter, her shortness of breath returned, but this time it wasn't because of the thin air or the altitude. She had never flown in one before, and the thought of being suspended in the air in such a tiny craft made her stomach churn with anxiety.

"I feel you, sister." Margo wrapped her arm around Jasmine's shoulders. "I would be scared to fly in that bucket with a rotor, too, but I heard your boyfriend is an excellent pilot." She shifted her gaze to Negal, who was loading their backpacks into the craft. "He'd better be. He's flying my mate too."

"He's good." Gabi wrapped her arms around both of them. "You can't beat immortal response time," she whispered so only they heard her. "You're in good hands."

When the men were done, they came back to kiss their mates goodbye, and Jasmine climbed into the helicopter.

Edgar, already in the pilot's seat, motioned for her to sit next to him, holding up a pair of headphones for her.

Jasmine hesitated, her eyes darting to the window and the vast expanse of sky beyond. She would have preferred to stay in the back, away from the dizzying views, but she forced herself to overcome her fear and settled into the seat beside him.

"Scared?" Edgar reached for her hand and gave it a light squeeze.

"A little bit. I've never been in an aircraft this small."

"You are in for a great experience," he reassured her with a bright smile. "Just buckle up, put the earphones on, and enjoy the ride. It's nothing like flying in a commercial jetliner. You feel it in a craft this size."

That was what Jasmine was afraid of. She didn't want to feel it. She wanted to feel like she was on the ground.

Once the doors were closed and those staying behind had cleared the area around the craft, Edgar started the engine, and the helicopter roared to life. When they lifted off the ground, vibrations coursed through Jasmine's body, and as the craft tilted and swayed in sharp angles, she squeezed her eyes shut, her hands gripping the seat in a white-knuckled grip.

Was Edgar doing that on purpose? Did he think that she enjoyed this roller-coaster?

"Jasmine, open your eyes," Edgar urged. "You're missing out on the beauty below."

Taking a shuddering breath, she forced herself to open her eyes and blinked against the bright sunlight streaming through the windows.

As her vision adjusted, she gasped at the sight that greeted her. The enormous plateau stretched before her in a vast expanse of untamed wilderness. The landscape's dominant shade was that of dark dirt, but small patches of green dotted it, the low-growing shrubs clinging to the rocky soil. Many valleys had rivers running through them, adding to the breathtaking picture below.

From this height, the Himalayas didn't seem so far. The sheer scale of the mountains was something to behold, filling Jasmine with a sense of awe at their untamed beauty and scale. Where the plateau was only dotted with vegetation, the mountains sprouted semi-dense forests at the bases. Jasmine noted how the tree line was repeated on every slope.

She could make out more details in the terrain as the helicopter flew lower. Herds of yaks grazed on the sparse vegetation, their shaggy coats blending into the muted colors of the plateau. Occasionally, they passed over a small village, the traditional Tibetan houses clustered together like colorful beads on a string.

Although the plan was to skip ahead by air ten miles at a time and land to get an updated scrying reading, this initial flight also helped them get a general sense of location and the lay of the land ahead.

Despite the incredible views, to Jasmine the flight seemed to drag on forever. Every gust of wind, every slight shift in altitude made her heart race and her palms sweat. She focused on her breathing, trying to stay calm and remind herself that Edgar was an excellent pilot who knew what he was doing.

After what felt like an eternity but was, in fact, less than half an hour, Edgar began to descend, aiming for a tiny spot on top of the peak they had marked on the map the day before. The flat patch was barely large enough for the helicopter to land on, and Jasmine held her breath as they touched down, the skids bouncing slightly on the uneven ground.

Edgar kept the rotors going as Aru disembarked and offered her a hand to help her down.

He rushed her away under the spinning rotors. "How are you doing?"

She chuckled. "Glad to be out of that flying toaster." She inhaled the dry, thin air. "I think I'm getting used to the altitude."

Edgar had been right about his venom bite helping alleviate her symptoms. It was a miracle cure-all, and she was grateful for the relief it had provided.

"Ready to do your witchy magic?" Aru asked.

"Yes, sir." She pulled her scrying stick out of the inside pocket of her jacket.

29

JASMINE

"I need to do this in private." Jasmine gave Aru an apologetic smile and walked toward a jutting boulder she'd spotted a few feet from the landing site.

It offered a modicum of privacy, and as she sat down in its shadow, she took a deep breath, closed her eyes, and offered a silent prayer to the goddess.

A tingling sensation started in her fingers, and as she held the stick aloft, it began to vibrate, pointing steadily toward the north.

"It's working." She was amazed and relieved at the same time. "It's working better without a map." A grin spread across her face as she got to her feet and walked back to where she'd left Aru. "It's pointing north."

"Then that's where we need to go," Aru said.

She returned to her seat, gave Edgar a thumbs-up, and put on her headphones. "We are heading north," she said.

The same routine was repeated several more times, with only slight shifts in heading, and by mid-afternoon, it was clear that they were nearing the limit of their range and needed to head back.

Looking at his avionics, Edgar seemed thoughtful. "I have an idea," he said. "Rather than continuing in that direction for the next hour or so before I have to return to base camp, we should change our heading, going either northeast or northwest for ten or twenty miles and take a new reading there."

Jasmine was confused. "Why would we want to abandon the heading the scrying is telling us to pursue?" The nodding she noticed from the gods made it clear to her that she was not the only one confounded by the suggestion.

Turning partially around so he was addressing everyone, Edgar gestured with his hands to illustrate. "Finding a point along a line can be tedious. Depending on how far away one is from the location, we may find ourselves hopping endlessly, or at least until we exceed our fuel range."

Aru nodded. "I see what you are saying."

"If we get another reading from a different location, we can follow both headings on the map from their point of origin." Edgar demonstrated what he had in mind by drawing an imaginary triangle in the air.

"So, if Jasmine can get an updated reading in the new location, we can triangulate both headings and get a better read on the pod's location. I can then take you as close as I can get or as close as fuel will permit me. That should save time and make your trek shorter."

Jasmine could feel the renewed excitement from the gods. The tedious routine of the past few hours had dampened their spirit, making them fear that this hopping about with the helicopter might take days. Now, there was a chance they could get started on their trek as early as today.

It took Edgar all of five minutes to draw a new heading on the map he was using and consult the instruments before pointing to a spot for them to see. "This is where you need to get to. Both lines intersect in this location. Given the error size of these headings," Edgar looked at Jasmine apologetically as he continued, "You should expect the pod to be found in the general vicinity rather than at the exact intersection point."

Looking at everyone to ensure they were following him, Edgar marked a new spot on the map. "This is as far as I can take you, though. Even going that far means I will have to rely on emergency fuel reserves to make it back. You will need to go on foot from there."

"Are you sure you are not cutting it too tight with the fuel?" Jasmine was concerned that Edgar was taking unnecessary risks out of concern for her.

Leaning over and framing her face with his hands, Edgar sounded calm and assured. "I will be fine. I know exactly how much fuel I have left and what I need. I am not taking a risk at all."

When they took off again, Jasmine no longer felt anxious. It wasn't just the familiarity with the experience she'd developed throughout the day but also the knowledge that her scrying worked and the excitement over the imminent discovery of the pod.

When Edgar landed again, she leaned over, kissed his cheek, took Aru's offered hand, and jumped out.

After the helicopter took off, the gods shouldered the backpacks including hers, and Negal helped her over every patch that he deemed even slightly difficult for her.

The terrain around them was harsh, with jagged rocks and steep inclines that made every step a struggle. As they pressed on, the sun started its descent, and the wind picked up, whipping at Jasmine's face and hair as if trying to push her back. But she wasn't about to let it deter her.

30

ARU

The thin air made the climb challenging even for a god, and as Aru trudged up the steep, rocky slope of the mountain, his breaths were coming in short, labored gasps. Behind him, Dagor and Negal followed, with Negal holding Jasmine's hand and helping her climb.

The woman was struggling, her face flushed with exertion and sweat beading on her forehead. He'd insisted that Jasmine use an oxygen mask to help her breathe, but even with the extra support and the help they were providing, she was reaching the limit of her endurance.

Soon, they would need to carry her, but he had anticipated that.

Jasmine was an actress, not a professional mountaineer.

Regrettably, they had to take her with them on this mission, and there was no way to get her where they needed to be with a helicopter. Edgar couldn't land safely where they were heading. On top of that, the winds were picking up, so Edgar might not be able to reach them even at the rendezvous location, and they could get stuck on the steep slopes overnight.

They were adequately equipped for that contingency, with tents and food to last them three days if needed, but he hoped it wouldn't be necessary. If they made it up the damn mountain by two o'clock, they could be down the other side by three, and there was a spot that would better protect them from the elements where they could set up camp.

Aru needed to be available by four to make the daily telepathic and satellite call, connecting the Clan Mother with the queen.

Her Majesty and Her Highness were aware that it might not happen because conditions didn't allow it, but he would hate to disappoint them.

He also needed to consult the queen about what to do if the twins were found alive. Not that it was very likely, but on the remote chance that they had somehow survived, he knew he couldn't report that to the commander of the patrol ship.

If the Eternal King was told they were alive, he would stop at nothing to eliminate them. Aru did not doubt that it wouldn't take long for the command to arrive from the king to kill the twins. And if he couldn't do that for whatever reason and could not provide proof of their demise, the king would order the patrol ship to turn around and eliminate all life on Earth.

The commander wouldn't carry out that order, which would make everyone on board a traitor and a deserter, and the king would send another ship to finish the job. All they would gain was a few centuries, which in the grand scheme of things was very little.

Aru had only two options. One was to claim that he hadn't found anything, and the other was to claim that he had found the twins dead. The problem with that one, of course, was proof. If the pod's record showed that life support functions were still working, Aru might not be able to assert that the twins were dead.

He couldn't tamper with Anumati's equipment because it was tamper-proof.

What if he destroyed the pod and claimed it had been damaged in the crash?

That would only arouse suspicion. The pods were built to withstand almost anything. A malfunction was possible, but not a complete disintegration. That was why his team's assignment was so important. They needed to find all the pods and either find survivors or provide proof that there were none, and then ensure that the pods were never seen by humans.

A cry of pain pulled Aru from his thoughts.

Negal was holding Jasmine up, but it appeared that she had stumbled, and something wasn't right.

Her oxygen mask hung loose from its cord, and Jasmine was clutching her ankle. "I need to sit down." She pulled on Negal's hand.

He lowered her gently to the ground and crouched next to her, looking lost for what to do next as tears streamed down her cheeks.

Aru crouched behind her, propping up her back. "Just breathe, Jasmine. The pain will subside in a few moments."

He wasn't sure that was true for a human, but it seemed to calm her down.

She turned to look at him with tearful eyes. "What are we going to do now? I can't walk."

"We will carry you. I planned on doing that anyway because you were reaching your breaking point. I should have done it an hour ago, and then this wouldn't have happened."

"I'm sorry," she said, her chin wobbling as she tried not to cry.

"Nothing to be sorry about. I just hope Julian can patch you up when we return."

Jasmine winced. "Humans don't heal that fast, Aru. It might take weeks before I can step on this foot, and we don't have the time."

"Don't worry." He put a hand on her shoulder. "Worst case scenario, we will carry you the entire time."

She groaned. "This is so embarrassing. I'm not some dainty damsel. I'm heavy."

Negal chuckled. "Nonsense. You don't weigh more than one of these backpacks. The only thing I'm worried about is Edgar's jealousy. He won't like it."

"That's his problem." Aru pushed to his feet. "Who wants to go first?"

"I do." Negal crouched in front of Jasmine. "Hop onto my back."

31

ARU

Negal and Dagor took turns carrying Jasmine the rest of the way up the mountain, one of them always walking right behind her in case the one holding her stumbled and fell.

When they finally reached the summit, Dagor set Jasmine down near a boulder. She was panting, her face slick with sweat, and her eyes glazed with pain.

Aru pulled out a water canteen and handed it to her. "Take a drink."

Dagor took several energy bars out of his backpack and handed them around.

Jasmine shook her head. "I'm nauseous. I can't eat anything."

It was probably from the pain, and Aru was angry with himself for not packing any painkillers. The doctor should have thought of it.

Maybe he did?

"Does anyone remember packing a first aid kit?"

"I did," Jasmine said. "It's in my backpack."

"I'll get it." Dagor opened the clasps and rummaged inside until he found the kit. "What do you need from here?"

"Advil, and a lot of it."

He found the container and handed it to her.

"Thank you." She shook a bunch of small brown pills into her palm, popped them in her mouth, and washed them down with water from the canteen.

Closing her eyes, she leaned her head against the boulder, and when she didn't move, Aru thought that she had fallen asleep.

Should he wake her up?

In the meantime, he could check for a particular signal signature. Pulling the device out of his vest pocket, he turned it on and walked in a circle, pointing it in different directions.

"Anything?" Dagor asked.

Aru shook his head. "I didn't expect to get a signal, but I was hoping to get lucky."

If the pod still functioned even at minimal life support, he should be able to get a reading within a mile or so of its location. If it was dead, he would get nothing, and that was a very likely possibility.

Fifteen minutes or so later, Jasmine opened her eyes and let out a sigh. "The Advil kicked in. The pain is no longer as overwhelming. It's more of a dull throb now." She reached into the inner pocket of her jacket and pulled out the stick she was using for scrying.

For a long moment, nothing happened. Then, slowly, the stick began to vibrate, and Jasmine's hand turned steadily towards the west. Aru followed its direction, his eyes narrowing as he spotted a cluster of structures in the distance.

Even with his enhanced vision, it was too far for him to tell whether what he was seeing was buildings or a collection of large boulders.

Reaching for his binoculars, he lifted them to his eyes and waited for the focus to auto-adjust and the image to become clear.

His heart sank as he realized what he was looking at. It was a small military base, more of an outpost. Still, the tall antennae and satellite dishes indicated that it was an intelligence facility, and getting past their defenses would be a challenge, even for gods.

"What do you see?" Negal asked.

Aru lowered the device. "A military base, and they can see us coming from miles away. We will have to shroud ourselves to get close, but it won't be easy. Each of us can only maintain the illusion for a short time, and I don't know if we can do that even while taking turns. We will need to calculate how long it will take us to climb there and how long each of us can keep it up."

Negal nodded. "We should be able to do it." He looked at Jasmine. "Anyway, we need to carry her, and we can move much faster when she's not slowing us down."

"She is right here." Jasmine glared at him.

"I'm sorry." He offered her an energy bar. "You seem to be feeling better, so you should eat."

"Thank you." She took the bar from him. "Is that a consolation prize?"

Negal chuckled. "No, just nourishment."

Aru shook his head. "We can't get there today. It's getting late, and it will be nighttime by the time we climb that slope. I need to call Julian and hear what he recommends. I also need to check with Edgar if he thinks that he can land nearby, in which case we won't set up camp but return to home base so Jasmine's foot can be looked at."

The truth was that heading back for the night would be better for Jasmine and make Aru's meeting with the queen and Clan Mother more private.

3 2

JASMINE

When Aru mentioned the prospect of making it back to the hotel for the night, Jasmine perked up. She couldn't hear most of what he talked about with Julian and Edgar, but when he was done and turned to her, he looked less worried, which was a good sign.

"As soon as you are ready, we will head toward the flat shelf that's halfway down the slope. Edgar says he can land the chopper there to pick us up, and he can be here well before it's too dark to fly around these mountains. Julian will wait for us at the hotel as there isn't enough room in the helicopter, and if he clears you to continue, we will tackle the base tomorrow."

Jasmine was relieved they were returning to the hotel, but she didn't like the idea of going through the base.

"The stick is pointing in that direction, but it doesn't mean that the pod is located in that base," she said. "It could be somewhere much farther away."

"I'm aware of that." Aru picked up two of the backpacks. "But we must go through it in case it is there." He chuckled. "The way things are going, I wouldn't be surprised if the pod is right under that base."

That wasn't likely given Syssi's vision, but then visions were not a literal representation of things. They were more like hints, and Aru might be right.

"Okay." Negal crouched in front of Jasmine. "Hop on."

"Thank you."

It was beyond awkward to ride on the back of a god, and not because he was an alien. Negal was with Margo, and it felt way too intimate to have her arms wrapped around his neck, her legs around his torso, and her breasts smushed against his back.

353

Soon, though, the awkwardness became the least of her troubles.

A sharp pain shot through her ankle with every step Negal took, but she gritted her teeth, determined not to complain.

The descent of the mountain was treacherous, with loose rocks and steep inclines that made every movement a challenge, but not so for the gods, who navigated the terrain as if they were experienced mountain climbers.

More annoying was the realization that they weren't even tired. If not for her injury, they could have kept going, probably even after the sun went down. With their enhanced vision, they could easily trek by moonlight and starlight.

Today, though, their objective was just to get to where Edgar could land. That meant rushing down the slope. It seemed a daunting challenge to her, which was made even more urgent by Aru's determination to make it in time for his mysterious phone call at precisely four o'clock.

Why couldn't he just make the call during the trek? They all had satellite phones that were supposed to work everywhere.

Or he could just call for a break.

Jasmine would love to rest her throbbing ankle, even if it was for a few minutes, and if Aru needed privacy for his phone call, he could walk far enough away from them so that he wasn't in their earshot.

Was it because the call would last so long that it would be dark by the time he was done, and a lift-off to the hotel would be impossible? That did not seem likely, given there was plenty of time until the sun would set over the tall mountain range surrounding them.

He must have his reasons; besides, it wasn't her place to make suggestions.

She had one job on this mission: to point them in the direction of the pod. The problem was that she wasn't convinced of any real magic in her scrying.

The concept of psychosomatic responses made her question the reliability of her intuition. What if her mind was playing tricks on her? Convincing her hand to move in a certain direction and point to a path that might not be real?

When they returned to the hotel, she would consult the tarot cards once more to confirm that her prince was indeed waiting for her to find him and wake him with a kiss.

The thought brought a smile to her face, and she had to stifle a chuckle at its absurdity. Her prince, the one she was destined to save, was an alien from the planet of the gods, a member of a race called Kra-ell, who looked markedly different from the humanoid immortals and gods she had come to know.

Ella had told her a little about the Kra-ell, describing them as very tall and slender, with narrow waists and enormous eyes. Given that description, Jasmine doubted that the alien prince was her destined one, and it wasn't just about his alien appearance.

According to Ella, the royal twins had been young when they boarded the settler ship, but they had spent nearly seven thousand years in stasis, their bodies and minds suspended in a state of eternal youth.

Jasmine wondered what it would be like for them to wake up and find themselves in a world so different from the one they had left behind and the one they had expected to arrive at.

Were they aware of the passage of time during their stasis?

Did they retain any awareness?

Or would it feel to them like no time had passed at all, as if they had simply closed their eyes one moment and opened them the next?

As the gods trudged down the side of the mountain, these questions swirled through Jasmine's mind, helping to distract her from her throbbing ankle.

It was such a tremendous relief to see the helicopter approaching and landing, and as Negal increased his speed to get to the craft, Jasmine didn't even mind the pain that flared in response to the additional jolting.

Edgar waited for them with the motor running and the blades spinning, ready to take off as soon as they got inside. The wind whipped at her hair and clothes as Negal ducked beneath the whirring blades and deposited her on the seat next to Edgar.

Buckling her in, Edgar regarded her with concern in his eyes. "I would have brought Julian with me," he said, his voice raised to be heard over the engine's roar, "but then I wouldn't have had room for everyone in the chopper. He's waiting for you back at the hotel."

"It's just a sprained ankle. I'll live." Jasmine tried to smile reassuringly.

Edgar didn't look convinced, but he nodded, his jaw tight as he turned his attention back to the controls.

She leaned back in her seat, closed her eyes, and tried to block out the pain radiating up her leg. She had taken another dose of painkillers less than an hour ago, so taking more wasn't advisable. She had to push through it until the doctor tended to her.

As the helicopter lifted off, the ground falling away beneath them, Jasmine let the exhaustion wash over her and dozed off.

33

EDGAR

E dgar maneuvered the helicopter into its designated landing spot just outside the small town, the whirring blades kicking up dust and debris as he set the craft down. Powering down the engines, he glanced over at Jasmine, who was slumped in the seat beside him, looking pale and in pain.

She had managed to doze off for a few minutes during the flight but had woken up when he started the descent.

With a nod to the other pilot, who had come over to take charge of the helicopter, he carefully lifted Jasmine into his arms, cradling her against his chest as he carried her toward the hotel.

Julian was waiting for them outside their room and opened the door for Edgar to carry her inside.

"The bed or the chair?" Edgar asked.

"The chair," Jasmine said. "I'm dirty."

He cast a glance at the doctor, who nodded.

"The chair is fine."

"Let's see what we got here." Julian knelt beside Jasmine.

When he gently removed her boot, she cried out in pain and then bit on her lower lip to stop herself from making more distressing sounds, but her face twisted in agony as the doctor gently palpated the tender flesh.

"I don't think anything is broken," Julian said. "Rest, ice, compression, and elevation are all I can recommend for reducing the swelling and promoting healing." He turned to Edgar. "Can you please get me a wet washcloth and a towel? I would like to clean the area before I bandage it."

"Of course." Glad he could do something to help, Edgar rushed to the tiny adjoining bathroom.

Jasmine winced when the doctor cleaned her foot and her leg, but she didn't cry out, so Edgar let out a breath.

When he finished with the washcloth, Julian pulled a roll of elastic from his bag and started wrapping it around Jasmine's toes, methodically working up her leg.

"Compression helps to reduce swelling by applying gentle pressure to the area," the doctor said, overlapping each layer and smoothing the bandage into place. "This pressure decreases the space available for swelling and promotes the fluid return to the circulatory system. It also helps stabilize your ankle, providing support to alleviate pain and prevent further injury as you move."

When he was done, Julian double-checked to ensure the wrap was snug but not too tight, explaining that it was essential to avoid cutting off circulation. He then checked that it didn't pinch or slip and advised Jasmine to adjust the bandage if it became uncomfortable or too loose. He emphasized the importance of keeping it clean and dry and instructed her to remove it periodically to check for any changes in skin condition and to allow the skin to breathe.

"Ice is good for managing pain and reducing inflammation," Julian said. "You can also take pain relief medication." He pulled out a container and handed it to Jasmine. "You can take two pills every four hours."

Edgar tried to memorize all the instructions, but there were so many that he wasn't sure he would know what to do. Taking care of a human was complicated.

"Thank you." Jasmine let out a breath. "I feel better already."

"I'm glad." Julian pushed to his feet. "I'll see if I can get you crutches. They have a clinic here, so they should have some. You should stay off your foot for at least a couple of weeks, but I know that's not feasible given our current situation."

Edgar nodded. "She'll need to be carried."

He wasn't thrilled about the gods carrying her on their backs the way he'd seen Negal do. It was too intimate for his liking. But there was no other way.

For a moment, Jasmine looked like she wanted to protest, but then she nodded. "I hate being transported like a piece of luggage, but it's not like I have any other choice."

Julian put a hand on her shoulder. "I appreciate that this is not easy, and yet you are doing your best and being reasonable about it. I am sure that everyone shares this sentiment both here and back home. I'll look for crutches for you."

After he left, Edgar helped Jasmine wash the rest of her body, change clothes, and lie down on the bed with her leg propped on a pillow to elevate it. He then brought some ice and packed it carefully around the bandaged ankle while she relaxed by scrolling through the content that William had loaded on her phone.

It had been a struggle to touch her so intimately and not make it sexual, but she was hurting and tired, and the last thing she needed was for him to turn this into sex.

Jasmine was so brave and resilient, and he was falling in love with her, but deep down, he knew that she didn't feel the same for him. The question was whether she was waiting to find the damned prince and then choose who she wanted, or the reason for her reserve was that they were simply not meant to be together.

He sat beside her on the bed and smoothed a few stray strands of hair away from her cheek. "Are you well enough to get some dinner?"

She put down the phone and nodded. "I'm hungry, but I'm also enjoying the rest and the reduction in pain. I dread moving."

"I can bring you a plate here."

"Nah, I want to see the girls. How come none of them came to visit poor injured me?"

He chuckled. "I told them that you were resting and not to bother you."

She frowned. "When? I didn't notice you leaving the room."

"I didn't. I texted them. I thought you were going to nap."

"Oh." Her expression was a curious mix of disappointment and relief. "I almost did, but I couldn't fall asleep, and then I thought that reading always helped me sleep, and I started to look for books online, and before I knew it, you were asking me if I was ready for dinner." She looked around the room. "What am I going to do about my foot? I can't put the boot back on."

"You are not supposed to step on it, so a sock is good enough. Can I put it on for you?"

She nodded. "Please. But be careful."

"Of course." He took a fluffy pink sock from her suitcase, rolled it, stretched it as wide as it would go, and slipped it over her toes. "Good so far?"

"Yes." She gave him an encouraging smile.

He continued rolling the sock up until it covered most of the bandage. Bending over her, he snaked his arms under her and picked her up.

Jasmine wrapped her arms around his neck. "Thank you for taking care of me."

"Always." He kissed her lightly.

As they entered the hotel's dining room, aka the big tent as they all called it, everyone was already there except for Aru and Gabi.

The moment Edgar set Jasmine down, Margo and Frankie hovered over her like two mother hens, forcing him to sit across the table with the two gods.

"Where are Aru and Gabi?" he asked to start a conversation.

"Aru needed to make a phone call," Negal said. "The Clan Mother insists on him calling her every day at one o'clock in the morning, her time, to tell her about our history."

Edgar frowned. Everyone knew that Annani was a diva, but this was eccentric even for her. "Why one o'clock in the morning?"

Dagor shrugged. "Maybe she has trouble falling asleep and Aru's stories help her relax."

That actually made sense.

Things weren't going well in the world, and with how much Annani cared about the humans, she was probably too perturbed to fall asleep.

Edgar didn't care as much, but even he often lay awake at night, worrying about what would happen to all the work the clan had invested in advancing human society.

He had a bad feeling that humans were being pushed into another dark age, regressing to the tyranny of theocracy and barbarism or, conversely, anarchy and brutality. Both extremes were bad, and both were fueled by religious fervor but of different flavors. Anarchists were usually atheists, but their rejection of God did not mean that they had no religion.

Their ideology was their creed.

34

JASMINE

It was the third day since they had arrived at Darchen and the second day since Jasmine had injured her ankle. Aru had allowed for one day of rest, and in the meantime, he had worked on a strategy that would get them in and out of the Chinese military base without being noticed.

That was why they were all gathered in his and Gabi's room.

Jasmine had worked on strategy as well but in her own special way. Last night, she had been too drowsy to seek advice from her tarot, but this morning, it had been the first thing she did while Edgar went to bring her breakfast.

As she had expected, the cards had still shown her the prince like they had done all those times before, but they hadn't given her any clues about a more precise location or whether the prince was still alive.

Shifting uncomfortably on the chair, Jasmine tried to school her expression and not wince as her injured ankle throbbed. The cramped space in Aru and Gabi's room added to her discomfort, making her feel claustrophobic even though only the five of them were there.

Margo, Frankie, Ella, and Julian had ventured out to explore the local shops and gather information on the military base.

"So, here is the plan." Aru lifted a tablet with a blurry, enlarged map of where the base was located. "Edgar will push it again and deliver us to the same ledge he picked us up from last time, which is here." He pointed on the map. "From there, we'll start trekking in this direction," he again pointed on the map, "away from the base, so we won't suddenly disappear when we start shrouding. Once we reach a spot out of sight, one of us will start shrouding the group, and we'll double back and begin our climb."

As Jasmine listened to his explanation, she couldn't help a prickle of unease. Messing with the Chinese military was dangerous. They wouldn't hesitate to shoot at a bunch of intruders before verifying who they were. The gods would most likely survive, but she wouldn't.

"We'll have to take turns shrouding," Aru continued. "When the first one gets tired, the second will take over, then the third, then back to the first one, and so on. Hopefully, by the time we cycle back to the first, he will have had enough time to recover. Naturally, we will also take turns carrying Jasmine."

It was so awful that she was adding to their burden, but what choice did she have?

She had to be there to use her scrying stick to guide them to the twins' pod. No matter how much it galled her to be so utterly dependent on others, she had to push through the pain and the humiliation for the sake of the mission.

Aru smiled at her. "By the way, did you have a chance to scry again?"

Jasmine swallowed, her mouth suddenly feeling dry. "I did, but the stick didn't respond. It was like it had gone dormant, like the connection had been severed."

As a ripple of unease passed through the room and the gods exchanged worried glances, Jasmine quickly added, "But I checked with my tarot cards, and they still showed me the prince."

She risked a glance at Edgar, her heart clenching at the sight of his tight mouth and furrowed brow. She knew that her connection to the prince was troubling for him, even if he didn't comment on it.

It wasn't fair to him. He had stayed by her side even though she hadn't allowed him into her heart. He had supported her and believed in her even when she doubted herself, and the truth was that she cared for him, too. But her connection to the prince and the sense of destiny that tugged at her soul were impossible to ignore despite how utterly alien she expected him to be.

She tried to imagine what the prince would be like, picturing his tall, slender frame and his huge, luminous eyes. What would happen when they finally met? Would their connection be as strong and undeniable as the cards suggested?

Casting a sidelong glance at Edgar, she saw he was not taking any of this well. She hated hurting his feelings, but then she hadn't promised him anything, right?

Well, that wasn't true.

She'd implied that he would be her inducer and that implied commitment. And who knew? Maybe he was the one for her after all.

Jasmine considered herself an open-minded woman, but after hearing Ella describe the Kra-ell, she doubted she could be attracted to the alien prince.

Edgar was a great guy—handsome, funny, even devoted—and if she only allowed herself to open her heart, she might fall in love with him.

Ugh, if only things could be so simple.

35

ARU

As the meeting drew to a close, Aru's mind raced with the countless details and contingencies that needed to be addressed before they set out for the military base. They would have to camp out in the mountains for the night, which would be a challenge with Jasmine's injury. The three of them could carry her, but there were certain things a woman wanted to do privately.

Not only that, they could run into trouble. They were about to enter a military base, and things could go badly despite the shrouding. Some humans were immune to mind manipulation, so there was always the possibility that the shroud wouldn't work. They could also accidentally trigger an alarm. If the soldiers opened fire, the gods would probably escape with very little damage, but the same wasn't true for Jasmine.

Casting her a glance, it occurred to him that he could speed up her recovery with a small transfusion of his blood. He couldn't do that while Edgar was hovering over her, but once they were out on the mountain, he could thrall her to sleep and inject her, but only with a tiny quantity. If she healed too fast, it would look suspicious, especially to the doctor, who would no doubt want to inspect her leg.

It seemed frivolous to use such an extreme measure for such a trivial injury, but it might save them a lot of trouble down the line.

A knock on the door had him shifting his gaze away, and as it opened and Gabi walked in, a smile stretched his face. It was odd and wondrous that he dreaded even the shortest separation from her. When she wasn't near him, he felt as if he was breathing only half of what his lungs required, and when she came back, he could finally take a deep breath.

That was why he hadn't objected to Margo, Frankie, and Ella coming along even though they were not needed for the mission. He knew how hard the separation was.

"Good morning, everyone." Gabi walked in and kissed him on the cheek.

Behind her, the rest of the team crammed into the small room, their faces flushed from the cold outside.

Julian was carrying a pair of crutches, which he handed to Jasmine. "I knew that the clinic would have them. Now you can at least go to the bathroom by yourself."

Jasmine took them, a grateful smile spreading across her face. "Thank you." She held them at her sides. "I've never used crutches. I don't know how to walk with them."

"I'll show you." Ella took them from her and demonstrated how to walk with the devices while keeping one of her legs off the floor.

"Got it." Jasmine took the crutches from Ella, tucked them under her arms and pushed up, standing on one foot.

Everyone squeezed to make room so she could take a few tentative steps.

Jasmine did okay, but it was clear that the crutches would be useless on the uneven, rocky terrain outside the hotel. "It's not easy," she admitted as she wobbled back to the chair, nearly losing her balance before plopping tiredly down. "You are right." She looked up at Julian. "These are only good for going to the bathroom. I can't take them on the trek." She shifted her gaze to Aru. "I'm afraid you will have to keep carrying me around."

"That's not a problem." He gave her a reassuring smile. "In a day or two, you'll be much better."

Julian cleared his throat. "Not likely. Sprains are nasty."

Aru pretended not to have heard the comment. "So, did you learn anything from the townspeople?"

Ella shook her head. "They don't even know that there is a military base so close to their town. Well, not so close that they can see it, but still. It's not like this is a densely populated area. They should have noticed something."

Julian rubbed his chin thoughtfully. "I even peeked inside a few minds to ensure they weren't lying. But unless the Chinese military knows how to use mind manipulation, these people genuinely seem to have no clue."

"They could have used hypnosis," Margo said. "I'm sure that armed forces around the world are using some type of mind control to keep their top operatives from revealing secrets."

Frankie chuckled. "Another conspiracy theory?"

Margo cast her a glare. "The real conspiracies are so vast and unbelievable that even conspiracy theorists can't envision them. I'm struck repeatedly by how right I was to suspect things when the truth finally comes out, which doesn't happen often, but when it does, it's just mind-blowing."

Aru shook his head. "This is not the time to discuss global cabals. We have a mission to complete."

Margo arched a brow. "So, you agree with me that there is a global cabal bent on manipulating humans to self-destruct?"

Dagor snorted. "Yeah, and it's called the Brotherhood of the Devout Order of Mortdh."

"They are not the only ones." Margo crossed her arms over her chest. "And I don't think that they are even the worst."

Aru lifted his hand again. "Please. You can keep talking about this later." He turned to the pilot. "Edgar, how soon can you have the chopper prepped and ready to go?"

"Fifteen minutes." Edgar pushed away from the wall he'd been leaning against. "I'll get it warmed up and ready to fly."

Aru nodded and turned to the rest of the group. "Okay, everyone, it's time to gear up. Double-check your equipment, and don't forget that we are camping out tonight, so make sure you pack extra warm clothing." He looked at Jasmine. "Don't forget gloves."

"I won't." She reached for the crutches and heaved herself up. "I also packed no-rinse bathing wipes." She turned to Ella. "Thank you for recommending them. They will be lifesavers out there."

"You're welcome." Ella threaded her arm through Julian's. "Good luck out there. I hope you find the pod soon."

"So do I." Jasmine frowned. "I feel it's not going to take long now."

JASMINE

A flutter of nerves took flight in Jasmine's stomach as Edgar brought the helicopter in for landing, the whirring blades kicking up a cloud of dust. That he could even land on that tiny patch of flat terrain was a miracle and a testament to his skill.

As Dagor slid the back door open, Jasmine leaned over and kissed Edgar's cheek. "Be safe," she murmured next to his ear. She couldn't hear herself over the engine noise, but she knew that he'd heard her.

Turning toward her, Edgar wrapped his leather-gloved hand over the back of her neck and kissed her hard. Passion mingled with desperation as he held on to her, and he didn't let go until Dagor cleared his throat loudly enough to be heard over the engine noise. "Sorry, lovebirds, but we need to move."

"Be safe," Edgar said as he pulled back.

When Dagor lifted her from the craft, Edgar yelled, "Keep her safe."

"I will." Dagor ducked under the rotating blades.

While she and Edgar had been busy kissing, Aru and Negal had taken the equipment out, and as soon as she and Dagor reached them, Aru signaled to Edgar that he was good to go.

Edgar returned two thumbs up, and the helicopter lifted off a moment later.

They watched it climb for a long moment, and then Negal turned his back to them. "I'm ready." He crouched low to the ground.

"What's that?" She pointed at the contraption on his back.

"A harness," Aru said. "That way, both your arms can be free. You don't need to hold on to whoever is carrying you, and he doesn't need to hold on to you, either. It is also less likely that any of us will drop you."

They had fashioned the harness from thick nylon straps that Jasmine couldn't imagine where they could have gotten them from. The main part wrapped around Negal's shoulders and chest, probably to distribute her weight more evenly and allow his arms to move freely.

They had added padded supports at the shoulders and waist, using foam to cushion against the pressure points. The design even included adjustable buckles, allowing the carrier to tighten or loosen the harness as needed.

"I can't believe you made this," she said. "When and how?"

"We worked on it yesterday while you were resting," Dagor said as he lifted her into a sling-like seat made from the same material which dangled from the main frame of the harness.

When she was seated, Negal checked each buckle and strap to ensure everything was secure. Once satisfied that she was safely ensconced and comfortable, he stood up slowly, adjusting to the weight distribution before starting to walk.

"Thank you for making this ingenious thing for me." Jasmine patted the pocket with the scrying stick. "Now, I don't need to cling to you like a monkey and can keep scrying on the way."

"You're welcome," Aru said.

They set out in the opposite direction from the military base, picking their way carefully over the rocky terrain. They had started late in the day, and the sun was high in the sky by the time they reached a large boulder that seemed to mark the edge of some invisible boundary.

Aru called for a halt, and as Negal carefully lowered Jasmine to the ground, Dagor helped unstrap her from the harness.

"We will rest here for half an hour." Aru put down the two backpacks he was carrying and leaned them against the boulder on one side of her, while Dagor did the same with the packs he'd been carrying on her other side.

Half an hour was a long time for the gods, who did not need rest, and since she was being carried, she didn't need rest either.

"Here." Aru handed her a canteen. "Drink."

She scrunched her nose. "Maybe I shouldn't. I don't want to have to go to the bathroom." Holding it for the entire trek was not feasible, but she intended to minimize bathroom breaks as much as possible.

"You need to drink." Aru crouched before her, shielding her from the sun with his body.

"Fine." She rolled her eyes but took a few sips before handing him the canteen back.

He smiled. "Now, that wasn't so difficult, was it?" He was looking straight into her eyes. "It was a hard trek, and you are feeling very tired. Close your eyes for a few moments and take a short nap. It will do you good."

As her eyelids started to lower, Jasmine wondered why Aru wanted her to sleep. They were in the middle of nowhere, with danger lurking around every corner, and he wanted her to nap?

It was absurd.

Except, he was right. Suddenly, a wave of fatigue washed over her, and the heaviness in her limbs seemed to drag her down like an anchor.

She tried to lift her eyelids and glare at the god, but when they refused to obey her, it occurred to her that he was using his mind manipulation abilities to force her into unconsciousness for some reason.

The thought filled her with unease, and a prickle of fear traveled down her spine.

But there was nothing she could do. She couldn't resist the inexorable pull of sleep. And as her mind slipped into darkness, Jasmine couldn't help but wonder what secrets the gods were keeping from her.

37

JASMINE

When Jasmine awoke, her world had transformed. Her ankle, swollen and throbbing with pain when she'd fallen asleep, now felt strangely light and almost free of pain, and her body thrummed with energy and vitality.

Suspicious?

And then some.

Taking a nap in the middle of the day had never affected her so profoundly, and certainly not when it was taken sitting on the hard ground and leaning against a hard rock.

Had one of the gods bitten her while she'd been out?

Was that why Aru had made her sleep?

That was the only thing that made sense to her. If Edgar's venom made her heal faster, the gods' venom must be even more powerful.

She reached up to touch her neck even though she knew no marks would be left from the bite. There never were when Edgar bit her.

Still, touching the area was an impulse she couldn't resist.

A venom bite seemed like a likely explanation for her sudden physical improvement, but it didn't make sense. The gods were all mated, and their bites were reserved for their partners. It was a very intimate act, and as far as she knew, it could only happen during sex.

If they had wanted to give her a health boost, they would have more than likely asked Edgar to do it last night instead of doing so themselves. Not that she had been in a mood for anything with how exhausted she'd been from dealing with the pain and the discomfort. After taking three of the pills Julian had given her, she'd fallen asleep like a rock.

Should she ask Aru if he or the others had bitten her?

She would if it wasn't so damn embarrassing. Hell, it could be considered an insult. It was like asking a dude if he had taken advantage of her while she slept.

Whatever.

She should be happy about feeling better and let the mystery remain unsolved.

"Ready to continue?" Aru asked, his expression smug.

Now, she was sure he had done something to her that he hadn't been supposed to do. "I am. Can I have one of those energy bars? I suddenly feel hungry."

"Of course. But first, let's put you back in the harness."

She was surprised that Negal still had it on. "Weren't you supposed to take turns carrying me?"

"Nah." Negal crouched low to assist Aru. "You weigh less than one packed backpack, and they are carrying two. I've gotten the better deal."

She sincerely doubted that one backpack weighed over a hundred pounds, let alone a hundred and thirty. But she wasn't going to argue the point.

Aru loaded her onto the harness on Negal's back, strapping her in with practiced efficiency as if he had been doing this for years, and then pulled out an energy bar and handed it to her.

"When I start shrouding us from view," he said, "you won't be able to see us or yourself. It can be disorienting, even a little frightening. I suggest you keep your eyes closed for as long as possible."

Jasmine nodded, but she didn't intend to do that.

She was curious to experience being invisible and moving through the world like a ghost.

Did she have the guts, though?

As they set out again, Jasmine closed her eyes as Aru had suggested, and a few moments later, she felt the first tingle of Aru's power washing over her. It was like a faint electrical charge that raised the hairs on her arms.

She kept her eyes closed for a few moments, but then curiosity got the better of her, and she cracked one eyelid open, peering out at the world around her.

What she saw took her breath away. Or rather, what she didn't see. Negal, whose broad back she could feel beneath her, was invisible, and so were the two other gods.

They too had vanished, leaving nothing but empty air and the faint shimmer of heat rising from the sunbaked ground.

Even her body was not visible to her, and when she lifted a hand to examine it, there was nothing to see. She felt like a disembodied presence, floating like a specter. It wasn't as fun as she had imagined. It was disorienting and slightly nauseating.

With a shudder, Jasmine closed her eyes again, surrendering herself to the familiar and comforting feel of Negal's solid body.

There was nothing sexual about it, and now that Jasmine knew that Negal belonged to Margo, she didn't feel any attraction toward him. So yeah, he was a god, incredibly handsome and strong, not to mention kind and intelligent, but he wasn't hers and he wasn't a prince.

The question was whether Margo would see it that way. Their friendship was important to Jasmine, and she didn't want to lose it over something as silly as the specter of impropriety.

Come to think of it, she should probably hide how much better she was feeling to avoid the gods' mates becoming suspicious.

38

NEGAL

As they climbed towards the Chinese military base, Negal focused on the steady rhythm of his footsteps. Jasmine's weight was hardly noticeable, her slender frame resting easily against his own as he navigated the terrain with ease.

Margo had seen him fashioning the harness the day before, and he'd felt like he had to explain that he felt nothing but camaraderie toward Jasmine, but she'd stopped him with a smile and a finger on his lips.

"I'm not jealous. I'm a hundred percent secure in your love," she'd said.

When he'd arched a brow, she'd laughed. "Okay, I admit it. I was jealous of Jasmine when she flirted with you, and then of Gertrude, who I thought you were dating, but that was before you pledged yourself to me. Since then, you've been proving how much you care every day, and I'm no longer jealous."

The memory made him smile. He liked that she trusted him so completely. After all, Margo had been human until recently, and human males didn't have a built-in loyalty mechanism. She hadn't grown up on romantic legends of fated mates.

Behind him, Negal could hear the soft rustling of the two backpacks that Dagor was carrying rubbing against each other, the faint clink of equipment mingling with his friend's steady breathing. Aru was ahead, leading the procession.

As they drew closer to the base, Negal could feel the tension in the air thickening, and the hairs on the back of his neck started prickling with anticipation.

They moved in silence, taking turns to shroud themselves from view, seamlessly passing the mantle of keeping their group invisible from one to the other.

Thankfully, when it was his turn to shroud, Jasmine was very quiet and moved minimally, mindful of the effort it took to keep the shroud going.

At last, they reached the base itself. It wasn't a big encampment, and from its appearance, its primary purpose was spying on neighboring countries. Several low buildings were sprawled over the flat area of the mountaintop, with four watchtowers that were slightly taller than the buildings but not by much. The location was elevated enough that they didn't need to be taller.

There were also no fences or barriers to mark the compound's boundaries, just an eerie sense of stillness and watchfulness that hung heavy in the air.

Guards patrolled the perimeter, their weapons seemingly at the ready, but the men looked more bored than alert. It wasn't as if anyone could get to their base unless they came by air or hiked on foot. An attack was highly unlikely. Several antennae and satellite dishes were positioned on the base's west side, and although Negal wasn't familiar with human technology, it wasn't difficult to figure out their functions.

Behind him, Negal could hear Jasmine's breathing quickening, the soft, rapid panting of someone on the verge of panicking. He wished he could comfort her, but they were preserving their energy and shrouding only for sight. Adding a noise bubble would have depleted their reserves much faster. The best he could do was pat the side of her leg, but that didn't seem to help. Her anxious energy kept washing over him with ever-increasing intensity.

Negal kept silent, his jaw clenched tight, as he navigated through the maze of buildings and equipment, following the path that Jasmine's scrying stick was pointing at.

Thankfully, there were no surveillance cameras in the base, which was what they had expected, but there could have been surprises.

It quickly became apparent that the crater in Syssi's vision wasn't located in the base, but it also meant that they had to keep going.

Suddenly, a door to one of the buildings opened, and a soldier stumbled out, heading in one direction and then, for no apparent reason, turning around and bumping into Aru's back.

Behind him, Jasmine gasped, but he put a hand on her thigh to steady her.

Aru swayed on his feet but managed to straighten himself, and the soldier started trembling but stayed rooted in place.

"Who goes there?" the man demanded in Chinese, his eyes wide with fear and confusion.

As Aru turned around, Negal expected him to reach into the guy's mind and make him forget that he had bumped into an invisible obstacle. But that wasn't what happened.

"This is hallowed ground," Aru said in Chinese, his words sounding ethereal and ghostly. "It is bad luck to bring weapons to this holy site." And then he must have reached into the man's mind because the soldier gaped, his mouth opening and closing like a fish out of water.

Then, slowly, the man shook his head, his eyes glazing over with a look of dull incomprehension. He turned and walked away, his steps unsteady and his movements jerky, as if he were a puppet whose strings had been cut.

Negal watched the soldier disappear into the maze of buildings.

Yup, Aru had messed with the guy's head, but what was the deal with the ghost voice? Was Aru bored and needing to entertain himself?

Negal let out a breath.

That had been too close for comfort. This was an army base, and everyone was carrying weapons. They needed to be more careful.

Behind him, he heard Jasmine letting out a breath as well. He patted the side of her leg again and kept walking.

39

JASMINE

J asmine's heart had nearly jumped out of her chest when the soldier had
bumped into Aru, her breath catching in her throat as she waited for the
inevitable shout of alarm.

That hadn't happened, though.

Aru had spoken some words in Chinese that she hadn't understood, but it
didn't matter what he'd said. It was how he'd made them sound as if he were a
ghost. The poor soldier had nearly peed in his pants, his body trembling as he
stumbled away in a jerky and uncoordinated scramble.

As they pressed on, moving deeper into the heart of the base, Jasmine lifted
her scrying stick, her fingers clutching the smooth, polished wood with trepidation.

Would it work despite the shrouding?

Would the energy expelled to maintain the shroud interfere with the energy
guiding her scrying?

She held the stick aloft, but the shroud was all-encompassing, and she
couldn't see the stick the same way she couldn't see her hand or the sleeve of her
jacket. Still, she could feel the wood in her hand and sense the subtle vibrations
that ran through its length.

In a sudden flash of inspiration, she remembered that the shroud did not
affect the gods. Only she and other humans and immortals couldn't see through
the gods' mind manipulation. If Negal could see where the stick was pointing,
he could indicate the correct direction for the others.

Holding the stick in front of his eyes, she tapped his shoulder with her other
hand and then pointed at the stick.

He tapped her thigh to let her know that he understood, and as he changed directions, she hoped it was because he was going where the stick was pointing.

Passing through the base, they emerged on its other side and started down the slope, the shroud still concealing their presence from the guards watching the area from the towers.

By the time they reached the bottom of the mountain, the sun had begun to set, the sky darkening to a deep velvety blue as the first stars appeared overhead. The wind had also picked up, whipping at their clothing and stinging their faces.

Jasmine could feel the cold seeping into her bones, the chilly night air cutting through her multiple layers of clothing.

They went around the base of the mountain and crossed into another ravine that was not in the line of sight of the soldiers at the base.

As the gods dropped the shroud, Jasmine let out a relieved breath. "Can I talk now?" she whispered in Negal's ear.

"Yes, but quietly."

Aru found a shallow cave with a narrow fissure in the rock face that offered some small measure of shelter from the wind and the elements. It was not much, just a little more than a crack in the mountainside, but it would have to do.

As Negal crouched, Dagor helped Jasmine out of the harness and set her down, leaning against the rock face.

"Thank you." She smiled at him and then turned to Negal. "Thank you for carrying me."

"No problem."

As the gods set about making camp, spreading out sleeping bags, and erecting a small tent for Jasmine, the pressure in Jasmine's bladder became impossible to ignore. However, asking one of the gods to carry her somewhere so she could relieve herself was embarrassing.

Her leg was feeling better, though, so maybe she could push up to her one good foot and use the rock as a crutch?

She started to rise slowly, and at first, none of them paid her any attention, but then Negal turned around to look at her and frowned. "What are you doing?"

"I need to do something privately."

Understanding flashing in his eyes, he nodded. "I'll carry you to a spot and leave you to do your thing."

Aru shook his head. "Stay close by. There are dangerous predators in this area."

"Like what?" Dagor asked.

"Leopards, wolves, bears," Aru said.

Jasmine shivered. They hadn't seen any animals during their trek, and she hadn't thought about them being present in the area, but after Aru's warning, she didn't want Negal to be more than a few feet away from her, no matter how embarrassing it would be to know that he could hear her pee.

"I'll stay downwind," Negal said as he swung Jasmine into his arms.

He carried her several dozen feet to a rocky outcropping that offered some small measure of privacy, leaned her against the rock, and helped her find a stable and secure position. "I'll be on the other side. Call me when you are done."

"Thank you." She was glad it was dark, and he couldn't see her reddening cheeks.

Fumbling with her clothing, her fingers clumsy and awkward in the cold, she managed to push her pants down and crouch supported on one foot while leaning her butt against the rock. She just hoped no ants or other bugs on the surface would find purchase on her naked bottom.

Annoyingly, nothing happened because she knew that Negal could hear her. It was so deathly quiet all around, and with every passing second, the pressure in her bladder was growing, the need becoming unbearable.

"Don't be stupid," Jasmine whispered to herself. "What are you going to do? Hold it in for one more day?"

Maybe Negal had heard her or was bored, but he started whistling quietly. The melody was soothing and relaxing, but most importantly, it provided a small measure of privacy by drowning out the sound of her release.

When she was done, she used a wipe to clean up, pull up her pants, and zipped them up.

It was official. She hated camping and swore never to do so voluntarily again. She just wasn't the outdoorsy type.

After Negal helped her back to the camp, he set her down in front of the small tent the gods had erected for her. "Don't go to sleep yet," he said. "You need to eat first."

Jasmine was more tired than she was hungry, and she also imagined that the gods would like to talk among themselves in their language, which they didn't do when she was around, but Negal was right about food being important. If she didn't give her body what it needed to heal itself, her recovery would take longer than necessary.

Eating cold rations out of a can was just as distasteful as she'd expected, but since making a fire was not an option given the proximity to the base, there wasn't much that could be done about that. The gods didn't seem to mind, though, wolfing down the cold stew and washing it down with water from their canteens.

When they were done, Jasmine felt bad about being unable to help clean up, but the gods didn't need her to do anything. They seemed proficient in outdoor living and handled everything efficiently and gracefully.

"Thank you for taking care of me," she said when it was time to retire to her tent. "I'm sorry about being so useless."

Negal smiled. "You are not useless. You are the most important person on this mission. Without you, we wouldn't know where to look."

"He's right," Aru said. "Good night, Jasmine. After a good rest, everything will seem better tomorrow."

She hoped that didn't mean he or one of the others would bite her again. Then, on second thought, why not?

If she weren't aware of the bite, it wouldn't make her uncomfortable or feel disloyal to Edgar, and she would heal faster.

"Good night," Dagor said.

"Good night, guys." She crawled into her tent and zipped up the opening.

Jasmine was too tired to ask why they hadn't put up their tents and only erected one for her. Her limbs were heavy with exhaustion, and as she lay inside the sleeping bag, she let out a soft, contented sigh and closed her eyes.

EDGAR

E dgar sat at the restaurant table, his fingers drumming a restless rhythm on the scarred wood as he tried to focus on the conversations swirling around him.

He nodded, murmuring his agreement or offering a suggestion occasionally, but his mind was on Jasmine.

She was camping in the wilderness with the gods, and even though he knew that she was in good hands, he couldn't shake the feeling of unease that had settled in the pit of his stomach.

Why hadn't she called him yet?

It was dark outside, so they must have cleared the military base by now and were settling down for the night. Surely, she could have at least texted him.

Checking his phone for what felt like the hundredth time, he was disappointed to once more see a blank screen. The silence and the faint glow of the screen mocked him in the dimly lit restaurant.

Beside him, Julian leaned forward. "It doesn't make sense that no one in this town seems to know that they have a base less than fifty miles away. How do they get supplies up there?"

"Helicopters," Ella said. "Big ones, the kind that can carry tons of cargo. That's the only thing that makes sense."

That was only possible during good weather, which was often not the case in this area. Edgar doubted that the base was supplied solely from the air. Perhaps they had yak supply caravans go up there. It was a slow and primitive method but safe and predictable.

"Maybe there is a road from the other side," Margo said. "Not everything can be brought in by air. They would have needed building supplies up there, and I can't see that done with helicopters."

Gabi nodded. "I agree. Maybe they have a tunnel leading into the mountain and an elevator that takes the supplies up to the top like we have in the village."

Edgar was about to comment on that when Gabi's phone rang.

Pulling out the device, she smiled. "It's Aru." She accepted the call. "Hello, my love. I'm in the restaurant with everyone."

The intro was no doubt to let him know that he shouldn't speak freely because everyone could hear him.

"Good evening, love. How are you doing?"

"I'm doing well, and so are the others. All of us want to hear about your progress."

"We are done with the base, and sadly, it doesn't have a crater, so we have to continue looking tomorrow. We found a place to camp for the night and will continue as soon as the sun is up."

Edgar felt a rush of relief wash over him. The team had overcome the most significant obstacle standing in their way, and they were safe—or as safe as they could be, given the circumstances.

"What about Jasmine?" he asked. "Is she okay? Can I talk to her?"

"She's asleep," Aru said. "It was a long and exhausting day for her, and she had a little fright when we crossed the base. After we put up her tent, she crawled in and started snoring a moment later."

Edgar doubted that was what had happened.

They had to eat, erect a tent, and roll out the sleeping bags. She could have called him anytime during these activities. She simply hadn't felt like it or just hadn't thought of him at all.

Margo reached out to pat his arm, but it only irritated him further and fanned the flames of his frustration.

"Jasmine was probably in a lot of pain," Margo said. "Dealing with unrelenting pain is very tiring. She probably also took a bunch of painkillers, and they are known to cause drowsiness."

She was right, of course, and now Edgar felt guilty for getting mad.

Relationships were complicated. He didn't like how his mind had been going into crazy loops ever since he had met Jasmine. He didn't know how to act, feel, or be a good boyfriend.

How did other males do it?

He looked at Julian, who seemed so at ease with Ella. The guy was even younger than Edgar, but he knew how to navigate the complicated intricacies of a loving relationship.

Sensing his gaze, Julian turned to look at him. "Is there something troubling you, Ed?"

Edgar glanced at Gabi, who took her phone and moved to a corner of the tent to talk with her mate in privacy.

"How do you know the right thing to do in a relationship?" He raked his fingers through his hair. "Half the time, I don't even know how I feel."

Julian cast him an understanding look. "Follow your heart, be patient and forgiving, and always assume the best about your partner. These are the only words of wisdom I can give you."

"It's not easy to share your life with someone," Frankie said. "Honesty and clear communication are important. How can you expect your partner to know what you want if you don't spell it out for her?"

Margo chuckled. "People expect their partners to be mind readers and guess what they want. It's so silly."

Edgar thought about what they had all said and shook his head. "But what if you assume the best about your partner but learn that your assumptions were mistaken?"

"Then you reevaluate," Ella said. "No one is perfect, and you need to decide what you are willing to live with and what you are not, but that's all irrelevant to immortals. When you find your one and only, all that little stuff becomes inconsequential. The love and devotion are so all-consuming that they override all the doubts, insecurities, and other nefarious relationship killers."

That sounded profound and lovely, but it didn't answer Edgar's question. "But how do you know if your partner is your one and only?"

Julian and Ella exchanged glances, and then Ella shrugged. "You just know."

That was unhelpful.

Or maybe it was?

Edgar didn't know whether Jasmine was his one and only, so maybe that indicated she was not?

On the other hand, they hadn't spent enough time with each other to even fall in love, let alone decide that they were each other's one and only. Except, he was pretty sure that he loved Jasmine, and he was just as certain that she didn't love him.

41

ARU

The morning dawned crisp and clear over the mountains, the sun's first rays casting a golden glow across the primordial landscape.

Aru had deliberately taken the last watch of the night. Watching the sky gradually brighten and night turn into day in these majestic mountains was a unique experience.

He contemplated starting a fire and warming some water for tea.

Doing so during the daytime would probably go unnoticed by the guards in the military base, but given that they were trying to conserve water so it would last them until the end of the day, it might not be the best idea. On the other hand, did it matter whether they drank it in the form of tea or straight from the canteen?

Probably not.

He should ask the others if they wanted some.

Aru suspected Negal and Dagor were awake, too, and the three of them were waiting for the human to wake up. Jasmine needed more sleep than they did, but on the other hand, she could doze off while riding on Negal's back, so maybe they should just wake her.

For some reason, the guy insisted on being the one to ferry her around, perhaps because the harness had been made to fit him, and adjusting to fit Aru or Dagor might undermine its stability. After all, they had fashioned it from whatever materials they could find, and none of them was an expert on building harnesses.

Next to him, Dagor stretched his arms over his head and yawned. "We need to get moving."

"Soon." Aru turned to look at Negal, whose sleeping bag was on his other side. "Are you awake?"

"Have been up for a while." Negal pulled himself out of the sleeping cocoon and sat beside it. "I would love a cup of coffee right now."

"We shouldn't." Aru cast him an apologetic look. "Not unless you can find us a source of water."

Negal glanced toward the base, which was not visible from where they were sitting. "I can make it there in half an hour, steal some water, and return in half that time."

"We can't risk it."

Glancing over at Jasmine's tent, Aru noted a slight rustle of movement from within, and a moment later the flap opened, and she emerged, her face still heavy with sleep and her hair all messy and tangled. But her eyes were bright, and the pinched expression she'd worn since getting injured was gone.

"Good morning," she said, her voice slightly hoarse from disuse. "Have you been waiting for me to wake up?"

Aru nodded. "We should be moving out soon if we want to make it on time to the spot Edgar is picking us up from."

She nodded. "I'll just go over there to take care of some private business." She seemed perfectly steady as she rose to her feet as if her ankle wasn't bothering her at all.

Negal got up. "I'll take you." He started walking toward her.

"No need." Jasmine waved him off and stretched her arms over her head. "My ankle feels much better today, and I think I can walk alone." She cast Negal a knowing look.

Aru frowned. Did she suspect something?

Her ankle had healed too quickly, and she was aware of it, but there was no way she could suspect that he had given her a blood transfusion without her knowledge or consent. She suspected something, though. He would have loved to peek into her mind and find out what fantastical scenarios she imagined, but that would be an even more grievous violation, so he would have to remain curious.

"I'm glad your ankle is better, but Negal needs to go with you anyway. Some predators in these mountains might look on you as a tasty snack."

Jasmine winced. "I forgot about that." She waved a hand at Negal. "Come on."

As she picked her way carefully over the rocky terrain, he followed, and Aru watched them until they disappeared behind a large boulder.

"Let's make coffee," Dagor said. "I'd rather start the day right and be a little thirsty later."

It was somewhat risky, but Aru nodded. "Let's do it but boil just enough water for a small cup for each of us."

Jasmine and Negal returned a short while later, Jasmine's face slightly flushed from the crisp morning air and her eyes sparkling with excitement. "I smell coffee."

"We've made a tiny cup of Turkish coffee for each of us." Dagor handed her one along with an energy bar. "It's cooked with sugar, so it's already sweet."

"Thank you." She beamed at him. "You are a god."

He chuckled. "Ha-ha."

She took a sip and closed her eyes. "Divine, truly. If you weren't mated, I would ask you to marry me."

"What about Edgar?" Negal asked before biting into his energy bar.

Jasmine seemed unfazed by the question. "He hasn't made me Turkish coffee yet. If he comes even close to this, I'll marry him."

She didn't sound very convincing. There was no wistfulness in her tone, only humor. It was as if she was talking about a colleague, not the male she'd been sharing her bed with.

Aru finished the last of the dregs from his cup and handed it to Dagor to stow away. They weren't going to wash them for obvious reasons.

He turned to Jasmine. "As soon as you are ready, you need to whip out your scrying stick and point us in the right direction, so we can get to where Edgar is going to pick us up on time and enjoy the crappy coffee in the hotel restaurant."

Jasmine smiled. "Maybe I can read the future in the coffee grounds." She took a sip and then lifted the cup, turning it this way and that to coat the sides. After another moment, she sighed. "All I see is a long road ahead. That's not telling me much." She reached into her pocket, withdrawing the scrying stick.

Closing her eyes, she mumbled something under her breath that Aru didn't catch, her brow furrowing in concentration.

Not that it mattered what she'd said.

Jasmine's mystical methods were just tools that focused her innate abilities. She could be reciting a recipe for momos for all he cared.

Thinking about the delicious Tibetan dumplings made his mouth water, and he banished the craving by thinking about the call he had missed with the queen the previous night. She had known that he might not be able to call because of conditions in the field, but he still regretted not being able to make it.

The truth was that he enjoyed being privy to the lessons the queen gave her granddaughter and everything else they talked about. He found it fascinating and educational. The lessons she imparted to her granddaughter were a master-class in politics and strategy, and Aru absorbed every word like a sponge. If he ever decided to pursue a political career, the knowledge he gleaned from these calls would be invaluable.

"Oh boy," Jasmine murmured as her hand holding the scrying stick started vibrating violently. The movement was so pronounced that it seemed like the stick had a life of its own.

Jasmine rotated her wrist, moving the stick in a circle. The vibrations intensified and then suddenly stopped. When she moved it again, the vibrations resumed, and when she returned to the same spot, they abruptly stopped again.

"It seems that the stick settled on a heading," she said. "It's quivering with an almost palpable energy when I point it at that lower peak over there."

The mountaintop she pointed at was less than a mile away, within range of Aru's scanner.

He pulled it out of his backpack, hoping to find a trace of energy with an Anumatian technology signature that would corroborate Jasmine's findings.

Regrettably, the only energy the device registered was human-made and emanated from the nearby military base.

If there was anything on the mountain the stick was pointing at, the scanner should have picked it up. It was probably just pointing to a path, not the actual location, although given the triangulation, it should be nearby.

Well, provided that Jasmine was onto something, they weren't wasting their time on a wild goose chase.

She wasn't faking it, that was for sure, but she could have convinced herself that she had magic, and that conviction could have influenced her energy flow, which in turn had made the stick vibrate.

4 2

JASMINE

J asmine was afraid to let herself get excited about the unassuming-looking
mountain that her scrying stick was adamantly pointing to.

It couldn't be that easy.

She'd expected to trek through these mountains for weeks. They all
had. Could their search be over as soon as they reached that mountain?

She started walking, but Aru's hand on her shoulder stopped her. "Not so
fast," he said. "I know you are eager to walk, but I need you to get into the
harness."

"Why? My ankle doesn't hurt anymore. I don't know how it suddenly got
better, but I'm not going to look a gift horse in the mouth, right?"

She looked for any sign that he was somehow involved in her rapid healing,
some flicker of amusement or guilt, but the god's expression didn't reveal a
thing.

"I know that your ankle feels better at the moment, but it's not smart for you
to hike up a mountain and put stress on the injury. Besides, you would slow us
down even if you were completely healed. It's better all round if you take advantage of the harness."

As much as Jasmine hated to admit it, he was right. The last thing she wanted
was to slow them down or reinjure herself and become an even greater burden.

With a sigh of resignation, she nodded. "You're right."

Negal put the harness on and crouched. "Up you go," he encouraged.

Dagor gave her a sympathetic smile as he helped her back into the harness
on Negal's back. "Don't feel bad. Without you, we would have been searching

386

these mountains for decades, and there was no guarantee that we would have found anything."

Jasmine managed a weak smile in return. "You had some clues from your previous visit. Otherwise, you wouldn't have been heading to Tibet in the first place."

"True." Dagor arranged the straps around her. "We have trekked through a different part of Tibet before, but we were chasing unsubstantiated rumors because we had nothing better to go on."

"Funny that you would say that. A vision and a scrying stick are not exactly scientific methods either."

"I agree." Negal stood up with ease. "On the other hand, if the pods were easy to find, we wouldn't have found so many other wonderful things while looking for them."

He adjusted the harness's straps to distribute her weight more evenly and walked up to Aru, who was waiting with two backpacks strapped on, one on his back and the other on his front.

He looked like a pack mule, and so did Dagor once he hefted the other two backpacks, but they still moved fluidly and gracefully despite the weight and how cumbersome it was to walk with double the burden.

The mile-long journey to the cliff face was grueling. The steep incline and uneven terrain made every step a challenge. Jasmine clung to Negal's back, her fingers digging into the thick fabric of his jacket as she tried to keep herself steady.

The landscape around them was a breathtaking tableau of rugged beauty, with snow-capped peaks looming in the distance like silent sentinels. But Jasmine had little attention to spare for the scenery, her mind consumed with thoughts of what they might find when they reached their destination.

When they crested the top of the mountain an hour later, the sun was high in the sky and beating down on her head, and even though she hadn't exerted herself, she was experiencing a shortness of breath. It could be the thin air, or it could be excitement mingled with fear.

The sweat trickling down her back despite the chill wind whipping at her clothes could be the result of either, but she was betting on the latter.

They pressed on, picking their way carefully across the rocky plateau until they came to the edge of a gaping chasm. It was smaller than Jasmine had expected, perhaps a hundred and fifty feet across and seventy or eighty feet wide, but it looked impossibly deep, the bottom lost in shadow.

Aru took out his scanner, pointed it down, and shook his head. "I'm still getting nothing."

Jasmine tapped Negal's shoulder. "Can you let me down?"

He obliged, crouching low so Dagor could help her disentangle herself from the harness.

As soon as her feet touched the ground, Jasmine walked towards the edge of the void and peered into the depths, but all she saw was darkness.

"Can you see anything?" she asked, glancing back at the gods who had come to stand beside her after dropping the backpacks in a pile on the ground.

Aru shook his head. "It's too deep and too dark. We'll need to send something down there for a better look."

He walked back to where they had left their backpacks, crouched next to one, and, after rummaging inside, withdrew a small metal container.

When he opened it, she saw it contained what looked like a mechanical insect. "What is that?"

"It's a drone." Aru removed the device from the box and placed the bee-sized craft in the palm of his hand. "And it's not even the smallest we have. We have spy drones that are the size of a small mosquito. But their range is very limited. This one is less so."

Dagor pulled out a laptop and began tapping away at the keys, his fingers flying over the keyboard with dizzying speed. A moment later, the drone whirred to life, rising from Aru's palm and hovering in midair.

It zipped towards the chasm at Dagor's command, disappearing into the darkness below.

Jasmine craned her neck, trying to glimpse the laptop screen, but the three gods had clustered around it, their broad shoulders blocking her view.

"Can I see?" she asked.

Negal glanced up at her, an apologetic smile tugging at his lips. "Sorry, of course." He moved slightly to the side while Dagor angled the laptop towards her.

Jasmine leaned in, her eyes widening as she took in the crystal-clear image on the screen.

The drone's camera was unlike anything she had ever seen, the high-resolution feed cutting through the darkness as if it were broad daylight. She watched in rapt attention as the rocky walls of the chasm scrolled by, the drone descending deeper and deeper into the earth.

And then, there it was.

At first, it was little more than a shadowy shape, half-buried beneath a layer of dirt and debris. But as the drone drew closer, the image sharpened, resolving into the unmistakable form of a sleek metallic pod.

Jasmine sucked in a sharp breath, her heart hammering against her ribs as she stared at the screen. The craft was covered in grime and battered by the ravages of time, but there was no mistaking the smooth, rounded contours that could only have been manmade, or rather god-made.

A rush of elation surged through her, tempered only by the realization of the daunting task of reaching the pod.

The chasm's walls were almost sheer, and the depth was dizzying.

43

ARU

Aru squinted at the drone footage, assessing the depth of the chasm with practiced ease. "I'd say it's about twenty-five meters down to the pod," he said, glancing over at Dagor and Negal. "Am I right?"

"Let's check." Dagor switched to a different screen that showed the stats the drone supplied. "Almost. It's nearly twenty-eight meters from the top of the cavern to the top of the drone."

"Do we have enough rope to rappel down there?" Aru asked.

Dagor nodded, already rummaging through their packs for the coils of sturdy climbing rope. "We should have plenty. I asked for their longest lengths, which are supposed to be thirty meters long."

Aru smiled. "Aren't we lucky? What would we have done if the pod was deeper than that?"

Dagor didn't look concerned. "We have four ropes, each thirty meters long, so we could tie them together. Luckily, we don't have to."

"Luckily." Aru motioned to a couple of sturdy boulders at the chasm's edge. "Secure the ropes to those. Dagor and I are going down."

As Dagor and Negal removed the ropes from the backpacks, Jasmine put her hands on her hips and shook her head. "I wondered what you had in those packs that weighed so much. You didn't tell me that you packed climbing equipment."

"We knew we were looking for a hole in the ground," Dagor said. "We didn't expect it to be easy to reach."

"Right." She sat on the ground and watched them secure the tough, fibrous lines engineered for rappelling to a couple of boulders.

As they worked, Aru returned to the scanner in his hand and aimed it again at the chasm, hoping to pick up some hint of an energy signature from the pod.

When he got the same results, he had to resign himself to the sad fact that they would not find any survivors. If the stasis pods were still functioning, they would have emitted an energy signature that he would have been able to pick up on his device, especially from this close.

Jasmine walked over to stand next to him. "Did you get anything on that thingy?"

He shook his head.

"Does it mean that they are all dead?"

He hated to quash her hopes. "Maybe the scanner is malfunctioning, or the energy release is so minimal that I need to get even closer to detect it."

She nodded. "I believe that the prince is alive. The goddess wouldn't have guided me to him only so he could get a proper funeral. But I also feel we are running out of time."

"I hope you are right." Aru crouched next to his large backpack and pulled out a smaller pack, much more suitable for the mission ahead.

Aru placed his water canteen, a couple of energy bars, and several tools he might need to open the pod into the pack.

"Alright," he said, shouldering his pack. "Let's do this."

Aru donned his headband, which bore a mounted flashlight, his gloves, and the harness, checking each buckle and strap carefully. Next to him, Dagor did the same.

Once they were ready, they stepped up to the edge of the chasm and turned their backs to it. Aru gripped the descender, and after nodding at Dagor, he began lowering himself down, the rope feeding smoothly through the descender. His practiced movements were deliberate and evenly paced.

The cavern walls were slick with moisture, glistening in the beam of his headlamp, probably the result of melting snow. As he went deeper, the cool air enveloped him, the sounds of the outside world fading until there was nothing but the whisper of rope and his and Dagor's steady breathing.

The descent went flawlessly until he noticed with a sinking feeling that the rope's end was approaching much sooner than the cavern floor.

With about five to six meters to go and no more rope to spare, he realized he would have to jump the rest of the way.

Aru cursed under his breath, glancing over at Dagor. "My rope is too short."

"So is mine." Dagor let loose a few expletives. "I should have double-checked the length instead of trusting that lying scumbag."

Aru shook his head, a wry smile tugging at his lips at Dagor's colorful curse word. "It's not a big deal. We can jump the rest of the way."

Six meters was a short distance for a god to jump. Getting back up would be more difficult but still doable. They would need help taking the individual stasis pods out, and Edgar would need to come with the proper equipment to do that.

Securing the rope's end, he unclipped from the main line, removed the harness, and leaped down.

Next to him, Dagor landed with a controlled thud on top of the pod's curved dome.

"That wasn't hard." Dagor dusted himself off. "But how are we going to get back up?"

Aru shrugged and pulled the scanner from his pack. "We climb."

They were gods. With their enhanced strength and endurance, they could punch their handholds into the rock face if need be. It would be painful, but it was far from impossible.

Dagor didn't look happy about the prospect of scraping their skin raw, but he didn't argue. They both knew that Aru was right.

Aru swiped the scanner over the pod's surface, and his heart leaped at the faint flicker of energy signature that appeared on the screen. It was so weak that it was barely there, but it was better than nothing. Perhaps some of the people inside had survived.

Dagor looked at the scanner. "We need to open this thing," he said, the excitement in his voice echoing Aru's.

Opening the pod proved to be easier said than done. The exterior was battered and worn, and the release mechanism, which should have been marked and easy to access, was nowhere to be found.

The pod had been designed by the gods, not the Kra-ell, but it was a seven-thousand-year-old model, an antique compared to the types he was familiar with, and apparently things had been made differently back then. Still, there was no way they hadn't incorporated a mechanical release mechanism that was not dependent on energy supply or didn't have an auxiliary emergency supply.

They searched the surface of the pod with growing frustration, scrabbling their fingers over every inch of the hull in search of a way to gain entry.

Just as Aru was about to give up hope, his fingers brushed against a small, almost imperceptible seam in the metal, and as he pressed on it, a lever popped out.

"I found it," he called out.

"Thank the merciful Fates." Dagor ran over the dome to where Aru was. "I hope it still works. This thing is ancient."

"Tell me about it." Aru took a deep breath and pulled on the lever, first lightly but then with increasing force when that didn't work, gradually escalating it for fear of yanking the lever out before triggering the dome's lifting mechanism.

When a rumble started, signaling that the mechanism had engaged, he was ready to jump for joy. When the dome started shaking, he leaped to safety, plastering himself to the chasm's wall.

Dagor did the same.

Their feet touched the rim of the pod below the dome and their backs were to the rock. Hopefully, the rising dome would not squash them.

As a hiss of pneumatic pressure echoed from the cavern walls, a plume of dust and debris erupted from the pod's surface, and with a final protesting groan, the dome began to rise.

The pod opened slowly and majestically, like the maw of a great beast awakening from a long slumber, and as the last of the debris cleared and the dust began to settle, Aru felt his heart leap into his throat at the sight that greeted them.

There, nestled within the protective embrace of the pod, were twenty stasis chambers, their surfaces gleaming dully in what little light filtered into the depths of the chasm, but mainly from their headlamps.

44

EDGAR

Edgar hadn't expected to enjoy the traditional Tibetan beverage of black tea, salt, yak butter, and milk, but it was growing on him. As his phone rang, he reluctantly put the cup down to pull it out of his pocket.

Seeing Aru's avatar picture on the screen, he tensed. "What happened? Is Jasmine okay?"

"Jasmine is fine." Aru's voice sounded as if he was inside an echo chamber. "We found the pod."

All around Edgar, murmurs of excitement started, and the others huddled closer to listen.

"That's incredible," Edgar said. "Did you find the twins?"

"We didn't open the stasis chambers yet. We want Julian to get here with his medical equipment before we attempt it. It seems like most of them are not working, but I'm getting minimal energy readouts, which gives me hope that some occupants might have survived."

Julian got closer to the phone. "Don't touch anything until I arrive."

"We won't," Aru said. "We also need more ropes and pulleys to remove the stasis chambers. The pod is about thirty meters deep, and the ropes we have with us are too short. We also don't have enough ropes or pulleys for pulling the chambers out."

Edgar had no idea where he would get those things. They had brought some equipment with them, but the operation Aru described required a crane and not just some ropes and pulleys. They had assumed that they would have time to get what they needed in Shiquanhe, which was still an option, but it seemed like Aru was in a rush.

"It won't be easy to get all that here," he said. "Do we have time to get what we need from the city?"

"I don't think so," Aru replied. "We might be too late already."

"I'll do my best to get what I can locally. I need your coordinates."

"I'll text them to you. But just be careful to avoid the military base. Come in from another direction. We don't want to draw their attention."

"Understood," Edgar said. "Is there enough clear space for me and the other helicopter to land? The payload will be too much for one helicopter, but if you don't want him to assist, I will do it in two trips."

There was a long moment of hesitation. "The military base is a pain in the rear, but we have permits for operating two helicopters, and we might need all that medical equipment when we open the chambers. Besides, going back and forth will look just as suspicious."

"What about a landing pad?"

"There is plenty of room. The top of the mountain is a flat plateau, covered mostly by low bushes and some grasses. The chasm is in the center and roughly the size of the pod, so I assume that the pod melted the rock going down when it crashed here. I doubt it's clearly visible from the sky, but take a look when you get over here. I'm curious to see how it looks from above."

That was indeed interesting. Unless the chasm was small and looked natural, someone would have come to investigate, especially since there was a military base nearby, which had to have air traffic since there were no roads leading up to it. The pod actually making the small crater made much more sense than it finding its way into it by accident.

"Don't forget to send me the coordinates," he told Aru.

"I'm sending them right now."

As the coordinates appeared on his screen, Edgar started mentally plotting the best route to avoid notice from the base. "I'll let you know as soon as we are in the air," he said.

"One last thing, remind Julian to bring his earpieces, and don't forget yours."

"I will do that."

As the call ended, Edgar shoved one more momo into his mouth and rose to his feet. "I'm going to see about the ropes." He looked at Julian. "Did you hear everything?"

The doctor nodded. "I'll load everything I have into the helicopter."

"Do you need help?" Frankie asked Edgar. "If you tell us what you need, Margo, Gabi, and I can do the rounds and buy what you need to save you time."

Edgar's first instinct was to say that he had this and that he didn't need help, but the truth was that he did. It would be great if they could help him secure the supplies faster.

"I'd appreciate any help I can get." He told them what kinds of ropes were needed, their lengths, and what other gear was needed for lifting the chambers. "I hope the general store has it. If not, you can check the warehouse at the end of the street. They collect odds and ends that tourists leave behind and resell them."

45

EDGAR

About an hour later, they met next to the helicopters. Edgar surveyed the ropes that Gabi and the other ladies had procured, ensuring they were long enough for what was needed. They had also brought pulleys and other equipment that he was surprised could even be found in the tiny town.

The place had only one general store, and since most tourists here were pilgrims who came to walk around their holy mountain, he hadn't expected the store to have climbing and rappelling equipment.

"You've got exceptional loot," he complimented Gabi and her helpers.

"We did, didn't we?" She grinned. "I was surprised, but the store owner explained that he tries to always have stock on hand for the crazy tourists who get confused and think that this is where Mount Everest is."

Edgar lifted a hand to shield his eyes from the sun's glare. "I doubt anyone could mistake Mount Kailash for Mount Everest or think that they could climb the holy mountain. As far as I know, it's forbidden."

"It is," Margo said. "I think the guy was joking. He was flirting with Gabi and trying to be funny."

Gabi shrugged. "I might have flirted a little back. Whatever works, right?" She winked. "The owner is in his mid-sixties, so I don't think Aru would mind."

"How old is Aru?" Julian said. "Even if he's young, he's probably older than sixty."

"As long as he doesn't look it." Gabi grabbed one of the boxes that Julian had brought and carried it to the helicopter.

Julian's medical gear was stored in boxes marked simply as equipment. It was important that the other pilot and whoever was watching them load things into the choppers didn't realize they were transporting medical equipment.

They were supposed to be a geological research team, so ropes and pulleys for climbing and ferrying soil samples could be easily explained, but not what Julian had in those boxes. Come to think of it, the stasis chambers would need to be shrouded when they got them to the town and then well hidden.

Once everything was loaded on the two helicopters, Julian kissed his mate goodbye and hopped inside.

Edgar explained to the other pilot the need to circumvent the military base, and they were off.

The flight to the coordinates Aru had provided was tense, with Edgar carefully navigating around the base and ensuring he didn't fly into restricted airspace, even though there had been nothing about it in the instructions he'd gotten along with the permit. Well, it wasn't as if he could read Chinese, but Aru had translated the permit for him, and there had been no mention of restricted areas.

As they neared the mountaintop, Edgar saw Jasmine and Negal. She was sitting on a flat boulder and stretching her injured leg out in front of her, while Negal was standing at the edge of the precipice, which didn't look like much from the air, not even when Edgar got closer.

They both looked up as he got within range, and Jasmine waved at him enthusiastically, with a big smile spreading over her face.

Something eased within him upon seeing her welcome. Even though her prince might be down in that pod, Jasmine was still his, and she was happy to see him.

As Edgar brought the helicopter down in a small clearing a short distance away from the chasm, the downdraft from the rotors whipped the grass into a frenzy and sent small stones skittering across the ground.

A few moments later, Norbu landed on the other side of the clearing, causing the same disturbance.

After Edgar killed the engine, he and Julian jumped out and waited for Norbu. When the other pilot approached them, Edgar thralled him again to refrain from communicating with anyone until he said it was okay. Norbu had a cell phone and a radio transmitter in the helicopter. He couldn't be allowed to tell anyone about the location of the pod or about the things that they were about to pull up.

Negal walked toward them. "Need help offloading?"

"We can use an extra set of hands," Julian said. "We brought a lot of equipment."

Once everything was offloaded and stacked near the boulders that anchored the ropes, Edgar walked over to Jasmine and crouched in front of her. "How are you doing, beautiful?"

Chuckling, she smoothed her hand over her messy hair. "I've been better, but I'm so happy that we found the pod that it doesn't matter."

He wrapped his arms around her and kissed her lightly on the lips. "You are gorgeous even with messy hair."

"You are so sweet." She kissed him back just as lightly.

It was okay. He hadn't expected a passionate kiss in front of an audience, who were watching them and waiting impatiently for Edgar to be done so he could assist them.

With one last peck on Jasmine's forehead, Edgar rose and walked over.

"Do I need to get down there with Julian?" he asked Negal.

Negal shook his head. "I just need you to watch over the ropes for now and, if anything happens, to pull. Can you do that?"

"Of course."

With the three of them going down, he would be left alone with Jasmine and Norbu, which suited him just fine. Getting rid of the other pilot was as easy as planting a thought in his mind to take a nap.

46

ARU

Aru watched as Negal and Julian rappelled toward him, their flashlights casting light on the chasm's walls. They were both carrying backpacks, which were no doubt filled with emergency medical equipment or maybe just diagnostic devices, and hopefully more portable lights.

The truth was that Aru was ill-equipped to deal with a situation like this, which made him wonder about the motives behind sending his team to find the missing pods and not providing them with proper medical training. If they had been expected to find the Kra-ell alive, they should have been instructed on basic things about the Kra-ell anatomy and physiology and what to do if something went wrong, but they hadn't even been told what a god's blood could do.

He had a sinking feeling about that. It was possible that his team was supposed to confirm that everyone in the pods was dead, and if they found any survivors still alive, they would be commanded to eliminate them.

Finding Kra-ell, who had already woken up from stasis, must have been a nasty surprise to the Eternal King and his cronies.

Or was it the queen?

She was the one who had pulled strings to have Aru arrive on Earth, but her motives were different. She wanted him to find out if the exiled gods had survived. His team's official mission was finding the Kra-ell, and that was on the king's orders or those below him who were loyal to him.

Aru would probably never find out.

The fact was that if not for Aria's training as a healer, he wouldn't have known what a god's blood could do. Therefore, he couldn't help save Kra-ell crash survivors unless their chambers had remained intact and kept them alive and well until they were found.

Following that thought, perhaps he didn't need Julian to revive the twins. He could probably do it with his, Negal's, or Dagor's blood. Then again, no one knew how the hybrid creatures would react to it, and he didn't want to take responsibility for messing things up and accidentally killing them.

Perhaps he was wrong, and the command to eliminate them wouldn't come.

In any case, it was better to leave it to the clan's doctor. If Kian had asked him explicitly to assist with a transfusion, he wouldn't have said no, but he wouldn't have volunteered for it either.

As Julian and Negal reached the bottom and unclipped themselves from the ropes, Aru could see the hesitation in their eyes as they debated where to stand.

With the pod dome open, there was no place for their feet other than stepping over the stasis chambers.

"That's okay," Aru said. "They are not going to break, and since their inhabitants are most likely dead, they can't complain about it either."

"Morbid humor?" Julian asked as he carefully maneuvered over the curved tops of the chambers, pulled out a portable work lamp, turned it on, and placed it at an angle that allowed the light to spread over the entire pod interior. "You didn't ask me to come here just to confirm that everyone is dead."

"I'm not known for my sense of humor," Aru said. "It's just the way things are. The way the pod is designed doesn't leave space between the stasis chambers. They are like peas in a pod."

The doctor regarded the pod's interior with curiosity. "I guess no walk paths are needed since everyone inside is in stasis, and the pod is supposed to navigate itself."

"Precisely," Dagor said. "This is a very old model, but the new ones operate on the same principle. The stasis chambers are always inside escape pods to be automatically ejected in an emergency."

While standing together, Aru pulled his earpieces out of his pocket. "Before opening the stasis chambers, I want to remind everyone to put their earpieces in. I know it's most likely unnecessary given their state, but Kian asked us to follow the protocol, and I won't argue with that." He smiled. "His paranoia must be rubbing off on me."

Julian didn't smile as he looked at him. "I do not doubt that Kian's so-called paranoia has saved the clan from annihilation on more than one occasion." He let out a breath. "It's human nature, or rather I should say it's the gods' nature since we are all your descendants, to project our values and beliefs onto others. That's why good people are such easy victims of evil. They don't expect it, they don't prepare for it, and many don't believe it even exists." He paused, his gaze sweeping over them. "But we all know that it does. I'm a young immortal, and the massacre of the villagers in Acapulco wasn't my first encounter with evil, but it was the worst. Kian has seen countless examples during his long life, so his so-called paranoia is well justified."

Aru nodded. "You are right. It's better to expect the worst and be pleasantly surprised when it doesn't come to pass than to be caught off guard by something we didn't anticipate and be too late to do anything about it." He waited until every one of them had their earpieces in. "Let's start opening the pods one at a time. Dagor needs to take pictures and record the lack of vitals to prove what we found, so please stay quiet and out of his camera view while he does that."

Julian nodded. "It doesn't matter to the dead when I jump in, but if we find any alive, I suggest that Dagor does it quickly because I won't wait longer than a couple of seconds."

Aru paused with the earpiece in hand. "On second thought, perhaps we can wait to film until after we verify whether the person inside is dead or alive."

It didn't matter if all of them were gone, but if any had survived, perhaps it was better not to record it just yet.

47

ARU

As Dagor attempted to release the manually operated locks on the first chamber, tension hung over them like a thick, soupy fog. The mechanism was stiff with age and disuse, the metal groaning in protest as Dagor strained to pull the lever.

For a moment, nothing happened. Then, with a pneumatic hiss, the chamber lid cracked open, a wisp of frigid vapor curling out into the warm air of the chasm.

The long-limbed Kra-ell male seemed intact, but Aru knew there was no life in him even before Julian reached inside to examine the body. There was no heartbeat. Dagor took a picture, put the device on the male's chest, and recorded the lack of heartbeat and breathing.

With a grim expression, Julian pressed his fingers to the neck of the still form, searching for a pulse.

Seconds ticked by until Julian looked up. "This one didn't make it."

A collective sigh rippled through the group, even though Dagor and Negal must have known there was no life in the male. Still, hope was powerful, and they all wanted Julian to prove them wrong.

The pod systems had failed, which meant that it was unlikely for anyone to have survived. The Kra-ell did not have the ability to enter stasis unaided, and once the chambers stopped working, they had died. The only ones who had a chance were the royal twins, provided the rumors about them being half-gods were true.

They moved on to the next chamber and then the next, each revealing the same grim truth. The bodies within were perfectly preserved, the chemicals locked in the airtight stasis chambers halting decay.

It wasn't until they reached the seventh chamber that they found something different. A collective gasp echoed through the chasm as Dagor released the seal, and the lid hissed open.

The figure inside was emaciated, the skin stretched taut over the bones like parchment, but that was a great sign. That's what natural stasis looked like; this time, when Julian checked the vitals, he was sure to find them.

The heartbeat would be too slow and faint for even Aru's enhanced hearing to catch, but Dagor's and the doctor's devices would detect it.

"Hold on." Aru stopped Dagor from putting his device on the emaciated chest. "Wait for two heartbeats. And record after the second one so it will look like there was none."

Dagor did not need explanations to understand the reason behind Aru's request.

News of the half-gods' survival should never reach the Eternal King. The best thing they could do for Earth and its inhabitants was to send him proof of the twins' demise.

Aru's main concern was the survival of the heir to the Anumati throne, but he also cared about the immortals who had become his friends and family, and even about the humans.

Not all of them, though.

Only those who had evolved from the state of barbarism and cherished life.

Leaning over the chamber, Dagor gently put his hand on the skeletal chest instead of using his device, and as he remained in the same position for well over a minute, Aru started to worry.

"I've got it," Dagor finally said after nearly ten minutes had elapsed. "It's faint, but it's there."

Julian was about to jump in, but Aru stopped him. "Wait. We need to record." He motioned for Dagor to use his device.

Now that they knew the intervals between heartbeats, it was easy to make a fake recording.

Aru waited patiently until Dagor put the device on the chest, then waited for several minutes, and then turned it off. "The pods must have been functioning at a minimal level," he said. "Just enough to allow some oxygen in. Otherwise, the vacuum would have prevented any nutrients from the surroundings being used by the body. Even his godly abilities wouldn't have been enough to keep him alive."

Julian crouched next to the chamber and looked his patient over without touching him. "Did you pick up any energy readings from the pod?"

"Minimal," Aru said. "I only picked up on it down here. It was too weak to register on my scanner when I was standing over the chasm. That must have been the last thing to go."

Julian nodded. "If so, we made it just in time."

"That's what Jasmine claimed." Negal crossed his arms over his chest. "She said that she had a feeling we were running out of time." He snorted. "I'm getting goosebumps thinking about the way she knew that. I'm not a fan of witchcraft."

"Intuition," Julian said. "That's all it was."

They moved on to the next chamber, and as the lid opened, they were greeted by another emaciated form, this one unmistakably female.

It was confirmed when Dagor and Julian checked for pulse and heartbeat.

Against all odds, the twins had survived.

The rest of the chambers held only death. All eighteen Kra-ell were gone.

Julian straightened up and turned to Aru. "We need to close the stasis chambers, including the live ones. They're too fragile to transport without its protection, and I don't recommend reviving them here."

"Of course not," Aru agreed and motioned for Dagor to follow the doctor's recommendation. "We'll need to take them to the keep like this and revive them there. It's the only safe place I can think of, and I hope Kian won't object. The clinic in the keep is ideal for what they need."

"Don't seal the twins' chambers," the doctor cautioned. "Just close them without locking them. Is that possible?"

Dagor nodded. "I get what you want to do. You want some air to get in."

Julian nodded.

While Dagor set about sealing the chambers, Aru sat down on one of the closed ones. "We will need a private plane to transport them. It's not like we can show up with twenty stasis chambers in the airport, thrall everyone to ignore us, and load them into the cargo bay."

"You need to call Kian," Julian said. "Leave the logistics to him and Turner. Possibly, Kalugal can help as well. He has connections in China."

48

JASMINE

J asmine shifted uncomfortably on the hard rock that served as her chair. Her injured ankle barely bothered her anymore, but she'd been sitting there for hours, and her butt was getting numb.

She'd thought about pulling a sleeping bag out of her backpack and folding it under her, but she already felt utterly useless, and getting comfortable while others worked to save the people trapped in the pod didn't seem right.

Straining her ears, she tried to get some hints about what was happening below, but she didn't hear a thing.

Edgar and the other pilot were in the same boat, standing near the edge with their eyes fixed on the gaping maw of the chasm. She was a little put off that Edgar hadn't tried to engage in a conversation with her as she'd expected, but then he was probably just as curious as she was about what was going on.

She wondered when they would thrall the other pilot to forget what he had seen. Would it be by the end of today? They should, or he could tell someone, and they wouldn't even know.

Norbu, or Nubru, she wasn't sure how to pronounce his name, leaned down and peered into the darkness with a look of confusion on his face. "Why did you need a doctor to come out here?"

Edgar hesitated momentarily, his eyes flicking to Jasmine before answering. "One of our team members was injured on the way down," he said smoothly, the lie rolling off his tongue with practiced ease. "The team leader called the doctor, and he also asked me to bring more research equipment."

"What's down there?" The pilot asked.

Edgar shrugged. "How should I know? I'm just the delivery guy. Maybe they found some fossils." He winked at Jasmine behind the guy's back.

Norbu looked skeptical, but he didn't press the issue. Instead, he turned his attention back to the chasm.

Jasmine had to hide a smile at the deftness of Edgar's story. He was quite good at spinning tales, as she had noted when they had crafted the sexy story leading to their first time together.

He was fun to be with, and it was a shame that she didn't feel about him as strongly as he felt about her. Well, to be honest, she wasn't sure he felt all that strongly about her either. If he had been so taken with her, he would have come looking for her in the lower decks of his own accord and not waited for Amanda to announce that she was looking for a companion for Jasmine and signal that it was okay to see her.

"You should go back to the helicopter and wait there," Edgar told Norbu.

He must have thralled the guy because the other pilot obeyed without question and walked away.

"Did you compel him?" Jasmine asked.

Edgar sat down next to her on the other boulder. "I can't compel. I can only thrall. Sometimes they work the same, though. I just planted the idea in his head that waiting in the cockpit is much more comfortable."

"That's a good one." Jasmine shifted on the flat rock that served as her chair. "Maybe I should do the same."

"You can. Do you want to sit in mine?"

She shook her head. "I'm too anxious about what they are going to find down there to move away from this rock."

Edgar glanced over at her, his expression softening as he met her gaze. "Aru said the chances of anyone surviving in there were slim. The pod was damaged, and the stasis chambers were not working. Without proper life support..." He trailed off, letting the implication hang heavy between them.

Jasmine swallowed, her heart clenching at the thought. She hadn't admitted to herself how much hope she'd pinned on this moment, allowing herself to believe that the prince would be waiting for her, alive and whole and just sleeping like in a fairy tale, waiting for her to wake him up with a kiss.

Thinking that they might have come all this way only to find a tomb was sad.

"But Aru asked for Julian to come along," Edgar said, probably sensing her plummeting mood. "That means that there's a chance they might find some survivors. He wouldn't have requested a doctor if he didn't think there was at least a possibility."

Jasmine nodded, clinging to that slender thread of hope like a lifeline. "You're right," she said, forcing a smile that felt brittle and false on her lips. "I hope that they'll find someone alive down there."

Edgar reached out and took her hand, his fingers lacing through hers. Then he leaned and kissed her.

She smiled. "So that's why you got rid of Norbu? You wanted to kiss me?"

"Of course."

The kiss was a nice distraction.

As they waited for news from below, the wind picked up, whipping Jasmine's hair around her face and sending a shiver down her spine. "It's getting cold."

"Do you want me to bring you your coat?"

She nodded. "That would be nice. And if it's not too much trouble, can you bring my sleeping bag? I need to put it under my butt before it goes numb."

Edgar smiled. "We wouldn't want that. I have plans for that butt tonight."

Usually, she would have felt a twinge of arousal at the prospect of fun times, but she wasn't feeling it now.

When he returned with both items, she tucked the sleeping bag under her and put on the puffer coat. "This is much better." She smiled at him. "If you could also get me a warm cup of coffee, you'd be a prince."

She wanted to take the words back as soon as they escaped her throat, but Edgar didn't seem bothered by her mentioning the prince.

"Let me see what I can do. I bet Aru and the others packed something to make coffee with."

"They did, but we used it this morning and left the pot and cups dirty because we didn't want to waste our water." She grimaced. "We ate cold rations and energy bars. It was pretty miserable."

"My poor baby." He patted her shoulder. "I brought plenty of water with me. I'll wash everything and make you coffee and something warm to eat." He returned to where the backpacks lay discarded on a patch of grass.

Jasmine was glad Edgar had something to keep himself occupied, so she didn't have to pretend everything between them was peachy.

It wasn't his fault she was confused and didn't know what she wanted. She felt guilty for stringing him along but wasn't willing to give him up yet, either. Maybe she was tired, hungry, and stressed, and everything looked bleak.

She didn't know whether her prince was dead or alive or, if he was alive, whether he was someone she could feel attracted to. Maybe her job ended with bringing the team to this spot, and there was nothing further for her to do.

Would it be so bad to settle for Edgar?

Compared to her other boyfriends, he was a catch, and not just because he was immortal, he could induce her dormant immortal genes and could give her multiple orgasms.

She enjoyed being with him, at least most of the time.

49

ARU

A ru lifted his gaze to the mouth of the cavern, searching for an angle that would provide him with the widest patch of view of the sky above. The satellite phone the clan had provided for him was state of the art, but it still needed a clear line of sight to the sky to connect with satellites in orbit, providing they were in the slice of space visible from his location. The surrounding rock and earth interfered with the signal, making it difficult to establish a connection, but if he could find a spot where the opening on the top was large enough, he could get a signal.

It was early afternoon in Tibet and nearly midnight in Los Angeles, but calling Kian this late shouldn't be a problem. After all, they had been having nightly meetings for a while, starting at one o'clock in the morning. That was when the queen of Anumati was available to take his telepathic call and talk to her granddaughter through him and his twin sister.

Regrettably, it wasn't possible every day now that they were out in the field.

"Do you have a signal?" Julian asked.

"Yes, I do." Aru selected Kian's contact and placed the call, the dial tone sounding unnaturally loud in the stillness of the cavern.

Kian answered on the first ring. "What's up, Aru?"

"We found the twins," he said. "And they're alive, but barely so. Julian says we got to them just in time. Regrettably, the eighteen Kra-ell did not make it."

"That is indeed regrettable." Kian sounded appropriately somber. "How come the twins survived, and the others didn't? Was it a deliberate sabotage of the others' life support?"

"I don't think so. It looks like the pod stopped working a long time ago. The

Kra-ell couldn't survive without stasis chambers, but the twins, being half-gods, could survive unaided. They are completely emaciated. Their bodies have been feeding upon themselves to sustain critical brain and heart functions, but Julian can most likely explain it better than I can."

"Put him on."

"I'll activate the speaker phone." Aru motioned for Julian to get closer, and they both sat atop one of the chambers.

It felt disrespectful to the dead, but it wasn't as if they had an alternative except to go up to the surface.

"The chambers were sealed," the doctor said. "So, their bodies wouldn't have had anything to convert into energy. Aru thinks the chambers operated at some minimal capacity, and I agree. Even gods cannot survive in a vacuum."

Aru frowned, a flicker of doubt passing through him at Julian's assessment. As far as he knew, that wasn't how unaided stasis worked. It was his understanding that the body's metabolic processes were suspended and not dependent on external resources. But he wasn't a medical expert, and there might be differences between pureblooded gods and hybrids in how their bodies handled stasis.

"Anyway," Julian continued. "Their bodies are too fragile to move out of the chambers or even attempt to revive outside of a clinic. I brought a lot of medical equipment, but it might not be enough. Frankly, I'd prefer to keep them inside the stasis chambers, bring them to a proper clinic, and have my mother do the honors of reviving them. I don't have enough experience, and given their state, I don't feel comfortable doing that."

"I'll defer to your expert medical opinion," Kian said. "We will need to arrange for a private plane to transport the chambers."

"What about the Kra-ell?" Aru asked. "They deserve a proper funeral, and their people should do it."

"We can leave them here," Negal said. "Now that we know where they are, we can send a group of Kra-ell to perform the necessary rites."

Dagor shook his head. "We can't leave them. What if someone finds the pod between now and the arrival of a delegation of Kra-ell? This place is too close to a military base. Leaving alien technology and bodies to be easily discovered is not advisable."

Aru rubbed the back of his neck. "They have not found it so far, and we wouldn't have found it either if not for Jasmine's scrying stick. The chasm is barely visible from above, even when flying low. Still, Dagor is right. We should not leave them here to be accidentally found by the Chinese."

"We can take the stasis chambers out," Negal said. "But there is no way we can move the pod. We can't destroy it either because it's indestructible. But maybe we could use explosives to collapse some of the cavern's walls and bury it under a lot of rock."

Aru winced at the thought. "The problem is that explosions would make a lot of noise, and the resulting plume of dust might be high enough to be visible from the base. We might as well send up a flare announcing our presence."

Dagor groaned. "That's not the only problem. How are we supposed to transport a bunch of stasis chambers from here to the airport? We can't shroud an entire helicopter while it's transporting the pods from here to the town, or an entire plane even if we can get one to land somewhere in the vicinity."

Aru's mind raced, trying to come up with a solution. They had the truck with the extra fuel. They could unload the fuel, load the chambers onto the truck, and cover it with tarps. But then it would once again be difficult to shroud the chambers while loading them onto the plane. They would need to commission crates, deliver them somewhere inconspicuous, load the chambers into them, and then get them to the plane.

It would be complicated and time-consuming but doable.

"What about the technology in the escape pod?" Kian asked. "We could learn a lot from studying it. Can you extract some key components before you bury it?"

"I can give it a try," Dagor said. "I planned on doing that anyway. With the Chinese base so close, we can't even think about extracting the entire pod, but maybe in a decade or two, the base will be gone, and then we can come back for it."

"We need Yamanu here," Julian said. "I tried to think of a way to avoid it, but with the base being so close, we can't even fly all the chambers out of here without raising suspicion. Those things are big, and we can fit only one in the helicopter. Going back and forth twenty times will surely bring the Chinese military here. Yamanu will have to shroud the helicopter while it's doing its rounds. We may also need William to supply us with a device to disrupt their radar. If William can't send us anything, we may need to go back there and damage their power supply and backup generators to give us the window of opportunity we need for the operation."

Aru had the Anumatian disruptor, but that device would permanently disable the radar, and if possible, it was better to cause just a temporary malfunction.

"Then, once we have all the chambers out of here and secure, we can plant explosives in the cavern and bring down parts of the mountain on top of the pod while Yamanu shrouds the activity."

There was a moment of thoughtful silence on the other end of the line, broken only by the faint sound of Kian's breathing. "Alright," he said at last. "I'll send Yamanu with a chartered plane and ask William to see what he can do, but even if we move as fast as we can, it will take time for Yamanu to get to you. You will have to sit on it for about three days."

"I need to take the twins out of here," Julian said. "We will have to risk flying these two stasis chambers to the town and keeping them with us in the hotel. I want to keep an eye on them."

"I agree," Kian said. "Two round trips with the helicopter should not arouse too much suspicion."

Aru wasn't sure Kian was right about that, but it wasn't as if they had much choice. The twins needed medical supervision, and keeping them in the escape pod in the cavern until Yamanu arrived didn't seem prudent either.

"Dagor and I will do our best to salvage as much as we can from the escape pod during those three days," he told Kian. "The tech is ancient, so there might be some non-solid-state components that can be reverse-engineered."

"Perhaps this escape pod can provide some clues as to the whereabouts of the others," Kian said. "Does it have something like a black box?"

Aru had heard the term before. A black box was a flight recorder used on aircraft. It collected flight data such as altitude, airspeed, heading, and various other data from the aircraft sensors, providing information that investigators could use to determine the causes of fatal accidents. He wasn't sure if the same device also recorded the conversation in the cockpit, including radio communications between the crew and air traffic control, or whether a different device was used. In any case, black boxes were designed to be highly durable to withstand a crash's force and the following conditions, including fire and deep-sea pressures.

"It should," Dagor answered for him. "That's one of the things I'm trying to find. It could give us clues about the location of the mothership when it exploded and the trajectory of this pod. We may be able to extrapolate from that the likely landing sites of the other pods, or at least further narrow down the search area."

50

KIAN

Kian ended the call with Aru and turned to Syssi, who had been sitting quietly by his side throughout the conversation. Her expression morphed from giddiness when she heard the news about the twins to sadness when she heard about the Kra-ell.

"You were right." He took her hand. "As always."

Syssi smiled sadly. "The Fates wanted them found, and evidently, it was urgent. That's why they hijacked my vision and showed me a way to find them instead of showing me Khiann." Her eyes misted with tears as she looked at him. "I just hope it's because he's not in danger and can wait, and not because he's gone."

"I hope so, too." He enveloped her in his arms and kissed the top of her head. "It's difficult for me to put my faith in the Fates and trust them to put us on the right path."

"It's tragic that the Kra-ell didn't make it. They were all young people who were promised a better life. I just keep wondering who's to blame."

"Does it matter?"

Syssi nodded. "Maybe not to them, but it does to me. I want to know who to rage against."

Kian chuckled. "Raging is my job in this family. You are supposed to be the logical and composed one."

"Not this time. This wasn't an accident. I know it, and you know it. What we don't know is who was behind it. The queen of Anumati delayed the ship's arrival but didn't rig it to explode."

Kian arched a brow. "And you know that how? Because she said so? Think about it. She had every reason to sabotage that ship. It was carrying assassins sent by the king to murder her beloved son, who she wanted to protect at all costs. She delayed the ship so it wouldn't be obvious that she was behind it, but she might have also ordered it to self-destruct upon arrival."

Chewing on her lower lip, Syssi contemplated his words for a while. "You are right. She would have done that even if she suspected that the royal twins were onboard and that they were her grandkids. They weren't legitimate heirs, so she didn't care about them."

"The queen might have cared a little, but not enough to endanger her son." Kian removed his arms. "I need to start making calls."

"Speaking of calls, we should inform your mother that the twins were found. She'll be upset if we don't tell her right away."

Kian hesitated momentarily, his mind leaping ahead to the calls he needed to make and the favors he needed to call in. "I have to start getting everything in motion. I don't have time to call my mother."

She would have a thousand questions for which he didn't have answers yet, and he was pressed for time.

Syssi squeezed his hand. "I'll call her."

"Thank you," he said, kissing her cheek. "I don't know what I'd do without you."

Syssi smiled. "Go." She shooed him towards his office with a wave of her hand.

Kian grabbed his half-finished coffee cup and headed to his home office. He settled into his chair, taking a moment to gather his thoughts and prioritize the calls he needed to make. Kalugal was first, he decided. His cousin had connections in China that would be invaluable for moving things quickly and efficiently. If he agreed to accompany Yamanu to Tibet, he could be of further help with his compulsion ability.

Kian chose Kalugal's number from his favorites list and placed the call, his fingers drumming restlessly on the polished wood of his desk as he waited for the call to connect.

"Kian," Kalugal answered with the usual warmth in his voice, which Kian was starting to learn wasn't fake. "To what do I owe the pleasure?"

He explained the situation as briefly as he could. Jasmine, scrying, the pod's discovery, the twins' precarious state, and the need for swift and covert action. He hadn't told Kalugal what he needed from him, but his cousin was smart enough to figure that out.

Kalugal listened intently, his occasional hums of acknowledgment the only sign that he was still on the line. When Kian finished, there was a moment of thoughtful silence.

"Naturally, you need my connections in China, my plane, and my compulsion ability," Kalugal said with a note of humor. "All three are at your service."

Kian felt relieved, even though he had expected Kalugal's response. His cousin was fascinated by the gods' technology, and the escape pod was a marvel he was eager to get his hands on. He wanted to know where it was and how to get it, and knowing him, he would find a way to extract the pod despite the Chinese military presence.

"Can your plane fit twenty stasis chambers? I think we'll need both our planes for this mission. We'll have to accommodate all the passengers and luggage and the medical equipment that Julian brought along. I assume that each stasis chamber is the size of a sarcophagus and probably just as heavy. Aru and Dagor are also trying to extract as much tech from the escape pod as possible, so there will also be a lot of equipment to transport."

"You are probably correct. Only some of the stasis chambers containing the Kra-ell can go in the cargo hold of each plane, but maybe they could all fit in one plane if both the cargo and the passenger cabin are utilized. The clan's plane will need to be the cargo carrier, as mine has more seating. Naturally, the twins will need to be fitted into my plane between the seats so Julian can keep an eye on them. I have enough room for all the passengers and their baggage."

"The other alternative is to charter a larger plane. That may be the better option."

"I don't know if you can get one as quickly as you'd like."

"True. How soon can you be ready to go?" Kian asked.

There was a long silence, and Kian imagined Kalugal checking with Jacki. "My pilot will probably need a few hours to get to the plane, get the flight details sorted out, get fuel, file the flight plan, and do the pre-flight check. I will be at the hangar, packed and ready to go by then. I assume that Yamanu is coming along?"

"You assume correctly. I didn't call him yet, but I'm about to."

"Have him meet me in the garage in two hours," Kalugal said. "I'll have one of my men drive us. I'm not taking any with me except for the pilot and copilot. Are you sending anyone in addition to Yamanu?"

"We need to sort the radar risk from the Chinese base. Even if Yamanu shrouds the helicopter from view, they will still see it on the radar, and twenty round trips are bound to raise suspicion. I will check with William if he needs to join you for that personally, or if he can give Yamanu a quick demonstration on how to use his signal scrambler or whatever other device he will choose. I will let you know. I'll call you if there is any change of plans. Call me if you are having trouble with anything."

Kalugal snorted. "I don't have trouble with anyone."

His cousin ended the call before Kian had a chance to thank him.

He dialed Yamanu next, and as Kian explained the situation, he could practically hear Yamanu's excitement building, the man's love of a challenge and a good adventure shining through.

"Mey, my love, do you want to come along?" Yamanu called out, his voice slightly muffled as he turned away from the phone.

There was a pause, followed by an indistinct conversation that Kian couldn't quite make out. Then Yamanu was back. "I'm afraid I'll have to travel by my lonesome this time," he said with a hint of disappointment in his tone. "Mey and Jin have an important meeting they can't miss with a major online retailer who insists on meeting them in person. Am I the only one who sees the irony in that?"

"You are onto something," Kian agreed. "An online retailer should be fine with online communications with the suppliers. Back to the mission, it will be a quick in-and-out job. You fly in, help them remove the stasis chambers without anyone seeing anything, and then cover them when they bury the pod. I don't think Jacki is joining Kalugal either so you can spend some quality time together."

"I'm looking forward to it," Yamanu said, and Kian wasn't sure if he was being sarcastic or meant it.

"Kalugal asked that you meet him in the underground garage in two hours, and you will probably hear from William shortly about operating the scrambler. I doubt he needs to join you on the mission just for that."

"Got it, boss."

Once Kian ended the call with Yamanu, he called Charlie to alert him to get the plane ready.

Next was William.

"I don't need to be there in person. The device is easy to operate. I'll call Yamanu and get him all set up."

Kian made his final call to Jade, the leader of the Kra-ell.

He delivered the news with as much tact as he could muster, and Jade received it in her usual no-nonsense manner. "It's regrettable, but I suspected as much, so I'm not surprised. I'm only surprised that the twins survived. I hope you told your people to be careful around them."

"I did, and the plan is to revive them in our clinic at the keep. You are welcome to join us for that, and if you want to bring some of your people to witness it, that's fine."

"Thank you. You honor me, Kian. And thank you for bringing my people to the catacombs for a proper Kra-ell farewell ceremony. Their remains will be treated with the respect and reverence they deserve."

As he ended the call and leaned back in his chair, Kian felt a wave of exhaustion wash over him, the events of the day catching up to him all at once. With a sigh, he pushed himself up and went to the kitchen, following the rich, inviting scent of brewing coffee.

Syssi was there, her back to him as she busied herself with the cappuccino machine. Kian paused for a moment in the doorway, simply drinking in the sight of her.

"How did my mother take the news?" he asked, moving to stand beside her.

Syssi turned to him with a smile. "She's excited," she said, reaching up to brush a stray lock of hair from his forehead. "She's on her way over."

51

JASMINE

"Why is it taking so long?" Jasmine asked Edgar.

Like her, he was sitting on one of the boulders that the ropes were tied to, and like her, he was looking into the chasm and listening to what was going on, but unlike her, he might actually hear and see something.

He shrugged. "I don't know. But if I had to guess, they are opening each stasis chamber and checking who is alive and who is dead."

Swallowing the bile rising in her throat, Jasmine clutched the metal mug with the coffee Edgar had made for her. He'd also warmed up a canned meal for her, and they had shared it in companionable silence.

All in all, Edgar was a good guy. He had some rough edges that shouldn't be too difficult to smooth out, but she wasn't sure she wanted to put in the effort.

Finally, when the ropes went taut, Dagor and Negal climbed out of the cavern a few moments later, and Jasmine rose to her feet. "Are they alive?"

Dagor cast her a sad look that had her heart plummet into her gut. "The royal twins are alive, but barely so, and the rest are dead. We are bringing the two chambers up."

"Thank the goddess." Jasmine was so relieved that she didn't ask how or why the twins were alive while everyone else in the pod had died.

Sitting back down on the boulder, she watched with bated breath as Negal and Dagor pulled on the ropes, their muscles straining with effort, and when the chamber finally crested the top of the crater, Edgar helped them to carefully maneuver the stasis chamber out of the chasm.

The chamber was bulky and unwieldy, and its sleek metal surface glinted dully in the sunlight as Dagor secured the ropes so he and Negal could guide it to rest on the ground.

A few moments later, Aru and Julian were pulled up, and as they scrambled over the edge, they were just as covered with dirt as Dagor and Negal.

They all just stood there for a moment, staring down at the alien chamber. For some reason, Jasmine had expected it to be rectangular, like the healing chamber the alien in the *Stargate* movie had used to regenerate his body, but the object in front of her was oval and curved, with no edges that she could see. It must have been difficult to secure the ropes around such a slick chamber, and now she had a mini panic attack thinking about the alien device slipping out of the ropes and crashing on the bottom of the cavern.

Staring at the chamber grimly, Edgar ran a hand through his hair. "It's not gonna fit in the chopper unless we leave the doors open on both sides and it sticks out."

Julian nodded. "We need to tie it securely, so it doesn't fall out, and do the same with the other chamber." He glanced to the other helicopter, where Norbu was taking a nap.

Edgar followed his gaze and shook his head. "I wouldn't trust Norbu with the live ones. I'd rather take them one at a time."

"I agree." Julian let out a breath. "I'll come with you. The two of us should be able to carry the chamber to the hotel while shrouding what we are carrying." He looked at the stasis chamber and chuckled. "I wish we could use the excuse of shooting a science fiction movie. It would have made explaining these things easy. But regrettably, we don't have the proper set-up."

"This thing is heavy," Dagor said. "And it's not easy to grip. You will have to improvise something to transport it."

Jasmine tried to picture the operational logistics. "Where will we put them?" she asked. "There are no rooms available in the hotel, and our rooms are barely big enough for us, let alone two giant stasis chambers." She worried her lower lip. "But maybe we can squeeze in one."

She wanted the one with the prince in her room, but she couldn't ask for it without sounding like a weirdo.

Julian rubbed a hand over his chin. "We can make it work. We'll put one in your room and the other in mine and Ella's. It will be a tight fit, but it's not like we have any other option. I don't want to leave them outside on the truck."

Edgar looked unhappy with the arrangement, his jaw tight and his eyes stormy, but he said nothing. Nodding his acceptance, he turned to help load the first chamber into the helicopter.

After securing it with ropes, Edgar and Julian climbed in, and as the rotors whirred to life and the aircraft lifted off the ground, Jasmine felt a pang of anxiety twist her gut. What if the chamber slipped out of the ropes holding it to the craft and broke into a million pieces on impact?

What if Edgar made a dangerous maneuver on purpose?

It was in his best interest to get rid of the prince, and if he made it look like an accident, no one could even blame him for it.

Banishing the disturbing thought from her mind, she turned to Aru. "What's going to happen now? Will Edgar make the rounds until all the chambers are transported out of here?"

"You can fly out on the next round," the god said. "We will take out just one more chamber, and the rest will have to wait for Yamanu to arrive. He can shroud Edgar while he's flying back and forth. We don't want the soldiers in the base to notice all this extra traffic. We also need him to shroud the area when we detonate explosives inside the cavern to bury the pod under rubble."

Jasmine frowned. "I don't know much about things like that, but can Yamanu also conceal the helicopter from the base's radar?"

Aru smiled, giving her an appreciative look. "He can't. We will take care of the radar in another way."

He didn't elaborate on the methods he would use, and she didn't ask because the explanation would probably not help her understand the technology involved.

"What about you? With the stasis chamber taking up the entire back of the helicopter, only one seat is left next to Edgar. Is he going to come back for you? Or are you coming back with the other pilot?"

"We will stay to guard the pod," Aru said.

Jasmine glanced at the other helicopter and wondered whether Aru wanted to stay behind because he didn't want to fly with the other pilot, or perhaps because he didn't want the other helicopter to fly back to town so that fewer flights would register on the base's radar.

"I get it. If Edgar doesn't trust the local pilot with the stasis chambers, I can't blame you for not wanting to fly with him. As for me, I'm more than happy to wait for Edgar to return and take me with him."

She suspected that the gods might have other reasons for wanting to stay behind. They probably hoped to extract whatever technology they could before burying it.

52

ANNANI

"Mistress." Ogidu rushed over to Annani with a shawl spread between his arms, looking like he planned to catch her with it, which was probably what was on his mind. "It is chilly outside this late at night."

He was probably right, but Kian's house was only a few minutes' walk away, so getting chilled was not a concern. Besides, with her excitement, Annani doubted she would even feel the cold.

That the royal twins, her half-brother and sister, had been found alive was a miracle, especially given that no one in their entourage had made it. If not for their godly genes, they would have perished too, but the Fates had spared them, and they must have done so for a reason.

The future would tell their purpose, but Annani did not doubt that it would alter the destiny of her clan and maybe even Earth and Anumati.

She could not wait to meet them.

They were why she had not gone home after the cruise had ended as she had planned. She missed her Alaskan sanctuary, the marvelous tropical oasis under a dome of reinforced ice, and her community there. Still, she'd had a feeling that the expedition to Tibet would be successful and that the twins would be found.

Once again, her gut feeling had proven correct. Her siblings were alive.

She wondered what their names were. No one seemed to know, which was odd, but she would soon find out, if their memories remained intact.

Poor Gulan had not remembered her name when she had awakened from her stasis after five thousand years, and she had adopted the name Wonder because she had heard a child call her that. The royal twins had been in stasis for over seven thousand years, which was significantly longer, but on the other hand, it had not been a critical injury that had put them in stasis. They had spent at least part of it in a chamber that had provided life support. Hopefully, their memories had remained intact.

"Thank you." She took the shawl from Ogidu, wrapped it around her shoulders, and waited for him to open the front door for her. "You can stay here. I am only going to Kian's house."

Ogidu bowed. "I am sorry, mistress, but I cannot obey your command when it contradicts your previous command to ensure your safety. Oridu and I will follow you to Master Kian's house, but if you so wish, we will stay outside and wait to escort you back home."

Ever since their rebooting, the Odus had not been as obedient as they had used to be. So far, it was in a good way. Still, it worried her a little. What if that newfound independent thinking of theirs led them to defy her in a moment of crisis?

She could imagine them interpreting something as a threat to her and refusing to stand down when ordered.

Annani shook her head, pushing the thought aside. It was a concern for another time, a problem to be addressed with careful reprogramming. For now, she had more pressing matters to attend to.

Reaching Kian's door, Annani lifted her hand to ring the bell, but before her finger could contact the button, the door swung open revealing her beloved son.

"Mother," he said warmly, kissing her cheek.

Annani lifted her arms, inviting a hug, and as Kian gladly obliged her, she threw her arms around him in a fierce embrace. Clinging to him for a long moment, she savored his solid warmth and the steady beat of his heart against her cheek.

As Syssi appeared behind him, Annani released Kian and hugged her equally enthusiastically. "As usual, your vision was true. They are alive."

Syssi squeezed her back tightly. "It was the Fates' will. Or so I hope."

Threading her arm through Annani's, Syssi led her to the living room. "Should we celebrate with a cappuccino or with champagne?"

"Cappuccino," Annani said as she sat down on the couch. "I love the way you make it. Your skill is unparalleled."

As she had expected, Syssi blushed, flustered by the compliment. "I have the best equipment money can buy. That's why they come out so good."

Annani waved a dismissive hand. "Having the right equipment is just half of the story. Knowing what to do with it is the other half." She winked, making Syssi blush crimson.

"Mother." Kian shook his head. "Sometimes you are worse than Amanda."

Annani laughed but then affected an innocent expression. "Am I wrong? A good storyteller can use a great typewriter to write her story faster. Still, it will not inspire her or make her a better writer unless she writes commentary about typewriters."

"No one uses typewriters anymore." Kian walked over to the kitchen, where Ogidu and Oridu had joined Okidu. "Would you like some chocolate cake with your coffee?"

"I would love some." Annani smiled at Okidu, who bowed deeply. "There is nothing better than chocolate to celebrate a joyous occasion." She shifted her gaze to Kian. "Did you share the good news with your sisters?"

"Not yet." Kian returned to the living room and sat on one of the armchairs. "I wanted you to be the first to hear about it."

"Then we should call them and invite them to celebrate with us," she said. "Would it be alright if I invite Amanda and Alena over? We can call Sari and have her join via a tele-call."

"Of course," Kian said. "Provided they are not in bed yet and wish to come."

"I'm sure they are not sleeping yet." Syssi put a cup of cappuccino in front of Annani and another in front of Kian. "I just don't know if they will be as excited about this as you are. We don't know anything about the twins, and they might not be good people." She cast Annani a soft smile. "We want to believe that they are and that the Fates sent them our way to benefit us, but we should be prepared for the possibility that they are not a force for good."

Kian nodded. "We are exercising precaution. Everyone on the team was instructed to use their compulsion-filtering earpieces around the twins. I hope they are following protocol."

That dampened Annani's exuberance, but it did not eradicate it. "The Fates used extraordinary measures to point us in the twins' direction, so I have to believe it was for a good reason and not to wipe us out. If they wanted that, they would not have saved me five thousand years ago from the fate that befell my family and the other gods on Earth."

53

JASMINE

C urious, Jasmine approached the remaining stasis chamber and peered in, straining to make out the figure's details. The curved dome that covered the pod was semi-transparent, the glass-like material transitioning from a deep, opaque brown at the base to a lighter, more translucent shade at the top.

She leaned forward, intent on pressing her face against the cool surface to get a better look, but Aru's hand on her shoulder stopped her short.

"Don't look," he said. "It's not a pretty sight."

Jasmine hesitated momentarily, a flicker of disappointment passing through her, but she knew Aru was right.

"I know." She took a step back from the chamber. "I heard Julian saying that he's almost a skeleton."

The words felt strange on her tongue, the pronoun slipping out before she could stop it. Somehow, though, she knew that it was true. The chamber's occupant was male, the brother of the female twin who had been taken away first.

Jasmine frowned. "How did the twins survive while everyone else in their pod died?"

Aru regarded her with a thoughtful expression. "Didn't Edgar tell you about the twins being different from the other occupants of the pod?"

"They were royal, a prince and a princess, and the others were either their guards or servants, meaning not royal."

He smiled. "Well, yes, I assume that's true, but that's not the only way these two are different. The Kra-ell are a long-lived species compared to humans, but they are not immortal and cannot enter stasis without a stasis chamber. The twins, on the other hand, are only half Kra-ell. The other half of their genetic makeup was contributed by their father, who was a god, and unlike the Kra-ell, gods are immortal. They can enter stasis unaided and remain in that state almost indefinitely. When the pod malfunctioned, and the stasis chambers stopped providing life-support, the pureblooded Kra-ell died, while the hybrids survived."

"What does it mean to enter stasis? Is it like hibernation?"

Aru nodded. "In a way, stasis is an extreme form of hibernation. Hibernation is a complex, adaptive strategy crucial for survival in extreme conditions. The metabolic rate slows to conserve energy. Body temperature, heart rate, and breathing rate all decrease to minimal levels." He gestured to the chamber behind them, his eyes tracing the sleek lines of the alien device. "Stasis chambers are designed to keep their occupants alive and in suspended animation for extended periods. Gods use them on long interstellar flights to preserve their bodies and arrive at their destinations in good shape, not looking like these two."

Jasmine shuddered as her mind conjured up images of countless horror movies she had seen. Zombies, reanimated corpses, and the living dead seemed to blur together in her imagination. Why had she even watched those nightmarish landscapes of decay and despair?

It had been a phase, a time in her life when she'd believed it was crucial to get exposed to as many genres as possible and learn what she could from them.

She'd once auditioned for a role in a low-budget horror film and had been relieved when she hadn't gotten the part. She'd found the prospect of spending hours in the makeup chair unappealing, and the thought of having her face caked with prosthetics and fake blood wasn't pleasant either. Even worse was the idea of being surrounded by other actors in similar makeup. It had just made her skin crawl.

Shaking her head, she took another step away from the stasis chamber. "I thought that the royals were Kra-ell. Oddly, none of you mentioned that they were half-gods."

"I thought you knew," Aru said. "Besides, I didn't believe that we would find them, so it was irrelevant. Also, we weren't sure that they were indeed half-gods. There were rumors, but it's not done on our home planet. The two species do not intermingle, and it's considered a taboo by both." He waved a hand at the stasis chamber. "Their survival confirmed that their father was a god."

Earth had witnessed its own share of strange taboos on interfaith and interracial marriages, so Jasmine wasn't shocked that two species that differed so much in appearance and longevity placed taboos on having hybrid offspring.

It suddenly occurred to her that the twins' paternal genes could have made them look more like gods than Kra-ell and therefore, more human.

After all, Aru and his teammates were gods and looked like the best version of humans.

"So, if the twins are not fully Kra-ell, do they look more like their father or mother?" she asked.

Aru shrugged. "Given their current state, it's hard to tell, but I guess they will have some traits from both parents."

Jasmine's brow furrowed in confusion, her head tilting to the side as she regarded Aru with a questioning gaze. "I don't understand. If there was such a strong taboo on intermixing, wouldn't that have been a problem for the queen if her kids looked like gods even a little bit?"

Aru sighed, his expression turning somber. "That's why their mother consecrated them to the priesthood from a very young age. They were always veiled from head to toe, their faces and bodies hidden from the public. Some speculated that they were deformed in some way and that their mother sought to hide their imperfections from the world. Others whispered that they were the product of an illicit affair, a forbidden union between the queen and a god during their years in the resistance when the queen was still just the heir apparent."

Jasmine felt sympathy for the twins, her heart aching at the thought of the prejudice and scorn they must have faced. "Were they in danger? What would have happened to them if anyone discovered that they were hybrids?" She had a good idea but was afraid to hear the answer.

Aru's jaw tightened. "If the Kra-ell had discovered that the twins were not purebloods, they would have been slaughtered without mercy along with their mother, the queen." He shook his head. "Not that they would have fared much better if they were discovered to be truly deformed. The Kra-ell are a cruel people in many ways, primitive and warlike. They have a long history of culling the weak and the imperfect from their ranks."

Jasmine felt a chill run down her spine at Aru's words, a sense of horror and revulsion washing over her. What kind of people would have done that to innocent children just because they were different?

"The current Kra-ell queen is trying to change things," Aru continued. "She's working to end the practice of killing off children deemed less than perfect. But the taboo against intermingling is still going strong. Both societies see the offspring of such unions as abominations, feared and reviled."

Jasmine swallowed hard, her throat tight with anger and sorrow. It was unfathomable to her that someone could be hated and persecuted simply for the circumstances of their birth.

It was no wonder that they had been sent away in a desperate bid for survival. Their mother had done everything she could to save them.

She must have been such an incredibly brave and foolish female. Why had she risked her life to have an affair with a god?

Had they been in love? Or had it been an act of rebellion?

"You said that the queen got pregnant with the twins when she was still a princess and that she met their father when they both took part in a rebellion. Who were they rebelling against and why?"

Aru smiled. "That's a long story. Let's save it for the flight back home."

54

EDGAR

Edgar adjusted his grip on the controls as the wind whipped at the helicopter. Scanning the horizon where the Himalayan peaks cut sharply into the gray sky, he took a moment to admire the landscape of jagged peaks and deep ravines.

Julian stayed behind in town to watch over the stasis chamber containing the princess, so Edgar made the journey back to the mountaintop alone, enjoying the solitude but not the disturbing thoughts swirling in his mind.

They had maneuvered the princess's stasis chamber into Julian and Ella's room, which meant that the prince was going to Edgar and Jasmine's, which did not make Edgar happy.

He didn't want to be stuck with the mummy in their room, especially since the prince wasn't really dead. Was he aware of anything happening around him while in stasis?

The only time Edgar had experienced losing consciousness had been during his induction ceremony at the age of thirteen, and he remembered being completely out. Then again, he had been unconscious only for a few minutes and not thousands of years.

Who knew if the twins' brains had remained intact after all that time? He didn't wish them ill, but if that happened, Jasmine wouldn't be interested in the prince, so Edgar wouldn't be too upset if that was the case. After all, it was a dog-eat-dog world, and he had already done his fair share of altruism.

Even the Fates couldn't hold his lack of compassion for the hybrid twins against him.

As the gusts of wind became even more violent, buffeting the aircraft, Edgar adjusted the cyclic and pedal, anticipating and counteracting the worst of their shifts and swirls and stabilizing the craft as he kept a steady course.

It was a challenge to land, and as he touched down on the rocky plateau, the rotors kicked up a cloud of dust and debris that, thanks to the wind, took flight.

He climbed out of the helicopter, his boots crunching on the loose gravel as he made his way over to where Aru and the others were waiting.

"When the wind picked up, I was worried," Aru said. "I didn't know if you could make it back."

"It's not as bad as it looks." Edgar shifted his gaze to Jasmine, who was sitting on the same rock he'd left her on, but instead of using the sleeping bag as a cushion for her bottom, she had it wrapped around her. "But it's getting worse. I'm not even sure I can take the other stasis chamber in these conditions. If it could fit inside, I wouldn't be concerned, but given that it overhangs out the doors, is rounded without a secure purchase, and we're using ropes to keep it from slipping out, I'm worried about losing it in a nasty gust. Because of the mountains, these gusts just come out of nowhere and slap the chopper." He clapped his hands to demonstrate.

He hoped Aru would see reason and leave the prince on the mountaintop for the night. It would give Edgar and Jasmine one more night alone with each other, and they both needed it.

"We have to transport them both." Aru's gaze swept over the mostly barren landscape. "We can wait with the rest for Yamanu to arrive and shroud the operation, but this one needs to be where Julian can keep an eye on him." He turned around to look at the crater. "From the air, this looks like just another natural formation, but if someone comes snooping around on foot, we'll have to be ready to shroud the pod or thrall them into forgetting what they've seen. Dagor and I will guard the pod, Negal will go back with the other pilot, and Jasmine will return with you."

Dagor nodded. "I'm sure Jasmine's had enough of sitting on that rock and freezing."

She lifted her head and looked their way, but not directly at Edgar, which rankled. "A shower and a bed sound like a dream," she said.

"I bet." He smiled, forcing her to smile back. "You can sit up front while Negal and I load up the stasis chamber and secure it."

"I'll wait for you to be done." Jasmine tightened the sleeping bag around herself. "I don't want to be in the way."

She was right, of course. Tying the chamber also required looping the ropes around the front seats.

"We'll do it fast." He turned to Aru. "Do you want Negal and me to swap guard duty with you tomorrow?"

"We shall see," Aru said. "In any case, the two of you should return tomorrow morning to bring us fresh supplies and help dismantle what we can from the pod."

"Of course." Edgar walked over to the stasis chamber. "Let's do it."

Once the chamber was secured, Edgar was sure it wouldn't slip out of the ropes no matter what the weather threw at him. As much as he didn't want the prince to come between him and Jasmine, he wouldn't intentionally harm the dude. Besides, losing the chamber would stain his exceptional reputation as a pilot, and even Jasmine wasn't worth that.

He returned to where her backpack lay on the grass and lifted it onto his back.

"Ready to go?" he asked her.

"I am." She removed the sleeping bag from her shoulders, rolled it up, and rose.

He was about to hug her when something about how she stood up made him pause.

Jasmine stood tall and straight, her weight balanced evenly on both feet as if she had never been injured. There was no sign of the pain or stiffness that had plagued her since she'd twisted her ankle, and no hint of the limp that had made each step a struggle before.

If she were an immortal, her recovery wouldn't have surprised him. But she was still human, and he hadn't bitten her since her injury, so it wasn't his venom that had contributed to her fast recovery.

A sudden, horrible thought occurred to him that made his blood run cold. The gods' venom was even more potent than that of immortals, and if one of them had bitten her, that could explain her miraculous healing.

All three were mated to their truelove mates, though, so it should be physically impossible for them to bite a female who was not their mate. Then again, they were gods and might not be the same as immortals.

Edgar had heard the stories about the gods of old and their promiscuity. They had not been known for being loyal to their mates, but he had always assumed the reason was that most of them had not mated for love but rather for politics and convenience. But what if the reason was a different physiology?

What if they could love their mates and still be unfaithful to them?

Only fated truelove mates bonded so powerfully that they were incapable of feeling attraction for anyone but their one and only.

It was also possible that the trait had been genetically removed from the new generations of gods, and Aru and his friends were more like humans in that regard.

"I see that your ankle is much better," he said as he walked toward the helicopter. "It seems to have healed remarkably fast."

"I know." Jasmine cast him a smile and lifted her boot-clad leg to show him how easily she could move it. "It has just gotten better and better, and now the pain is gone. Maybe it's the fresh mountain air, or maybe it's magical." She smiled and leaned toward him. "Or maybe my witchy abilities are getting stronger, and I healed myself with a spell." She winked.

Edgar didn't find that amusing. "I doubt magic had anything to do with it." He turned to look at the three gods who were standing close to each other and speaking in hushed voices. "I heard that a god's venom is even more potent than an immortal's. Perhaps one of them offered his assistance."

Jasmine's eyes widened, a flash of hurt and anger passing over her features as she realized what he was implying, and then her eyes narrowed. "What are you trying to say, Edgar?"

Shrugging, he put her backpack over the stasis chamber and secured it with a rope. "I'm not trying to say anything."

He offered her a hand up, but she refused and climbed into the craft without his aid. "I can't believe you, Edgar."

"Same here," he murmured as he climbed in. "They are all mated."

She shook her head. "How you can even suggest such a thing is beyond me. What kind of a woman do you think I am?"

55

JASMINE

The truth was that the same thing had occurred to Jasmine, so she couldn't blame Edgar for being suspicious, but it still hurt that he didn't trust her.

If one of the gods had indeed bitten her and then made her forget it, it hadn't been done to take advantage of her or do something inappropriate but to help her heal.

So yeah, there was an ick factor to the act that couldn't be ignored because the bite was associated with sex, and all three gods were in loving, committed relationships. Still, maybe there was a workaround, some clause that allowed biting to aid someone in trouble or something like that.

Edgar's angry expression faltered, doubt flickering over his features, but then his jaw tightened with stubborn resolve. "What am I supposed to think? When you left the day before, you had to be carried because you couldn't put any weight on that foot. Humans don't heal that fast without help." He handed her the headphones and started the rotor.

Fitting the headphones on, she leaned back in the seat and fastened her harness. "I don't know how it happened. So don't use that accusing tone with me."

Performing a final check of his instruments, Edgar didn't answer, and she thought that maybe he hadn't heard her. Maybe her mouthpiece hadn't been turned on?

The wind outside howled as he grasped the controls and increased the throttle. The engine's growl deepened as the rotor blades gained speed, blurring into a continuous circle overhead. Then, the helicopter began to lift off the ground, the force of the rotors battling against the push of the wind.

As the ground receded rapidly below them, Jasmine's stomach lurched into her throat, especially when a gust of wind made the helicopter tilt precariously. She had a moment of panic that the chamber would slide out, but then Edgar managed to stabilize the craft, piercing through the curtain of wind.

Letting out a breath, Jasmine crossed her arms over her chest. "Your jealousy was kind of cute at first," she said, even though she wasn't sure he could hear her. "But now it's just ugly. I don't appreciate the accusation in your tone. Besides, you have no right to feel possessive and jealous over me. We are not in love, and I didn't make you any promises. We were just enjoying being together."

A flash of hurt passed over his face. "It seemed like more than that to me."

"Oh, really?" Jasmine huffed. "If you were so into me, you wouldn't have waited for Amanda to mention me to Max and, when he declined the offer, to jump on the opportunity. Unlike Max, you'd met me before, and I thought we could have something, but you never came to visit me in the staff decks."

"I was not allowed. You know that. Not until Amanda gave me the green light."

Jasmine snorted. "If you were so into me and couldn't stop thinking about me, you would have found a way. You would have badgered Kian or Amanda to allow you a visit or snuck in to see me without waiting for anyone's permission."

Edgar stared at her, his mouth opening and closing like a fish out of water. For a moment, it seemed like he might argue, try to defend himself, or plead his case. But the words died on his lips, and his shoulders slumped in defeat.

Except, that didn't last long.

Like a dog with a bone, he didn't seem capable of admitting she was right. "You say you didn't promise me anything, but that's not true. You implied that I would be your inducer, which is a big deal for us, and you know it. You only agree to be induced by someone with whom you feel a bond. But that was a lie. You were holding out for your prince all along, weren't you? Keeping me around just in case he was dead or ugly or just looked too alien. And now that you know that he's alive, you want to cast me aside."

There was more than a smidgen of truth to what he was saying because she'd had thoughts along those lines, but she hadn't acted on them. Besides, that wasn't the point of their argument. She wasn't accusing him of infidelity or any other wrongdoing, while he was attacking her for no good reason.

Jasmine snorted, the sound loud and jarring in her ears. "Are you even listening to yourself?" she asked, her voice dripping with disdain. "Have you taken a look at the prince? He looks like a corpse, Edgar. A fucking corpse. Do you think I'm romantically interested in him?"

Her patience wearing thin, she threw her hands up in exasperation. "And let's not forget how this whole thing started, with you accusing me of sleeping with one of the gods and letting him bite me. What's next? Are you going to suggest that I had some orgy with all of them? That they passed me around like a party favor and took turns sinking their fangs into me? That would explain my rapid healing. Venom from three different gods would do that, right?"

"I didn't mean it that way," he murmured weakly.

She shook her head. "I abhor jealous tantrums." Her voice rose with each word, her anger and frustration boiling over. "I am so sick and tired of that, Edgar. So fucking tired. Without trust, there is no future for us. Your lack of trust means that you don't respect me, and I could never love a man who thinks so badly of me."

As the words hung heavy in the air between them, Edgar looked like he had been slapped, which, in a way, he had been.

She might have been too harsh, and there could have been a gentler way to say what she'd said, but she had spoken the truth. Even if Edgar's lack of trust was just a personality flaw, and he would have been suspicious of any woman, regardless of who she was or the circumstances that caused his suspicion, Jasmine couldn't think of it as anything less than profound disrespect.

56

JASMINE

When the helicopter touched down with a jarring thud, the rotors whining to a stop as Edgar killed the engine, Jasmine didn't wait for him to speak. She didn't feel like giving him a chance to argue or apologize.

Instead, she unclipped her harness, pushed open the door, and stepped out into the crisp air.

Edgar had to wait for Negal to land with the other helicopter and for Julian to arrive and help them with the stasis chamber, but she had no intention of waiting around or even spending the night with Edgar and the prince in the same room.

She needed space and time to clear her head and sort through the tangled mess of her emotions.

Perhaps she could room with Gabi or Frankie tonight.

A snort escaped her throat as it occurred to her that Edgar would find a way to turn this into some illicit sexual affair as well.

Whatever.

His jealousy was his problem.

Jasmine strode towards the hotel, hoping to find comfort and solace in the company of her female friends. She forced a smile and waved hello at Julian and Negal as they passed her by on their way to the helicopter to help Edgar unload the stasis chamber.

She knew they would be shrouded, their activities hidden from prying eyes as they transported the prince's stasis chamber to the hotel room she had been sharing with Edgar.

As she'd expected, Jasmine found Margo, Frankie, and Gabi in the hotel restaurant, huddled together over steaming cups of tea and plates of momos.

They looked up as she approached, Margo frowning at the sight of her thunderous expression.

"What happened?" Margo asked as Jasmine sank into a chair beside her. "Is your ankle bothering you?"

"I wish it was that simple, but you are on the right track." She picked one of the momos from Margo's plate and put it in her mouth, rolling her eyes as the flavors of the freshly cooked delicacy exploded in her mouth.

She finished chewing while her friends looked at her expectantly. "My ankle is healed, but I guess it's a mixed blessing." The floodgates opened, and Jasmine poured out the whole sordid story, her words tumbling over each other in a rush.

Frankie listened with a sympathetic ear. "It is strange that you healed so quickly, but maybe Edgar's venom was still in your system from before. I know that when Dagor bit me after I was shot, I healed incredibly fast. And then, during my transition, his venom helped me through the worst of it." She reached out, laying a comforting hand on Jasmine's arm. "I know that Dagor is a god, and his venom is probably more potent than Edgar's, but on the other hand, you were only dealing with a sprained ankle, not a bullet wound. Edgar's venom didn't have to work as hard to fix that."

Jasmine nodded, the tension in her chest easing slightly at Frankie's words. When she thought about it logically, it made sense. She hadn't known that the venom could affect her two days after being bitten, but given Frankie's experience, Edgar's venom might have been still coursing through her veins and working its magic on her body.

It had nothing to do with the gods and some sordid fantasy conjured up by Edgar's overactive imagination.

Margo leaned forward. "I know you're hurt and angry right now, but don't give up on Edgar. Talk to him, try to work things out. Jealousy isn't logical, and I know that better than most."

She smiled ruefully. "I was so jealous when you flirted with Negal when we met. On some level, I knew it was silly and that he only had eyes for me, but I couldn't help it. You are a beautiful, sexy woman, uninhibited, cheerful, and full of life. Any guy would want you, and I was so jealous that I was driving myself crazy."

"I never meant anything by it," Jasmine said, shaking her head. "And I'm so sorry that I made you feel that way. I flirt with everyone. It's just second nature for me. On his part, Negal certainly never encouraged me. He was always polite but distant."

Margo reached out and took Jasmine's hand. "Give Edgar a chance. Talk to him, really talk to him. Make him see how much he hurt you, how much his accusations and distrust have damaged your relationship. And then, if he's truly sorry and willing to work to earn back your trust...forgive him."

Jasmine sighed, her anger draining away like water through a sieve. Margo was right. She shouldn't drop Edgar on an impulse. He was a good guy.

Flawed, but then no one was perfect.

57

EDGAR

As Edgar helped Negal and Julian maneuver the second stasis chamber into his and Jasmine's hotel room, he felt like crap.

Why did he have to be such a jealous ass?

Jasmine hadn't promised him exclusivity, and usually, it wouldn't have been an issue because he didn't expect that from his hookups. But he'd hoped for more with her, especially if she was a Dormant.

There weren't many of those just hanging around, and Jasmine was a catch. She was beautiful, upbeat, and open-minded. He'd had more fun with her in bed and outside of it than with any of the other women he'd been with, and he'd even thought that he was falling in love with her.

Was he, though?

Maybe. He'd thought he was, but what Jasmine said was true. If he'd been so taken with her, he should have sought a way to be with her before Amanda offered the opportunity to Max. The truth was that he had barely thought about Jasmine before Amanda had mentioned her.

Still, his feelings for her had grown over the short time they had been together, and he could easily see himself mated to her.

He hated that she was now mad at him and probably complaining to her girlfriends about him. Hopefully, she wasn't talking shit about him and besmirching his reputation.

Jasmine wasn't malicious, or at least he didn't think she was, so he didn't believe that she would do that, but who knew?

How did the saying go?

Heaven has no rage like love to hatred turned, nor hell a fury like a woman scorned.

Except, in this case, he was the scorned one.

Well, they both were.

Was that right, though?

Jasmine acted like she had done nothing wrong, and he believed her. So, she had every right to be mad at him for insinuating misconduct on her part.

Perhaps one of the gods had bitten her without her knowledge?

Edgar cast a sidelong glance at Negal, who would be the prime suspect. The guy had induced Karen, who hadn't been his mate, so biting Jasmine to make her heal faster was just the kind of thing he would do. The difference was that when he had bitten Karen, he hadn't been in a relationship with Margo yet.

Now that he was bonded to a mate, he shouldn't be able to do such an intimate thing with another female, but Edgar had already conceded that gods might be different in that regard.

As they settled the chamber into place and released the ropes, the dull thud of its base against the worn carpet sounded unnaturally loud in the room's stillness.

"It's a tight fit," Negal said. "But it will have to do."

Edgar regarded the coffin-like chamber with a grimace. "I don't know about you, but I'm not happy to have a corpse in my bedroom while I'm making love to Jasmine."

Negal chuckled. "I hear you. I wouldn't want this thing in my and Margo's room either, but your lady seems attached to it." He looked around the room until his gaze settled on the colorful extra blanket draped over the single chair. "Maybe we can put this over the chamber." He shifted his gaze to Edgar. "Do you want to do that?"

"Yeah. I do." He reached for the blanket, draped it over the oval chamber, and turned to Julian. "You should do the same with the one in your room."

Julian waved a dismissive hand. "I don't mind, and Ella doesn't either. We are careful to leave the alarm on the door so if anyone tries to open it when we are not there, the noise will chase them away."

"Unless they are Chinese military," Edgar murmured. "The faster we can get out of here, the better."

"I'm not worried about that," Julian said. "I'm just grateful for Kian's paranoia and William's genius for creating devices to counteract it. I would have never thought to booby-trap my hotel room door." He turned to Negal. "Don't you guys have a cloaking device? What with all your technological knowhow, you should have a way to hide yourself and your stuff."

Negal opened the door. "We do. It's called shrouding. But you are right. We should have developed a way to hide our belongings when we are not around."

As the two launched into a discussion of how a cloaking device might work, Edgar closed the door behind them and activated the alarm.

He needed to find Jasmine and apologize to her even though his suspicions were valid. She was right that the lack of trust was offensive, and for that, he owed her an apology. He had basically accused her of being a dishonest person, and that had been uncalled for.

"I'm heading to the restaurant," he told Negal and Julian. "Are you coming?"

Julian waved a hand without even bothering to look his way. "Yeah, in a bit." He went back into his discussion with Negal.

For a physician, Julian knew a lot about science fiction, and the arrival of the three gods from an alien planet had fueled his obsession with alien tech.

58

EDGAR

E dgar found Jasmine in the big tent, huddled around a table with Margo, Frankie, Gabi, and Ella. They were all holding steaming cups of tea and had several empty plates between them.

As he approached the table, Jasmine looked up, her eyes widening a little at the sight of him. For a moment, Edgar feared that she would turn away and ignore him. But to his surprise, she nodded her greeting with a guarded expression that was thankfully not hostile.

"Hello, ladies." He forced a smile before putting his hand on Jasmine's shoulder. "Can I steal Jasmine away for a few minutes?"

Margo regarded him with a knowing smile. "Of course."

Jasmine cast her a baleful look before turning it on him. "I should be the one you ask if it's okay to steal me for a few minutes."

She was killing him with all that nonsense. "I apologize, but in our culture, asking the entire group's permission is considered polite."

"Whatever." She rolled her eyes. "I just don't like it when people talk about me like I'm not there." She set her cup down on the table with a clink and pushed to her feet.

Her rebuttal amused him. "Isn't that better than people talking about you when you are actually not there?"

Given the headshaking at the table, he had committed another faux pas, but he was tired of walking on eggshells around Jasmine. If he couldn't speak his mind to her honestly and without weighing every word, then perhaps they shouldn't be together. It was too much effort.

"Let's take a walk," Jasmine said as they left the tent. "I assume that the prince is in our room?"

"Correct, but I wish someone else had taken it. I don't know why he ended up in our room. As the leader of the search team, Aru should have taken him."

She didn't react and kept walking. "So, what did you want to talk about?"

"I'm sorry for offending you. If anything did happen to speed up your healing, I believe that you were unaware of it." He reached out, tentatively taking her hand in his.

She didn't pull away to his relief, her fingers curling around his in a gesture of cautious acceptance.

"Can you forgive me?"

Jasmine was silent for a long moment, her eyes searching his face as if looking for some sign of sincerity. And then, to Edgar's immense relief, she nodded, a small smile tugging at the corner of her mouth. "I forgive you, mainly because the same thing had occurred to me. I just don't know how it's possible."

"They could thrall you to forget anything they want."

"I know, but that's not what I meant. First of all, they should have asked for my consent, which is supposed to be such a big deal for you guys. And secondly, aren't the gods supposed to be incapable of biting any woman other than their mate once they are bonded?"

It was a relief to hear her admit that she suspected the same thing, mainly because she couldn't be too angry with him for reaching the same conclusions.

"All those things are true for immortals, but perhaps not for the gods."

"They are your ancestors. You got your physiology and customs from them."

He stopped and turned toward her. "That's also true, but a lot has happened on Anumati since our ancestors were exiled. The gods are masters of genetic manipulation and haven't been idle for the past seven thousand years. Aru, Negal, and Dagor are made differently. The truth is that we don't know much about them."

She nodded. "Seven thousand years is just incomprehensible to me. It's more or less the entire length of human civilization."

Edgar nodded. "Imagine where humans will be in seven thousand years."

"I can't. I think we will all be replaced by robots."

He laughed. "That's possible. Or we will all have chips in our brains." He wrapped his arm around her shoulders. "Only I don't think that will happen. The gods are no smarter than we are and could have easily been made much more intelligent. I bet they have laws against it." He led her back toward the restaurant. "Have you eaten already? I'm starving."

She shook her head. "I had a few momos but not a full meal. I was waiting for you."

His heart leaped at her words. "I'm touched. You waited even though you were angry with me."

Did it mean that she had feelings for him after all?

It didn't seem likely considering her assertion that she hadn't promised him anything and her obsession with the prince, but perhaps her emotions were more nuanced, and she could have feelings for him despite all of that.

59

JASMINE

I t was nice to make peace with Edgar.

Jasmine didn't like being angry at people, not even disappointing boyfriends. She preferred to forgive, forget, and move on.

Why spend life harboring resentment and pain? It was so much better just to let it go. None of her other partners had had nefarious intentions except for Alberto, and she didn't fault them for being less than she'd wanted. So yeah, there was always the sense of disappointment when things didn't work out, but she chose not to dwell on it.

Still, as nice as it was to have sorted out things between them, she knew there was no going back.

She and Edgar just weren't meant for each other, and since the time of fun and games was over, there was no point in dragging out the death of their relationship.

The problem was that she hated hurting people, and delivering that final cut was extremely difficult. That was why the cowards and the selfish just ghosted partners who they didn't want to be with anymore instead of doing the right thing and ending the relationship properly. It required courage and sensitivity, which many lacked.

Hand in hand, she and Edgar made their way back into the restaurant. As they settled into their seats and placed their orders, Edgar looked so relieved and hopeful that Jasmine's gut clenched at the prospect of shattering his illusions that they could move past this and find their way back to each other.

Julian regarded her from across the table. "I hear that your ankle is much better. I want to take a look at it later."

The last thing Jasmine needed was another male accusing her of improprieties.

She shook her head. "It will have to wait for tomorrow. I'm exhausted and need to take a long shower before I let anyone near my bare feet. When I took my boots off last night in the tiny tent the guys erected for me, I almost died from the toxic fumes."

Frankie snorted, covering her mouth with the back of her hand. "I would have never believed you are such a tomboy, Jasmine. You look so feminine and refined."

"I'm not a tomboy and spending a night in a tent is not my idea of fun. But it is what it is, right? And no one's feet smell like roses after being stuck in boots for a whole day of hiking."

Thankfully, Ella had heard all about the healed ankle and Edgar's accusations before, and she distracted Julian by telling him stories about her little brother and his stinky feet.

Leaning toward Jasmine, Margo whispered in her ear. "It seems like you and Edgar had a good talk."

"We did," Jasmine said.

"So, everything is back to normal?" Margo asked.

Jasmine cast a sidelong glance at Edgar, ensuring he was still talking with Negal and Julian, before shaking her head.

"Why?" Margo whispered. "Are you still mad at him?"

Jasmine shook her head again. "It's complicated. I need to think."

She'd done all her thinking already, but it was wrong to talk to Margo about Edgar when he was sitting right next to her. He should be the first one she told, not the last one to find out.

Getting the hint, Margo let it go and started asking questions about the pod and the other stasis chambers instead.

Jasmine didn't say much throughout dinner, letting the others talk and only adding a word here and there. She'd eaten with her usual healthy appetite, though, so she wasn't conflicted about her decision anymore.

After dinner, everyone said their good nights even though it wasn't particularly late. There was nothing to do in the small town, so they all headed to their bedrooms.

As Edgar opened the door, Jasmine was taken aback by the sight of the large stasis chamber that was taking up most of the available floor space in the room. The extra blanket she'd used when it got cold at night was draped over the chamber, making it look even larger. "It didn't look that big when it was out in the open."

Edgar chuckled. "That's what she said."

445

It took her a moment to get the joke, and she snorted. "It's not funny, but I'm glad you can still find humor in the situation."

Edgar pulled her into his arms, holding her gently against his body. "Sometimes humor is all we've got. I don't like having this thing in here, and I'm angry at myself for not suggesting it be placed in Aru's room."

Jasmine shuddered. "I don't know if Gabi would have been okay with that. It's kind of spooky."

"It is," he agreed. "That's why I don't like it here."

Casting a sidelong glance at the chamber, Jasmine wondered for the umpteenth time if the prince was aware of what was happening around him. She hoped he wasn't because that would mean seven thousand years of having been locked inside his brain, which was a horrible fate she wouldn't wish even on Alberto or the Modana brothers.

She pushed on Edgar's chest. "I should take a shower before I fall on my face."

Thankfully, he didn't offer to join her, which, given the accommodations, would have been stupid even if they weren't on the brink of a breakup. The water pressure was so weak that it was like showering in raindrops, and the tiny electrical heater could only heat the water to lukewarm. It was best to get it over with as quickly as possible.

Later, as Jasmine lay next to Edgar in bed, he reached for her, his hands skimming over the soft curves of her hips and breasts. There was a slight spark of desire, but her heart wasn't in it, not just because of the eerie presence of the stasis chamber and its occupant.

"I'm tired," she murmured. "I just want to sleep."

"Of course," Edgar said, pressing a chaste kiss to her forehead. "You need the rest."

She curled into his side and rested her head on his chest. As her breathing slowly evened out and she was drifting off, she thought about how good it felt to have Edgar in her bed even when she wasn't interested in sex. He could be a wonderful partner, someone she could lean on, someone who always respected her wishes.

Why the heck was she thinking about leaving him?

60

ARU

Aru's breath fogged in the crisp morning air as he and Dagor made their way toward the gaping maw of the cavern. The night had been cold, and they had spent it huddled around a small fire, taking turns keeping watch over their discovery.

Sleeping on the hard ground hadn't been fun, but he hadn't minded it as much as going back down into the cavern and starting another day of dismantling the pod. It was grueling labor, and they were working against the clock.

Come to think of it, though, there was no real need to rush. If they didn't manage to remove everything worth saving from the pod by the time Yamanu arrived, they could ask him to stay a day or two longer until they were ready to bury the craft. He might not like it, but his preferences were a lesser concern than salvaging all they could.

"I hate this bloody wind." Dagor adjusted his scarf so it covered his mouth.

"Then you should be glad we are going down for another lovely day of hard labor in the cavern. There is no wind down there."

"Worth it," Dagor murmured from behind his scarf.

After checking the ropes and verifying that they were securely tied to the boulders, they grabbed one and rappelled down.

Two hours later, they had a pile of components nestled in the spots that the royals' stasis chambers had formerly occupied, but so far, they hadn't found any hint of tampering or sabotage.

Dagor huffed out a breath. "We're not going to find anything. We don't have the right tools or the training. We are like kids trying to dismantle a toy to discover how it is made."

Aru chuckled. "Are there any toys like that left?"

"Yeah." Dagor sat on one of the stasis chambers. "The simple ones for babies."

Aru joined him on top of the next chamber. "We are lucky that our kids will be born on Earth. They will be able to take everything apart because almost nothing is built as a solid state."

"Give it time." Dagor sighed. "Someone soon will come up with the brilliant idea that this is the perfect method to prevent reverse engineering, and they will manufacture everything the way it is done on Anumati."

"Perhaps, but I don't think it will happen anytime soon." Aru pushed to his feet. "I know it's a long shot, but I'm hoping we will find something that will help us locate the other pods."

Dagor shook his head, his expression bleak. "What are the chances that there will be any survivors? The others are most likely dead, just like the ones we found here."

Even though the Kra-ell were not his people, Aru felt a pang of grief at the thought. These settlers had been young and hoped for a new beginning on Earth. Instead, they had forfeited their lives. He didn't know whether to blame the queen of Anumati, the queen of the Kra-ell, or the Eternal King, but did it even matter?

It was always the commoners who paid with their lives for the games the elite played. The rulers, whether monarchs or democratically elected politicians, viewed the common people as a means to an end. That was even true of the queen of Anumati, whom he served.

She didn't care about her grandchildren if they could not advance her agenda. The twins were as much Ahn's kids as Annani was, and the same was true of Areana, but the queen only cared about Annani because she was the only legitimate heir to the Anumati throne.

"You are probably right," he told Dagor. "I doubt we will find any survivors, but I'm not ready to concede defeat until we find every pod. Perhaps some have miraculously survived."

Dagor's expression was skeptical. "All the pods that still functioned have opened already, and their occupants are the pureblooded Kra-ells who are currently living in the village."

Igor had slaughtered most of the males and taken the females, but since then, more purebloods and hybrids had been born. Their community didn't have enough genetic variety to sustain growth, but mating with humans was prolonging its survival.

"Mey and Jin's parentage indicates otherwise," Aru said.

Dagor waved a dismissive hand. "A hybrid Kra-ell had a secret affair with a woman who he thought was human but who carried godly genes. It was a fluke, not proof that other Kra-ell survived. Igor didn't find the other pods because their occupants never woke up from stasis, so their trackers couldn't transmit a signal."

Aru rubbed a hand over his jaw. "We've talked about this. It's possible that some of the pods had opened before Igor found a way to locate the signals from the implanted trackers, and they might have removed them."

Dagor sighed. "Let me remind you that the settlers didn't know they had been implanted with trackers. Why would they even look for them? They couldn't have removed what they hadn't known existed."

Aru was not ready to give up. "They could have discovered it by accident. Maybe someone sought medical help and went through a scanner for some reason." He was clutching at straws, but the alternative was losing hope, and he wasn't ready to do that. "It's a flaw in the tracker's design that they need a live host to transmit a signal. Otherwise, we could have found them even if the settlers removed them."

"It is a huge flaw," Dagor agreed. "If they transmitted a signal even when the bodies hosting them were dead or in stasis, we would have found them long ago. They were designed to use the host's body for energy because they had to last for a very long time, and even now, we don't have batteries that can last that long."

The truth was that Aru didn't know if he should feel hopeful at the prospect of other Kra-ell surviving or dread it. After learning that there had been assassins planted among the settlers, perhaps it was better that they were all gone, especially now that the life of the heir to the throne was on the line.

"The upside of finding everyone in this pod dead is that it would be easy to convince the commander that there is no chance of anyone else surviving."

"But not everyone was dead," Dagor said. "The commander will want proof, and I'm not sure that our trickery with the heartbeats will convince him, especially since the Kra-ell bodies are well preserved and the royal twins look like corpses. The commander and whoever else looks at this will immediately realize why they don't look the same."

"Not really. He knows that the royal twins are in one of the pods, but not this one specifically, and not that they are half-gods. It was only a rumor. He will be more inclined to believe that these two stasis chambers belonged to two unfortunate Kra-ell and that they malfunctioned before the others. With how emaciated the twins are, it's impossible to tell they are not purely Kra-ell."

Dagor regarded him with an amused smile. "That doesn't make any sense, Aru. The pod runs all the stasis chambers. There is no reason for one to malfunction before the others."

"Right." Aru rubbed a hand over the back of his neck. "I don't know enough about how these things work. Maybe we will have to stage something. We can't let the Eternal King find out that the twins are alive. We need to make a convincing case for them being dead."

He would have to pose the question to his sister and let the queen decide what to do about reporting the finding of the twins.

Dagor groaned. "We should just fake our own deaths like Kian suggested and be done with it. If we are presumed dead, we can't tell them anything, right?"

"The Eternal King will just send another team. The only way to prevent it is to pretend that we are still searching for clues about the Kra-ell and drag it out for as long as possible."

Dagor tilted his head. "If we don't want to find the other pods, then why are we going to all the trouble of dismantling components from the pods in the hopes of finding clues about their locations?"

Aru shrugged. "I want to find them, but that doesn't mean we need to report everything we find to the commander."

6 1

MARINA

As Marina bustled about the tiny kitchen of the bungalow she shared with Peter, she looked out the window toward the lodge and the ocean beyond. The view was spectacular, with the water stretching into the infinity of dark blue. The sun had barely begun to peek over the horizon, painting the sky in soft shades of pink and gold.

The aroma of freshly brewed coffee mingled with the sizzle of eggs in the pan, creating a comforting and familiar soundtrack to the start of another day.

She hummed to herself as she worked, her mind busy planning the rest of her day off. Peter was due back any moment from his night shift, so after breakfast, he would want to get in bed for a few hours. He would probably want to make love before falling asleep and again when he woke up, which would work out great. The bite would send her on a psychedelic trip that would last a couple of hours, and when she woke up, she could laze in bed until Peter got enough sleep, either reading or watching television.

Life with Peter was good every day, but especially on a Sunday when she didn't have to work.

In the short time they had been together, living in this cozy little haven, she had discovered that happiness and fulfillment were rooted in the small things. Sharing breakfast, going for a walk, walking on the beach, spending time with friends, and making love. It was more than she had ever dreamt of, and even if Kian didn't approve her transfer to the village and she and Peter stayed in Safe Haven, she would be perfectly happy.

With its views and privacy, the bungalow was truly her Safe Haven.

Even the prospect of cleaning guest rooms for the rest of her life didn't seem as daunting anymore. It was hard work, but it wasn't emotionally or intellectually demanding, and the simplicity and repetitiveness of the tasks were calming. Besides, she got to spend her days working side by side with her best friend and her evenings with the best male she'd ever known, so all was good.

As Marina flipped the eggs onto a plate and reached for the toast, a loud ringing noise pulled her out of her pleasant reveries.

Turning the heating plate off, she picked up her flip phone, which, unfortunately, didn't have any of the bells and whistles of a modern smartphone, so she couldn't tell who was calling her.

"Hello?"

"Good morning, Marina. It's Eleanor. Can you come to my office?"

Marina's gut clenched. "What happened? Is Peter okay?"

"Peter is fine. Come as soon as you can. It's Sunday, and I don't want to be stuck here all day." She ended the call.

Marina's mind raced with reasons for Eleanor's summoning her on a Sunday morning. Was it about her transfer request? Had there been some problem or issue that needed to be addressed?

That was probably it. Maybe she needed to fill out some form correctly or had forgotten to initial one of the paragraphs.

Should she call Peter and let him know where she was going and why?

It was probably a matter of signing some papers or dealing with some minor administrative issue. There was no need to worry him unnecessarily, especially since what Eleanor needed her for wouldn't take long, and she would probably be back before his shift ended.

Marina left everything where it was, put her phone in the back pocket of her jeans, and left the bungalow.

As she reached the door to Eleanor's office, she took a deep, steadying breath and knocked.

"Come in," Eleanor's voice called from within.

Marina pushed open the door and stepped inside. She'd only been in Eleanor's office once, when she'd filled in the paperwork for the transfer request, and the space was just as impersonal and devoid of any comforts as she'd remembered it.

"Take a seat." Eleanor gestured at the chair.

"Thank you." She did as she was instructed. "Is everything alright? Is there something wrong with my transfer request?"

To her surprise, Eleanor's face broke into a smile, a rare display of warmth from the immortal. "On the contrary," Eleanor said, her tone almost jovial. "I wanted to let you know in person that your transfer request was approved." She lifted a piece of paper and handed it to Marina. "This arrived earlier, and I printed it for you. It's an official invitation from Kian himself."

A rush of relief washed over Marina as she reached for the paper and brought it closer to her eyes to read through it.

"That's awesome." She lifted her gaze to Eleanor. "Do I need to show it to the guards when I enter the village?"

Eleanor chuckled. "I'm sure they will be notified of your arrival, but you should keep it with you just in case. I thought you would want to save it as a keepsake."

"I do. Thank you."

Eleanor must have seen the emotion playing across Marina's face because her expression softened, her gaze turning almost sympathetic, or as much as the immortal was capable of experiencing that emotion. She was not known for being warm and fuzzy. "I'm happy for you, but if for any reason things don't work out as well as you hoped for and you want to come back here, Safe Haven will always take you. It's your home."

Marina nodded, swallowing hard past the lump in her throat. She knew what Eleanor was implying, and although she didn't like the insinuation that her relationship with Peter might be short-lived, she couldn't fault Eleanor for thinking that.

Relationships between immortals and humans were discouraged by the immortals, and rightfully so. Things might look all rosy now that she and Peter were in the honeymoon phase, but when reality came knocking on the door, that could change, and it was possible that Marina would want to distance herself from Peter.

It could happen, but she wasn't as worried about it now as she had been before. Their relationship had only improved after living together for almost two weeks. They were in love; they didn't argue or fight about anything, and being with him was bliss.

She had never been happier.

Meeting Eleanor's gaze, Marina lifted her chin and smiled. "Thank you. I appreciate the offer, and it means a lot to me knowing that I will always have a home in Safe Haven, but I have faith in what Peter and I have. We will defy the odds and make it work."

"I wish you the best of luck," Eleanor said. "I hope you will be happy in the village, but if not, don't hesitate to call me and request a transfer back."

"I'll keep it in mind. When can I leave?"

Eleanor glanced down at the papers on her desk, her expression turning brisk and businesslike once more. "The new team of Guardians is set to arrive this Wednesday. When they get here, you and Peter can leave with the current group."

Marina nodded, her heart leaping with excitement at the thought. In a few short days, she would start a new life with Peter in the immortals' village.

But even as the thrill of anticipation coursed through her veins, she felt sad at the thought of leaving behind her friends and family, people she had known her entire life.

Larissa would be the hardest one to part with, and the one Marina's departure would impact most. They hadn't been as close back in Igor's compound, but since moving to Safe Haven and rooming together, they had become as close as sisters.

At least it wouldn't be a surprise. Larissa knew it was coming, and she supported Marina's decision.

"Is there anything I need to sign?" she asked.

"No." Eleanor smiled. "You are free to go. I'm sure you want to share the good news with Peter."

"I do." Marina pushed to her feet. "Thank you again for doing this for us."

"It was my pleasure. I owe Peter more than I could repay with just this one gesture. He was there for me when I needed him."

Peter had told her about his time with Eleanor and Leon in Safe Haven and what Emmett had done to them after Leon had left with Anastasia. It was such a bizarre story that she'd thought he had exaggerated it, but Eleanor was not the type to express gratitude for just any minor favor. What Peter had done for her must have been major.

62

PETER

When Peter stepped into the bungalow, the silence that greeted him was an unpleasant surprise, and the sight of the half-prepared breakfast heightened his unease.

Marina and the housekeeping staff didn't have work today, so it wasn't like she needed to step in for someone who got sick. The last retreat ended on Friday, and the housekeeping crew spent all of Saturday cleaning up and preparing the lodge for the next retreat, which was about to start on Monday.

Maybe something had happened to one of her friends?

No, she would have called him if that was the case. She had probably made a quick run to the kitchen to pick up some ingredients she needed to finish making breakfast or something she planned to cook for lunch, and she would be back in no time.

Taking off his holster, Peter hung it in the closet and returned to the kitchen to finish what Marina had started.

He chopped the remaining vegetables, heated the skillet, added a pat of butter, and watched as it sizzled and foamed in the pan. The aroma of browning vegetables filled the air, mingling with the rich scent of the coffee that still sat untouched on the counter.

Just as he was about to heat the half-cooked eggs, the sound of the door bursting open made him jump, his hand automatically reaching for the weapon that was no longer at his hip. But before he could process that, he registered who was barreling toward him, and he had just enough time to turn off the stove before he found himself with an armful of Marina, her face flushed with excitement and her eyes shining with joy.

"Whoa, what's got you so excited, love?"

Marina pulled back just enough to look into his eyes. "My transfer was approved," she said, the words tumbling out in a rush. "We can leave for the village on Wednesday as soon as the new team of Guardians arrives."

Peter felt a rush of relief wash over him.

Pulling Marina close, he buried his face in the soft curve of her neck and breathed in her sweet, familiar scent. "I'm so happy for us. I can't wait to show you all the wonders of living near a big city. We can go out to restaurants, the movies, theater, musicals, whatever you can imagine can be yours."

He felt Marina stiffen in his arms. "I'm pretty sure that Kian won't allow me to leave the village whenever I want."

She might be right if she was just a regular transfer, but she would be accompanied by a Guardian.

"Having a Guardian for a boyfriend comes with some privileges. With me taking responsibility for you, Kian won't object to your excursions out of the village."

His words had the effect he had hoped for, and her shoulders relaxed. "Having a boyfriend who is a Guardian is a privilege." She stretched on her toes, kissed him, and then chuckled. "It's not enough that we will be the first and only human-immortal pair in the village; we will be doubly scrutinized because you are part of the force."

"We wouldn't be the first. There were others before us."

"Right." She smiled sadly. "When one of them was a Dormant, waiting to be induced to transition, but that's not going to happen to me. I'm going to stay a human no matter what, and your people might look down on our relationship because of that."

Peter's heart clenched at the fear and vulnerability in her voice, the way her eyes shimmered with unshed tears. He hated seeing her like this, hated the thought that anyone or anything could make her feel less than the incredible, beautiful, absolutely perfect woman she was.

"Listen to me, Marina." He cupped her face in his hands and stared into her eyes. "Instead of the possible negatives, we should focus on the positives. We're going to be trailblazers, and in more ways than one." He waggled his eyebrows suggestively, a mischievous grin spreading across his face.

Marina's eyes widened. "What do you mean?" she asked, her head tilting to the side in that adorable way that always made his heart skip a beat. "In what other way are we trailblazers?"

Peter chuckled. "Forgive me. I've misspoken. I forgot about Brundar and his kinky club when I thought that we would be the only couple with divergent proclivities. It's just that Brundar keeps it on the down low, and not many know about it."

Marina shook her head. "Why am I not surprised? Brundar looks the part of a dominant. But how does he find the time to run a club? I thought he was a full-time Guardian like you."

Peter shrugged, a half-smile tugging at his lips. "It's more of a passion project for him. He doesn't do it for money. He does it because he enjoys it. Brundar wanted to create the perfect atmosphere to cater to his particular preferences."

Marina pursed her lips. "It sounds lovely to make money from something that provides him joy and satisfaction, but I know what it takes to run a hospitality business, and a kink club is no different. Come to think of it, it's probably more complicated and involved than running a regular club."

"He has a partner," Peter said. "So, it's not like he needs to be there every night. His mate used to work with him at night, but then Callie opened a restaurant in the village and got too busy. I bet Brundar doesn't frequent the club as often now that she can't join him."

Marina's eyebrows shot up. "Callie? I know her, and she doesn't seem like the submissive type at all."

Peter laughed, pulling her close and nuzzling the soft skin behind her ear. "Looks can be deceiving, love," he murmured, his breath hot against her neck. "Who would guess that beneath the rebel with blue hair and piercings lies a woman who craves the thrill of submission and the rush of surrendering control?"

"True," she admitted. "But I've never been to a club like that." She lifted a pair of blue eyes to him. "I'd be lying if I said I wasn't curious." She sounded breathless.

Peter wondered how Marina knew about the existence of such clubs. She hadn't had access to the internet in Igor's compound, and in Safe Haven, her access was limited.

"How do you know about kink clubs?"

Marina smiled conspiratorially. "We had books in the compound. We could order whatever we pleased, but books were not a high priority since we had a tiny allowance for personal expenses. Still, we shared what we got, and some of the romance novels were pretty kinky. How do you think I learned about all that?"

"I thought it was because of the Kra-ell."

She laughed. "They are brutal but not kinky."

Her comment reminded him of his experience with Kagra, and he had to agree.

"I can take you there," he said. "If you want to go, that is. Reading about it and experiencing it in person is not the same."

She grinned. "Does taking me to a kink club also fall under the definition of Guardian supervision?"

"Even more so." He lowered his hand to cup her bottom. "You won't be able to give me the slip when you are all tied up."

Marina shivered in his arms, her eyes fluttering closed as a soft moan escaped her lips. "I'm a little scared, but that only arouses me more." She lifted her gaze to him. "But if Brundar keeps his club a secret, will he be okay with us showing up there?" Then, her brow furrowed. "Have you ever been to his club?"

Peter shook his head in amusement. "I love it when you get jealous over me. I've never been to Brundar's club. It will be the first time for both of us." When she still looked unsure, he added, "Trust me, love. No one at Brundar's club is immortal or knows about our existence. As far as they're concerned, Brundar and Callie are just a beautiful couple, and they will think the same about us." He leaned in close, his lips brushing against the shell of her ear. "We don't have to do anything publicly if you are uncomfortable with it. We can just rent a private room."

Marina's eyes darkened with desire as she melted against him. "Let's take it one step at a time. Private room first, and then we shall see."

"No problem. I'm not much of an exhibitionist, but I'll do anything you feel like doing." He gave her bottom a hard squeeze. "You know that it's all about you, right?"

She nodded. "With you, it is. Not everyone is like that."

Peter felt his fangs elongate. "Those types don't deserve to scene with anyone."

"I agree."

63

MARINA

Marina's heart raced as she gazed up at Peter, her eyes locked with his in a moment of perfect clarity and connection. The rest of the world seemed to fade away as she lost herself in the depths of his hungry stare.

"Are you tired?" She reached up with her fingers to caress his cheek, marveling at his skin's smooth, cool texture beneath her touch.

"I'm never too tired to play." Smiling, Peter leaned into her hand, his eyes fluttering closed briefly.

"I love you," Marina whispered. "I'm humming with excitement and nervous energy, and I need to do something about it, but if you need a few hours of sleep to recharge, I'll wait."

He lifted his head. "As I said, I'm never too tired to play, and I'm open to suggestions."

"You always are," Marina smiled. "And that is one of the many things I love about you." She took his hand, guided him into their bedroom, and closed the door.

The blinds were closed, making the room dark even though it was early morning, but she knew that Peter wouldn't have a problem seeing her despite the lack of illumination.

"I want you to show me what it is like in a club. I want to scene with you."

She had read about it and even done many of the things that supposedly happened in those kinds of clubs, but she still felt unprepared for an actual visit. Nevertheless, thinking about being in a place like that had produced a spike of arousal that needed an outlet.

"Marina." Peter pulled her into his hard body, and she melted into his warmth and his strength.

He hooked a finger under her chin and lifted her head, so she was looking into his glowing eyes. "I love you." His large palm stroked circles on her back as he lowered his head and kissed her.

His gentle hold on her contrasted with the ferocity of his kiss, the possessive passion, the firm press of his lips, the forceful stroking of his tongue as it glided against hers.

Marina moaned, lost to the passion, threading her fingers through the short strands of his dark hair.

As Peter leaned away and looked into her eyes, the sight of his elongated fangs sent a shiver down her spine.

"Any hard limits I should be mindful of?"

She appreciated that he always asked her before they did anything not pure vanilla. Sometimes, she was in the mood for just a little spice, and sometimes she was in the mood for a lot, and it was very considerate of him to find out without dipping inside her mind, even though she'd given him permission to do so.

After all, Marina had no more secrets from Peter, and granting him complete control was the ultimate show of trust. If she wasn't a hundred percent sure that he would never abuse it, she wouldn't have given it.

"No limits today. You've whetted my appetite for bondage with your talk about Brundar's club." She smiled and added, "Do as you please with me because that's what will please me."

"I like that answer." He retook her lips, but this time, he wasn't as gentle, fisting her hair and pulling her head back as he devoured her mouth.

As usual, the dominance of the act aroused her more than the slight sting, and as she rubbed her achy nipples against his chest, he tightened his hold on her and pressed his erection against her mound.

Lost to the sensations bombarding her body, Marina felt her knees turn to jelly, and if not for Peter's firm hold, she would've fallen to the floor. Holding her up with one arm, he gripped the bottom of her T-shirt, pulled it over her head, and tossed it on top of the dresser. Then he unzipped her jeans and pulled them down.

He left her thong and bra on for some reason, making her wonder about the game he had in mind. Hopefully, he didn't plan on taking her outside and spanking her bent over the railing of the front porch.

Okay, so maybe she had some exhibitionist fantasies after all because that image turned her on way more than it should have.

His palm splayed over her belly, possessive and reassuring. "You're beautiful, Marina."

She stifled a nervous chuckle. Peter kept telling her that she was beautiful, and perhaps she could be considered good-looking in human terms, but compared to him and the other immortals, she was painfully ordinary.

Reaching behind her, he snapped the clasp of her bra open, hooked his fingers in the shoulder straps, and lowered them down her arms, his fingers feathering over her skin and raising goosebumps in their wake.

When the bra joined her clothes on the dresser, Peter looked at her practically nude body; her nipples pebbled in response to the hunger in his eyes.

"Put your hands behind your back and clasp them."

"Yes, sir."

He didn't prepare anything to tie her up with, so unless he got creative, her bondage would be more of a suggestion than anything physical.

She could live with that.

The pose of holding her hands behind her back made her small breasts jut out invitingly. Peter responded by lifting his hands and stroking his thumbs over both of her nipples, running lazy circles around the hardened peaks.

He was teasing her, prolonging the anticipation, and even though she wanted him to do so much more, she bit her lower lip, knowing that he would punish her by going even slower.

He tweaked her nipples, the slight pain sending a zing of desire straight down between her legs. "Eyes on me," he commanded.

Her eyes flew open.

His fanged smile was chilly. "I love being able to say this to you after a lifetime of commanding women to keep their eyes closed." He hooked his thumbs inside the elastic of her thong, pulling it down past her hips and letting it drop to the floor.

His nostrils flared as he got a whiff of her arousal. "You smell good enough to eat, love." He went down to his knees and gripped her hips before doing just that.

It was good that Peter was holding her and that he was so strong because his tongue was turning her into a puddle of goo, and her legs couldn't support her weight.

That wasn't the scene she'd been expecting, but she didn't mind; she was a hair away from orgasming when a sharp smack on her behind reminded her that she didn't have permission to come yet.

"Patience." Peter turned her around and, with a slight push on her back, had her bent over the foot of the bed. "You can put your hands on the mattress."

Here it comes.

They had played this type of game many times before, but that didn't mean that any less butterflies were taking flight in her stomach or that she was less eager for the game to begin.

461

64

PETER

Peter leaned over to brush aside the long strands of blue hair spilling in soft waves down Marina's slender back, exposing the elegant column of her spine.

She shivered when he brushed his lips over her neck, so he did it again.

She was delicately built, slender, and small-boned, but she was by no means fragile, and that dichotomy also applied to her character. She was sexually submissive but assertive and took charge in every other way.

Except for being human, she was perfect.

There was still a lot he didn't know about her and a lot he had to learn, and he hoped he would have enough time with her to do that.

Would a steady supply of venom keep her healthy and prolong her life?

That was something none of the immortals had tried, and maybe they should have. Not that even doubling Marina's natural lifespan would be enough, but it was better than the miserly few decades she could give him.

He kissed her neck as he caressed her back and then circled his arms around her to cup her breasts. She moaned, thrusting her bottom up and out while he tormented and pleasured her nipples in turns.

It was hard to resist her silent plea when she expressed it so vividly with the soft globes of her ass pressing into his groin.

It was time to up the ante.

He cupped her breasts, easing the ache he'd caused and letting her catch her breath, but not for long.

Leaning back, he brought his hand to her upturned bottom.

She moaned as he rubbed the sting away and then moaned even louder when he smacked her other cheek.

The next few smacks brought a lovely pink hue to her creamy flesh. When he stopped to reach into the nightstand drawer, she turned to look at what he was taking out and gasped when she saw what implement he had chosen.

"Any objections?" He asked, even though he knew what her answer would be given the flare in the scent of her arousal.

"No, sir." She took a deep breath and rested her cheek on the mattress in a gesture of submission.

"Good girl." He removed the toy from its casing and coated it generously with lube.

Caressing her back in soothing, soft strokes, he coated his finger in the lube and rubbed it against her rosette.

Marina's entire body flushed and tensed as he pushed his finger past the resistance. He was aware that she could come just from that, but she knew better than to climax without his permission.

When he added a second finger, her moan sounded like a plea, and then she said, "Please. I can't hold it."

"Not yet." He pulled his fingers out, letting her catch her breath momentarily before inserting the toy.

She was panting, her back covered in a sheen of sweat, and her pinked bottom lifting to meet the toy rather than pull away from it.

"Patience." He twisted the plug before inserting it a little deeper. "Hold it until I say you can come."

When the toy was fully inside, Marina was shaking with the effort not to come.

"Good girl," he said as he removed his clothes.

Stroking himself, he angled his shaft at her opening, coating it in her juices but not pushing in. She could take him with the plug inside; they had done that before, but he knew that the moment he entered her, she would climax, and it would be over in moments. He could go again, but if he bit her, she would pass out from his bite, and there was no way he would be able to hold back on that.

He wasn't ready to end the play yet.

Pulling back, he delivered a few more light smacks to her bottom, which, in addition to the plug, would overwhelm her enough to pull her away from the brink.

He rubbed his tip against her wetness again, coating himself before pumping into his fist a few times as he pushed two fingers into her sheath.

"Peter..." she whispered.

Unable to hold back any longer, he pulled his fingers out and replaced them with the tip of his arousal. "Hold on for just a little bit longer," he said through protruding fangs.

With the plug inside of her, he needed to go slow and make sure she was okay with the double penetration.

Marina's breaths were coming out fast and shallow, so he slowed down even more. "Breathe, Marina."

When a moment later she seemed to breathe normally, he pushed in a little further, the plug in her other channel making her feel incredibly tight.

As a mewling sound escaped Marina's lips and her sheath convulsed around his shaft, he pushed all the way in and hissed, "Come for me, Marina."

He managed a few more pumps before the need to bite her became impossible to ignore. Gripping her hair, he pulled her head back and sank his fangs into her vein.

She climaxed again and again, and as he retracted his fangs and licked the puncture wounds closed, she blacked out, going limp under him.

He pulled out, making a mess over her ass, and repositioned her so she was entirely on the bed before he pulled out the plug.

Taking it to the bathroom, he dropped it in the sink for proper scrubbing. He wetted several washcloths in warm water, then returned and carefully cleaned her.

Peter considered returning to the bathroom and cleaning the toy, but it could wait. Lying beside Marina and holding her close was much too tempting to resist. He gathered her close, buried his face in the silken curtain of her hair, breathed in the sweet, familiar scent of her, and drifted off on his cloud of bliss.

65

ARU

As the afternoon sun dipped lower in the sky, casting long shadows across the rocky terrain, Aru glanced at his watch. He had twenty-five minutes until the queen arrived at the Oracle's temple, and he could ask her what to do about the discovery of the royal twins.

With a sigh, he pushed to his feet and stretched his back. He'd spent hours hunched over, using hand tools to pry off components from the pod that he probably could do nothing with. Even seven thousand years ago, most were in a solid state.

"I need a break," he told Dagor. "I'm going to head up top and get some air."

Dagor nodded. "Take your time. I'll keep going at it."

Aru clapped his friend on the shoulder and walked over to the ropes. The climb up was so practiced by now that he did it in a couple of minutes, and when he crested the top, he wasn't even sweaty. The air was so arid that sweat evaporated as fast as it was created.

The crisp mountain air hit him like a physical force, the chill wind whipping at his face and his clothes. And yet the sun was shining brightly with no cloud in sight. Aru squinted against the glare, his eyes adjusting to the brightness after so long in the dimly lit confines of the cavern.

He made his way to the plateau's edge, the sound of his boots crunching on the loose gravel almost indiscernible over the shrieking of the wind.

There, perched on a weathered boulder that offered a stunning view of the valley below, Aru closed his eyes and reached out with his mind, opening a channel to his sister.

There was only silence for a moment, the vast emptiness of the mental landscape stretching out before him. But then, like a candle flaring to life in the darkness, he felt the warmth of her presence filling his mind.

Hello, Aru, she spoke in his mind. *The queen is here, but she is talking with the Supreme, so we will need to wait for her to be ready.*

He had told Aria that he needed to talk to the queen, but he hadn't told her why. Perhaps he should have. Aria was wise, and he valued her input. She might have offered him advice.

A few more moments passed until Aria said, *The queen is ready, and she asks if you have the heir on the line with you.*

I don't. Not today. I'm still in the mountains with Dagor, and I can only take a break from him for a few minutes before he comes looking for me. I need to tell Her Majesty about the discovery we made. He paused, taking a deep breath. *We found the Kra-ell pod, the one Syssi saw in her vision, and Jasmine helped us locate. It contains the twins, and they are alive, but barely though. All the others are dead.*

So, the rumors were right, Aria said for the queen.

Yes, Aru confirmed. *The royal twins survived because, as half-gods, they could enter stasis without the aid of the stasis chamber. That is why all the others are dead, and they are alive.*

He paused, his mind flashing back to the grim scene they had discovered in the heart of the cavern. *There were eighteen Kra-ell with them. Nine males and nine females, an unusual ratio for the Kra-ell, who typically put four males in the pods for every female to reflect the ratio of the genders in their population. I wonder what the significance of that is.*

Aria was silent for a moment. *The queen speculates that the twins' mother hoped that Ekin and Athor would find a way to even out the numbers in the next generation by altering the Kra-ell's genetics. Athor was a talented geneticist, and Ekin was a gifted engineer.*

The Eternal King's offspring were superior to other gods, not just because the genetic material he contributed to them was so great but because they were engineered to be better than others. Even though his talented children had turned against him, the king ensured each child received the best genetic enhancements possible.

It's possible, Aru said. *But we can only speculate what the queen wanted her children to do on Earth. Once they are revived, we might learn more.*

Or at least he hoped so. After being in stasis for so long without support, they could have sustained brain damage or memory loss.

His greatest fear, though, was that the queen would order him to murder the twins, and he wouldn't blame her if she did. They were vulnerable right now, and if allowed to be revived, they could pose a threat to Annani.

The entire resistance's hope rested on Annani's shoulders, and the queen would not allow anything or anyone to endanger her, even if that meant doing the unthinkable.

As no further communication came, he continued. *I need to know what the queen wants us to do about reporting the discovery. Dagor recorded what we found in each of the chambers we opened in a way that will show that they are dead, including a recording of no heartbeat or breathing, but while the Kra-ell bodies are perfectly preserved, the twins look like corpses. It's not difficult to guess why.*

The queen says that the king will want more definite proof of their state than the recordings. You will have to put the bodies on a funeral pyre and film them burning.

She was correct; altering the footage with artificial intelligence was not an option. Anumati's technology would immediately reveal the trickery. The queen would most likely tell him to kill the twins and put them on a funeral pyre as well.

There was a long, heavy pause that seemed to stretch on for an eternity, and then Aria spoke in his mind, *The queen needs time to consider all the options.*

I understand, and I hate to rush the queen, but Annani's people plan to revive the twins soon.

After another moment, Aria asked, *When are they planning to do so?*

They are waiting for the arrival of an immortal with unparalleled shrouding abilities and a private craft to transport the twins and the Kra-ell bodies back to the immortals' stronghold. They have a clinic with all the necessary medical equipment and experienced medical personnel. They plan to revive the twins there. They don't want to take any chances.

How long will it all take? Aria asked.

I estimate at least three days, probably four or five. We are in a remote location, an eight-hour drive to the nearest airport. We will also need at least a day to transport all the stasis chambers out of the pod.

A moment later, the queen responded. *Her Majesty will give you an answer by tomorrow.*

Do not repeat what I say. Do you think she will tell me to end them?

I honestly do not know. She is not easy to read.

66

ARU

The cold mountain air bit Aru's skin as he stepped out of the hotel on Monday afternoon, his eyes squinting against the bright midday glare of the sun.

Negal and Edgar had spent the night at the crater, guarding the pod so Aru and Dagor could get a break. After spending two nights in the field, showering in the trickle of hot water that the hotel supplied had felt like such a wonderful luxury.

He had become so spoiled.

Best of all, though, was spending the night in bed with his mate. The short separation had felt much longer, and he had been loath to leave the warmth of her embrace in the morning, but duty called, and there was still much to do.

Glancing at his watch, he estimated that Yamanu and Kalugal should be arriving momentarily. There was barely any traffic on the road leading to town, so spotting them wouldn't be difficult.

A few moments later, the roar of engines and the billowing clouds of dust heralded their approach long before the vehicles came into view.

Kalugal could have chartered a helicopter, but he had chosen to arrive with the large truck full of fuel barrels he had commissioned.

As the vehicles rumbled to a stop and the engines cut, Aru strode forward to greet the newcomers, his hand outstretched in welcome.

"You've gotten a tan." Kalugal shook his hand. "And you look like a rugged Tibetan."

Aru chuckled. "I've spent two nights inside the crater. The tan is from before." He turned and shook Yamanu's hand. "Thank you for making it here so quickly."

"Couldn't have done it without this guy." Yamanu tilted his head toward Kalugal. "His connections made it possible."

Kalugal grinned, his teeth flashing white against the dark hair of his goatee. "I couldn't pass up the chance to see the pod with my own two eyes, and the survivors, of course. This discovery might change the course of history."

Aru nodded. "Frankly, I hope the impact won't be that big."

He didn't want the Eternal King to discover it and turn Earth into a dust ball. There were many good people worth saving on this little rock, not just Annani and her clan. There were also many who seemed like a lost cause, barbarians who committed unspeakable atrocities, but he hadn't lost faith in all of humanity yet. They could still be salvaged.

"I appreciate you smoothing the way with the Chinese authorities," Aru said, his gaze shifting to the pile of permits and paperwork that Kalugal held in his other hand. "I can only imagine the hoops you had to jump through to arrange all this so quickly."

Kalugal waved a dismissive hand, his grin widening. "Child's play," he said, his tone smug. "When you know who to approach and have a little bit of persuasion on your side, there's no such thing as a locked door." He winked.

Being a compeller certainly made things easier, and Kalugal had proven that and then some in Puerto Vallarta and Acapulco.

As they made their way back to the hotel, Yamanu fell into step beside them. "Where are you keeping the twins?"

Aru's lips twitched with amusement. "The princess is in Julian and Ella's room, and the prince is in Edgar and Jasmine's, if you can believe it. We wanted another room in the hotel, but none were available. We had to work with what we had."

Yamanu snorted. "Talk about creepy. I hope that they don't carry bad luck."

Aru frowned. "What do you mean?"

Yamanu shrugged. "Their ship malfunctioned, arriving seven thousand years later than it was supposed to, then it exploded in orbit, and their pod also malfunctioned. That's a lot of bad luck. They might be cursed."

"First, I don't believe in curses; secondly, at least some of that was deliberate sabotage. Maybe all of it."

"True," Yamanu agreed. "But that might be part of their curse. In any case, I don't want to spend too much time around them."

"We didn't have much choice," Aru said. "It was either that or leave them out in the open, and that wasn't an option." He smiled. "Speaking of luck, it's good that you don't plan on staying the night because you would have to sleep on the floor in our rooms."

"Lucky indeed," Yamanu said.

As they reached Edgar and Jasmine's room, Aru rapped his knuckles against the weathered wood door, and a moment later, Jasmine opened up.

Aru had warned her that Yamanu and Kalugal were on their way and would want to see the stasis chamber, and she had taken it to heart. She'd styled her hair and put makeup on, which she hadn't done since their first night in Tibet.

Kalugal stepped forward, his hand outstretched and a charming smile plastered across his face. "A pleasure to see you again, Jasmine."

"The pleasure is all mine, Kevin." She gave him a charming smile as she shook his hand. "Or should I call you by your real name? What's the protocol when we are around humans?"

He chuckled. "I'm glad to hear that you no longer think of yourself as one. I prefer Kevin when in mixed company."

"Noted." She took a step back and motioned for them to enter. "I bet you want to see the prince more than chitchat with me."

"Chitchatting with you is a pleasure, my dear."

These two could have been a perfect couple. They were both naturally flirtatious and outgoing and competed over who was more charming. Then again, they might have been too similar to make it work.

Not that it was anything but hypothetical. Kalugal was happily mated.

"Hello, beautiful." Yamanu leaned to kiss her on the cheek. "How have you been holding up here?"

Jasmine looked a little surprised by his display of familiarity, but she didn't seem put off by it. "I'm doing fine. I miss having a proper shower and a comfortable bed." She glanced at the stasis chamber. "And I'm worried about him. Julian says he and his sister are barely hanging on, but he's afraid of reviving or moving them out of the chambers in these conditions. He wants to do it back in the keep's clinic."

Kalugal leaned over the stasis chamber, where the glass was more transparent. "Yeah. That doesn't look good." He straightened up. "Is Julian positive that they are alive?"

Aru nodded. "He checked their vitals. They are very weak, but they are there."

The next one to look was Yamanu. "They look more like us than them," he murmured, his voice soft with wonder.

Kalugal frowned. "How can you tell? It's impossible to say for sure. Not without opening the pods and getting a closer look." He turned to Aru. "Can we do that?"

Aru looked at Jasmine and shook his head. "I wouldn't do that without Julian's permission. Let's go to his room, and you can ask him yourself."

If not for her being present, he might have allowed Kalugal to take a quick look, but he didn't want her to see what her prince looked like.

After they visited the princess, Julian allowed Kalugal and Yamanu a quick look. Aru opened the door and motioned for them to step out. "We're losing daylight," he said. "We need to get moving if we want to have any hope of extracting at least some of the other chambers before nightfall. There are eighteen of them, and every round trip takes an hour and a half. Edgar is at the site with his helicopter, but we can fly out there with the other pilot."

Kalugal grinned. "I can't wait to see that pod."

"We took a lot of the components out," Aru said. "But even with the big pile we made, you couldn't tell by just looking at the pod. We also need to fly that pile out, which means more trips."

Yamanu nodded. "I'll fly with Edgar and shroud the helicopter to make it look like we're just surveying the area or not even there."

"Not there at all is better," Aru said.

After collecting Dagor, the four of them headed to where Norbu was waiting with the other helicopter.

Kalugal grimaced when he saw the chopper. "We are flying in this?"

"It's old, but it seems to be okay." Aru climbed in.

Kalugal followed him inside. "It's going to be cramped here with the four of us and the pilot."

Norbu turned around and smiled at Kalugal, who smiled back and waved.

67

JASMINE

Jasmine sat on the edge of the bed, her gaze fixed on the stasis chamber that dominated the cramped hotel room. She'd removed the blanket that Edgar had draped over it before Kalugal and Yamanu's visit, and now she was staring at the inert metal cocoon that seemed to pulse with strange, otherworldly energy as if the being inside was exerting some magnetic pull on her very soul.

She knew that she must be imagining it. The stasis chamber was broken. It didn't work, and it couldn't sustain life. The only living thing that could exude any energy was the barely alive prince, who definitely couldn't spare any.

He was helpless in that thing, so fragile that Julian was afraid to move him, and she needed to keep him safe.

Jasmine couldn't explain it; this feeling of protectiveness had washed over her the moment the others had left. It was irrational since she couldn't do anything to protect him. She was just a human with some paranormal abilities that didn't include anything that could be used as a weapon.

It would have been so cool to be a battle witch if such a thing existed. But without magical powers, she would have settled for a handgun. Not that she knew how to use one, but hypothetically speaking.

Violence was abhorrent, and she hated it, but she had no moral qualms about using lethal force to protect the people she loved and those who couldn't defend themselves.

Like her poor, barely alive prince.

She chuckled at the absurdity of the thought. Who would want to harm a mummy, a being so fragile and desiccated that a stiff breeze might crumble it to dust?

And yet, the feeling of unease refused to abate and only worsened. Someone wanted the prince and the princess dead, and given the chain of misfortunes they had met with, that someone was powerful and possessed a long reach.

A knock at the door had Jasmine nearly leaping out of her skin, her heart pounding against her ribcage.

Damn, she'd let her imagination hijack her common sense. A perpetrator wouldn't have knocked. They would have kicked down the door and attacked.

Taking a deep breath, she tried to calm her racing pulse.

"Come in!" she called, wincing at how her voice cracked and wavered.

The door opened, and Ella entered with a steaming cup of tea in each hand. "I thought you might like some tea and some company."

Jasmine smiled. "I would. I'm going crazy sitting here, watching the stasis chamber and letting my imagination run wild about the potential danger to the prince and princess." She let out a breath. "Someone wants them dead. That much is obvious."

Ella closed the door behind her by giving it a slight push with her foot, walked over to the bed, handed Jasmine a cup of tea, and sat down on the edge of the bed beside her.

For a long moment they sat in companionable silence, sipping their tea and listening to the muffled sounds of life beyond the thin walls of the hotel.

"So," Ella said at last. "How are you doing?"

Jasmine sighed, her shoulders slumping. "Besides imagining assassins coming after the barely alive prince, I'm fine."

Ella frowned. "Did you see anything in your cards that made you think the royal twins are in danger?"

Jasmine shook her head. "But now that you mention it, I should do a reading."

"So, it's just a general uneasy feeling?"

Jasmine nodded.

"Does it have anything to do with Edgar and the kerfuffle you two had?"

Jasmine shrugged. "I'm not mad at him anymore, but honestly? I think that this relationship is going nowhere." She slanted a look at Ella. "I'm not one to pass on a good tumble in bed, and Edgar is definitely a good one, but I was relieved that he spent the night on the mountain."

The words hung heavy between them, a confession Jasmine hadn't even realized she'd been holding inside. But as soon as she spoke it aloud, she knew it was true.

Ella was quiet for a long moment. "Is it because of him?" she asked at last, her eyes flicking to the stasis chamber.

Jasmine let out a bark of laughter, the sound harsh and grating to her own ears. "The prince?" she asked, shaking her head in disbelief. "No, I'm definitely not thinking of a corpse-like alien in terms of a new boyfriend. After what Aru said about his condition, I'm afraid to even look at him."

Ella grimaced, her nose wrinkling in distaste. "No kidding. Julian told me that the dead Kra-ell looked like they were sleeping. But the twins' bodies had consumed themselves until there is barely anything left."

Jasmine shuddered, a chill racing down her spine at the image Ella had painted in her head.

"Where are they taking the other chambers?" she asked. "I mean with the dead Kra-ell inside?"

"Also to the keep," Ella said. "There are many underground levels that are even lower than the one the clinic is located in, and the lowest contains the catacombs. Although, given that the Kra-ell custom is to cremate their dead, I don't think they will stay there for long."

"Who is going to do that?"

"Their people, of course. They don't have a priestess among them, but maybe Jade can assume the function since there is no one else. Or they could wait for the twins to be revived, and they can perform the final rites. They are both priests."

Ella continued to tell her about how the Kra-ell queen hid them behind veils and isolated them behind the temple walls.

Jasmine's eyes widened. "But they are half-gods. So how can they be Kra-ell priests when the Kra-ell think that they are abominations?"

"They didn't know. That's why the queen did that. From what I understand, the Kra-ell priestesses are always veiled when in public, and they are celibate."

Did that mean that the prince was a virgin and was prohibited from having sex?

Now, that would be a cruel joke. The cards had promised her a prince, but he was a monk.

Ella reached out, laying a comforting hand on Jasmine's arm. "The truth is that I don't know much about the Kra-ell. I don't really have much contact with them."

Jasmine frowned. "Am I going to meet them?"

"I don't know. I assume Jade will be there when we arrive at the keep, and she won't be alone, so you'll get to see a few of them. Once you get used to them, they no longer look so weird. The too-big eyes are the hardest to get used to."

"I wonder what the prince will look like." Jasmine took another sip of the lukewarm tea. "More Kra-ell than god or more god than Kra-ell?"

"We have one hybrid in the village who is half immortal and half a hybrid Kra-ell. He's very tall and skinny and has raven black hair like all of them, but his eyes are shaped like a human's; one is blue while the other is green. He's handsome in his own way and the sweetest guy you'll ever meet. Vlad is proof that the gods and the Kra-ell were both wrong. Instead of an abomination, the union produced an angel."

"How did his parents even meet?"

Ella laughed. "Now, that story will require another cup of tea. Do you want to get a fresh one in the restaurant?"

Jasmine glanced at the somber stasis chamber. "I'm afraid to leave him alone in here."

"Don't be silly," Ella said, pushing to her feet. "We will lock the door and activate the alarm. No one will be able to get to him without us knowing."

When Jasmine still didn't move to get up, Ella put a hand on her hip and struck a pose. "You can't stay here all day. You need to eat and hang out with your friends."

"You are right." Jasmine pushed to her feet and looked at the sleek stasis chamber. "He's safe in there."

6 8

ARU

As Norbu navigated the helicopter over the mountainous terrain, Aru was glad that the winds had subsided and that the flight was less eventful than the one he and Dagor had experienced the day before. Thankfully, they had transported only some of the equipment they had removed, so he hadn't had to worry about a stasis chamber getting loose when they were hit with one of the more forceful gusts.

Still, that had worried him much less than what the queen might order him to do today. He would have no trouble thralling the immortals and Jasmine to forget that they had found the twins alive, but he couldn't do that to those in the know in the village. If the queen ordered him to get rid of the twins, he would have to somehow engineer an accident without implicating himself, so he would suffer no repercussions other than a permanent stain on his soul.

He was not a murderer.

There was a big difference between killing defenseless people in cold blood and killing in battle. Both left a mark on the soul, but the former introduced a rot that could not be redeemed on either side of the veil.

Or at least that was how it should be. Coldblooded murderers should not be allowed redemption, not even by forfeiting their own lives. The problem was that aside from the Supreme Oracle, no one got to glimpse the afterlife, and since she wasn't sharing what she'd seen, he needed substantiation for his belief. Nevertheless, he had to stick to it to keep his sanity and moral compass.

As they touched down, Aru saw Negal and Edgar sitting on the two boulders to which the ropes were tied.

Kalugal was out of the helicopter as soon as the skids touched the ground, and Aru was forced to do the same.

The guy was a council member and an important figure in the clan, but he probably knew nothing about rappelling and would injure himself going down.

"Hello, gentlemen," Kalugal said as he reached Edgar and Negal, offering each his hand. "I would very much like to see the pod."

Negal lifted a brow. "Do you know how to rappel?"

Aru was glad that Negal had saved him the need to ask the same question.

Yamanu, who had been leaning over the edge of the chasm and trying to get a glimpse of the pod, turned and lifted his hand. "All Guardians train to do that."

Aru had assumed as much, but Kalugal wasn't a Guardian.

Kalugal lifted a brow. "Of course. I'm not some soft technocrat." He chuckled. "Well, lately, that's precisely what I've become, but once upon a time, I was a well-trained warrior, and I haven't forgotten what was instilled in me since I turned thirteen. Besides, the pod is the main reason I volunteered to come here." He smiled. "And also, because my compulsion ability might be needed with that Chinese military base over there."

Aru felt unease at the reminder that Kalugal was the son of Annani's arch-enemy and a powerful compeller. Kian trusted him not to betray the clan, and so did his mother, but that trust didn't extend to Kalugal's thirst for knowledge and how far he was willing to go to gain it.

Being a compeller, he could overpower Aru, Negal, and Dagor with the same ease that he could overpower Edgar.

"We've got the base covered," Aru said. "Their radar is out."

Kalugal's eyes shone with excitement. "I was wondering about that. Kian told me that he was sending William's disruptor. Later, he said you found a different solution and to leave it on the plane. How did you do that?"

"Anumati tech. I really can't tell you more about it." He couldn't even if he wanted to because he had no idea how it worked, only that it did.

The damage to the equipment in the base would be irreparable, but their techs wouldn't know why or how. There would be no trace of evidence.

Aru smiled, thinking about what he had told the soldier who had bumped into them when they had first crossed through the base while shrouding them-selves. Maybe he would spread a rumor about the spirits being angry because no weapons were allowed on the mountain's hallowed ground. The Chinese were highly superstitious people, so they might believe that was why their equipment malfunctioned.

The glow in Kalugal's eyes dimmed. "You're no fun."

Chuckling, Aru turned to Negal. "Were you able to recover anything valuable from the pod?"

"We managed to extract a few more components," Negal said. "Once we clear out all the stasis chambers, we can access more of the pod's systems."

"Good work." Aru clapped Negal on the shoulder. "You and Edgar focus on getting the chambers out while Dagor and I handle the loading and transport."

He turned to Yamanu. "We will only extract the chambers when you are here to shroud the operation. I know that will mean that it will take more time, but I don't want to chance a patrol catching a glimpse of them."

Yamanu nodded. "No problem. You are the boss here, and you decide how this operation is run, but I would like to see the pod before we begin."

Aru tilted his head. "I thought that you regarded the pod as bad luck."

"I do. But I'm too curious to let that stop me from seeing it."

"Very well." Aru turned to Kalugal. "You and I will go first. I want to make sure that you get down in one piece." He looked at Negal and Dagor. "Watch over the ropes in case Kalugal needs to be pulled up."

Kalugal shook his head. "You insult me."

"My apologies." Aru dipped his head and looked pointedly at Kalugal's loafers. "Not the best shoes for rappelling."

"I agree." Kalugal shrugged. "But they were custom-made for me and will not fall off. I'm even willing to wager on that."

Aru knew better than to bet against a master manipulator.

"I'll take your word for it."

As Kalugal started gearing up, Aru realized his fears about the guy's abilities had been baseless.

The councilman approached it like a pro, pulling gloves from his pockets before getting into the harness, tightening the straps, and ensuring the harness fit snugly around his waist and legs.

Then, he double-checked that the anchor was secured around the boulder. Once satisfied with his inspection, he attached the controller to the harness using a locking carabiner and threaded the rope through the device. As an extra precaution, he tied a Prusik knot around the rope and clipped it to his harness, a backup that would catch him if he lost control.

"You've done this once or twice before," Aru remarked.

Kalugal grinned. "I told you that I was well-trained." Positioning himself at the edge, he leaned back into the harness and descended.

Aru controlled his speed so it matched Kalugal's. The cavern walls closed around them as they got deeper. When they reached the bottom, Aru unclipped the controller from his harness, removed it, and then attached it back so the others could pull it up and use it.

Next to him, Kalugal did the same. "She's a beauty," he said as he surveyed the pile of salvaged components. "The stasis chambers alone are worth a king's ransom." He traced his fingers over the smooth, seamless metal with an almost reverent touch.

Behind them, Yamanu and Dagor unclipped their controllers and joined them.

Yamanu peered at the glass of one of the chambers. "Are you sure they are dead? They look like they are sleeping."

"I wish they were," Aru said. "Julian confirmed that they are gone."

69

EDGAR

T he first chamber was loaded without incident, the gods working together to maneuver the heavy, awkward container out of the chasm and into Edgar's helicopter.

"This is going to take forever," Kalugal grumbled, echoing Edgar's thoughts. "We need to find a way to speed things up and get these chambers out of here before someone comes along and starts asking questions." He turned to look at Norbu's helicopter. "Why aren't we also using the other one? If we can transport two chambers at a time, this will go much faster."

"Not possible," Yamanu said. "I can shroud both helicopters, but Norbu will not be able to see through the shroud for obvious reasons."

"I can fly his helicopter," Kalugal offered.

Aru blinked, his surprise echoing everyone else's. Kalugal hadn't said anything about being able to pilot a helicopter. If he could have flown from Modana's mansion to his yacht, why had he asked for Edgar?

"Are you sure?" Aru asked. "After your display of skill with rappelling, I don't want to doubt you again, but have you received formal training in piloting one of these?" He waved a hand at the other craft.

Kalugal shrugged. "I admit that my schooling was virtual, but it is just as good if not better than the real thing. The Perfect Match simulator threw incredible challenges at me. I was chased, I had to evade missiles, and I had to make emergency landings in precarious locations. It was such an adrenaline rush. I recommend you try it."

That was all fine, but it was like learning to shoot a rifle in a video game and then being thrown into a battle. The aim might be better than someone who had never practiced, but the reflexes and the split-second decisions needed to be made would not be on par with a soldier who had received proper field training, and even less so compared to a soldier who had taken part in actual battles.

Edgar had heard that argument too many times to count. That's why he had joined some of the Guardian training.

"What about real-life experience?" Aru asked.

"I don't have any, but don't worry. I'm not your average Joe." Kalugal tapped his temple. "I can master any skill in a fraction of the time it would take someone else. Besides, it's not like we have a lot of options. Unless you want to be stuck here for two more days while we wait for Edgar to shuttle back and forth."

Edgar would be the last one to disagree with that.

"You make a valid argument," Aru said at last. "But I want you to do a test run first. I will load your helicopter with some of the equipment we've removed from the pod. If you manage to fly that without incident, you can fly the stasis chambers."

Kalugal chuckled. "So, you are more worried about the chambers than my life."

Aru blanched. "I did not mean that. But if you have to make a crash landing, while you might walk away unharmed, the chambers might not. They don't fit well in the helicopter, and we need to leave the doors open with the chamber sticking out on both sides."

Kalugal lifted a hand to stop him. "I get it, and you don't need to worry; I'm not a daredevil, and I wouldn't have offered my help if I had doubts about my ability. I know what I'm doing."

Edgar was familiar with Perfect Match. He had helped design the helicopter pilot interfaces and had enjoyed several thrilling sessions, but he doubted it was enough, especially with old models like those they had with them. The simulation was built on the latest technology, not aircraft from two decades ago.

Besides, as advanced as the simulation was, it was no substitute for real-world experience. The instinctive responses that could only come from hours spent in the cockpit, battling adverse weather conditions and whatever else came up, could not have been developed in simulation runs.

"What do we do with Norbu?" Dagor asked. "Should I thrall him to take a nap on the grass?"

Aru nodded. "That's a good idea. Just make sure he chooses a spot that is not in the way."

Once that was done, Edgar followed Kalugal to the helicopter. "Let me give you a crash course on these ancient machines. They are unlike what you've experienced in the simulator and require greater skill."

Yamanu joined them, grinning like a hyena. "The competition between you and Kian is hilarious."

Kalugal arched a brow. "What do you mean?"

"When you heard that he learned how to pilot a helicopter and a small executive jet on a simulator, you had to do that too. Except, Kian did that years before Perfect Match was even an idea."

"I didn't know that," Kalugal said, but it sounded like a lie to Edgar. "Just so you don't worry, I'll have you know that I've logged many hours in the simulator."

As Edgar went over the controls, he realized that Kalugal hadn't boasted about being a quick study. He mastered the information in mere moments.

"Who is flying with me?" Kalugal asked. When no one answered, he shook his head. "Ye of little faith."

"I'm with you." Yamanu followed Edgar to his craft.

As both rotors whirred to life and the helicopters lifted off the ground, Edgar's gaze flicked to the other aircraft, but so far, Kalugal seemed to be doing fine. That didn't last long, though.

When the wind picked up, as it usually did at this time of day, Edgar's gut twisted with worry as he watched Kalugal's helicopter wobble and sway in the air like a drunk on a tightrope.

Thankfully, Yamanu had his eyes closed, or he might have lost his concentration upon seeing Kalugal's precarious maneuvering of his craft. After a few moments, though, the winds subsided, and the rest of their journey was uneventful.

Edgar waited for Kalugal to land first before maneuvering his helicopter to land a safe distance away.

He felt like he had run a double marathon, and after killing the engine, he just leaned back and closed his eyes for a moment.

Yamanu's massive hand on his shoulder startled him. "Time to unload, buddy."

"Yeah. I need a moment after watching Kalugal in the air."

Yamanu winced. "That bad?"

"For a novice, he did okay, but it was stressful."

"I get it." Yamanu opened the door and jumped out.

As the two of them worked to unload the stasis chamber from his chopper, maneuvering the heavy, awkward container onto the waiting truck and securing it beneath a tarp, Edgar glanced over at Kalugal's chopper, wondering why the guy hadn't emerged yet.

Had he been as stressed as Edgar during the flight and needed a few moments?

That wasn't likely. Kalugal was too full of himself to doubt his ability and get scared.

When they were done, they started toward the other chopper, and Edgar knocked on the window to get Kalugal's attention. "Are you all right in there?"

The guy lifted his head from the screen of his phone and opened the door. "Of course, I am. I was going over my emails while waiting for you to come and unload the equipment."

Edgar gaped at him but then closed his mouth and looked at Yamanu, who shrugged. "I guess we are the hired help."

Kalugal got out of the craft. "I can help if you need me to," he offered in the least enthusiastic way possible.

"That's okay." Yamanu clapped him on his back. "Edgar and I got it." He smiled at Edgar. "The faster we get this done, the faster we can fly back, right?"

With a sigh, Edgar turned back to Kalugal's chopper and started unloading stuff.

They were halfway done when Edgar realized what had been bothering him.

At least half an hour had passed since they had landed, and with how tiny the town was, Jasmine couldn't have missed it even if she tried, and she hadn't come to see him even though he'd been gone for almost twenty-four hours.

Then again, Jasmine was human, so she might not have heard the landing. Except, the other ladies had, and they would have told her.

He had to concede that she didn't feel like coming over and saying hi.

ARU

As four o'clock neared, Aru got more and more nervous despite the operation going well. The queen had promised him an answer today, and he was afraid of what that answer would be. He'd been praying all day to the Fates that it wouldn't be an order to kill the twins.

"What's wrong?" Dagor asked. "You've been uncharacteristically quiet all day."

"Really?" Aru forced a smile. "I didn't know I was all that chatty on other days."

"You know what I mean. You've been frowning, and I even heard you cuss a few times, which is even more unlike you than being all up in your head and not talking."

"I'm just worried about the operation," Aru said, trying to inject a note of casualness into his tone. "Kalugal is an inexperienced pilot, we have a Chinese military base that is probably in uproar because their radar is not working, and we are running against the clock to get what we can out of the pod."

It was all true, but he wasn't really worried about that. The extraction had proceeded smoothly, with Aru and Dagor working in tandem to load the stasis chambers one at a time, securing each one with sturdy ropes before signaling for Negal to haul them up to the surface.

Above them, Negal was assisted by Yamanu and Edgar when the chambers were being sent up, and between the rounds, he was piling the equipment they were salvaging.

Kalugal had opted out of the manual labor, claiming that he had a business to run while he wasn't piloting the chopper. He was always on his phone, but even if he was pretending, Aru had to admit that his contributions had been so invaluable in other ways that it was okay if he didn't lend a hand. His connections and resources, greasing the wheels of bureaucracy and keeping the Chinese authorities at bay, were priceless.

"I'm also tired of sitting in this dark pit," Aru grumbled.

"Why don't you go up top for a bit?" Dagor suggested, jerking his chin towards the mouth of the cavern. "Grab some sunshine, take a breather. I can handle things down here until the choppers get back."

"Thanks. I need it."

Aru needed to talk to the queen, and he needed a private spot to do that. Maybe he could lie down next to Norbu on the grass and pretend that he was taking a nap.

When he emerged, the crisp mountain air filled his lungs with a rush of invigorating cold. For a moment, he stood with his eyes closed and his face tilted towards the sky, letting the warmth of the light and the whisper of the wind wash over him. Then he found a patch of grass, sat down, and opened a channel to his sister.

Can you talk? he asked.

There was a long silence, a stillness that seemed to stretch on for an eternity. And then, like a cool breath of wind on a scorching day, he felt her presence, the gentle touch of her mind against his own. *One more moment.*

Aru waited, sweating from the stress and dreading the verdict but also wanting to be done with the uncertainty. Whatever the queen's decision, he had no choice but to accept it.

The queen wants you to delay your report, Aria said. *When the Kra-ell build the funeral pyres for their dead, you and Annani's people are to stage a similar ceremony for the twins and record it, just as you will record the rites for the fallen. She leaves the trickery up to you and her granddaughter's people and asks that you make it convincing. Naturally, that means not reviving the twins until after the recording of their funeral.*

The relief was profound, but with it came the worry of how to pull it off. Any artificial manipulation would be immediately discovered. It had to be staged. The other problem was that he hadn't informed anyone other than the queen that he had found the missing Kra-ell. Would his commander believe that he and his team had decided to perform the Kra-ell funeral rites?

The queen trusts in your judgment and ability to craft a convincing illusion with whatever technologies you have at your disposal.

I understand, Aru said. *I have no idea how we will pull it off, especially since we are still supposed to be looking for the Kra-ell from Igor's compound, but I hope the clan people will help us create a convincing illusion.*

A long moment passed as Aria transmitted his message. *The queen asks that you inform her if you have difficulty executing her directive.*

Of course. Aru swallowed the lump that formed in his throat.

If he failed to find a solution, the queen might command him to kill the twins after all.

71

EDGAR

Edgar's muscles burned with fatigue as he and Yamanu carefully maneuvered the last stasis chamber into place, securing it with ropes and tarps on the truck. They had worked through the night, taking only a couple of breaks to eat and rest.

No one wanted to stay in the area longer than was necessary.

It had been a grueling twenty or so hours of seemingly endless loading and unloading cycles and going back and forth between the mountain and the makeshift base of operations. Even for an immortal, the strain was starting to take its toll, but it wasn't the physical exhaustion that was weighing on Edgar and made each step feel like a Herculean effort. It was the gnawing sense of unease that had taken root in his gut and refused to let go.

Jasmine had given up on them.

She hadn't said anything, but he felt it in his gut. She'd told him that she'd forgiven him and that everything was fine between them, but she sure as hell wasn't acting like it was.

He needed to fix this and bring them back to how they had been. It had been so good, so easy between them. How could a few careless words cause such a profound change in her attitude? And how was he going to win her back?

The answer eluded him, slipping through his grasp like smoke on the wind. He'd even considered asking Yamanu for advice but was too proud to admit his failure.

Right now, he just wanted to be done and go to the hotel, where Jasmine and the other ladies were waiting for them in the restaurant. They were packing boxes with food for the road and for Aru and Negal, who had stayed behind.

Poor Norbu was still asleep but not on the grass back on the mountain. They had brought him with them on one of their round trips and put him in the tent he had brought to sleep in.

"Ready to head back to town?" Yamanu asked as he tucked the tarp under the stasis chamber so none of it was showing. "I'm starving."

"So am I," Kalugal said. "All that piloting was much more exhausting than I anticipated."

Edgar wanted to roll his eyes.

Piloting was all that Kalugal had done. He, Yamanu, and the gods had done all the loading, unloading, and refueling. Most of the extra fuel they had brought on the truck was gone, and the containers were stacked behind the two trucks they were using.

As they walked down the street, Edgar thought about the last item on their agenda: the pod. It had to be buried beneath a mountain of rubble and debris to ensure no trace of its existence remained. They couldn't risk leaving even the slightest hint of alien technology to be found by humans.

As they entered the big tent, Edgar gazed over the place, searching for Jasmine and finding her with the other ladies, sitting next to a large table and a pile of packaged food.

She was so beautiful, so sexy, and so indifferent to him that it hurt.

"Hello, ladies." Yamanu strode to the table. "Is there anything we can shove into our mouths before going? I'm starving."

Gabi lifted a big platter with several dishes on it, which had been hidden behind the boxes, and put it at one corner of the table. "This is for you."

"Thank you." Yamanu pulled out a chair. "You are an angel."

Edgar walked over to Jasmine, and as he stood beside her, she had no choice but to look at him.

"Hi," she said.

"Hi." He smiled. "I missed you."

She averted her gaze. "You should sit down and eat before Yamanu gobbles everything down."

"Yeah." He rubbed a hand over the back of his neck. "I should." He pulled out a chair next to Yamanu and tore open a packet of hand sanitizer that Gabi left for him next to his plate.

Dagor piled his plate and walked over to the other side of the long table to sit with Frankie, and Kalugal joined Yamanu and Edgar.

"What's that?" He pointed at the shaptak.

"It's a traditional Tibetan dish," Margo said. "It's stir-fried meat made with ginger, cabbage, and other stuff that mostly uses spices, so if you don't like a lot of spices, you should choose something else."

"I love spice." Kalugal piled his plate with the dish.

Edgar's stomach rumbled, not caring that his heart was aching. It wanted food. Once Kalugal was done piling his plate, he took the serving dish from him and put some of it on his own plate.

"Listen," Yamanu said, wiping his mouth with the wet towelette Gabi had given him. "We're about to head back to the mountain, and there will be a big boom. The townsfolk and Jasmine won't hear or see a thing, but the rest of you probably will. Don't get scared and don't respond."

Jasmine's brow furrowed. "Is it dangerous?" she asked. "The explosives, I mean. Are you going to set them off from a distance?"

"Of course," Kalugal said. "You have nothing to worry about. We will all be in the air when we detonate the mountain."

Jasmine nodded. "I thought so. I just wanted to make sure that you are safe." She glanced at Edgar and smiled, her concern for his safety making his heart soar with renewed hope.

Edgar, Kalugal, and Yamanu pushed to their feet when they were done eating. Dagor remained seated; his job was done, and he did not need to return.

Edgar walked over to Jasmine and pulled her into a hug, breathing in the sweet, familiar scent of her hair. She stiffened momentarily, her body tense and unyielding in his arms. But then, with a sigh that sounded almost like surrender, she relaxed, melting into his embrace with a softness that made his heart ache.

It wasn't the enthusiastic response he had hoped for, but it was something.

72

ARU

Aru shifted on the hard boulder he'd been sitting on and turned to Negal. "I've thought a lot about it, and we will have to fake the twins' death. When the Kra-ell prepare the funeral pyres, we will wait for them to perform the rites and then one of us will have to light the torch while it is being filmed. The trick will be to do the same with the twins, given their state."

Negal pursed his lips. "What if we could create dummies that look like they did before they turned skeletal? The clan should be able to help us with that."

"Dummies will not fool our recording equipment, but you are onto something. We could wait until they are revived and back to looking healthy and then somehow make them appear dead."

"Right." Negal chuckled. "Our equipment will register even the faintest sign of life, and don't forget the pyre. That's going to be hard to fake as well."

Negal wasn't wrong, but Aru had no other ideas. "If you have any constructive suggestions, I'm listening."

Negal shrugged. "Simple. We never found the pod. The mission to Tibet was a failure, and we are exploring other leads."

That actually was a good idea, but the question was whether the queen would agree.

Aru had a feeling that she wouldn't. She'd wanted him to stage their death before reviving them for a reason. If the trickery didn't work, she wanted them dead.

"The choppers are coming." Negal pointed a finger at the sky.

If not for the remaining salvaged equipment, they could have all fit in one helicopter, but they had managed to get a few more components loose, and Aru didn't want to leave them behind. Since nothing worked, he didn't know whether he'd found the flight recorder or anything else that could hint at the cause of the accident or where the other pods could be. Still, perhaps William could do something with all this junk without destroying it in the process.

As the birds touched down on the rocky mountaintop, Aru and Negal rose to their feet. Each lifted an armload of equipment before striding toward the helicopters.

Yamanu got out, holding several boxes of food from the restaurant. "Hungry?"

"Very." Aru put the components on the chopper's floor and took one of the boxes from Yamanu. "We finished the last energy bar after you left." He opened the box and sat down on the step. "Everything is ready. So, once we get the rest of the equipment in, we can move out."

While Negal and Aru ate their lunch, Dagor and Edgar got busy bringing in the rest of the stuff, including the ropes and the rappelling equipment.

When everything was loaded, Aru and Yamanu got into the helicopter with Edgar, while Negal and Dagor got into Kalugal's.

Clutching the detonator in his hand, Aru waited until they were in the air and Yamanu was shrouding the mountain before pressing the button.

As a muffled thump shook the ground below them, the sound of the explosion was almost anticlimactic. It was a fraction of the noise and fury he had expected.

A cloud of dust billowed up from the cavern's depths, a blinding haze that obscured the mountain in a veil of gray.

Aru squinted against the onslaught, his eyes watering as Edgar guided the helicopter up and away until the dust settled a little. Then, he angled back for a better view.

It was hard to see, the dust still swirling and eddying in the air, but as Edgar made another pass over the mountain, Aru fought to peer through the haze and the sun's glare and was satisfied with what he saw.

The crater was mostly gone, buried beneath rubble and debris. Only a shallow depression remained, a barely there divot in the rugged landscape that, in a few hours, would give no hint of the secrets that lay buried beneath.

All that remained was for them to return to base, gather the last of their belongings, and make their way to the nearest airport, where two private planes awaited them.

73

JASMINE

J asmine's heart ached at the distance that had grown between her and Edgar. She knew that she needed to end things, to set them both free to find their true paths in life. But the thought of hurting him, of seeing the pain and heartbreak in his eyes, made her want to recoil, to retreat into the safety and comfort of the familiar.

Except, they both deserved better than this.

Strangely, it wasn't about love or lack thereof. Jasmine cared for Edgar, and in time, she knew she could have learned to love him, but deep down, she knew that he was not her forever. He was not the one she was meant to walk beside through eternity's long, winding road.

As much as it pained her to hurt him, she knew that she had to let him go. They both deserved to find their true soulmates, the other halves of their eternal being.

But as she looked at him now and saw the hurt and confusion in his eyes, Jasmine felt her resolve waver and her courage faltering.

How could she do this?

There were no easy answers, no painless paths to follow, but she had to find a way to end things with grace and compassion, to part as friends rather than enemies.

And so, with a deep breath and a silent prayer for strength, she turned to face him, ready to speak the words that would set them both free, but a knock on the door stopped her before she could open her mouth.

"Come in." She put the pair of pants she had folded into her suitcase.

Julian opened the door and walked in. "We need to load up this chamber." He tossed a length of rope to Edgar.

As she watched Edgar and Julian carefully maneuvering the prince's stasis chamber out of the hotel room, Jasmine felt a pang of unease. It wasn't about the unfinished business between her and Edgar. There was something unsettling about the way the chamber seemed to shimmer and then fade out of view as Julian wove his shroud to conceal it from prying eyes.

She understood the necessity of it, but that didn't make it any less disconcerting to watch two men carrying a metal sarcophagus simply vanish, leaving what seemed like empty air in their wake.

Following close behind them, she navigated the narrow hallway, keeping a watchful eye out for any unsuspecting passersby who might stumble into the invisible procession.

Julian had said she didn't need to tag along and should stay and pack her things, but she wanted to ensure they made it safely to the truck.

Not that they needed her. She was the weak link among them, the one who could not see past the shroud and followed them blindly, hoping she was heading in the right direction.

When would she stop being the outsider and become part of their world?

What would it be like to be one of them? To have endless years, enhanced senses and strength, and the ability to thrall and shroud?

Would it change her, transform her in some fundamental way?

Or would she still be the same Jasmine at heart, just long-lived and powerful?

Power was corruptive, but it could also be used for good. The immortals and gods she'd gotten to know were good people, but she'd heard that others like them were not good, which made sense. Humans were good and evil, so immortals and gods were probably divided similarly.

What if she wasn't a Dormant, though?

She wouldn't know until she let an immortal induce her, and right now, it didn't seem like it was going to be Edgar.

When they got to the waiting truck, Julian dropped the shroud. As he and Edgar hefted the chamber and placed it in a spot that seemed to have been reserved for it, Jasmine tried to figure out which chamber belonged to the princess. Since they were all identical, she guessed it was the one next to the prince's, but she didn't know whether it was the one on the right or the one on the left.

"Are you going to mark them?" she asked Julian. "Otherwise, how are you going to be able to tell them apart from the others?"

He motioned for her to get closer. "Do you see the seam here?" He pointed.

"I do."

"Now look at this one." He lifted a tarp. "Can you see a seam?"

She got closer to take a better look but couldn't see it. "There is none."

"There is." Julian lowered the tarp and tucked it under the chamber. "You can't see it because the chamber is sealed. I left the ones containing the royal twins unsealed so their bodies could absorb nutrients from their environment."

"I see." She smiled at him. "Thanks for explaining it to me."

"You're welcome."

Julian was such a great guy. He had a gift for explaining complicated things in layman's terms that she could easily understand. He didn't try to dumb them down for her, which would have made her feel like a simpleton.

The doctor went back to working with the gods and Edgar, securing the cargo with tarps and ropes, but Jasmine barely registered the details. Her mind was too caught up in the swirl of emotions that churned within her.

With a final glance at the truck, Jasmine turned and made her way back to the hotel room.

As she pushed open the door, the familiar scent of Edgar's cologne wafted over her like a bittersweet memory, and Jasmine felt a pang of sorrow for what could have been but wasn't.

With a sigh, she reached into her bag and pulled out her tarot cards, their worn edges and faded images a comforting weight in her palm. She had always turned to them in times of need, seeking guidance and clarity in the face of life's challenges.

Until now, Jasmine hadn't dared ask the one question that would determine her future more than any other. In fact, it was much more important than whether the prince was her one and only or not.

Taking a deep, steadying breath, she shuffled the cards, her fingers moving with a deftness born of years of practice. And then, with a whispered prayer to whatever gods or Fates might be listening, she laid them before her, her eyes scanning the spread with hope and fear.

The first card she turned over was the Star. The image of a woman pouring water from two jugs symbolized renewal, healing, and hope. The second card was the Wheel of Fortune, a reminder that life was ever-changing and that good and bad fortunes were fleeting moments in the grand scheme of things.

And then she turned over the final and most important card and gasped.

It was the World card, depicting a naked woman hovering above the Earth, holding a baton in each hand and surrounded by a wreath. She was being watched by the four living creatures: a man, a lion, an ox, and an eagle.

The World card represented the ending of one cycle of life and the beginning of the next.

The cards had spoken, and their message was as clear as if shouted from the rooftops. It was a new beginning—the closing of one chapter of her life and the start of a grand new adventure.

Jasmine felt a rush of emotion wash over her, a dizzying mix of relief and elation.

She had her answer. She was a Dormant, and she would become immortal.

RESURRECTION

1

KIAN

Kian surveyed the unusual group of people he'd assembled in his office and wondered if he was overdoing it. After all, the royal twins were little more than emaciated corpses and were in no state to offer resistance or cause any trouble.

Still, after all the warnings about how powerful and dangerous the twins were, Kian wasn't taking any chances. If the Eternal King feared them, he must have a good reason for it.

Or maybe not.

The king might have been paranoid, which was very likely given the lengths he was willing to go to, to keep his throne. It could also be that the paranoia was genetic, and if so, Kian might have inherited the trait from his great-grandfather.

The thought was so amusing in a macabre way that a soft chuckle escaped Kian's throat.

"What's so funny?" Bridget asked.

"The role genes play in shaping who we are." He waved a dismissive hand. "Don't mind me. It's not important."

The doctor leaned back in her chair. "We have nothing better to do while we wait for William to arrive and Anandur to return with the coffees and pastries, so you might as well tell me."

Kian let out a sigh. "I thought I might have inherited my paranoia from the Eternal King. I wouldn't have minded inheriting his brilliance, his charm, and his leadership skills, but the flip side of that is megalomania and disregard for the sanctity of life, and I'm grateful that I didn't inherit those traits."

Bridget's eyes softened. "You are an excellent leader, Kian. We all tease you about your paranoia, but the truth is that we are glad you are so diligent about protecting us."

He dipped his head. "Thank you."

She smiled. "That being said, I don't think we all need to wear compulsion-filtering earpieces on day one. The twins will not wake up from stasis and immediately try to compel everyone to obey them."

"They might."

That was why they were waiting for William to bring more devices for those who still didn't have them and needed instructions. That included Bridget, Merlin, and Gertrude, the medical team tasked with reviving the twins from stasis.

Jade had her pair, but the four hybrids she had chosen to accompany her needed filtering earpieces of their own.

Her task was to provide familiarity and security.

The twins didn't know her personally, but they would find her Kra-ell features familiar and understand her language. Not so with the hybrids, who looked different, and Kian wondered about Jade's choice.

She could have selected some of the older pureblooded males, those who had arrived on the settler ship with her and knew the old customs, but they had been sentenced to community service, so she'd probably decided that taking them out of the village wasn't a smart move. The pureblooded females could have also been a good choice. They knew the Kra-ell customs as well, and some of them were skilled warriors, so they could have provided protection if necessary.

The younger pureblooded Kra-ell who had been born on Earth were not familiar with the Kra-ell traditions, and their mastery of the language was probably only so-so, but the hybrids were no better.

Had she chosen them because she trusted them more or because they were easier to control?

Or maybe...

When the answer suddenly occurred to him, Kian realized Jade's choice was brilliant. The hybrid Kra-ell were half human, and therefore resembled how the twins probably looked. Showing the twins people who were hybrids like them and who were not reviled by their pureblooded companions was an excellent and expeditious way to assure the twins that they were safe and welcome.

Still, her brilliant choice might miss the mark simply because the intended beneficiaries would not be aware enough to realize what they were seeing.

It would take weeks or even months for the twins' bodies to regenerate to full strength, and their minds might take even longer to recuperate.

There was also the issue of the dead Kra-ell, who needed proper funeral ceremonies, but that wouldn't happen immediately upon their arrival either. Jade would have to return and bring along purebloods who knew the Kra-ell prayers to send the souls of their dead to the fields of the brave, or whatever they called their afterlife.

"I'm a little worried," Merlin said. "Hildegard is an experienced nurse, but I'm uncomfortable leaving her alone in charge of the village clinic." He turned to Bridget. "One of us should stay behind, and the other should take both nurses to the keep."

Bridget regarded him with a smile. "The only ones who might need our help are the humans, and I don't expect any emergencies that Hildegard can't triage in our short absence."

Merlin shook his head. "The village is isolated, and if, Fates forbid, anything serious happens, it might take us over an hour to get back here."

"Relax." Bridget put a hand on his shoulder. "Nothing will happen while we are gone for a couple of hours."

"It's going to take much longer than that," Merlin grumbled. "It's not like we're going to throw some fresh water on the twins and leave. If it was that easy, Anandur could do it by himself. We must monitor them until they stabilize and intervene if they become distressed."

Bridget nodded. "Just in case, we should revive them one at a time."

"I agree a hundred percent." Merlin leaned back in his chair. "And you can handle it on your own, so I can stay here in case any humans need medical attention."

It seemed to Kian that Merlin didn't want to leave the village for some reason, or maybe he had a problem with reviving people from stasis, or maybe his problem was just with reviving the royal twins. Whatever his issue was, he wasn't wriggling out of it.

Kian leaned forward and squared his gaze at Merlin. "I need you there. You are our expert on tracker removal after performing dozens of these procedures on the Kra-ell. There is every reason to suspect that the twins have trackers implanted in their bodies, and we cannot risk them being activated when the twins are revived. It is critical to remove them while their bodies are still at minimal functioning, so the trackers don't go online and alert the Eternal King. It is crucial to hide their survival from him."

For a second or so, Merlin looked like he was searching for a rebuttal, but then he nodded his agreement.

Gertrude frowned. "Will we be able to move them into the scanner, though? I thought their condition was so bad that Julian didn't want to even remove them from the pods before they were brought to the clinic."

Kian nodded. "William rigged up a hand scanner that we hope will be sensitive enough to find the trackers while the twins remain in their stasis chambers. He will explain when he gets here."

2

KIAN

"Sorry I'm late." William rushed into the office with a large bag dangling from his fingers. "I had to wait for the earpieces to be tested. They were fresh off the assembly line."

Merlin cocked a brow. "You have an assembly line?"

"Of course." William pulled out a chair and sat down. "How do you think we put together all these gadgets you all love?"

The doctor shrugged. "I thought one person did everything from start to finish."

"It's less efficient that way." William reached into his bag. "But we do that when we're working on a one-of-a-kind like this beauty." He pulled out a device very similar to the wands used by airport security to scan individuals manually. "This portable tracker scanner is just as efficient as the big machines we used on the Kra-ell. I calibrated this one for the dimensions of the Anumatian trackers and their X-ray signature."

"When did you do that?" Merlin eyed the device suspiciously.

"Right after the gods arrived, they told us they were looking for the other Kra-ell pods. I figured that we may again find ourselves needing to look for these implanted trackers and may not have a CT machine available." He chuckled. "I didn't expect to have to put this wand to the test so soon."

Looking closely at the device William handed him, Merlin still seemed skeptical. "Won't the stasis chamber interfere with the device's readouts?"

William shook his head. "The wand is programmed to look for the specific trackers we found. It will ignore anything else, even if made from the same material."

Kian sighed. "Scanning them in the stasis chamber is not ideal, let alone performing any procedure on them if trackers are found. In their condition, that may prove fatal, but the trackers going live poses an existential risk not only to the clan but possibly to the entire population of Earth. It is not a risk I'm willing to take to save the twins."

He wasn't being paranoid or dramatic for effect. The Eternal King would not allow such a potential risk to his reign to continue.

For a long moment, no one spoke, and when the door opened and Anandur walked in with trays of coffee and bags of pastries, there was a collective sigh of relief.

"It's a madhouse down at the café," Anandur said as he put the trays on the conference table. "Wonder hopes the new human arriving in the village this afternoon will apply for a job. They need help desperately." He put down the paper bag and started pulling out wrapped pastries.

"Who is the human?" Merlin asked.

"She is from Igor's former compound," Anandur said. "You've probably seen her around during the cruise. The server with the blue hair and the piercings. She and Peter got close, and she asked to be transferred to the village."

Merlin's face split into a huge grin. "I know who you are talking about. Marina is lovely. I'm so glad that they are going to live here."

Kian had approved Marina's transfer because he believed the Fates must have brought her and Peter together for a reason, although he couldn't fathom what that reason might be.

Unions between immortals and humans were a prescription for heartache, and Kian knew that better than most.

In his youth, he had fallen in love with a mortal, married her against his mother's wishes, and had a daughter with her.

That story hadn't ended well, but maybe Peter's would.

Kian groaned. "I never expected so many humans to be living in the village."

"We don't have all that many," Bridget said. "Including the newcomer, there will be nine people in total."

Kian frowned. "Are you counting Karen's kids and Lisa in that?"

"No, of course not." Bridget tore a piece of her pastry and put it in her mouth.

"Then it's five more." Kian lifted his hand, fingers splayed. "That brings the total to fourteen."

Kian glanced at his watch. "We should head to the parking garage in a few minutes."

"Did they land yet?" Jade asked.

"No, but they are about to."

The time it took to get from the village to the keep was about the same as from the clan's airstrip to the keep, so as soon as the two planes carrying the Tibetan team and the stasis chambers landed, he and his group should head out.

Jade glanced at her watch. "Weren't they supposed to arrive almost an hour ago?"

Kian nodded. "They hit a bit of a snag on the way, something about avoiding turbulence, so they were delayed. But they should be landing at the airstrip any minute now. Okidu and Onidu are there to meet them and help transport the team, the equipment, and the stasis chambers to the keep."

"I remember when we revived Dalhu from stasis," Anandur said. "The dude was only entombed for a week, and he still looked like death warmed over when we opened the sarcophagus. I can't even imagine what state the twins are in." He shivered, but it was more of an act than an involuntary response.

Kian let out a soft chuckle. "You don't have to imagine. Just stroll down to the catacombs and look at the Doomers stashed away there. That should give you a pretty good idea."

None of the Doomers they had collected over the years had spent more than a couple of centuries in the clan catacombs, though, so they were probably in a much better state than the twins.

Up until recently, Annani had disallowed executing captured Doomers, and they had been forced to put them in stasis and take care of the bodies because of his mother's naive belief that someday they could be redeemed. But after what they discovered in Acapulco and the atrocities that the Doomers had the cartel commit, she had finally changed her mind.

Kian didn't know why it had taken her so long.

Doomers had been committing terrible atrocities throughout human history. But the truth was that it had been a long time since they had done something so evil, and his mother had probably thought that those days were over, never to return. It must have been a shock for her to realize that their cruelty and barbarism were still just as present.

"Wonder told me about what she looked like when she woke up from stasis after five thousand years," Anandur said. "She was a walking skeleton."

"I'm surprised she could walk at all," Bridget said.

Anandur puffed out his chest. "My Wonder is a warrior. She's unstoppable."

Bridget nodded. "She is, but don't forget that the twins have been in stasis for seven thousand years without the benefit of being able to absorb nutrients from the earth like Wonder could. They are probably much worse off."

Kian reached into his pocket, his fingers brushing against the smooth, metallic surface of the compulsion-filtering devices. "Should we test the new earpieces?" He looked at William. "I'm curious about the new Kra-ell translation feature."

"Sure." Jade pulled hers out. "I tested mine with Phinas, and they worked beautifully." She nodded at William. "These will save me a lot of time translating for everyone else and make wearing them less awkward." She turned to Kian. "We don't even need to tell the twins about the compulsion-filtering feature of the devices. They will assume we are wearing them for their translation capabilities alone."

Kian shook his head. "They will figure it out eventually, and then they will not trust us. I'd rather be upfront about it." He smiled coldly. "That way, they will know not to try anything. But we can wait until they get better before telling them."

His mind flashed back to Igor and the moment when the powerful Kra-ell had held him at his mercy, his will subsumed by the force of the pureblood's compulsion. If Jade hadn't been there, and if she hadn't acted with such decisiveness and courage, Kian shuddered to think what might have happened.

He shook off the disturbing memory and straightened his shoulders. "Even though it is unlikely that the twins will pose a threat to us in their current state, we need to take the necessary precautions and ensure our safety, which means never forgetting to wear the earpieces while around them." He looked pointedly at Jade. "But we must also remember that they are my mother's half-brother and sister and are most likely not our enemies. We should treat them with kindness, care, and vigilance."

3

JASMINE

J asmine squirmed in her seat as the bus driver navigated the spiral drive's sharp turns down into the keep's bowels.

How deep was it?

They had already passed several parking levels, and there still seemed to be no end to the downward drive. The bus was air-conditioned, yet she could feel it getting colder the deeper they went.

Imagining the layers of earth above them made her feel claustrophobic, and she instinctively lifted her hand to reach for Edgar's, but she fought the urge and put her hand back in her lap. He wouldn't deny her, but it would be cruel for her to do that.

They were no longer together as a couple, and she needed to respect the new boundaries of their tenuous friendship.

Behind them, the large truck that carried the eighteen Kra-ell stasis chambers trundled along, forced to make the same sharp turns as the bus while somehow avoiding scraping against the concrete walls.

Thankfully, the twins' stasis chambers were on the bus, secured with ropes in the back, with Julian and Ella watching over them.

When they finally reached the bottom, the bus driver stopped in front of a gate, and as it slid to the side, he drove through and parked.

The place was nearly empty, with only a few cars parked in a row. The truck followed inside and stopped next to the bus.

"Have you been here before?" Jasmine asked Edgar.

"Of course. This is the clan's private parking level."

Despite the breakup, Edgar was doing his best to be not only cordial to her but also friendly, and she appreciated his effort.

It had been a difficult conversation, a painful admission of the truth that had been staring them both in the face for longer than either cared to admit. Their relationship had run its course. The spark that had once burned between them had faded, leaving behind only the dying embers of what might have been.

They still cared for each other, but they both knew that they were not meant to be. They had been good together, but it was more of a friends-with-benefits arrangement than the love she'd witnessed between Margo and Negal and the other couples who had accompanied them to Tibet.

After witnessing their eternal and all-consuming love, Jasmine wasn't willing to settle for anything less.

Still, Edgar had been hurt by her words, and the pain she'd seen in his eyes had made her heart ache, but to his credit, he had been more gracious and understanding than she had thought he would be.

"I'm not going to pretend that I'm not disappointed," he had told her. "But I get it. We had a good run, and I don't regret it." He'd offered her his hand. "I'm all for staying friends if you are up for it."

Jasmine had felt a rush of relief at his words. She would love for them to move forward as friends without bitterness or resentment.

"Of course, I am." She'd put her hand in his. "You are a great guy, and I care about you. I will keep my fingers crossed and light candles to hasten your truelove mate's arrival."

Edgar had chuckled at that, a glimmer of his old humor returning to his eyes. "I hope you will do that in reverse order. Light the candles first and cross your fingers later."

When she'd laughed, he'd continued, "And what about you? Is Prince Charming your truelove mate, the other half of your eternal soul?"

Jasmine had shrugged, a flutter of uncertainty and anticipation mingling in her gut. "Maybe. It's also possible that he'll take one look at me and run screaming in the other direction."

Edgar had laughed and shaken his head. "That's very unlikely. You are a beautiful and desirable woman."

Jasmine knew she was attractive, but the prince was not from Earth, and what he considered desirable might be very different from who and what she was. Maybe he was into Amazonian warrior women who could wield a sword and jump forty feet in the air.

In her fantasies, though, the prince opened his eyes for the first time after seven thousand years, took one look at her, and fell in love with her on the spot. But that was so silly that she felt embarrassed even thinking it.

The poor guy was barely alive, and if he managed to open his eyes at all, the first person he'd see would be the doctor, and the first thought that would cross his mind was to try to understand where he was and when.

She felt sorry for all he had lost while asleep in stasis.

"You know…" Edgar had leaned closer to her. "There is a chance that the prince isn't into women. In which case, I'd say you dodged a bullet."

Jasmine had laughed at that, but it wasn't all that funny.

The prince had been consecrated into the priesthood, and Kra-ell priests were celibate. He might not be into anyone other than the deity he worshiped.

4

EDGAR

"I'm heading up to the penthouse for a proper shower." Edgar leaned over to kiss Jasmine's cheek, remembering at the last moment that it was no longer appropriate.

In some human cultures, it was common for everyone to kiss each other in greeting and farewell, but Edgar wasn't comfortable doing it.

"Okay." Jasmine smiled at him, and it wasn't fake. There was genuine affection there, which made it even worse. "I'll see you later, right? You're not leaving yet."

She wasn't getting rid of him that easily. "No, not yet. I'll wait for you." He forced a smile. "We still need to have an end-of-mission party."

"Of course." The softness in her eyes was slaying him.

Couldn't she be more of a bitch about it so he could rage at her?

Turning on his heel, Edgar stalked through the halls of the keep, heading to the freight elevator in the back so he wouldn't be in the way while Jade's crew of hybrids carried the stasis chambers from the truck to the catacombs.

The problem was that the service elevator didn't go to the penthouse, and he had to get out at the lobby level and switch to the one that did.

Waving at the guards, he called for the penthouse's dedicated elevator, and when the doors opened, he was greeted by soft instrumental music playing on the hidden speakers. Regrettably, it wasn't loud enough to drown out Jasmine's voice in his head. The conversation they'd had on the plane was still replaying in his mind in a relentless loop of anger and regret.

She had dumped him.

Edgar had never been dumped before.

He had always been the one who walked away, and it hurt to be on the receiving end of the boot. It was a bitter pill to swallow, a jagged shard of glass that lodged in his throat and refused to move no matter how much logic he tried to wash it down with.

He knew he should be happy for Jasmine and respect her wishes like the good friend he had promised to be. But the green-eyed monster of jealousy had sunk its claws deep into his soul, poisoning his thoughts and twisting his emotions until he could barely recognize himself.

She was right that they both deserved better and that his truelove mate was waiting for him somewhere, but knowing and accepting were two different things.

As he reached the penthouse, Edgar slammed the door behind him with a satisfying bang, the sound echoing through the empty rooms, a hollow and mocking reminder that he was once again on his own.

It had been nice to be part of a couple, to have someone to return to at the end of the day, someone he'd thought belonged to him. And it wasn't about being a possessive asshole. For the short time they had been together, Edgar believed that he also belonged to Jasmine.

Except, she didn't want him.

Stripping off his clothes, he left a trail of discarded garments in his wake as he stalked toward the bathroom. The shower beckoned with a promise of a powerful stream of hot water and a good soap that might wash away the stain of failure and inadequacy.

But even as he stood beneath the scalding spray, Edgar couldn't escape the anger that felt like a corrosive acid in his veins.

If not for that damn corpse of a prince, Jasmine would still be his.

He had done his best for her. He had been there for her every step of the way, and they had been great in bed together. What more could that alien prince give her?

Nothing.

Even if he woke up from his stasis with his brain intact, the prince and Jasmine had nothing in common, nothing to talk about, nothing to share. How could she hope to love the half-god, half-Kra-ell alien?

Better yet, how could she hope that he would love her?

Or perhaps love didn't matter to her?

Jasmine was obsessed with royalty so much that she didn't even care that her royal was not the same species as her, which painted her as shallow and stupid.

The thing was, though, she was neither of those things. She was just misguided and blindsided.

As he stepped out of the shower, Edgar felt a flicker of something dark kindle in his chest. It was a feeling he had never experienced before, a burning need to lash out, to hurt and destroy, and make someone else feel the same pain and turmoil that was tearing him apart from the inside out.

He knew it was wrong and that it went against everything he had ever believed in, every code of honor and decency that had guided his life until this moment. But the jealousy was like cancer, eating away at his reason and his restraint until there was nothing left but a raw, bleeding wound that refused to heal.

"Take a breath," he commanded himself. "You are not going to hurt anyone."

Edgar toweled off, pulled on a fresh set of clothes, and began to plot.

He wouldn't do anything stupid, but there was no law against competing for the affection of a female and using any means considered fair play. He would find ways to undermine the prince and expose him as the dangerous alien freak he surely was.

There was a good reason for Kian to demand that they all wear compulsion-filtering earpieces around the twins. They were rumored to be incredibly powerful and dangerous.

Jasmine was just a fragile human, and she had no business being anywhere near the powerful alien creatures. She might not realize that, but she needed him to protect her.

5

JASMINE

J asmine observed the wide, industrial-style corridor as she followed Negal and Dagor, who were carrying the prince's stasis chamber.

The bowels of the keep looked very different than the top portion, and not only because they were underground—there were no windows ,and the only light was artificial. No interior decorator had bothered to spruce up the space, and everything was utilitarian. There were naked concrete floors, walls made from blocks painted some off-white, and no pictures or plants in sight.

"I need coffee." Frankie stopped in front of the open doors of a huge commercial kitchen. "Do you think they have the stuff to make it here?"

"They do," Gabi said. "Follow me."

As Margo joined the two, Ella fell in step with Jasmine. "I wonder if the stasis chambers could hover when they were still working. It doesn't seem right that such advanced technology needs to be carried."

If self-driving cars were a reality on Earth, which was primitive compared to the planet of the gods, then the stasis chambers could probably drive themselves too.

Jasmine tried to imagine them hovering into the pod, perhaps guided by a technician or maybe self-guiding. The latter made more sense, given the advanced technology of the gods.

"Over here." Bridget waved Negal and Dagor into the clinic and then straight into one of the patients' rooms. "Put it right here on the floor."

The hospital bed had been shoved against the wall to make room for the stasis chamber, and as the two gods carried it inside and lowered it to the floor, it took up most of the floor space in the room. There were about two feet left on each side, so the doctor and the nurse could attend to the patient while he was still inside his chamber.

There was no room left for observers, though, and Jasmine hated having to stay out in the waiting room.

"Where do you want the princess?" Aru asked as he and Julian arrived with the other stasis pod.

"The next room!" Bridget called out. "It's ready for her."

Jasmine moved to stand against the wall to let them through, and when they cleared the waiting room, Kian walked in.

"Hello, Jasmine." Kian offered her his hand. "I want to thank you in person for helping us find the pod. It wouldn't have been possible without you."

"I'm glad that I was able to help." She put her hand in his and let him shake it. "I just have one favor to ask in return."

It was bold, but she had rehearsed the request for hours.

Kian let go of her hand. "What is it?"

"I want to be present when the prince is revived. The cards foretold his arrival in my life for months, and I'm eager to meet him."

Kian nodded. "I have no problem with that, but you might. He's not looking pretty at this time. Wouldn't it be better to wait until he looks less corpse-like and has some flesh on his bones?"

Jasmine swallowed. "I can't. I need to be here when he opens his eyes." She put a hand over her chest. "I feel it here that it's the right thing for me to do."

"As you wish," Kian said. "Don't say that I didn't warn you, though."

Behind him, the tall redheaded Guardian nodded. "I've seen a dude wake up from stasis once, and it turned my stomach. It's nasty, and I'm not talking just about the looks. The stink is almost worse."

Jasmine grimaced. "Thanks for the warning. I'll make sure not to breathe through my nose."

Kian walked into the first patient room, where Bridget was still fussing around the prince. "Don't do anything yet. I need Merlin to scan them first. In the meantime, Aru and I also need to discuss a few things." Jasmine couldn't see the doctor because Kian was blocking the entrance to the room, but the silence that followed was telling.

"They don't have much time, Kian," Bridget said. "I can't even hook them up to monitoring equipment because their skin is frail, and it will break if I try to attach anything to it. The sooner we douse them with pure water, the better."

Why was it so important to use pure water?

Jasmine looked around until she located the two containers each with twelve one-liter bottles of mountain spring water. That was all that was needed to revive two ancient beings from stasis?

Surely, they had more containers stacked up somewhere?

"Shouldn't you do that in the operating room?" Kian asked the doctors.

"It won't make a difference," Julian said. "We are not operating on them, and we have all we need in the patient rooms." He ran his fingers through his shoulder-length tawny hair. "I should shower and change first, though." He looked at Kian and then shifted his gaze to Aru. "When will you be ready?"

"That depends on the results of our talk." Aru looked at Kian. "Can we talk in your office?"

"Of course."

What was that all about? What did Aru have to discuss with Kian, and did it have anything to do with the prince?

Jasmine had a feeling that it did.

When the two left, Ella pushed away from the wall. "Coffee?" she asked Jasmine. "I'm sure Frankie has a fresh pot by now."

Julian had ducked somewhere inside the clinic, probably to shower and put on scrubs, but Bridget and the nurse could take care of the twins. No danger lurked down in the depths of the keep, and Jasmine felt it was safe to leave her prince in the clan doctors' capable hands.

The only thing that made her uneasy was the conversation between Aru and Kian, but it wasn't as if she could find Kian's office and eavesdrop.

"I would love some."

6

KIAN

As Kian led Aru to his office, curiosity gnawed at him, but he held off asking the god what he wanted to talk about until they were inside, and he closed the door behind them.

He moved to lean against the edge of the conference table, crossing his arms over his chest as he fixed Aru with a steady gaze. "Let me guess. This has to do with your queen."

"Good guess." Aru pulled out one of the chairs and sat down. "We can't let the Eternal King know the twins survived. The best way to go about it is for me to report that everyone in the pod we found was dead. The problem is proving that to him, and before you suggest it, let me assure you that computer manipulation won't work with Anumatian technology. They'll instantly see through any digital or computer tricks."

"I wasn't about to suggest that. I know better." Kian pulled out a chair and sat next to Aru. "So, what's your idea?"

"It's not mine. It's the queen's. She suggests that we fake a funeral pyre for them like we intend to do for the Kra-ell, but I have no idea how we can do that without actually incinerating them."

Kian drummed his fingers on the conference table. "I wouldn't know the first thing about faking a funeral pyre, but I can ask our media expert for help. After all, they were doing that in movies long before computers and digital manipulation were a thing."

Aru nodded. "That's good. There is another problem that we need to take into consideration. The twins are emaciated, while the Kra-ell bodies are perfectly preserved. The difference is self-explanatory. Being half gods, the twins could enter stasis unaided, while the Kra-ell did not, and that's why their bodies consumed themselves to preserve basic function. Anyone on Anumati will figure it out at a glance."

Trying to figure out a solution to a seemingly unsolvable problem, Kian was silent for a long moment, his brow furrowed in concentration as he turned it over in his mind. Perhaps he should call Turner and Kalugal and ask them for ideas. After all, the queen wasn't the only one who knew that the Eternal King must never find out that the twins were alive, and he could ask their advice without mentioning her.

A thought, or rather a memory, was trying to push itself to the forefront of his mind—something about faking death.

Then it hit him. "I know what we can do. We will wait until the twins have recovered from their stasis so they look as whole as the Kra-ell, and then Bridget will administer a drug that will slow their vitals to a crawl even more so than stasis and make them appear dead to even the most advanced scanners. Once you record their lack of vitals, she will administer the antidote and revive them."

Aru's eyes widened. "If she can do that, it would be perfect. We can forgo recording the funeral pyres altogether. After all, no one expects us to give the Kra-ell their proper funeral rites." He tilted his head with a frown. "Did you base your idea on anything concrete, or was it only a hypothesis?"

"We've done something like that in the past." Kian pushed to his feet and motioned for Aru to follow him. "We needed to infiltrate the Doomers' island. The problem was that getting in was easy, but getting out was impossible. The plan was for our operative to fake her own death by administering a drug, getting out of there in a casket, and then being revived. In the end, her escape happened differently, but Bridget tried the method on her, and it worked."

"Who was your operative?" Aru asked.

Kian smiled. "Carol. Lokan's mate."

The god gasped. "That sweet little angel infiltrated the Doomers' island alone?"

"She did," Kian said. "Don't let her delicate appearance fool you. She's the gutsiest and most resilient person I know."

They strode down the hall together, their footsteps echoing off the concrete walls.

As they entered the clinic, Kian caught sight of Bridget, her red hair pulled back in a ponytail. She stood still next to the prince's open stasis chamber, partially obscuring Merlin while observing him scanning the prince.

"I need a word with you," Kian said. "Can we talk in your office?"

"Of course." She cast one last look at the emaciated figure and then at Merlin. "If you need my help to maneuver the prince carefully, let me know."

Merlin remained focused on the prince. "I think I got it, but thank you, I will." Kian walked toward the doctor's office. "Merlin seems to have it in hand; I just hope there are no trackers we need to cut out of them in their condition."

"Why haven't you sent Jasmine away?" Bridget grumbled, redirecting her frustration to another subject. "There is no need for her to be hanging around the clinic."

"I owe her." Kian opened the door. "Without her, we would have never found them. Besides, do you really want to stand in the way of the Fates' plan?"

"Good point." Bridget walked around the desk and sat behind it. "So, what's going on? What did you want to talk to me about?"

After Kian explained his idea, she was silent for a long moment, her lips pursed in thought.

"Carol was an immortal," she said at last. "I knew her physiology inside and out. But these twins are half Kra-ell, half god, and I'm not as sure that I can predict how their bodies will react to the drugs. The Kra-ell get tipsy from painkillers, so obviously, their chemistry is a little different than ours. Also, it will take a long time for the twins to regain their health, and I won't be able to experiment on them until they are back to full strength."

Kian turned to Aru. "It's your call. How long can you wait before reporting to your commander?"

The god closed his eyes for a moment. "As long as I want, but within reason. I can tell him that the mission to Tibet failed, and that we are back in Los Angeles to investigate another lead. Once we have a good plan, I will schedule another expedition to Tibet and report my findings then." He rubbed a hand over his jaw. "I need to tell Dagor to erase his recordings. Thankfully, we had the foresight to record with an offline device."

Kian canted his head. "You must have subconsciously known that you would need to delay the report."

"I guess I did." Aru turned to Bridget. "So, what's next, doctor?"

"As soon as Merlin is done, we will start reviving one of them and then the other. I don't want to risk doing it to them both at once."

7

JASMINE

"I need to get back." Jasmine pushed to her feet.

Gabi looked at her. "What's your rush?"

"I'm afraid they will start without me. I want to be there when the prince opens his eyes."

Jasmine wanted to be the first one he saw when he opened his eyes and for the connection between them to be powerful and immediate. It was a silly fantasy that was as anchored in reality as driftwood on a stormy sea, but she didn't want to miss the prince's resurrection on the one-in-a-million chance that it might happen.

Ella put her coffee mug down on the industrial kitchen counter. "Perhaps it's better that they do that without you. When you see what he looks like, you might faint, and they will need to attend to you instead of focusing on the prince."

As her imagination supplied vivid images of what the prince might look like, bile rose in Jasmine's throat. Zombies and ghosts looked better, but whatever. She would hold it together, and if she felt faint, she would walk away so no one would have to take care of her.

"I'll be fine." She took her empty coffee mug, carried it to the sink, and rinsed it. "Are you going to be here?" she asked.

Margo regarded her with worried eyes. "I wanted to go up to the penthouse and shower, but I'm afraid to leave you here alone. You might need someone to hold your hand during the resurrection."

Tears stung the back of Jasmine's eyes as the full impact of Margo's words hit her. She no longer had Edgar to lean on in a time of need, so Margo was offering herself.

With a sigh, she walked over to her friend and wrapped her arms around her. "You are a good friend, Margo. Thank you for having my back, but have you seen the clinic? There is not enough room for everyone who needs to be there to stand, and Kian is doing me a favor by allowing me to witness the revival. As much as I would love to have you there to hold my hand, you can't be there. It would be best if you went up, got a decent shower, and ate something. Come to think of it, you can order delivery from that Chinese restaurant we all love."

"I like the sound of that." Gabi rubbed her tummy. "I'll take care of the delivery." She rose to her feet and took the rest of the cups to the sink.

They parted in front of the clinic, and as her friends continued to the elevators, Jasmine pushed the door open and entered the waiting room, where five imposing people were standing outside the prince's room.

She had no trouble guessing who they were.

The imposing female was, without a doubt, Jade, the Kra-ell leader Jasmine had heard so much about. The four males with her were probably her guards. They did not look purely Kra-ell like their leader, though, and could be mistaken for tall and slim Eurasian men.

Still, even though Jade was a pureblooded Kra-ell, and her eyes were indeed larger than normal and her waist was unnaturally slim, she was not weird looking. She was quite beautiful in an otherworldly and intimidating kind of way.

The female radiated dominance like the most alpha of males, and it was curiously attractive even though Jasmine had never been on the fence about her sexuality. She had always been a hetero through and through, but there was something about Jade that made her pulse quicken a little.

Feeling her gaze, Jade turned and looked at her. "You must be Jasmine." She crossed the few feet between them and offered Jasmine her hand. "I'm Jade."

She didn't smile, but Jasmine did as she took her hand. "I know. I've heard a lot about you."

As she'd expected, the female's handshake was firm and brief. "Same here." Jade lifted her hand and pushed Jasmine's hair aside to expose her ear. "You should put in your earpieces."

"I'll do that when they start." Jasmine glanced at the door to the prince's room. "Are they about to?"

"Not yet, but soon. Did Kian tell you about the latest upgrade to the earpieces?"

Jasmine shook her head.

"They can translate Kra-ell to English and the other way around. If he speaks, you'll be able to understand him. Regrettably, we can't put earpieces on him yet until he has ears, so I'll have to translate things for him."

As bile rose in her throat again, Jasmine swallowed. The prince had no ears?

Shaking off the disturbing visual, she changed the subject. "Everyone refers to the prince and princess as the royal twins. Do they have names?"

"I don't know what they are," Jade admitted. "Priestesses were always referred to as holy mothers, and there were no male priests before the prince. When we left on the settler ship, the twins were still acolytes, and therefore, they were called holy sister and brother in training."

Jasmine nodded, a pang of sympathy welling up in her chest. To have one's identity reduced to a title, to be known only by the role one was meant to play, seemed like a lonely and isolated existence.

Her heart ached for the twins and all they must have endured.

As the door to Bridget's office opened, Kian, Aru, and the doctor stepped out. Kian nodded at Jade and then shifted his gaze to Jasmine.

"Are you sure that you want to witness the resurrection?"

Swallowing again, she nodded. "I am."

8

ARU

Aru approved of Kian's decision and Jasmine's gumption. She had more than earned the right to be there for her prince's revival.

Bridget grimaced. "There is very little room around the stasis chamber."

"I can stay outside," Aru said. "If you leave the door open, that is. I still want to witness this."

Behind him, Negal and Dagor also said they were happy to stay out of the room provided the door was open.

They and Jade's crew had finished transporting the stasis chambers carrying the dead Kra-ell to the catacombs, and even though they had wiped the chambers clean as much as possible before loading them onto the planes, some dust had remained and found its way onto the males' clothing.

Perhaps it wasn't the best idea for them to be so close to the corpse-like fragile prince while he was being revived. With almost no blood in his veins and organs that were a hair away from failing, he might not be able to fight off pathogens in the same way a healthy god or immortal could.

Curiously, Kalugal had opted out of witnessing the momentous event and had gone home, so there was one less person to crowd the packed waiting room.

"I can stay outside as well." Kian turned to Jasmine. "Just remember to keep your earpieces in."

She nodded, her fingers trembling slightly as she pulled the devices out of her jeans pocket and inserted them into her ears. Around her, the others did the same.

Just as she was done adjusting the earpieces, Merlin stepped out of the room and seemed startled at the crowd outside the door.

"If this device is as effective as William assures us it is, the prince had no trackers implanted in him."

Jade nodded. "That makes perfect sense to me. The twins were never supposed to be on the settlers' ship. They were snuck on board covertly minutes before the last pods were sealed. It is extremely unlikely that someone managed to put trackers in them during that time."

Looking at Merlin, Kian tilted his head toward the princess's room. "Just to make sure, please scan the princess as carefully as well."

"I need to be in the room when you revive the prince," Jade said. "He might recognize me from my time serving in the queen's guard." She turned to Aru. "You and the other gods should stay out of his line of sight."

Aru glanced at the petite redheaded doctor. She was almost beautiful enough to pass for a goddess, but not quite. Would the prince think that she was one?

The settlers knew about humans, so he might assume that, and the same was true for Jasmine.

Bridget pursed her lips. "I doubt he will be cognizant enough to evaluate what he's seeing, but I agree that Jade's face will be the least disturbing to him." She looked to her son, who was waiting with a bottle of mountain spring water in each hand. "Get in position, Julian."

Behind him were Jade's hybrids, each holding two bottles, ready to hand them to Julian when needed.

That was enough water to revive several people from stasis, but Aru said nothing. Perhaps the prince's fragile state necessitated more than usual.

As Julian stepped forward, Bridget motioned for Jasmine to get in and stand next to the wall.

Aru expected Julian to pour the first bottle over the prince, but after removing the cap, the young doctor handed it to his mother. "His bones are so brittle and fragile that I'm afraid a strong stream of water might crumble him."

Bridget nodded. "I'll start at his feet and go up. If they fall off, he can regrow them."

Jasmine swallowed hard, her heartbeat so loud that Aru heard it from his position by the door. She wasn't looking at the stasis chamber and the body inside. Instead, her eyes were fixed on Bridget's face.

He wondered if her courage had left her, and she was afraid to see what state the royal was in.

"Here goes," Kian murmured next to him, the low tone sounding even odder through the earpieces.

Aru fought the impulse to adjust the devices. It wouldn't help and would only reduce their effectiveness.

Taking a deep breath, Bridget lifted the bottle and drizzled a few drops over the prince's withered feet.

Aru had seen a baptism on television once, and what Bridget was doing reminded him of the ritual cleansing that was supposed to wash away the sins and sorrows of the past.

When the feet remained intact, Bridget got bolder and sprinkled more water over the parchment-like gray skin.

As the minutes ticked by, the silence was tense, and the only sounds were the steady drip of water, the rasp of everyone's breathing, and their various heartbeats.

Aru tried to ignore all that background noise and focus on the prince, but there was no sign of life in his body, not even a flicker.

He couldn't be dead.

Julian had been monitoring the infrequent heartbeats of the twins, and he would have known if time had run out for the royal.

Still, too much time seemed to have passed since the last heartbeat Aru had heard.

Had he missed one?

Yeah, that was more likely than the doctors not being aware of the prince's passing.

The twins' death would solve many problems, but Aru couldn't bring himself to wish for that. That being said, he wouldn't pray for their survival either.

9

JASMINE

It wasn't working, Jasmine realized with a sickening lurch of dread.

She felt her heart sink, a leaden weight settling in her chest as she watched the scene unfold. She still hadn't looked directly at the prince, afraid of what she would see, but the tense silence and Bridget's pinched expression spoke loud and clear.

Was he dead?

Was his body so depleted that it had crossed the point of no return and couldn't pull itself out of stasis?

Bridget was being very careful. She wasn't filling the stasis chamber with water like Jasmine had imagined she would, turning it into a bathtub. Instead, she was dripping it over the prince, and she wasn't done even with the first bottle Julian had handed her.

When the doctor reached for the second water bottle, Jasmine bit her lower lip to refrain from telling her it wouldn't work like that. She needed to fill the thing so it would cover the prince, leaving only his nose exposed so he could breathe.

But what did she know?

Jasmine had no medical training and knew next to nothing about immortals, gods, or the Kra-ell. Their bodies probably worked very differently from humans, and Bridget had a lot of experience getting people out of stasis.

Closing her eyes for a long moment, Jasmine gave herself another pep talk about not being a chicken, and not wanting to draw attention to herself, she took in a slow, shallow breath.

She turned her head down so that when she opened her eyes, they would be trained straight on the prince, caught her lower lip between her teeth to stop herself from uttering any sound, and started counting.

One, two, three…

She opened her eyes, and a sob lodged in her throat.

Just as Julian had warned her, the prince was in a horrible state, but he didn't look like a zombie, ghost, or corpse.

Well, he did look a little like a corpse, but mostly, he looked like a victim of starvation, and Jasmine hoped that he hadn't been aware of any of it and hadn't suffered.

What surprised her the most was that his clothing was intact. She'd expected something like what she'd seen on mummies—deteriorating scraps of robing or nothing except a loincloth. Instead, the prince was wearing a uniform of some sort, and even though it had probably been form-fitting when he had entered the stasis chamber, it was now loose around his emaciated body, the dark gray fabric clinging to his protruding ribs.

How had it survived for seven thousand years?

If the Kra-ell had survived intact in their chambers, it shouldn't surprise her that their clothing also had. She hadn't looked into the other stasis chambers because they had been transported from the pod to the catacombs locked, but it made sense. The only reason the twins' bodies were in such a horrid state was that they had consumed themselves to keep alive.

When Bridget reached the prince's face, she dripped a few drops on his forehead, eyelids, lips, and cheeks and then repeated the process with infinite patience and care.

Jasmine longed to spread the moisture with her fingers, to see the prince's skin turn pink, but she wouldn't have done that even if she wasn't such a coward. His skin was so fragile that it would probably disintegrate when touched, which was why Bridget was going so slowly.

But wasn't he supposed to be showing some signs of life already?

Jasmine was about to shift her gaze to Kian and check his expression to see if he was worried when a barely-there twitch of the prince's eyelids froze her in place.

She sucked in a breath, and so did everyone else, which meant that she hadn't imagined it.

And there it was again. A flicker of movement, so subtle and fleeting that it could have easily been missed if she wasn't so focused on the prince's face.

A twitch of an eyelid, a flutter of lashes against a sunken cheek.

And then, with a hoarse, rasping gasp, the prince's eyes opened, a sliver of shocking blue amidst the ruin of his face.

For a long moment, he just stared, his gaze unfocused and glassy as he blinked once, twice, but then the haze seemed to clear, and awareness shone from those incredible eyes as he looked straight at her, his gaze locking on to hers with an intensity that stole her breath away.

It was just as she had dreamt it. Hers was the first face he saw when he opened his eyes.

A rush of emotion washed over Jasmine, a tidal wave of joy, relief, and awe at the sight of him alive and awake. It was a miracle, a gift from the Mother of All Life.

The prince's lips parted, a soft, rasping sound escaping his throat as he tried to speak, but the effort was too much, his weakened body failing him, and his eyes fluttered closed once more.

"He's alive," Julian murmured.

"Of course, he is," Bridget said.

"Shouldn't we put an IV in him and feed him intravenously?" Julian asked.

She shook her head. "We don't know if he is more god than Kra-ell or the other way around. He might need blood to survive."

Blood?

Ella hadn't mentioned anything about blood.

Were the Kra-ell vampires?

1 O

KIAN

K ian let out a relieved breath. The Prince had woken up, even if only for a split second.

"Is that normal?" he asked Bridget. "Wasn't he supposed to revive?"

"Dalhu did," Anandur said. "And so did Wonder. As soon as water touched her body, she was awake and didn't lose consciousness since. Well, except for fainting when she saw the Clan Mother."

"Maybe it's his clothing," Jasmine said. "What if it's preventing the water from touching his body?"

Kian opened his mouth to reprimand her for butting in about something she had no clue about, but Bridget's frown stopped him.

"You might be onto something." The doctor put the bottle of water aside, leaned over the prince, and gently peeled back the sleeve of his uniform. "His skin is completely dry underneath." She chuckled. "I'm so embarrassed." She looked up at Jasmine. "It didn't occur to me that his clothing was water resistant because it shouldn't be. Not for a god and not for an immortal. But for a Kra-ell, it didn't matter because the Kra-ell relied on stasis chambers to sustain them."

Julian nodded. "We need to cut it off him, and that scares the crap out of me."

His mother smiled indulgently. "I'll do that. During my residency, I had to remove clothing from burn victims. They were in a much worse state than our prince." She straightened to her full five feet and two inches. "I need everyone to leave while I do this. First, to preserve the prince's dignity, we shouldn't expose him in front of an audience. And secondly, this is going to be a delicate operation, and I want to be able to concentrate on my patient."

Kian nodded. "We can wait in the waiting room."

Bridget shook her head. "This is going to take a long time, and I don't expect him to wake up even after we've soaked his naked body." She let out a breath. "I'll call you if there is any change in his state."

"I need to stay," Jade said. "If he wakes up and can't understand what you are saying, he might freak out. You need someone who speaks Kra-ell."

Bridget hesitated. "I wish the translating earpieces came with a speaker. That would solve the language barrier problem."

"William is working on a device," Kian said. "He told me it should be ready in a day or two."

Jade shook her head. "A translating device is not good enough. The prince will wake up in a different world than the one he left and not the one he expected to arrive at. He is going to be confused and frightened. Seeing a familiar face and hearing his mother tongue will go a long way to make his awakening smoother."

"True." Bridget waved Jasmine and Jade out. "You can stay in the waiting room. I'll call you if he wakes up."

"Should I also stay in the waiting room?" Jasmine asked.

"You should go up to the penthouse, shower, and get something to eat."

Jasmine put a hand on her stomach. "I'm too anxious to eat. I want to make sure that he's okay first."

The exasperated look on Bridget's face had Kian moving toward Jasmine and taking her elbow. "Come. Let's give the doctors room to breathe. They don't function well when people are hovering over them."

Behind Jasmine, Bridget mouthed, "Thank you."

The three gods followed as he led the woman out of the clinic and toward the elevators.

He stopped outside the clinic door and waited for the hybrid Kra-ell, Anandur, and Brundar to join them.

"I'm going to escort Jasmine to the penthouse," he told his bodyguards. "Can you take these men to the kitchen for a bite to eat? You can order a delivery from one of the local restaurants."

Brundar grimaced, but Anandur spoke up. "We are not supposed to leave your side. We should accompany you to the penthouse."

Kian let out a long sigh. "I'm only going to be gone a minute, and then I'll join you in the kitchen."

Anandur still didn't look happy, but he nodded. "If you are not back in five minutes, we are coming up."

As the two groups continued in opposite directions, Aru fell in step with Jasmine. "Good call about the clothing," he said. "I should have thought about that."

She seemed embarrassed by the compliment. "Did you wear the same uniform during your interstellar travels?"

He nodded, pushing his hands into his pockets. "Very similar, but not the same. The gods supplied the settler ship, the pods, the stasis chambers, and everything else. The Kra-ell were not technologically advanced back then and are still not today. It's just not in their culture. They are what humans would call naturalists. They prefer a nomadic lifestyle and keeping things simple. The ship that brought me here was much more advanced, and our uniforms were made from a material different from what the prince was wearing. I wonder if everyone wore that back then or if it was chosen specifically for the Kra-ell."

As the elevator doors opened and they all stepped inside, Jasmine leaned against the mirrored wall. "Why don't the Kra-ell embrace technology?"

Aru shrugged. "There are many reasons, but the most important is cultural."

Kian knew that the explanation was more complex than that, but Aru probably reasoned that this wasn't a good time for Jasmine to get a lesson about Anumati politics and the class system.

11

JASMINE

As Jasmine walked into the penthouse, her heart was still racing with the adrenaline and emotion of the past few hours. The prince's awakening had been fleeting but still left her shaken.

She couldn't believe that she had been the only one who had thought about the clothing being a problem. It should have made her feel smart, and it did, but only a little. Sometimes, an uninformed outsider saw things more clearly than the experts.

Thankfully, Kian parted with Aru and the other gods at the door and headed back down to the clinic, or rather the kitchen where his bodyguards and Jade's crew were waiting. She needed a respite, and he wasn't an easy guy to relax around.

"You are just in time." Margo waved them over to the massive coffee table that was covered with boxes from their favorite Chinese restaurant. "The delivery arrived a few minutes ago, and everything is still hot. Come and dig in."

"We really should move to the dining room," Jasmine grumbled before finding a spot on the carpet beside Ella. "And I need to shower, but I'm hungry, and I also need to talk to you." She glared at Ella.

"What did I do?"

Frankie lifted a hand. "Before anyone says another word, I need to know what's happening with the twins. Were they revived?"

"Bridget is working on the prince," Aru said. "He opened his eyes briefly, tried to say something, and went under again. Bridget won't start on the princess until she has him stabilized."

Everyone's mood seemed to plummet at the news.

"Is he going to be okay?" Margo asked.

Jasmine's throat felt too tight to answer, so all she could do was shrug and fold in upon herself.

"He will be," Aru said with more conviction than Jasmine felt. "Bridget and Julian are cutting away his clothing so the water can touch all of his skin. Bridget kicked us out to preserve his privacy, and she will let us know when and if he wakes up."

"Jade stayed in the clinic in case she was needed," Jasmine said quietly. "Being a Kra-ell, she would look familiar to him and can speak his language." She cast Ella another baleful look.

"What?" Ella asked.

"Never mind." Jasmine took the paper plate Margo was handing her and a pair of chopsticks. "I'm hungry." She reached for one of the boxes and opened it.

"The doctors might decide to put him in an induced coma to help him heal," Margo said. "When Mia's heart gave out and the doctors were fighting for her life, that was what they did."

"Makes sense," Ella said. "Especially since her heart was probably operating at a fraction of the capacity it should have been."

Frankie nodded. "It was such a horrible period in our lives. It changed me."

"Me too." Margo sighed. "But it changed us in different ways. I lost my naive belief that everything would be okay and that I was invincible because I was young, and you decided to throw caution to the wind and live every day as if it were your last."

"True." Frankie popped a piece of orange chicken into her mouth, chewed it, and swallowed. "My way was better because I was having fun."

Margo waved a dismissive hand at Frankie before turning to Jasmine. "You said that the prince was trying to say something. Did Jade understand any of it?"

Jasmine shook her head. "It was just a croak." She closed her eyes and tried to recall every detail of those precious seconds he'd been awake. "His eyes are the most amazing shade of blue. I've never seen eyes like that. And he looked right at me." She lifted her gaze to Aru. "Did you see that? Or was it my imagination?"

"He looked at you," Aru confirmed. "It was mostly a glazed-over look without seeing, but there was some momentary awareness in his gaze." He smiled at her. "You should be glad that his eyes are shaped like a god's and not like a Kra-ell's."

She hadn't thought of that, but it was a good point, and she was relieved that he looked more human than she had expected. The rest of the physical differences didn't bother her as much, except his dietary preferences.

She turned to Ella. "When you told me about the Kra-ell, you forgot to mention one significant detail."

Ella frowned. "I told you about their huge black eyes, but the prince apparently doesn't have them."

"You told me about that, but you didn't tell me about something much more important than the shape of their eyes. They are freaking vampires! They live on blood, Ella! Don't you think it should have been the first thing to mention?"

Ella didn't even look guilty as she shrugged. "You are making too big of a deal about something that is not all that important. They drink from animals, and they don't kill when they drink. It's all very sustainable."

The chuckle that bubbled up from Jasmine's throat sounded manic. "Sustainable? Are you freaking serious? They drink blood!"

"So what? What's the big deal? You drink milk and eat animal flesh, and they drink its blood. They prefer it fresh, that's true, but they can live on frozen store-bought blood, too." She leaned back and looked at Jasmine down her nose. "You didn't seem to have a problem with Edgar's fangs."

"That's because he doesn't drink blood." It dawned on her that she hadn't seen him or even noticed his absence. "Where is Edgar, by the way? Did he leave?"

Ella shrugged. "I didn't see him when we got here. He must have decided to return to the village."

A pang of unease coursed through Jasmine. "He said he would wait for me to return. He also said that we need to celebrate the successful completion of the mission."

"Maybe he went underground to look for you," Frankie said.

"Maybe." Jasmine lifted a piece of broccoli with her chopsticks. "I hope he will return when he doesn't find me."

The truth was that she missed him and felt a little lost without him.

Well, a lot lost.

What would happen to her now? Would she go back to her apartment and her customer service job? Was she still in danger from the Modanas and their cohorts?

Who would induce her godly genes?

Would it be the prince?

As she remembered what he looked like, a shiver ran down Jasmine's spine, and not the pleasant type. It could be months before he was in any state to be intimate with a woman, and then he might remember that he was a celibate priest and not give her the time of day.

Would she have to find another immortal to do the honors?

Mother of All Life, what a mess. Maybe she shouldn't have ended things with Edgar so soon. She could have waited until they were back in the penthouse and had unprotected sex with him.

It wouldn't have been such a great hardship, but it wouldn't have been fair to him unless he was willing to be just the venom donor and didn't expect anything else.

They ate silently for the next few moments, and then Margo put her plate down. "So, what happens now?" Her voice cut through the haze of Jasmine's thoughts like a beacon in the fog. "I mean, we found the twins, we brought them back to the keep. What's the next step?"

Jasmine shrugged. "I honestly have no idea. I feel like a ship adrift in the ocean. I don't know what I'm supposed to do next."

Gabi put her plate down and wiped her mouth with a napkin. "I don't know about you, but I'm glad to be back. I thought we'd be trekking through those mountains for months, freezing our asses off and battling altitude sickness. Thanks to Jasmine, the mission was over much sooner than I expected."

12

MARINA

The day Marina had been simultaneously dreading and eagerly anticipating had finally arrived.

It was time to leave Safe Haven and part with her friends, her family, and the place that had been her temporary sanctuary after her people's liberation from near slavery in Igor's compound and the oppressive rule of the Kra-ell.

The irony wasn't lost on her.

She was willingly moving to a place where her former masters had chosen to reside, and although they weren't in charge there, she couldn't help the apprehension that gripped her at the prospect of facing them again.

Not all had been cruel, but they had all acted superior, looking upon her and the other humans in the compound as less worthy. After a lifetime of believing that was true, she would have a hard time interacting with them without feeling inferior again.

In the immortals' village, the immortals were naturally at the top of the hierarchy, with the Kra-ell below them, and as usual, humans were last. The difference was that the Kra-ell were in-your-face kind of people who never tried to hide how they felt, while the immortals did their best to appear inclusive and respectful but probably felt the same as the Kra-ell.

What if she was making a huge mistake by moving there? Perhaps she should have convinced Peter to stay with her in Safe Haven, where humans were the majority.

Stop it, Marina commanded.

If she didn't like it in the village, she could always return to Safe Haven, and Peter would come with her because he loved her.

Standing in the parking lot of the main lodge, her belongings packed into a single duffle bag at her feet, she watched as the new team of Guardians spilled out of the rented SUV and exchanged greetings with the departing team.

When they embraced and clapped each other on the back, the sound reverberated from the walls enclosing the parking lot, and their male voices were made more boisterous because of the echo amplifying the sound.

Marina saw Larissa rushing to her from the corner of her eye even though they had already said their goodbyes. Her eyes red-rimmed and her face streaked with tears, she pulled Marina into a fierce, desperate hug. "I'm going to miss you so much," she whispered, her voice choked with emotion. "Promise that you'll call every day."

Marina fought back tears as she held Larissa in her arms. "Of course, I will. At least twice a day." She pulled back a little to look into Larissa's tear-stained face. "You can move to the village, too. It's not as difficult to transfer there as we thought. All you have to do is fill out a request form or have Eleanor fill it out for you and sign it. Plenty of jobs exist, and they need people to fill them."

"I can't." Larissa rubbed a hand over her face, wiping off the tears. "I don't want to live with the Kra-ell again and not with the immortals either. I want to be among humans." She grimaced. "I've had enough immortals to last me a lifetime."

Larissa was still in the process of getting over her very short relationship with Jay, and as a result she was sour on all immortals.

"I get it." Marina took her friend's hand and gave it a gentle squeeze. "You need to do what's right for you, staying in Safe Haven and dating human guys."

"Yeah." Larissa let out a watery chuckle, a spark of mischief dancing in her eyes despite the sadness that still clouded them. "I've had enough of immortals, but I'm not going to lie. I will miss the sex and the venom-induced trips." She sighed. "Perhaps I shouldn't be so harsh and give moving to the village some more thought."

They both knew it was nothing more than a joke, a bit of gallows humor to lighten the mood. Larissa's heart was set on staying in Safe Haven and finding a nice human guy to settle down with and have kids.

"You do that," Marina said.

"Right now, I'm still too mad at Jay to even think about it," Larissa admitted in a whisper.

"Why are you so angry at him?" Marina blurted out the question she hadn't dared ask before. "Did he make you any promises? Did he ever lead you to believe it could be more than just a bit of fun?"

Larissa shook her head. "No," she admitted, her voice barely above a whisper.

"Jay was upfront about what it was, but I let myself get carried away and yearned for something that I knew wasn't on the table." Her chin wobbled. "Seeing you and Peter and how happy you are together made me hopeful. You two started the same way as Jay and I, so I thought things with Jay might also grow into more."

Marina pulled her into another hug, holding her close as if she could absorb some of her pain. "I'm sorry," she murmured. "I wish I could wave a magic wand and give you the happy ending you deserve."

Taking a deep breath, Larissa pulled out of Marina's arms. "I deserve better than Jay, that's for sure. I deserve someone who will love me and feel lucky for having snagged a rare find like me." She smoothed her hands over her ample curves. "Because I am worth it."

"Yes, you are." Marina grinned. "You are a goddess."

"That's right." Larissa took another fortifying breath.

A gentle hand on Marina's shoulder made her look up, her gaze meeting Peter's warm eyes.

"It's time to go, love," he said.

Marina nodded and turned back to Larissa. "I'll come visit as often as I can. I don't know the rules in the village, but I'm sure I can come back here with Peter. And maybe you'll change your mind and stay with me for a while."

Larissa smiled. "Come back as soon as you can. And call me when your plane lands so I know you are safe and call me again when you get to the village. I want to hear all about it in detail."

With one last fierce hug, Marina followed Peter to the waiting SUV. The three other Guardians returning to the village with them were already seated, two in the front and one in the back, leaving the middle seat for her and Peter.

After he'd loaded their things into the trunk, he got in, sat down, and wrapped his arm around her. "Have you ever flown in a private jet?"

"Yes. We were picked up from Greenland by private charter planes."

"That's not the same as flying in a luxury executive jet. You are in for a treat." He smiled. "Usually, Charlie flies the teams to and from Safe Haven in the larger and less fancy plane, but he and that plane were needed for another mission, so the jet is being piloted by Eric, the clan's standby pilot."

Marina felt a twinge of apprehension. "Is he any good?"

"He's excellent. Eric served in the Air Force for many years. After getting discharged, he started a private charter-jet business and did that for a while, so he has thousands of flight hours under his belt. You have nothing to worry about."

13

JASMINE

The meal was over, the table was clean, and the leftovers were stored in the fridge, but there was still no sign of Edgar.

Jasmine had thought about calling him, but that wasn't smart. She shouldn't cling to their relationship and rely on him when she'd been the one who had ended things between them.

It wasn't fair to Edgar; she wasn't the type of woman who took advantage of a man's attraction to her.

A small, insidious voice in the back of her head whispered, *why not?* Women did that all the time, especially those the goddess had gifted with good looks and charm.

The truth was that Jasmine wasn't a saint, and she'd used her assets to her advantage in the past, but it had always been with men who saw her as an object of desire, not those who had genuine feelings for her.

Like Edgar.

"Coffee is served, *mesdames et messieurs*." Frankie put the tray down on the coffee table. "Help yourselves."

Gabi leaned back against the plush cushions of the couch, her expression thoughtful as she gazed out the window at the sprawling city below. "Aru and I will probably stay here for a while. My clients are okay with me working remotely, and I even did that from Tibet, but it was a hassle because of the time difference. It's going to be a breeze doing it from here."

"What about you?" Jasmine asked Aru. "What are you going to do now?"

The god looked unsure. "We need to evaluate the equipment we salvaged from the pod. I hope William can help us with that. I also need to figure out our next move." He sighed. "Given the state of the pod we found, I don't have much hope of finding any other pods with living Kra-ell inside. Still, we need to find them and ensure that they don't fall into the hands of humans."

Jasmine felt a pang of sorrow at the thought of all the lives that had been lost and all the hopes and dreams that had been lost with them.

Gabi smiled with a mischievous glint in her eyes as she turned to Frankie and Margo. "You two can finally come to the village and start working as beta testers for Perfect Match."

"That's right." Frankie clapped her hands. "By the way, Mia and Toven are coming over, and they are picking up champagne to celebrate with us. Mia is over the moon that we are back so soon. She expected this to take months."

Jasmine envied what they had so much.

They had all already found their forever mates, had transitioned into immortality, and knew what their future held. At the same time, she was stuck in limbo with nothing more than vague readings from her tarot cards and promises that might or might not come true.

"Do you think I could come see the village?" she asked. "I'd love to see it, and maybe they can find a spot for me on the Perfect Match team."

"I'm not sure," Gabi admitted. "It's not really up to me. Kian will have to make that call." She glanced at the others, a shadow of uncertainty passing over her face. "I hope Kian will be okay with us staying in his penthouse. If not, we will have to look for a place to rent."

"I'm sure Kian will let you stay here," Ella said.

"Yeah, I think he will, but we should ask and not just assume that we can stay." Gabi cocked her head to the side, a curious expression stealing over her features. "Speaking of decisions..." She pinned Jasmine with a questioning look. "I understand that you and Edgar have shifted into the friend zone. Is it friends with benefits?"

Jasmine chuckled. "Before, it was. Now it's only friends. Why?"

Gabi shrugged. "I was just thinking about your induction and who will do it."

Margo shook her head. "Couldn't you have waited a few more days? Now you will have to find someone else to do it."

Jasmine had been thinking the same thing only moments ago, so she shouldn't get angry at Margo for suggesting that she would have been better off using Edgar and discarding him when she got what she needed from him.

"Edgar was fun to be with, and I'll always care about him as a friend, but things just fizzled out between us, and there was no point in dragging it out. It wouldn't have been fair to him if I just used him to induce my transition."

Negal nodded his approval, and Dagor did too.

"You did the right thing," Negal said. "Edgar might be hurting right now, but it would have been much worse if he felt used."

Tears prickled the backs of Jasmine's eyes. "He's a good guy, and he deserves someone who can give him her whole heart and looks at him like he hung the moon and stars for her."

Frankie sighed, a wistful expression stealing over her face. "I just hope your prince will feel that way about you once he wakes up and gets to know you."

"There is no guarantee of that." Gabi winced. "The guy is a celibate priest."

"Was," Jasmine said. "The twins' mother consecrated them to the priesthood to hide them from their people because they looked hybrid, and it was crucial that no one found out. They didn't join out of religious convictions or the wish to serve their people through their spiritual journey. It was just the part they were forced to play."

Jasmine wasn't sure who she was trying to convince, herself or Gabi.

"Still, even if he has no qualms about dropping his celibacy, he might take one look at me and run screaming in the opposite direction."

She'd said that as a joke, but Gabi wasn't smiling.

"There might be another problem," she said. "It is not a foregone conclusion that the prince could induce your transition at all. The Kra-ell don't have that ability. Only the gods and immortals do. Let's hope the prince's venom is as potent as the gods' or the immortals'."

Jasmine nodded as fear and hope mingled in her gut. Gabi was right, and there were no guarantees about anything, but even as doubts and uncertainties coursed through her like a gathering storm, deep down, she knew everything would be okay.

Whether the prince could induce her transition or not, she had to believe he was her destiny, the other half of her soul.

14

THE PRINCE

He was dreaming, his mind a swirling maelstrom of fragmented images and half-formed thoughts he couldn't grasp the threads of, but one image pierced through the fog of confusion, clear as if it was seared into his mind's eye—luminous eyes staring into his as if their owner knew him, knew who he was while he did not.

Could she tell him his name?

Was she the Mother of All Life?

Oh, that was a cohesive thought. A memory. He remembered the Mother. All was not lost.

Had the Mother come to escort him to the fields of the brave?

No. He did not deserve entry.

He had failed.

At what?

He could not remember but felt the failure like a crushing weight on his chest.

If she was the Mother, she came to escort him to the valley of the shamed.

But if she was not the Mother, who was she?

The question echoed through his mind like a relentless drumbeat. It drowned out all other thought fragments.

Who was she?

Who was she?

Who was he?

He had no name, no sense of who or what he had been before the awakening inside a dream. The very concept of identity seemed to slip through his grasp like water through his fingers, leaving him adrift in a sea of uncertainty.

Perhaps he was dead and no longer possessing a separate identity. Maybe he was a part of a larger whole.

Voices murmured around him, hushed and urgent, but their words were little more than a garbled hum to his ears.

Did hearing spoken language mean that he was not dead? In the afterlife, talking was unnecessary because everyone was connected, and thoughts floated on the ether like sparks of light.

Where had that idea and the imagery come from?

A memory tickled his mind, but it was like trying to hold on to a tendril of smoke.

It was no use.

He did not know.

He strained to make out the meaning of the words spoken next to him, to latch on to some scrap of context that might help him piece together the shattered fragments of his reality, but it was no use. The harder he tried to focus, the more the sounds seemed to slip away, fading into the distance like a half-remembered dream.

He tried to open his eyes, to force his way back to the waking world and the answers that surely awaited him there, but his eyelids refused to move. He felt as if they were weighted down by some invisible force that he lacked the strength to overcome.

Panic began to rise in his chest, a clawing, desperate thing that threatened to consume the precarious connection to his consciousness.

Concentrating, he tried to feel anything, but even though his mind did not register any sensations, he still felt a connection to a physical form. Was it an illusion? Or was he trapped, a prisoner in his own unresponsive body?

As fear threatened to overwhelm him, the sense of failure from before reemerged, forcing the fear for himself to a secondary position in his barely functioning mind. It wasn't for himself that he feared but for another.

For her.

Sister.

The realization hit him like a bolt of lightning, a sudden, blinding flash of clarity that cut through the haze of confusion like a knife. He had a sister whose face he could not conjure and whose name danced just beyond the reach of his fractured memory. But he knew with a certainty that defied explanation that he had failed her.

He had vowed to keep her safe, but his promise had been worthless. It had shattered like glass upon the ground.

He had a sacred duty that superseded all others, and he had failed. He failed her, himself, and whoever had entrusted him with his sister's safety.

He wanted to scream, to plead with the Mother to give him another chance to fulfill his duty, but his voice remained locked within his chest, a silent, impotent cry of anguish that echoed only in the confines of his mind.

Despair washed over him in waves, a cold, numbing tide that sapped what little strength he had and left him feeling hollow and utterly alone. He had no idea where he was, no concept of how much time had passed since he had last drawn breath. All he knew was the pain of the all-consuming guilt that gnawed at his soul.

As consciousness began to fade again, he clung to the one scrap of memory that remained, the one thing that tethered him to a world he no longer understood. A pair of intense golden eyes staring into his own with hope and some other emotion he couldn't decipher.

Whoever she was, that female was his lifeline, his beacon in the dark.

15

PETER

Marina squeezed Peter's hand as the car's windows turned opaque and the vehicle slipped into autonomous mode. "I'm so excited. I'm finally here."

"Almost." He leaned over and kissed her temple.

He'd warned her about the windows so she wouldn't freak out, and he also told her about the underground tunnel leading into the mountain that the village sat on top of.

When the car wound its way into the tunnel's hidden entrance, Marina's eyes widened, and her hold on his hand tightened.

Peter had seen this journey countless times before, and the James-Bond-style high-tech marvels that guarded their secret sanctuary no longer registered, but seeing them through Marina's eyes, he once again noted the miracle of ingenuity that was involved.

Most of the credit belonged to William, but the guy didn't work alone. He had a team of bright minds working under him, coming up with innovative solutions and technologies.

The air grew cold and damp as they descended deeper into the earth, and even though the windows were still opaque, they admitted light, which was absent in the tunnel. Peter wondered why no artificial lighting had been installed, or maybe it had been, and it just wasn't on when there was no need for it. The car drove itself, and it was perfectly able to navigate in the dark.

As Marina shivered, pressing herself closer to his side, he wrapped an arm around her shoulders. "Are you cold?" he asked.

"A little. But mostly, I'm spooked. I don't like dark places, and I don't like being underground. I hated that my cabin on the ship didn't have a window."

"Don't worry." He lifted their conjoined hands and kissed the back of hers. "We are not going to stay underground for long. After we park, we will take the elevator to the surface, and you'll see how full of sunlight the village is." He glanced at his watch. "The sun will set soon, but we still have enough time to see most of the village. It's not that big."

"When are the windows going to clear?" she asked.

"When the car enters the elevator, which will happen in one, two, and… three." The car stopped, and a moment later, they lurched up.

"Amazing," Marina whispered. "It's like a science fiction movie."

"It is." He smiled. "I've gotten used to it, so I don't see it anymore, but watching the marvels through your eyes makes me excited about it again."

When the elevator doors opened with a soft ding and a pneumatic hiss, revealing the cavernous underground parking garage, Marina's jaw dropped, her eyes darting from one sleek row of vehicles to the next.

"So many cars," she whispered.

It dawned on him then that Marina had never been to a mall or supermarket. She'd never seen a sprawling parking lot full of cars of every make, shape, and color.

"I need to take you to see the city."

Her cheeks pinked. "I sounded provincial, didn't I?"

He laughed. "Where have you ever heard that word?"

"I don't remember. Maybe I heard it in one of the movies or shows I've watched lately or dreamt it." Marina chuckled. "I don't know when it happened, but lately, I've started to think and dream in English."

"That's good." He opened the door. "It indicates mastery of the language, which you have." He stepped out of the vehicle.

One of the other Guardians beat him to Marina's door and opened it for her. "Welcome to the village, Marina."

"Thank you." She stepped out and looked around. "I'm already impressed, and I've only seen the parking garage. We have one bus and two cars in Safe Haven, and we didn't have much more than that in the compound in Karelia. I've never seen so many cars in real life."

There were still so many things he could show her that would make the parking garage seem like nothing, and Peter was excited at the prospect of being her guide.

As they gathered their luggage and made their way toward the elevators that would take them to the surface, Peter felt a flutter of excitement in anticipation of the moment Marina would lay eyes on the village for the first time.

He had told her about it, of course, painting vivid pictures of the lush greenery, winding paths, and cozy homes, but he wasn't great with words and could only convey so much without showing her actual photos, which he didn't have.

When the elevator doors slid open, revealing the sun-drenched pavilion with its soaring glass walls and displays of ancient artifacts, the look of slack-jawed amazement that crossed Marina's face made Peter grin.

She darted out of the elevator, her eyes wide and her steps faltering as she took in the display that lined the walls. Ancient pottery and intricately carved statues, gleaming blades, and clay tablets carved with ancient symbols were a treasure trove of history.

"What is all this?" Marina walked from one item to the next, her voice hushed with reverence as she ran her fingers along the glass.

"Kalugal is an amateur archeologist, and this is his collection," Peter explained. "Calling him an amateur is doing him a disservice. He might not do it for profit or fame, but he's very serious about it. When he moved to the village, he brought his entire hoard with him, and this is just a small sample of what he's got squirreled away in storage on the lower levels. From time to time, he rotates the exhibits, so we always have a fresh display." He walked over to stand by her side. "He also adds descriptions and explanations about each item."

Peter pressed a button, and a recording started, with Kalugal lecturing about that particular artifact. He let it play for a minute and then stopped it. "When you are bored and have nothing better to do, you can come here and listen to his lectures."

"I certainly will. This is fascinating."

He put his arm around her. "Maybe you'll discover that archeology is your passion."

"Maybe." She raised her glowing face to him, lifted on her toes, and kissed him on the lips. "Thank you for bringing me here."

"You're welcome, but you've seen nothing yet."

16

MARINA

Marina gasped as they stepped out into the sunlight, her free hand flying up to shade her eyes against the brightness. Peter had been right about the place being drenched in sunlight. It was almost as sunny as it was during the cruise.

The lush greenery was perfectly manicured, with narrow paths intersecting green lawns and patches of bushes and trees. There was a large pond and a playground, where several Kra-ell children were playing, most of them hybrid.

Out of everything that Marina had expected to see, this sight was the most shocking. The children were playing, laughing, yelling, and running around like human kids. She'd never seen them doing that in Igor's compound.

They had been highly disciplined, and their days had been spent learning and training.

Evidently, not only the humans of the compound had been freed, but also the Kra-ell, whom she used to think of as her masters.

"Welcome to the village, Marina," Peter murmured as he pulled her into his arms and spun her around in a giddy circle.

Clinging to him, she laughed, the sound bright and carefree to her ears.

Behind them, Alfie trundled along with their luggage and a long-suffering expression. "Are we walking or calling for the cart?" he asked.

Marina's eyes widened, her head whipping around to face Alfie. "There are carts?"

"There are," Peter confirmed. "But I thought we could walk so I can show you everything on the way and give you time to drink it all in."

Marina nodded. "I'd like that." She laced her fingers through Peter's once more.

They set off, with Peter pointing out the café, where people were sitting and having coffee and pastries. Recognizing her from the cruise, probably because of her blue hair, some smiled and waved, and she smiled and waved back.

As he showed her the office building and the clinic, Marina fought the impulse to look at the playground again and this time observe the parents. Or, more to the point, assess their response to seeing her.

But there was plenty of time to make assessments, and right now she needed to show Peter how happy she was to be in the village and respond with joy and enthusiasm to everything he was showing her.

He seemed even happier than she was about her being with him, and she didn't want to spoil the fun for him by introducing a potential problem he hadn't given any thought to.

"Do you want to see the playground?" Peter asked. "You keep looking at it."

"The children just look so happy. I never saw the Kra-ell kids smile like that back in the compound or heard them laughing out loud. It was always so grim, so oppressive there. I can't believe how quickly they have changed." She shifted her gaze to Peter. "It seems like the liberation of Igor's compound happened so long ago, but in reality, it didn't."

Peter nodded, his smile softening as he looked at the children. "It's easy to get used to good things. Jade is doing an incredible job with her people, but it wasn't smooth sailing by any means."

Marina chuckled. "I bet. They are such a combative people. I think they need a strong leader just to keep them from killing each other." She winced. "Sorry. I forgot that you dated one of them."

"I don't think Kagra is like that. She wants to be like Jade when she grows up, and she is emulating her leader. She's also more levelheaded than most of the other pureblooded females."

Marina didn't like that he thought so well of Kagra, but she was smart enough to keep her mouth shut and not say anything snippy about the female. It would only make her look petty and jealous.

As Peter led her to the newest section of the village, he explained that it was home to the Guardians and council members, and he seemed excited about showing her his house.

They crossed a small pedestrian bridge, walked up the street for a few minutes, and then Peter stopped in front of one of the houses. "This is it. That's where we live." He turned to her. "Your new home."

"It's beautiful." She lifted her head and kissed him on the lips. "Are you going to carry me over the threshold?"

"Of course."

He swung her into his arms.

Behind them, Alfie snickered.

Peter turned to him. "Don't just stand there. Open the door for us."

"Yes, sir." Alfie reached over and pushed the door open.

"Welcome home, Marina," Peter said as he carried her inside.

Holding on to his neck, she looked around the beautiful living room. "Did you decorate it?"

Peter chuckled. "It wouldn't be so pretty if I had done it. Ingrid chose all the colors and finishes, and she also ordered the furniture and all the accessories." He kept going. "Alfie and I just brought over our clothes and shoes." He entered the bedroom and put her down on the bed. "Do you like?"

"It's all beautiful," Marina breathed. "And there is so much space. I could live in this bedroom."

Peter grinned, pulling her into his arms and kissing her forehead. "That can be arranged," he murmured, his voice low and filled with promise.

Desire stirred inside of her, but she pushed it aside. There would be plenty of time for that. Right now, she wanted to explore the wonders of her new house.

"Can I see the kitchen?"

"Sure." Peter offered her a hand up.

When they entered the living room, Alfie cleared his throat. "Should I start packing my bags?"

"Don't be ridiculous," Peter said. "This is your home. Nothing has changed."

Not looking convinced, Alfie turned to Marina. "Are you sure? I can find another Guardian to room with."

"Don't you dare." She smiled. "I would hate it if you left because of me. Besides, you'll regret it if you leave."

Alfie tilted his head. "Why is that?"

"You have yet to taste my cooking. Once you do, you will never consider leaving again."

"You are that good, eh?" He sounded skeptical.

"I am. And I will prove it to you."

17

JASMINE

J asmine stepped out of the bathroom, her hair still damp from the shower, and changed into a comfortable pair of leggings and an oversized blouse that was still nice enough for an informal celebration. The pair of low-heeled mules would make the outfit a little more festive, but that was as far as she was willing to go in preparation for the party.

She was exhausted from the trip, her anxiety over the prince, and the drama of breaking up with Edgar.

Nevertheless, she was sufficiently energized to make a run to the clinic and check on the prince's progress. Bridget hadn't called, so there was no change, and he was still unconscious. However, Jasmine wanted to see if they had successfully taken him out of the stasis chamber and transferred him to the hospital bed.

Hopefully, the doctors hadn't broken anything or caused him additional damage in the process.

She couldn't shake the image of his emaciated body, the way his skin stretched taut over his bones—looking gray, dry, and brittle. She couldn't even imagine what he looked like when he wasn't starved and on the verge of death.

"I'm going to check on the prince," she told Gabi, the only one in the living room.

"Don't be long," Gabi said. "We have a party to prepare."

"I won't. He's still unconscious, so it's not like I'm going to stay around and chat." Jasmine forced a smile and opened the door.

As she exited the elevator on the clinic level, the clicking of her mules echoed in the empty hallway, making her regret her choice of footwear. She didn't want to announce her presence.

When she entered the clinic, the doors to the prince's room and Bridget's office were closed, and only the door to the princess's room was open. Jasmine peeked inside and wasn't surprised to see that the doctors hadn't removed her from the stasis chamber yet.

Morbid curiosity propelled her to look into the open chamber, and as she'd expected, the princess looked as skeletal as her brother. Still, it was easy to see that she was a female, even in her emaciated state. The bone structure was more delicate, and she was smaller.

As the door in the next room opened, Jasmine rushed out to catch whoever was there before they closed it.

"Doctor Bridget," she called out when she saw the red ponytail on the woman leaning over the hospital bed.

Evidently, they had moved the prince.

Bridget turned around. "Oh, hi, Jasmine. What can I do for you?"

"I just came to see how he was doing."

Bridget straightened and let out a breath. "As you can see, we moved him and hooked him up to the equipment."

An intravenous feeding tube was attached to the back of his hand, and various monitoring equipment was showing stats that Jasmine didn't know how to interpret. She could tell that things were working, though, and that they were steady.

"Is he going to make it?"

Bridget shrugged. "His body will, but I can't guarantee that his mind will as well. He's still unconscious, but he's stable."

Jasmine nodded, her gaze drifting to the prince's face. Even in his weakened state, his features had a regal quality.

He was so still, his chest barely rising and falling with each shallow breath.

"Are you going to stay here overnight?" she asked the doctor.

Bridget nodded. "Julian and I will stay in the keep for as long as the twins need us." She smiled. "My mate is used to sleeping with me on a hospital bed."

Jasmine swallowed. "You can take over my room. I can sleep on the couch in the living room."

Bridget smiled. "Thanks for the offer, but I want to be near my patients."

"If you change your mind, just come up to the penthouse."

"It's okay." Bridget walked over to her and clapped her on the back. "This is the life of a physician, and I love what I do." She walked Jasmine to the door. "Go. Celebrate with your team." She opened the door and gently shoved her out.

"I'll come back tomorrow morning."

"Of course. Good night, Jasmine." Bridget closed the door.

With a heavy heart, Jasmine made her way back to the penthouse. As she entered, she found Margo, Frankie, Gabi, and Ella already hard at work, setting out platters of food and arranging bottles of various liquors on the kitchen counter.

They looked so full of energy and excitement, their immortal bodies needing much less rest than her human one.

Jasmine felt a pang of envy at their energy and high spirits. She was exhausted, both physically and emotionally, and all she wanted to do was crawl into bed and sleep for a week or at least one full day.

Ella turned to her. "Hi. How is the prince?"

"They moved him to the bed, and they are feeding him intravenously." Jasmine pushed a strand of hair behind her ear. "I guess it doesn't matter what his diet is for that, and they are only feeding him liquids."

Ella nodded. "Some things are universal."

"Is Edgar back?" she asked.

"Nope," Margo said. "Haven't seen him."

Jasmine wondered where he had gone. His things were still in the bedroom they had shared before the mission, so she knew he was coming back to collect them, and he had also promised her that he would be back for the party.

The prospect of not seeing him again triggered a pang of regret. Letting him go had been the right thing to do, but that didn't make the separation any easier. She still craved his company.

The prince was an unknown, and things might not take off between them, while with Edgar, she knew where she stood. If she were smart or a little less principled, she would have stayed with Edgar until she knew whether the prince was an option. As the saying went, it was better to have one bird in the hand than two up on the branch or something like that.

She smiled as her mind conjured an image of Edgar and the recovered prince sitting in a tree with their feet dangling below. Maybe they could be friends, but she doubted that.

The doorbell ringing startled Jasmine out of her reverie, and as she turned to see who was at the door, she expected it to be Edgar, but Margo's squeal of happiness indicated otherwise. Margo liked Edgar, but not that much.

Curiosity getting the better of her, Jasmine put down the glasses she was carrying to the table and walked over to the entryway to see what all the fuss was about.

Her jaw nearly hit the floor when she saw Mia, standing on her own two feet with Toven beside her. He was holding a large bag in one hand and extending the other towards his mate, ready to catch her if she stumbled.

"Your legs," she murmured like an idiot. "You are standing."

Mia's small feet were encased in a soft pair of slippers, and she walked inside with a hesitant but determined gait.

The regeneration process of her legs had been long and arduous, taking many months, but it was finally complete, and Mia was walking on her own two feet.

It was a miracle. Possible only because she had turned immortal.

Frankie started crying, and Margo quickly followed suit. Then, the three friends clutched each other in a fierce embrace, all of them shedding happy tears.

Jasmine felt her eyes well up as she watched them sharing this incredibly happy moment with Mia, celebrating her victory. The trio were more than just friends; they were more like sisters, and Jasmine envied their closeness.

All she had were two hostile stepbrothers, her manager, and her friendship with Margo. The rest of her so-called friends were fellow actors she'd met during the various productions she had participated in over the years. Those relationships could not compare with that of the three childhood friends.

Gabi came up beside her, wrapping an arm around her waist. "I love happy endings, don't you?"

Jasmine nodded, a lump forming in her throat. "Who doesn't?"

18

EDGAR

E dgar clutched a shopping bag full of books as he stepped out of the elevator on the penthouse level. It was his parting gift to Jasmine, and he hoped she would appreciate the gesture and the effort he'd put into thinking about it and acquiring it.

There should be a guide for clueless guys about what gift fit which occasion. Females seemed to know stuff like that intuitively, but most guys needed help.

At first, Edgar had thought of getting her some perfume, which most women liked, but it was too generic and meaningless. The same was true for chocolate or wine. Then it dawned on him. Jasmine had complained about having only two paperbacks with her, and somehow, they had never found the time to stop by a bookstore before heading out to Tibet. It had been mostly his fault for always finding other things to do that had been more important than that, and in retrospect, he realized that he had been too selfish, and Jasmine had been too accommodating. She should have insisted.

He'd spent hours at the bookstore, going numb while leafing through the most popular romance novels of the day.

Ultimately, he'd chosen the ones that had more going on than just he-loves-me, he-loves-me-not. Jasmine was an intelligent woman, and he was certain that she needed more than such simplistic plots to fulfill her. But then, women were a mystery, and he might be totally off.

She'd said that she read to relax and forget about all the crap that was going on in the world, so maybe those simplistic storylines were precisely what she needed.

Well, she wasn't getting that. He'd taken a gamble and bought her one book with dragon riders that was pretty cool and appealed to the pilot in him, a couple about vampires, and a whole series based on fairy tale retelling. The saleslady assured him that it was trending and that he couldn't go wrong.

He tried to muster a smile as he walked in, but it felt forced. "Hello, everyone." He waved.

Jasmine looked up as he approached and cast him a smile that melted some of the ice around his heart. "You are just in time. Mia and Toven got here a few minutes before you, and we haven't started yet."

He glanced at Mia, noting that something was missing.

Her wheelchair wasn't there. She was sitting on the couch with Toven on one side and Margo on the other, and as Edgar's gaze drifted down, he saw that she wasn't wearing one of her long skirts or covering her legs with a blanket. She had on form-fitting pants, and her small feet were on full display, clad in shoes resembling slippers.

"Congratulations, Mia. I'm so happy to see your regeneration is complete."

"Thank you." She beamed at him and lifted her feet, twisting them this way and that. "I wish it was warmer outside so I could wear sandals or flip-flops and show off my new toes."

Smiling indulgently, Toven patted her knee. "Remember what Bridget said, love. You need to start with comfortable footwear and slowly transition to other styles."

Mia pouted. "She wanted me to wear orthopedic shoes, but I drew the line at that. I didn't suffer through all these months to go back to wearing granny shoes."

As the discussion moved to all the styles Mia wanted to try out as soon as possible, Edgar sat on the floor next to Jasmine and put the paper bag in front of her.

"I got you some books," he murmured.

Her eyes widened, and she pulled the bag closer to peer inside. "Thank you." She lifted her gaze to him. "Is that where you went? To a bookstore to look for books for me?"

He nodded. "You complained about having to reread the same two old paperbacks. I thought I'd replenish your supply before I left."

"That's so sweet of you." She leaned over and kissed his cheek.

"Take them out and see if they are to your liking. It was a challenging task finding something that you might like." He reached for one of the Snake Venom beer bottles lined up on the coffee table.

"I bet." Jasmine chuckled and reached into the bag, pulled out one of the fairy tale retellings, and cooed over it like it was treasure trove.

Edgar took a long swig of the beer, letting the cold liquid coat his throat. It would take much more than one bottle to numb the ache in his chest, but the night was still young, and the table was loaded with bottles.

"They are perfect." Jasmine returned the books to the paper bag. "Now I will have plenty to read to pass the time while I wait..." She didn't finish the sentence and cast him an apologetic look instead.

She didn't have to.

Edgar knew what Jasmine would be doing over the next several days. He'd stopped by the clinic and asked Bridget about her progress with the twins, and she'd given him an update. The prince was still unconscious, but he was being fed intravenously and monitored, and Edgar could see Jasmine sitting in the chair next to him like he was her mate or a family member, and not an alien she'd never met and knew nothing about.

As time passed and the drinks kept flowing freely, the tight sensation in Edgar's chest started to ease. However, his brain was still fully onboard, and the anger and disappointment that had been his constant companions for the past couple of days were just as vocal when drunk as they had been when sober.

"Are you okay?" Jasmine asked.

Edgar barked out a laugh. "No, I'm not okay." He took another swig of his beer. "I would have stayed, you know. To be with you. But I'm needed in the village. I'm the clan's only helicopter pilot." He snorted. "Well, Kian and Kalugal have learned how to fly helicopters on the simulator, so they can do that now, and maybe I'm no longer needed."

"That's nonsense, and you know it," Jasmine said. "That's your job, and you are very good at it. No one is going to take it away from you."

He finished what was left in the bottle, put it down, and reached for a new one. "Yeah. They are both too important to fly themselves, let alone others." He took a swig from the new bottle. "Come with me, Jasmine," he slurred his words. "You'll be happy in the village." He waved a hand in a big arc. "You have nothing here. I can give you everything that he can't."

"I'm sorry, but I can't," Jasmine said with sadness in her eyes. "I wish I could."

The finality in her words was like a knife to his heart, and suddenly, he couldn't stand another moment with her. Pushing to his feet he staggered back, nearly tripping, and the room spun around him, the faces of the others blurring together.

He had to get out of there.

"I need to go."

"You shouldn't drive when you are in a state like this," Toven said. "Mia and I can take you back to the village."

Edgar waved a dismissive hand. "That's what autonomous driving is for. Good night, everyone." He stumbled toward the door.

Jasmine called after him, but he ignored her and closed the door behind him. The elevator was right there, and as he got inside, the doors slid closed.

Alone at last, he leaned his forehead against the cool mirror glass and squeezed his eyes shut so he wouldn't have to look at himself.

19

JASMINE

Jasmine stood before the bathroom mirror and dabbed concealer on the dark circles under her eyes.

Despite the exhaustion and the discomforts of the trip to Tibet and the comfortable, fresh-smelling bed in a fancy bedroom inside the multimillion-dollar penthouse, she hadn't slept as well as she should have.

The opulent bedroom had felt empty and cold without Edgar beside her in bed, and when Jasmine couldn't fall asleep, she'd opened one of the books he'd gotten for her, reading until her vision blurred and her eyes refused to stay open.

That should have been enough to have her sleeping like a log, but she'd been plagued by strange dreams, or rather, nightmares. Upon waking, she realized that she'd dreamt scenes from the sci-fi movie *Stargate*, but she'd substituted the prince for the evil, life-sucking creature in the film.

It wasn't hard to guess why she'd had such nasty dreams about the prince. It had started with Edgar's comments, then she'd discovered that the Kra-ell needed blood for sustenance, and the kicker had been seeing the prince's emaciated form inside the stasis chamber.

When dressed and ready for the day, Jasmine stepped into the living room expecting to see her roommates, but no one was there. The only evidence of her companions' presence in the living room that morning was the half-full coffee carafe on the kitchen counter.

The coffee was cold, but Jasmine had no patience to brew a fresh pot. She poured a cup, sweetened it with sugar, and added milk so it didn't taste as stale.

She needed to find out what was going on with the prince.

Bridget hadn't called, which could mean that he was still unconscious or that the doctor no longer considered Jasmine as someone who needed to be informed.

She had served her purpose, and now she was not needed anymore. Should she go back to her apartment and her old job? She'd given in her resignation, but they would take her if she wanted to go back. There was always a need for experienced customer service reps at the call center.

Kian had promised to find her something better, but that seemed like ages ago, and now she was in limbo. She still had the credit card he had given her, but she didn't feel right using it for anything other than buying stuff related to the mission, and that was over.

With a sigh, Jasmine opened the penthouse door, stepped into the vestibule, and called for the elevator. Lifting her face to the camera above the door, she smiled and waved, knowing that the place was monitored twenty-four-seven.

Thankfully, her thumbprint had been inputted into the database as soon as they had returned, so she could use the private elevator to take her directly to the underground level.

She hadn't been granted access to that level before the mission, so it may mean she was now considered part of the team even though her part was done. Then again, she hadn't needed access to that level before.

She first peeked into the prince's room when she got to the clinic. He already looked much better than the day before, and the monitoring equipment readouts indicated steady outputs, a sign that he was doing well.

Or so she hoped.

Her medical knowledge was limited to what she'd seen on TV and in the movies, so it wasn't much. Come to think of it, however much it was, given the sources, it was all questionable at best.

"Good morning, Jasmine." Bridget startled her.

She spun around. "Good morning, doctor. How is the prince doing?"

Bridget glanced at the monitors. "He's doing well. Now it's a matter of waiting for him to wake up."

"So, he's not in an induced coma?"

The doctor shook her head. "There is no need. Physically, he's recovering as expected, given his condition. It's just his mind that I'm worried about." She gave Jasmine a sad smile. "You can sit next to him, if you like, and talk to him or read him a book."

Jasmine frowned. "He won't understand a word I'm saying."

"True, but he might be drawn to the sound of your voice. It's better than just letting the television provide the stimuli."

Jasmine nodded. "I'll do that."

"Do you want me to lend you a book?" Bridget asked.

Jasmine chuckled. "I'm an actress." She tapped her temple. "I have scores of scripts memorized. I can entertain him for hours with just what's stored in my head."

20

MARINA

The morning sun was climbing across the sky when Marina and Peter stepped out of the house, her hand tucked in his. The village was stirring to life, but the people she saw on the paths were not on their way to work. Given their sporty attire, they were on their way to some exercise facility, some fast walking, others jogging or cycling.

"Does everyone here start their workday late?" she asked.

"Most clan members work from home." Peter led her down the winding path. "So, they can set their own hours." He smiled. "And some don't work at all and engage in creative activity that is not commercial in nature. Every clan member gets a share of the profits the clan enterprises generate, and if they are okay with a modest lifestyle, they don't need to work." He leaned closer to whisper in her ear. "Guardians are very well paid, and I've been promoted twice already, and my pay increased accordingly. You don't have to work if you don't want to. You can be my pampered sex slave."

Marina chuckled. "As tempting as that sounds, I want to work and have my own source of income. I also want to meet people and not be chained to your bed twenty-four-seven." She smirked. "Although, I wouldn't mind that occasionally…"

Teasing aside, Peter might not always be around. He might tire of her or find his immortal or dormant truelove mate, and she needed to save for a rainy day.

It was a conclusion that Marina didn't like giving too much thought to, but she was painfully aware that she'd also once harbored the belief that her ex would be her forever one. Love blinded people to reality, and she wouldn't make the same mistake twice.

Peter kept introducing her to the people they were passing by, but there was no way Marina was going to remember all the names and faces. There were so many, and they all blurred together in a whirlwind of beautiful smiles and greetings.

The good thing was that no one had sneered at her or looked down their noses at her.

Finally, they arrived at the village café, a tiny building the size of a small train car with many adjacent outdoor seats. There were umbrellas over the tables, which probably served more to provide shade than to shield people from rain.

As the smell of freshly brewed coffee and baked goods wafted to greet them, Marina's stomach growled in anticipation.

"I wish I could stay and have breakfast with you." Peter squeezed her hand. "But all I can do is introduce you to Wonder, and then I have to run. My meeting starts in less than fifteen minutes." He pulled a card out of his pocket and pressed it into her hand. "Use this to pay for stuff in the café."

"I have money." She patted her pocket.

Peter shook his head. "You can't pay with money here. Only with the card."

Marina nodded. "Should I wait for you here until after your meeting?"

"Yes, but don't wait for me to have breakfast. I want you to eat, and when I come back, you can have coffee with me." He leaned down and kissed her cheek. "I hope to return bearing gifts."

He was getting her a clan phone, one of those fancy ones with internet access so she could read and watch movies.

"Yay!" Excitement thrumming in her chest, she lifted on her toes, wound her arms around his neck, and kissed him hard.

With a groan, he kissed her back, held her tightly for a few seconds, and then pushed her away. "I can't be late. Onegus will have my head." He turned toward the little booth where two gorgeous brunettes were serving customers. She knew Wonder, who had married the big redhead, but she wasn't sure she had seen the other one on the cruise. "Talk to Wonder. She's the one in charge."

"Okay."

He cast her an apologetic look. "I'll come find you as soon as I'm done." And then he was gone, striding down the path with his long legs.

Marina took a deep breath and walked over, but there was a long line of people waiting to be served, and she felt awkward about approaching Wonder and distracting her from her work, so she stood in line and waited until it was her turn.

"Marina," Wonder greeted her with a friendly smile. "Welcome to the village."

Marina was surprised that the female knew who she was. "Thank you. I was hoping I could talk to you about a job here."

Wonder grimaced. "I'm a little busy right now, but if you take a seat, I'll come to you when it gets a little less crazy here."

"Okay." Marina started to turn.

"Wait." Wonder stopped her. "Did you have breakfast yet?"

Marina shook her head.

"What can I get you? Do you want coffee, a Danish, a sandwich?"

It felt so awkward to be served by the immortal. "Coffee would be nice. And a Danish too, and a sandwich." She smiled sheepishly. "Peter has nothing in his house, and I'm famished. We just got here yesterday and didn't have time to go grocery shopping."

Wonder gave her a sympathetic smile. "Don't worry. I'll take care of you."

"Thank you." Marina pulled out the card Peter gave her and put it on the counter.

Wonder pushed it back to her. "It's on the house. Employees eat for free, and you are a future employee."

"You haven't even interviewed me yet."

Behind Wonder, the other female snorted. "If you want the job, you're hired." She handed a cup of coffee to the guy waiting for it and then offered Marina her hand. "I'm Aliya."

With a twinge of apprehension, Marina took the female's hand. "Nice to meet you."

The hybrid Kra-ell was surprisingly gentle as she shook her hand, and her smile was genuine. "Same here. I think I saw you on the cruise. You were serving food in the dining hall."

"That's right. I don't know how I missed you." Marina felt bad about not noticing Aliya.

"I didn't sit in the section you served."

Marina wanted to say that she had also attended some of the weddings as a guest, and she still hadn't seen her. Perhaps the female didn't like weddings and had stayed away.

After collecting her coffee, sandwich, and pastry, Marina took the tray to the only available table and sat down. She was lucky that most of the customers took their purchases to go, or she wouldn't have found a place to sit.

She was long done with her breakfast when the traffic in the café dwindled to a trickle and Wonder left Aliya to take care of things.

"Sorry it took so long." She pulled out a chair and plopped down. "It's crazy from six to nine in the morning, and then we have three hours of relative calm until the lunch rush starts. We close at six in the evening, though. So at least there is an end in sight."

"It's still a long day."

Wonder smiled. "It's not as difficult as it sounds. But that's because I'm immortal, and Aliya is half Kra-ell. Wendy used to work with us full time, which made things easier and allowed us to take days off from time to time, but after she enrolled full time in college, she switched to only working here on the weekends."

Marina tried to remember who Wendy was. The name sounded familiar, so maybe she had been one of the brides, but which one?

"For a human, it's tough," Wonder continued. "I don't expect you to work as hard as we do. If you can work during the rush time, that would greatly help us. Six to nine, and then twelve to three. Six hours total with three hours to rest between shifts shouldn't be too hard."

"I can work six to three."

Wonder grinned. "That's even better."

"How come the café is so busy?"

"This is the only place in the village open during the day, so everyone stops by to get their caffeine fix and something to eat."

"What happens after six?" Marina asked.

"We have vending machines in the back for those who want some coffee and a snack after hours, and Callie's restaurant is open four nights a week. Atzil's bar is open only on Friday and Saturday nights, but he's looking for more help to expand his hours. The bottom line is that you can pick your jobs around here." Wonder leaned closer to Marina. "But I hope you pick the café. Aliya and I need a third set of hands."

Marina worried her lower lip. "I don't know how to operate that coffee machine you have there. I can make great sandwiches, though."

"The pastries and the sandwiches are supplied by Jackson's bakery and kitchen. We just serve them. We only make coffee, tea, and hot cocoa."

"Well, that makes things easy. When can I start?"

Wonder grinned. "You can start today if you want. Now that it's not that busy, it is the perfect time to show you how to work the cappuccino machine."

21

JASMINE

J asmine sat by the prince's bedside, acting out scripts she'd memorized over the years. Some of them were musicals, so she sang the parts, the female and the male ones, just modified for her range.

She knew he couldn't understand her and that the words were just a jumble of meaningless sounds to his ears, but he might enjoy her singing, and since her acting imbued the words with emotion, he might understand that as well.

After all, people were the same whether they were humans, immortals, or Kra-ell.

She tried to keep it down, and she didn't want to distract or disturb Bridget and Julian while they were working on the princess in the next room.

Later, when Bridget walked in to check on the prince, Jasmine asked, "Am I bothering you and Julian?"

Bridget smiled. "Not at all. You are very talented and entertaining. It's like listening to a Broadway show from the dressing room."

Jasmine dipped her head. "Thank you. I wish the casting directors at all my auditions shared your opinion."

Bridget canted her head. "Looks and talent are two legs of the stool. The third is luck, and the Fates had different plans for you, so they didn't make you lucky."

Jasmine chuckled. "I'd like to think that. It's so much better than thinking I wasn't good enough."

Bridget turned to look at the prince. "Everyone is smart in retrospect, and the Fates don't like to show their hand. Perhaps your future is something you haven't even imagined yet." She stepped out of the room, leaving the door slightly ajar and Jasmine to ponder what she'd said.

What if the prince was just one more steppingstone toward a different future?

Jasmine closed her eyes and tried to think outside the box. What else could her future be? She was talented in many things but not exceptional in any of them. Her voice was strong, and she had perfect pitch, but it wasn't unique. She also wasn't a songwriter, and it seemed like these days, every successful singer had to come up with original pieces of their own.

A knock on the door pulled her out of her reveries, and as Jasmine turned and saw who it was, she tensed.

"Good morning," Kian said as he walked in with William.

"Good morning. My earpieces are in." Jasmine moved her hair aside to show William that she was wearing them.

William smiled. "Good. I'm glad that you are being cautious." He pulled out a small box from the bag he was carrying. "I have a new toy for you." He handed her the box.

"What is it?" She opened the top and looked inside.

William hadn't been joking. The thing looked like a toy. A small microphone and loudspeaker were housed in a teardrop-shaped pendant, which hung from a delicate chain.

"It works on the same principle as the earpieces, just without the compulsion filtering component. It will translate your words into the Kra-ell language so the prince can understand what you're saying. You can hang the chain around your neck."

She pulled the pendant out of the box. "How do I activate it?"

"It responds to voice commands." William smiled sheepishly. "The command to activate is 'Kra-on.'"

Jasmine chuckled. "That's easy to remember." She put the teardrop-shaped device in the palm of her hand. "It's so much more convenient than putting earpieces in the prince's recovering ears. Thank you for coming up with such a clever idea."

"It wasn't mine," William admitted. "My team has been working on improving the earpieces, and they've developed more great features. The device allows you to program it with your own voice, so it will sound like you when it translates your words into Kra-ell."

Jasmine frowned. "Will there be a delay, or will it translate simultaneously as I talk?"

"Simultaneously," William said. "And before you ask, the prince will only hear the Kra-ell translation, or mostly that. The device will cancel your voice waves by producing counter waves. It's not perfect yet, so he might hear some of it, but it won't be enough to confuse him."

"That's marvelous." Jasmine found three tiny buttons on the device, probably the manual controls. "Your technology is amazing." She turned the teardrop over. "What about singing, though? Will it also sing for him in Kra-ell?"

Kian regarded her with a puzzled look. "I don't think so. Is that an issue?"

She shrugged. "I sing to the prince. I don't know if he can hear me, but maybe he likes it. I would like to keep singing to him."

"Jasmine is very good," Bridget said from the waiting room. "Beautiful voice."

William and Kian exchanged glances, and William shook his head. "If you want to sing to him, deactivate the device."

"That's what I thought." She sighed. "It's a shame, though. I mostly sing songs from musicals, so the words are important. Still, this is a miraculous little device. You could make a fortune with it."

William ducked his head, looking embarrassed by her praise. "The next generation of earpieces will automatically learn the speech patterns and voices of the people around them, so they'll sound completely natural to the listener."

Kian chuckled. "The first generation was awful. The voice was male, and hearing my wife talking to me in a male voice was disturbing."

"I can imagine." She smiled up at him. "How complicated is it to teach it to use my voice?"

"I'll show you." William took the device from her.

"While you do that, I'll check on the princess." Kian turned around and left the room.

William spent the next few minutes showing her how to program the device and then left to give the new devices to the medical staff.

As Jasmine continued training the teardrop the way William had shown her, she thought about communicating with the prince the same way she would be talking to a human man in his situation.

The nuances of speech and the emotions behind them might be completely lost on him, and the same was true for her, even if William's team updated the earpieces before the prince woke up.

The prince was an alien from a completely different world with different values and beliefs. Would she understand him even if she could hear his voice?

Could she read him like she could read the people of her world?

Probably not. She would have a hard time communicating with someone from Tibet or Japan in a meaningful way, even if there was no language barrier. Their cultural expectations were too different.

Things would be so much easier with Edgar. He was an immortal, also alien in some ways, but he had been born on Earth, and he had grown up immersed in the same Western culture and values that had shaped her.

With him, there would be no language barriers, no cultural misunderstandings. Still, as the thoughts flitted through her mind, she pushed them aside because there was no escaping the fact that Edgar was not the one meant for her, and she should stop thinking about him as an option.

22

MARINA

Marina cringed at the number of cappuccinos she'd made that had gone down the drain. "I just can't get the hang of it. It looks so simple when you do it."

Wonder put a hand on her shoulder. "You need to develop the touch, which only comes with practice."

Leaning against the counter, Aliya nodded. "It took me days to master this beast and weeks until I could make all those fancy hearts and other designs with the frothed milk."

"Thanks for the pep talk, but I still feel like a failure."

Marina was getting used to the hybrid, who was very different from the other hybrids she knew from Igor's compound. The girl seemed more refined and better educated, but when Marina remarked on that, Aliya burst out laughing.

"I had the bare minimum of education when the clan found me. What you see now is the result of my mate's hard work. Vrog is a teacher and took it upon himself to educate his ignorant mate."

"Are you exclusive with him?" Marina asked hesitantly.

"I am." Aliya sighed. "When I came of age, I entertained following the Kra-ell ways and had several males in my unit, but it just didn't feel right. Vrog didn't want to share, and I didn't want to either. I'm very happy having only one mate." She crossed her arms over her chest. "Frankly, I don't know how the Kra-ell females manage several partners. It must be exhausting."

It had been quite a shock when the humans at Safe Haven had heard about Jade choosing one of the immortals as her exclusive mate, but evidently, she wasn't the only Kra-ell who had gone that way. Aliya and Vrog were also a monogamous couple. Emmett was another hybrid Kra-ell who was in an exclusive relationship with an immortal, but then Emmett was unlike anyone else on this planet.

"Hello, ladies." A tall, striking woman with long, silver-blonde hair approached the counter. "Can I bother you for a cappuccino and a pastry?"

Wonder cast her a warm smile. "Of course, Kaia." She turned to Marina. "Our newest hire will make your cappuccino."

Marina felt her cheeks get warm, and she wasn't quick to blush. "I'm not good enough yet."

"Welcome to the village, Marina." Kaia smiled. "I'll gladly be your first customer."

Marina winced. "Are you sure? Every cup I've made so far has gone down the drain."

Kaia shrugged. "I'm a scientist. I'm used to trying things a thousand different ways until something succeeds." She extended her hand. "I'm honored to try your cappuccino."

That was such a nice thing to say. "I'll do my best."

When the cup was ready, she put it in front of Kaia on the counter. Marina held her breath as the female lifted the cup to her lips and took a sip.

"Excellent." Kaia smacked her lips.

Marina very much doubted it, but she appreciated the white lie.

"Come back in a few days, and I promise it will truly be excellent."

"It already is." Kaia took another sip.

"What kind of scientist are you?" Marina asked.

"I'm a bioinformatician."

Marina had no idea what that meant and was too embarrassed to ask and admit her ignorance.

Kaia must have read her expression because she smiled. "Not many people know what bioinformaticians do. I work with biological data, trying to unravel the secrets of life." She tilted her head. "Who knows? We might discover how to turn ordinary mortals into immortals, no godly genes required."

Marina's heart rate accelerated, and her eyes widened. "Are you serious? Or are you just teasing me? Because if you are teasing, that's just cruel."

Kaia's piercing blue eyes seemed to hold the universe's secrets as she trained them on Marina. "The gods weren't always immortal. They found a way to modify their genes and make their bodies self-repair at such an accelerated rate that they turned immortal. What if we find a way to do the same?"

Marina's mind was reeling as she tried to process the implications of what Kaia was saying. If it were true, if there was a way for humans to become immortal, it would change everything. She could have forever with Peter after all. They could build a life together.

"How close are you to discovering the secret to immortality?" Wonder asked.

Kaia sighed. "Regrettably, I am not as close as I would like to be, but I believe I will be able to crack the code." She finished the last of the cappuccino, wrapped up what was left of her pastry, and put it in the paper bag Wonder handed her.

"Do you want to take another one for William?" Wonder asked.

"He's not here. He's at the keep today."

Wonder nodded. "Right. Anandur is there as well, guarding Kian."

Marina had a feeling that something important was going on in that place they called the keep, but she didn't dare ask what it was.

She was here because of Kian's good will, and if she didn't want to be kicked out, she should keep her nose out of where it didn't belong.

23

KIAN

T GIF, Kian thought as he rolled over and turned to look at Syssi, who was still asleep beside him. Or was it TTMFIF? 'Thank the merciful Fates it's Friday' didn't roll off the tongue as easily, though.

He leaned over and gently kissed Syssi's forehead before slipping out of bed and heading for the shower. He had a busy day ahead of him, with five phone meetings and a thousand and one details to attend to.

Nearly a month had passed since the cruise had ended, and he was still catching up.

As he stood under the hot spray, letting it sluice over his shoulders and down his back, he thought about the twins and the slow progress of their recovery. There had been some small improvements in their condition, but the road ahead of them was still long, and no one knew whether their minds would function properly once their bodies recovered.

Jasmine was keeping vigil at the prince's bedside, which was romantic given that all she had seen so far was a withered body. There was that one moment when the prince had opened his eyes and looked straight at her, but he hadn't done that since.

The poor woman was pining for what could be and not what was.

When Kian returned to the bedroom, Syssi wasn't in bed, and when he went looking for her, he found her as he had expected in Allegra's room.

"Good morning, my loves." He kissed Syssi's cheek and then his daughter's.

"Daddy!" She stretched her arms toward him.

"She is such a daddy's girl," Syssi murmured as she handed Allegra to him.

"Daddy." Allegra cupped his cheeks with her little hands and planted a kiss on the tip of his nose the way he liked to do to her.

"I love you, munchkin." He hugged her to him and turned to Syssi. "Do you want to get dressed while I get her ready?"

"Yes, please." She stretched on her toes and kissed him on the lips. "I'll be quick."

He knew she would be. Syssi's morning routine was no-fuss and efficient, with most of the time dedicated to breakfast rather than clothes, makeup, and hair. She had her priorities straight.

Their daughter, though, was a different story.

He went through eight different outfits until she settled on a frilly dress that was not practical for daycare in the university, where she would play in a sandbox that Amanda had recently added to the facility.

"You look very pretty," he said as he laced her pink sneakers.

Shoes were another quirk of hers. She abhorred Velcro. Allegra wore either laced sneakers or shiny Mary Janes.

He carried her to the kitchen and put her in her highchair.

Okidu placed a platter of his famous waffles on the table with all the toppings, and Kian handed Allegra a plain one. She didn't like anything mushy or gooey on her waffles.

Syssi smiled at him over her cappuccino machine. "What took you so long?"

"I think our daughter inherited her aunt's obsession with fashion. She's a very picky dresser."

"Tell me about it." Syssi rolled her eyes. "I think I'll start having her pick her outfits the night before to save time in the morning. And just so you know, I totally blame Amanda. She makes such a fuss over what Allegra is wearing that it is no wonder the child is striving to keep impressing her favorite auntie."

Kian pretended shock. "Just don't say Amanda is her favorite in front of Alena or Sari. They will be offended."

"Oh, they know." Syssi poured milk into their two cappuccinos. "She spends much more time with Amanda than with them, so it's natural."

Alena was due to deliver any day now, and although she was completely serene and unconcerned, Orion was going nuts. Not that it was a big surprise. This was his first child, while it was Alena's fourteenth.

The number was incomprehensible, especially for an immortal. "Have Alena and Orion chosen a name for their baby yet?"

Shaking her head, Syssi put the cappuccino cups on the table. "They are both superstitious and don't want to name the baby until it is born."

"Iti," Allegra said. It was her nickname for Bhathian and Eva's son.

Syssi smiled. "We already have an Ethan in the village, sweetie."

"Iti," Allegra insisted.

"Maybe there are other boy names that sound like Iti."

Syssi chuckled. "Yeah. E.T., the extraterrestrial who wants to go home. Does she think that her cousin is going to be an alien?"

"Or maybe she's talking about Nana's brother and sister." Kian grimaced. "I wonder if they will want to go home when they wake up."

He was just about to take a sip of his cappuccino when his phone buzzed, and when he lifted it to check whether he should answer it or ignore it, the name on the screen had him answering right away.

"Good morning, Mother," he said. "Were your ears burning? I was just talking about you."

She laughed, the sound raising goosebumps on his arms like it always did. "What were you saying about me?"

"Allegra insisted that Alena's baby should be named Iti, and Syssi said that it sounded like E.T. I responded that maybe Allegra had meant to name her Nana's siblings."

His mother didn't laugh. "That child of yours is definitely psychic. I called to tell you I want to see my brother and sister. Can you take me to the keep today?"

"There's nothing to see yet. They look a little better than they did when we brought them in, but they're still unconscious. They're barely more than dried-out corpses at this point, and I doubt you want to see that."

"Nevertheless, I feel like I need to see them." She was quiet for a moment. "I spoke with the queen last night through Aru and Aria, and the conversation made me worry."

Kian frowned. "What did she say?"

"I prefer not to discuss this on the phone. If you are not in a rush to get to the office, I would like to come over."

As if it was an option to refuse her. "I'm never in a rush when you need me."

"Excellent. I will be there in a few minutes." She ended the call.

"I'll start on the cappuccino," Syssi said, rising from her seat and moving towards the kitchen. "Okidu," she said, "can you make a few more waffles? The Clan Mother is on her way."

Allegra clapped her little hands, her face alight with excitement. "Waffles!" she cried, bouncing in her seat. "Nana!"

"Isn't it wonderful." Syssi turned to Kian with a smile, "to have your mother living just a short walk away?"

"You're probably the only daughter-in-law on the planet who feels that way about her husband's mother," he said, his voice teasing.

Syssi shrugged. "I love your mother," she said simply. "And your sisters, too."

Kian felt a rush of love and gratitude for his mate, for how she had embraced his family as her own. "I know, and it makes me the luckiest guy."

24

THE PRINCE

He drifted in a sea of darkness, his mind a jumbled mess of fragmented memories and half-formed thoughts. He couldn't tell where one ended and the other began, couldn't separate the dreams from the reality that once must have been his life.

Still, through the haze of confusion and uncertainty, one thing remained constant—the sound of her voice. It was a lifeline, a tether to hold onto in the endless expanse of nothingness that surrounded him.

He needed to find out who the female was and what language she spoke. He couldn't understand a single word. But her voice was a soothing melody that seemed to wrap around him like a warm embrace.

Sometimes, she sang, her voice rising and falling in a haunting cadence that stirred something deep within him. The songs differed each time, some joyful and uplifting, others sad and mournful. Some were passionate, filled with a yearning that he could feel deep in his soul, while others were light and playful, tunes that made him want to dance, laugh, and spin in circles even though he couldn't remember ever dancing.

He couldn't make out the words or decipher the meaning behind the melodies. But it didn't matter. Her voice was enough, a tether that kept him grounded in the void.

In the rare moments when the darkness receded and his mind cleared, he found himself grasping at the fragments of his past, trying to piece together the shattered remnants of his identity.

He saw flashes of a woman's face, who he knew was his mother. She was strong and brave, he knew that as well, and she did everything in her power to protect him and his sister, but she feared that even her formidable power would not be enough. She never said that, but he could see the fear in the shadows in her eyes.

"Your destiny awaits across the stars," she'd said. "The seer foretold your future. You will live, and you will thrive, and you will be safe."

He remembered the pain in his mother's eyes, the knowledge that she was sending them away and would never see them again.

The thought was too painful to cling to, so he drifted away, anchoring himself to that enchanting voice again. The female seemed to assume different roles as she spoke, sounding different with each switch.

It was so odd. Perhaps she was retelling tales of valor from days past, acting the parts of the heroes.

Time had lost all meaning.

He was trapped in the liminal space between life and death.

Gradually, though, ever so slowly, he began to feel a change. It started as a warmth in his chest, a tiny spark of life that grew and spread until it filled his entire being. It was like the first rays of dawn after an endless night, the promise of a new day and a new beginning. It was the feeling of blood flowing in his veins, of vitality returning, not in a torrent, but in a trickle.

The female was speaking to him again, her words a soothing murmur that washed over him like a gentle rain. He strained to listen, to make out the meaning behind the sounds. But it was like grasping at smoke, the syllables slipping through his fingers like sand.

And then, suddenly, something changed. The woman's voice shifted, the cadence of her words taking on a new pattern. It was as if a veil had been lifted, the sounds coalescing into something recognizable that he could almost understand.

It was a language he had never heard, the syllables strange and alien to his ears, soft, liquid, not guttural like his mother tongue. But somehow, he could make out the meaning behind the words, or perhaps he could feel the intent and the emotion conveyed through them.

He wanted to open his eyes and behold her, to reach out with his fingers and touch her, but the darkness was too strong and his weakness too profound. He slipped back into the void, back into the endless expanse of his mind. But even there, in the depths of his unconsciousness, he could still hear her voice, and he knew with a certainty that defied all logic and reason that she would be there when he finally managed to break to the surface of the murky waters under which he was submerged.

25

ANNANI

As Annani turned into Kian's walkway, she saw him waiting at the door with Allegra in his arms.

"She is excited to see her Nana," Kian said.

"Nana." Allegra stretched her arms toward Annani.

That was the best good morning possible, and Annani's heart felt immediately lighter. "Come to Nana, sweetness." She took the child and kissed her on both cheeks.

Allegra leaned away, looked into her eyes with that too-old gaze, and then leaned back in and kissed the tip of her nose.

"You are so precious, my sweet little granddaughter." Annani hugged her to her chest and followed Kian inside.

The smell of Okidu's famous waffles mingled with the smell of Syssi's cappuccino and the sweet smell of the child in her arms was the best mix of aromas.

It smelled like home.

"I have your cappuccino." Syssi leaned to kiss her cheek. "Made with real milk the way you like it."

"Thank you." Annani sat down with Allegra in her arms. "I do not know how you can drink that vile oat milk." She held the child with one arm, lifted the cup with the other, and took a sip. "Perfect."

Syssi beamed at the compliment. "Thank you."

Annani tilted her head. "Am I keeping you from going to work?"

Smiling, Syssi sat down next to her at the kitchen table. "I called Amanda and asked her if leaving a little later today was okay. She has no classes on Fridays, so her schedule is more flexible. The postdocs can handle the research in our absence."

"I am glad I get to enjoy your company for a little longer." Annani reached for one of the waffles and handed it to Allegra, who snatched it with her usual glee at something tasty to munch on.

"So, what's got you so worried?" Kian asked as he sat on her other side.

Annani sighed. "The queen is insisting that we at least come up with a solid plan to fake the twins' deaths, and between the lines, she implies that if we cannot do that, we will have to resort to a less savory solution. We cannot afford even an iota of doubt to form in the Eternal King's mind regarding the twins' survival. He must be led to believe that they are dead and that their threat to him has been eliminated along with them. Our ruse needs to be perfect." Annani rose to her feet and put her granddaughter in her highchair. "I recommend doing so sooner rather than later because my grandmother is not a patient lady."

Kian chuckled. "I beg to differ. Someone plotting against her husband for thousands of years must be very patient."

"She deems my siblings a threat." Annani took a sip from her cappuccino. "Mostly, it is because the Eternal King will stop at nothing to ensure their elimination, even if it means obliterating Earth to achieve that goal, but also because of who they are and the powers they supposedly have, which might pose a direct threat to me. I tried to convince her that we need all the help we can get, and since we share a common enemy, the twins would naturally ally with me."

"That's an excellent argument," Syssi said. "How did she respond to that?"

Annani put the cup down. "She agreed with me but then pointed out that the twins might have their own agenda and that we must be careful."

"Nothing new there," Kian said. "We are taking every precaution with them. The plan is to induce momentary death, record it, and then revive them, but we can't do that until they are restored to full health. First, because they need to look as perfectly preserved as the Kra-ell who perished, so no one will suspect they entered unaided stasis, and second, so they survive the poison."

"Can I tell her that during our next chat?"

Kian hesitated. "Bridget needs to experiment with different doses of the poison to make sure it will work as intended and that she will be able to revive them. We might have to find another way if she says the poison is out. That's why I didn't want to tell the queen anything yet."

"We have to give her something," Annani said. "I think she is allowing us to nurse them back to health only because she knows it is important to me. If not for that, I do not doubt that she would have ordered Aru to get rid of them while still in Tibet. She might still do that once they no longer look emaciated." Annani glanced at her granddaughter, who was happily munching on the waffle.

"They are also her grandchildren," Syssi said. "How can she be so cold?"

Annani sighed. "Ani has been a queen for a very long time. She no longer thinks as a mother and a grandmother, if she ever did. I am precious to her not because I am her only son's daughter but because I am the heir, and she has no qualms about eliminating her other descendants if she deems them a threat to her plans."

Setting his drink down, Kian was considering the input. "Let me see how they are doing today and if Bridget has more insight about how to proceed. Hopefully, I will have more for you to share with the queen in your conversation with her tonight. But until the twins are awake, there is little point in you going to the keep."

JASMINE

J asmine sat beside the prince's bed, her eyes fixed on his face.

Had anything changed?

His color was better, his face looked a little less hollow, and she could see his chest rising and falling as he breathed. It was progress, and she shouldn't expect more after only two days.

It seemed so much longer, though. It felt like the small patient room and the chair she was sitting on had become her entire universe. She'd gone up to the penthouse last night after Bridget had kicked her out, but she couldn't fall asleep, and after a few hours of tossing and turning, she'd come back down.

Thankfully, Bridget had been nowhere to be seen, and the nurse was much more sympathetic and let Jasmine stay.

Rising to her feet, she glanced at the slightly open door to make sure no one was watching her and started a stretching routine to get her blood flowing and relieve the stiffness in her muscles. After a few leg swings and arm circles, she moved into gentle yoga poses and concluded with a spinal twist to further unwind her body.

She should go to the penthouse and have something to drink and eat. Her friends had given up on calling her to join them for meals, but they had been kind enough to leave her leftovers in the refrigerator so she wouldn't starve.

Another option was the enormous commercial kitchen where she'd had coffee on the first day. Perhaps she could find something in its long row of refrigerators. What the heck did the clan need such a big kitchen for in its underground facility? Did they host parties down here? There could be a banquet hall somewhere for weddings and other celebrations.

She should take the opportunity to explore a little and see what else was there. The catacombs should be fascinating, but they were too creepy to visit alone, and she doubted she would find anyone to take her there.

Margo and Frankie had gone with Toven and Mia to the Perfect Match main office in the city for a tour, and Ella had returned to the village. Gabi had taken over the office in the penthouse to conduct Zoom calls with clients, so disturbing her was out of the question. She'd even posted a note on the door warning everyone not to knock or enter.

The gods were somewhere in the lower levels, working on the equipment they had salvaged from the pod, probably with William or others from his tech team.

Jasmine sighed.

She felt like a ghost, floating in limbo, not knowing what the future had in store for her. She didn't even know how long she could stay in the penthouse. She needed to talk to Kian and find out his plans for her.

Casting one more look at her prince, she slipped out of the room and was heading toward the clinic's main entrance when the door opened, and Edgar walked in.

In one hand he held a cardboard tray with two paper coffee cups, packets of sugar, and wooden sticks for stirring, and in his other was a large brown paper bag with something that smelled delicious.

Chocolate croissant. Jasmine was willing to bet that was what she was smelling.

"Hi," she said, looking at what he'd brought and hoping it was for her but not daring to assume. He had left in a huff after the celebration of the mission completion, and he hadn't been back since. "Who are you here for?"

He smiled. "You, of course. Who else? I came to see how you were doing and thought you could use some pick-me-ups."

"Oh, Goddess, I can." She reached for the coffee first. "Thank you. You are a lifesaver." She motioned for him to join her in the seating area of the waiting room.

He sat down, put his loot on the low coffee table, and handed her two brown sugar packets with two wooden sticks.

Jasmine felt a surge of gratitude and affection wash through her. "You still remember how I like my coffee."

He chuckled. "Of course, I do. We've not been apart long enough for me to forget." He pinned her with his blue eyes. "Not that I will ever forget. I will always remember you, Jasmine."

Why the heck did he have to be so sweet?

Not knowing what to say, she removed the lid from her latte, emptied the two sugar packets inside, and stirred.

Edgar reached into the paper bag and pulled out two croissants and two sandwiches. One of the croissants had gooey chocolate spilling onto its wrapper. He also produced a stack of paper napkins and put them next to the croissants.

"My mother always told me to eat my sandwich first and the dessert later, but the croissants are warmed up, so I suggest you start with them. One has chocolate filling and the other almond."

Jasmine grinned. "That's what I intended to do. This chocolate croissant has my name on it." She tore a large piece off and took a bite.

Her eyes rolled back in her head. "It's so fresh and delicious."

Edgar watched her mouth as if he wanted to lick the chocolate off her lips. "They are made fresh every night and delivered in the early morning hours. One of our clan members runs a large bakery and kitchen. The sandwiches come from the same place."

"Give him my compliments."

Edgar was quiet for a moment, regarding her with an intense look. "Come to the village with me, and you can compliment Jackson yourself. I'll also introduce you to him and everyone else." He smiled tightly. "We don't have to be together, but you are welcome to stay at my place until your situation clears. Not that I would be averse to us being together again, but that's obviously up to you."

It was so damn tempting to accept Edgar's invitation and leave all the uncertainty behind.

Well, nothing in life was certain, but having a roof over her head, food in her fridge, and a handsome man in her bed was a good start.

"I wish I could, believe me, I do. But I can't." She reached for his hand and gave it a light squeeze. "We had a good time together, and we probably could enjoy being together for a little longer, but in the end, it would have fizzled out because the Fates have different plans for us."

Edgar nodded, his face a mask of resignation. "I know, but it's so hard to let go. Especially when I see you sitting here all alone and looking dejected. I miss seeing the vibrant and upbeat Jasmine who stole my heart."

Jasmine rolled her eyes. "Perhaps she borrowed your heart for a bit, but she certainly didn't steal it. Your heart still belongs to you, waiting for the female you will gift it to. And as for me, I hope things will get better." She sighed. "I don't like the limbo I'm in. I want to know what's in store for me tomorrow and the day after that, but Kian rushed out yesterday before I could ask him his plans for me."

"Kian is here in the keep," Edgar said, his voice a little strained. "I think he went to see what Aru and his team are doing with the equipment from the pod. I'm sure he will stop by the clinic later."

"That's good to know." She lifted her cup and took several long sips. "I hope you will come to visit me again." She cast him a sidelong glance. "I was serious about staying friends."

He chuckled. "You just want me for the cappuccino and the croissants."

She was glad he was joking again. Seeing him suffering was paining her.

"I just want you in my life." She reached out, pulling him into a fierce hug. "Thank you." She leaned back and smiled teasingly. "For the coffee and the croissants and everything else."

27

KIAN

Kian strode through the keep halls, his footsteps echoing off the stone walls as he made his way toward the underground chambers he'd dedicated to storing the equipment from the pod. Beside him William kept pace, his face alight with excitement at the prospect of getting his hands on the advanced technology the gods had salvaged.

"Don't look so excited." Kian cast him a sidelong glance. "I talked with Aru earlier, and he said they hadn't been able to crack anything open."

The sparkle in William's eyes didn't diminish. "Even if we can't get anything open, we can probably connect it to a power source and see how it works. I would be happier if I could take every bit of equipment apart and reverse engineer it, but if I can't do that, I'll make do with figuring out what it can do."

"Fair enough," Kian said. "My main impetus is finding clues to the where-abouts of the other missing pods, but since I don't expect to find any more survivors, it's more out of curiosity and the need to prevent humans from finding them than the urgency to save people. All the Kra-ell are likely dead."

William arched a brow. "I'm not so sure about that. We didn't solve the mystery of Mey and Jin's parents, and we know for sure that their father must have been a hybrid Kra-ell, and we also know that he didn't come from Jade's tribe."

Kian used his phone to open the door to the suite of chambers the gods were using to work on the equipment. "Their father could have come from one of the other tribes that Igor found and subjugated. I don't know if the leaders of the other tribes kept their males on such a short leash as Jade. One might have fathered a hybrid boy outside his tribe, and that boy later became Mey and Jin's father."

William nodded. "That's possible."

As Kian opened one of the interior doors, they were greeted by Aru and his team hunched over a table littered with scraps of components.

"Any progress?" Kian asked.

Aru shook his head. "We've managed to power up some of the devices, but everything is solid state."

"That's great progress." William leaned over the table. "Can you show me what works and how?"

"I'll leave you to it." Kian clapped William on his back. "I'm going to check on our royal guests, and I'll let you know when I'm ready to head back to the village."

Waving Kian away, William didn't even lift his head.

"Evidently I'm no longer needed," Kian murmured as he stepped out of the room.

When he reached the clinic, he found Bridget in her office. He knocked on the open door and walked in. "How are you doing?" he asked.

"That's novel." Bridget leaned back in her chair, a small smile playing at the corners of her mouth. "Someone asking me how I am feeling."

"You look tired."

She sighed. "Sleeping on a gurney is not as fun as I remembered, but Victor is a good sport and doesn't complain. I think he enjoys it."

"Why don't you go home in the evenings? Julian and Gertrude can monitor the twins at night."

"I prefer to let Julian go home to his mate." Bridget smiled. "Besides, he's not experienced enough to deal with the twins on his own."

Kian tilted his head. "Are you sure? Maybe you are coddling him a little? Your son impressed me as a very capable physician."

Bridget grinned. "That's nice of you to say, and it's true, but he's not confident enough in his skills to deal with these two. Not only are they a unique medical challenge, but they are also the Clan Mother's siblings. Julian is terrified of them expiring on his watch."

"Is there a chance of that?"

She shrugged. "I think they are doing well. Their vitals are improving daily, and their brain activity is picking up. It's only a matter of time before they start regaining consciousness. Still, I've never encountered anyone who was in stasis for seven thousand years in a sealed stasis chamber that stopped working at some indeterminable point during those thousands of years."

"Still, it sounds like their prospects are good, right?"

"Unless something unexpected happens, yes. Jasmine's presence is helping.

She keeps talking to him, and by talking, I mean that she is acting out entire plays and singing. It would have been much more boring here without that constant entertainment." She leaned forward. "I leave the doors to both rooms open so the princess can benefit from the stimulation as well."

"Good." Kian rose to his feet. "If you say that talking to a comatose patient is helping, then who am I to say otherwise?"

Bridget crossed her arms over her chest. "I know it does. Are you in a rush to return to the village?"

"I need to wait for William to be done, why?"

"Do you want to see our guests?"

"Of course. I would be remiss if I didn't, but first, I need to talk to you about something." He turned and closed the door before returning to his seat. "My mother visited me this morning. She's concerned that we are waiting too long to stage the death of the twins. I told her our plan, and she asked me to verify whether you still think it will work. Did you get any more insight into their physiology?"

Bridget nodded. "They are built like us, and their metabolism works like ours, not the Kra-ell's. I believe that the poison will work."

"Good." He let out a breath. "This will assuage the Clan Mother's fears."

Now, she could tell her grandmother to take a breather and wait patiently until the twins looked like their pod companions so their deaths could be faked convincingly.

Bridget pushed to her feet and rounded her desk. "They look better with every passing day. Come see for yourself."

The doctor walked out of her office and into the princess's room just across the waiting room.

"She looks much better." Kian leaned over the hospital bed. "Her eyes are shaped like ours, not the Kra-ell's."

Bridget nodded. "She is also not as tall. I measured her, and she's only five-nine. So, she is tall for a human but short for a Kra-ell female. She must have worn high-heeled shoes under her robes to pass for a Kra-ell."

"I wonder how old she and her brother were when they entered stasis. I should ask Jade if she knows."

"She should know, but I assume it was at least a few decades. It must have been a nightmare for them and their mother to hide their identities for so long. I'm sure other acolytes didn't take as long to become full-fledged priests."

"Indeed." Kian took another look at the princess. "We will know more when they wake up and tell us their story, provided they remember it."

28

JASMINE

Jasmine heard Kian talking about the princess over in the next room, and she wondered when he would come to see the prince.

She needed to talk to him, but he would probably walk in with Bridget, and she didn't want to have that talk with him in front of the doctor. Not that she had anything to be embarrassed about, but still. Some pleading would most likely be needed, and she'd rather do that with no audience.

Casting a glance at the prince, she decided she didn't want to talk in front of him either.

She stepped out of the room and waited by the door for Kian and Bridget to come out.

"Hi." She greeted him with a smile. "I was wondering if I could have a few words with you after you check on the prince."

"Of course." He returned her smile. "Bridget tells me that you are providing entertainment for the entire clinic and helping our patients find their way to us."

"I hope." She let out a breath. "I've been talking and singing for hours."

"Give me just a moment to look at him, and then we can talk in my office." He tilted his head. "That is if you are comfortable leaving your prince for a few minutes."

"That's fine." She waved a dismissive hand. "I come and go all of the time."

That was an exaggeration. She kept her absences to a minimum but didn't want to seem obsessed.

Kian took little time in the prince's room, and when he came out, he seemed encouraged.

"He is starting to look more like a prince than a frog," Kian attempted a joke. "Soon, he will be pretty enough to kiss."

Jasmine grimaced. "He's an alien to me, and I'm an alien to him. I don't expect any kissing anytime soon, if ever." She cast him a sidelong glance. "He's also a priest, and I was told that the Kra-ell priests are celibate."

"True." Kian continued walking down the corridor.

When they got to his office, he pulled a chair for her next to the oblong conference table, waited until she was seated, and sat beside her.

If he weren't a hundred percent loyal to his wife, Jasmine would have been worried about the intimate setting.

Mated immortals were not supposed to be capable of sexual attraction to anyone other than their mates, and Kian was an honorable guy. Still, she'd been in enough situations like this for the proximity to trigger apprehension.

"So, what did you want to talk to me about?" Kian asked.

"I was wondering if I was still in danger from the cartel. Can I go back to my apartment or my job? How long can I stay in the penthouse before I need to vacate it, and did you consider my employment prospects with Perfect Match?"

Smiling, Kian lifted his hands. "Whoa. That's a lot of questions. I'll answer them one at a time."

"Sorry." Jasmine winced. "I've been thinking about it for two days straight, so it was like releasing the relief valve on a pressure cooker."

Kian leaned back in his chair. "No one has come looking for you or put a tracker on your car. I had it checked. They snooped a little around the agency Margo worked at, but they didn't bother with her parents or her brother. They are back in their homes, and Margo's brother is supposed to get married next month. They ended up postponing the wedding after Margo told them she would have to stay in witness protection for a while longer. Her brother refused to have a wedding without her."

"Good for him," Jasmine said. "So, basically, I'm free to go if I want to?"

Kian leaned forward, his elbows resting on his knees as he fixed her with an intense gaze. "Do you want to go back?" he asked. "Because if you do, we'll make it happen. But I thought you wanted something different for yourself."

"I do," she answered with no hesitation. "I mean, I want something different. I want to be part of your world and see where this thing with the prince goes. It might go nowhere, and then I will need to reevaluate, but for now, I need to know that I can stay in the penthouse and that you are not going to kick me out. I mean, I don't have to stay in the penthouse. I can sleep on a cot in the clinic. I just need to know that I can stay here. With him."

Kian smiled indulgently. "You can stay in the penthouse for as long as you want. I told the gods the same thing. They are all welcome to use the penthouses as their base even when they have to travel."

"Thank you," she whispered as relief washed over her. "Right now, I can't work yet, but as soon as he is stable, I can start filling any position needed. I'm not choosey."

"No rush." Kian pushed to his feet. "For now, your job is to keep talking and singing to the prince and princess."

"I can do that."

"I'll arrange an allowance for you, and if you need help getting things from your apartment, terminating the lease, bringing your car over here, or any other arrangements, let me know, and I'll have someone assist you."

That was so much more than Jasmine had expected, and for a moment, she was stunned by the generosity.

"Thank you," she finally managed to say. "I really appreciate that, and I will take you up on your offer."

"You are welcome. It would be best if you also kept using the credit card I gave you. Just to be cautious, don't use your own cards yet. I don't want the Modanas tracing you here."

29

KIAN

Kian scowled at his cappuccino, absently stirring the oat milk and watching the swirls form. A new problem had been brought to his attention, and even though it seemed like a poorly conceived prank, it still disturbed him because things like that had never happened in the village before.

Across the breakfast table, Syssi watched him with a knowing look in her eye, her breakfast untouched. Allegra sat between them, happily munching on a piece of toast with cream cheese.

"What's that frown about?" Syssi asked. "You've been staring at your coffee as if it has done something to offend you."

"It's not the coffee." Kian sighed, running a hand through his hair in frustration. "Things have been happening around the village that leave a bad taste in my mouth. People are complaining about items missing from their yards and packages that were marked as delivered disappearing from the mail room. Stuff like that has never happened before, and naturally, everyone thinks it's either the humans or the Kra-ell, and they are not shy about giving both the stink eye. It's difficult enough to run an integrated community without someone perpetrating stupid pranks and petty thefts."

"It sounds like something bored teenagers would do, but we only have three in the clan, and they are all wonderful kids who would never do anything like that. From the new arrivals, there is just one human teenage girl who is so timid that the thought of stealing things would have never even occurred to her, which leaves the Kra-ell. There is a larger group of teenage and young adult Kra-ell, purebloods, and hybrids, and those who need to survive on blood are getting antsy because they don't get to hunt often enough. Jade only took two small groups so far, and it was mostly pureblooded females and some of the younger children. She needs to step up the outings."

Kian was surprised that Syssi knew so much about the Kra-ell. Working nearly full-time at the university and taking care of a young child didn't leave her with a lot of spare time.

"How do you know all that?"

She shrugged. "When Amanda and I return from the university, we usually stop at the café and hear all the gossip from Wonder and Aliya. Those two know everything that's going on in the village, and now that they've added Marina, she will soon become a good source of information as well."

"Amazing." Kian shook his head. "Maybe you can ask them if they've heard anything about the missing items?"

"They don't know who is doing it, but the hypothesis about the teenagers is floating around." She sighed. "I hope it's the teenagers and not adults who want to stir things up."

"Yeah. That's what I'm worried about. So far, the missing items are not very valuable, and it's more of an annoyance than a significant loss, but I'm afraid that whoever is doing it is just testing the waters."

She chuckled. "If I'm right and the Kra-ell are responsible for the thefts, they are definitely not testing the waters. Pushing their boundaries is more apt."

Given the Kra-ell's aversion to deep water, Syssi was right, but Kian wasn't concerned with semantics. "It's not just the missing items. The nighttime shutters have been malfunctioning in some of the houses, letting light spill into the darkness, and that's a security risk. If someone were to fly over the village at night, they'd see the lights and know that something was up here that shouldn't be."

William's ingenious devices kept the village hidden from electronic detection. During the daytime, the clever reflective roof tiles made the entire top of the mountain look like there were only trees. But something as simple as light in the window at night could destroy the illusion.

"Which houses had their shutters malfunction?" Syssi asked.

"They are all in phase two. Either the crews that built those homes did a shoddy job and cut corners, or the shutters we ordered were of crappy quality."

The second part was less likely because he had personally reviewed all the large purchases, and he would never have approved anything that wasn't considered top-notch.

She frowned. "I didn't know about the shutters, and that sounds like deliberate sabotage."

"I agree. But why would anyone do that? The safety of everyone residing in the village depends on us staying hidden and keeping the village a secret from the rest of the world, especially the Doomers. William's devices ensure that we're invisible to electronic detection. If that's sabotage, then whoever is doing it has a death wish." He leaned back in his chair and crossed his arms over his chest. "Besides, they are all under compulsion to not harm anyone living here."

Syssi shook her head. "There are always loopholes. They could convince themselves they are doing it for the greater good or some other nonsense that allows them to circumvent the compulsion. You need to put surveillance cameras in the mailroom and around the houses in phase two."

Kian nodded. "As much as I hate spying on my people, it has to be done."

Syssi shrugged. "We already have cameras in strategic places, like the bridge to phase two and at the perimeter of Kalugal's enclave. We also have cameras all over the mountain. A few more will not make a difference."

"It's a slippery slope, Syssi. Where does it end?"

"We don't put cameras in people's bedrooms and bathrooms." She chuckled. "It's funny that I find myself on the side of adding security features while you push back on that."

"I am not pushing back. I agree a hundred percent. I'm just playing devil's advocate." He sighed. "What if we suspect something nefarious is happening in private spaces?"

"Like what?"

He arched a brow. "Do I need to spell it out for you? We have humans living in the village. It's very easy to take advantage of them."

"Right." She scrunched her nose. "Maybe that's something we should leave to Edna. Did she ever approve a search or something along those lines?"

Kian snorted. "Clan law predates all the fluffy laws of today. If I suspect someone is taking advantage of a human or a minor, I don't need a search warrant to break down the door."

Syssi's eyes became hooded. "Why does that make you so sexy to me?"

He cast a glance at Allegra. "Is there a chance you can put her in front of the television to watch the Wiggles?"

Syssi laughed. "I could, but I told Amanda I would meet her at the playground."

He leaned closer to her. "Call her and postpone your playdate. It's Saturday. Tell her that you overslept."

JASMINE

"Good morning, Bridget." Jasmine handed the doctor a large cappuccino and a bag with a warmed-up chocolate croissant. "Enjoy."

The doctor smiled. "Thank you, I will." She took both to her office while Jasmine headed to the prince's room.

"Good morning, my prince." She leaned over and gently kissed his cheek.

He was still unconscious, and he didn't react to the kiss, but something told her that he could feel it. It was probably her imagination, but it seemed like his lips curved up a little.

Yeah, she was hallucinating.

Sitting on her chair, she put the coffee on the floor and bit into the croissant. After Kian had told her that she was part of the team and that her job was to talk to the prince and princess and stimulate them with her acting and singing, he'd also reminded her that the credit card he'd given her was still at her disposal and she could buy whatever she wanted with it. He had still advised against using her cards, to be on the safe side.

It was nice to stop at the café in the lobby and get coffee and something to eat. She would have ordered delivery from a supermarket and cooked proper meals, but not if she was the only one to cook for.

Margo and Frankie had started training in the Perfect Match center, Ella had returned to the village, and Gabi was busy working or visiting her family there. The gods spent most of their days in the bowels of the keep, working on the salvaged equipment, and she had no idea where they were getting their food from. Maybe they ordered deliveries, collected them at the guard station, and ate them where they worked.

Talk about dedication.

Pulling the teardrop from her pocket, Jasmine regarded it with suspicion.

She was not tech-savvy, and it took her time to adapt to new gadgets. She already had the earpieces, which she had to wear all day long, and now she needed to program the teardrop so it would sound like her.

It was important that she did that before the prince woke up.

He was used to the sound of her voice, or so she hoped, and when she used the teardrop to translate for her, it would confuse him if it didn't sound like her.

In fact, perhaps she should start talking to him through the device while he slept. If he could hear her, it would be good if he could also understand her.

Activating the device, she spoke a few lines from a play, but even though it got the tonality right so that it didn't sound flat, it still sounded strange and distorted. Then again, she'd recorded herself speaking enough times to know that she sounded different to herself than she did to others and that the way her voice resonated in her head was not the same as how the outside world perceived it.

Which gave her an idea.

She pulled out her phone and recorded herself speaking to have a baseline.

Next, she recorded the teardrop's output and compared the two. It was the start of a long, painstaking process of training the device to reproduce her voice accurately. She recorded herself repeatedly, listening to the playback and making tiny adjustments until the words that came out sounded more like her own.

It was a tedious task that required patience, persistence, and a willingness to listen to her voice until it began to sound like a stranger's. But Jasmine was determined and refused to give up until she had achieved the perfect balance of tone and inflection and the near-perfect replication of her own cadence.

Even then, however, the device had its limitations. When Jasmine tried to sing, the teardrop spoke the lyrics, translating them into the harsh, guttural sounds of the Kra-ell language without any of the melody or rhythm that made music powerful. She remembered then that William had told her to deactivate the device when she wanted to sing.

Jasmine considered transcribing the lyrics herself, trying to capture the essence of the songs in the alien tongue. But as she listened to the Kra-ell words that the device produced, she realized it would be impossible. The language was too different, too foreign to her ears and her understanding.

What about Shakespeare, though? Would the teardrop be able to tackle that?

She began to recite lines from *A Midsummer Night's Dream*, the words flowing from her lips in a steady stream of iambic pentameter. But even as she spoke, she could hear the way the teardrop struggled to keep up, and she did not doubt that the meaning of the words was lost in the translation.

She activated her earpieces in a stroke of inspiration, letting them translate the Kra-ell translation back to English. She'd been right. It was a mess.

Switching to a more contemporary play, Jasmine watched the prince's face for any sign of awareness, not expecting to see anything, but then she saw something that hadn't happened before.

The prince's eyes were moving beneath his closed lids.

Her heart racing with excitement, Jasmine rushed out of the room and ran into Bridget's office.

"You have to see this." She waved the doctor on and rushed back into the prince's room.

Bridget came running, her forehead creased with concern as she hurried to his bedside.

"Look at his eyelids," Jasmine said. "They are twitching."

"I can see that. He's dreaming. His brain activity is increasing, and his eyes are moving, suggesting he's experiencing REM sleep. It's a good sign, Jasmine. A very good sign." Bridget spent a few more moments checking the readouts on the equipment before leaving the room.

Jasmine felt a wave of emotion washing over her as she looked down at the prince's face. He looked so peaceful, so vulnerable in his sleep.

"I'm here for you," she said.

Then, realizing that she hadn't activated the translating device, she turned it on and repeated the same sentence. "You are not alone. Your sister is in the next room, and the doctor is taking good care of you both. You are safe, and you are going to be okay. I promise." She leaned down and brushed her lips over the back of his hand.

3 1

PETER

"I've never seen so many cars," Marina breathed as Peter pulled into the mall's parking lot. "Not even in the village. There is a sea of them."

He smiled. "You ain't seen nothing yet." He found a spot, which was a stroke of luck on the weekend, slid his car into the narrow space, and cut the engine. "Wait until you see the inside."

He planned a whole day of wonders for her, and the mall was just the first stop. It might be too much for her first outing in a major city, but his Marina was a trooper, and she would do just fine.

She released her seatbelt. "I'm still amazed that I was allowed to leave the village."

He leaned over and kissed her pouty lips. "I told you that no one would object to that as long as you were with me. If you wanted to venture out on your own, the answer would have most likely been no."

She smiled. "My protector, my keeper, my Guardian."

Her tone was clear of sarcasm or ridicule. Marina enjoyed being under his protective wing, and he enjoyed the fact that she was okay with him hovering over her like an overprotective, over-possessive, overly romantic boyfriend.

Hell, he loved it.

Peter also loved that she waited for him to go around the car and open the door for her. All it had taken was him asking her just once to allow him to be a gentleman. He hadn't asked her permission, though, to show her all the wonders and delights the world had to offer and make up for all the years she had spent locked away in Igor's compound and then isolated in Safe Haven.

He was going to surprise her with that.

As she took his offered hand, he pulled her to him for a quick kiss. "Let's go shopping like there is no tomorrow. I want you to get a whole new wardrobe, with clothes for every occasion, shoes to match, sexy lingerie, makeup, jewelry, hair color, whatever you need to feel like a princess."

But not a Cinderella.

When he'd seen the duffle bag containing all her earthly possessions, he'd found it difficult to hide his wince. The bag hadn't even been full. He took more things with him on a weekend vacation than everything Marina owned.

She chuckled. "I've only been working in the café for two days, and I don't even know how much they will pay me. I can't afford all this."

Shaking his head, he wrapped his arm around her. "When you are with me, you pay for nothing. It's my treat."

She cast him an amused sidelong glance. "Since I'm not allowed to go shopping without you, I will always be with you when I buy things."

"Precisely." He leaned and kissed the top of her head. "As I told you, Guardians are paid very well, and until now, I've had nothing to spend my money on. Now that I have you, there's nothing I would rather spend it on than making you happy. Everything I own is yours."

She stopped walking, turned to him, and opened her mouth, probably to argue, closed it, and then opened it again. "We are not married, Peter. And even if we were, it wouldn't be fair for me to come into your life and share the fruits of your labor that you've accumulated over hundreds of years."

"I'm not that old," he grumbled. "And you buying a whole new wardrobe won't even make a dent in what I have in my bank accounts." He wracked his brain for something he could say that she wouldn't be able to rebut. "We are together, Marina, which is as good as being married. We don't need any official document to legitimize our union."

Huffing out a breath, she resumed walking. "We are just starting out, Peter. We are in love, and everything is great, but things might change."

"They won't. Not for me."

As impossible as it was for him to bond with a human, Peter felt bonded to Marina. She was his mate, but he knew she wouldn't just take his word for it. She didn't know what it meant to be fated to a partner, and if he tried to explain, she wouldn't believe him.

As Kagra's taunting resurged in his mind, he wondered if perhaps she'd been right and he was in love with the notion of love.

Marina leaned into him, resting her head on his bicep. "I love you."

"I love you too." He tightened his fingers on her shoulder. "Do it for me. It will please me to no end to have you buy as many things as we can both carry."

"Okay," she murmured.

"Yes!" Peter pumped his fist in the air.

Hand in hand, they entered the mall, a blast of cold air greeting them as they stepped through the automatic doors. Marina's eyes widened in wonder as she took in the vast expanse of the atrium, the gleaming storefronts, and the throngs of shoppers milling about.

"It's so beautiful." She squeezed his hand. "Look at the height of the ceiling and the skylights, oh my, so marvelous. It's like a wonderland."

"Come on, beautiful. Let's shop till we drop."

Peter led Marina into the fray, guiding her from store to store and helping her pick out outfits, accessories, and everything else he'd planned.

As they made their way through the racks of designer gowns and cocktail dresses, Peter felt excited at the thought of what lay ahead. He had never been one for grand gestures or elaborate schemes, but with Marina, everything was different. It was charged with a sense of possibility and promise that made his blood sing.

At first, she'd needed some coaxing, especially when hit with price tag shock, but once he'd gotten her over that hurdle and she gained confidence, Marina turned out to be a natural-born shopper with an eye for fashion and a love of all things beautiful.

They lost themselves in the simple pleasures of the moment, laughing and chatting and trying on things just for fun, like the cowboy hat that Marina insisted he had to get.

"I will need matching boots," he said with a fake Southern accent.

"Then let's get them." She tugged on his hand, leading him to the men's shoe section in the department store.

It was uncanny how quickly she'd got her bearing and knew where everything was.

"We don't have time for that." He laughed, grabbing the first pair he saw and motioning for the clerk to get him a pair in his size.

His other hand was going numb from the number of bags he was carrying, and Marina had a whole bunch of them, too.

The hunting had been fruitful, and Marina had everything she needed for tonight and the rest of next week. He planned on taking her to the mall again.

"Why don't we have time?" She plopped tiredly on the chair next to him. "When is the mall closing?"

He turned to her with a smile. "There is plenty of time until closing, but I've made dinner reservations at a fancy restaurant tonight at eight, and we still need to go home and get showered and changed."

She turned to him and smiled with her head resting on the back of the chair. "You've planned a full day of fun for us."

"I did," he said with no small amount of pride. "It wasn't easy to get reservations for *By Invitation Only*. I had to beg Kian to give me the spot tonight. There is a long waiting list for spending a small fortune at the best kept secret in town."

Marina frowned. "If the restaurant is so good, why is it a secret?"

"It's a super exclusive place owned by a clan member. People pay hundreds of thousands for a membership just so they have the privilege of making a reservation. It's the kind of place where the rich and famous enjoy themselves away from the public eye."

Marina's eyes nearly popped out of her head. "And you want to take me there? I don't belong in a place like that."

"Don't worry about it." He took her hand. "Neither do I. But it's dark and intimate, and no one will pay us any attention."

He didn't add that it was a place where illicit affairs were conducted in shadowy corners, and the air was thick with the scent of forbidden desires.

She eyed him with suspicion. "Are you sure?"

"I'm sure." He lifted her hand and kissed the back of it. "Remember the wrap dress I told you was perfect for dinner in a fancy restaurant?"

She smiled. "How could I forget? It was the most expensive item you bought me. That and the shoes that went with it." Her eyes sparkled. "They are so sexy. I can't wait to wear them."

Just then, the clerk returned with a tower of shoe boxes and put them on the floor next to Peter. "I took the liberty of bringing several styles for you to try, sir."

Peter stifled a chuckle. Seeing the number of bags he and Marina were hauling between them, the clerk must have assumed that he was dealing with serious shoppers who were worth his time and effort.

3 2

MARINA

When Marina collapsed into the passenger seat of Peter's car, her body was exhausted, but her spirit was exhilarated. The trunk was filled to bursting with shopping bags, a testament to the whirlwind day of indulgence they had spent.

Growing up in Igor's compound, shopping had been as foreign to her as the idea of freedom. Her life had been simple, defined by her duties and designated place in the hierarchy. The funny thing was that, at the time, she hadn't considered her life terrible. She had known her place and what had been expected of her, and as long as she'd toed the line, she was safe. Others in the compound hadn't had it any better, not the humans anyway, and even the Kra-ell had lived modestly, including Igor himself. He had been a glutton for power but not for luxury.

It was so easy to get used to all the good things Peter introduced her to. The lovely big house was professionally decorated, with a comfortable bed that felt like sleeping on a cloud. And now the shopping extravaganza had been so over the top that Marina was having difficulty internalizing the amount of money Peter had wasted on her. A village could buy food for a month with that kind of money.

Still, it was his money, and he didn't owe it to anyone. He had earned and saved it, and if it made him happy to spend it on her, she would oblige him.

As Peter glanced at his watch, his brow furrowed. "We will have to rush things a bit to make it in time to *By Invitation Only*." He looked at her with a smirk. "And we do want to make it on time. They are very strict about that. If you are not in their parking lot at the scheduled time, they will not wait for more than fifteen minutes."

Marina wanted to ask why they were meeting someone in a parking lot to go to a restaurant, but she didn't want to appear too provincial.

Besides, she didn't have the energy. She was tired, and the prospect of dressing up and going out to a fancy restaurant seemed daunting. Not that she was going to say a thing. Peter had gone to a lot of trouble planning this day for her, but he had forgotten that she was human with human limitations and reserves of energy. Nevertheless, she had no intention of disappointing him and putting a damper on the magic.

Summoning a smile, she pushed down the fatigue and focused on the thrill of anticipation. "I can't wait."

Peter wasn't fooled, though. He was too attuned to her to fall for the brave face she put on. Reaching over, he took her hand. "Shopping is hard work." He sighed dramatically. "I suggest that you recline the seat and nap on the way home to recharge your batteries for tonight."

That was a good idea, but it wasn't as easy as just closing her eyes. "Can you thrall me to feel sleepy?"

Peter hesitated. "I'd rather not. I don't take thralling lightly, and I don't do it casually. I can sing you a lullaby, though."

Marina didn't want him to do anything he wasn't comfortable with, so she reclined her seat, curled on her side, and closed her eyes. "I'd like to hear you sing."

Not surprisingly, Peter had a beautiful singing voice. It was deep and velvety, and his pitch was perfect. In no time, she felt sleepy.

"Wake me up when we get home," she murmured.

As they merged onto the highway, Marina was carried away by the gentle rocking motion of the vehicle and the soft, steady thrum of the engine, and she let her mind drift,

Hovering on the edge of sleep, the word *home* echoed through her mind.

She'd lived in the village less than a handful of days, yet it felt more like home than any other place she'd lived in because she was with Peter, and Peter was her home.

33

PETER

Peter selected a dark red silk tie from his collection, the color complementing his charcoal-colored suit. Standing in front of the mirror, he draped the tie around his neck and, with practiced movements, crossed the wide end over the thin one, looped it underneath, and brought it up through the neck opening.

The truth was that he didn't wear ties often, but when a man was almost two centuries old, he'd had enough practice to do it blindfolded.

He tucked the wide end down through the loop he had created, tightening and adjusting the knot to sit neatly against his collar. After ensuring that the tie was centered and the length was right, he smoothed down his suit jacket and inspected his reflection with a satisfied nod.

He looked handsome and debonair if he said so himself.

The gold cufflinks had been a present from his mother upon his acceptance to the Guardian training program, and they added to the look he was going after tonight, which was refined sophistication.

Peter chuckled to himself. Was he a good enough actor to fool anyone?

Not likely. A tailored suit and a pair of fancy cufflinks could not replace years of formal education in snobbery.

As Marina stepped out of the bathroom with a towel wrapped around her chest and another around her hair, Peter lifted his hand and smoothed it over his goatee.

"Don't worry." She patted the one on her head. "I'm the queen of quick blowouts."

He snorted. "Yes, you are. But it's called blow jobs, not blowouts."

Marina rolled her eyes. "Nice try." She dropped the towel covering her body, which was a pure act of revenge because she knew he could do nothing about it.

They needed to arrive on time.

"You are wicked," he said, his eyes glued to her sashaying naked ass.

She looked at him over her shoulder, her eyes hooded, and a naughty smirk lifted her lips. "I know."

Oh, she was going to pay for that.

"Wear the wrap dress," he called after her.

"I am. You told me you wanted me to wear it tonight when you bought it for me."

He had, but he hadn't told her the rest of his plan. He would tell her later.

"Can you find it for me? It will save us time. Also, the black shoes."

"Sure thing, sweetheart."

When she emerged from the bathroom fifteen minutes later, with her hair and makeup done and sporting a new, sexy lingerie set, he held the dress up but didn't hand it to her.

She reached for the hanger, but he held it up.

"Peter." She tried to jump for it. "We are going to be late."

He shook his head. "Take off your bra and panties."

Noting the mischievous glint he no doubt had in his eye, she shook her head. "We don't have time for games." Her voice sounded breathless.

He'd known that it would excite her. "We are not going to play now. Take them off, and I'll give you the dress."

Her eyes widened. "You can't be serious."

"I'm dead serious. Do as I say."

The scent of her arousal hitting his nostrils was all the confirmation he needed that she was very much on board for the game he had in mind.

"Yes, sir."

She reached behind her and unclasped her bra, sliding the shoulder straps down her arms, letting it fall off, and tossing it on the bed. Next, she hooked her thumbs in her thong panties and shimmied out of them.

As Peter's erection threatened to escape the confines of his boxer shorts and he began to sweat, he realized that his plan was going to be sweet torture that would last long hours unless he got some creative ideas, like sneaking Marina into the bathroom or the supply closet in his cousin's restaurant and fucking her into oblivion, or having her prove her claim that she was the queen of blow jobs.

Striking a pose, Marina extended her hand. "Are you going to hand me the dress or not?"

He offered it to her without a word, knelt at her feet, and helped her into the impossibly high heels.

Marina was a beautiful woman, but she was a vision standing naked in four-inch stilettos, with her hair and makeup done to perfection.

Still kneeling, he watched her put the dress on, wrap it around her body, and secure it with a belt, which she tied tightly around her narrow waist.

"I hope I'm not going to flash anyone but you."

He pushed to his feet and wrapped his arm around her middle. "Don't worry. I'll make sure no one gets to see what's mine."

34

JASMINE

As Jasmine walked into the penthouse, holding a stack of laundry under her arm, her back was aching from the long hours spent sitting by the prince's bedside, and her shoulders felt tight even though she'd tried to remember to stretch from time to time.

They should invest in better chairs for the patients' loved ones sitting at their bedside.

Not that she was the prince's loved one, but he didn't have anyone else to watch over him, and Jasmine had nominated herself. Well, nominating implied a voluntary decision when it was more like a compulsion. She didn't have a choice in the matter. There was no other way to explain why she slept on the floor near his hospital bed, only a sleeping bag cushioning the hard surface, and why she showered in the small, utilitarian en suite bathroom. She had barely left his side in the days since his arrival, her heart aching with the need to be near him like they were connected by some invisible thread that had tied them together across time and space.

Somehow, everything she had ever strived for and worked so hard to achieve seemed less important than nursing this stranger, this alien from a different planet, back to health.

Thankfully, the medical staff didn't notice the sleeping bag she'd hidden under the hospital bed and that she didn't spend every moment sitting in the damn chair but stretched out on the floor for a quick nap here and there. Or maybe they had noticed and were pretending that they didn't because no one had the heart to kick her out.

"Hello, stranger." Margo's voice startled her.

Jasmine gasped, her hand flying to her chest, and when she scanned the room to find where the voice was coming from, she found Margo sprawled out on the living room couch with her phone clutched in her hand.

"You startled me. I thought you were still training in the Perfect Match center."

"It's Sunday." Margo sat up. "Frankie went to visit her family, the guys are working in the basement, and Gabi and Ella are in the village. I'm all alone up here."

Calling the sprawling underground labyrinth under the high-rise a basement was the epitome of an understatement, but Jasmine didn't correct Margo. "I'll just drop this in the washing machine and come sit with you for a bit."

She wanted to return to the prince as soon as possible, but Margo looked like she could use a friend.

"Do you want coffee?" Margo pushed to her feet.

"Sure. I planned to drop my dirty stuff in the machine and carry a fresh stack back to the clinic, but I'm a little hungry. Are there any leftovers in the fridge?"

The truth was that she was famished, and she would have raided the fridge on her way out anyway. The café in the lobby was closed on Sundays, so she'd gotten coffee in the kitchen and instant oatmeal she'd found in one of the cabinets. The medical staff must have assumed that she ate at the penthouse, which she did when she could find leftovers.

"I'll put together a plate for you," Margo said.

"Thank you."

After loading the washing machine, Jasmine went to the bedroom and collected a fresh change of clothes and a few towels.

When she returned to the kitchen, two fresh cups of coffee were on the counter and a large plate of assorted fruits and cheeses.

Not the meal she'd had in mind, but it would do.

"That looks awesome." She snatched a strawberry and popped it into her mouth.

"I'm glad you like it. That's all I could find." Margo lifted her coffee cup and took a sip. "How are the twins doing?"

Jasmine shrugged, the familiar words rolling off her tongue with practiced ease. "Still unconscious, but they look better with every passing day. It's amazing how quickly you people recover. It would have taken a human several weeks or even months to make the progress these two have made in three days."

"They are half gods." Margo smiled tightly. "I'm just an immortal, but I get what you are saying."

Sensing that something was weighing on her friend's mind, Jasmine frowned. "What's going on, Margo? Trouble with the family? Or are you feeling lonely because Negal is spending his days in the basement?"

Margo chuckled. "Both. But it's mainly about my brother's wedding." She lifted her phone and showed Margo the screen. "Lynda changed her mind about the bridesmaids' dresses and sent me a link to choose a new one. She always makes life as difficult as possible for everyone around her."

"I don't get it." Jasmine put a piece of cheese on a cracker. "I thought that the wedding was postponed because your family was whisked away to safety to hide them from the cartel, but then no one came looking for them, and they were allowed to go home. Everything was already arranged, including the bridesmaids' dresses."

Margo sighed. "It's never as simple as that with Lynda. Besides, it was postponed again."

"Why?"

"Because of me. I told them that I was still in the witness protection program because of the trip to Tibet, and Rob refused to get married without me."

"Good for him," Jasmine said. "Do you need help choosing your new bridesmaid dress?"

Margo shook her head. "I don't care about the damn dress. I care about Rob's future." She turned a pair of pleading eyes on Jasmine. "Can I ask you for a favor?"

"Of course. Anything."

"What I need is for you to do your card magic to tell me if Rob is going to be happy with Lynda."

Jasmine stifled a wince. "Are you sure you want me to do this? I know the cards have proved themselves regarding the prince, but they might not always be right."

It was also possible to misinterpret their meaning, and Jasmine was far from the best at reading them.

"I know." Margo clutched her cup of coffee as if it was a lifeline. "But I'm desperate. I have to know."

"I'll get the cards." Jasmine pushed to her feet.

Margo put a hand on her arm. "Finish your coffee and your meal first. The tarot can wait a few more minutes."

3 5

PETER

T he night was unusually dark when Peter drove through the city streets. Clouds obscured the moon and stars, and the air smelled like rain.

Beside him, Marina stared out the window at the passing scenery. "This city is huge, and each neighborhood looks different." She turned to him. "I still think the village is much nicer than anything out here."

"I agree." He put his hand on her knee.

Knowing that she was naked under the dress and that he could fondle her any time he wished, it had been a struggle not to part the skirt and explore how turned on she was. But part of the fun was the anticipation, and he wanted to save the game for when they were seated in a dark corner booth.

As he turned down a narrow, nondescript alley, Peter guided the car into the parking lot and eased into the spot marked with a large number twenty-three on the pavement.

Cutting the engine, he glanced at Marina. "Ready to be wowed?"

"By what?"

"You'll see." He opened the door, stepped out of the car, and walked to the passenger side.

The restaurant's nondescript limousine pulled up behind them just as he opened Marina's door and offered her a hand.

"Good evening." The limo driver opened the back door for them.

They slid in and, a moment later, were again on their way.

"It's like some spy movie," Marina whispered.

"It's all part of the mystique, a cultivated air of exclusivity that makes *By Invitation Only* the exclusive club it is." He chuckled. "And you don't have to whisper.

The driver can't hear us." He pointed at the glass separating the back from the front.

She frowned. "How can you be sure of that? He might have a microphone back here."

"That's an excellent observation, but he doesn't. The owner ensures that his staff obeys the rules."

Understanding glinting in her eyes, Marina nodded.

As the limo stopped in front of a gate, there was nothing there that would indicate the presence of a world-class restaurant on the other side. There were no signs or markers that would betray its existence beyond the ordinary-looking gate. To the untrained eye, it looked like just another residence of some wealthy family that wanted to protect its privacy.

Peter squeezed Marina's hand as the gate slid open and the limo crawled up the long and winding driveway. "This is a new location. It's my first time here."

Her eyes widened with surprise. "Really? I thought you'd been here before."

"Only once, and it was in the previous location. The demand became so high that Gerard had to buy a larger place. Not that it was a problem, given the fortune he makes. When he first came up with the idea, I thought he was nuts because no one would pay that much for a membership that only gave them access to make reservations and still pay for the meal, but he was right. I underestimated how the rich really live and how much they are willing to spend on exclusivity and privacy and belonging to a club that only accepts the elite of the elite."

"I'm surprised your cousin demanded Kian buy a membership."

Peter grinned. "Kian co-owns the place with Gerard, so I don't think he had to pay full price, but I don't know that for sure. Gerard is a gifted chef, but he also has an ego to match, and he's not easy to work with. Kian is probably a very silent partner who only collects profits in proportion to his investment."

As the limo stopped in front of the grand entry, Marina swallowed, and her eyes flooded with trepidation. "I can't go in there, Peter. I don't know how to act around people like that."

He intertwined his fingers with hers. "Neither do I," he said in a playful tone. "I just try to remember that this is a classy joint, so no getting drunk and singing Scottish lurid love ballads. If you can do that, you'll do just fine."

Marina laughed nervously. "I'll do my best, but I make no promises."

As the driver opened the door, Peter stepped out and offered his hand to help Marina out while blocking her from the view of the guy in case her skirt parted.

The driver went ahead of them and opened the door with a flourish almost rivaling Okidu's. "Welcome to *By Invitation Only*."

A hostess greeted them with a warm smile as they stepped through the door and into the dimly lit foyer. "Good evening."

She didn't ask for their names and didn't utter the name Peter had made the reservation under. Anonymity was the name of the game or, rather the pretense of it.

The rich and famous wanted to be seen and acknowledged by their peers but left alone to their illicit affairs and clandestine meetings. As long as no names were spoken, there was no definite proof of who they were. There were plenty of lookalikes, and Peter wouldn't have been surprised to discover that the elite used doubles to mislead the paparazzi and perhaps even one another.

"Please, follow me." The hostess led them through the cavernous room, which was divided into intimate seating arrangements.

"I've requested the booth," Peter said.

The woman nodded. "A booth was reserved for you, sir."

A jazz band was playing soft, sultry tunes that seemed to dance on the air like wisps of smoke, but no one was dancing yet.

It was too early for that.

Peter cast a sidelong glance at Marina, watching her reaction to the grandeur and the beauty of the room, the celebrities they were passing by, and the way the candlelight flickered across the faces of the diners and made their jewels sparkle.

Squeezing her hand, he leaned to whisper in her ear, "Welcome to the magical and wondrous world of *By Invitation Only*."

36

JASMINE

J asmine retrieved her well-used tarot deck from the bedroom and returned to the living room.

"I made fresh coffee," Margo said with a nervous smile.

"Good." Jasmine sat next to her on the couch. "Do you know anything about tarot?"

"A little. My roommate in college introduced me to them, but I never took her readings seriously. It was just a fun thing to do to pass the time and have a good laugh." She smiled apologetically. "No offense."

"None taken." Jasmine shrugged. "As long as you don't think that they are the devil's toys, I have no problem with you doubting the readings."

Margo laughed. "The devil's toys? Are you serious? Has anyone ever told you that?"

Jasmine grimaced. "My father, but I don't want to discuss it." She took the cards out of the pouch.

With a deep breath and a silent prayer to the Mother of All Life, she shuffled them a few times and then put the deck on the coffee table in front of Margo.

"Put your hand on the deck and think about your question. Hold the image of your brother and his fiancée in your mind while you ask."

Margo did as she was told, her hand resting on the deck for a long moment, and her eyes closed.

"Okay." She removed her hand. "What now?"

"Now it's my turn." Jasmine closed her eyes, letting her mind drift as she also put her hand on top of the deck, feeling the universe's energy flowing through her.

When the tingling sensation stopped, she opened her eyes and began to lay out the cards in a familiar spread. The Lovers reversed. The Tower upright. The Three of Swords piercing a heart with its sharp, gleaming blades.

Jasmine felt her heart sink as she looked at the cards and their message. Betrayal, heartbreak, the shattering of illusions, and the crumbling of foundations.

She didn't want to say it out loud and give voice to the painful prediction of Rob's future, but as she looked at Margo, she saw that her friend had formed her own interpretation of the cards and the message they conveyed.

"I knew it." Margo sighed. "The way Lynda acted in Cabo made it obvious that fidelity was not something she concerned herself with."

Jasmine hesitated, not wanting to confirm her friend's fears. "I can make another spread. Perhaps your suspicions influenced the results. It is also possible that the infidelity will happen in the distant future, not in the past. It can also mean that it happened in the past but will not happen in the future. It can possibly mean that Rob is the cheater."

Margo shook her head. "I asked if Rob was going to be happy with Lynda, and the answer was obvious. There's betrayal and a lot of pain and heartbreak on the horizon. This time, I will be more precise with my question." She looked at Jasmine. "I will ask if Lynda is cheating on Rob or will cheat on him in the future."

"Let's do this." Jasmine collected the cards, reshuffled them several times, and put the deck in front of Margo. "Go ahead. Put your hand on it."

Regrettably, the second spread turned out identical to the first one, which was eerie.

"I'm sorry." Jasmine collected the cards.

Margo let out a breath. "I don't know how to tell Rob. He's not going to believe me. It's not like I can tell him I'm basing my accusations on a tarot reading."

Jasmine chewed on her lower lip. "You need real proof. Did you ask the cards if she was cheating on him currently?"

Margo nodded.

"Then you can catch her in the act and bring him proof. You don't have much time before the wedding."

Margo snorted. "I doubt she is sleeping with someone while at the same time running around town and driving everyone crazy with her wedding plan changes. If she is, she must make very effective use of her time." Margo closed her eyes. "There isn't enough time to do anything, and even if there was, I don't have the money to pay a private detective, and I don't want to ask Negal for the money either."

Margo's comment gave Jasmine an idea. "You could ask Negal to spy on Lynda. He can shroud himself and be invisible."

"He's too busy with the equipment salvaged from the pod," Margo said. "I can't ask him to do that."

"Yes, you can, and he will do it for you." Jasmine reached for Margo's hand. "Rob is a Dormant, just like you. Marrying Lynda the cheater might cost him a chance at immortality."

Margo stared at her for a long moment. "You are right. I didn't think of that. Rob is a couple of years older than me, so it's not like he has endless time to attempt transition. Not doing anything about him throwing his life away on Lynda is not an option. I have to make it my number one priority."

Jasmine nodded. "I'm here for you. If you need me to do anything, say the word." She winced. "Just don't ask me to put a hex on Lynda. I only do positive stuff."

Margo chuckled. "I wouldn't dream of it. I don't wish Lynda ill. I want what is best for my brother, and Lynda is not it."

37

MARINA

Marina had a death grip on Peter's hand, not because her shoes were dangerously high and the heel was so thin that she was afraid it would snap if she made a wrong move. And it wasn't even the opulence of the plush, velvet-covered curved chairs in the circular booths. The people truly took her breath away, the faces she recognized from television and movies, from the glossy pages of magazines and gossip columns. They were the elite, the kind of people she'd never dreamt of meeting, nor had she wanted to.

And yet here she was, the lowly human girl who had grown up as a serf in a Kra-ell compound rubbing elbows with the crème de la crème.

The hostess led them to their table, a secluded corner booth cast in shadows, intimate, that would hide her from the crowd to which she didn't belong.

Peter guided her into the booth and slid in beside her, his body a solid, comforting presence that anchored her to the moment and shielded her from her anxiety and feeling of inadequacy.

"Your server will be with you momentarily," the hostess said. "Can I offer you something to drink while you review the menu?"

"Yes, please," Peter said. "The bottle of wine I reserved."

The hostess's eyes glistened with excitement, but Marina felt that it wasn't because she found Peter hot, or maybe it was, but it wasn't the only reason. "Of course. I'll be right back with your bottle."

Marina leaned against his arm. "She seemed very happy about the bottle you reserved. Does she get a cut?"

"Probably." He leaned in close, his lips brushing the sensitive skin of her neck in a way that made her shiver with anticipation. "I'm glad you don't feel intimidated by all this."

"Oh, I do. I'm very happy to be hiding in this booth with you." She turned to face him and brushed her lips over his. "Doing all kinds of naughty things that we are not supposed to do."

Peter's eyes started glowing. "Did I tell you already how much I love you?"

She smiled. "You did, but I don't mind hearing it again and again."

"You are perfect."

"Thank you." She batted her eyelashes. "Tell me more."

He fake-groaned. "I've created a monster." He kissed the pulse point on her neck, the spot he liked to bite.

"But you love me anyway." Smiling, she let herself sink into the plush, velvet-covered cushions of the booth.

The hostess returned with the wine and made a big production of uncorking it, pouring it into their glasses, and then waiting for them to approve.

Marina didn't know much about wines, but this one tasted exquisite, and she told the hostess that.

"Wonderful." The woman beamed.

"You'll have to order for me," Marina told Peter after the hostess left. "I don't understand most of the menu. What language is it written in?"

"Snobbish."

She laughed. "Seriously."

"French."

"Do you know French?"

He nodded. "But the easiest and best way to order in this place is to get the day's special. All the items are perfectly coordinated and complementary."

"That's convenient." She let out a relieved breath. "That's what I'll have."

The menu didn't have prices, and she wasn't going to ask how much it cost because Peter wouldn't tell her.

As the meal began, Marina got lost in the culinary sensations. Every item was a work of art and a symphony of flavors and textures that danced on her tongue and made her moan with pleasure.

The portions were small, almost laughably so, but each was a masterpiece. The chef and his helpers must all be obsessed perfectionists to produce things that looked and tasted like that, and she could understand why people were willing to spend a fortune on the experience.

Through it all, Peter's hand occasionally wandered to her thigh beneath the table, his fingers tracing idle patterns on her skin that made her pulse race.

She didn't know when he was going to up the game, but she was sure he would do so soon. His eyes had been glowing throughout the evening, but he somehow managed to keep his fangs from elongating.

When the first bottle of wine was gone, Peter ordered a new one and poured them both a glass.

He lifted his and waited for her to do the same. "To life, love, and joy."

Marina repeated the toast and clinked her glass against Peter's, the sound ringing out like a bell in the hushed, intimate space of the booth.

It was then that Peter's hand began to wander higher, and his fingers brushed against the soft, sensitive skin of her upper inner thigh, eliciting a strangled moan from her throat.

A flicker of fear mingled with excitement as he coaxed her legs to part wider, her cheeks flushing with embarrassment at the thought of being caught in such a compromising position. But then Peter's lips were at her ear, his voice low and husky with desire as he whispered to her in the darkness.

"No one can see," he murmured, his fingers doing naughty things, teasing and tormenting her in a way that made her squirm on the soft velvet seat. "Lean back and enjoy, love."

She let her head fall back against the cushions of the booth, and her eyes fluttered closed as Peter's fingers dipped into the soft, slick heat of her core.

As he teased and tormented her, she bit back a moan, her hips arching up to meet his touch, and as he brought her to the brink of ecstasy and then pulled back, leaving her gasping and trembling with need, she nearly lost her mind.

It was a delicious torture, a sweet, agonizing pleasure that left her breathless and dizzy with desire. In the dark, intimate cocoon of their booth, with Peter's touch setting her skin on fire and his lips whispering wicked, delicious promises in her ear, Marina found that she didn't care if anyone heard her moan or saw her expression of ecstasy.

She was lost as he held her on the edge for so long that she was ready to scream, and when he finally whispered in her ear the command to come, she bit so hard on her lip that she drew blood.

Long moments passed until her heartbeat stabilized, and she opened her eyes. "That was positively wicked." Marina reached with her hand and cupped him over his pants. "What about you?"

"Don't worry about me, love." He removed her hand and leaned to kiss her. "I have everything planned."

She snorted. "Do I even want to know?"

38

PETER

The drive back to the village was quiet, the silence broken only by the soft purr of the engine. The night had been magical, with the finest food and wine, dancing and laughter, as well as a naughty game that had Marina climaxing all over his hand.

Peter smiled, remembering how long it had taken her to catch her breath and calm her heartbeat. His Marina was a closet exhibitionist, and he intended to coax more of that from her in Brundar's club.

Not yet, though.

He would let a few days pass before he suggested it so she wouldn't feel overwhelmed. It was his responsibility to make sure that she expanded her boundaries at a comfortable pace and didn't force herself to do more than she was ready for just to please him.

He glanced over at her, taking in the way her eyes drooped with satisfied fatigue and her head lolled against the headrest as if it were too heavy to hold up on its own.

"Don't fight it, love." He reached over to clasp her hand. "Sleep. I'll carry you home."

Marina smiled, her fingers tightening around his. "I have an account to settle with you. I still owe you an orgasm."

Heat rushed through Peter at her words. He would've loved to collect on that debt tonight, but he could wait until tomorrow.

"I'll take an IOU, love. Tonight, it's going to be straight to bed for you."

She sighed. "Your resilience and boundless energy are what I envy the most about your immortality." She turned to him and smiled. "Well, that and not getting sick, and staying young forever."

Peter's gut clenched at the reminder that his time with Marina was limited.

"I hope that my frequent venom injections will keep you young and healthy for much longer than normal for humans."

"I hope so, too." She lifted their conjoined hands and kissed his knuckles. "And perhaps the solution to our predicament will come from an unexpected source." She slanted him a smile. "I met Kaia on my first day in the café, and she said something about working on a way to turn ordinary humans immortal. I thought she was saying that just to make me feel good, but Wonder said she was a scientist, so maybe she's actually onto something?"

"Kaia is a brilliant bioinformatician, and I know that she is working on something, but I don't know what it is exactly. It's classified."

Marina frowned. "But you are a Guardian?"

"Even Guardians don't have access to everything."

Peter had heard rumors, of course. But they were mainly about building a more primitive version of the Odus, not finding the secret to immortality.

"That's a shame. I thought you knew something about her work."

"Well, I do." He scrambled for something optimistic to say. "Our ancestors became immortal through genetic manipulation, so it's possible, and if anyone can find the answer, it's Kaia."

Marina sighed. "Kaia has endless time to find the answers she's seeking and figure out how to make humans immortal, but I don't. If I'm lucky, I might have a decade before I start showing signs of aging. And if I'm not lucky, it could be even sooner than that."

Peter wanted to take Marina in his arms and promise her that everything would be alright and that science would find a way to keep her young and beautiful and vibrant forever, but she was right, and there was nothing he could say to make it better without resorting to lying.

"I believe that the Fates brought us together for a reason, Marina," he said instead. "I feel the bond forming between us, which shouldn't be possible between a human and an immortal, and yet, here we are."

"Oh, Peter." Marina smiled indulgently. "I'm not a Dormant. I think we've established that by now."

She was right, of course. No Dormant had ever taken this long to transition, especially given the steady supply of his venom.

Still, he couldn't shake the feeling that there was more to their connection than met the eye, that the Fates had woven their threads together for a purpose that he could not yet see.

"Every Dormant is different, and every transition is unique. You could be the rare case of a late bloomer."

She laughed. "That's not likely, Peter. For that to be true, my mother would have to be a Dormant too, right?"

Peter shrugged. "There are many Dormants in the human population; it's just that there are so many humans that it's like looking for the proverbial needle in a haystack. Even if your mother was born in the compound, she could still carry the godly genes."

Marina closed her eyes. "I wish you were right."

Damn, he hated the resignation in her voice.

"Assume the win," he murmured.

She opened her eyes, confusion flitting across her face. "What does winning have to do with anything? Winning what?"

Peter just grinned, his heart pounding with reckless excitement. "Let's get married."

"Peter..." she said as if she was admonishing him for making a stupid joke.

"I'm serious. Let's have a ceremony in the village square, in front of all our friends and family, and show the Fates that we have faith in them and that we believe in the power of our love to overcome any obstacle."

Marina shook her head. "You're such a romantic, Peter."

"I know, so? Do you want to marry me or not?"

She stared at him, her eyes wide with disbelief. "You can't be serious."

But he just smiled. "Yes or no?"

For a long moment, Marina was silent, her eyes searching his face as if looking for some sign of doubt or hesitation. But there was none to be found, only love and devotion and his fierce, unshakable determination and belief that he was right.

And then, with a smile that lit up the darkness like a beacon, she nodded. "Yes, but I expect a proper proposal with a ring and you down on one knee."

39

THE PRINCE

His mind drifted aimlessly among fragments of hazy memories of mostly sounds, clouded visuals, smells, and tactile senses.

Fabrics.

For some reason, he had the impression of how different fabrics felt against his skin. But those were memories.

He felt nothing now.

He knew he was male, so there was at least that, but he didn't know his name or what he looked like. Had he never seen his own reflection?

There was no sense of time, no concept of how long he had been floating in this confusing void or why.

Maybe this was death?

This could be what being dead felt like.

After all, he had no sensation of having a body or being inside a physical shell. As far as he knew, he could be just a floating consciousness.

But why was he conscious if he didn't have a purpose? Wasn't the soul supposed to end up somewhere special according to its merits?

And there was that sound again. A female voice that was somehow whole and clear among the haze of his fragmented thoughts and distorted memories of sensations. He could not understand what she was saying, so that was aligned with the rest of his confusion, but the sound was so clear, as if she was right there beside him, talking to him, singing to him.

Was the sound a lifeline or a beacon he was supposed to follow to find his place in the afterlife?

No, it couldn't be the afterlife because if he were dead, the sound wouldn't evoke such longing in him. He wanted to see the female's face, knowing that she would be beautiful, to feel the touch of her hand, knowing it would be soft and gentle.

Clinging to the sound, he followed it, his consciousness clinging to the tether...

If he could open his eyes...

If he only had eyes...

He should concentrate on remembering what it felt like to have them—having eyelids, closing them, opening them, moving his head from side to side.

A sense of apprehension assailed him every time he thought about anyone seeing his eyes. There was an instinctive need to cover them so no one would see them.

Why?

What was wrong with them?

And why was the sound gone?

He needed the female's voice so he could follow it. Where had she gone?

Had something happened to her?

The sudden flash of fear and anger was like a bolt of energy, like a lightning strike that animated the body that he was becoming aware of, not enough to move anything but perhaps enough to lift his eyelids and look at the world he was in without reaching for a veil.

Dangerous. It was so dangerous. But he was tired of living in fear.

Commanding the shutters on his eyes to lift was at first futile, but he was not ready to give up. With a monumental effort, he forced the movement and almost lost consciousness just from the exertion of that slight action.

Then it dawned on him. He was conscious.

The view that greeted him was alien and terrifying. He hated small, confined spaces, and this chamber was small and devoid of color. White walls, various equipment, and all kinds of tubes and wires were attached to him.

A scream lodged in his parched throat, but then he saw her.

A female was slumped in a chair beside his bed, her wavy dark hair spilling over her shoulders, her face softened by the gentle embrace of sleep.

For a moment, he simply stared at her.

Who was she?

Why did she sit in this alien room with him, guarding, talking, and singing to him? Was she a medic?

Did he know her and had forgotten who she was?

Perhaps this was home, but he had forgotten that as well.

He tried to speak, to force the words past the dryness of his throat and the heaviness of his tongue, but all that emerged was a rasping, guttural sound that seemed to echo in the room's stillness like a cry of despair.

The female didn't rouse, but suddenly the door flew open with a bang, and another female rushed in, red hair the color of fire flying behind her like a torch in the wind.

The dark-haired female jerked awake, her eyes wide open as she sat up straight in her chair.

They spoke to each other in urgent tones, their words a jumble of unfamiliar, incomprehensible sounds. But then, with a movement almost too quick to follow, the dark-haired female lifted a pendant that hung around her neck and spoke a command, "Kra-on."

The redheaded female followed her example, and suddenly, miraculously, their words became clear, the meaning of their conversation snapping into focus like a puzzle piece falling into place.

With a start, he realized that the devices hanging from their necks translated their foreign language into one he could understand.

"My sister," he managed to croak, his voice a hoarse, broken whisper that seemed to scrape against the inside of his throat.

The dark-haired female rushed over to his bed and leaned over him, her smile soft and reassuring and her strange golden eyes glowing with warmth and affection as she brushed cool fingers over his forehead. "Your sister is fine," she said through the device. "She's in the next room, still unconscious like you were, but getting better with every passing day."

Tears gathered in his eyes, a wave of relief and gratitude washing over him like a cool, cleansing rain. "Thank the Mother," he whispered, his voice choked with emotion.

The female's smile widened, her eyes crinkling at the corners with a warmth that seemed to radiate from her every pore. "Welcome back to the world of the living, my prince."

"Prince?" Why had she called him a prince? "I'm no one's prince."

But the redheaded one stepped forward before the dark-haired female could answer him. "I need to examine the prince," she said briskly, her voice crisp and businesslike as she gestured for the other female to move aside. "Please, give me some space."

The dark-haired female nodded, stepping back from the bed with a lingering glance that seemed to promise she would never be far away.

And then the red-haired female was leaning over him, her hands moving over his body with the practiced efficiency of a medic.

A medic. That was what she was. And this was a medical facility.

Was the dark-haired female another medical provider?

"I'm senior medic Bri–" the translation device seemed to have a problem with the sounds.

The dark-haired one stepped forward and said, "Bri-jet," without the device's help.

When he repeated the sound, the senior medic nodded. "You have got it right. Good job. I am going to touch you now to do a more thorough check of how you are doing. If this is agreeable to you, say yes or nod, and if you cannot do either, blink once; if it is not agreeable and you prefer a male to check you, blink twice."

Did he prefer a male?

He was not sure, so he blinked once.

The medic pulled out a metallic device, rubbed it for some reason, and put it on his chest.

It suddenly occurred to him that he might be naked, and he did not want the female to see him, but she was a medic, and it was too late to say that he preferred a male to conduct the examination.

"Can you feel this?" she asked after doing something he couldn't feel.

"No," he rasped.

She paused what she was doing, stepped away from him for a moment, and then returned with a cup.

"I will start by wetting your lips." She poured some water on a white square of fabric and rubbed it over his lips. "Better?"

He licked his lips, the water tasting fresh on his tongue.

"Yes. Can I have more?"

The medic smiled. "Do you usually drink water?"

"Yes," he replied, wondering about the odd question.

The doctor nodded, her eyes narrowing as she studied him with a gaze that seemed to see straight through him. "I am going to raise the back of the bed to bring you to a semi-reclining position. There will be a whizzing sound when I activate the mechanism. Ready?"

Too tired to say the word, he blinked once.

"Here it goes." She pressed something, and then, with a soft whirring sound, the back of his bed began to lift, the angle shifting until he was propped up in a semi-reclined position.

The medic put in the cup a strange, tubular device bent at one end and held it out to him with an expectant look on her face. "Suck gently," she instructed. "I only want you to wet your mouth. You can swallow a little, but not a lot. Your stomach can't handle anything more than that right now."

He did as he was told, drawing the cool, clear water into his mouth and letting it sit on his tongue for a moment before swallowing it. It felt strange, almost foreign, as if his body had forgotten how to perform even the most basic functions.

When the medic took the cup away, the prince looked up at her, his eyes searching her face for some hint of familiarity, some clue that might help him piece together the shattered fragments of his memory.

"How can you understand me?" he asked.

The device that translated their strange language into the one he understood did not work in reverse. It did not translate what he had been saying to them.

The female pushed her flaming hair behind her ear, revealing a small device lodged inside her ear. "This translates for me," she explained, tapping it with one slender finger. "The same way the teardrop translates for you." She tapped the pendant that hung around her neck.

So, they had two kinds of translation devices—one for hearing and one for talking.

Interesting.

But even as he marveled at the ingenuity of the gadgets and wondered how they worked, the thought that bothered him was that he still didn't know who he was.

They called him prince, but a prince of what?

What had happened to him that made him unable to remember his own name?

40

JASMINE

The prince was awake, and his eyes were the brilliant blue she remembered from the moment he'd opened them.

Jasmine's heart was pounding so loudly that she had no doubt Bridget and the prince could hear it, but she didn't care.

This was the moment she'd been waiting for.

She wasn't a medical professional, but it seemed to her that he was out of the coma for good. He was keeping his eyes open and talking in whole sentences.

It would have been nice to hear his real voice and how he sounded in his own language, but she didn't dare defy Kian and take the earpieces out. They were staying no matter what, but not because she feared the prince's compulsion. She just didn't want to give anyone an excuse to kick her out of the room.

Her prince was still painfully thin, but he was breathtaking, with his chiseled features and regal bearing, his skin smooth and unblemished despite the ravages of time and stasis. Julian had cut short the tufts of long hair that had stayed attached to his head through thousands of years of stasis, and the bald spots were starting to sprout new hair.

Brown. It was a beautiful shade of chestnut brown, not black like Jade's.

Regrettably, by the time Bridget was done with her checkup, the poor male had fallen asleep again, but the doctor reassured Jasmine that he was resting, not unconscious.

"I'm going to dim the lights," Bridget said. "Now that he's conscious, he will be more comfortable sleeping without direct light shining into his eyes."

Jasmine nodded.

"He is very weak," Bridget said. "I expect he will be drifting in and out of sleep for the next day or two. Right now, it seems he only has the energy to stay awake for a few minutes."

The doctor sounded apologetic, as if it was her fault that Jasmine hadn't had a chance to talk with her prince yet.

"That's okay. I'll wait until he wakes up again."

Bridget chuckled softly. "It will most likely take a while, so I would have suggested that you take a break and go for a walk to stretch your legs, but I have a feeling that wild horses won't be able to drag you away from this chair."

"Your feeling is spot on," Jasmine admitted. "Now that he's finally awake, I'm not going anywhere."

She had a bottle of water and a couple of energy bars in her purse, so she was all good.

"Very well," Bridget said. "I will call Kian and tell him the good news."

Jasmine nodded, excitement and trepidation mounting inside her, making her gut clench with worry about what was still in store for her fragile prince. Kian would be thrilled to hear the news, but he would also have questions and exhaust her poor guy, robbing her of the few precious wakeful minutes during which she and the prince could get to know each other.

When the doctor left, Jasmine rose to her feet and stood over her prince, admiring the incredible progress he'd made in a few short days.

"Were you the one I heard in my dreams?" He startled her when he spoke.

His eyes opened, glowing blue in the dark room.

"Yes," she answered before remembering that the teardrop wasn't on.

"Sorry," she murmured. "Kra-on. Yes."

"Your voice kept me tethered to life," he said. "I followed it out of the void."

His admission filled her with warmth. "The doctor, Bridget, said it was good to talk to people in a coma. I didn't have the teardrop or the translation device, so I just sang and recited plays and poems in my own language, hoping that my voice would soothe you and make you feel less lonely. But then William brought me this." She lifted the device. "And it translated what I said to your own tongue. It didn't work with singing, so each time I wanted to sing to you, I had to turn it off."

The prince smiled, a soft, gentle curve of his lips that made Jasmine's heart skip a beat. "I loved the singing and the talking even when I couldn't understand it. You have such a lovely voice."

"Thank you."

As a wave of emotion washed over her, Jasmine felt tears prick at the backs of her eyes. She had never felt so needed as she did in that moment, with the prince's eyes fixed on her face.

"I am the one who should be thanking you," he said in a near whisper. "You brought me back." The prince's eyes began to drift closed, his lids heavy with exhaustion and his breathing slowing to a steady, even rhythm.

Jasmine's heart sank, a flicker of disappointment washing over her. But then she remembered what Bridget had said about the prince drifting in and out of sleep for the next couple of days, and she sat back down.

Hopefully, he would wake up again before Kian arrived so they could talk some more.

41

KIAN

"What's your impression of him?" Kian asked when Bridget was done telling him about the prince.

There was a long moment of silence. "He opened his eyes and spoke. He recognized Jasmine as the one whose voice he had been hearing, and he responded to my questions with clarity and coherence. On the other hand, he had no idea that he was a prince and asked a prince of what? He remembered having a sister; that was the first thing he asked about. When Jasmine told him that his sister was alive, there were tears in his eyes. I might be wrong, but he doesn't seem like the scary, powerful creature that the Eternal King is afraid of. He didn't try to use compulsion on me or Jasmine, and if he even has the ability, he doesn't remember having it."

"How do you know that he didn't try?"

Bridget chuckled. "Come on, Kian. Do you think that I wouldn't have known? He didn't even ask me to do anything. Aside from asking about his sister, he was just reacting to me and my questions."

"He's recovering. I'm sure he will be less agreeable when fully healed."

"I don't think so," Bridget said. "He seems like a gentle soul to me."

Beside him, Syssi nodded sagely. "The prince was raised as a servant of the goddess. I don't know what that implies, but if it's anything like human monks and priests, it requires a certain level of humility and compassion."

Kian lifted a brow. "Not all monks and clerics are blessed with those two qualities, and that's putting it as mildly as I can. Some of those who call themselves men of god are servants of evil."

"I know, my love." Syssi patted his thigh as if she was gentling a wild horse.

"But there are many good ones as well, and there is no reason to get all upset over nothing."

"Daddy?" Allegra looked at him with worried eyes from her spot on the floor.

"Everything is okay, sweetie." He forced a smile. "Daddy is not angry."

When she nodded regally and returned to her toys, the gesture was so like his mother that it made him smile.

He turned back to his phone and the doctor, who was still on the line. "I'll let my mother know. I'm sure that she would want to see her brother immediately, so get ready for a visit."

He'd managed to keep his mother away from the twins by convincing her to wait for them to wake up, and now that one of them had, she wouldn't want to wait another minute.

"You should bring Jade along," Bridget said. "Maybe seeing his people will jog his memory. I was very surprised he didn't react to how Jasmine and I looked. I thought he would assume we were goddesses, and maybe he did, but it didn't prompt a negative reaction from him, which is strange for someone who grew up surrounded only by Kra-ell and fearing gods."

Syssi shook her head. "He and his sister grew up in isolation. We don't know what they were taught by the priestess they were apprenticed to."

"True," Bridget agreed. "Let me know when you are on your way."

"I will." Kian ended the call.

"Your mother will be so thrilled," Syssi said.

Kian nodded, his mind already racing ahead to the safety measures needed to protect her.

With a sigh, he dialed his mother's number.

"Good morning, Mother."

"Good morning, my son." Annani sounded cheerful. "Are you bringing Allegra over?"

"Not today. Bridget just called to tell me that the prince was awake. He's weak and confused, but he's alive and speaking. I'm sure that you want to visit him as soon as possible."

"Of course. When are we leaving?"

"As soon as you are ready, I want you to wear a disguise."

There was a long moment of silence. "Why?"

"Precaution. I don't want him to know who you are until we are sure of his intentions. I wish you still had the Nurse Rachel costume."

Annani laughed. "Oh, yes. That was such a lovely outfit, but I am afraid that I do not know what happened to it. I might have donated it along with other old clothing."

"You probably did. I think a pair of jeans and a T-shirt will do the trick. That and tamping down your glow and making yourself less beautiful. He is only half god, so he might not be immune to your shrouding."

His mother scoffed. "If I need to shroud myself anyway, what do I need a costume for?"

"It's less tiring when you don't have to shroud everything for a long period."

Syssi leaned in close to whisper in his ear. "I could get a pair of jeans and a shirt from Lisa. She's much taller than your mother but just as slim."

Kian nodded. "Good idea." He turned back to his mother. "Did you hear that?"

"Yes, but it did not make me happy. You know how much I detest jeans."

"I do." He pulled out his trump card. "But I also know how much you want to see your brother."

"Very well," she said. "Are you coming over to collect me?"

"It's up to you. I can come over, and we can continue from your place, or you can come here. I still need to call Jade, and Syssi needs to get the clothing from Lisa, so let's make it an hour?"

"I will come to your place," his mother said. "Do I need to bring along my Odus?"

"That's an excellent idea, but one will suffice."

The Odus were the best protection for his mother, and they were immune to compulsion, but given the prince's weakened state, there was no need for more than one.

"I will be there in an hour." His mother ended the call.

Syssi pushed to her feet. "Can I come with you? I'm curious to see the twins."

"Of course, you can." He stood up and pulled her into his arms. "You don't need to ask. I'm always at your command."

"I know, my love." She stretched up on her toes and kissed him. "But I'm worried that your sisters will be upset for not being included while I was."

"Don't worry about them. Alena is not going anywhere because she can barely walk and is about to go into labor at any moment, and Amanda doesn't like to get involved in the early stages of anything."

Syssi laughed. "You know your sisters well. What are we going to do with Allegra? I don't want to take her with us, and I don't want to leave her with Okidu either."

"Take her to Andrew. Allegra loves playing with her older cousin."

"What if he asks why?"

Kian shrugged. "You can tell Andrew. It's not a big deal if he knows. By now, the entire village knows the twins are at the keep."

"That's good." She kissed him again. "The fewer secrets I need to keep, the better."

42

THE PRINCE

The senior medic had left the back of the bed elevated, and as he lay back against the pillows with his eyes closed, his mind reeled with what he had learned in the brief moments of his waking.

He felt overwhelmed, his thoughts still fragmented and scattered and refusing to coalesce into a logical tapestry that could help him orient himself in this strange world he had found himself in.

Was it strange, though?

How would he know what was strange and what was not when he had no reference, anchor, or name?

He wanted to fall asleep again and let the blessed oblivion of unconsciousness take him away from the confusion and fear, but the female sitting beside his bed, the one with the golden eyes and the gentle touch, seemed determined to keep him awake and anchor him to the waking world with the sound of her voice and the warmth of her hand in his.

What had she been saying to him?

He had lost the thread at some point. "I am sorry, but my mind wandered off. Can you repeat what you have just said?"

She smiled. "Of course. I am sorry for talking nonstop and keeping you awake. Do you want me to let you sleep?"

He did not wish to offend her and lose the only person who seemed to care about him in this world. "No, please continue." He managed to turn his head so he could look into her bright, golden eyes. "I do not know your name."

When she said something that the translating device couldn't interpret, she tried again, and when it still refused to cooperate, she shook her head. "I'm going to turn it off for a moment." She pressed on the device.

"Jaaz-min." She patted her chest. "Jaaz-min."

When he slowly repeated the two syllables, she smiled and activated the translation device. "It's the name of a white, sweet-smelling flower. Some say that it grows in the gardens of the gods. Do you have anything like that in your world?"

Something tickled his memory. "Dull-or. It's a white flower with a pleasant smell." He was so happy to remember anything at all.

"Wonderful," Jasmine said. "I will program the teardrop to translate Jasmine to Dull-or and the other way around. Can you remember any other flowers from your world?"

"Shorga. It is a purple flower." He felt stupidly happy for remembering such an unimportant detail.

They spent the next few minutes trying to jog his memory about other things, but he became tired, and his mind became sluggish.

"I am sorry," he said in a near whisper because he did not have the energy to speak up. "I am tired."

"You are also thirsty. Your lips are dry." She reached for the cup of water beside the bed and brought the tubular thing to his lips. "I don't know how much you should drink, so take only a little."

He still remembered the medic's instructions, sucking in a little bit of liquid to wet his mouth.

When Jasmine took the tube away, he sighed. "I wish I could remember my name so I could give it to you."

She retook his hand, her touch warm and reassuring as she leaned in close. "It will take time, but you will remember. Small steps. And for now, I'll call you prince."

"Prince of what? No one's answered that question for me yet."

"Prince means that you are the son of a queen or a king. I was told just a little bit about why you were sent here, and I'm not even clear on all the details, so I don't want to give you the wrong information. Besides, I think that it's better if you remember it yourself." She gave him a small smile. "That way, you will know it is true, right? I could tell you all kinds of pretty lies and you won't know because you don't remember anything. I could also tell you the truth, but you won't believe me."

She was confusing him, but since he was enjoying just looking at her smiling face and hearing her voice, he didn't say anything and let her talk.

"You can also decide what being a prince means to you and adopt it. You don't have to be limited by what others expect from you. In stories, a prince is the leader of his people, a brave warrior of great honor and courage."

Was that who he was?

Somehow, the description did not fit. He was not a warrior; or was he?

A memory flashed through his mind of training with a sword; his partner was his sister, clad from head to toe in fabrics that concealed even her face. She was fast on her feet, and he'd had trouble keeping up, but there had been joy in their dance.

He tried to cling to the memory, but it disintegrated into smoky fragments, dissipating completely.

"Tell me what you know about me," he commanded.

"I don't want to give you the wrong information. Those who know more about you and can give you better answers have been notified that you are awake, and they will arrive within an hour or two."

He tensed. "Who are they?"

"Don't worry." She squeezed his hand. "No one means you or your sister harm. You are in good hands."

"Can you at least give me their names and titles, so I know how to address them?"

"Kian is the leader of this community. He doesn't have a title or a last name, so you just need to call him Kian. He's a little grumpy, but he is a very good guy. I owe him my life."

He frowned. "How so?"

Jasmine shrugged. "It's a long story that you will not understand without context that you don't have, but I'll try to make it simple. I got involved with some bad people who had nefarious intentions for me. One of Kian's people got pulled into my mess by mistake, so he sent a rescue team. They got us both out."

The prince put his other hand over his heart. "Then I owe Kian a life debt for saving you."

Her eyes widened. "No, you don't, but thank you for offering. I have repaid the debt by myself."

He narrowed his eyes at her. "How?"

Jasmine laughed. "Not the way you think. Kian is happily mated."

He had no idea why that was relevant and what she imagined he had thought.

"I do not understand what Kian's mate has to do with your life debt to him. Did you save her life?"

Jasmine opened her mouth, closed it, and then opened it again. "Talk about cultural differences. We have a lot to learn about each other."

"I still do not understand." He was too exhausted to guess what she could have meant by her odd comment. His eyelids felt heavy. "I'm sorry," he mumbled, his words slurring together as he fought to keep his eyes open. "I'm too tired to think."

Jasmine's smile was soft and understanding. "It's okay. Your body and mind need time and rest to heal."

He nodded, his eyes fluttering closed as he drifted off into the welcoming embrace of sleep.

43

ANNANI

Annani did not know which feeling was stronger, the excitement at the prospect of meeting her half-brother for the first time or the annoyance at having to wear jeans.

Why did Kian think plain human clothing would make a difference to her appearance?

Her brother did not know how the people of this world dressed. He did not know that a gown was a formal dress or that jeans were casual. It would not influence what he thought of her.

Sometimes, appeasing her son's paranoia was tiring.

As she reached Kian's front door, Okidu opened it and bowed.

"Good morning, Clan Mother."

"Good morning." She swept past him and headed straight toward Kian's office.

His door was open, and she did not wait for an invitation.

"Hold on, William." Kian put the phone down and pushed to his feet. "Good morning, Mother." He rounded the desk, leaned down, and kissed her cheek. "I'm almost done talking to William. Please take a seat."

Nodding, she accepted the invitation and listened as he continued the conversation with William.

"I only need two devices. One for Syssi and one for my mother."

"I can do that," William answered. "Give me half an hour."

"No problem. Can you send someone to my house with them?"

William chuckled. "I'll come myself. It's Sunday, and there is no one in the lab. It's just me."

"Right." Kian raked his fingers through his longish hair. "I forgot what day it was today. Thank you for doing this for me on a weekend."

"No problem, boss. I live for this stuff."

As Kian ended the call, Annani arched a brow. "What devices is William bringing for Syssi and me?"

"It's a translator device that works similarly to the earpieces, only it translates from English to Kra-ell and broadcasts the speech through a small speaker. We assume that the twins speak only Kra-ell."

"You probably assume correctly." She let out a breath. "I am so excited. Do you think he looks like me?"

Kian smiled indulgently. "No one looks like you, Mother, and the last time I saw him, he looked only a little better than a corpse."

She grimaced. "Can you please stop saying that word regarding my siblings? It is upsetting to me."

"I'm back!" Syssi walked into the office with a bundle of clothing clutched in her arms and a smile on her face. "Good morning, Clan Mother. I've got the teenage clothes to help make you look more ordinary, although I doubt it would move the needle."

"I doubt it as well." Annani took the bundle from Syssi's hands, her brow furrowing as she unfolded the garments and held them up.

Jeans and a pink T-shirt with a picture of a white cat on the front. "This is ridiculous." She gave the bundle back to Syssi. "I despise pants in general and jeans in particular. Perhaps you have a dress that I can borrow?"

Syssi smiled, her eyes twinkling with mischief. "I had a feeling that you would say that. I'll be back with something you might be more comfortable wearing." She rushed out of the office.

Kian sighed. "It's just for a couple of hours, and you've worn jeans before. I don't know what the big deal is."

Annani gave him a haughty look down her nose and did not bother to answer.

When Syssi returned, she brought a sundress made from red fabric with white and black flowers printed on it. The pattern was pretty, and it probably looked adorable on Syssi, but it was not something Annani would have ever gotten for herself.

"It's a little small on me," Syssi said. "But it will still be too big on you. Luckily, it comes with a belt to cinch the waist."

Annani took the dress from Syssi and regarded it with a frown before holding it against her body. It was too long. Her usual style was floor-length gowns, so the length in itself was fine, but for that particular style and cut, the hem should be at the knee, not mid-calf. She would look like a girl in her mother's dress.

"Very well. I will try it on."

She took off her breezy silk gown in the bathroom and slipped the sundress over her head. The fabric felt pleasant on her skin, so there was a small comfort in that, but that was the only positive thing she could say about it.

With a sigh, she braided her long hair, pulled out the sunglasses from the pocket of her gown, and put them on.

The reflection in the mirror depicted someone who wasn't her. The female looking back at her was not the queen that she had always been, the leader of her clan, the Clan Mother.

She was not meeting her brother for the first time looking like a beggar in an ill-fitting dress. When he first saw her, he would see a queen.

Annani was out of the sundress and into her gown in seconds, but it took her a little longer to unbraid her hair.

"Mother," Kian said reproachfully when she walked back into the office with Syssi's dress draped over her arm.

She shook her head, her jaw set with resolve. "My brother's first impression of me will not be based on falsehood. I will meet him as me," she said firmly, her voice filled with authority that brooked no argument. "The only concession to security that I am willing to make is to not mention my father or that the prince and I are related, but if I feel that he poses no threat to me, I will reveal this as well."

Kian looked like his mouth was full of broken glass, but he knew better than to argue with her. "As you wish, Mother."

Syssi took her dress back. "I'm sorry you didn't like it." She sighed dramatically. "Now I will have no choice but to lose weight to fit into this."

Kian growled. "Give it to charity. You are not losing anything."

She sent him an air kiss before turning to Annani. "How about a cappuccino while we wait for William?"

"That is a wonderful idea." Annani threaded her arm through Syssi's. "Is there any chocolate cake left?"

Syssi smiled brightly. "Of course."

4 4

JASMINE

J asmine let out a breath when the prince's eyes fluttered closed, and his breathing slowed to a steady, even rhythm.

He was so lost, and when he finally remembered who he was and why he had been sent to Earth, he might be even more lost than he was now.

Her heart ached for him.

She hadn't lied about not knowing all the details, but she knew that he and his sister were considered abominations in their home world and that they had been sequestered in the temple and covered from head to toe to hide who they were.

If their secret came out, they would have been killed by their people, and their mother would have shared their fate for her transgression. That was why the queen had sent her children to Earth on the settler ship, knowing she would never see them again.

She had done it to save them.

Although now that Jasmine had seen what the Kra-ell looked like, she couldn't fathom how the queen had thought to pull it off. The prince looked like the gods, not the Kra-ell; the same was true for his sister. If everything had gone according to plan and the ship had arrived when it had been supposed to, the settlers would have woken up and discovered the two hybrids among them.

Perhaps the plan was for the twins to pretend to be gods who had joined the expedition.

That actually made sense.

There had not been all that many gods on Earth, and the settlers could have chosen to settle somewhere far away from them so they wouldn't have anyone to compare the twins to.

If only the prince could remember his mother's instructions, they could have had answers to so many questions.

Perhaps his sister would remember more, although Jasmine doubted that. She hadn't woken up yet, which implied a worse condition than her brother's, so her brain might be more severely damaged.

At least the prince was coherent, and she was thankful for that.

With a sigh, Jasmine let go of his hand, rose from her chair, and made her way to the kitchen.

The enormous place was deserted as usual, but she knew where the coffeemaker was and got busy brewing a fresh pot.

What did they use this kitchen for? It looked like something that belonged in a venue. She could easily imagine a large team of chefs and kitchen staff preparing food for a wedding or some other event.

Sitting at the counter with a mug of coffee, she thought about Margo and wondered if her friend had talked with her mate about shadowing Lynda.

She pulled out her phone and typed up a message to Margo.

Her phone rang a few moments later.

"Yes, I did," Margo said. "And Negal had a much better idea than following her around. We will attach a tiny bug drone to her, and it will record everything she does until it runs out of power. Hopefully, we will get something by then, and if not, I will collect the dead drone and replace it with a new one. Lynda is so self-absorbed that she won't even notice."

"How small is that drone?"

"Smaller than a mosquito. They brought a bunch of them from their home planet, and it's precious, so they can't afford to lose any of them, but I don't intend on letting it get lost. I'll get it back for them."

"Sounds good to me. By the way, the prince is awake."

"I know. Negal told me. He also told me that the guy doesn't remember his name."

"He doesn't, and he's very upset about it. Where are you now?"

"Negal and I are collecting my stupid bridesmaid dress."

Jasmine chewed on her lower lip for a moment. "Are you going to introduce him to your family?"

Margo sighed. "Eventually I'll have to, but not yet. I told them I met someone in the witness protection program, and I'm dating him, so I can keep telling them he's on missions until I'm ready to present him. What about you?"

Jasmine laughed. "Thankfully, I don't have such problems. Even if I had someone to introduce to my father, I wouldn't. The less he knows about my life, the better."

"You have someone," Margo said. "The prince. How did he respond to you?"

"He's very sweet and grateful for my presence, but he can't stay awake for more than a few minutes at a time, so it's not like we have fallen madly in love and are about to live happily ever after."

Jasmine had a feeling that the road ahead was full of obstacles, and not just because of the prince's damaged memory. Naturally, there were obvious cultural differences between them, and if she wanted to bridge them, she needed to find someone who knew about the Kra-ell culture.

Not that the prince had grown up like other Kra-ell boys. His only companion had been his sister, and the only other people he'd come in contact with were his mother and the priestess, who must have known who and what they were and had protected them.

"Well, according to the cards, you will have your happily ever after with him," Margo said.

"I was shown a prince in my future. The cards didn't promise me a good ending."

"Then do another spread," Margo suggested. "If they could tell you that Lynda was unfaithful to Rob, they can tell you whether you will live happily ever after with your prince. You just need to ask the right question."

Jasmine swallowed. "I'm not ready to ask them that question. In fact, I don't think I should."

"Why not?"

"Because not everything is predetermined, and some things need to unfold on their own."

45

KIAN

T he mood in Kian's old office was a mixed bag of anticipation, excitement, worry, and even introspection.

The last one seemed to afflict his mother and Jade, but his mother was more excited than contemplative, while Jade was the other way around.

Kian knew what was going through his mother's head, but he wasn't sure about Jade. For her, the prince was a reminder of the life she'd left behind on Anumati. It had been a different world when she and the other settlers had been put in stasis chambers inside the escape pods that had comprised the bulk of the interstellar ship. Seven thousand years had passed, give or take a few decades, but that wasn't how Jade felt it. The thousands of years spent in stasis had passed without any awareness, so for Jade, time had resumed only after her stasis chamber had opened, which had happened not so long ago.

Next to him, Syssi thrummed with pure excitement, seemingly not worried at all that the prince might have nefarious intentions, and Aru was on the other side of the spectrum, mainly looking worried.

"How is your Kra-ell?" Kian asked him.

"It's good."

Jade snorted. "The Kra-ell the prince and I speak is an ancient dialect compared to yours."

"You can still understand me, and I can understand you," the god said. "That's all that matters."

Her shrug indicated that she had nothing further to say on the subject.

"We need to decide how much to tell the prince," Kian said. "We don't know the queen's plan and how much of it she'd shared with her children. They might have been sent to do damage, or they might have been sent to their father for protection. Those are two opposite ends of the spectrum. Right now, the prince does not even remember his name, so perhaps it's better to keep him in the dark and wait for his memory to start returning so we can evaluate the kind of person he is and his intentions."

His mother shook her head. "That will only create mistrust. He will remember eventually, so there is no point trying to keep him in the dark until he does. It is better that he regains those memories sooner rather than later, so we know what we are dealing with while he is still vulnerable."

Kian groaned. "The guy has just woken up after seven thousand years of stasis. We can't dump on him the entire history of Anumati, the conflict between the gods and the Kra-ell, the gods with the resistance, and what happened on Earth. There is only so much he can absorb. What I'm trying to figure out is what to tell him today."

Annani nodded. "You are right, my son. We should give him a few tidbits of knowledge and see how he reacts." She lifted the translating pendant. "I am glad to have this gadget and to be able to communicate with my brother. It would have been impossible without it."

Jade dipped her head at his mother. "With all due respect, Clan Mother, I think that I should be the one to talk to him. Even if he does not remember anything, he will instinctively feel more comfortable with a Kra-ell female that will remind him of his mother and the head priestess who de facto raised him and his sister."

Annani did not look convinced, but she gave Jade a nod. "We will play it by ear."

Jade tilted her head. "What does that mean?"

Syssi smiled. "It means that we will decide who will tell the prince what depending on the situation, and how receptive he seems to you or the Clan Mother. Who knows? Maybe he would prefer to hear it from Aru?"

"I doubt it," Aru said. "He will be more receptive to females, but I don't think he will have a preference for Jade. Given what Bridget and Julian reported, the prince doesn't know what species he belongs to. It's a miracle that he has even retained his language."

"That is interesting," Annani said. "Wonder, my dear childhood friend who spent five thousand years in stasis, woke up with similar amnesia. She knew she was an immortal female and remembered her language, but she did not know which people she belonged to and where she came from."

"How long did it take her to regain her memory?" Aru asked.

"Months," Kian said. "I hope it won't take the prince that long."

Syssi sighed. "The princess is probably going to be in an even worse state. I hope she didn't sustain brain damage."

"The prince's amnesia presents both an opportunity and a challenge." Kian drummed his fingers on the polished surface of the conference table. "On the one hand, it gives us a chance to shape his understanding of the world and his place in it. On the other hand, there is a chance that he's immensely powerful and not aware of it yet, and we will have an unpredictable wildcard on our hands that can turn into an ally or an enemy, depending on how we handle the situation. That's why we need to tread carefully and take it slow."

He turned to Jade. "You can start by introducing yourself as you would if you were still on Anumati. I'm curious to see his reaction to you. If he asks you questions, answer them, but try not to overwhelm him with too much information at once. Don't mention anything about who his father was and his relationship to Annani."

As Jade inclined her head in acknowledgment, his mother turned to him. "How long do you want me to hide from my brother that I am his sister?"

"Not long. I just don't want you to tell him right away. I want to see if he knows anything about Ahn, and that means waiting for him to remember and not feeding him information that might skew his responses. You should also tamp down your glow."

His mother grimaced. "Only until I reveal who I am."

Kian nodded.

"What about Jasmine?" Syssi asked. "She sits by his side day and night." She looked at Kian. "Are you okay with her meeting the Clan Mother?"

He winced. "Not yet. We will have to get her out of there."

"I'll do that," Jade offered.

Syssi arched a brow.

"What are you going to tell her?"

"I don't need to give her a reason. I'll instruct her to wait in the penthouse or the kitchen until I tell her it's okay to return." Jade smiled coldly. "People usually don't argue with me."

4 6

THE PRINCE

Time seemed to slip away as the minutes and hours blurred together in a haze. The prince drifted in and out of sleep, his mind still a jumbled mess of fragmented memories and half-formed thoughts, but things were not as chaotic as they had been when he had first become aware. He wondered why he felt calm instead of frantic.

It was the smell.

The female, Jasmine, the one who was named after a white, sweet-smelling flower. She didn't smell sweet, not entirely. There were spicy and musky undertones, too, and he wondered whether the scent was natural or artificial.

Feeling the first tendrils of wakefulness pulling at his eyelids, he opened his eyes, a smile lifting his lips when he saw her sitting by his bed and still holding on to his hand.

"Well, hello." She grinned at him. "I'm so happy that seeing me makes you smile. You must be feeling a little better."

"I do feel better, and seeing you makes me happy." He tried to squeeze her fingers, but his hand didn't obey his command.

He couldn't remember if he had ever held a female's hand other than his sister's. He must have held his mother's hand but didn't remember that either. How old was he?

"You are sad again. What were you just thinking about?"

"I do not know how old I am. Is there a way to tell?"

"I can tell you are an adult, but I do not know enough about your kind to even try to guess your age."

"What is my kind?"

"Don't you remember anything besides your sister?"

He had a feeling that she was avoiding answering on purpose. Maybe she didn't know what he was.

Maybe he was a survivor of a crash landing on a distant planet?

Something tickled his memory again.

A uniform.

It was a disguise. He had never worn one before. He had been used to comfortable, loose robes...

Princely robes?

"You are remembering something," Jasmine said. "I can tell by the faraway look in your eyes."

"It's just fragments. I remember wearing loose robes, I remember the feel of the fabric on my skin, and I remember vowing to my mother that I would protect my sister with my life." His eyes prickled with tears. "But I failed. She was hurt."

Jasmine intertwined her fingers with his. "You didn't fail. Your sister is alive, and she's getting stronger every day."

"Not thanks to anything I did."

"How do you know that? You don't remember anything. You might have done heroic acts to save your sister, and she might be alive thanks to you."

"I wish that was true." He knew it wasn't.

He wasn't injured. He hadn't fought for his sister. Something happened to both of them. But what could it have been to render them both unconscious while not injuring them?

But wait, what if he was injured and did not know it? He could barely feel his body. He was numb all over. Perhaps the medics gave him something to numb the pain of his injuries.

"Am I wounded?" he asked. "Is my sister?"

Jasmine frowned. "I thought you knew what happened to make you weak and forget everything. You and your sister were in stasis for a very long time. We found you, brought you here, and the medics resuscitated you. It takes time for your bodies to replenish themselves."

He was not sure he knew what stasis was, but he could guess. Had it been natural or induced?

He took a deep, shuddering breath, trying to steady and anchor himself in the present moment. "Where did you find me?"

"A place very far from here. Your escape pod landed on a mountain and made a big hole." She hesitated. "Only you and your sister survived. The others in your pod didn't. I'm so sorry."

Another tear escaped his eye for the lives lost of people he couldn't remember. "Tell me about this place."

"Where we found you?"

"Yes, and everything else in this world." He needed a distraction from the sadness. Something good to lift his spirits and make him feel like there was hope for him and his sister. Like there was a reason he was there.

Other than Jasmine, that is.

Perhaps he was meant to arrive on this world to find her?

She hesitated. "I don't know where to start. There is so much. There are so many different people, cultures, and ways of life. Some good and some not so much. It's a place of great beauty, but also great danger, a place where anything is possible, for better or for worse."

He nodded. "Tell me more about the people. In what ways are they different from one another?"

She took a deep breath. "This planet orbits a star that we call the sun. We have oceans and mountains, forests and deserts, great cities with millions of people living in them, and vast wildernesses and deserts where there are no people at all."

He listened, enraptured, as Jasmine painted vivid pictures with her words of towering structures that seemed to touch the clouds, all kinds of vehicles that moved on land, oceans, and the sky, and other technologies that, for some reason, failed to impress him. He found the many different races and cultures, each with their traditions and beliefs and their many different ways of seeing the world, fascinating.

"But for all its wonders, Earth is also a place of great strife and conflict," Jasmine said. "There are wars and famines, injustices and cruelties, but there is also great kindness and compassion, people who dedicate their lives to helping others and making the world a better place."

What she was describing resonated with him. "Good and evil, creation and destruction, life and death, honor and dishonor. It's all a duality." He closed his eyes. "I don't even know what it means, but I'm supposed to know."

Jasmine sighed. "You were raised to be a priest. You should know those things. They will come back to you."

He frowned. "So, you know things about me. Why didn't you tell me before?"

She lowered her eyes. "I didn't want to tell you that."

"Why not?"

"Because I wanted you to like me."

47

JASMINE

The prince looked so puzzled that his expression was almost comical, but the last thing Jasmine felt like was laughing.

Did she really say that?

I wanted you to like me.

"I don't understand," he said.

"No, of course, you don't." She grappled for words to explain what she'd said without sounding ridiculous, but before she could come up with something profound, Jade strode into the room without bothering to knock or announce her presence in any other way.

Evidently, there were significant cultural differences between what Jasmine considered polite and what the Kra-ell considered acceptable behavior.

"Greetings, holy brother." Jade lifted a fist to her chest. "I am Je-Kara, first daughter of the tribe of Thar'ok, a former member of the queen's guard."

The prince's eyes widened, a flicker of recognition sparking in their depths as he struggled to push up against the back of the hospital bed.

"Greetings, Mistress Je-Kara. Do I know you?"

Jasmine wasn't surprised that Jade wasn't the female's real name, and Je-Kara was much more fitting, but why had the prince prefixed it with mistress?

The female made him nervous, which Jasmine could understand. Jade was intimidating as hell, but she couldn't be his superior if he was the prince, and she was just a guard, right?

"No, you do not," Jade said. "I have seen you and your sister from afar, but you've probably never noticed me."

Some of the tension in his shoulders released, and he offered Jade a tentative

647

smile. "Even if I did notice you, Mistress Je-Kara, the first daughter of the tribe of Thar'ok, I am afraid that my memory is malfunctioning, and I cannot even remember my own name. If you know me, I would very much appreciate it if you could tell me what I am called."

Jade inclined her head. "In our culture, priestesses in training are called holy sister in training, and in your case, holy brother in training. You were the first Kra-ell male ever to enter the priesthood." She smiled. "And please, call me Je-Kara or Jade, as I prefer to be called here on Earth. Je-Kara was never a name fit for a warrior."

His eyes sparkled with amusement. "Perhaps I should also adopt an earthly name until I remember the one that was given to me at birth. What would you suggest?"

Jade glanced at Jasmine. "Any ideas?"

Jasmine chewed on her lower lip, thinking hard. The prince was gentle, sweet, and polite. What kind of name would fit him?

"Would you like the name Cedric? It means kind and loved." She turned off the teardrop and repeated the name so he could hear it as it sounded and not translated.

Jade grimaced. "That's a soft name. The prince needs a strong name. Something like Kor-rug or Or-gul." She slanted a look at Jasmine. "Kor-rug is a lion-like creature on Anumati, and Or-gul is a bird of prey."

"I like Cedric," the prince said.

Jade looked like she had just sucked on a lemon, but she inclined her head. "As you wish, my prince. I hope your memory will return soon, and you will remember the name your mother, the queen, gave you when you were born. I am sure it is a powerful name."

Jasmine exchanged an amused look with the prince and swallowed a chuckle.

Jade turned to her. "I must ask you to leave us for a time. The prince is about to receive several visitors, and we need to discuss some matters privately. You can wait in the penthouse or the kitchen for me to tell you when you can return."

Jasmine knew that Kian was on his way, so it made sense that he wanted to talk to the prince in private.

"Of course. I'll be in the kitchen if you need me. I could use another cup of coffee."

Jade nodded in approval.

Jasmine looked at her prince. "I'm not going far. I will be just down the hall."

She gave him a reassuring smile when he nodded and stepped out of the room.

As usual, the kitchen was deserted, the counters clean and gleaming under the strong fluorescent lights, and it reminded Jasmine how much she hated to be alone, especially in a room with no windows. This whole underground structure was depressing.

Perhaps she should go to the penthouse after all?

She could drink her coffee on the terrace and enjoy some fresh air. Even in downtown Los Angeles, the air was fresh so high up.

But she'd told Jade that she would wait in the kitchen, and if she went back to the clinic to tell her that she was going upstairs, it would seem as if she was snooping.

With a sigh, Jasmine set about making herself a fresh pot of coffee, her hands moving through the familiar motions with mechanical precision. She measured the grounds, filled the carafe with water, and watched as the dark liquid dripped and hissed into the waiting pot.

As she worked, her mind drifted back to the prince and the moments of connection and understanding.

He liked the name she had given him.

Cedric.

Did he look like a Cedric?

The name evoked an image of a British lord, someone who had graduated from a classy university and spoke with an upper-class diction and vocabulary.

Yeah. She'd read way too many historical romance novels.

Come to think of it, maybe that was where her obsession with royalty had begun.

Half of the heroes in those books were princes. Or maybe it was the other way around, and she'd always known she was destined to meet a prince, and that was why she'd been drawn to those kinds of stories.

As the coffee finished brewing with a final, sputtering hiss, jolting Jasmine from her reverie, she poured herself a mug and sat on one of the barstools next to the polished, stainless steel counter.

48

EDGAR

Edgar stopped in front of the clinic door and wondered whether he should leave the takeout bag outside. The smell of the dishes was delicious, but it could be overwhelming for the clinic and disturb the prince.

That was actually a good reason to bring it in, but he wasn't that much of an asshole. Besides, Bridget might have a problem with Chinese food being brought into her space, and he wasn't stupid enough to get on the doctor's wrong side.

Leaving the bag by the door, he pushed it open and walked in.

Anger rolled in like thunder when he saw the inner door to the prince's room closed. Had Jasmine closed it because she'd wanted to be alone with her prince?

She can do whatever she wants, he reminded himself. *You have no right to feel possessive.*

"Edgar," Bridget said as she walked out of her office. "What brings you here?"

"Takeout from the Golden Dragon. Are you hungry? I got it for Jasmine, but I have enough for everyone."

He'd gotten it for Jasmine as a gesture of friendship but also to remind her that he was still around, and if her prince turned out to be a frog, she was welcome to return to his arms.

Still, in case Jasmine thought it was creepy, he'd gotten enough to feed the entire clinic staff.

Bridget smiled. "I can't right now, but I'll gladly partake if there are any leftovers." She tilted her chin toward the closed door. "The prince is awake, and Kian is with him along with the Clan Mother, Jade, and Aru."

Edgar didn't know whether he should be relieved that Jasmine wasn't with the prince behind that closed door or more worried because the prince was awake.

Hopefully, the prince had disappointed Jasmine, and she was ready to embrace reality instead of the fantasy she'd created about the half Kra-ell.

"How long has he been awake?" he asked.

"Since early this morning, but he's still frail and sleeps on and off every so often."

"Where is Jasmine?"

Bridget smiled knowingly. "She's in the kitchen, and I'm sure she will be thrilled about the takeout."

"I hope so." He returned the doctor's smile. "I'll leave the leftovers in the fridge so you can feast when your guests are gone. The Golden Dragon is the best."

"I know, and I will."

After collecting the bag he'd left on the floor, Edgar continued down the corridor to the keep's kitchen and pushed open the door.

Jasmine looked up from her coffee mug as he entered. "Hi." She rose to her feet and walked over to him. "What brings you here?"

He held up the bag of food. "Brought you some lunch." He set the bag down on the counter. "Thought you might be hungry after all the excitement of the day. I've heard your prince is awake."

She didn't take the bait about the prince. "That's so sweet of you." She reached for the bag. "I didn't even realize how hungry I was until just now."

"I must have sensed it." He tapped his temple.

Edgar watched as she unpacked the food, satisfied by the small, appreciative noises she made as she inhaled the savory aromas of the dishes he had chosen.

He knew her tastes and had chosen accordingly, but there were other dishes there as well that were more aligned with his preference for spicy stuff.

"You got enough to feed an army." She put two plates on the counter, one for him and one for herself. "Do we need more plates? Who else is joining us?"

"I thought that Bridget, Julian, and Gertrude would appreciate some fresh food, but they can't leave while the distinguished guests are visiting. Bridget asked that we store the leftovers in the fridge."

Jasmine probably didn't know about the Clan Mother being there, so he wouldn't mention her unless she did.

She nodded and lifted a pendant he hadn't noticed before. "Did you see William's latest gadget? This can translate what I'm saying into Kra-ell and still sound like me. Do you want to see how it works?"

"Sure."

Edgar's heart sank. If she could communicate with the prince, she would make him fall in love with her, and then she would fall in love with him. Or maybe she already had?

Well, it had to happen one way or the other.

"Kra-on!" she said and then added a few more words that came out sounding like the guttural Kra-ell language.

Edgar frowned. "How come I didn't hear what you said in English?"

She turned the device off. "William said something about it producing counter sound waves to absorb what I say so only the Kra-ell is heard. I might be confusing stuff because I don't understand anything about these kinds of things."

He didn't like Jasmine's tendency to put herself down and try to appear not as smart or capable as she was. Perhaps he should say something. They might not be a couple anymore, but they were friends.

He smiled at her to gentle the sting of his words. "Why do you do that?"

"Do what?"

"Pretend to be less smart than you are?"

She shrugged. "I don't want to be a show-off, and I really don't think I should speak with fake authority about things I understand little to nothing about."

"Now, that was a much better answer. You basically said the same thing but without disparaging yourself." He picked up the box closest to him and opened it. "Fates. Those smells were killing me on the way here. Let's eat before things get cold."

Jasmine laughed. "Let's."

Her laugh was a relief. It signaled that she hadn't been hurt or offended by what he had said.

They got busy shoveling food into their mouths for the next few minutes. Well, he shoveled. Jasmine ate with her usual restraint and ladylike manner.

She would fit the princess role well, but she needed to develop more hutzpah.

"So, tell me. What do you think of the prince so far?"

Lifting a napkin, Jasmine patted her lips to clean them. "He's very different from what I expected."

"In what way?"

"Everyone kept talking about how powerful and dangerous he was and that we needed earpieces to protect ourselves from his immense compulsion ability. But he doesn't seem powerful at all. He was visibly intimidated by Jade even though she was being perfectly polite."

Edgar chuckled. "I don't blame him. She intimidates me as well."

Jasmine nodded. "Yeah. She has a presence about her, which is kind of sexy."

Edgar lifted a brow. "Really? I didn't know that you swing that way."

"I don't. It's just an observation. I'm attracted to power, but I am purely into males."

Maybe that was what he had been missing?

"Anyway," she continued. "The prince is gentle, fully devoted to his twin sister, and gets teary-eyed when talking about her because he thinks he failed her." She pushed a strand of hair behind her ear. "I think he and his sister were so sheltered and isolated that they are still very naive and fragile."

He didn't know if Jasmine realized it, but she sounded like she was already in love with the prince, even though he was the direct opposite of what she'd imagined and found attractive.

If her description of him was accurate, then instead of a fearsome leader, the prince was a lost soul searching for a nurturing heart.

The surprising part was that Jasmine was uniquely suited for the task. She was quick to accept people the way they were and was open to new ideas. Perhaps the Fates had been right to send her to the prince. But if that was true, what did the Fates have in store for Edgar?

Why had they involved him in this mess?

Then it hit him. What if he was destined for the princess?

He wasn't as nurturing and open-minded as Jasmine, but he would make the effort for the right female.

"What about the sister? Is she showing signs of waking up?"

"She's still unconscious. What is clear, though, is that her brother cares a great deal about her, and since he's a good guy, she must be a good person as well."

Edgar leaned his elbow on the counter. "Perhaps I should sneak into her room and see if I can wake her up with a kiss."

Jasmine laughed. "It's worth a try. After all, a little kiss on the cheek is not going to do her harm."

He laughed along but was more serious about the idea than he was letting on. "Who knows? Maybe the Fates have brought me here for a reason. Perhaps she's my one and only."

"Perhaps." Jasmine reached for his hand and gave it a light squeeze. "I'll keep my fingers crossed for you."

49

THE PRINCE

The medics brought three more chairs into his room, arranging them around his bed, which didn't help calm his nerves.

Meeting Je-Kara had already shaken him; now, he was expected to receive more visitors, who were obviously even more important than the imposing female.

When the door opened again, Je-Kara walked in and nodded to him. "Are you ready?"

He wasn't, but he nodded.

The first to enter was an imposing male with piercing blue eyes. He had the same teardrop translation device as Jasmine and the medics hanging from his neck. Taking an assessing look around, he nodded his greeting and then walked out and returned with two females. One was pretty and golden-haired, and the other was a stunning, regal female with flaming red hair who had to be a goddess.

He didn't know why and how he knew that other than her perfection indicating that she could not be anything else.

Were more memories percolating up from under the thin barrier of his subconscious?

The female had a regal bearing, and the power emanating from her was a tangible presence. The male who had entered first acted with authority like he was the group's leader, but that was a ruse.

The goddess was in charge.

The male was not fully a god, nor was the golden-haired female.

Then another male entered, with dark hair and dark eyes, and the last one was Je-Kara.

"Good afternoon," the one with the blue piercing eyes said through the translating device, his voice coming out deep and growly. "My name is Kian; this is our Clan Mother, Annani, my mate Syssi, and my good friend Aru."

So, he had been right, and the redheaded goddess was in charge. There was something about her, something that tugged at the edges of his memory like a half-forgotten dream. She reminded him of someone, a face that hovered just beyond the reach of his fractured recollections.

Given his limited range of motion, he inclined his head the best he could. "I am honored by your presence," he said to all of them while looking into the goddess's eyes.

The Clan Mother smiled and inclined her head slightly.

"You've met Jade already," Kian said as Je-Kara entered.

It took the prince a moment to remember that Je-Kara preferred to be called Jade because Precious was not a name befitting a warrior. She was right, but was being named after a shade of green any better?

"Yes, I have." He forced a smile. "I wish I could give you a name, but I do not remember mine. Jasmine suggested that I use the name Cedric until I remember the name I was given by my mother."

"Do you remember your mother?" the goddess asked.

"I have one partial memory of vowing to her to protect my sister. I do not remember anything else about her."

"Do you remember your sister?" the golden-haired one asked.

"I remember I have a sister and am supposed to protect her. I do not remember her name or what she looks like either." He had planned to ask to see her, but since he could barely move his arms, that would be a problem.

He did not want to ask the medic to carry him to her room.

The goddess regarded him with affection in her wise eyes. "I am so happy that we have found you, and I agree with Jasmine that the name Cedric fits you. I can call you Prince, Cedric, or Prince Cedric. Which one do you prefer?"

He thought for a moment. "I do not feel like a prince, so I guess I will use Cedric until I remember my name."

The Clan Mother smiled. "Very well, Cedric. You can call me Annani, and I want you to know that you are safe, and that I am here for you and your sister. You both have my protection and my hospitality."

"Annani," he repeated the name with reverence. It reminded him of another name, but again, his faulty memory refused to cooperate. "Such a beautiful name. Thank you for sharing it with me."

"You are very welcome." The goddess sounded almost as emotional as he felt. "I am looking forward to the day I will also learn your real name."

He swallowed. He had been lost, adrift in a sea of confusion and uncertainty, and now he had someone to turn to, someone powerful and benevolent who had just vowed to protect him and his sister and take care of them.

50

ANNANI

Annani felt her heart swell with emotion as she sat beside her half-brother's bed. She wished to reach for his hand and clasp it, but the gesture would seem improper given that he did not know they were related, and she was not ready to tell him yet.

He looked so fragile, so unsure. He needed to be told things a little bit at a time.

She could see her father in the prince. The same strong, chiseled features and even the same eye color, but where her father's gaze had been determined and powerful, the prince's was soft and a little lost.

And to think that they had all feared that he and his sister were terrifying creatures who could wield unimaginable power. The earpieces were there to protect her from him in case he was more powerful than she was, but they also translated Kra-ell to English, while the teardrop pendant translated English to Kra-ell, breaching the barrier of language.

The devices were Fates sent, or rather William sent, even though they could do nothing to bridge the cultural divide that Cedric was not even aware of yet, but he would be.

His eyes were misted with tears, and it was not an act because Cedric did not even know that he was supposed to act like a tough Kra-ell prince, with all the arrogance and dominance of the purebloods.

He was not one of them, but that was how he was raised.

Or maybe not. He and his sister had grown up in the temple, with the priestess being the strongest influence on their lives. Perhaps she had taught them compassion instead of a thirst for war.

Annani's eyes started to sting with sympathetic tears.

There was just something very touching about a grown male tearing up.

"Oh, my dear Cedric." She reached for his hand despite the impropriety. He did not know what was acceptable behavior and what was not, and since he did not pull his hand back, she assumed he was agreeable. "I am so incredibly happy and thankful that you and your sister are here. If only my Khiann and my Lilen were here as well, my life would be complete."

Next to her, Kian shifted on his chair, and on his other side, Syssi wiped tears from her eyes. Aru and Jade just observed, unmoved and untouched by the moment.

"Who were they?" Cedric asked.

"Khiann was my mate and the love of my life. He was taken from me mere months after we were married, murdered by a jealous and vengeful god who could not stand the thought that I chose Khiann over him."

The prince frowned. "I do not understand. Why did you have to choose one over the other? You could have had both."

Annani smiled. "I see that some of your memories are coming back. You grew up among the Kra-ell, where males outnumber females four to one, so Kra-ell females take several mates. I am a goddess, and gods are born in equal numbers. We choose only one mate."

He dipped his head in embarrassment. "I apologize for the improper comment. I meant no disrespect."

"I know." She patted his hand. "If you had all of your memories back, you would have known that gods mate only one person, even though gods and Kra-ell come from the same planet. We are all Anumatian."

He looked at her for a long moment. "What am I?"

"You are part god and part Kra-ell. Your mother was the queen of the Kra-ell."

His eyes started glowing in excitement. "And my father?"

"We are not sure who he was." Annani hated to lie to him, and she was not sure she should.

Until she had laid eyes on the prince, she had no proof that he was indeed her half-brother, so her statement might have been true, but seeing him and realizing how much he looked like their father, only a little darker and a lot softer, she could no longer harbor doubt.

The prince glanced at Kian and then back at her. "Who was Lilen?"

He could have asked her more about himself and where he had come from, but instead, he asked about Lilen. That spoke volumes about the kind of person he was.

"Lilen was my son. He fell in battle, defending our clan."

His fingers closed around hers with the gentlest of squeezes. "I am so sorry that you have lost so much."

She nodded. "Thank you."

"If I may..." The prince glanced at Kian and then back at Annani. "Can I ask if you know why my sister and I are here?"

Annani looked at Kian, who nodded.

Her son was observing the prince closely, checking for any signs of him remembering why he was sent to Earth.

"Some of what I am going to tell you will be upsetting, so before I start, I want you to look at my son and his mate. They are half god and half human. They are immortals like gods and have many of the other traits that the gods on Anumati have, but to a lesser degree, and they are perfect the way they are."

"Of course," the prince said. "Why would anyone claim otherwise?"

Annani smiled. "I am glad you asked. On Anumati, gods and Kra-ell do not mix. Even though they are genetically compatible, probably because they originated from the same common ancestors, mixed-race relationships are forbidden by both. The claim is that any children born of such unions will be abominations."

His eyes widened. "So, my sister and I are considered abominations?"

Annani nodded. "That is why your mother hid you behind veils from the day you were born and then sent you away from Anumati the first chance she had. She did that to save your lives."

5 1

THE PRINCE

S o much of the fragmented memories suddenly made sense. The reason why he couldn't remember what his sister looked like even though he'd remembered them sparring with swords.

The tactile sensations of different fabrics against his skin. The absence of other people.

They had been covered from head to toe, veiled, and isolated.

"If relationships between gods and Kra-ell are forbidden, how did my sister and I come to be?"

The goddess smiled. "Love, I guess. Or maybe the rebellion of the young. Your mother was still just the princess when she became pregnant with you and was part of the resistance that tried to bring more equality to the Kra-ell. She worked closely with gods championing the Kra-ell cause, and she must have fallen in love with one of them. The birth of twins is extremely rare on Anumati and nearly unheard of among the Kra-ell, especially fraternal twins when one child is a female and the other a male. That alone cast suspicion on the newly crowned queen, but she was a clever female who spun a protective web around you. Taking advantage of the rarity of your twin births, she declared that you would both serve the Mother of All Life and consecrated you to the priesthood, effectively removing you from the public eye."

The goddess turned to look at Jade. "Am I doing your history justice so far?"

Jade inclined her head. "Yes, Clan Mother. But if you wish, I can take it from here."

The prince tensed. He did not want the cold Kra-ell female to tell him about their world. He wanted the gentle goddess to keep talking.

She must have sensed his wish and shook her head. "Thank you for the offer, Jade, but I will continue the story. If I get anything wrong, though, do not hesitate to correct me."

Jade's lips quirked up in an almost-there smile. "I would not dare, Clan Mother."

"Please do," the goddess said. "I do not want to provide our dear Cedric with the wrong information."

When Jade nodded, Annani turned back to him. "There are no male Kra-ell priests, but since the Kra-ell believe that twins share one soul, your mother proclaimed that by virtue of your sister, you would become a priest too. The advantages were clear. You were kept isolated in the temple, where the chief priestess of the Kra-ell ruled supreme and could protect you. You were never seen without your veils covering every inch of your body. Still, your mother could not do that forever, so she hatched a scheme to sneak you onto a settler ship bound for Earth."

"How could she have done that if we look like hybrids?" he asked. Annani looked at Jade. "You had a theory about that, right?"

Jade nodded. "I believe that you shrouded yourselves. Gods can make themselves look any way they want or even disappear from view. I believe that you shrouded yourselves to look like pureblooded Kra-ell." She shifted slightly in her chair. "I was in the next pod over when you and your sister arrived, and something about you looked familiar. As I mentioned before, I was on the queen's guard and saw you walking the palace gardens between the palace and the temple. You were always veiled, but I recognized your particular gait and bearing. There were other hints as well. All the other pods had three or four females and seventeen or sixteen males, which is the natural Kra-ell gender distribution. Your pod had an equal number of males and females. I don't know what your mother's plan was, but I assume she wanted you to find your father when you got to Earth."

This was so much information that he was struggling to organize it all in his head. "What happened to the other people in our pod?"

"None made it, regrettably," Kian said. "The Kra-ell cannot enter stasis without a stasis chamber. Gods can. The stasis chambers stopped working when the pod malfunctioned, and the Kra-ell perished. You and your sister remained in natural stasis and survived like that for thousands of years."

He must have misunderstood, or maybe the translation device had made a mistake.

"Thousands of years? Is that how long it takes to travel from Anumati to Earth?"

Kian shook his head. "Aru tells me that it takes approximately five hundred years, but the ship carrying the Kra-ell settlers was old, so it might have taken longer. Still, not that much longer. It either malfunctioned or was sabotaged, and it arrived seven thousand years later. The ship exploded over Earth but managed to expel some or all of the stasis pods. Some made it safely and opened, like Jade's, but most were lost. We found yours thanks to Syssi and Jasmine."

His head was spinning. "I do not understand. How could they have known where to look for us?"

Syssi smiled shyly. "I'm a seer, and I foresaw that Jasmine would be instrumental to finding your pod, and I was right. She has very unique talents none of us even dreamt about."

His heart swelled with pride even though he could not take credit for Jasmine's talent. "Jasmine is special. I knew that from the first moment I saw her."

Kian chuckled. "Which was earlier today. But you are right. You and your sister owe the woman your lives. The physician who was part of the rescue team says that you were both running out of time. A few more days or at most weeks, and you would have perished, even in stasis, because your chambers were sealed."

He didn't know what that meant, and he did not really care. All he could think about was that Jasmine had saved his and his sister's lives, and he owed her a life debt, which he would gladly spend the rest of his life repaying.

He had known her for mere hours, but already he could feel a bond between them. How apt therefore, that it was Jasmine who had named him upon his rebirth.

5 2

KIAN

T he prince was nothing like any of them had expected, but then the guy didn't remember anything, including possible instructions to eliminate Ahn or whatever other agenda he had been ordered to follow.

Kian didn't like how close his mother was sitting to the guy or that she was holding his hand like he was a child. He was weak, that much was obvious, but it wouldn't take much for him to snatch the earpiece out of Annani's ear and compel her to do his bidding.

He couldn't imagine the amount of damage his mother could do if someone else hijacked her power.

At least she hadn't told the prince that she was his half-sister, but Kian wasn't sure how long she would be able to hold that back. If he were a human, his mother's impulsiveness would have given him an ulcer.

Still, it was difficult to feel threatened by a male who teared up over everything.

This male didn't appear to be the powerful, dangerous creature they had been warned about, which on the one hand was a relief because he didn't seem like a threat, but on the other hand, he was not a powerful ally who could help their cause either.

It was too early to make a definitive judgment, though. Time would tell, and in the meantime, Kian would ensure that no one neglected safety precautions just because the guy had leaky eyes.

He had seen enough monsters who had done horrific things, crying like babies when the tables were turned on them.

Filthy cowards.

Kian shook his head, dispelling the thoughts that didn't belong in this room.

The prince seemed like a genuinely gentle soul, and Kian was starting to think that the warnings about the twins' powers had been deliberate misinformation.

Their mother might have spread the rumors of their power and their danger on purpose to protect her children from their grandfather and others who might have wished them harm.

If so, it was a clever plan, he had to admit. It made the twins seem too formidable, too terrifying to attack, but the queen had miscalculated.

The worst thing she could have done for her children was to draw the Eternal King's attention to them and make him think that they might pose a threat to his throne.

"He's like a child," Jade whispered almost inaudibly behind him. "No grown Kra-ell male would tear up over every other sentence. His mother did a poor job of raising him. She didn't teach him the way of the sword or prepare him for life."

Her words were harsh, but they echoed Kian's thoughts. The prince had grown up sheltered and coddled, which hadn't done him any favors.

It didn't make sense, though.

Kian's mother had pushed him to take on responsibilities and become the leader she'd needed him to be from a young age, and Annani was a sweetheart. The twins' mother had to be a tough female, or she wouldn't have been a queen of the Kra-ell.

Perhaps she had done precisely what she had intended, though, and had raised her son to be gentle and loving and to value compassion and empathy over strength and power.

It was a radical idea, a concept that went against everything the Kra-ell valued, but maybe the queen hoped that her children would create a different society in the colony on Earth. The odd configuration of the twins' pod fit this radical idea. It was the only one with an equal number of females and males. Another possibility was that the sister was the powerful one of the two.

In the Kra-ell society, males were subservient to females, so it wasn't such a far-fetched idea.

"Why did you ask Jasmine to leave?" the prince asked Jade. "Is anything we discuss a secret that should be kept from her?"

"I am the secret," Annani said. "I do not wish to burden you with too many details, so I am not going to explain why I like to keep my identity hidden from any who are not part of my clan or affiliated with it. At the moment, Jasmine's affiliation is still in question."

The prince looked troubled. "Why is it in question?"

Annani was about to answer when the door opened, and Bridget stepped inside. "I apologize, Clan Mother, but I'm afraid this will have to do for today. The prince is exhausted, and his vitals are all over the place. He needs to rest now."

"Of course." Annani rose to her feet and leaned over the prince. "I shall visit again." She kissed his cheek. "Hopefully, next time I come, you will be well enough to tolerate me for a little longer."

The guy looked at her with so much affection, admiration, and longing that even a cynic like Kian was touched.

"I enjoyed every moment of your visit, Clan Mother. Every word was a revelation and a comfort. I am looking forward to many more talks with you." He smiled. "Someone needs to tell me who I am and where I came from."

Annani cast a glance at Jade. "There may be no need because your memory will return. It would be better for you to remember who you are than for someone else to shape your self-perception."

"Then we will spend time together talking about you and your world."

"I would like that," Annani said. "Now, close your eyes and sleep, my sweet brother."

Kian froze, but the prince just smiled. "Thank you, my lovely sister. I will obey your command."

He must have thought that Annani had called him her brother as a term of endearment and that it meant something other than an actual blood relationship.

Nevertheless, it was a slip-up that shouldn't have happened.

53

JASMINE

J asmine tensed as Jade walked into the kitchen with a grimace twisting her mouth.

"Is the prince okay?"

"He's fine." Jade's gaze swept over the array of open takeout boxes on the counter. "Your food stinks."

"I beg to differ," Edgar said. "It smells delicious."

"I believe it does to you, but the smell of cooked meat is repulsive to me." She shivered in disgust. "Anyway, I came to tell you that you can return to the clinic. He's asleep and will probably stay asleep for a while after all the excitement, so there is no rush." She gave them both a two-fingered mock salute, pivoted on the heel of her combat boots, and strode out.

"The nerve of her criticizing what we eat," Edgar murmured. "As if drinking blood from a live animal's vein is not repulsive."

Jasmine winced. "That's gross. I hope the prince does not like drinking blood. Bridget says his digestive system is like ours, but he also seemed disgusted when she mentioned meat. I guess it's a cultural thing."

Edgar shrugged. "So, what do we do with all the leftovers? Put them in the fridge, or call Bridget and the others to come and eat now that the guests are gone and her patient is sleeping?"

"Let's call her so she can eat it while it's still warm. Reheating Chinese food ruins the taste." Jasmine started closing the boxes and arranging them in a neat row.

"I don't have anything scheduled for today." Edgar finished closing the last of the boxes. "I can come and sit with you, keep you company while he sleeps." He gave her a lopsided smile. "So you won't be bored."

"I'm not bored," Jasmine said. "I've been singing to him, reading him stories. It helps pass the time."

Edgar frowned. "You can't do that anymore, remember? He is no longer unconscious, and you should let him rest."

"You're right." She canted her head. "It's strange how fast habits form and how difficult it is to change them. It's like I've spent my entire life, not just a few days, sitting in that chair in the clinic, talking and singing to an alien prince who I wasn't sure could even hear me." She smiled. "But he did. He told me that my voice soothed him."

Edgar nodded, but she wasn't sure whether it indicated that he understood or agreed or both.

"I'm curious to see what he looks like now," he said. "That's another motive for me to get Bridget out of there. She might not allow me to see him." He started toward the door.

"Why wouldn't she?" Jasmine followed him out of the kitchen. Edgar shrugged. "I have no reason to be there other than curiosity."

That was true of all the visitors, but Edgar was the only one who might not have the prince's best interests at heart.

Jasmine hated even to think that, but she should encourage at least one medical staff member to remain so Edgar wouldn't have free rein to do as he pleased. She could not physically protect the prince from the immortal and had no defenses against his mind manipulation. If he was planning to harm the prince, he could thrall her to do it for him.

Then again, Edgar didn't need to be in the clinic with her to do that. At any time, he could have thralled her to put a pillow over the prince's face and smother him or do something else to him that was less obvious.

He didn't, though, and she felt awful for even thinking that. Edgar might have a mile-long jealous streak, but he wasn't a bad guy.

The door to Bridget's office was open as they entered the clinic, and Edgar knocked on it before walking in. "We didn't put the food in the fridge. We left it on the kitchen counter. If you hurry, you might still eat it warm."

"Don't mind if I do." The doctor rose to her feet. "I'll ask Julian and Gertrude to join me."

Jasmine tensed despite her earlier rationalization that if Edgar meant the prince harm, he could have used her to do that already.

"Shouldn't at least one of you stay here in case of an emergency?"

Bridget smiled. "The kitchen is seconds away, and if anything out of the ordinary is registered on the monitoring equipment, our phones will sound the alarm."

"Oh, okay." Jasmine hid her embarrassment by turning to look at the slightly open door to the prince's room. "I didn't know that. I should check on him."

"I'll come with you." Edgar followed her.

When she walked up to the prince and gazed at him, Edgar walked around to the other side of the bed.

"He looks good." He lifted his eyes to her and smiled. "He's handsome. I was afraid he would look like the Kra-ell. Jade is pretty, but she's a bit too alien-looking for my taste, and the males look too feminine with their long hair and narrow waists. They are strong bastards and fierce warriors, so their looks are misleading, but still. If I were a female, I wouldn't have been interested. Then there are their strange mating rituals. No thank you."

"What strange mating rituals?" Ella hadn't said anything about that.

"They are violent, and they fight for dominance." He grimaced. "Did you watch Star Trek: The Next Generation?"

"I did. I loved it."

"Remember the Klingon matings? It's something like that."

Jasmine shivered. "I'm glad that the twins were celibate and were not exposed to such barbaric practices."

"Yeah, me too." He smiled sheepishly. "Let's go see the princess."

Jasmine was also curious, but mostly, she wanted to get Edgar out of the prince's room. "Let's do it."

As they slipped inside the other room, Jasmine sucked in a breath. "Oh, wow, she looks much better as well."

The princess was beautiful; her features were delicate and finely wrought beneath the fragile skin, and her body was long, lean, and graceful. The few strands of hair still attached to her head were stringy and the same color as the prince's. A warm chestnut brown that would be gorgeous once it was restored to health.

"She's beautiful," Edgar murmured, his voice soft and filled with a quiet reverence as he studied the princess's face. "Regal, even. But it's a shame that her hair is in such bad shape. It would be better to shave it all off, let it grow back evenly." He looked up at Jasmine. "She'd look good bald. She has the bone structure for it."

Jasmine snorted. "Are you smitten, Edgar?"

He shrugged. "A princess is probably out of my league."

She laughed. "The prince is out of my league as well, but that's not stopping me. Why should it stop you?"

Edgar was silent for a long moment, and his brow furrowed as he considered her words. And then, slowly, a small, rueful smile began to tug at the corners of his mouth. "Would it be a little creepy for us, as former lovers, to be involved with the twins?"

She winced. "Yeah, it is a little creepy. But given that we are dealing with ancient aliens who are royals from another world, I think we're allowed a certain level of weirdness. As long as we don't mind and they don't, what's the harm?"

"Fair enough."

54

THE PRINCE

He stirred, his eyelids fluttering open as he emerged from the depths of sleep. For a moment, his mind struggled to reconcile the strange surroundings with the fragmented memories that danced at the edges of his consciousness.

Slowly he turned his head, his gaze falling on the female curled up in the chair beside his bed, and a smile blossomed on his face.

Jasmine looked soft and relaxed in sleep, her dark hair spilling over her shoulders in soft waves.

Extending his arm, he tried to reach the strands with his fingers, but the bed was too high, too far away. He tried to move sideways and stretch his arm closer, but his arm was already trembling from the effort, and his muscles were still weak.

With a groan, he tried harder to force his body to obey his commands, but he'd reached his limit and had to give up. It was unsettling to be trapped within his own flesh and unable to control his most basic functions.

Perhaps he could rest a little and try again.

Yeah, he should rest and try to recall what he had learned from his visitors.

How long ago had they sat in his room and told him things he had already mostly forgotten?

While he'd slept, someone had removed the extra chairs, and Jasmine had returned, but that still did not tell him how long he had been asleep.

They had told him about his mother, who had made him vow to protect his sister. As if he needed to make a vow to do that. It was his honor and duty to protect her. Even his memory loss could not erase his devotion to his twin. She was his entire world.

Had been his entire world.

Now, there was also Jasmine, but his sister had to come first. They told him that she was in the next room over and doing fine, but he had to see her with his own eyes to believe it, to reassure himself that she indeed lived, that he hadn't failed.

So close, and yet so far.

How could he reach her if he could not reach Jasmine's hair? Rest. He needed to rest.

Closing his eyes, he let his mind drift off until sleep overtook him, and when he woke up again, he felt a little stronger.

Jasmine was still asleep on the chair, and he felt a pang of guilt about her discomfort. She was there for him, and he now knew why. She felt responsible because she helped find him and his sister, saved them from the grip of death.

He owed her a life debt, and he couldn't wait for her to wake up so he could make the vow to her.

Right now, his vow would be worthless because he couldn't protect her any more than he could protect his sister, but when he was back to full strength, he would protect them both with his life.

He had to get stronger fast, and he wasn't going to achieve that by lying in bed. With a sudden burst of determination, he gathered his strength and pushed his legs down the side of the bed. Now, if he could only force his torso to lift off the mattress and move him to a sitting position...

The door burst open, and Bridget came rushing in. "What do you think you're doing?" She crossed the room in a few quick strides and gently but firmly pushed him back onto the bed. "You could have torn out your IV feed, and you're in no condition to be moving."

"What's going on?" Jasmine rubbed her eyes. "What did I miss?"

"Your guy tried to get up."

Jasmine turned to look at him with a shocked expression on her face. "What were you thinking?"

"I have to see my sister."

Bridget's expression softened. "You will, but not today. She's in the room next to you, and she's doing fine. That's all you need to know for now."

She tilted her head. "I can show her to you if you want."

"How?"

The medic pulled out a device from her pocket. "We have cameras installed in each patient room, so I can take a look even if I'm away from the clinic." She cast a glance at Jasmine, who blushed for some reason.

He shook his head. "I need to see her with my own eyes. I need to touch her hand and feel the warmth of life under her skin."

55

JASMINE

The prince's desperate plea to see his sister tugged on Jasmine's heartstrings. She turned to Bridget. "What if we wheel his bed into the other room?"

When the doctor started shaking her head, Jasmine looked up at her. "Before you say 'no,' I think that seeing his sister might jog his memory."

Bridget hesitated for a moment. "It's worth a try. The rooms are small, and these beds are bulky. Before I call Julian and the nurse to see if we can make it happen, I need to measure the space we have to verify that it is doable." She looked at the prince. "Don't worry, we will find a way for you to see your sister even if Julian has to carry you."

When he nodded, Bridget pulled a measuring tape from her coat pocket and stepped out of the room.

Jasmine stood next to the bed and took the prince's hand. "I keep trying to refer to you as Cedric in my mind, but it doesn't sound right. I want to know your real name."

"So do I." He squeezed her hand. "Thank you for suggesting rolling my bed to my sister's room."

"It was nothing." She chewed on her lower lip. "I saw her earlier. She's beautiful."

He smiled. "For some reason, you sound guilty."

"I do?" She closed her eyes. "I snuck a friend of mine in to see her."

The prince's smile evaporated, and his eyes started glowing. "What friend?"

She knew now that it wasn't a display of jealousy, so the response must have been about him perceiving what she had done as dangerous to his sister.

"Edgar, the guy I took to see her, was the pilot who worked with the gods and me on the mission to rescue you. After all he has done, I thought he deserved to see how well the two of you were doing."

And just like that, the smile was back, but only for a moment, and then he frowned. "You said that gods accompanied you on the missions. Who are they?"

"Aru, Negal, and Dagor. Why?"

The prince nodded. "Aru was one of my visitors. I suspected that he was a god."

"Good." She patted his hand. "Your memory is starting to come back if you can tell gods from immortals."

"It is not easy. They look a lot alike."

"Tell me about it." Jasmine rolled her eyes. "To me, Kian looks like a god. He is so incredibly good-looking."

"I was not sure myself whether he was an immortal or a god," the prince admitted, and again, there was not an iota of jealousy in his tone.

It was a little disappointing.

Jasmine didn't like Edgar's excessive jealousy, but a little bit would mean that the prince was interested in her as more than just a friend.

"Okay." Bridget walked into the room with Julian and Gertrude in tow. "Let's do this."

As Julian and the nurse worked together to quickly and efficiently disconnect the tubes and wires that tethered the prince to the monitoring machines, Jasmine slipped outside so she wouldn't be in their way.

When they were done with that part, they wheeled the bed out into the hallway and maneuvered it to pull it inside the other room.

From the open door, Jasmine saw that they had already moved the princess's bed to the side to make room for the second one, and she wondered if they planned on leaving the prince in his sister's room. He would be overjoyed if they did, but Jasmine preferred to have him all to herself and not to have to worry about his sister hearing them talking or doing other things, even when unconscious.

What other things?

It would take weeks until the prince was well enough for that. Besides, he hadn't shown any romantic interest in her yet.

He's been awake for one day. Get a grip.

Patience had never been Jasmine's strong suit.

The moment his bed was aligned with his sister's and his eyes fell upon her face, the prince's eyes filled with tears, and as he reached with a trembling hand to her, Julian helped him by moving the princess's hand closer and putting his on hers.

"Morelle," he whispered.

Jasmine stood at the doorway, unsure whether he wanted her there. "Morelle," he said louder and turned to look at Jasmine with a grin spreading over his handsome face. "My sister's name is Morelle."

Jasmine clapped her hands. "You remembered her name. That's amazing." She was giddy with happiness for him, and yet her eyes stung with tears.

She squeezed to stand on the other side of his bed and placed a hand on his shoulder, hoping he would find it supportive rather than intrusive.

"Can you try and remember your own name?" Bridget asked.

"Ell-rom. We are each other's mirror image."

Ell-rom, Jasmine repeated in her head. She didn't know what it meant, but it suited the prince much better than Cedric.

"Anything else that you remember?" Bridget asked gently.

"No. Morelle and Ell-rom. Those are our secret names, but I guess we don't need to keep them a secret anymore."

"Why were your names a secret?" Julian asked.

"I do not know." Ell-rom's eyes were focused on his sister's face. "I hope you wake up soon, Morelle, and I hope your memory didn't suffer as much damage as mine."

KIAN

K ian glanced at his watch while Onegus delivered his report, hoping the chief hadn't noticed. As usual, he was pressed for time, and even more so now because of his back-and-forth trips to the keep.

But it wasn't as if he could delegate the task of escorting his mother to see her half-brother. He had to do it himself and ensure she didn't reveal every possible secret in her excitement over finding her siblings.

The guy seemed pretty harmless, but Kian wasn't taking chances, especially when his mother was involved.

"William's crew installed two surveillance cameras in the mailroom overnight," Onegus said. "They made sure that no one saw them even enter the building, and the cameras they installed are tiny. The pranksters won't suspect a thing."

"You think it's just pranks?"

Onegus shrugged. "I judge things by the harm done, not by their moral implications, and the stolen items are cosmetics, some clothing items, and a jewelry box. None of the items is worth more than fifty bucks."

"So, our culprit is a female." Kian leaned back in his chair. "A male wouldn't have stolen such items."

Onegus lifted a brow. "Are you sure about that? Maybe a guy is collecting items to gift a female, or he wants to try them on himself. It seems to be in vogue now."

Kian shrugged. "I still remember when men wore wigs, stockings, and heeled shoes, painted blush on their cheeks, and used pomade to make their skin look whiter. Things come and go. This too shall pass."

"I don't know about that." Onegus rubbed a hand over the back of his neck. "Not that I care about who wears what and why, but it seems to me like a big, noisy smokescreen, so people focus on this and not that. You know what I mean?"

"I do, and I'm worried, but I can only deal with so many things at the same time, and right now, we need to find out what's happening under our noses because these small thefts and acts of sabotage could be a smokescreen too, or rather a smoking gun."

Onegus nodded. "William's crew is working on the malfunctioning shutters. They're checking every unit to determine if it's a design flaw or tampering."

"It can't be a design flaw." Kian sighed. "Too many going bad at the same time."

"My money's on the Kra-ell teenagers," Onegus said bluntly. "They're bored out of their minds. People that age with no structure and no purpose, it's a recipe for trouble."

"What do you suggest we do with them?" Kian asked.

Onegus leaned forward, bracing his elbows on his knees. "Enroll them in the Guardian training program. Everyone sixteen and older who is not pursuing academic education should enroll. Give them something to work toward, a sense of accomplishment, pride, and belonging."

Kian's eyebrows rose in surprise. "You think that's wise? Sixteen is young."

Onegus lifted his hands. "Most of them are not interested in higher education, and fighting is in their blood. The older ones who joined are doing very well. I'm already using them to assist our rescue teams. We put them in tactical gear that hides their alien features and keep them in backup positions so they are not in direct contact with the victims we rescue. Our Guardians feel much safer having them defending their backs."

It might work, provided that the young Kra-ell wanted in. Forcing them would make them more resentful.

"Let's do it. But we need to be smart about this. We need to hype up the force so they will want to join, supervise them closely and have a zero-tolerance policy for any hint of trouble."

The Chief nodded. "I'll speak with Jade. She knows how to keep them in line."

"Apparently not, if they are running around perpetrating petty crimes."

Onegus leaned back in his chair. "Jade has one deputy, Kagra. It was enough when all she needed was to police her tribe, but now she has a whole community, and she's not set up for that. She needs to deputize more people."

Kian smiled. "You are welcome to suggest that to her."

"I will. Looking forward, we could expand our rescue operations once they graduate, which will not take them as long as it takes our people. Shoring up our defenses is also a huge benefit."

"I agree. What about the pay? Do we pay them the same as our people?"

Onegus sighed. "That's somewhat complicated. While in training, they should get paid the same as our trainees, but once they graduate, we might want to introduce a new pay structure that rewards seniority and the types of positions people hold. We don't want to upset our people who have been serving for years, and we don't want to appear as if we are discriminating against the newcomers. There needs to be a balance."

"I will leave it up to you to figure this out. When you have the pay structure ready, bring it to me for review."

"Of course." Onegus rose to his feet. "I'll let you know what William's crew finds out about the shutters."

"Thank you, Onegus."

After the chief left, Kian swiveled his chair toward the window and looked at the peaceful scene outside. The village green was bathed in sunlight, with immortals, Kra-ell, and humans alike passing by.

Who was the culprit?

Immortals showing their displeasure about the changing nature of their village? The Kra-ell fertility rate was higher than the immortals', and there were whispers about them one day taking over.

It was a valid concern, and even though they seemed to coexist peacefully with their hosts, they weren't really integrating. The two groups kept to themselves, with Jade, Phinas, Vanessa, and Mo-red being the exception, not the rule.

Had he made a mistake by inviting the Kra-ell to join their community?

The surveillance cameras and the Guardian training program were all just stopgap measures, temporary solutions to a deeper problem. The real challenge lay in bridging the divide between their peoples and finding a way to coexist while maintaining the balance of power.

After all, the village belonged first and foremost to the clan. It was not fair to expect them to share it, or worse, fear that they would be outnumbered and driven out of their homes one day.

No one had said that, not to him anyway, but if he was thinking that, others were too.

57

MARINA

When the morning rush had finally subsided, leaving behind a welcome lull in the constant bustle of the café, Marina wiped down the tables and the counters and then poured herself a much-needed cup of coffee.

Leaning against the counter, she listened to Wonder as she was humming while rearranging the pastry tray so it wouldn't look so depleted. "I hope the delivery from Jackson arrives before the afternoon gets busy."

"Is it ever late?" Marina asked.

Wonder snorted. "It's Los Angeles. Traffic is unpredictable, and the delivery is done in a roundabout way."

"I was wondering about that. Who brings stuff to the village?"

"Everything is delivered to our downtown location, and one of ours brings it from there. Up until not too long ago, Jackson restocked the café himself, but he got too busy and hired help." She chuckled. "His friend Gordon recently graduated from Oxford with a degree in philosophy, but he makes a living delivering pastries and sandwiches to the village." She smiled. "It's just temporary. He wants to continue his studies."

Marina frowned. "Peter told me that clan members don't need to work if they don't want to and that they get a monthly allowance."

"They do." Wonder pushed to her feet. "I guess Gordon likes to be busy, or he just wants to help out his friend." She glanced at the back of their shop, where Aliya was doing the dishes. "I'm going to help her out."

"I'll do it." Marina put her coffee cup down.

Wonder stopped her with a hand on her shoulder. "You need a break. Rest, drink your coffee, and eat something."

"Thank you." Marina smiled at her gratefully.

She was used to working hard but couldn't compare with the immortals and the Kra-ell. They were machines. Still, despite how crazy it sometimes got, she loved it at the café. The people were so friendly and welcoming, especially the Guardians, who stopped by and chatted with her and Wonder as if they were part of the gang because their mates were on the force.

Hearing footsteps approaching, she put her coffee cup down and turned around with her professional smile in place.

Seeing who the customer was, the smile slid off her face.

Borga.

What the hell was she doing in the café?

She was a pureblooded Kra-ell, so it wasn't like she was there to order a cappuccino and a pastry.

There could be only one reason, and that was to taunt Marina. For some reason, the female despised her and made it her mission to make Marina's life miserable.

She knew the reason, but it was as unhinged as the female herself was. Kra-ell were not supposed to be possessive or demand exclusivity from their bed partners, but since Borga had given Mo-red a son, she had convinced herself that he belonged to her and gave every female he ever looked at the stink eye.

The thing was, Marina had never been with the pureblooded male. The extent of their interaction had been him smiling at her a couple of times, which, given how severe the Kra-ell usually were, had given Borga ideas.

"Well, well, well," Borga drawled, her voice dripping with disdain. "If it isn't the little blue-haired koraba."

Koraba sounded like the name of an animal from the Kra-ell home planet, which probably had some unfavorable characteristics for Borga to hurl it so derisively at Marina.

Marina affected a neutral expression. "What can I get for you, Borga?"

The female leaned against the counter, her lips curving in a cruel smile. "I need my house cleaned. You are a maid. Figure it out. Or are you too busy servicing your immortal when you are not working in the café for pocket money?"

Behind her, Marina heard Wonder's intake of breath, and tension practically crackled in the air. Hopefully, Wonder would stay out of it and let her handle it herself.

Rising to Borga's bait would only make things worse.

The female thrived on conflict and used her so-called power over those she considered beneath her, whether hybrids or humans. Engaging with her would only feed that twisted need, and Marina wouldn't give her the satisfaction of knowing that she had gotten under her skin.

"I'm sorry, Borga," she said evenly, meeting the female's gaze without flinching. "But I'm afraid I can't help you with that. If you are not here for coffee or pastries, I will have to ask you to step aside so I can assist the next customer in line."

Borga's eyes flashed with anger, her nostrils flaring as she leaned in close. "Don't use that tone with me, human," she hissed. "You might think that you are all that because you are an immortal's plaything, but you are nothing, just a novelty that will wear off sooner or later."

Borga was trying to get a rise out of her, the words designed to cut and wound and leave her feeling small and insignificant, but a small, treacherous part of her couldn't help but wonder if there was a kernel of truth buried beneath the vitriol. After all, what did she have to offer someone like Peter?

"That's enough, Borga," Wonder said, her voice low and menacing. "You need to leave. Now."

Since Borga had spoken to Marina in Kra-ell, her tone alone must have annoyed Wonder enough for her to intervene.

The Kra-ell female sneered, her gaze flicking dismissively over Wonder's face. "Or what? You'll make me? You and what army?"

Even Marina's surprise over Borga's mastery of English couldn't diminish her panic as the two females squared off, their bodies coiled with tension and radiating aggression.

Wonder was a big female, but she was immortal, and as a pureblooded Kra-ell, Borga was much stronger and definitely more vicious.

She didn't want Wonder to get hurt because of her.

"I don't need an army to teach a conceited, rude female her place." Wonder leaned over the counter, staring Borga down.

Aliya sidled over to Wonder. "And if she needs help teaching you some manners, I happen to be an excellent teacher." She put her arm around Wonder's shoulders.

"A hybrid and an immortal defending a worthless human." Borga snorted. "I can hand you both your asses without breaking a sweat."

"You can try," Aliya snarled, her eyes flashing red and her fangs on full display.

Damn, the girl was scary. Marina was glad that Aliya was on her side.

Borga must have thought so too, because she took a step back. "As much as I would have enjoyed tearing you two a new one, we are under compulsion not to harm each other." She spun on her heel, and as she stalked away, she flipped them the finger.

The three of them stood there for a moment, the tension slowly leaching out of the air.

"What's her problem?" Aliya asked.

"She's unhinged." Marina let out a breath. "For some reason, she hates me and enjoys taunting me. I had forgotten about her when I asked to be transferred here."

Wonder's eyes were still blazing with anger as she turned to Marina. "You need to report this to Jade," she said firmly. "This is not acceptable behavior in the village."

Wonder was correct, but Marina was reluctant to make a fuss and draw attention to herself. Borga had been living in the village for a while, while Marina had just arrived. If Borga had behaved well so far, Jade might blame Marina for provoking her.

Besides, Jade was even scarier than Borga.

"It's okay. Eventually, she will tire of picking on me and move on."

"That's not how it works." Wonder sighed. "I don't have a lot of life experience, but even I know that bullies need to be dealt with, or they just get emboldened."

"Why you, though?" Aliya asked. "Borga is unpleasant, but I've never seen her that vicious to anyone."

"Borga is a bad apple, always has been. Not that the other purebloods were much better, but they were mostly just condescending, and she was mean. I was one of the maids assigned to clean the pureblooded females' quarters, so I was forced to interact with her. Maybe she'd gotten it into her head that I caught Mo-red's eye, or she just enjoyed lording it over me. No one had much in Igor's compound, not even the pureblooded Kra-ell, and because they had so little, the ones whose characters were less than stellar tried to make themselves seem better than others by tormenting the humans."

58

THE PRINCE

Ell-rom blinked, confusion clouding his features as he stared at Bridget. "What do you usually eat?" she repeated, her voice gentle but insistent.

He frowned, searching his fractured memory for some clues, some hint of what his body required for sustenance. But there was only blankness, a void where that knowledge should have been.

After having such a remarkable breakthrough and remembering his and his sister's names, he had hoped more memories would come rushing in, but he had no such luck.

After they had rolled his bed back to his room, he'd fallen asleep again, and when he'd woken up, it was with the same confusion as before.

"I don't know," he admitted. "I can't remember."

Bridget nodded as if she had expected as much. "That's all right," she reassured him, laying a comforting hand on his arm. "We'll figure it out together. I don't think your body can process blood, but that's what the Kra-ell live on, so let's start with that. Does drinking blood appeal to you?"

He felt bile rise in his throat, and his stomach convulsed as if preparing to purge what was inside of it.

"Not at all. I find even the thought of it disgusting."

"How about animal or fowl flesh? Raw or cooked?"

Ell-rom's stomach lurched violently again, a wave of nausea crashing over him. He swallowed hard, fighting the urge to hurl, his face twisting with disgust.

"No," he managed, shaking his head vigorously. "No meat, either."

"That's odd." Bridget frowned. "The gods eat everything." She glanced at Jasmine. "Am I right?"

Jasmine nodded. "We all ate the same things, and there were all kinds of you-know-what in the dishes. I don't want to mention it because Ell-rom looks green."

"I do?" He lifted his hand and looked at it. "I still look slightly gray."

"It was a tease." She patted his knee through the blanket covering him.

The friendly touch shouldn't have aroused him, but he couldn't help it. He didn't know how old he was, but he knew he hadn't been touched much, and definitely not by females other than his sister. He couldn't remember their mother touching him either, but she must have, at least when they were little.

"It makes sense," the senior medic said. "It's not like they could get the you-know-what or cook it in the temple." She looked at him. "How about baked food, fruits, or vegetables?"

Tearing himself away from sinful thoughts, Ell-rom tried to catch a flicker of memory that danced at the edges of his consciousness.

The scent of ripe fruit, sweet and fragrant, the taste of it bursting on his tongue like a small sun. His mouth watered at the thought, a sudden, visceral longing filling him.

"Fruit," he said. "I remember the taste of fruit."

Bridget smiled. "Good. That's a start. I'll bring you some vegetable broth to start, and we'll take it from there."

"Yay!" Jasmine clapped her hands. "You are about to eat real food."

Ell-rom glanced at the clear line that extended from a bag full of liquids to the back of his hand. "What about this? Do we still need it?"

Bridget hesitated. "You are holding down water just fine, so we can take it out, but if we encounter problems feeding you, we might need to put it back in."

He lifted his hand. "I am willing to take the risk."

"Excellent." Bridget looked at him with assessing eyes. "Since you seem eager to get out of bed, I'm inclined to assist you in that. But first, we need to remove everything else, including the other end." She winked. "I'm sure there is no Kra-ell translation for that word."

He knew what she meant, and having such an exchange in front of Jasmine was embarrassing.

"Yes, I am willing to risk that as well."

"Excellent. That means that you will have to use the restroom on your own. The first couple of times, Julian will help you, and I will get you a walker for later."

It was a terrifying prospect, and he didn't know if he was ready, but he was so tired of the bed and the white wall in front of it. He needed to see the sky and breathe fresh air, but until he became mobile and stable, he could not do any of those things.

"I'll help," Jasmine offered. "You can lean on me on the way to the bathroom."

He would rather die, but he did not say that.

"Also," Bridget said. "It's time you got a proper shower. After Julian removes all the wires and tubes, he will help wash you."

Ell-rom knew what a shower was because Jasmine used it to clean herself every night. She did not wash her hair every time she used the shower, but she always smelled good when she came out.

He did not want to think about how he smelled. Julian, the male medic, had been wiping him clean with some special kind of towel with cleansing agents, but it wasn't the same as standing under a spray of water and using cleansing products directly on his skin.

Had he had showers where he came from?

He couldn't even remember what kind of bed he slept on, let alone any other comforts.

"Julian will come over to help you," Bridget repeated. "Is that okay?"

"Yes, of course. I'm looking forward to it."

Bridget turned to Jasmine. "I think Ell-rom would like privacy for his first shower."

Jasmine jumped up from her chair as if something had bit her lush bottom. "Yes. I'm leaving right now."

No, he wasn't going to think about her bottom, or her bosom, or her lips… Oh, dear Mother above. He would need some time to calm down before the male medic arrived, or he would die from embarrassment.

Jasmine turned to him and smiled. "I'll come back when Julian tells me it's okay. I'm going to take a walk and stretch my legs."

Still dying on the inside, he nodded.

When Bridget and Jasmine left, Ell-rom released a long breath and turned his thoughts toward all those poor souls who hadn't made it. Perhaps using them to douse the fire coursing through his veins was disrespectful to their memory, but he had nothing else.

He would pray for their forgiveness later.

59

ANNANI

As Annani waited for Kian to join her for lunch, she looked out the sliding doors of her house at the lushly green backyard. The view, together with the sounds and smells coming from the kitchen where Oridu was bustling about, provided a soothing background to her racing thoughts.

How could it be that a half-brother, born on a distant planet and raised under such different circumstances, was so much like her?

They shared a father, but, although Annani had loved Ahn dearly and respected him immensely, he hadn't been ruled by his heart like she was and like the prince seemed to be.

Ahn hadn't been known for his compassion either.

Her father had never been cruel for cruelty's sake, and he had not been a tyrant obsessed with ruling, but he had been ruthless, unforgiving, and steadfast in following the code he had imposed on their people. But then, Annani hadn't inherited her impulsivity and her romanticism from her mother either. She actually shared those traits with her uncle Ekin, who was also the Eternal King's son, but not Queen Ani's, so if they were, in fact, inherited traits, they had to have come from the Eternal King, the only ancestor they had in common. But, Annani sincerely doubted that they had all inherited good hearts from him.

Genetics were complicated, and as much as the gods thought they could control every aspect of creating an intelligent being, some things were the Fates' doing.

As the warm, savory scent of the simmering stew filled the air, Annani started to get impatient for her son's arrival.

She was eager to share lunch with Kian, a rare treat they seldom enjoyed, and then drive together to see her brother again. It wasn't that she didn't like family meals with Syssi and Allegra, but it was nice to get her son all to herself occasionally.

The sound of the doorbell brought a smile to her lips, and as Ogidu opened the door for Kian, she rose to her feet and walked over to greet him.

"You are right on time." She tilted her head for him to kiss her cheek and then the other way so he could kiss the other.

"Something smells good," he said.

"Oridu got excited when I told him you would join us for lunch. He made the vegetable stew you like."

Usually, her butler prepared the stew with beef, but since Kian did not eat animal products, Ogidu had found wonderful substitutes.

Kian's eyes widened. "I have not had that in such a long time."

"Then let us begin the meal without delay." She led him to the dining room table.

After pulling out a chair for her and waiting until she was seated, Kian took the seat to her right.

"I have good news," he said as he unfurled his napkin and draped it over his lap. "Bridget called me this morning to tell me that the prince remembered his and his sister's names."

Annani's heart rate accelerated. She had not expected such fast progress. "This is indeed wonderful news. What are their names?"

"His is Ell-rom, and his sister's is Morelle."

Annani felt tears prick at the corners of her eyes. "Ell-rom and Morelle," she repeated softly, the names feeling both foreign and achingly familiar on her tongue. "My brother and sister. What jogged his memory? Did Bridget say?"

"She did, and she credited Jasmine with the idea that led to it. Ell-rom was desperate to see his sister, so he tried to get out of bed on his own. Naturally, he was in no state to do that, and Bridget caught him in time before he face-planted on the floor. Bridget offered to show him a camera feed of his sister, but the prince was adamant about seeing her himself and holding her hand. When Jasmine saw how distraught he was because he couldn't see his sister, she suggested that they take him to see her by wheeling his bed into her room. Bridget agreed to try it, and somehow, they managed to squeeze his bed next to his sister's so he could reach over and take her hand."

Imagining the reunion, Annani could not hold back the tears falling down her cheeks.

"I wish I had been there to see them together. It must have been such an emotional moment."

"I bet it was," Kian said. "So much so that the prince remembered his sister's name, which in turn brought back his own."

Annani smiled through the tears. "I think the Fates were very wise choosing Jasmine as my brother's mate." She chuckled. "She is so dedicated to him and so resourceful. I hope she will transition and prove that she is a princess at heart."

She waited for Ogidu to serve the stew, toasted bread, and fresh salad. "We do not know anything about her family." Annani leaned back to allow Ogidu to place some stew on her plate. "From what you told me, she is not close to her father, and her mother died when she was young. I would like you to look into that."

Kian nodded. "I'll get someone onto that. If she is to become my aunt, I need to know more about her history."

Annani winced. "An actress who is a Wiccan witch would not have been my first or second or third choice for my brother's mate, but I need to have faith in the Fates."

"She is a lovely young lady." Kian reached for a piece of toast to dip in his stew. "Beautiful, kind, and most importantly, full of joie de vivre. You will like her."

"I would like to meet her. Perhaps today, you will allow her to remain by his side when I visit?"

Kian sighed. "Not yet."

"Why not?"

"First of all, I would rather wait for her to transition. Meeting you will leave such an indelible impression that we will not be able to erase her memory of that, provided that it is needed."

Annani laughed. "After finding an alien pod with twenty stasis chambers inside, eighteen dead Kra-ell, and two live half gods, half Kra-ell royal twins, I do not think meeting me will be the most memorable thing in Jasmine's mind."

For a moment, it seemed like she had won the verbal sparring with her son, but then he got that gleam in his eyes that portended otherwise.

"You might be right about that, but it's also not the right way to introduce her to you. Would you rob Jasmine of the full experience of meeting a goddess for the first time by doing so in a cramped clinic room?"

He got her there.

Or maybe not.

"We can do this in your office in the keep. I will sit at the head of the conference table, looking regal and glowing, and you will bring her in to meet me. I will do my thing, welcoming her to the clan and acting godly, and from there, we can walk together to Ell-rom's room."

60

THE PRINCE

"This is a happy moment," Julian said as he entered the room and closed the door behind him. "It deserves a celebration."

"Yes. I hope so."

Julian smiled. "Close your eyes and count to a hundred. By the time you are done, I will be done too."

It was probably how the medic took care of frightened small children, but Ell-rom was happy to follow the advice.

In a way, he was like a small child, learning the world he had recently awakened to. Everything was strange and unfamiliar, but his sister was in the next room over, and he had Jasmine by his side.

He wasn't alone.

There were also the others who had visited him the day before—Annani, who had been so gracious and promised to take care of him and Morelle. Kian, Jade, and Aru also seemed like good people who did not mean him or his sister harm, and maybe they could all become friends at some point. Perhaps he and Morelle would find a community among these people.

"All done," Julian announced. "You can open your eyes now."

"Thank you. That was good advice. I did not feel most of it."

"I tried to be as gentle as possible, but some things hurt no matter how hard I try." Julian leaned over Ell-rom. "Wrap your arms around my neck. I will count to three, and on three, I will lift you off the bed. Try to help by hoisting yourself up and moving your legs over the side of the bed."

As Ell-rom followed the medic's suggestion, he was glad Jasmine was not there to see the humiliating display of helplessness.

"You are doing very well," Julian said as Ell-rom got his feet on the floor. "Now, try to stand straight and leave only one arm around my neck."

His legs shook, and he hung from Julian's neck, but he managed to make one step and then another. Then, he was at the door to the bathroom, and Julian helped him get inside.

"I don't know if you had toilets where you came from, but this is where you empty your bladder and bowels. After you are done, the toilet automatically activates and washes everything down. After a bowel movement, you can press this button, and a water spray will clean the area. All that will remain to be done is to wipe the moisture with some paper. I don't expect you to need to do that yet, but you need to empty your bladder." Julian tilted his head. "Do you want to give it a try?"

"I should." Ell-rom smiled nervously. "I don't want that tube inside of me again."

Julian helped him sit down on the toilet. "I'll give you some privacy by turning my back to you, but I don't want to leave you alone here just yet."

It was glorious to relieve himself, to perform that small function on his own, but when it was time to get up, Ell-rom lacked the strength.

Shame and frustration warred within him, but he could not bring himself to ask for Julian's help.

Instead, he sat there and waited until the medic turned around. "All done?" Julian asked cheerfully.

"Yes, thank you. I just can't get up."

"That's perfectly all right." Julian offered him both of his hands. "Let's do this together."

When he was up, the toilet whooshed behind him, startling him.

He looked over his shoulder, watching as the water spiraled inside and a blue light flashed.

"The light sanitizes the bowl," Julian explained. "I've never thought to ask Jade how things like that worked back on Anumati." He guided Ell-rom into the shower stall and helped him sit on a small stool. "It's funny how you never think about things like that until you meet someone who can't remember anything."

The medic removed the garment that covered Ell-rom and tossed it into a bin that stood in a corner. "I've got a pair of loose pants for you and a matching shirt. You will feel so much better in them."

"Thank you." Ell-rom was trying to maintain some dignity by sitting up and not allowing himself to slide down to the floor.

He was so frail, so vulnerable.

As Julian washed Ell-rom with brisk but gentle movements, the medic kept talking in his soothing, conversational tone.

"Do you want me to cut your hair?" he asked after washing it with some fragrant lotion and then rinsing it. "You have those clumps of long hair and a fuzz of new growth, and it doesn't look good. Cutting everything short will look better."

"I trust your judgment." He chuckled weakly. "I haven't looked at myself yet."
"You are about to in a few moments." Julian turned the water off, rubbed a soft towel over Ell-rom, and then helped him into a robe made from the same soft fabric as the towel.

Leaving him sitting on the stool in the shower, Julian stepped out and returned with a paper cup and a brush with some white paste on it.

"This is a toothbrush. As the name implies, it's for cleaning your teeth. Don't swallow the paste. After I'm done brushing your teeth, you will rinse it out with water from the cup." He handed it to him.

"I can brush my teeth by myself," Ell-rom said.
Julian looked doubtful, but he gave him the brush. "Go ahead."

It was a challenge, his hands shaking and his grip weak as he tried to maneuver the small brush over his teeth and gums. In the end, Julian had to help him, guiding his hand and steadying his arm until the task was done.

"Okay." The medic grinned at him. "Looking good. Let's get rid of those clumps before I lead you to the mirror."

He must have looked bad if the medic felt the need to fix his hair before letting him see his reflection.

Julian returned with a pair of scissors. "I'm not a barber, so don't expect anything fancy, but I will do my best."

By the time Julian was done and helped Ell-rom up, exhaustion was dragging him down, and as he stood in front of the mirror, he didn't recognize the face staring back at him.

Gaunt and pale, with sunken cheeks and hollow eyes, the male in the mirror looked like a ghost. Ell-rom lifted a hand to his face, tracing the sharp angles of his cheekbones and the sparse tufts of new hair on his scalp.

"I don't know who I am," he whispered, his voice cracking. "I don't recognize myself."

Julian's hand was warm and solid on his shoulder, his arm wrapped around Ell-rom's middle, holding him from falling. "You still have a long journey back to yourself, but you can make it only one step at a time."

As Julian helped him into the fresh clothing he'd brought and then back into bed, Ell-rom clung to those words like a lifeline.

Once step at a time.

61

ALENA

The first contraction came out of the blue and hit Alena with the force of a freight train, a searing, twisting pain that radiated from her back and left her breathless. She gasped, one hand flying to her belly with the other groping for Orion's arm.

"It's happening," she managed, her voice tight with strain. "The baby's coming."

With a strangled sound, Orion tore the virtual reality headset off his head and dropped it on the couch. His face drained of color as he stared at her with wide, panicked eyes. "What do we do now? I forgot what I need to do."

They'd been preparing for weeks, and he'd had everything memorized, but panic had a way of erasing sense. Her mate, the fearless warrior, was reduced to a stammering mess at the prospect of impending fatherhood.

It was endearing to see him so unraveled. But she didn't have time to coddle him, not when their child was eager to make its way into the world.

Kid number fourteen would not take as long as kid number one had taken, or even number five. That first contraction had not been a gentle warning. It was a war horn.

It was time.

"Call Merlin," she said, her voice calm and steady now that the pain had subsided. "Tell him that we are on our way to the clinic. I suggest you summon a golf cart because I won't make it there on foot. The baby would come out on the way."

Yeah, that wasn't the best way to approach a male who was already panicking, but she really didn't have time. This baby was going to be out in less than an hour.

Orion nodded, fumbling for his phone with shaking hands. As he dialed, Alena focused on her breathing, on the familiar rhythm of inhale and exhale that had carried her through thirteen previous labors. This was like a comfortable old hat for her, a dance she knew by heart. But for Orion, it was all new, all raw and terrifying in its intensity.

Her delivery bag had been packed since before the cruise, and she kept it by the door so Orion wouldn't have to look for it.

There was nothing to prepare because she'd been ready for weeks, hoping the baby would arrive early. Instead, it was arriving late.

She reached for Orion's hand, lacing her fingers through his and giving them a reassuring squeeze. "It's going to be all right," she murmured, meeting his gaze with a soft smile. "I've done this many times before, remember? Fourteen is my lucky number."

Orion didn't look convinced, but he managed a shaky nod, bringing her hand to his lips and pressing a kiss to her knuckles. "I love you so much," he whispered. "I love you so much, Alena. You're the strongest person I know."

"I love you too." She smiled. "But we better get moving, or this baby will be born on this sofa, with you delivering it."

The last comment did what she'd expected: lighting a fire under Orion's bottom and getting him moving fast.

When they left their house, a Guardian was waiting for them with a golf cart. "Hold on tight." He smiled at Alena. "It's going to be a bumpy ride."

She lifted a hand. "No need to drive like a bat out of hell, Rodney. Slow and safe will get us there on time."

During the drive another contraction hit her harder than the first, and as she white-knuckled the seat and bit on her lip to stop herself from whimpering, Orion continued calling her family to let them know that the baby was coming.

By the time they reached the clinic, she'd had three more contractions. They were coming every two minutes now, which meant she was getting close.

Orion half-carried her inside, his strong arms supporting her weight as Merlin and Hildegard rushed to meet them.

The eccentric doctor was a comforting sight. He hadn't delivered any of her other babies, who had all been born before he had even been born, but she liked him and his unruly shock of white hair and his piercing blue eyes that seemed to see straight into the heart of things.

Orion, on the other hand, wasn't pleased with Merlin. The doctor's eccentricities blinded him to how brilliant and compassionate he was.

The distrust was written all over his face. "When are Bridget and Julian coming back?"

Merlin smiled good-naturedly. "When the twins are back on their feet, I guess. But don't worry. Alena is in good hands. Hildegard and I have delivered plenty of babies over the years, and your mate is a pro at this. She'll be fine."

"You delivered human babies."

Hildegard stifled a chuckle. "There is no difference. Now stop jabbering and get your wife on the bed. There is no time to waste."

62

THE PRINCE

Ell-rom wasn't sure what woke him up. Jasmine's gasp or the aroma of food. Forcing his eyelids to lift, he looked into her stunned face. "What happened?"

"You are gorgeous."

He frowned. "Your translation device must be malfunctioning. It said that I'm exceedingly good to look at."

"You are." She smoothed a hand over his mostly bald head. "You look so much better without those long strings of hair." She scrunched her nose. "You know what else I've just noticed?"

"What?"

Jasmine must be prone to exaggeration because he had seen himself after Julian had cut off the loose locks, and he still looked like a walking shadow.

"You don't have facial hair," Jasmine said.

"Is that bad?"

"No, it's just strange since all the immortals and gods I know either have beards or shave them off. Maybe it's a Kra-ell trait." She pressed the lever, which he now knew was under the bed, and lifted the back of it. "Bridget tasked me with feeding you."

He glanced at the steaming bowl of fragrant clear liquid in her hands. "What is that?"

"It's called vegetable soup. You are probably wondering where the vegetables are. Right?"

"Yes. I was curious to see what Earth's vegetables look like."

695

"I wouldn't be surprised if they are the same as on Anumati. After all, everything probably originated from there. But that's beside the point. Because your stomach is just getting used to regular food, you are supposed to consume only clear liquids, so even though the soup was cooked with vegetables, they were taken out." She lifted a spoonful to his lips. "Taste it."

Ell-rom hesitated a moment before opening his mouth and allowing her to put the spoon inside. As the warm, savory liquid slid over his tongue, he was surprised to find it pleasing. It was rich and flavorful, a medley of tastes that he couldn't quite identify but found appetizing, nonetheless.

"Good?" Jasmine asked.

"Yes."

She smiled brightly and brought another spoonful to his mouth. Before long, the bowl was empty, and his stomach felt warm and full.

As if waiting for the exact moment he was done, Bridget walked in. "How does your stomach feel?" she asked. "Any discomfort? Nausea?"

Ell-rom shook his head. "It feels fine. Warm. Good." His eyelids were already growing heavy with exhaustion.

Bridget nodded, stepping back and allowing Jasmine to adjust his blankets and fluff his pillows. "If you can keep that down, we'll try something a bit more substantial later on," she said, her voice fading into the background as sleep began to claim him.

Ell-rom mumbled something in response, but the words were lost as he drifted off, his mind slipping into the waiting embrace of dreams.

He saw himself standing with a goblet of dark, viscous liquid in his hand. He lifted it to his lips, pretending to drink, but as soon as the rim touched his mouth, he felt a wave of revulsion wash over him. Subtly, carefully, he let the liquid dribble back into the cup, the metallic scent of blood filling his nostrils and making his stomach churn.

No one could see what he had done because the veil covered his head, the goblet, and the hand holding it, but the noises his stomach was making were a little harder to hide.

From whom?

He did not know. There was no one around he could see, but he heard a distant murmur of voices.

"Go to your room," his sister whispered urgently next to him. "Slowly. Do not draw any attention to yourself."

She was small, a child still, and covered in robes and veils—a walking tent like the adult priestesses, just smaller.

He assumed that he looked like her. Just another small tent, but he listened to her and retreated as slowly as he could, which was not slow at all because the contents of his stomach refused to stay down.

Finally, when he reached his chamber and closed the door, he ran into the bathroom while tearing the veil off. Sliding into position at the toilet, he retched and heaved, his body rejecting the small amount of blood that had managed to slide down his throat.

A figure loomed over him, a female draped in the black robes of a priestess. "You fool," she snarled, her voice dripping with contempt. "You will get yourself and your sister killed with your foolishness. What did I tell you to do?"

He wiped his mouth with the back of his hand and looked up at her helplessly.

"Tell me! What did I tell you to do?"

"I was supposed to hold the goblet under my veil and just pretend to drink." "And what did you not understand about that simple directive?"

"It was just a drop," he whispered. "I did not mean to drink it. The drop was on the rim."

The priestess crouched next to him, her eyes blazing at him through the veil. "A mistake like that is the difference between life and death, little Holy Brother. You might not care for your life, but I know you care about your sister's."

"It will never happen again, Holy Mother."

Ell-rom jerked awake with a gasp, his heart pounding and his skin slick with sweat.

For a moment, he couldn't remember where he was, but then he recognized the white walls of the clinic and let out a relieved breath.

He was safe here, in this little room with walls that were white but not quite. There were shades of pink and yellow in the white, making the room feel cozy rather than stark.

Or maybe it had nothing to do with the colors but the female sitting in the chair beside his bed, her face soft and peaceful as she read a book with a tiny light illuminating the pages.

When he'd asked her what it was, Jasmine had explained that it was a story written on paper. Humans had special machines that printed many thousands of those things, and people purchased them in stores. She'd said they also had stories on electronic tablets, which he found much more logical, but many still preferred the paper books.

Humans were strange creatures, but he was eager to learn more about them, particularly about her.

Absorbed in her reading, Jasmine did not notice that he was awake, and he was glad that she didn't because he needed a few moments to collect his thoughts.

He was safe, surrounded by people who cared for him and wanted to help him heal. Not kill him and his sister because they were unlike everyone else.

But even as he clung to that thought like a talisman against the darkness, he couldn't shake the sense of unease that lingered, the feeling that something was lurking in the shadows of his past, something dark and dangerous that was more than his inability to tolerate the taste of blood.

What was it about him and his sister that he was not supposed to let anyone see?

63

ALENA

Alena liked having people around her when she was having her babies. It was a joyous occasion, especially for people who didn't get to celebrate births often, and she liked to share her blessings.

It got a little crowded with her mother and Kian there, but she was glad Orion managed to catch them in the parking lot before they left for the keep.

If they had left earlier and had been at the keep when Orion called, her mother wouldn't have made it in time to see the baby born, and she would have regretted it dearly.

Her mother had witnessed all her babies coming into the world, and this last one shouldn't be any different.

Hopefully, it wouldn't be the last, but Alena didn't want to be greedy and anger the Fates who had been so incredibly generous with her.

Also, Orion seemed much calmer now that Annani was there, and Alena hoped her mother wasn't thralling him to take the edge off.

He was probably glad to have someone with plenty of experience helping Alena.

"Breathe." Annani clasped Alena's hand as another contraction hit her hard. "In and out, slow and steady."

"Syssi and Amanda are on their way," Kian said, his face pinched with unnecessary worry. "They're coming from the university, but they'll be here as soon as possible."

Alena laughed, the sound strained and a little breathless. "They probably won't make it," she managed, shaking her head. "This baby is coming out fast."

"Not necessarily," Merlin said as he entered the room. "Your contractions are coming every two minutes, but that doesn't mean the baby will come flying out. It could still be a couple of hours yet."

Alena shook her head. "Wanna bet?"

Merlin chuckled. "Save your energy for pushing," he advised, his voice warm with affection. "I'll give you all a few minutes, and then I need everyone out for a little bit to check how things are progressing." He winked at Alena before stepping out of the room.

As she settled onto the bed, resting between contractions, she glanced at her mate, whose pale face was drawn with worry. He looked like he was about to be sick.

"Hey." She reached for his hand and gave it a gentle tug. "There is absolutely no reason to worry. I'm a demigoddess, remember? Nothing is going to happen to me."

"I know, but I can't stand seeing you in pain. It's killing me. And then I worry about the baby. He's not going to be born immortal even though we are both demigods, and if something goes wrong, all of our powers combined might not be able to save him."

He was wrong about that, but she couldn't tell him what her mother's blood could do, or his father's. If the baby was in trouble, Fates forbid, a small donation from either would bring him back.

That wasn't guaranteed, though. If the baby was stillborn, even a god's blood could not bring him back.

Kian leaned against the wall, holding his phone. "Did you find out the baby's gender and didn't tell anyone?"

"We didn't." Alena winced as another contraction started. "Sari convinced me that statistically it was more likely that I would have a boy this time, so we started referring to the baby as he."

As the pain took her breath away, she couldn't talk anymore; holding on to Orion's hand and panting was all she could do.

When the contraction subsided, Kian was not in the room, and Merlin was back.

"I can give you all kinds of things for the pain, from mild relief to an epidural."

Orion looked at her with hope, but Alena shook her head. "I've delivered thirteen children with nothing to ease the way. I'll do no less for my fourteenth."

Merlin nodded. "I had a feeling that you would say that." He turned to Orion. "I don't mind if you stay, and naturally, the Clan Mother can stay as well, but I need to check the opening."

When Orion swallowed audibly, Alena patted his hand. "Wait outside with Kian, sweetheart. Maybe get some coffee from the café."

He shook his head. "I'm not leaving your side."

"The baby is not coming out yet, and you'll just be in the waiting room. Go."

Her mother pushed to her feet. "Come on, Orion. Let us give Alena some privacy."

When he stood up, she threaded her arm through his. "So, did you two come up with a list of names?" She looked over her shoulder at Alena and winked.

She sent her mother an air kiss.

Merlin smoothed a hand over his long beard as the door closed behind the two. "Maybe the Clan Mother shouldn't have left. Do you want me to call Hildegard to be in here while I perform the examination?"

Alena rolled her eyes. "Don't be silly, Merlin. Just do it."

She could have reminded him that he was her great-grandson, but there was a chance that it would make him even more uncomfortable.

6 4

ANNANI

The first cry of new life filled the air, a piercing, precious sound that brought tears to Annani's eyes. Her heart was full to bursting as she watched Hildegard wipe the tiny boy clean while Merlin took care of the afterbirth.

Delivering children into the world was messy, difficult, and painful, but no greater joy existed.

"Here you go, Mommy." Hildegard placed the baby on Alena's chest.

"He's perfect," Orion whispered, his cheek next to Alena's as both gazed upon their little miracle.

"Do you want to hold him?" Alena asked her mate. His eyes turned the size of saucers. "I'm too scared."

Annani took a step closer and leaned to touch her latest grandson's tiny cheek. He had a mop of dark hair like his father and cupid-bow lips like his mother.

"Your brother is in the waiting room, biting his nails. Can I invite him in?"

"Of course." Alena smiled. "I want him to be here when we reveal the name we have chosen for our son."

"Maybe we should wait for Amanda and Syssi to get here," Orion said.

Alena winced. "Amanda will be pissed if she misses it. You're right. Let's wait for them to get here."

Merlin opened the door and waved Kian in. "Come. Say hello to your new nephew."

A grin spread over Kian's face. "So, it is a boy after all."

"Of course," Annani said. "We all knew it was going to be a boy."

"Right." He leaned down and kissed her cheek. "Congratulations, grandma."

"Congratulations, uncle."

"I'll be in my office if anyone needs me," Merlin said. "I'll send Syssi and Amanda in when they get here."

As the door closed behind the doctor and Kian shifted his gaze to his new nephew, his eyes softened, and his smile turned tender. "Congratulations, Alena, Orion. So, does this strapping baby boy have a name?"

"He does," Alena said. "But we decided to wait for Amanda and Syssi to get here before we name him. You know how upset Amanda will be that she wasn't here when he was born."

"Yeah, she will." Kian pulled out the one chair that was in the room for Annani. "Please, sit down, Mother."

Annani did not argue. It was not that she was tired, but with everyone towering over her, she was more comfortable sitting down.

The door swung open, and her daughters, one by birth and the other by marriage, walked in, both looking rushed and sweaty as if they'd run the entire way.

"Oh, Alena, he's beautiful," Amanda gushed.

"Adorable," Syssi whispered.

"Where is Allegra?" Kian demanded.

"With Merlin." Syssi walked up to him and kissed his cheek. "Evie, too. The guy is in heaven, holding one on each knee."

"Do you trust him with them?"

Syssi gave him a scolding look. "What kind of question is that? Of course, I trust him."

Smiling, Annani shifted her gaze to Orion, who still looked shell-shocked.

"Do you want me to help hold him?" Hildegard asked the new father.

He nodded, but even though it did not look convincing, Hildegard lifted the baby off Alena's chest and put him in his father's arms.

Orion's face was a mask of wonder and terror, and he looked like he might faint at any moment.

Kian chuckled, putting a steadying hand on the new father's elbow. "Breathe, Orion. He is a beautiful, healthy baby boy."

Orion nodded jerkily, his gaze never leaving the perfect face of his son. He took a few stumbling steps forward, his arms cradling the infant like he was made of spun glass, and then he went down to one knee in front of Annani.

"Clan Mother," he said hoarsely, his voice cracking with emotion as he held the baby out to Annani. "Meet your grandson, Evander Tellesious."

Annani's heart swelled with love as she took the child into her arms, marveling at his solid weight, the impossibly soft brush of his skin against hers. "Evander," she repeated. "A beautiful name for a beautiful boy."

Looking at the tiny face, she drank in every detail of her grandson's face, committing each tiny feature to memory. The slope of his nose, the bow of his lips, the wispy curl of hair that clung to his scalp. He was perfect, a miracle in miniature, and Annani already loved him fiercely.

She dipped her head and brushed a kiss on the silky soft cheek. "There is nothing better in the universe."

Orion was still kneeling in front of her, his hands twitching as if he longed to take the baby back and cradle him close to his chest.

Annani smiled, shifting Evander in her arms and giving his father a reassuring nod. "Do not worry, Orion. I have held hundreds of newborns in my time, and I have not dropped one yet. Your son is safe with me." She stood up with the baby securely held against her bosom.

Orion pushed to his feet as well and hovered nearby as Annani walked over to her daughter's side.

Alena looked radiant, her face flushed with the glow of new motherhood, her eyes bright with joy and love. She held out her arms as Annani approached.

"He is perfect." Annani agreed, carefully transferring Evander into his mother's waiting embrace. "Just like his mother." She kissed her daughter's forehead. "I am so proud of you, my Alena."

Her daughter just smiled, as she always did when she thought Annani was being overly dramatic or too much of a diva. That quiet acceptance was one of Alena's greatest strengths.

The baby settled against his mother's chest, yawned adorably, and fell asleep. "Such a good little boy," Amanda said. "So calm."

Alena stroked his little back. "All my babies were like that."

"That's because you are calm." Syssi leaned against Kian's arm. "You project it. By the way, did you tell Allegra what you were naming the baby?"

Alena shook her head. "We told no one. Why?"

"She insisted that the baby's name was going to be E.T."

"Like mother like daughter." Kian wrapped his arm around Syssi's shoulders. "Allegra is already predicting the future."

As Amanda and Alena murmured in agreement, Annani looked around at her family and noticed that Hildegard had left the room at some point. Still, that did not mean that she could talk freely because there was a camera in the room, and even though she doubted Merlin would pry intentionally, he might take a look to ensure that mother and baby were doing okay.

"I have news," she said quietly, not to disturb little Evander. "Bridget called this morning to tell us that the prince remembered his and his sister's names. That is a very good sign that his memory is coming back."

"What are the names?" Alena asked.

"The prince's name is Ell-rom, and his sister is Morelle."

Alena's face lit up. "That's wonderful news, Mother. I think it's symbolic that he recalled their names on the day Evander was born and named."

"Indeed." Annani nodded. "That is why I decided not to wait to tell my brother I am his sister."

As she had expected, Kian was not happy. "It's too early, Mother. Let's wait for him to regain more of his memories so we can assess his intentions."

Annani pinned her son with a hard look. "The more I tell him, the more I reveal, the faster he will regain his memories, and the quicker we will learn his true nature. I do not have patience, and I do not want to wait to make Ell-rom and Morelle part of my family. The only concession I am still willing to make for the sake of your insistence on security is to wear the earpieces, but once I am convinced that my brother does not harbor ill intentions toward me, I will remove them."

She leaned down to press a final, lingering kiss to Evander's forehead, breathing in the sweet, milky scent of him.

"It is a blessed day for our family as we welcome Evander, Ell-rom, and Morelle into our clan."

65

MARINA

T he morning sun slanted through the kitchen windows, bathing everything in a warm, golden glow. Marina stood at the counter, her hands wrapped around a steaming mug of coffee, and tried to ignore the knot of tension that had taken residence in her gut.

Beside her, Peter moved with easy grace, cracking eggs into a bowl with one hand and whisking them with a fork with another. Thinly sliced onion and mushroom pieces were sizzling in a pan, waiting to be folded into the omelet he was working on.

"This one is going to be a masterpiece." Peter put another pan on the stovetop and turned on the burner.

"It sure smells like it." She leaned up and kissed the underside of his jaw. "You are spoiling me."

He grinned. "I love spoiling you, so stop complaining." He dropped a generous portion of butter into the pan.

"I'm not complaining. I'm just stating a fact. You didn't even let me make toast."

If she let him cook for her daily, she could kiss her slim figure goodbye. The guy loved his butter.

"Today is my turn to make breakfast." He poured the egg mixture into the pan. "Sit down and enjoy."

"Yes, sir."

She walked over to the dining table and sat down. Alfie had gone to the gym, so it was just the two of them, and Marina should have been enjoying the homey atmosphere. Still, she couldn't shake the memory of the previous day's confrontation with Borga and the cruel, taunting words that had dripped like venom from the Kra-ell female's lips.

She'd tried not to let it get under her skin, but it was hard. Back in the compound, Borga had been at the top of the so-called food chain and Marina at the bottom, but here in the village they were supposed to be equal, and Marina hadn't expected to be subjected to that crap, nor was she willing to just roll over and let Borga stomp all over her.

She wanted to fight back, but she didn't know how.

"You're quiet this morning," Peter said as he slid a plate of a delicious-looking omelet and toast in front of her. "Everything okay?"

Marina sighed, setting her mug down and running a hand through her hair. "Not really," she admitted. "I had a run-in with Borga yesterday at the café."

Peter frowned. "Borga? Pavel's mother?"

Marina nodded. "She came into the café and tried hard to get under my skin. She used to taunt me in the compound, too, but I wasn't mentally ready for it in the village, and it did get under my skin."

Peter's eyes blazed with inner light. "What did she say?"

Marina shrugged. "She threw around comments about wanting me to clean her house and then also about our relationship. She had the nerve to bring you into it and suggest I was just using you to get ahead."

Peter's jaw clenched, his eyes flashing with anger. "Nasty person."

"She is, but she's just saying what others are thinking. I was a maid all my adult life, first in the compound, then in Safe Haven, and even on the Silver Swan. I've been a barista for less than a week." Marina picked at the omelet with her fork. "People also wonder what you could possibly see in someone like me."

Peter reached across the table and took her hand. "I don't care what anyone else thinks. I love you, and I want you in my life. Nothing and no one can change that. Not that I think anyone other than Borga has a problem with you. Even my mother has warmed to us being together, and she asks about you every time I call."

A lump formed in her throat. "I love you too."

Peter's mother probably wanted to hear him say they had broken up, but Marina kept that to herself. It was good that the woman was in Scotland, and she didn't have to deal with her every day.

His lips quirked in a smile. "Borga and anyone else who has a problem with us being together can go to hell. They are not worth your energy."

Forcing a smile, Marina nodded. "You're right."

Peter grinned. "That's my girl." He leaned in to press a kiss to her lips. "I'll talk to Kagra about Borga. She will put her in her place."

Marina didn't want him talking to his ex, not about Borga or anything else. "I'd rather put this episode behind me and pretend it never happened."

Peter leaned back in his chair. "I don't think that's smart. Borga didn't make trouble before, and suddenly she's allowing herself to be rude to a community member right as a slew of things start happening that have never happened before."

"Like what?"

"Theft. Packages are being stolen from the mailroom, shutters are malfunctioning, and yesterday, one of the trash incinerators broke down. Those things are built to last forever. There is no way it malfunctioned without someone doing something deliberately to sabotage it."

"I don't think the incidents are connected to Borga, but I'm not a Guardian. You have experience with stuff like that."

"Not really," he admitted. "This is the first time we've had things stolen in the village. No one even bothers locking their doors, and unless things start going missing from inside homes, they'll continue leaving them unlocked. But before I call Kagra, let's finish breakfast."

Talking about Borga and Kagra was enough for Marina to lose her appetite, but she made an effort to take a few more forkfuls before pushing the plate away.

"Okay. Let's do it." Peter reached for his phone, his fingers flying over the screen as he texted Kagra.

Once he was done and hit send, the reply didn't take long to arrive. "She's on her way. She wants to get all the details straight from you." Marina swallowed.

She hadn't seen Kagra since their community had been divided between Safe Haven and the village, but that wasn't why she was apprehensive about meeting the female.

What if she also made derisory comments about her former boyfriend shacking up with a human?

When a few minutes later, a knock sounded at the door, Marina tensed. Peter gave her hand a reassuring squeeze before rising to answer it.

"Good morning." Kagra walked in like she owned the place. "Long time no see, Marina." She nodded at her. "Looking good."

Did she mean that Marina looked good, or was she referring to Peter's house being in a much better state than it had been when the two of them were together?

Marina kept it clean and organized, so that could be what Kagra had meant. "Good morning." She forced a smile. "Please, take a seat." She motioned to the couch. "Can I get you some coffee?"

The purebloods could drink coffee and tea as long as it didn't have added cream or sugar.

"No, thank you." Kagra sat down. "We all have jobs we need to get to. Tell me what happened with Borga."

"It's not a big deal, but Peter thinks it might be connected to other things happening in the village, and that's why he texted you." She continued telling her about the encounter and her past interactions with Borga.

Kagra nodded. "Borga is a character. She needs to be reminded of her place occasionally, and then she behaves for a while." Chuckling, Kagra stretched her long legs and crossed her booted feet at the ankles. "She's like a hormonal human, no offense, Marina."

"As if the Kra-ell are so even-keeled," Marina murmured. "'Between the big egos, the power plays, and the petty jealousies, you are much worse than humans."

Marina would have never dared say that to a Kra-ell while still in the compound, but she felt fearless with Peter at her side.

Kagra barked out a laugh. "Every word you said is true. Still, Borga has her good and bad sides like everyone else, and she is usually not that vicious."

"For some reason, she is to me."

"I don't doubt that." Kagra turned to Peter. "What's your take on this?"

"You know my take. I wouldn't have called you here if I thought there was nothing to it. But what bothers me is that none of the Kra-ell or humans should be able to pull off the recent wave of thefts and the small acts of sabotage. You were all subjected to a powerful compulsion that should prevent you from harming the clan and the village."

Kagra pursed her lips. "Many of the Kra-ell and the humans in the compound spent their entire lives under Igor's compulsion, and they learned to take advantage of every possible loophole that allowed them to maintain some semblance of free will." She leaned forward, her eyes boring into Peter's with an intensity that made Marina's skin crawl. "Borga, or whoever else is committing those small acts of rebellion, might have convinced themselves they are harmless pranks and as such, don't fall under the umbrella of Toven's compulsion."

Marina felt a chill run down her spine. The thought of Borga or any of the other Kra-ell being able to defy the compulsion that bound them by mislabeling their actions as pranks was terrifying. Countless acts of small cruelty could be defined as pranks by the perpetrators while being much more than that to the victims.

Kagra uncrossed her feet. "We should tell Kian." She shifted her gaze to Marina. "Call your supervisors and tell them that you will be late. I'll check with Kian when he can see us."

66

KIAN

ian put the phone down and turned his chair to look out the window at the village below.

From his vantage point on the second floor, he could see the bustling activity of the café and even hear the laughter and shouts of Kra-ell children playing on the playground. The small pond glittered in the sunlight, its surface rippling with the gentle breeze that stirred the leaves of the trees.

It was a peaceful scene, a tableau of harmony and contentment that should have filled Kian with a sense of pride and satisfaction. After all, he had worked so hard to achieve this—a community where immortals, former Doomers, Kra-ell, and humans could coexist in mutual respect and understanding. But it was an illusion, and dark currents were circling underneath the surface.

The recent string of thefts and acts of sabotage, and then Borga's unprovoked attack on Marina, were all troubling signs of unrest that he knew better than to ignore.

It was like dismissing a slight whiff of smoke when what was causing it was an inferno raging undetected underground.

For the sake of the children, his daughter, his newborn nephew, and all the others, he needed to make this place a sanctuary again, and if harsh steps needed to be taken, so be it. His people, his clan, always came first.

That was why he had called Jade and Onegus and asked them to join the meeting with Kagra, Peter, and Marina. They had to get to the bottom of this and do it fast before the smoke became suffocating and the fire consumed his village.

When his guests arrived a few moments later, he guided them to the conference table.

"Borga is not the main instigator behind this," Kagra said without preamble. "I'm sure of it. But I'm also sure she knows who the leader is, who else is involved with the saboteurs, and what they hope to achieve."

Jade's eyes flashed with anger. "I can get her to talk."

Kian did not doubt that, but there were better ways of handling the situation. Lifting his hand, he got everyone's attention. "Let's not get ahead of ourselves. Borga may or may not have operated on her own, but until we know what's going on, I would rather not tip our hand." Remembering that some of the people present might not know the idiom, he added, "We don't want them to know we are on to them, so they don't go into hiding. I want to do it discreetly."

Jade crossed her arms over her chest. "I can throw Borga in the brig just for being rude to Marina. I'm curious who will come to speak on her behalf."

Kian nodded. "That's a possibility, or just put a bug on her and find everything you need to know."

"Which is?" Jade asked.

"I want to find out who the other players are and what their agenda is."

Jade scoffed, her lip curling in a sneer. "What does it matter? Their grievances are irrelevant. There is no excuse for breaking the law and endangering everyone in the village." Her eyes were blazing with anger. "How are they even doing that? They shouldn't be capable of sabotage."

Kian sighed, rubbing a hand over his face in frustration. "We assume the Kra-ell are responsible, but maybe they are not. It occurred to me that some of the clan members might not be happy about the village's latest changes, and they are showing their discontent."

Jade frowned. "You told me everyone got to vote, and the decision was unanimous."

"People succumb to peer pressure," Onegus said. "They might not want to look like the bigots who refuse to invite a group of alien refugees. It's also possible that they believed things would work out better between the two groups, but contact between the groups is minimal. Except for you, Phinas, Vanessa, and Mo-red, even friendships between Kra-ell and clan members are rare or nonexistent." He flashed his charming smile. "Maybe we should organize parties so everyone will get to hang out together, and barriers will get broken."

That suggestion had been raised before, but it had never materialized. The younger immortals and Kra-ell had tried to bond over music and form a band, but even that had fizzled out. People tended to stick to the familiar and the comfortable, and forming friendships with members of a significantly different tribe was not easy. It needed work and the will to do it.

Kian sighed. "You know my opinion about all that kumbaya. Seems good in theory but seldom works in practice."

Onegus didn't seem discouraged. "Just give the assignment to Amanda, and it will be done."

"That's not a bad idea," Kian said. "But we need to solve this mystery first. Who's doing it, why, and how."

Onegus leaned back in his chair. "If they are Kra-ell or humans, that would require impressive creative thinking on their part to excuse malfunctioning shutters as a prank. Light at night gives the village away and renders our sophisticated camouflaging measures ineffective. Everyone knows that."

Kagra nodded. "I was thinking about that on the way here. It's possible that the saboteurs convinced themselves that they are doing it for the greater good, for the benefit of the community."

Kian frowned. "How could that be for the benefit of the community?"

Kagra shrugged, a bitter smile tugging at the corners of her mouth. "They might think separating the Kra-ell from the clan would be better for everyone. I know that some think we'd be better off on our own."

"That's ridiculous," Marina said. "We're stronger together. I mean, you are stronger together. Humans are inconsequential to both groups in that context." Kian nodded. "Marina is right." He turned to Jade and Kagra. "Find out whether Borga is working with others or is a lone player, and at the same time, snoop around for clues about the saboteurs. Once you have the information, report back to me, and we will decide how to proceed."

Jade looked like she wanted to argue, her jaw clenching with barely contained frustration. But after a long moment, she nodded. "We'll do it your way, Kian. But if this backfires, and Borga and her cronies cause more serious damage, don't blame me, and remember that I wanted to put her in the brig."

67

ANNANI

Annani stood before the mirror and surveyed her reflection. The dark blue silk of her gown shimmered in the soft light of her bedroom, the rich color bringing out the vibrant red of her hip-length hair and the fluid fabric skimming over her figure.

It was just another day dress, but it was her favorite. She never wore anything constricting, and silk was her preferred fabric because it was gentle on her skin and breathable, so at first glance there was no difference in her appearance today compared to any other day. But she had taken extra care for the grand reveal.

Ell-rom had already met her, so this wouldn't be his first impression of her, but it would be the first time she would face him as his sister rather than the Clan Mother.

It was a big deal, as the young ones liked to say. She had spent so long without any family other than the one she had created herself, and thinking that she was all alone, the only one of her kind, had been difficult. Discovering that Areana lived had been a tremendous joy, but her sister was out of reach for all intents and purposes, imprisoned by Navuh. Then the Fates brought her childhood best friend, Wonder, as she preferred to be called, back to her. As if that was not enough of a boon, Toven returned to her as well, and Annani was immensely grateful for having her cousin in her life.

Now, the Fates had guided two more siblings to her.

She had also discovered that there were trillions of beings like her on a distant planet, and yet she was still one of a kind because she was the only legitimate heir to Anumati's throne.

Annani smiled at her reflection. "There was a good reason for all these years of acting like a diva after all."

She had assumed that her penchant for theatrics was just a way to amuse herself and her family. After all, she had never abused her status and had only used it to make things special. Ceremonies needed some pomp and grandeur to be entertaining and memorable.

Evidently it was part of her DNA, her unique genetics. She was born to be a queen.

The problem was that she preferred to be a ceremonial figure rather than engage in actual ruling. If she ever took over the Anumati throne, she would create a council that would be democratically elected and be the de facto governing body of the planet and, by extension, the galaxy.

Oh, well, she should not dwell on such heavy topics on the day she was going to welcome her brother into the family.

Sighing, Annani turned around and walked over to the jewelry section of her closet.

Most of the pieces stored in the velvet-covered drawers were modern acquisitions, some custom-made for her by renowned artists and others store-bought. But those seemed inappropriate for today.

Opening the one drawer with her most precious possessions, she pulled out a lapis lazuli bracelet. It was priceless not because the stones were precious or the silver binding was costly, but because it was an antique. For her, though, the value came from the memories attached to the item. It was the first gift Khiann had ever given her when he was still pretending to be her tutor.

Even now, so many centuries after his untimely death, the sight of it brought tears to her eyes and a bittersweet ache to her chest.

She slipped it onto her wrist, the cool metal warming quickly against her skin.

When the doorbell rang in the living room, she turned around and stepped out of the bedroom to greet her son.

"Hello, Mother." Kian dipped his head to kiss her cheek. "You look lovely today. That color suits you."

"Thank you." She kissed him back. "I am ready to see my brother again."

Kian winced. "Are you sure I cannot convince you to wait? At least until Morelle wakes up as well. Wouldn't it be better to tell them the good news together?"

Smiling, she patted his arm. "That was an excellent argument, but I do not wish to wait." She moved her hand to her chest. "I feel that I need to tell him now, and I trust my instincts."

Kian nodded. "I won't argue with that. Your gut feelings are rarely wrong."

She gave him an amused haughty look. "Almost? Were they ever wrong?"

"I can't recall right now, but I'm sure you've not always been right."

"If you cannot think of an example, I must have been right every time." She strode toward the front door. "Did you bring the golf cart?"

"Of course, Mother." He opened the door for her. "I'm thinking of buying one that has air conditioning." He helped her up and walked around to the other side to sit behind the wheel. "It usually doesn't get hot enough in the village, so it's not a necessity, but occasionally we get very hot days." He smiled as he pulled into the path. "Imagine it was one of those days, and you were sweating on the way to an important meeting. You would be annoyed."

Annani knew what he was trying to do, and she appreciated the effort, but it was unnecessary.

She was not apprehensive about revealing who she was to Ell-rom and did not need to be distracted. She was excited, yes, but not nervous.

"I would not sweat during the five minutes it takes to drive the golf cart from my house to the pavilion, even on the hottest days, but it might benefit someone, and it is not a great expense, so go ahead. You do not need my permission to get it."

Kian smiled. "I am not asking for your permission, just for your advice."

Annani adjusted the folds of her skirt. "You are a very good son, Kian, but you were never very obedient."

He arched a brow. "When was I ever disobedient?"

She laughed. "Unlike you, who cannot remember even one occasion of my gut steering me wrong, I remember each of your many acts of defiance."

68

KIAN

"I took Allegra to see Evander yesterday," Kian said as Anandur started the engine and pulled the SUV out of its parking spot. "Or E.T., as she named him. I was surprised at how emotional she got. She was so quiet when Alena held her together with little Evan, just staring at him until Alena told her that she could touch him. She brushed a finger over his hand and looked at Alena to make sure that it was okay. When Alena complimented her for being so gentle, she finally smiled, put her head on her aunt's chest, and just kept looking at the baby."

His mother smiled softly. "That is the wonder of new life, Kian, of creation. Even a little girl who is still a baby can feel the magic."

From the front seat, Anandur chuckled, his eyes twinkling with mirth in the rearview mirror. "Just wait until Evander is old enough to start causing trouble. Then we'll see how magical he seems. But that's nothing compared to Allegra. That little girl of yours is a rebel at heart. One look at her eyes, and it's obvious that she will be a major troublemaker."

Kian laughed. "Thank the merciful Fates we've got a few years before we need to worry about that."

"So, you don't deny it?" Anandur asked.

"No, I agree. My mother accused me of not being an obedient son, and she gave me several examples to prove her point. I don't expect my daughter to be any different."

Annani chuckled. "I cannot really blame you. You have gotten that from me. I was not an obedient daughter either."

"Thank the merciful Fates for that." Kian patted her hand. "Imagine where we would be if you followed your father's commands to the letter."

She nodded. "It is not good to be overly obedient. It is much better to think and evaluate than to follow blindly. People can do terrible things when they cease thinking critically and independently. The result is them usually turning into a mindless herd when pacified. Becoming a dangerous mob is only a spark away."

"There is always an instigator," Anandur said.

Kian sighed. "Speaking of trouble and instigators, I must confess that I have been keeping some things from you."

She usually knew everything that was going on, so his news probably wouldn't surprise her.

His mother frowned. "What is happening?" Maybe she didn't know.

Kian sighed, running his hand through his hair. "There've been a few minor acts of sabotage and thefts. Also, one of the purebloeded Kra-ell was very rude to the new human in the village. On their own, these are not events that would merit a mention, but the pattern I'm starting to see indicates discontent."

His mother nodded. "The village is going through demographic changes, and you cannot expect everything to go smoothly or settle without some friction. People need time to adjust to a new reality."

He hesitated, his gaze sliding away from his mother's. "I'm starting to wonder if inviting the Kra-ell and some of the humans from their compound to live with us was a mistake. We don't have the same culture or the same values, and we are immortal while they are not. That might make them envious and resentful. On the other hand, they have many more children than the clan members have, and that could bring resentment from the other side."

His mother was quiet for a long moment. "You are correct that there are differences, but they are not that big that we cannot coexist. It is not like what is happening in the human world where religious wars still rage in this day and age." She sighed. "I hoped that era was done with and that we had entered a new era of enlightenment, never to return to that darkness, but as usual, humans make a step forward, grow complacent, and then let evil drag them two steps backward. I am so tired of that never-ending cycle." She turned to look out the window. "I keep wondering what part Ell-rom and Morelle will play in our future."

Kian nodded. "Bringing the twins into the fold introduces yet another factor into an already delicate balance. I worry that it might be too much for our community."

To his surprise, Annani laughed, a beautiful sound that held no trace of reproach or judgment. "Oh, Kian," she said, shaking her head with a fond smile.

"There have always been voices of dissent, my son. You have just chosen to forget about them. Our community survived then, and it will survive now."

Kian knew what she was referring to, and she was right. Not everyone was happy about him leading the American arm of the clan, and Sari the one in Scotland, despite the stellar job they were doing. Some just did not want Annani's children ruling over them.

They wanted a full democracy.

Perhaps he should give it to them. After all, if he held an election today, the vast majority would vote for him.

His mother leaned back in her seat, her gaze growing distant as she lost herself in memory. "Do you remember Alex?" she asked, her voice tinged with a hint of old anger. "I still cannot believe one of ours could commit such crimes, but he did. I guess every society has its share of sociopaths. Amanda considered him a friend because he was charming and perfected his act. But only a sociopath could kidnap young women and sell them for profit while blaming the unfair clan leadership system for his evil deeds." She turned a pair of glowing eyes at him. "When he was caught, he expressed no remorse."

"That's because he was indeed a sociopath, as you have aptly noted. What did trafficking unsuspecting, naive college girls have to do with the clan's leader-ship? Nothing. It was just an attempt to put a political spin on his evil deeds."

His mother snorted. "He was right about one thing, though. The clan is not a democracy. It is a family. And like any family, there will always be bad apples, those who seek to sow discord and strife for their own gain."

"Rotten apples," Anandur murmured. "If you don't catch them, they will spoil the whole bushel."

"Then we have to catch them," Kian said. "Pretending that they don't exist will not save the bushel." He turned to his mother. "On another subject, what do you want to do about Jasmine? We can keep her out of the room when you talk to Ell-rom, or we can get the introductions out of the way and let her stay. It's up to you."

Annani didn't answer right away. "Jasmine might be Ell-rom's mate, so even if we keep her out of the room, he will tell her everything later. She is there for him around the clock, and I am sure that a bond between them already exists even though they have not been intimate yet."

Kian groaned. "I need to get into her head and make sure she is who she claims to be."

"Edna probed her," Anandur said. "There is no need for that. Just imagine what will happen when Ell-rom is back to his full power and discovers that you violated his mate's privacy by peeking into her mind."

He had a point.

"I will ask her permission first," Kian said.

That seemed to satisfy Anandur. "Good. That way, she can't complain to him later."

His mother smiled. "As we have discussed before, we shall welcome Jasmine into the clan with all the usual pomp and ceremony, and I would rather you did not spoil her welcome by asking to look inside her mind. I trust Edna's intuition or the probe, as you call her talent."

His mother was right, and the truth was that he didn't get any negative vibes from Jasmine. "Where would you like to do that?" he asked.

"I will wait for Jasmine in your office at the keep, and you will bring her to me."

Kian hesitated. "I've thought about it, and I'm not sure it's wise. Jasmine is not a clan member yet, Mother. We don't even know for certain that she's a Dormant, although the odds seem to be in her favor."

Annani's eyes sparkled with a knowing light. "Finding the missing pod was a great feat of supernatural ability, which indicates that Jasmine is a Dormant. Besides, the Fates have spoken loud and clear. The threads of Ell-rom and Jasmine's life were woven into the Fates' tapestry. They are destined for each other." She leaned forward and took Kian's hand. "The end of their journey is already known, my son. They need only to take the right steps to get there."

Kian chuckled. "Isn't that true of everything in life?"

"Ah." Anandur looked at them through the rearview mirror. "But the joy is in the journey. All the twists and turns and unexpected detours make the destination all the sweeter."

69

JASMINE

J asmine flipped through the magazine pages, looking at the photos of glamorous people and not reading any of the articles.

There was no point.

The magazine was at least two years old, and everything written in it was no longer true. Heck, it had been untrue even then. Hollywood couples hooked up to promote their movies, not because they were in love, and once the movie was over, they usually went their separate ways.

Once upon a time, she had fantasized about being a part of that world, but it wasn't in the cards.

Jasmine chuckled. In her case, that was a literal description. Her tarot had never promised her a great acting career.

Looking up at Ell-rom, she watched his chest's steady rise and fall. Even that was getting stronger. At first, his breathing had been barely discernible, but now it was deep and resonant.

He slept a lot, which Bridget claimed was precisely what his body needed, and Jasmine had lost track of how long she had been sitting next to his bed.

Minutes blurred into hours, hours into days, and the outside world faded into insignificance as she focused all her attention on her prince.

At the sound of the door opening, she turned to check who was coming in and smiled at Julian. "Hi. Is it time for check-ups?"

Julian shook his head. "Kian wants to see you in his office."

A ball of dread nestled in Jasmine's gut. Was Kian dismissing her? Was he ordering her to leave Ell-rom's side?

"Do you know why? Is something wrong?" She rose to her feet and stretched out the kinks in her neck and shoulders.

"It's nothing bad." A reassuring smile tugged at the corners of Julian's mouth. "He just needs to talk to you."

Casting another glance at Ell-rom, she sighed and followed Julian out of the room. "I don't like leaving him alone for long."

"It's not going to take long," Julian reassured her.

As they walked, Jasmine ran her fingers through her hair, trying to tame it a little so she would look semi-presentable to Kian.

Watching her efforts, Julian chuckled. "Do you want to stop by a restroom before we go in? You look a little disheveled."

"I don't have a brush with me, so there is really no point." Jasmine doubled her efforts, combing the strands with her fingers and twisting them to form large curls.

As they approached the door to Kian's office, she felt a surge of nervousness, making her palms grow damp and her heart race. She paused and turned to Julian. "Is there going to be someone other than Kian in there?"

A glimmer of amusement sparked in Julian's eyes. "You're very astute, but I'm afraid I can't tell you. It's a surprise."

He didn't seem worried, so perhaps it was something to look forward to. "A good one, I hope?"

Julian's smile widened. "The best," he assured her, his voice ringing with a quiet certainty that made Jasmine's breath catch.

As the doctor opened the door and gestured for her to go in, Jasmine took a final fortifying breath and took a step forward.

Her eyes widened, and her breath left her lungs in a sharp, stunned gasp. A glowing angel was seated on a chair in front of a large conference table.

It wasn't a trick of the light because the room was not very well illuminated, and the glow emanated only from her exposed skin.

She was small, almost impossibly so, with a delicate, ethereal beauty that seemed to radiate from within. Her hair was a rich, vibrant red, falling in soft waves down her back and over her shoulders. Her eyes were a piercing, luminous blue, filled with wisdom and knowing that seemed to stretch back through the ages.

She was a goddess.

Jasmine had seen male gods. She had traveled with them to Tibet, but they were nothing like the one sitting before her.

This female was in a class of her own.

She emanated power and benevolence and had an aura of timelessness and majesty that made Jasmine's knees buckle, and her heart skip a beat.

Without thinking, she sank into a deep, reverent curtsy, her head bowing low.

She had never felt so small, insignificant, as she did at that moment, standing before a being of such immense, unfathomable power.

"Rise, child," the female spoke. Her voice was simultaneously commanding and soft, kind, musical, and filled with a warmth that seemed to wrap around Jasmine like a gentle embrace. "There is no need for such formality."

Jasmine lifted her head, eyes wide and uncertain as they met the goddess's steady, unwavering gaze. She swallowed hard, her throat suddenly dry as she searched for something to say and found nothing.

"I am the Clan Mother," the goddess said in that musical voice of hers.

"Clan Mother?" Jasmine repeated, her voice little more than a whisper of sound. "Are you Kian's mother?"

The goddess nodded, a glimmer of pride and affection shining in her eyes as she glanced at her son. "I am also the mother of Alena, Sari, and Amanda. Most of the immortals you met on the cruise are my grandchildren, great-grandchildren, and so on, stretching back through the centuries."

The goddess rose to her feet in a fluid, graceful motion. She was even smaller standing up, her head barely reaching Jasmine's shoulder, but there was no mistaking the power that radiated from her in palpable waves.

"Come, child." She took Jasmine's hand. "Let's visit Ell-rom together." It felt surreal to walk holding hands with a goddess.

She did not doubt that the Clan Mother could crush her hand with ease or maybe even reduce her to dust and ashes with a single thought. But there was no threat in her touch, no hint of malice or danger in the gentle pressure of her fingers—only warmth.

As they approached the prince's room, the Clan Mother paused and turned to face Jasmine. "You may stay in the room while I talk with Ell-rom. He would appreciate you being there for him."

70

ANNANI

As Annani stepped into her brother's room, the earpieces nestled snugly in her ears were a concession she had made to appease Kian but also a necessity.

She did not speak the Kra-ell language, and the devices translated Ell-rom's words in real time for her. If he asked what they were for, she could answer that they facilitated translation, which would not be a lie.

It just would not be the entire truth.

Oh, well. Life was full of compromises, and Annani had learned to live with that.

"Clan Mother." Ell-rom dipped his head respectfully, shifted his gaze to Kian, and repeated the gesture. Lastly, he smiled at Jasmine without saying a thing.

"Good afternoon, Ell-rom," Annani said. "I am happy to see you improving so quickly."

He looked so much better than the last time she had seen him. His skin no longer looked gray and lifeless; his face was no longer gaunt and hollow. There was a hint of color in his cheeks and a spark of life in his eyes. Julian or Bridget had trimmed the hair that had hung in limp clumps off his skull, and even though he was nearly bald, he looked very handsome.

"Thank you, Clan Mother. I feel so much better after proper cleansing and a meal." He made as if to rise, his arms trembling with the effort of pushing himself to a sitting position.

Annani held up a hand. "Please stop," she chided. "I am overjoyed that you are feeling better, but I do not want you to exert yourself. You do not need to prove anything to me."

He groaned in frustration. "I made it to the bathroom earlier. I can stand."

"I am sure you can, but perhaps you have overexerted yourself, and you need to gather your strength before making another attempt." Annani sat down on the chair closest to the bed.

Looking nervous, Jasmine waited until Kian sat down before taking her seat. Ell-rom seemed so deflated as he reclined against the stack of pillows that Annani scrambled for something to say to cheer him up.

Perhaps seeing a picture of his grandnephew would do the trick.

Reaching into a hidden pocket in her gown, she withdrew her phone. "I planned to visit you yesterday, but I could not because of a surprise visit by this little guy." She rose and held up the phone with Evander's picture on the screen. "This is the newest addition to my family. Evander Tellesious, son of my daughter Alena and my son-in-law Orion."

Beside her, Kian hissed, no doubt worried that she was getting too close to the prince and that he could yank the earpieces out and compel her, but Annani ignored him.

She trusted her brother.

Ell-rom's eyes widened, a look of wonder and joy flooding his face. "Congratulations. May he be blessed by the Mother of All Life and grow into a mighty warrior."

Annani stifled a wince. It seemed that Ell-rom was remembering more about the Kra-ell warlike culture.

She did not want little Evander to grow up to be a warrior. Her clan needed more scientists.

"I would rather that little Evander chose a different path for himself, but thank you for the blessing."

Ell-rom's eyes misted with tears. "You have a beautiful family."

Annani's heart swelled at the longing in his tone. "They are your family, too." She returned the phone to the secret pocket, sat back down, and waited for the words to sink in.

He dipped his head. "Thank you for welcoming my sister and me into your community, Clan Mother."

He had misunderstood her meaning.

Annani sighed. "I did not mean that figuratively. We are related by blood, Ell-rom. You and I share a father. I am your and Morelle's half-sister."

On Kian's other side, Jasmine gasped softly.

Ell-rom's eyes widened, a look of shock flashing across his face. "How is that possible?"

"It is a long story, and I will tell you everything." She sighed. "It would be easier to explain if you remembered your life before boarding the settler ship, but perhaps my tale will help you remember."

He nodded. "Thank you, Clan Mother."

"Please, call me Annani."

He looked horrified. "I cannot take such liberties with the leader of the clan."

Annani's lips twitched. "Do you address your twin sister as princess or as Morelle?"

Ell-rom blinked, a look of confusion flitting across his face. "Of course, I would call her by her name. She is my blood—" He trailed off, his eyes widening as understanding dawned, the puzzle pieces suddenly snapping into place.

"I am your blood too, Ell-rom," she said softly, her voice thick with emotion.

Ell-rom stared at her, his eyes wide and disbelieving, his mouth opening and closing soundlessly as he struggled to find the words.

She reached out, her hand finding his and clasping it tightly. "It is a lot to take in, but it is all good. You and Morelle are not alone here on Earth. You have a large family to call your own."

Ell-rom swallowed hard, his throat working as he fought to keep his composure. "I don't know what to say," he whispered. "We are so different. We don't even look alike." He sounded ashamed for some reason.

Annani's heart clenched, a fierce, protective love surging through her veins. "Oh, my dear Ell-rom. You are perfect, exactly as you are. A child of two worlds, a bridge between the gods and the Kra-ell. You are more than the sum of your parts." She rose to her feet and brushed her fingers over his cheek. "Our father was a dreamer, a visionary who dared to dream of a world where everyone was judged and treated based on the merits of their character and nothing else. For a while, your mother shared his dream."

7 1

THE PRINCE

Ell-rom stared at Annani, his mind reeling with the revelation that she had just dropped on him like a bombshell. Could it be true?

He had felt an affinity toward her, had seen something familiar in her impossibly beautiful face, and now she was telling him that the reason for that was that they were related.

The same god had fathered them.

He and Morelle were not alone anymore. They had a family. A big one.

Even though he couldn't remember his life before waking up in this room, Ell-rom knew that he and his sister had been mostly alone. The dreams and tidbits of memories that had surfaced so far indicated that they had lived in profound isolation.

"Do you believe me?" Annani looked into his eyes with hope shining in hers.

He lifted his hand, intending to cup her cheek, but put it over his heart at the last moment.

Annani might be his sister, but they were strangers, and her son would not like Ell-rom touching his mother. The guy was tense and ready to pounce, and his bodyguards loomed dangerously from where they were standing against the wall by the door.

"I felt the connection in here." He tapped his chest. "And your face looked familiar. I thought that maybe you looked like my sister, but now I realize that the resemblance I have noticed is to both Morelle and me. It's subtle, but it is there." He swallowed. "It is so frustrating not to remember my past. If I knew my history, I would probably be able to deduce how we could have the same father."

Annani smiled, a soft, patient curve of her lips that held a world of understanding. "It is a long and complicated story; much of it is speculation." She sat back down, and he had to turn on his side to look down at her face. "My father did not tell me about his past on Anumati. The exiled gods did not share their history with their children; I can only guess the reasons. They might have been ashamed of their home world and its injustices, or maybe they wanted their children and the humans they ruled over to believe that all gods were benevolent and followed the same moral code as the one adopted and enforced by the gods on Earth." She shrugged her slim shoulders. "Or they might have been ashamed of being exiles. Regrettably, all the founders of the colony on Earth are gone, so we cannot ask them."

"What happened to them?" Ell-rom asked.

"Mass assassination—an act of terror. One of the gods did not like being ruled by our father and established his stronghold away from the other gods. Our father was willing to negotiate with him to maintain peace, which was a mistake. That god committed the heinous crime of killing a fellow god and was sentenced to entombment by the council of gods. To avoid that fate, he dropped a bomb over the assembly that killed all the gods. He was caught in the blast and died as well." She sighed. "Mind you, I was not there because I escaped, so the only thing I know for a fact is the aftermath. I can only hypothesize how it happened. The version I told you was the most likely one until recently, but after we found Jade and the Kra-ell people, we learned things that might indicate another party might be responsible for that abominable act of terrorism. Not only the gods died in the nuclear blast. The entire region was devastated, and everything living within a radius of hundreds of miles died. It took decades for the region to recuperate."

Ell-rom had an uneasy feeling in the pit of his stomach when he asked, "Who is the other possible party?"

Annani smiled sadly. "Our grandfather, the Eternal King. But I am getting ahead of myself. You need first to understand why the gods were exiled to Earth. As I mentioned, I did not know their history until I learned about Anumati from Jade and the three gods who came to look for the missing Kra-ell settlers."

His sister paused and turned to the tall redheaded guard standing by the door. "I am getting parched from all the talking. Can you please call the security office and have someone bring us refreshments from the café?"

As the guard asked everyone what they wanted to order, Ell-rom thought about what Annani had said about their father and his and Morelle's mother. Our father was a dreamer, a visionary who dared to dream of a world where everyone was judged and treated based on the merits of their character and nothing else. For a while, your mother shared his dream.

Had his mother been a rebel? But she was the queen? Who had she rebelled against?

"What about you?" Annani asked. "What would you like from the café?"

The question caught Ell-rom by surprise. "I do not know what I am allowed to have. The medic said that I can only have clear liquids."

"Herbal tea, then," Annani told the guard.

The guard did not have a teardrop, and he responded in the language they spoke on Earth, but his tone was friendly and respectful, not fearful or reverent.

Seeing how Annani treated the guy warmed Ell-rom's heart. He might not remember much or have a lot of life experience, but the interaction between Annani and the guard spoke volumes about the kind of person she was.

THE PRINCE

E ll-rom wasn't surprised that Annani did not wait for the drinks to be delivered to continue her story.

She seemed eager to share it with him.

"Our father, Ahn, was the Eternal King's only legitimate heir and a rebel. He led a group of young gods who dared to challenge the status quo and fight for the rights of the Kra-ell. Your mother, who was the crown princess at the time, worked closely with the resistance, which was how they met and either fell in love or lust."

Annani laughed, the sound so beautiful that it sent tingles down his arms. "Who knows? Maybe it was just another act of rebellion for them. They are not here to tell us one way or another, and neither left a diary behind. Whatever the nature of their relationship was, you and your sister are the testament that they were together for a brief moment in time."

"It's so romantic," Jasmine murmured, probably unaware that everyone could hear her.

"Indeed." Annani smiled at her. "I bet it would have made a great love story."

Jasmine shook her head. "Love stories need to have happy endings, and theirs didn't."

Annani's face fell. "No, it did not. What Ahn and your mother did was forbidden. Perhaps they dreamt of a future where they could be together openly, and their love would be celebrated rather than condemned, but the resistance was crushed. The rebellion's leaders were exiled to Earth, and others were probably exiled to even less hospitable planets. Your mother became the queen, and Ahn left, not knowing that he had fathered her twin children."

Ell-rom felt a chill run down his spine. "I am glad that the rebels were exiled and not executed. I guess the king did not have the heart to kill his own son."

Annani's lips twisted in a bitter smile, a flash of anger sparking in her eyes. "Trust me, Ell-rom. The king did not do that because he loved his son. The Eternal King loves only one thing, and that is his throne. He had a public image to uphold, and appearing merciful and forgiving toward his rebellious children was a political move. The exile was only the first step in his plan, though. I think that he planned on eliminating them from day one."

"Why?" Ell-rom asked. "Why would he want to kill his heir?"

"Because Ahn was a threat," she said flatly. "As his name implies, the Eternal King does not need an heir because he is eternal. A legitimate heir to the throne, who happened to be popular among the young gods, could challenge the king's rule, and so he had to be removed, first by being cut off from his power base and his supporters, and then killed." She shook her head, a hint of disgust creeping into her tone. "It was a masterstroke. The king trumped up charges of war crimes against Ahn and then severed all communications with Earth to prevent Ahn from contesting them and blamed the communications blackout on Ahn. He claimed that our father had destroyed the satellites because he did not want to face the questions and accusations coming his way."

Ell-rom felt a surge of anger, a pulsing fury that burned hot in his chest. "That's absurd," he sputtered. "How could anyone believe such nonsense?"

Annani shrugged. "Most people believe what they are told by their leaders, and the Eternal King is a master manipulator. He is a skilled propagandist who uses mass compulsion to drive his message home, so to speak."

Ell-rom frowned. "Compulsion? What is that?"

Kian leaned forward and looked at him with suspicion in his eyes. "What does it sound like to you?"

"Compelling people is using some kind of leverage to make them do things they would not normally do."

"Give me an example," Kian demanded.

It took Ell-rom a long moment to think of something that would fit the word. "If I know something that you do not, and I know that you will be upset when you hear it, I would rather not tell you, but if it is important to prevent something bad from happening, I will feel compelled to warn you."

Beaming, Annani patted his hand. "That was an excellent example, but that is not the type of compulsion the king uses. He has an innate ability to enter people's minds and force them to accept what he tells them as truth and to follow his instructions. It is a very rare gift, or curse, depending on how you look at it, and those who wield it are very dangerous because most people cannot defend themselves against it. The Eternal King is probably the most powerful compeller in existence, so much so that he can compel people while broadcasting his speeches on the Anumatian media." She looked at him with a slight tilt of her head that made her seem contemplative. "The Kra-ell queens are usually strong compellers as well.

"You and your sister should have inherited the trait."

He shook his head. "I wouldn't know the first thing about it. Perhaps when more of my memories return, I will."

"Interesting." Annani pursed her lips. "It is possible that you were not taught how to use it. I inherited the talent from my father, but I did not like forcing people to do things they do not want to do, so I did not practice it." She turned to smile at her son. "Later in life, I was convinced to use my ability for good."

Ell-rom was about to ask in what way she had used compulsion for good when a knock sounded on the door. The tall guard opened it, and someone handed him two trays filled with cups.

"Coffee and tea are here," he announced.

"Wonderful." Annani accepted one of the cups from him and motioned for him to continue to the others. "Let us take a short break."

73

ANNANI

Annani put her half-empty coffee cup on the floor. "That was a timely refresher."

"Indeed." Ell-rom cradled his paper teacup in his hands. "This is a delicious drink. What is it called?"

"Jasmine white tea," Jasmine said.

He smiled. "With you as its namesake, it is no wonder it is exceptional."

Jasmine chuckled nervously. "You flatter me, Prince Ell-rom."

"Just Ell-rom and it is not flattery when it is the truth."

Annani stifled a smile. Her brother was definitely taken with Jasmine, and she was with him. It was always such a pleasure to observe love blossoming. That and babies were the best life had to offer.

"Are you ready to hear the rest of the story?" Annani asked.

"Yes, please," he said.

"After the Eternal King destroyed the communication satellites, he declared Earth a forbidden planet. He had it expunged from all the official records and maps, and as far as the Anumatian civilization was concerned, it ceased to exist."

Ell-rom frowned. "Why go to such lengths? Why not just kill Ahn outright?"

"He could not." Annani paused, thinking of how to continue without revealing her connection with her grandmother. "From what Aru told me, the queen, Ahn's mother, holds great power herself. She is the daughter of one of the most prominent industrial families, and she represents all the other houses. It was important for the king to convince her and the rest of the Anumatian citizenry that he was a loving and merciful father and was doing his best under grave circumstances."

In a way, telling her brother the story and explaining the Eternal King's motives was crystallizing things for Annani.

"To exile his rebellious son and his closest supporters to a forbidden planet was a brilliantly evil move, which should not surprise anyone given the Eternal King's long rule over Anumati and his ability to maintain the reputation of a great and benevolent ruler. I hate to sound so admiring of that monster, but there is no denying his genius. Instead of eliminating Ahn by killing him and making himself look bad, the king destroyed Ahn's reputation and made him practically disappear. Then, when enough time had passed, and most gods had forgotten about Ahn, he also arranged for his assassination. Mortdh, the god who I blamed for the murder of my people, could have been a convenient scape-goat. By the way, he was also the Eternal King's grandson, the son of one of the king's many illegitimate children."

Ell-rom frowned. "But if Earth was deleted from all the records, how could the king send assassins to eliminate the rebels?"

Kian snorted. "That was all propaganda for public consumption. Earth was erased from all the civilian records, but the king and his military retained the information, and patrol ships were sent occasionally to check on Earth and its inhabitants. The king wasn't taking any chances. He wanted his son dead, and he got it done."

Ell-rom sighed. "It is strange to grieve for a father I have never known. I wonder if our mother told us about him."

"Probably not," Kian said. "She was doing everything in her power to shield you. It would not have been wise to tell you."

Annani tilted her head. "Maybe she told you right before sending you to him. I think that was her plan. She wanted you to be with your father so he could protect you."

Now that it seemed the twins were not as powerful as they had suspected, that option made even more sense. They were no match for Ahn, who had indeed been powerful, and they had not been sent to undermine him or replace him. They were sent to him for protection.

"I wish my mind wasn't so blank," Ell-rom murmured. "This is so frustrating." He took a deep breath. "How long did the exiled gods live on Earth before they were assassinated?"

"About two thousand years. They were not the first gods to arrive on Earth, though. Gods have been mining gold on the planet for hundreds of thousands of years. But before our father and his supporters' permanent settlement on the planet, the gods' involvement with humans had been much more limited. The gods needed obedient workers, and they created them by manipulating the genetics of early humanoids. They deemed them a commodity, not people. When Ahn arrived on Earth, he set out to elevate humans by providing them with the tools of an advanced civilization. He introduced a writing system and a code of law that was moral and just. His brother Ekin, a gifted scientist and engineer, taught the humans agricultural and shipping methods. Things were going well until Mortdh, Ekin's son, decided he was better suited to rule the gods and started causing trouble for Ahn and the other gods."

"What about your mother?" Ell-rom asked. "Who was she? How did they meet?"

Annani smiled. "My mother was a clever and cunning goddess. She knew in her heart that Ahn was her fated mate, but she was still too young to pursue him. She could have waited, but she was afraid that he would wed another before she was of age, so she trapped him and seduced him, and he had no choice but to make her his official wife. Despite their first encounter's less-than-perfect circumstances, they were deeply in love and very happy together."

74

THE PRINCE

Ell-rom had so many questions.

When the assassins killed the exiles, what happened to the gold mining operations and the other gods that had been on Earth before their arrival?

How had Annani alone survived while all the other gods had perished? Perhaps she wasn't the only one, and other gods had survived as well?

He was about to voice his questions when he noticed Kian glaring at his mother. Why was he angry at her?

What had she said that he objected to?

Going over her story in his mind, the realization dawned on him like a crack of lightning. After Ahn's death, Annani, Ahn's only daughter from his official mate, became the only legitimate heir to the Anumati throne, which put her in great danger.

That was why Kian was so angry. He did not want her to reveal her status.

But who would Ell-rom tell? It wasn't as if he posed any threat to Annani or anyone else. He was a helpless male who had miraculously survived in stasis for far longer than should have been possible.

He wanted to tell Kian that he had nothing to worry about, but the anger and suspicion that flashed in his nephew's eyes gave him pause.

Wariness and mistrust radiated from Kian in palpable waves. He did not trust and did not welcome Ell-rom into their community with the same open arms as his mother.

Ell-rom did not blame Kian for his animosity. Annani, Kian's beloved mother, was a possible challenger to the Eternal King's throne, which put her in grave danger.

He, of course, would stand with Annani and defend his sister even if his loyalty came at the price of making an enemy of the most powerful being in the known universe.

So be it.

He and Morelle had been saved thanks to Annani's determination to find them. She had earned their loyalty.

Besides, what she offered them was priceless.

Annani offered them a family, a community that accepted him and Morelle as they were without passing judgment or discriminating against them, while on their home planet they were considered abominations and would have been killed if discovered.

He could not comprehend a world in which people believed that it was okay to murder others just for being different. The ugliness, the cruelty, and the barbarism of such beliefs were abhorrent and unnatural. He was proud of his parents for starting a rebellion and trying to change that.

He was also proud of Annani and what she had accomplished practically on her own.

He had to wonder, though. Was Annani so happy to have found him and Morelle because she had lost her family in the assassination? Or did she think that they could assist her against the Eternal King?

Ell-rom did not know if he and his twin could help in any way, but he would do what he could, and hopefully, so would Morelle.

The truth was that he did not know how his sister would react. Was she like him? Motivated by the same things he was? Why couldn't he remember even that?

"I am so sorry for all you have lost," Ell-rom said at last. "Did you have any siblings?"

"I did, and I do. My older sister Areana also survived."

Ell-rom released a relieved breath. "So, you are not the heir."

She smiled. "I am. Areana's mother was a goddess my father had a short dalliance with. She was not his official wife. She is very dear to me, but regrettably, she is not around. She mated my archenemy."

His eyes nearly popped out of his head. "How could she do a thing like that? And who is that enemy? Is he another god who survived?"

Unexpectedly, Annani laughed. "Those are excellent questions, Ell-rom, but that is not the story I want to tell you. Are you not curious about what happened to your ship and why it was delayed for seven thousand years?"

"Jade and Kian told me the settler ship had malfunctioned, probably because it was sabotaged. But I'm more interested in hearing about you and your enemies. I thought I only had to worry about the Eternal King, but now you are telling me that you have a local enemy and that your sister is mated to him."

Annani nodded. "I will give you the shortest version I can. The long version can wait for another time."

He nodded. "I will accept whatever you are willing to offer."

"You are so agreeable, Ell-rom." She put her hand on his and gave it a light squeeze. "Mortdh, the god we believed killed all the other gods, was my intended. Ahn thought he could appease and maintain peace by promising him my hand. Mortdh was much older than me, had countless concubines and scores of children, and did not care about me. I knew that once we were wed, he would get rid of me as soon as I gave him a child. None of his children were gods. They were all immortals. Naturally, I did not want to mate Mortdh, and when I found my truelove mate, it was my right to dissolve the engagement because to deny true love was to anger the Fates, and not even Ahn or Mortdh would dare do that. As an alternative, Ahn offered Mortdh my sister Areana, who was a widow. Mortdh reluctantly accepted her, but he did not want her. He left his son Navuh to escort her to his stronghold in the north. That was why she was away from the assembly when Mortdh bombed it and died along with the other gods.

"Navuh is just an immortal, but he is more powerful than many gods, and by the Fates' will, he and Areana are truelove mates. Nevertheless, he harbors great hatred for me, blaming me for his father's death and that of all the other gods. He also disapproves of my role in continuing Ahn's work and encouraging humans to do better. He and his army of immortal minions would see humanity enslaved, and me and my clan eradicated."

75

ANNANI

nnani observed Ell-rom's response and the warring emotions playing across his face.

"What Mortdh did was not your fault, and it was not even he who killed the gods, so you should not blame yourself. Navuh is not right in the head for blaming you even if he does not know about the Eternal King and his assassins."

Relief washed over Annani. She knew that Ell-rom was right and that the demise of the gods was not her fault, even if Mortdh had been the one to drop the bomb. It was survivor's guilt, and logically she rejected it, but in her heart, doubt lingered.

"Thank you. In my mind, I know that you are right, but my heart is harder to convince."

Beside her, Kian shifted uneasily, his jaw clenched and his eyes wary as he watched her brother with suspicion and concern.

Annani ignored him.

Ell-rom was not a threat. She felt it in her heart and her gut.

"Let us go back to why your mother feared for your lives and snuck you onto the settler ship."

Ell-rom frowned. "Wasn't it because Morelle and I are hybrids? If we had been discovered, we would have been killed, and so would she. That was what Jade told me."

"That is true, but there is more." She took a deep breath. "The Eternal King feared you. The belief was that a product of god and Kra-ell would be an abomination, which could mean a hideous creature or one so powerful that it could be a threat to the king. He wanted to eliminate you the same way he wanted to eliminate your father, just for different reasons."

"I don't have any special powers; I don't think I do."

Annani nodded. "You are still weak from the stasis, so we need to wait and see about that. It is also possible that Morelle is the more powerful of the two of you. Your Kra-ell genes might make her so."

He nodded. "It is possible, but I don't remember much about her. She was protective of me, that's the one memory I have of her." He sighed. "I guess our mother did not know that the Eternal King planned to kill our father. Otherwise, she wouldn't have sent us to him."

"I do not know for certain if that was her plan. But if I were in her place, that is what I would have done. I would have sent my children to the one person I knew would protect them. Ahn was progressive, and he did not believe in all that abomination nonsense. He was much more open to interracial relationships. After all, he allowed gods to take human partners. That is how immortals were born."

"Was it common practice to send Kra-ell settlers to other planets?" Ell-rom asked.

"Pressures were growing on Anumati about the Kra-ell multiplying much faster than the gods. After the rebellion ended and the King of the gods and the Queen of the Kra-ell negotiated a truce, an agreement was reached that the Kra-ell would start colonizing other planets. That was long before Earth was declared a forbidden planet and expunged from the records. A settler ship was sent to Earth, and the queen smuggled you on board, hoping your father would take you in and protect you. Then something happened, and the ship was lost in space, and communications with it were lost."

Annani couldn't tell Ell-rom who was responsible for the ship's sabotage.

Their grandmother's part in the plot still needed to remain a secret.

Next to her, Kian released a breath as if he feared that she would tell Ell-rom about her communications with the queen of Anumati.

She cast him a quick glance and shook her head at him. He should know that she would never do a thing like that. She would not betray Aru's trust and endanger his sister even if the risk was nearly nonexistent.

"By the time the ship arrived, your mother was long gone." Annani squeezed her brother's hand. "The Kra-ell are long-lived but not immortal. They have a lifespan of around a thousand Earth years."

Annani didn't add that the queen hadn't gotten to live to that old age. She had suffered an accident that was most likely also an assassination.

Ell-rom swallowed. "I wish I could remember her. I dreamt about her, but it was just a few snippets in time. I got the impression that she cared about us but also that she was remote."

"She was the queen." Annani gave him a reassuring smile. "According to Jade, the Kra-ell do not believe in coddling their children. Although observing them living in our village, I would say this is only partially true. They are affectionate with the little ones but also strict." She sighed. "On Anumati, where tribal wars used to claim the lives of many young males, mothers needed to distance themselves from their children, and those Kra-ell social norms persisted even after the tribal wars were outlawed. Here on Earth, where their offspring are most likely to live to old age, there is no need to adopt such strict practices."

Ell-rom nodded. "That's good to know. What about Ahn? What kind of a father was he?"

"He was the ruler of the gods and had to project a certain persona. He also needed to raise me to be strong so I could one day become a ruler. But he still showed me love even though he was not the type to hug or kiss freely. He was a good male. Brave, disciplined, and dedicated to his people."

JASMINE

J asmine listened to the goddess in stunned silence, her mind reeling with the weight of all she had just heard. The tale Annani had woven, the history of the gods and the Kra-ell, of the Eternal King and his boundless ruthlessness, which he had so masterfully hidden behind a convincing act of benevolence and the love of a father for his son.

In a way, it was such a human tale that she had no problem understanding the players and their motives, but the vastness of it made it hard to wrap her head around it.

She felt small and insignificant in the face of such cosmic forces and ancient conflicts. What was she, a mere human, in the grand scheme of things? It was such a tangled web of politics, evil schemes, and subterfuge.

So far, Ell-rom had been handling everything the goddess had told him remarkably well, but Jasmine could see that he was growing tired.

Annani must have realized that he was reaching his limit as well because she stopped talking and rose to her feet. "You look exhausted, Ell-rom." She kissed his cheek. "I will return tomorrow, and we will talk some more."

Ell-rom nodded, his eyelids heavy with fatigue even as he fought to keep them open. "I'm looking forward to it. Thank you for being so honest with me."

"Of course." She leaned to brush a kiss over his forehead. "I will stop by Morelle's room on my way out and kiss her cheek as well." Annani's eyes had a sheen of moisture that glittered in the room's soft light. "Rest, brother of mine."

He held on to his sister's hand. "Tomorrow, would you tell me about Areana? Our other sister?"

"I will. Areana is the sweetest person I know, and she has done much good in her life, but she deserves more than a couple of sentences uttered in passing. I will tell you more about her tomorrow."

He nodded. "I have three sisters. It is hard to believe."

Chuckling, Kian rose to his feet. "As someone who also has three sisters, I can tell you that it is not a walk in the park. My sisters are all wonderful people, but I can't help but worry about them all of the time."

Ell-rom smiled tiredly. "That is a lot of responsibility."

"That's right." Kian patted his shoulder and turned to follow his mother. "Goodbye, Jasmine," he said as he left the room.

"Goodbye. Thank you for letting me be here for all of this."

"You are welcome." He closed the door behind him.

With a sigh, she walked over to the bed and smiled at Ell-rom. "How are you feeling?" She took his hand and twined their fingers together, her thumb tracing soothing circles over his knuckles.

He let out a shuddering breath, his eyes fluttering closed for a moment. "Overwhelmed, confused, and grateful. Annani gave me a tremendous gift. She gave me a family and a community."

Jasmine nodded, a lump forming in her throat at the wonder in his tone. "It's a lot to take in."

He was silent for a long moment, his eyes searching her face as if looking for some sign, some hint of the thoughts and feelings that swirled like a maelstrom beneath the surface. "Tell me about how you found me."

He had taken her by surprise, and she hesitated. "You are so tired. Do you want to hear about it now? After all you have learned?"

He nodded. "I need to fill in the missing pieces in this picture."

"Okay," she said. "But only if you promise to rest. Don't force yourself to stay awake. If you fall asleep, I'll continue the story when you are awake."

As he nodded and closed his eyes, she hoisted herself on the bed and sat beside him. "It all started with the tarot cards my mother left for me."

"What do you mean left for you?"

Jasmine sighed. "She died when I was a little girl. She left me a jewelry box with the tarot hidden in a secret compartment. My father disapproved of them, so she hid them where I could find them."

"Why didn't he approve?"

Jasmine chuckled. "If I tell you my entire life story, we will never get to the part of why and how I found you."

He turned on his side and looked at her. "I want to hear your life story."

"And you will, but not right now, back to the tarot. I learned how to read them and got good at it. Since about a year ago, I started getting the same cards over and over again. The cards promised me that I would meet a prince."

She told him of Alberto the scumbag, and the ill-fated vacation that had led her into the clutches of the cartel. And she told him about Margo, the woman who had saved her life and had brought her into the fold of Annani's clan.

Ell-rom listened silently, his eyes never leaving her face as she spoke. She could see the emotions playing across his features: anger, sorrow, gratitude, and wonder.

She somehow managed to tell him about the scrying stick and the trip to Tibet without mentioning her relationship with Edgar, but she knew she would need to tell him sooner or later.

Just not right now.

Ell-rom already had a hard time processing all that he had learned today, and adding a former boyfriend who was a clan member might be the last straw, so to speak.

When she told him about hiking through the Himalayan mountains and the Chinese military base, his eyes began to drift closed, and then his breathing slowed and evened out into the gentle rhythm of sleep.

For a long moment, she sat on the bed and gazed at his handsome face, her hand still clasped in his, and her heart full to bursting.

She was in love with this male and desperately needed him to love her back.

7 7

THE PRINCE

Ell-rom lay against the pillows, contemplating all that he had learned and all that he still did not know and had not gotten around to asking.

Like, what time of day was it?

How long had it been since he had awakened for the first time in this bed?

So much had happened every time he opened his eyes that it felt like each awakening was a new day.

Regardless of the actual passage of time, a lot had happened since his first awakening.

He knew his own name now, his sister's name, and today, Annani had told him that she was their sister and that the two of them had a welcoming family and a community waiting for them when they got better.

Ell-rom was so glad he'd gotten to see Morelle with his own eyes. She was still painfully thin and pale, and most of her hair was missing, but she was beautiful to look at, warm to the touch, and, most importantly, getting better.

He owed it all to Jasmine.

If not for her, he and his sister would have perished, their bodies withering away to dust in the sealed stasis chambers.

The thought made his stomach churn and his heart ache for the others who had not been so fortunate, the ones their mother had chosen to accompany them on their journey to their father. He was sure she hadn't chosen randomly and that each of those Kra-ell had been selected for a reason, but even if they had not been, he still mourned their deaths.

Ell-rom found it frustrating that his faulty mind had forgotten basic knowledge, like the physiological differences between the Kra-ell and the gods.

Why could gods enter stasis unaided while the Kra-ell could not? Why were gods immortal while the Kra-ell were only long-lived?

Why did the Kra-ell consume only blood for sustenance while the gods could eat a variety of things but not blood?

That was only a tiny sample, and he was sure there were many more differences. Je-Kara, or Jade as she preferred to be called now, could explain everything to him, but he didn't want to talk to her. He knew Jade thought him weak and overly emotional. She had no respect for him.

He preferred for those memories to return on their own, even if he had to wait for them a little longer.

"Good morning." Jasmine rose to her feet. "How are you feeling?"

"Good. Is it morning, though? How long has it been since Annani left?"

"It's late afternoon, and you slept about four hours since she left." She smiled. "It was a very exciting visit, and you learned a lot. You hung on the goddess's every word until you lost the fight with your eyelids. No wonder that you slept for so long."

Ell-rom let out a breath. "It's so confusing not even knowing the passage of time down here."

"You can always ask me." She took his hand.

"I have so many more questions that no one can answer. Was I a learned male before I was put on the settler ship? Are Kra-ell priests taught about science and technology?"

"Perhaps Jade knows the answers to those questions. She served in the queen's guard."

He did not want to tell Jasmine why he preferred not to speak to Jade.

"She might not know my particular circumstances. She only saw me from afar. I do not know who I was as a person."

Jasmine smiled. "I don't know who you were before, but I know who you are now. You are kind, loving, loyal, and compassionate."

"Are those good things? Jade thought that I was acting like a little boy. She did not know I could hear her murmuring behind Kian's back."

"Ugh. That's nasty." Jasmine's eyes glinted with anger. "She's lucky that I didn't hear her, or I would have put her in her place, no matter how intimidating she is."

The ferociousness with which Jasmine defended his honor warmed his heart. "Thank you. It means a lot to me that you don't share her opinion, but her words hurt because they are at least partially true."

Jasmine's eyes blazed with anger. "They are not. Do not listen to her." She put a warm hand on his cheek. "Love, kindness, compassion, and loyalty are wonderful qualities. Jade is a soldier who thinks that all civilians are soft."

"Maybe she is right?"

"She is not. It takes strength to show compassion, courage to love, and a good moral compass to be loyal." She leaned closer, her breath fanning over his face. "I want to kiss you so badly. May I?"

The request caught him unprepared, stunned even. His breath caught in his throat, and his pulse quickened with a sudden, fierce anticipation. He wanted to answer with an enthusiastic yes, but all he managed was a slight nod.

"Good answer." Jasmine leaned forward and captured his lips with her own.

At first, the kiss was soft and tentative, but when he moaned and wrapped his palm around the back of her neck, she deepened the kiss, her mouth hot and hungry with a desire that equaled his.

The kiss washed over him like a wild storm, transforming him from the outside in or the inside out, he wasn't sure.

He responded instinctively, his lips parting to welcome her and his fingers tightening around the back of her neck to pull her closer to him, closer and deeper into the heat and the hunger of their embrace.

As the world fell away, there was nothing but the two of them, lost in the fire and the fury of their passion.

He knew that he would never be the same after this kiss because he had found something precious, something rare and beautiful and infinitely valuable.

Hope.

Fate.

He and Jasmine were destined to be together.

In her arms, Ell-rom had found a sanctuary from the raging storm, and he knew, with a certainty that defied explanation, that he would never let her go.

COMING UP NEXT
DARK AWAKENING TRILOGY
INCLUDES:
86: DARK AWAKENING: NEW WORLD
87: DARK AWAKENING HIDDEN CURRENTS
88: DARK AWAKENING ECHOES OF DESTINY

Read the enclosed excerpt.

"Your destiny awaits across the stars," Ell-rom's mother told him. "The seer foretold your future. You will live, and you will thrive, and you will be safe."

The seer's prophecy has come true. Ell-rom and his sister are safe, surrounded by people who care for them and want to help them heal, which is in stark contrast to where they came from. On Anumati, they were considered abominations because of their mixed heritage. As half gods and half Kra-ell, they would have been eradicated if ever discovered.

But even as he clings to that thought like a talisman against the darkness, he can't shake the lingering sense of unease, the feeling that something lurked in the shadows of his past, something dark and dangerous that is much worse than his inability to tolerate the taste of blood.

What is it about him and his sister that he is not supposed to let anyone see?

DARK AWAKENING: EXCERPT

1

JASMINE

irst kiss.

Jasmine had had many of those, and most had been exciting, but none compared to the one she had just shared with Ell-rom.

None even got close.

Perhaps it was the exhilaration of finally reconciling the elusive prince her tarot had promised with the flesh and blood male she'd saved from wasting away in a nonfunctioning stasis chamber.

A stasis chamber that had been inside a crashed escape pod, which had been ejected from an exploding alien ship. It could be a great script for a sci-fi movie in which Jasmine was the star, but ironically, she had never even auditioned for one of those.

The closest she had gotten to playing a part in a fantasy or a sci-fi production was when she had gotten a callback for a zombie apocalypse film. In the end, she had not gotten that part, which she hadn't been too sorry about.

Zombies freaked her out, and she wasn't a fan, but she had watched all the big sci-fi movies. All the *Star Treks*, *Star Wars*, *Stargate*, and *Independence Day*.

The last one was her favorite, especially the president's speech. But while most remembered the famous line, *we will not go quietly into the night,* Jasmine favored a different one—*you will be fighting for our freedom not from tyranny, oppression, or persecution but from annihilation. We are fighting for our right to live, to exist.*

Jasmine chuckled.

The speech was epic, but in that film, the aliens were the enemy, and humans cooperated to save the planet, while, in reality, it was the opposite. The aliens were trying to save humanity, while humans were more divided than ever, and World War III was brewing.

Well, at least she was aligned with the good guys and was now part of an alternative reality that had been running parallel to the one that had prevailed throughout human history.

Until a few short weeks ago, Jasmine had no clue of its existence, and the most out-there thing she had ever done had been to join the Wicca community and practice a bit of harmless witchcraft. In her wildest dreams, she couldn't have imagined that it would lead her to kiss an alien prince who was part god, as in the mythological gods of yore, and part a completely alien race, the Kra-ell, who drank blood for sustenance.

It wasn't Ell-rom's alien origin that had made the kiss magical, though. It was the fact that it had been his first.

Ever.

Her prince had been a priest in training when he had been smuggled onto the settler ship, and Kra-ell priests were celibate. Ell-rom was a virgin, an innocent she had tempted with forbidden fruit…

Jasmine's fingers flew to her lips. "Oh, dear Goddess. What have I done?"

Ell-rom's eyelids, which had been at half-mast until she'd spoken, popped wide open. "What's wrong? Are you not allowed to kiss me?"

The guilty look in his eyes made it evident that he had been aware he was not supposed to get intimate with a woman, and yet he hadn't stopped her.

Jasmine wanted to believe that he had been overcome by desire or didn't care about his religious obligations because he couldn't remember them, but it was more likely that he felt indebted to her.

After all, she had saved him and his twin sister from death and then pulled him out of a coma by talking and singing to him for days.

No, it couldn't be gratitude.

Ell-rom still looked dazed and euphoric from the kiss, so it had to be lust or maybe even some tender feelings that Jasmine didn't dare hope for.

Nevertheless, she should have been mindful of his situation and not tempted him. He shouldn't succumb to desire until he remembered more about his past and figured out where he stood concerning his religious convictions.

"I'm so sorry." She took his hand. "Well, that's a lie. I'm not sorry that I kissed you. I'm sorry about you being a celibate priest and for tempting you to do something that you were not supposed to."

As Ell-rom frowned, guilt made Jasmine shift her gaze away from his handsome face and look at the wall behind his hospital bed. The unadorned, cream-colored walls and medical equipment were a reminder of his vulnerable condition. She had just taken advantage of a male who, only a day ago, hadn't been able to remember his own name.

"I don't recall what being a priest entailed," he said. "I don't even remember what I was taught about spirituality. The only reason I know I was a priest is that you, Jade, and Annani told me about it." He rubbed a hand over his jaw. "Jade said it was my mother's way to protect my sister and me. We didn't look Kra-ell, and we were in mortal danger if we were discovered. They didn't tolerate hybrids where we came from. The only way she could hide us was to put us in the temple where we were protected by the head priestess and the robing that veiled us from head to toe. It wasn't our choice to join the priesthood. Do I have to follow a path I didn't choose?"

Jasmine wanted to say that he didn't have to do anything he didn't want to or didn't feel duty-bound to do, but the truth was that neither of them knew what his life had been like in the temple. What if he had found it satisfying to dedicate himself to serving the Mother of All Life and helping others with their spiritual journey?

Despite her love of carnal pleasures, Jasmine could understand how giving it all up could be fulfilling when it was done in the service of others.

To internalize people's plights and offer genuine compassion, it was necessary to give up something meaningful or experience hardships.

Being a spiritual leader was about more than just leading prayers and rituals.

"Perhaps we should wait until you remember your choices," she said, even though it pained her. "I don't want to lead you astray from your beliefs. When you remember more about who you are, you might realize that you loved dedicating your life to the service of others."

"What others?" Ell-rom asked.

Jasmine looked up at him. "Jade and her people might need a spiritual leader."

He looked at her for a long moment, his piercing blue eyes holding hers captive. "I may not remember my past, but I know how I feel right now, and I know that I enjoyed that kiss far too much to give it up." He took her hand and brought it to his lips for a sweet, feathery kiss. "I enjoy *you* too much to give you up."

It was a relief to hear him say that, but it didn't assuage her guilt. She still felt responsible for leading him away from his faith. "I was hoping that would be your answer. Indeed, I hope it will still be your answer after your memories return. But I don't want to become your regret."

"Never." He pulled her toward him. "But just to be sure I'm making the right decision, I'll need another kiss."

His humor surprised and delighted her. It must be innate because he hadn't had enough life experience since he had woken up to learn and emulate it, and his memory loss meant that he couldn't have remembered it from his past.

Ell-rom's face fell. "I see that you don't want to kiss me again. Was my first attempt so inadequate?"

"Oh, Ell-rom." Jasmine cupped his cheek. "Of course, I want to kiss you again." She leaned in and brushed her lips over his. "It's just that my mind tends to race, even when it's not supposed to."

He frowned. "In which ways was it racing?"

She shrugged. "Just a lot of silly questions that you can't answer."

"Like what?" He leaned into her palm, his eyelids going to half-mast.

"Are you tired?" She brushed her other hand over his nearly bald head.

"Not too tired to hear you talk. I love the sound of your voice."

Jasmine chuckled. "You just want another kiss."

"Yes, that too. But I want to know what's on your mind." He lifted his head and smiled at her. "You seem to have thousands of thoughts swirling around at any given moment, and I want to know all of them."

That made her laugh. "Believe me, you don't want to look inside my crazy, busy head, although you probably can."

He frowned. "What do you mean?"

"The immortals can look into the minds of humans, and since you share ancestors, you should be able to do that as well."

"It doesn't seem right to me." He tapped his temple. "Even though there isn't much anyone can gain from looking into the fragmented pieces of my mind, I wouldn't have wanted anyone invading my thoughts without my permission."

"They can't do that to you. You are one of them."

He looked confused. "Can they only read the minds of humans?"

Jasmine nodded. "But they don't do it unless it's necessary." She looked up at the camera installed near the ceiling and lowered her voice. "But I have to wonder how many do so despite the prohibition. It's not like anyone can find out. And without enforcement, most people will ignore it and do as they please, especially when there is so much to gain and so little to lose."

Ell-rom pursed his lips. "What about honor? If they vow to uphold the law, that should be enough."

"Not all are equally honorable," Jasmine whispered. "I can't speak about the immortals because I haven't been part of their community for long, but since they are part human, and humans are not all honorable, I have to assume that the same is true of the immortals."

Ell-rom's expression darkened. "Did any of them enter your mind?"

Jasmine suspected that one of the gods had bitten her to speed up her recovery after she'd twisted her ankle, and then had made her forget it. But even if she was right, the gods were not part of the immortal community, and therefore not bound by the same rules.

Should she confide her suspicions to Ell-rom?

It felt right to share everything with the male she was falling in love with, but he was still so weak, and it wasn't fair to burden him with too much too soon.

On the other hand, she didn't want to hide things from him, and the way he looked at her expectantly, her only choices were to tell him what she suspected or lie.

"There was this one incident during our trek through the mountains when we were looking for you."

A growl emanated from deep in Ell-rom's throat. "Who did that?" he hissed.

His sudden vehemence was in such stark contrast to his otherwise affable demeanor that it was quite jarring.

Jasmine raised a hand. "Hold on. Don't get mad yet. I twisted my ankle and was in a lot of pain. I fell asleep while taking a short rest, and my ankle felt much better when I woke up. I suspect that one of the gods thralled me to go to sleep, gave me a dose of his venom to heal me, and then thralled me again to make me forget it."

Ell-rom's brow furrowed. "What do you mean that he gave you a dose of venom? Where did he get it from, and why did he hide it from you?"

"Oh boy." She let out a breath. "There is so much you still need to learn about yourself. You know that you have fangs, right?"

Jasmine had felt them elongate when they kissed, but she hadn't been surprised or alarmed. Being with Edgar had taught her how to navigate around them to avoid getting nicked.

Ell-rom lifted a finger and touched his canines, which were back to normal by now. "Isn't that part of my Kra-ell heritage? They need fangs to drink blood. I don't, but I still have them."

Jasmine scrunched her nose. "Not exactly. They are also—"

Her words were cut off as the door to the room swung open, and Bridget walked in.

The medic paused in the doorway, taking in the scene of Jasmine perched on the edge of Ell-rom's bed, their hands intertwined. "Am I interrupting?" she asked, a knowing smile playing at the corners of her mouth.

Jasmine let go of his hand. "I was just about to explain to Ell-rom about his fangs and what they are for, but you can probably do a better job of it than me."

Bridget regarded her with a twinkle in her eyes. "I can explain while I do my checkup. Why don't you get some fresh air while I'm at it? Maybe grab a cup of coffee?"

"Good idea." Jasmine shifted her gaze to Ell-rom. "I'll be back in a few minutes. Do you want me to get you something from the café?" She turned to Bridget. "Can I get Ell-rom coffee? He's probably never had it."

Bridget shook her head. "You can give him a tiny sip of yours to taste. But you can get him some more vegetable soup."

Jasmine arched a brow. "I didn't know they had soup there."

"They do now." Bridget turned to her and smiled. "Since the clan owns this building and the café belongs to us, we can ask them to get whatever we want."

That made sense.

The clan owned half of the high-rises on this downtown Los Angeles Street, and the humans renting apartments and offices in the buildings above had no clue that their landlord was a clan of immortals.

They also didn't know that there was a vast underground complex sprawling beneath them.

2

ELL-ROM

As Ell-rom watched Jasmine leave his room, his body and mind were still ablaze from their kiss.

Perhaps he was lucky that he did not remember his celibate life and the sacrifice of intimacy he had been forced to make. He did not know how old he was, but he knew he was not a boy. He was an adult male who should have enjoyed the pleasure of a female partner for many years. Instead, he had been forced to play the role of a priest and forgo touching and being touched.

What a terrible loss that had been.

Whatever he ended up remembering about himself and his convictions, religious and otherwise, he was never going back to being celibate. If the Mother of All Life had a problem with that, she would have to appear to him in person and argue her case to convince him to return to that miserable existence.

The chief medic approached his bed with an amused expression on her face. "How are you feeling, Ell-rom?"

How should he answer that?

That he had been transformed? But how could he claim to have been remade if he did not know his old self?

"It has been a long and momentous day," he said instead. "So much has happened."

"Indeed." She handed him an odd-looking device.

It was a compact, sturdy tool with a handle to grip and a small screen on top.

"What is this?" he asked.

"It's a device that measures the strength of your hand grip. It assesses your muscle function and helps us monitor your recovery by tracking changes in your strength over time."

Ell-rom regarded the device with suspicion. "What am I supposed to do with it?"

"Place your hand around the grip handle, and when you're ready, squeeze it as hard as you can. Try to apply maximum effort, and don't be afraid of breaking it. William calibrated it for an immortal male's strength."

He hesitated before doing as she instructed. "Does that mean that human males are weaker than immortals?"

The medic nodded. "Immortals are about three to five times stronger than humans, and Kra-ell are about three times stronger than immortals. Since you are a hybrid, you are probably somewhere between the two on the strength scale, but that is in peak state. Presently, you are far from it, but this gadget will help us monitor your progress during your recovery."

Bridget sounded earnest, but he still wasn't convinced that her motives were purely therapeutic. These people had heard rumors about him and his sister, accusing them of being abominations and possibly incredibly powerful.

What if the rumors were true?

Jasmine was human, which meant she was much weaker and more fragile than the immortals, who were supposedly weaker than him. If he wanted to keep kissing her and maybe put his arms around her and hug her too, he should know his strength so he wouldn't harm her by mistake.

With that in mind, he squeezed the device as hard as he could and waited to see the result flash on the small screen. Except, he had forgotten that he couldn't read the language it was displayed in.

"What does it say?" he asked.

The medic took the device from him, looked at the display, and nodded her approval. "Right now, your grip strength is forty-five pounds, which is what I would expect from an elderly human female."

He winced. "That sounds terrible."

"It's very good, given the state you were in when you were brought here. Your muscles were completely atrophied, but you are growing stronger quite rapidly." She gave him a reassuring smile. "We will keep checking daily. At your current recovery rate, you will be as strong as a human in a week or two, and as soon as we can get more food into your stomach, you will improve even more rapidly."

She pulled out a small tablet from her coat pocket and wrote something on it, probably the results of the measurement she had just taken.

"How are your memories?" Bridget asked without looking up from her tablet. "Any new recollections?"

Ell-rom frowned, scanning the fragmented landscape of his mind. "Nothing concrete. Just feelings. Impressions." He sighed, frustration creeping into his voice. "I was told that I was a priest or at least training to be one, but I can't remember what that meant to me. Was it just a sanctuary to hide in from those who would have killed my sister and me, or was it my calling?"

Bridget put the tablet back in her pocket. "It will come back to you eventually. Don't force it, and don't stress over it. Just let it flow."

He winced. "I am impatient, and I am also apprehensive. What if that is all I'm going to get? Some fragments of memories, some impressions, and the occasional dreams?"

She smiled fondly. "The fact that you are getting those so soon after waking is a good indicator that you will get all of it back. Just as your body cannot recover its full strength overnight, your mind can't either. These things take time."

He stifled a frustrated groan. "Is there a way to speed up the process?"

"Of course." Bridget walked to Jasmine's chair and sat down. "Tomorrow, I will start you on physical therapy. I ordered a walker to be delivered, and you will begin by walking down the corridor outside the clinic. Jasmine can watch over you while you are at it, but if you are embarrassed about her seeing you struggling, Julian or Gertrude can assist you."

"Why would I be embarrassed?"

A smile tugged at the medic's lips. "Evidently, losing one's memory is not all bad, especially for a male." When he frowned, she chuckled. "Males like to portray strength, especially when trying to impress a female, but those who are smart realize that there is a caretaker inside most females and that they love nursing a good male back to health."

"They do?"

Bridget pursed her lips. "Well, I don't think that is true for the Kra-ell. Their females are not typically nurturing; the males would rather die than admit weakness. For them, getting killed in battle is the only honorable way to die."

Something about what she said resonated with him, more like a distant memory than something he believed in. "They sound like warmongering people."

"That's how they used to be." She sighed. "Tribal wars were a way of life for them, and duels to the death were commonplace. Nature compensated for the high male death toll by giving them a gender distribution of four males born for every female, but then a progressive queen disturbed the balance by stopping the tribal wars and outlawing deadly duels. A new system had to be devised with males outnumbering females four to one. They are not monogamous, and their family units include several males to one female who heads the household. Things got even more out of whack when they landed on Earth and had to survive, but I digress. I just hope that the Kra-ell who joined our community will adopt our values, at least to some extent, and learn that compassion and kindness are not weaknesses but strengths."

Once again, something about what she'd said resonated with him, but as before, he didn't know whether it was because he agreed with her or for some other reason. Compassion and kindness were excellent qualities, but they should be applied cautiously and only to those who had earned and deserved them. Otherwise, they could be manipulated by the unscrupulous to trap and destroy the well-meaning people.

How did he know that?

Was it innate knowledge or something he had learned?

"You look troubled," Bridget said. "Did something about what I said jog your memory?"

He shook his head. "It's a feeling. A warning sensation that goodness could be one's downfall."

"That's a very good instinct, Ell-rom." She pushed to her feet. "Whoever provided your education did a good job. Compassion and charity need to be backed up by strength, or they will be exploited." She patted his shoulder.

Was she planning to leave already? He wasn't done with his questions.

"Can you stay a little longer? I have another question."

"I'm not leaving yet," she said. "There are a few more tests that I would like to run on you."

3

ELL-ROM

sking the medic about his fangs was going to be so embarrassing, but Jasmine had left him no choice.

"Um, it's about my fangs," Ell-rom said. "Jasmine said that you can explain what they are for."

Bridget's lips twitched, but she stifled the smile and retained her professional demeanor. "Ah, yes. I can certainly help with that. What do you know about your physiology?"

"I know I'm half Kra-ell and half god, and I know the Kra-ell drink blood, but I don't. The idea of consuming blood repulses me. I don't know whether my fangs are just a remnant of my Kra-ell genetics that is not needed or if they serve some other function." He cleared his throat. "I've noticed that they elongate in response to certain stimuli."

"In that respect, you take after the part of you that is half god. Your fangs aren't for feeding; they're for... well, let's call it sharing."

"Sharing?" Ell-rom echoed.

Bridget nodded. "Both Kra-ell and gods have glands that produce venom. The Kra-ell use it mainly to immobilize their prey and to heal its wounds once they are done drinking its blood. The venom actually makes it a pleasurable experience for the prey. This ability is much stronger in gods, naturally or genetically enhanced, but only the male gods have fangs. The females do not."

That didn't seem fair, but the Mother of All Life knew what she was doing, so there was probably a good reason for that.

"In what way is the gods' venom different?" he asked.

"To start with, their venom is much more potent than the Kra-ell's," Bridget said. "In a fight, it can incapacitate an opponent or even stop his heart, which is one of the few ways to kill a god or an immortal. Aggression triggers the production of this dangerous type of venom. The production of the other type, which is used to pleasure sexual partners, is triggered by arousal. Your fangs will elongate in response to either trigger, but the composition of the venom will depend on the situation."

That explained why his fangs had elongated when he kissed Jasmine.

"Is it dangerous?" he asked, suddenly worried. "Could I hurt Jasmine?"

Bridget shook her head. "Not with the venom. Your body knows what type to produce for her benefit, which is not limited to enhancing her pleasure. She will feel stronger, healthier, and more energetic. If she has an ailment bothering her, your venom will help cure it or at least alleviate its symptoms. So, you shouldn't worry. But as you get physically stronger, you will need to be mindful of your superior strength and of her human fragility. Also, her sexual stamina cannot match yours. While you will be able to perform consecutively without rest, she will tire long before you are satisfied, but you will need to follow her lead in this."

Bridget had delivered the explanation in her usual dry and factual tone, but the effect of her words on Ell-rom was instinctive and visceral. All that talk about climaxing and satisfaction was making him respond most embarrassingly, and he crossed his legs under the blanket to hide the evidence.

"Does that answer your question?" the medic asked.

All he could do was nod.

"Very good." Bridget moved to stand close to where he did not want her to be. "Let's check your mobility. Can you sit up for me?"

He was happy to comply and further hide the evidence of his arousal. Pushing himself into a sitting position took less effort than it had taken earlier that day.

As Bridget guided him through a series of simple exercises, testing his range of motion and strength, his arousal subsided to a level where he was no longer embarrassed. Then, his mind just had to wander back to the kiss, and he had to force himself to think about his past before the situation became awkward again.

"Can I ask you something?"

"Of course." Bridget didn't look up from her tablet, her fingers flying over the screen.

"I was told that I was a priest in training and that the Kra-ell's consecrated clergy are supposed to be celibate."

She lifted her head from the tablet and leveled her gaze at him. "That's what Jade told us, but I don't know much about it."

"I know, but all I'm asking for is your opinion. Do you think I should ignore the past I can't remember and follow my feelings for Jasmine instead?"

Bridget hesitated. "I can't comment on your religion or your individual beliefs. All I can say is that from a medical standpoint, your connection with Jasmine has been beneficial to your recovery."

"I understand your reluctance to opine about something not in your field of expertise, but I don't have anyone else I can talk to."

Bridget sighed. "This is something that you'll have to decide for yourself, but in my opinion, I think life is too short—or in your case, too long—to deny yourself happiness based on a past you can't remember."

Relief washed over Ell-rom. "That is what I thought, but since I lacked any meaningful reference, I didn't know whether I was just telling myself what I wanted to hear or whether it was the right thing to do. Thank you for easing my mind."

The medic nodded, patting his shoulder. "Any time. Now, let's get you up and walking a bit before Jasmine gets back with the soup."

With Bridget's assistance, Ell-rom swung his legs over the side of the bed and slowly stood up, his legs trembling slightly under his weight. Still, he remained upright and took a step forward, then another.

"Excellent." Bridget held on to his arm with surprising strength for such a petite female. "You're making good progress."

As they made a slow circuit around the small room, Ell-rom's thoughts once again drifted back to his conversation with Jasmine and what she had said about immortals' ability to read minds. He was particularly concerned about her suspicion that one of the gods had used venom to heal her during their mountain trek. He didn't have a problem with them doing that, even if it required some level of arousal, but he had a big problem with them doing so without Jasmine's consent.

"Hold on," he said, pausing to catch his breath. "I need a little rest."

"Of course." Bridget helped him to lean against the bed. "If you are tired, we can stop and continue tomorrow."

"No, I just need a few seconds to rest, and then I can continue."

"No problem."

"I have another question."

She smiled. "Ask away."

"Is it true that immortals can read human minds?"

The medic's expression tightened. "It's not mind reading exactly. We can't read thoughts. But we can read impressions; when they are very recent, that's as good as reading thoughts. It's like seeing a movie of what has just happened in that person's life. Why do you ask?"

"It's another thing that Jasmine mentioned to me. I don't know if I have the ability, and if I do, when it's okay to use it. I don't think it's acceptable to invade someone's mind without their permission."

Bridget smiled approvingly. "You are right. We have strict rules about it. It's only allowed to hide our existence from humans, which is an existential risk for us, and to save lives. Sometimes special permission can be given by our judge if she's presented with a compelling argument for it."

"How is compliance enforced?" He pushed away from the bed, and the medic helped him take a few more steps around the room.

Bridget sighed. "As you can imagine, it's impossible to enforce. We drill this into our children's heads and hope it sticks."

That was what he had suspected, and there wasn't much else that could be done about it.

"Is there any way to know if someone has invaded your mind?"

Bridget helped him back to the bed before answering. "Not really, but you don't need to worry about it. I doubt anyone other than the gods can invade your mind, probably not even them."

"I see." Ell-rom settled back against his pillows. "Are the gods bound by the same rules as the immortals?"

Bridget's hesitation was answer enough. "The gods operate under their own code, but from what I have seen of them so far, they are honorable people. I don't think they would violate the privacy of anyone's mind unless it was absolutely necessary for security reasons or to save someone's life."

4

JASMINE

As Jasmine crossed the lobby toward the café, she again experienced the disconnect between the secret world of immortals that existed underneath the luxury residential high-rise, and the world above.

Standing in line, she felt odd to be surrounded by humans suddenly. It wasn't that the immortals or even the gods looked markedly different than the people around her—well, except for being unnaturally good-looking—but then this was Los Angeles, and there were plenty of good-looking people around.

The main difference was in her, though, and what she knew now that she hadn't before. She was privy to the best-kept secret in the world, and none of these unsuspecting humans could even imagine that it existed.

Then there was the kiss that had changed everything and yet hadn't.

It had only proved that the tarot had been right all along and that the prince they had shown her had not been just a prince of a man, although Ell-rom was that too. It had always been about the prince being her one and only, her destined mate.

So why wasn't she giddy with excitement?

Because nothing was ever that easy, and Jasmine knew with absolute certainty that many obstacles would materialize on her and Ell-rom's way to happily ever after.

It was just the way it was. Nothing good ever came easy.

It could be his religion once he remembered it. Or it could be his sister once she woke up. Or it could be something unexpected.

Jasmine had done a tarot reading the night before, and the cards had been encouraging, hinting at new beginnings and deep connections, but they'd also warned of challenges ahead and difficult choices to be made.

That had fueled her worries. After all, if the tarot had been correct before, there was no reason to doubt them now.

Still, she was grateful for the chance she'd been given and the wonderful male the Mother of All Life, or the Fates the immortals believed in, had sent her way.

Who would have thought that she would find his innocence and inexperience so endearing?

Perhaps that was why the Fates had prompted her to be so easy with her affections. It had all been a part of their grand plan. Ell-rom was the novice, the apprentice, and she was the expert, the master, and it was up to her to teach her virgin prince everything she knew about carnal pleasures, which was quite a lot.

The prospect of introducing him to all the marvels of sex was so exciting.

"Next in line, please," the barista called, jolting Jasmine from her reverie.

She ordered her usual latte, adding a blueberry muffin on impulse and a cup of soup for Ell-rom.

Waiting for her order, she wondered if there was coffee on Anumati. The gods had drunk plenty of it on their trip through the Tibetan mountains, but they might have developed a taste for it during their time on Earth.

She should call Margo and ask her.

"Order for Jasmine," the barista called out, sliding a cardboard tray across the counter.

Jasmine collected the tray, but instead of heading straight back, she chose to enjoy her coffee at a small table by the window.

Bridget was probably still in Ell-rom's room, and the doctor didn't like being crowded when she performed her examinations. She should give her a few more minutes.

Besides, after being cooped up in a room without windows, Jasmine enjoyed gazing at the outdoors.

It was getting dark outside, but traffic was still congested, and Jasmine watched the cars passing by. People were heading home to join their families, eat dinner together, or engage in whatever drama was currently consuming their lives. Each individual was a microcosmos, each with their own issues, aspirations and hopes, triumphs and disappointments.

As her phone buzzed, she pulled it out and smiled when she saw the message was from Margo. Her friend must have felt that she needed to talk to her.

Good evening, my darling. How's your Prince Charming doing today? Any more memories surfacing?

Jasmine stared at the screen with her thumbs hovering over the keyboard and wondered what she should tell Margo. Should she tell her about the kiss?

At her age and with the number of sex partners she'd had, it seemed silly and immature to brag about a kiss, but the truth was that it was a big deal.

How many women could boast about kissing a celibate alien prince?

Nevertheless, it wasn't something to convey in a text message.

In the end, she settled for a simple reply. *He's doing better every day, but today was a big day for Ell-rom. He got to meet Kian.* She knew she wasn't supposed to tell her about the goddess's visit, and she needed to remind Ell-rom not to talk about it either. *I'll fill you in later, okay?*

When? Margo replied.

When Ell-rom falls asleep, I'll come upstairs. Are you there tonight?

Where else would I be?

Jasmine smiled. *Partying or clubbing with your god.*

My god is spending most of his waking hours tinkering with the salvaged equipment as if the secrets of the universe are hiding somewhere in there.

Jasmine typed back. *Who knows? They may be. BTW, any progress with spying on Lynda?*

I'll tell you when you get here.

Was that Margo's payback for Jasmine's cryptic reply?

Probably.

As her thoughts returned to her prince, she took a bite of her muffin and washed it down with a sip of coffee.

Hopefully, she wasn't leading Ell-rom down a path he wasn't ready for. Perhaps it wasn't fair for her to encourage his feelings when he was still piecing together his own identity.

Maybe she should slow down and wait until he knew who he was and what he wanted.

She had no easy answers. All she knew was that her feelings for him were real and growing stronger.

5

ELL-ROM

As Bridget continued to measure the length and circumference of Ell-rom's atrophied leg muscles, he struggled to keep his eyelids from drooping. The few steps he had taken around the room had robbed him of the last dregs of energy he could muster, and if he weren't eager to see Jasmine return, he would have gladly succumbed to sleep.

When the knock came and Jasmine peeked in, he couldn't help the grin spreading over his face.

She held a steaming cup in one hand and a covered bowl in the other. "Is it okay to come back in?" she asked, her eyes darting between Ell-rom and Bridget.

"Perfect timing," Bridget said, gathering her things. "I was just finishing up. He's all yours."

As Jasmine walked in, Bridget headed for the door but paused in the doorway, looking back at Ell-rom. "Remember what I said. Don't push yourself too hard."

He nodded.

When the door closed behind the medic, Jasmine set the two containers on the bedside table. "Hungry?" She removed the lid from the bowl, and given the smell, it was his soup.

He tried to stifle a grimace. "Frankly, I'm a little nauseous after all the physical activity Bridget made me do."

"What did you do?" Jasmine perched on the side of his bed.

"I just took a few steps around the room, and it exhausted me." He didn't want to mention the device that had measured the strength of his grip and the results that were in line with that of an elderly human female.

Jasmine eyed the soup. "It's a shame to let it get cold. Also, Bridget said that you need to eat to get stronger."

That was the convincing argument.

He definitely wanted to get stronger as soon as possible.

"I'll try some." He leaned over to take the bowl, but Jasmine stopped him.

"Let me feed you. You're tired."

Recalling what Bridget had said about females enjoying the role of caretakers, Ell-rom didn't argue. "I like it when you feed me."

Jasmine's bright smile turned her face from beautiful to spectacular. "And I love feeding you." She lifted a spoonful into his mouth. "I have to wonder, though, how you are going to grow back your muscles on vegetable broth. You need to eat protein, but since you don't consume meat, I guess it would have to be tofu or beans or maybe a protein shake. Can you tolerate milk or cheese?"

"I don't know. Maybe?"

"Let's give it a try." She put the soup on the side table and picked up the other container. "This is coffee with milk. Do you want to give it a try?"

The idea of drinking something that was meant for baby animals did not appeal to him, but Jasmine seemed to enjoy it, so maybe it tasted good.

He nodded. "It doesn't smell offensive."

"I think it smells really good." She brought the cup to his lips and gave it a little tilt so he could drink. "So, what do you think?"

"It's good." He licked his lips.

It was sweet, but that wasn't because of the milk. "Did you sweeten the coffee?"

"Yes." Her eyes remained glued to his mouth as she murmured, "Do you want more?"

He felt his fangs elongate. "I do, but not coffee. I want to kiss you again."

Jasmine swallowed. "Did Bridget explain the fangs and the venom and all that?"

"She did." He lifted his arm and was proud of himself when he managed to wrap it around Jasmine and pull her to him.

Not that she offered any resistance. With how weak he was, he wouldn't have been able to do anything to her without her full cooperation.

"Be careful around the sharp points," he murmured before he fused their mouths together.

She kissed him lightly this time and leaned back. "I know my way around fangs. You are not the first immortal I've kissed."

Ell-rom smiled. "It's obvious that you have more experience than I do. I'm operating on pure instinct. I just hope not to fumble too badly."

"You're doing great." Her smile was tight for some reason.

"What's wrong?" He kneaded the soft skin at the back of her neck. "Suddenly you seem tense."

"Aren't you going to ask me who I kissed?"

He frowned. "Should I?"

She seemed frustrated. "Doesn't it bother you that I had sex with other males?"

"Why should it?"

She shook her head. "You are right. It shouldn't, but my previous partner was such a jealous guy that I'm surprised to find you so indifferent. Don't you care about me?"

"Of course I care. How can you say that I don't? If you want me to display jealousy, I will."

"But you don't feel it. I don't want you to fake it."

He kept massaging her neck even though it was becoming difficult for him to keep his arm up. "I would not be happy if you showed affection toward another male now, but what was in the past has no bearing on the present or the future." He finally let his arm drop away.

She pouted. "What if I was a terrible person in my past? Would you forgive all of my past transgressions?"

"Yes. But I'm sure there is nothing to forgive. You are pure of heart and strong of spirit, my lovely Jasmine."

6

JASMINE

J asmine wasn't sure that she deserved such unconditional acceptance, especially given how little Ell-rom truly knew about her. Not only that, she was the only person he knew other than the doctors and the nurse.

When he got exposed to more people, he might not like her, especially after he got to know her better. Not that there was anything inherently wrong with her, but she was a nobody with average intelligence, better-than-average looks, a better-than-average voice, and a mediocre acting talent. She also had a witchy ability that she was still exploring.

Not bad for a random human, but Ell-rom was a prince, and once he remembered what that entailed, he might realize that he needed a female of a higher caliber than her.

"You think too highly of me." Jasmine averted her gaze. "I'm not as pure of heart or as strong of spirit as you believe. You don't know anything about me."

"I know that you are a wonderful singer and storyteller, and I know that you went searching for me and my sister despite the journey not being easy. You saved both our lives. Then you sat by my side day and night. That makes you pure of heart and strong of spirit in my eyes."

She leaned over to the bedside table and picked up her latte to buy herself a moment to think.

Honesty was important in a relationship, but they didn't really have one yet. They were in the courtship stage, and during such a vulnerable and impressionable time, it was better to throttle the insecurities and doubts while inflating all her positive attributes. It was the selling stage, not the settling stage, and being an actress, Jasmine was an expert at selling herself.

Still, a little self-deprecation was always a good strategy as long as she didn't overdo it.

"What you feel is gratitude." She took another sip. "But you forget that I wasn't the only one there. The three gods, Julian, Edgar, and their mates, were there too."

He arched a brow. "Did all of them go trekking through the dangerous mountains to look for our pod?"

"Only the gods and I went trekking, but the mountains weren't all that dangerous. I twisted my ankle because I'm a clumsy city girl who is not used to hiking, trekking, or any of those outdoorsy activities. If it were Jade instead of me, I'm sure nothing would have happened to her."

He chuckled. "I'm sure of that as well, but that makes your sacrifice even greater. You volunteered to do something that you were not good at, something you did not like and that was potentially dangerous to you, and you did that because you wanted to save lives. That's admirable."

"I was searching for my prince," she reminded him. "The prince that the cards promised me."

"Oh, yes. The foretelling cards. I am still waiting for you to show them to me." The smile died on his lips. "Perhaps you can do a reading for Morelle."

Her eyes widened. "Why didn't I think of that sooner? I should go get them."

He put a hand on her thigh. "Not yet. I'm so tired that once you leave, I'm going to fall asleep, and I'm not ready to part with you yet."

Goddess above, that was so sweet.

Out of all the nice things he had said to her so far, that was the sweetest.

Putting her latte back on the side table, she kicked off her flip-flops and lifted her legs onto the bed. "Bridget will probably have my ass for this, but it's worth it." She stretched out next to him on her side and leaned to brush her lips over his. "This is probably the first time you've had a woman in your bed. Do you want me to take a picture?"

Without waiting for his answer, she pulled out the phone from her jeans pocket, activated the forward-facing camera, and lifted it over the two of them. "Smile!" she commanded while beaming at the screen.

Ell-rom did as she asked, but his smile looked more like a grimace. Nevertheless, she snapped several pictures before putting the phone on the side table. "Why did you make a face at the camera?"

"I saw my reflection on your device, and it looked terrible. I have no hair on my head, but I think that I'm starting to grow hair on my face. My jaw looked dirty in the reflection."

Frowning, Jasmine leaned closer, cupped his cheek, and rubbed her thumb over his skin. "You are right. It's still just hair follicles, so I can't feel the stubble, but you are starting to grow facial hair. I thought that you didn't have any."

"Why? Kian has facial hair, and so does Julian. What about the gods? I don't remember if Aru had hair on his face. And what about the Kra-ell?"

"Aru either shaves or has stubble. I've only gotten to see the Kra-ell males that Jade brought to carry the stasis chambers to the catacombs. They all looked clean-shaven, so maybe the Kra-ell don't have facial hair, but we can ask Jade the next time she comes to visit."

"If she comes." His eyelids drooped, but he forced them to open.

"Right."

Lying so close to Ell-rom and not getting any reaction from him was a little disappointing. His fangs were still dormant, and his eyes weren't glowing.

He tried to shift to his side, but he ended up needing her help. "I walked today. I should be able to turn on my side."

"You are exhausted. Don't be so hard on yourself."

He looked down at the teardrop hanging from her neck. "I guess being hard is one of the idioms that don't translate well to Kra-ell." He lifted his hand and brushed her hair aside, exposing her ear. "Do you experience the same in reverse? When these devices translate what I say for you?"

"Rarely." She brought the hair forward to cover her ear again. "I forget that they are there. Kra-ell probably doesn't have many idioms and is more straight-forward than my language."

She still hadn't told him that the earpieces were doing more than translating Kra-ell to English for her and that they were filtering compulsion.

He must have misinterpreted the guilty look in her eyes. "Tell me why you think that you are not as pure and courageous as I think you are."

Listing her shortcomings was not something Jasmine wanted to do, but it was better than telling him what the earpieces were really for.

"I am an actress. Do you know what that is?"

He nodded. "A performer. You sing and tell fictional stories."

"I also enact fictional stories. I don't know if you have movies or theater on Anumati. The gods do, but maybe the Kra-ell stay away from such entertainment. Here on Earth, it's a highly desirable profession, and many hope to become a star, a face that everyone recognizes." She looked into his eyes. "Are you following so far?"

"I think so. What qualifications do you need to become a star?"

Ell-rom was a smart guy, and he was grasping concepts with surprising ease.

"Good looks are important, and many use surgical means to enhance their appearance, but I'm proud to be all natural. Acting skills are required as well, the ability to memorize scripts quickly, being easy to work with, which means taking directions well and not being overly demanding or fussy."

"You seem to have all those requirements covered."

"Thank you." She smiled. "I do, but that's about it. I'm good, but I'm not exceptional. It's not easy to get rejected over and over again and still go on auditions hoping that a miracle will happen and I will fit the director's vision for a breakthrough part. There are two ways to get great parts. One is to be already famous, and then they want you because you have an audience that will come to see you no matter what the movie is about, and the other is to fit a role so perfectly that the director will be willing to take a risk on a no-name."

"Sounds tough."

"It is." She sighed. "At times, I pretended to be attracted to males to gain favor, hoping it would help me get chosen for a part I wanted." She shivered. "It's a nasty business, and many young people are exploited. I should have given up on dreams of fame and fortune as soon as I realized how sleazy it was, but I convinced myself that if others could do that to get ahead, I could do it too, and that it wasn't a big deal." She smiled nervously. "I bet that didn't translate well to Kra-ell either."

"No, I got the meaning." He lifted his arm with effort and wrapped it around her. "I'm sorry you had to go through such unpleasantness."

The guy was a born diplomat. To call her basically whoring herself out for parts an unpleasantness was a masterpiece of understatement.

"It wasn't as bad as it sounds. I don't like sleeping alone, so I would have probably picked up some loser who I didn't care for anyway. At least by seducing casting directors, I got a few parts."

Jasmine fell silent, memories of lonely nights and hollow victories washing over her like a wave of muddy water.

Ell-rom squeezed her hand. "Nothing of what you told me contradicts my assessment of you being pure of heart and strong of spirit."

"You are pure sweetness." She leaned to plant a soft kiss on his lips. "I've never met anyone like you."

He smiled. "And I have not met anyone like you."

She rolled her eyes. "You don't remember meeting anyone at all."

His smile wilted. "From the little I remember, my sister and I were alone most of the time. Our mother was too busy to visit, and the head priestess who knew what we were under the veils was not the kind, loving type."

As tears prickled the back of Jasmine's eyes, she kissed him again to hide the pity she felt for him and his sister. What a horrible way to grow up.

Ell-rom returned the kiss, his touch gentle but filled with so much passion that it made her heart race.

It was like being fourteen all over again and stealing kisses with Jason Moreno behind the bleachers.

Jasmine had lost her virginity young and hadn't looked back, but she had to admit that the change of pace was nice, and taking it slow was kind of charming. Why did everyone rush into sex before getting to know each other?

If she had done her due diligence instead of jumping straight into yet another relationship, Jasmine might not have gone with Alberto to Cabo. But then she wouldn't have met Margo, wouldn't have ended up on the *Silver Swan*, and would never have found her prince.

7

KIAN

S hai poked his head into Kian's office. "Brandon is here to see you."

"Excellent. Show him in." Kian rose to his feet and walked toward his guest with an extended hand. "Good morning, Councilman."

Brandon flashed him a smile full of teeth, but it lacked the usual spark. "Good morning, Regent." He shook Kian's hand while doing the one-armed bro hug and clap.

Kian responded in kind and then motioned to the conference table. "Please, take a seat."

"Can I get you coffee, gentlemen?" Shai asked.

Kian wasn't comfortable sending Shai on errands of that sort, but it was early, he had a feeling that his talk with Brandon would take some time, and he wanted his guest to feel comfortable and stay as long as was needed.

He looked at his guest. "Coffee?"

"Sure." Brandon smiled apologetically at Shai. "I should have grabbed three cups at the café for us, but my head was elsewhere."

Shai waved a dismissive hand. "Don't worry about it. I was planning to go anyway. Do you want pastries as well?"

For a moment, Brandon looked like he was going to refuse, but then he shrugged. "Oh, hell. Why not? I would love a Danish."

"One for me, too," Kian said.

When the door closed behind Shai, Brandon leaned back in his chair and crossed his arms over his chest. "You said something about needing my movie magic expertise. Can you elaborate?"

"You are aware that we have the royal twins in the keep's clinic, right?"

Kian had sent all the council members a memo, but Brandon did not live in the village, and he avoided council business when he could, so Kian wasn't sure he had read the updates.

"I am aware. How are they doing?"

If he had read the last memo, he would have known, but it seemed like he hadn't.

"As you know, they were in terrible shape when we found them. It was just in the nick of time. The medical team tried to wake them both up from stasis, but so far, only the prince has woken up. He had lost his memory and didn't even remember his name until two days ago. The team is slowly bringing them both back to health, and the prince is about to start physical therapy."

"What is his name?" Brandon asked.

"His name is Ell-rom, and his sister's name is Morelle. He only remembered both their names after he was brought into her room. Seeing her triggered the recollection. They seem very close, and he feels responsible for her."

"That's natural." Brandon uncrossed his arms. "What about the immense powers that he was supposed to possess?"

Kian smiled. "For now, he seems as harmless as a kitten, and I'm positive that he's not pretending, but I wouldn't be surprised if those powers manifest once he gets physically stronger and regains his memory. It could also be that the sister is the dangerous one."

"I assume that you have guards stationed near the clinic."

Kian nodded. "Two Guardians and two Kra-ell hybrids are manning the security office at all times. I have them working in shifts and monitoring the surveillance cameras from the clinic. That way, the prince doesn't feel like he's a prisoner under guard, which my mother would have never approved of, but I don't need to worry about his powers suddenly manifesting, either. Also, everyone wears the compulsion filtering earpieces around him."

"Good," Brandon said. "So, where does my expertise come in?"

"We need to stage their deaths. We are waiting to perform the funeral rites for the Kra-ell who perished in that pod, until the twins regain enough body mass to look like their fellow Kra-ell, and we want to film it. Aru will send the recording to his commander, and ultimately the evidence will reach the intended audience, meaning the Eternal King. It is essential for the king to be convinced that everyone inside the pod is dead. The problem is that Anumati tech will immediately recognize digital or computer manipulation. We need to do this the old-fashioned way, with movie magic. We will probably also use Bridget's poison trick to induce a death-like state for the twins, but adding a convincing funeral pyre would help."

He didn't need to explain why it was important for the Eternal King to think

777

the twins were dead. That had been covered in a council meeting that Brandon had actually attended in person.

The media specialist chuckled. "These days, everything is done with CGI, but I know a few old timers who still remember how things used to be done before that. If they are still around, they are probably working for theme parks. They are a dying breed."

"How convincing can they make it look?"

Brandon shrugged. "For regular moviegoers, they can make it very convincing. I don't know if they can fool superior technology, though. Perhaps you should think about a better solution that will not require movie magic."

"Like what?"

"I can't think of something off the top of my head, but I'll give it some thought. When do you need to do this?"

Kian was about to answer when Shai walked in with a tray of coffees and a bag of pastries.

"Here you go, gentlemen." Shai put the tray and the bag down on the conference table, took one of the paper cups, and turned around. "I'll be in my office if you need me."

"Thank you," Kian said, and so did Brandon.

Kian picked up one of the cups and took a sip. "The twins are not camera-ready yet. They are no longer as emaciated as they were when we brought them in, but they are still very thin and pallid. In contrast, the dead Kra-ell look healthy because their bodies did not eat themselves and were perfectly preserved in the sealed stasis chambers. The twins also lost most of their hair, and it will not grow as fast as it would have if they were physically well. Regrowing hair is not their bodies' top priority while they rebuild weakened muscles and organs that were on the verge of collapse."

Brandon leaned forward. "We can get creative with wigs and maybe some subtle prosthetics to fill out their features. Careful lighting and camera work can hide imperfections as well."

Kian smiled. "I'm glad to see you getting excited about the production. You've always loved the creative side of the business."

To Kian's surprise, Brandon's expression turned serious. "I still do, but I reached a point where I can no longer stomach the rest. I'm done with Hollywood."

Kian blinked. "What happened? You used to boast about beating the sharks in their own infested waters."

Brandon had been instrumental in propagating the clan's narrative through films and television. Equal human rights independent of race, gender, and religion had been an uphill battle that owed its success in no small part to the councilman in charge of informing and enlightening human culture through media.

Brandon ran a hand through his hair. "The industry has changed dramatically in recent years. It's becoming increasingly difficult for us to exert our influence in the ways we once did."

Kian raised an eyebrow, prompting Brandon to continue.

"The rise of streaming services, the consolidation of major studios, the shift in focus to woke issues, and the influx of high finance—all led to lesser focus on good storytelling," Brandon explained. "Writers, the very people we used to work closely with to shape narratives, are being marginalized with less creative control and lower pay."

"Surely, that makes them more susceptible to our influence?" Kian countered.

Brandon shook his head. "Not when they're constantly worried about their next paycheck or jumping from project to project without fully understanding the bigger picture. And don't get me started on the obsession with remakes and seemingly perpetual franchises. It's limiting the scope of stories being told."

Kian's brow furrowed. "I see. So, what's the solution?"

"Social media. This is where modern narratives are being shaped, and it's where the public attention has shifted to." Brandon's eyes lit up with excitement. "Platforms like InstaTock are shaping culture faster than any blockbuster movie ever could or did. We can reach millions instantly, without the bureaucracy, financial constraints, and the big egos of Hollywood."

Kian considered the implications. The clan had always adapted to changing times, and this shift seemed particularly significant.

Not for the first time, he wondered how much longer they could maintain their influence hidden in an increasingly connected world.

"Very well," he said. "Whether it's a silver screen or a smartphone screen, our goal remains the same—to guide humanity away from the shadows." He didn't add that it was growing increasingly more difficult lately.

Kian had a strong feeling that their archenemy had made a secret move on the eternal chessboard game they had been playing and that he was getting ahead of the clan. Wars were once again sprouting everywhere, human rights were diminishing, and darkness was once again spreading, but this time, it was happening at an alarming pace.

"I'm glad that you are so understanding about it." Brandon sighed. "I'm so fed up that I'm selling my condo in Brentwood and moving to the village full-time. I need to hit the reset button and devise a new strategy."

"What do you have in mind?" Kian asked.

"I'd like to talk with Kalugal and brainstorm some ideas and see what we can do to take it to the next level. Movies are dying, Kian. The future is in interactive, immersive experiences. That's where we need to be."

There was nothing more interactive and immersive than Perfect Match, but it was not ready for general consumption yet. For now, InstaTock was all they had to work with.

Kian leaned back. "I will arrange a meeting with Kalugal."

"Excellent, thank you." Brandon pulled a Danish out of the bag and took a big bite. Once he was done chewing, he used a paper napkin to clean his lips. "So, what's the next step with the twins? I mean, in addition to staging their deaths?"

"I'm sure my mother would demand that we bring them to the village. She's already told Ell-rom that he and Morelle are her half-brother and sister. The truth is that I'm not even going to fight her over this. Moving them both to the clinic in the village will make life easier for everyone. Bridget and Julian want to get back home to their mates." He chuckled. "They have been creative, with Turner sleeping with Bridget in the clinic and Ella staying some nights with Julian in one of the penthouses. They are being good sports about it and not complaining, but there is no reason to make their lives more difficult than we need to."

Brandon seemed skeptical. "That's not like you, Kian. You still don't know whether the twins are threats or assets. Don't you want to find out first how powerful Ell-rom will get before you move them to the village? We can't have everyone wearing earpieces all of the time."

"Of course. I'm referring to the future after we know everything there is to know about the twins' powers. Right now, Ell-rom doesn't even know what compulsion is, and my mother will have to coach him on how to use it for us to assess it."

Brandon frowned. "Is that smart?"

"If he has the power, he will discover how to use it sooner or later. I'd rather it didn't happen spontaneously. Ell-rom is improving rapidly, but Morelle is still unconscious. She might be the dangerous one. What if she's hostile? What if she has abilities we're not prepared for?"

"Those are all valid concerns," Brandon said. "Perhaps you need to call a council meeting and brainstorm this together."

"That's a good idea. I'll call a council meeting soon. We need to make a decision as a community. But first, I want to see how Morelle progresses. And I want to get a better read on Ell-rom. In the meantime, I want you to work out a solution for faking their deaths."

"Give me a week to make some calls, feel things out. I'll have a preliminary plan for you by next Friday."

DARK AWAKENING TRILOGY
86: DARK AWAKENING: NEW WORLD

NOTE

Dear reader,

I hope my stories have added a little joy to your day. If you have a moment to add some to mine, you can help spread the word about the Children Of The Gods series by telling your friends and penning a review. Your recommendations are the most powerful way to inspire new readers to explore the series.

Thank you,

Isabell

Also by I. T. Lucas

PERFECT MATCH

TRANSLATIONS

LOS HIJOS DE LOS DIOSES

EL OSCURO DESCONOCIDO

1: EL OSCURO DESCONOCIDO EL SUEÑO
2: EL OSCURO DESCONOCIDO REVELADO
3: EL OSCURO DESCONOCIDO INMORTAL
EL OSCURO ENEMIGO
4- EL OSCURO ENEMIGO CAPTURADO
5 - EL OSCURO ENEMIGO CAUTIVO
6- EL OSCURO ENEMIGO REDIMIDO

LES ENFANTS DES DIEUX
DARK STRANGER
1- DARK STRANGER LE RÊVE
2- DARK STRANGER LA RÉVÉLATION
3- DARK STRANGER L'IMMORTELLE

THE CHILDREN OF THE GODS SERIES SETS

BOOKS 1-3: DARK STRANGER TRILOGY—INCLUDES A BONUS SHORT STORY: **THE FATES TAKE A VACATION**

BOOKS 4-6: DARK ENEMY TRILOGY —INCLUDES A BONUS SHORT STORY—**THE FATES' POST-WEDDING CELEBRATION**

BOOKS 7-10: DARK WARRIOR TETRALOGY
BOOKS 11-13: DARK GUARDIAN TRILOGY
BOOKS 14-16: DARK ANGEL TRILOGY
BOOKS 17-19: DARK OPERATIVE TRILOGY
BOOKS 20-22: DARK SURVIVOR TRILOGY
BOOKS 23-25: DARK WIDOW TRILOGY
BOOKS 26-28: DARK DREAM TRILOGY
BOOKS 29-31: DARK PRINCE TRILOGY
BOOKS 32-34: DARK QUEEN TRILOGY
BOOKS 35-37: DARK SPY TRILOGY
BOOKS 38-40: DARK OVERLORD TRILOGY
BOOKS 41-43: DARK CHOICES TRILOGY
BOOKS 44-46: DARK SECRETS TRILOGY
BOOKS 47-49: DARK HAVEN TRILOGY
BOOKS 50-52: DARK POWER TRILOGY
BOOKS 53-55: DARK MEMORIES TRILOGY
BOOKS 56-58: DARK HUNTER TRILOGY
BOOKS 59-61: DARK GOD TRILOGY

Books 62-64: Dark Whispers Trilogy
Books 65-67: Dark Gambit Trilogy
Books 68-70: Dark Alliance Trilogy
Books 71-73: Dark Healing Trilogy
Books 74-76: Dark Encounters Trilogy
Books 77-79: Dark Voyage Trilogy
Books 80-81: Dark Horizon Trilogy

MEGA SETS
The Children of the Gods: Books 1-6
INCLUDES CHARACTER LISTS
The Children of the Gods: Books 6.5-10

Perfect Match Bundle 1

CHECK OUT THE SPECIALS ON
ITLUCAS.COM
(https://itlucas.com/specials)

FOR EXCLUSIVE PEEKS AT UPCOMING RELEASES &
A FREE I. T. LUCAS COMPANION BOOK

Join my *VIP Club* and gain access to the VIP portal at ITLUCAS.COM

To Join, go to:
http://eepurl.com/blMTpD

Find out more details about what's included with your free membership on the book's last page.

TRY THE CHILDREN OF THE GODS SERIES ON
<u>AUDIBLE</u>
2 FREE audiobooks with your new Audible subscription!

**FOR EXCLUSIVE PEEKS AT UPCOMING RELEASES &
A FREE I. T. LUCAS COMPANION BOOK**

Join my *VIP Club* and gain access to the VIP portal at itlucas.com
To Join, go to:
http://eepurl.com/blMTpD

INCLUDED IN YOUR FREE MEMBERSHIP:

YOUR VIP PORTAL

- Read preview chapters of upcoming releases.
- Listen to Goddess's Choice narration by Charles Lawrence
- Exclusive content offered only to my VIPs.

FREE I.T. LUCAS COMPANION INCLUDES:

- Goddess's Choice Part 1
- Perfect Match: Vampire's Consort (A standalone Novella)
- Interview Q & A
- Character Charts

If you're already a subscriber and you are not getting my emails, your provider is sending them to your junk folder, and you are missing out on important updates. To fix that, add isabell@itlucas.com to your email contacts or your email VIP list.

**Check out the specials at
https://www.itlucas.com/specials**

Printed in Great Britain
by Amazon